WOLFBORN

WOLFBANE SERIES: BOOK 3

CELIA HART

Celia Hart LLC

Wolfborn
Wolfbane Series: Book 3
by Celia Hart

Copyright © 2023 by Celia Hart

All rights reserved.

Edited by Corbeaux Editorial Services
Cover design by Emily's World of Design
Chapter heading artwork by Studio Saturno

Print ISBN: 979-8-9864024-4-4
E-book ISBN: 979-8-9864024-5-1

Content Warning

These content notes are made available here so readers can inform themselves, if they want to. Some readers might consider these "spoilers." If you don't like spoilers, look away. You've been warned.

- **Bad language**: strong and frequent

- **Sex**: several fully described and explicit sex scenes, including cunnilingus, fellatio, and some kinks

- **Violence**: several graphic and explicitly violent scenes, including torture

- **Other**: body-shaming, bones, bullying, childbirth, death, domestic abuse, fatphobia, homophobia, mentions of rape, murder, panic attacks, poisoning, pregnancy, slut-shaming

If you'd like more information on any of the above content notes prior to reading, please reach out (celia.hart.author@gmail.com) and I will be happy to elaborate so that you may make a fully informed decision before choosing to turn the page!

For Christina & Melissa, my potluck "sisters".

Chapter 1

Ginger

Secrets. Everyone had at least one, right?

Mine was that I lost my wolf. It happened a long time ago. It was an accident, one of those moments in life that changed everything. You know what I mean. One day, everything was normal, great even, and the next thing I knew, my life was destroyed over one bad decision.

Yep, all it took was one stupid decision and my wolf was gone. I kept crossing my fingers that there was a chance she might come back—that she was still somewhere deep within me, stagnant, in a coma, just needing a little shove to wake up. That was why I went to see a witch on a regular basis.

That was my *other* secret.

My parents were suspicious of witches. Werewolves and witches didn't exactly have the best relationship. Lots of old wives' tales, I think—that whole "be careful what you wish for" thing. Apparently, when a witch granted a wish, it never quite worked out like expected. But I was desperate. It was the only hope I had to ever be whole again.

My family told me they still loved me, told me that I didn't need a wolf to be happy. I mean, sure, there were tons of humans populating the planet, and they seemed to be doing okay without wolves. But I didn't *want* to be a human! I wanted to be a werewolf, like everyone else I grew up with. Most of all, I wanted to meet my mate. Every werewolf had a mate out there they could innately sense after turning eighteen. Well, except me, probably. I mean, I still thought I had a mate, but could you even recognize your mate without a wolf?

That was why in early May, at the tail end of my freshman year of college, I found myself taking the commuter rail to Salem, Massachusetts, to meet with my witch doctor. During the school year, while far away from my parents' prying eyes, that was what I did—made a monthly trip from my college campus in Boston to the suburbs of Massachusetts with what little money I was able to earn working part-time at the school cafeteria.

Luckily, the train station in Salem wasn't far from the downtown area. I was easily able to make my way to the small shop on foot, and it was actually quite a pleasure to do so that day with the most gorgeous spring weather. As soon as I stepped off the train, I pulled off my hoodie, allowing the sun to warm my shoulders, and wrapped the sweatshirt around my waist.

Unsurprisingly, the downtown area was very lively that day. Not quite as lively as it was in October but still very busy with tons of people crowding the brick roads, ducking in and out of shops, and eating outdoors. People suffered through long, cold winters waiting for nice weather in New England, and we all loved taking advantage once it finally came.

I quickly made my way to the familiar fortune-telling shop, a front for what it really was. But they certainly made coin off that business as well, especially judging by the tourists sitting in the waiting area of the small shop that day—or at least I assumed they were tourists. Not having a wolf, I couldn't distinguish between our kind and humans because I also lacked all the other benefits, such as a heightened sense of smell, night vision, and an extraordinary immune system.

"Sit, please," Helena, a woman who looked to be in her late twenties with curly, black hair, said to me, gesturing at a cushioned chair by the entrance. She'd never been particularly friendly, even after knowing me for nine months now. I took a seat, leaving a chair empty next to a couple who was really into PDA and turning away from them.

Since the shop usually wasn't too busy, I hadn't been expecting to wait. I pulled out my phone to mindlessly scroll through Instagram when the chime of the door distracted me. Not that I cared much who entered, but I still looked up on impulse. And *damn*, the guy who entered was F-I-N-E with a capital *F*! *Holy fuck*. I didn't think I'd ever seen such a drop-dead gorgeous man in my life.

He brushed his huge, tanned hand through his dark hair in a je ne sais quoi fashion as he entered the small shop. If I were at a party right then, I would have totally crossed the room to chat him up, and I definitely *definitely* would not have left without taking him home.

It probably would have been a disappointment, to be honest. Most hot guys sucked in bed, and they were usually dicks, especially to girls like me. Not that there was anything wrong with my body per se—there wasn't—but I also wasn't svelte like the women they seemed to prefer, kind of like my twin sister. But still, I wouldn't have minded taking a look at what he had going on under that clothing. Based on how his arms strained against the sleeves of his T-shirt, and how the thin fabric of his shirt fell against his pecs, he clearly had a nice body. Even if I were a shame fuck to him.

"What are you looking at?" he snapped at me, catching me off guard. I hadn't even realized I'd been staring. Of course, just as I thought—he was a dick. A ridiculously good-looking one though.

"That huge zit on your face," I snapped back.

He narrowed his eyes at me. "That's not even possible."

Damn, so he must have been a werewolf. Although I, personally, couldn't distinguish between our kind, they could recognize I was one of them. I apparently still smelled like one even without my wolf.

"Guess you must be growing weak then," I came back quickly. "Too weak to fight off acne now! Before you know it, your hair will recede, and you'll get scrawny. Then you'll be just as ugly as your personality!"

"Do you know who you're talking to?" he growled at me, crossing his arms, his nostrils flaring, and his very distinct amber eyes taking on a cold, hard, evil appearance. And then I realized his eyes looked familiar somehow. I'd definitely seen them before.

"To be quite frank, I don't give a shit who you are. You're a huge dick, clearly to overcompensate for the small one in your pants." Everyone in the small shop was staring at us now. "It's probably so small you need a magnifying glass to see it. You probably fuck chipmunks you're so small. Your pickup line to them is, 'Wanna nut?' and they go for it, not knowing they're being lured in by a predator." I didn't know what came over me, but I was on a roll now, just spitting out anything that came to my mind. "Does that make you feel powerful? Taking advantage of small, weak animals, you perverted chipmunk fucker!"

His mouth was agape, eyes wide, staring at me. Okay, I literally had no idea what came over me. I had not only body-shamed this dude, something I was adamantly against, but also made a rape joke as casually as if I were telling a knock-knock joke. Heat swarmed my cheeks from the shame of what had inadvertently come out of my mouth. He blinked a few times and then finally spit out, "Who the fuck are you?"

His eyes were even more intense now. He had the look of someone ready to pounce on his prey. I'm pretty sure the only thing preventing him from shifting into his wolf to claw me to death was that we were in the presence of humans.

"Someone who wishes she never wasted her breath on you, you useless tool!" I retorted, knowing an apology was probably in order. My overreaction was completely unwarranted. And I should've really been more scared, knowing he had a predator inside him and I'd be entirely defenseless if he snapped. But something about him put me on edge. Don't get me wrong, I was excellent at comebacks and insults in the worst and best of circumstances—bully-victim survival—but he really, truly had brought out my worst.

"What?" he responded.

"You heard me! Get on the other side of that door and stop using up all my oxygen. You think you're so great, but you're not."

"Rich coming from someone like you. Typical chubby girl with a chip on her shoulder."

"You fucking douchebag!"

"You're the one who went low first."

"You're the one who came in here ready to bite my head off."

"That's enough!" Helena came over to us. "No more arguing. You're ruining the energy of our sanctuary. Our mediums cannot concentrate in such an environment."

"My apologies." The douchey dude's whole demeanor changed as he gave Helena an award-winning smile. "We didn't mean to interrupt your activities. But I do hope one of your mediums has time for me. I have some very important business to take care of." I didn't fail to notice how he brought his hand forward, lightly touching Helena's arm. Goddamn manipulator.

"Oh, of course, sir." Was she blushing? "We can fit you right in. Actually, I think our best medium is almost done with her clients. Why don't you go in right after they come out?" She winked at him.

What? You have to be kidding me! My eyes burned into his back.

"Great. Perfect." He smiled even more widely. "I was going to say I'm in a bit of a rush but looks like you already sensed that." He winked at her. "Clearly this place is legit."

"Best in the business." She smiled back at him.

Gross! I couldn't believe that not only had she allowed him to cut everyone in line, but he also agreed to do it. This guy was a total prick. I took back that I owed him an apology. I owed him nothing—fucking ridiculously good-looking douche. Why were all the pretty ones always the ones with the worst personalities?

I seethed in my seat as his infuriatingly nice ass made itself comfortable in the one next to me, which was, unfortunately, the only open chair left in the place. *Ugh.* The day had started out so well!

"I see I'm not your type," the jerk said.

"What?" I turned to glare at him. Why was he still speaking to me? He gestured toward my phone where I glanced back and found that I had absentmindedly scrolled onto a lingerie ad.

"Man-hating bitch."

"Dude, just shut up," I snapped at him quietly so I wouldn't get kicked out. Helena made it clear who was getting voted off this island if we started arguing again.

"Nobody tells me what to do. Least of all some bitch with a stick up her ass," he said in a quiet, menacing tone. At that moment, a couple of girls walked out into the main shop area, giggling. They stopped and looked at him on their way out, their eyes lingering on him. Goddess, I fucking hated him.

"Okay, Mister, come right this way!" Helena called out to him. He strolled over to her without a second glance back at me. And I hoped to Artemis that that was the last time I'd ever see him again. As nice as his ass was, it had clearly become a part of his personality. Ew.

It felt like I was sitting there for an hour as I watched person after person, group after group exiting before it was finally my turn to go. He was still back there by the time I was called. I wondered what was taking so long, but I was also relieved I didn't have to see his smug face again as he exited.

"Gigi, darling, welcome back." An older version of Helena welcomed me into a small room done up with rich purple and gold drapes, a crystal ball at the center of a small table, and decks upon decks of tarot cards behind her. "Has it been helping? Tell me. Tell Sybil everything." I took a deep breath, inhaling the subtle smell of incense, gripping the faux leather and wood of the chair I was seated in.

"I think so," I squeaked. "I sometimes feel something within me stirring." Okay, maybe it was how nauseous the herbs made me, my stomach shuddering with the need to reject them as soon as they were swallowed, but still!

"Give me your hand." I placed my small hand into Sybil's larger one. She closed her eyes and began humming. I scooched forward in anticipation. Suddenly, her eyes shot open. "Yes, it's definitely working. I sense it more today than I ever have previously. You must have been more diligent than usual."

I tried to think back. I was always very diligent. I couldn't recall being any more so this last time. But maybe I had been. The weather had been better, which always put me in a better mood, so perhaps my enthusiasm had translated into the spells as I chanted them.

"Yes, she wants to come alive. Something has called to her. Something is pulling her from the abyss. Her spirit wants to return and reclaim her body."

"Really?" I asked, my heart racing and stomach fluttering.

"Yes. I recommend a double batch this month. You're getting close."

"Yes, please. I'll do anything!" My eyes brimmed with tears. I almost never cried, but my emotions were now going into overdrive. My wolf wanted to come back. She wanted to return. This was actually happening!

"Next full moon, do the spell twice."

I nodded my head vigorously.

"Since you're buying a double batch this time, we'll even give you a 10 percent discount." She smiled, her eyes glistening. I didn't care what it cost. I was willing to go into severe credit card debt over this. There was nothing that mattered to me more than getting my wolf back.

"What about three times?"

"Not yet. Better to ease into it. We'll check you over again after the next full moon and see if you're ready."

I enthusiastically followed her to the front where she placed a jar with the herbs by the register and gestured to her daughter. As I turned to go check out, I was dismayed to find that the douchebag was back.

"So, how long are you in town for?" Helena looked up at him with doe-like eyes.

"Not long. I have business up north. But I'll be back again soon." He grinned at her.

"If you need someone to show you around when you come back, I'd be happy to give you my number. Lived in Salem my whole life. And I know the whole underground scene. I'm sure someone like you would be interested."

"Someone like me isn't usually welcome in the types of places someone like you frequents."

"I'm sure we could get you in. I'm well-connected around these parts."

"Sure, why don't I take your number? Next time. Today I've got somewhere to be."

"Great!" She pulled the receipt out of the printer and scribbled some numbers on it. As she did that, he sniffed the air and then turned to come face-to-face with me, his eyes piercing into mine.

"What do you want?" I snapped at him, not much differently than he had when we first met.

"Nothing from you, clearly," he said, turning back around to take the receipt from Helena. He then rushed out of the tiny little shop. And something inside me did stir at that moment. Almost like a rumbling, scratching in my stomach and chest. It was working!

"Four hundred and thirty-two dollars," Helena said unenthusiastically as I approached the register. I pulled out my credit card. When I'd first learned the price, I'd almost had a heart attack. As a college student who was perpetually racking up student loans and living expenses, coming up with the money wasn't exactly easy. They claimed these herbs were difficult to get. They had to import them illegally from somewhere in Australia, where they had found the perfect climate and soil for growing them.

But I didn't even care that I had met the douchiest guy ever and spent almost everything in my checking account at that moment. Nothing could ruin my good mood.

I stepped back outside into the warm afternoon and made my way back to the train, checking my phone to see when the next one would be coming. Another few days and I'd be done with school, moving back to my pack for the summer. And then next weekend was the next full moon. One moon phase closer to my wolf coming back.

Chapter 2

Ginger

"Gigi!" My sister Paige wrapped her arms tightly around me as soon as I entered the house. I hugged her back, so appreciative to be reunited with her again since I returned to my pack in northern Vermont after finishing up the school year. Being twins, we had a special connection. It had been much stronger when we were younger. A lot of my own resentment toward her pulled us apart over the years. It wasn't her fault, but I couldn't help but feel envious that she was able to accomplish all my dreams. An unsettling feeling that someone else was living my life constantly choked me, salt rubbed into the wound.

The thing was, becoming a warrior was always *my* dream. Our dad was a warrior, and I was always way more into it than Paige. I'd loved to go with Mom to watch him spar on nice days out. I'd prized the time he spent training me to fight and defend myself in the backyard. Yes, I was a daddy's girl through and through. And the way I hung on to my dad was the way Paige hung on to me. Even though she was born only fifteen minutes after me, she still always acted very much like the baby sister.

Before long, my dreams became her dreams. And not long after that, we started competing in everything—especially who did better in training at school. While, okay, my sister was pretty good, I still think I was better. "She has heart." That's what trainers used to say about me.

Of course, that dream was abruptly stolen from me the night I lost my wolf. How could I fight without my most prized weapon? Before I even had the chance to train as a wolf, she had disappeared. And now, well, now my dreams consisted of doing human things like going to college, getting a desk job, and maybe even having a human husband one day. After all, how could I have a mate without a wolf? And what kind of werewolf would want a wolfless girl?

"Peachy Gigi!" my dad sang out, pulling me in for a hug next, using his nickname for me. I snuggled into him, inhaling the Dove soap he used, freshly showered after warrior duty. The smell brought a feeling of familiarity and comfort. While I'd come to understand that my sense of smell wasn't as acute as my other family members', different scents did still bring back different memories and feelings. I liked to believe more so than for humans, but I had no way of knowing whether that was true.

My mom and older sister, Heidi, who had brought me home from school, were now making themselves busy in the kitchen preparing dinner. Heidi had always been the most domesticated out of the three of us, and none of us were surprised when she found her mate not long after coming of age, got married almost immediately, and was now trying to start a family.

If I was being completely honest, there were often days I felt sick with envy looking at her life. I had never been a hopeless romantic, nor had I ever wanted to be a housewife like my sister, but something about the ability to meet my mate being taken away from me just made me bitter about the whole thing. She was all blissed out, living with her mate, while I was slaving away in school and fucking around with fuckboys who wanted nothing to do with me between the hours of six in the morning and ten at night.

Before long, we were all seated at dinner, the OG members of the family reunited. "So, Gigi, how are you feeling after completing your first year of college?" my dad asked.

"Good. All As of course." I stuck my tongue out at my twin.

"She clearly didn't get my brains." My dad chuckled. "Looks like I picked a good mate for breeding." He winked at my mom. She fluttered her eyelashes at him like a teenager. My parents were so vomit inducing most of the time. Okay, I totally wanted it for myself one day. They were proof the mate bond worked.

"It's so funny how Paige and Gigi ended up doing completely the opposite of what I would have thought," Heidi said. "Like, if you'd asked me ten years ago who I thought would have ended up as a warrior and who would have ended up as a student, I would have totally put down a hundred bucks that Paige would be the student and Gigi would be the warrior."

The whole table was silent. Heidi had decided to go there. The place the family knew not to go. It was a soft spot for me, and she had pushed on it. And she said it, too, as if it were my choice. As if Paige hadn't gone on to do what had always been *my* dream.

"Gigi was always smarter than me, so it makes sense," Paige quickly responded. Always the fucking diplomat trying to smooth things over. Always the one who didn't rebel or make waves. The one who played it safe. The one who made the right choices and didn't lose her wolf. Boring, in my opinion. But I'm also the one who lost my wolf, so the jury's out on whether being boring is a bad thing.

"Gigi, you're doing so great. Your mom and I are so proud of you." My dad patted my leg.

"Very proud." My mom smiled at me. Goddess, I couldn't take their pity.

"Can I be excused?" I asked, not wanting to sit with my family anymore.

"If you want." My mom gave me a pained glance and a clenched half smile.

"Yes, I do." I pushed my chair away from the table, the legs scraping against the tile floor. Before anyone could stop me, I ran up to my room, my safe place. When we were kids, Paige and I shared a room out of choice. But after the whole losing-my-wolf thing happened, we separated our bunk beds, and I moved into my own room.

I pulled out the jar and rotated it in my hands, memorizing every detail of the crushed, dried herb that was contained within. Hope—that was what it signified. Maybe I wouldn't be stuck like this forever. Maybe it would work. No, that was the wrong attitude. It *would* work. My wolf *would* come back to me. *I just need to think it into existence.*

The full moon was a few days later. Just as I'd done during each prior one, I made my way outside close to midnight. In school, no one paid attention to what I did, so it was easy enough to take an Uber out to the Fells in Medford, where I'd make my way into the woods to perform my ritual. Okay, it was probably pretty crazy considering how vulnerable I was without a wolf, without night vision, and without a powerful sense of smell to alert me to predators. But I threw all caution to the wind out of desperation.

Now, in my pack, I was much safer. Werewolves guarded the border to keep intruders out. But I didn't exactly want my family to know what I was up to. They'd certainly try to talk me out of it. So I waited until everyone was asleep and snuck out, making my way on foot with a tote bag filled with my supplies.

I walked all the way to the outskirts of the pack to the lake that was historically known for parties before they were banned at least a decade earlier. I quickly ran to the lake to fill my jar with water, then screwed the cap back on and shook it, allowing it to dissolve the herbs inside. I then entered back through the tree line, walking into the forest until I found a small clearing that would be perfect.

I dropped my tote onto the ground and pulled out the crystals inside. After drawing a circle in the pine needles using my foot, I used a compass app on my phone to place one crystal in the most northern point and then placed four more to indicate the other four points of the pentagram. After completing this task, I checked the time. Five minutes to.

I stripped myself completely naked as I'd been directed, folding my clothes neatly and leaving them on a nearby rock. Then I stepped into the pentagram and waited, cell phone and concoction in hand. At one minute to, I unscrewed the top. Once my cell phone indicated 12:00, I went through the ritual I had now memorized, chanting the words the witches had taught me, then instantly throwing back half the concoction. It burned as it went down my throat, practically making me gag with how horrible it tasted—something like spoiled yogurt mixed with vinegar. But it didn't deter me. I did the same thing again, throwing it back a second time. Then I spread my arms and legs and turned in circles, allowing the moonlight to hit every inch of my skin.

My stomach grumbled murderously, rejecting every bit of what I'd swallowed. But I would rather die than throw it up. This was my only hope. I incessantly swallowed my saliva, indicating to my body that the only direction was down, and it had another thing coming if it even thought about sending anything up.

But although I had always been successful when I took just one dose, the double dose was too much for me to handle. Before I knew it, my whole body was convulsing with agony, my insides burning. My vision blurred. I was sure I'd poisoned myself. I probably needed to go to a hospital. But I stayed there, unmoving, allowing the poison to overtake my body as I fell to my knees and tears spilled from my eyes, a silent plea for help.

Chapter 3

Tyson

If I was being honest, it was nice being away from my pack for once. That place could be so suffocating most of the time. I mean, my grandfather was a complete dick, and my dad wasn't much better. It was like they said, alphas always have to be in charge, and more than one alpha is volatile—an explosion just waiting to go off. In the case of my pack, there were three of us, which made the whole thing pretty combustible. I was actually surprised we hadn't battled it to the death yet.

Granted, things weren't exactly smooth sailing coming to Alpha Blake's pack either. While we weren't rivals, we were still two alphas with strong, competing personalities. But it was better than dealing with my father and grandfather. Blake was at least reasonable and wasn't hell-bent on making my life miserable. Although, I was pretty sure Blake wanted nothing to do with me coming to his pack to "check things out." But he was desperate to make his mate's family happy, so he agreed to the arrangement for the summer. That worked out great for me. I got a vacation from the fam, and I had some things I needed to take care of on the East Coast anyway.

I was technically supposed to be reviewing all of Blake's training programs and warriors to make sure they were up to par. But I didn't really give a shit. I was much more interested in getting some fresh meat.

I couldn't lie, Blake's pack had some really nice pussy. I hadn't been here long, but already I'd met plenty of girls who were more than willing to spread their legs for an alpha. That guy must have really slain before he met my cousin. These girls were so slutty, especially for religious girls, and especially compared to my pack, which was a lot stricter and more conservative. Girls back home at least liked to pretend they were pure. Challenges were fun, but there was something so sweet about a girl who was easy.

I loved uninhibited girls, especially if they were thick and curvy. That was the other thing—I liked a little cushion for the pushin' as they say. I loved meeting a woman with T and A, and thighs I could grab on to. Goddess, was there anything nicer than that, than a woman who could keep you warm all night?

One Saturday night in mid-May, while in my wolf form, I was deep in thought about such intellectual subject matters when a familiar scent cut through the woodsy scent of pine, moss, and wet wood and entered my nostrils. It both delighted and infuriated me simultaneously. If I had to be honest, it was the kind of scent someone dreamed about, better than anything I'd ever smelled before—a sweet, musky scent, maybe patchouli or cinnamon . . . No, something very unique. Some sort of amazing perfume that I had to know the name of. But it also reminded me of the biggest bitch I'd ever met in my life—the cunt who'd been wearing it the day I first smelled it.

Still, I followed the fragrance, intoxicated by it, especially in my wolf form when I was more driven by instinct than logic. Where was it was coming from? I abandoned my run of the patrol stations as it led me through the woods until I spotted her—her strawberry blonde hair and pale skin illuminated by the moonlight—completely naked. Not wanting to approach her in that state, I instead acted like a creepy peeping tom and hid behind some pine trees, unable to pry my eyes away. *Shit.* If there was a perfect female body that existed, I was suddenly in the presence of it. Her ass was big and round—better than ones I'd seen in rap music videos and on Instagram models. Her tits were spectacular—probably too large for even my large hands to handle. And she had a perfect hourglass shape with a soft belly that dipped inward on the sides, proportionate to her thick, beautiful thighs and hips—the type of hips I could just imagine grabbing on to as I took her from behind.

Goddess, as infuriating as she was, she was also mesmerizing. I didn't know why she had ended up here, completely bare in the middle of the woods at midnight, but Goddess, what a sight. This had to be a dream. I had never seen such a perfect woman in my life.

And—*fuck*—I was such a creep, just staring at her, unable to avert my eyes. It wasn't like me to do this. Yes, I was a horndog, but I wasn't the type who did things without consent. I'd been raised better than that. I had a mom and a sister. And if some creep was staring at one of them like I was at her at that moment, they'd be lucky to be alive.

I was about to turn away when she suddenly fell to her knees, the metallic smell of blood blowing toward me and drawing my eyes to a red stream trickling from her nose. What was happening to her? Tears spilled from her eyes, an agonized expression on her face as her limbs trembled.

Without thinking, I rushed to her, needing to make sure she was okay. Something deep within me compelled me. I was no longer myself but my wolf, my protector instincts in full gear.

Unable to mindlink with someone not in my pack, I quickly shifted into my human form, got down on my knees, and pulled her body toward mine, cradling her. "Are you okay?" I asked, locking eyes with hers.

Her hazel eyes widened, and her mouth fell open, a quiet gasp fleeing her mouth. It didn't escape me that we were both completely naked while I was holding her in a very intimate way, the clammy skin of her torso against mine.

"Please don't hurt me," she cried out, her eyelids sagging. Something about holding her felt so natural and so perfect that I almost forgot how much she'd pissed me off that day I'd met her and she'd called me a chipmunk fucker. I mean, seriously, who does that? And who the fuck would say that to an alpha? But now she was so vulnerable, I found myself both deeply sympathetic to her situation and oddly endeared.

"We need to go to the clinic." My heart beat frantically, a protective feeling emerging from deep within.

"No!" she screamed out, feebly pushing her palms against my chest.

"You're hurt, though." I tried to reason with her.

"Please don't take me to the clinic," she slurred. "Please. My mom's best friend is a nurse there, and she'll know."

"Know what?"

"Please, just leave me here. I'll be okay."

"I can't just leave you." As I said that, her eyes drooped closed, and her body went limp in my arms. I checked to make sure she was still breathing. Should I follow her request? As I weighed the pros and cons, I noticed a jar on the ground next to us. I stretched my arm out to bring it to my nose and smelled it, but I was unable to distinguish what it was. Some sort of plant, maybe? Nothing I'd ever smelled before. Had she eaten whatever had been inside?

I sighed to myself. There was clearly something she didn't want her mom to know. I could relate, constantly keeping secrets from my own overbearing parents. In the end, I decided to just take her back to the packhouse, not knowing where else I could bring her. Certainly, her wolf would heal her of whatever ailment had been inflicted on her.

I found her clothes lying on a rock nearby, and I put them back on her. As I slid her panties up her thighs, I again felt like such a creep, especially as I couldn't help but be completely turned on by what I was doing.

But, still, I had to get points for being a gentleman. I had dressed her. Certainly, it would have been much worse had I left her naked.

I shifted back into my wolf form and flipped her on my back into a wolfman's carry before running her back to the packhouse. Everyone was already asleep when I got there. Not knowing where else to deposit her, I brought her into my room and placed her on the guest room bed. I then wet a washcloth and gently wiped the blood that had trickled out of her nose from her face. She did have a very beautiful face, with cute little freckles dotting her nose and pouty pink lips—very kissable lips.

While indoors, her perfume penetrated the air around me, so much stronger, like the first time I saw her. When she woke, I'd have to ask her what it was. It had to be the most amazing thing I'd ever smelled. I leaned closer, getting a good sniff of her neck, and then forced myself to walk away. I had to stop being creepy, taking advantage of a passed-out girl. I mean, seriously, I was a lot of things, but a rapist was not one of them.

I then sprinted back out of the packhouse and continued my patrol run, not able to stop thinking about her. I'd never obsessed over someone so much in my life. Even after that day in that witch shop. After all that shit she'd spat at me—normally I just forgot someone worthless like that immediately. But something about her had buried itself within me, her words cutting much deeper than they should have. And now—*fuck*! Now I wanted nothing more than to, well, bury my cock inside her, fuck her in every position that was physically possible, defile her amazing body, come on her size G tits. (Oh, did I mention I snuck a peek at her bra size? Yep, total creep! But holy shit, I didn't even know such a bra size existed!)

And as much as my whole body was begging for me to crawl into bed with her when I got back, already imagining how nice her soft curves would feel against my torso, I stayed the gentlemanly course and instead crawled onto the alpha living room couch, falling asleep there. But not before my hand found its way to my cock, rock-hard from the evening. I rubbed it vigorously, playing out all my fantasies in my mind. And even after I came on my abs and wiped it off with one of my socks, it wasn't long before the dirty thoughts entered my mind again.

The only thing I knew for sure was that this fucking infuriating man-hating bitch had gotten me obsessed and horny as hell in a way no other woman ever had.

Chapter 4

Ginger

Oh Goddess, fucking Artemis. My head hurt, my stomach burned, my chest wheezed. The sun was so bright. I kept trying to open my eyes, but the light streaming in through the window made it very difficult. I moaned, in terrible pain, my whole body sore. This was worse than my worst hangovers. Even when I blacked out, it was never this bad. I really did need to go to the pack clinic. I'd cry out for Paige to carry me there. She was a full-time warrior—her muscles were definitely strong enough by now.

I finally forced my eyes open and was instantly confused by my surroundings. This wasn't my bedroom. I'd never been in this room before at all. Had I hooked up with someone the prior night? I tried to think back. What had happened?

The full moon! It all hit me at once. I'd taken the double batch of the potion and then everything got blurry. And, oh my Goddess, was that a dream or had that douchebag from the fortune-telling shop really appeared? It had to have been a dream, right? But where did I end up? I thought I'd passed out in the forest, but maybe not?

Suddenly the door to the bedroom swung open and a woman entered with a bunch of cleaning supplies. "Oh, sorry!" she shouted and exited, slamming the door.

"What happened? Are you okay?" I heard someone's voice outside. Someone who sounded very much like Alpha Blake. He had a very distinct voice that really commanded your attention, so it had to be him.

"There's a girl in there!" the women responded.

The man who had spoken chuckled. "Fucking Tyce. It's okay, you can go home for the day, Wendy. Thanks for coming on your day off. I appreciate you coming in this morning to clean up after last night's big dinner."

"Of course, Alpha," the woman responded.

Fuck, it was Blake. Was I in the packhouse? Why? And who was Tyce? He couldn't be the douchebag, could he?

"Blake!" I heard another voice that also sounded very familiar, recognizing it as Paige's new friend, the new luna of the pack.

"Yes, babe?" Blake replied in a very tender voice.

"Paige just called me, hysterical. Her twin sister is missing. Can you get the warriors to put in a lookout for her?"

"Shit, when was the last time they saw her?"

"Last night. She says they all went to bed like normal, but she's missing from her bed and the house this morning, not answering her cell phone, and they can't mindlink with her."

"Can't mindlink? Like she's blocking them out?"

"I don't know. Maybe she's too out of range."

"Fuck, well, I'll get them right on that, Jaz. Tell Paige not to worry." There was a pause, and then he continued, "You know, you don't have to go through me to command the warriors anymore. You're the luna now, and you have the power to give them orders yourself."

"I know." Her voice trailed off. "But I still feel weird about it."

"You'll get used to it, Mrs. Alpha."

Shit, Paige and my family were worried about me. I had to get out of here. But I didn't want to be noticed. The alpha and luna clearly didn't know I was here, also meaning they weren't the ones who brought me here. Then, I remembered something else. Hadn't I been naked when I passed out? And that guy—wasn't he naked too? Shit, did he take advantage of me? I peeked under the sheets to find all my clothes were miraculously on. Had I gotten dressed?

"Also, have you seen Tyce anywhere?" Jasmine asked. "My parents want to invite him over for dinner tonight before the service."

Blake snickered. "That kid. Reminds me of me. Before I met the best thing that ever happened to me, of course."

"What do you mean?"

"He's getting very familiar with what the pack has to offer."

"What does that mean?"

"Of the female variety."

"Oh!" Jasmine said in a very *duh* kind of way, finally understanding what Blake was insinuating.

Wait, but who was this Tyce guy? And how was he related to our alpha?

"Anyway, I don't know where Tyce is. But he's definitely not in his room." Blake chuckled.

Haha, so funny. I couldn't help but feel annoyed by how funny Alpha Blake was finding all of this. Some pervert had dragged me back to his bedroom while I was blacked out and did who knows what to me while I was unconscious. Okay, I wasn't sure that was actually what happened. Judging by the fact that I was fully dressed, that was probably not what happened. But this Tyce guy did sound like a serious player, whoever he was. Even his name sounded like a fuckboy name.

I forced myself out of bed, feeling unsteady on my legs, a migraine pounding in my skull. I looked around—my shoes nowhere to be found.

And, damn, I really had to pee. My bladder was throbbing. What time was it?

As soon as I heard footsteps disappear down some stairs, I finally exited the room, stumbling down the hallway, opening doors until I found one that led to a bathroom. I quickly peed, and then my stomach, again, violently rumbled. I bent over the toilet, just in time for bright green vomit to explode from my throat. I moaned again, in so much pain, then washed my hands and rinsed out my mouth, grabbing a bottle of mouthwash to rinse it some more. Goddess, I felt so gross. I had to get home. At least now that I'd rid my stomach of those herbs, I was feeling somewhat better. A tear escaped one of my eyes as I once again mourned the loss of my wolf. I tried to sense her, but still nothing. Another month that it hadn't worked.

I tried to console myself—these things took time. She'd been dead for six years before I had started doing the spells. Who knew how long it would take to bring her back to life? I just hoped that the herbs had had time to take effect before I threw them all up.

I then spotted some large Adidas pool slides on the floor of the bathroom by the shower. They were probably at least double the size of my feet but better than nothing. I slipped my feet into them and then snuck out quietly, trying my best not to allow them to clack on the floor from how awkward it was walking in them. They were fucking huge. I thought back, and that guy from the fortune-telling shop was quite large and imposing. Was he Tyce? But no, there was no way that he and Tyce were the same person. I mean, what were the odds? I randomly met some douchebag in Salem and now he was staying at the packhouse? Seeing him last night had to have been a dream. And these slides were probably Alpha Blake's anyway.

I quietly made my way down the stairs, one slow step at a time, keeping an eye out. Once I was satisfied no one was around, I sprinted out the front door. The fresh air felt nice as I did my walk of shame. We lived a fair bit away from the packhouse, but I probably needed the walk anyway.

I hadn't gotten far before a group of wolves swarmed me. Terrified, I waited until one of them transformed, approaching me completely naked, his muscles on full display. "Gigi?" he asked.

I knew nudity wasn't taboo in our pack, but I still had to get used to it since I'd never really had the opportunity to shift between human and wolf. I nodded back at him, speechless.

"Alert Alpha." He turned to the other wolves.

"Can I go?" I asked.

"We'll escort you."

"Oh . . . okay," I replied. Just as we were all about to start walking down the street, a wolf who was so dark brown he was practically black sprinted over, then quickly shifted into Alpha Blake, also completely naked. And, holy shit, he was fucking hot. I mean, he was hot while he was dressed, but damn. I blushed, feeling my face burning red hot. I was gawking at my sister's friend's mate. I had to get a hold of myself.

"Gigi, are you okay?" He approached me with concern. "What happened?"

I stuttered, "Ye-yeah, I-I'm fine."

"You're not hurt, are you? Your family's worried about you."

"I-I'm fine . . . just going home now."

He looked down at my feet and back up at me, his intense blue eyes piercing into me, a smirk on his face. Fuck, was he going to recognize his own sandals? Or, shit, they might be Tyce's, whoever he was. He'd totally caught me as the girl who was in his bed that morning.

"Good night?" He had a mischievous smile on his face.

"Something like that," I replied, sick with shame. But I also didn't want to explain what had actually happened. Somehow, him believing I'd hooked up with this Tyce dude seemed like the better option. "Can I go please, Alpha? Alone?"

"I'll mindlink your parents so you don't have to change forms," he said, turning to leave.

"Thanks," I replied, thinking, *More like because I can't change forms.* Everyone then dispersed, and I was left on my own to make my way home.

It took me about twenty minutes to finally get to my house, ready to take an Advil and pass out again. My parents kept them on hand just for me, since clearly no one else in the family needed them. As soon as I entered the house, I was bombarded, everyone shouting at once, their voices blending together, all concerned.

My mom finally quieted everyone and asked, "Gigi, where were you? We were all so worried. You're so vulnerable." She pulled me in for a huge hug, squeezing me against her.

Suddenly I heard obnoxiously loud laughter escape Heidi's mouth. "What shoes are you wearing, Gigi!?" Everyone's eyes turned to my feet. Shit, I should have kicked them off before I entered.

"Whose shoes are those?" My dad appeared ready to murder someone.

"Calm down, Dad!" Heidi laughed some more. *Haha, so funny!* "That's just what Gigi does."

"What does that mean?" my mom and dad both asked at the same time, pursing their lips and raising their eyebrows. Oh, did I mention that my family was very religious? This wasn't exactly a laughing matter. But I hadn't thought of any other excuse. Fuck. Why hadn't I kicked the shoes off before I entered the house?

"I hope you met your mate and you're not acting inappropriately, especially around our pack." My mom's eyes burned into me.

"We raised you better than that, Gigi." My dad grimaced and shook his head, a deep crease embedding itself in his forehead, making me feel even sicker than I already did. I couldn't stand the fact that I had disappointed him.

"It's fine. Gigi wouldn't act inappropriately. Right, Gigi?" Paige elbowed me. "You just went to a party and got so drunk you lost your shoes, right?" Hey, Paige actually wasn't so bad with this whole excuse thing. Was there a rebellious side of her I didn't know?

"Yeah, that's exactly what happened. I wouldn't ever be with anyone who isn't my mate, Daddy." I gave my dad my best puppy eyes, and remorse shot through me for all my bitterness toward Paige. She did always have my back.

"Of course you wouldn't, Peachy Gigi." He smiled. I knew parents weren't supposed to have a favorite, but I was definitely my father's favorite. "But I don't like how you're going out and not telling us where you are. We were really worried about you."

"I'm sorry, Daddy. I wasn't planning to stay out all night, but it was a really good party, and I lost my cell phone and ended up at Jocelyn's house. Her brother let me borrow his sandals since Jocelyn's feet are too small."

"Okay. Be careful, Gigi. You know you're really vulnerable. I don't like how you're underage drinking, but I'm glad you're okay. I'll let it slide this time." He paused. "Also, next time, don't just sneak out of the house without telling us where you're going. I know you're an adult now, but we worry about you when we don't know where you are."

"Okay, Daddy," I replied, trying to appear as remorseful as possible.

After my parents were finally satisfied that I was okay, I went upstairs, my sisters following me right into my bedroom. Sometimes I hated having sisters.

Heidi laughed like a hyena. "Those are some big shoes on your feet. He must have been huge! What are those, like size 16, 17, bigger? So is it true? Are feet and, you know, proportional?"

"Ha ha ha," I said sarcastically.

"Come on, you can tell us! You've never been shy about it before," Heidi hounded me, taking a seat next to me on my bed.

"Why'd you basically tell Dad that I sleep around?" I glared at her, very angry with my sister for her disloyalty.

"Yeah, that was mean, Heidi," Paige agreed. "You wouldn't have liked it if Gigi did that to you."

"Come on, it was hilarious." Heidi laughed again.

"No, it wasn't!" I yelled back. "You know how Mom and Dad are. That was really fucking rude. Now get out of my room."

Heidi rolled her eyes at me but followed my instructions and left. Thank Goddess. I didn't have the patience for her that morning. I was still processing everything.

"So what really happened?" Paige sat down next to me as soon as Heidi was gone. She sniffed me and then said, "You do smell like a guy, but he's not from our pack. You're lucky that Dad just believes everything you tell him."

"Really?" I asked. "What pack does it smell like he's from?" And then I realized that Blake had likely smelled him on me too. So he definitely had no doubt about whose bed I'd slept in.

She sniffed again. "I don't know. I don't think I've ever smelled whatever pack it is."

"Oh." I slumped my shoulders. I'd hoped Paige would offer me some helpful information.

"So what really happened?"

"Just a rough night," I replied, not ready to tell Paige my secret. I knew she'd try to talk me out of doing what I was doing, and I didn't want to hear it.

"You know you can tell me anything." She took my hands in hers. "I'd never tell Mom, Dad, or Heidi."

"I know, but I'm just not ready to talk about it."

"Okay." She slumped her shoulders.

I wanted to ask her if she knew of anyone staying at the packhouse. She would definitely have heard, being friends with the luna. But then she might put two and two together, so I kept my mouth shut. Whoever this Tyce guy was, I was going to find out and also find out what really happened after I passed out.

Chapter 5

Tyson

"Good night?" Blake smirked at me as he caught me entering the pack-house after I'd gone for a run. His eyes crinkled in an amused expression.

"What?"

"I saw that girl you had here last night doing the walk of shame this morning. Don't worry, your secret's safe with me." He chuckled. "I see you're enjoying everything my pack has to offer."

"You saw her?" I asked.

"Yeah, her family was worried about her, so we put out a search. Like the pack security? Make sure you report that back to your family."

"Do you know who she was?"

"You dog!" Blake pushed on my shoulder with an amused smile. "You didn't even get her name? I always at least got the name."

"Well, what's her name?" I kept my expression neutral, not sure whether it was better for Blake to think I'd banged her or not. I still needed to find out what she was hiding from her parents. As much as she infuriated me, I didn't want to blow whatever cover she had for whatever the fuck she was doing—which I also wanted to know.

"Gigi."

"Gigi? Is that a nickname?"

"Not sure. Only met her once before. But that's what Jasmine and her sister call her."

"Jasmine knows her?"

"She's friends with her twin sister."

She has a twin? Well, damn, I'd always fantasized about sleeping with twins. "Are they identical?" I asked, my mind instantly going into the gutter. Damn, two curvaceous miracles existed. And maybe her twin wasn't so prickly. Maybe her twin actually liked men.

"They look alike, but not sure they're identical."

"Hmm," I responded, trying to decide whether this was a good or bad thing.

"Oh, by the way, Jasmine was looking for you earlier. Her parents wanted to invite you over for dinner before the service tonight."

"Oh, I'll text her and let her know I'll be there," I replied, turning to go upstairs. Now that my mind was in the gutter, I couldn't get it out. Just like last night, I was quickly becoming hornier and hornier, my cock hardening in my pants. Goddess, that girl had me so worked up. And now that I knew she was a twin, all my twin fantasies started playing out in my head.

I fell into my bed, which still smelled like her perfume, only putting me more on edge. I pulled off my shorts and angrily stroked my cock. Goddess, the way she wouldn't leave my mind was pissing me off, but damn it, I wanted to fuck her so badly. Her and her twin.

Ginger

By the time we were on our way to the Sunday temple service, I'd had a chance to get cleaned up and collect my phone, shoes, and crystals from the place where I'd left them. I was feeling much better at this point, having finally recovered from the terrible hangover the herbs had caused. Thankfully Heidi had gone home, so I didn't have to deal with her. I was still angry about what she'd done. Although, she'd definitely be at the service that night, being just as religious as the rest of our family.

We took our normal seats by my parents' other temple friends. I relaxed into the pew, thinking the day would soon be over. The service started as normal, with a sermon from our priest, Bernard, and him leading us through different prayers, chants, and meditations. Since I'd attended my whole life, I could basically do everything in my sleep.

As the service was wrapping up, I was surprised when Bernard called Blake to the podium for an announcement. I sat up from the slouching position I'd been in. My muscles went weak, and my skin tingled with discomfort at the sight of someone else following him to the front of the congregation, someone just as tall and muscular, someone with intense amber eyes. It was *him*—the guy from the fortune-telling shop. The guy whom I thought I'd dreamed about the prior night.

"Good evening, Midnight Maple Pack!" Blake's voice boomed as everyone quietly listened. "As many of you already know, we have a very special guest in our pack visiting us for the summer. Luna Jasmine's cousin Alpha Tyce has come all this way from the Jade Moon Pack in Alaska so that we can build our alliance. This is very important to me and an honor for our pack as this alliance was built not due to politics but blood. I hope all of you will treat Alpha Tyce with the utmost respect, as if he is your own alpha, while he is here with us. He will be leading in many of our pack activities such as training and patrol duty. So, please, everyone, give Alpha Tyce a warm welcome."

The whole congregation applauded loudly, and my mouth fell open. My face burned as I realized that all those things I'd said in the fortune-telling shop had been directed at an alpha. No wonder he asked me if I knew who I was speaking to. Oh Goddess, I couldn't believe I'd done that. And not only that, but he was from an ally pack, a pack that we were aligned with due to familial relations. He was the cousin of our very own luna! I'd totally put my foot in my mouth.

"Very good-looking young man." My mom winked at my sisters and me. She had always had a thing for alphas. When he was still alive, my mom had had a schoolgirl crush on the late Alpha James, Blake's father. She'd cried all day when she found out he'd passed in battle over a year ago.

After the service, everyone fell into conversation with the others in attendance. My parents instantly went over to greet their own group of friends. Paige pulled my hand, heading toward the front. "C'mon, Gigi, let's go meet to the new alpha! Jasmine will introduce us!" I didn't know what to do, horrified by the idea as if I were witnessing an oncoming trainwreck.

"Hey, Paige!" Jasmine pulled her in for a hug as soon as we approached. "And nice to see you again, Gigi," she said, wrapping her arms around me. I just let her hug me, frozen in place.

"So, any chance to meet the new alpha?" Paige elbowed Jasmine.

"Of course!" Jasmine brightened. "Hey, Tyce!" He was distracted by whomever he was talking to, but he turned to face her before excusing himself.

"Hey." Tyce approached our group, glancing at Jasmine first and then turning to look at us, his amber eyes locking with mine. And then I realized exactly whose eyes his reminded me of. I couldn't believe I'd forgotten Jasmine had the same eyes, recalling how distinct I'd thought they were when I first met her.

"This is my friend, Paige." Jasmine introduced my sister to him first.

"Nice to meet you, Paige." He smiled, shaking her hand.

"Pleasure's all mine, Alpha!" she squeaked out. Don't tell me that she was getting a crush on him now! She did always take much more after Mom than I did.

"And this is her twin sister, Gigi." Jasmine introduced me next. My heart was beating so loudly in my chest I was sure everyone could hear.

He reached out his hand as if this was totally normal, grasped my small hand in his huge one, and gripped it tightly, practically crushing it. "Nice to meet you, Gigi. I heard you have a lot of opinions about chipmunks." His eyes twinkled with amusement as he smirked at me.

"Chipmunks, what?" Jasmine laughed. "What does that mean? You've heard things about Gigi?"

"Yes, I have." His smile widened. "I've heard she has many opinions—not just about chipmunks, also about magnifying glasses, predators, and receding hairlines. Maybe you should share them with the group, Gigi."

My face burned. Goddess, what had I done?

"What!" Paige was joining in with Jasmine's laughter. "Is this some sort of joke? Gigi, what is he talking about? Have you two met already or something?" Then something flashed across her face, and she glanced down at his feet.

Fuck!

"What size shoes do you wear? Your feet are really big," Paige remarked innocently, leaning closer to him, nostrils flared. Paige wasn't stupid.

"You like them big?" His eyes were really twinkling with amusement now as he showed off his shoes. Locking eyes with me again, he said, "If you're wondering, the answer is yes. They are proportional to everything else. I'm definitely not chipmunk size." His eyes never left mine. I wanted to die. Goddess, why hadn't those herbs just killed me yesterday?

"Why do you keep talking about chipmunks?" Jasmine giggled. "I feel like you have some inside joke with Gigi that we're not privy to."

"Oh, Gigi and I have shared many jokes, mostly at my expense. And I haven't forgotten. Now, if you'll excuse me, ladies, I have an entire pack to meet tonight."

I let out a deep breath as soon as he left, relieved he was gone. But the way he said he hadn't forgotten, it was chilling. He clearly wasn't someone I should have fucked with. Not knowing what he had planned completely terrified me.

"So, spill, Gigi! How do you know Tyce?" Jasmine asked brightly. She did seem much livelier than when I'd met her five months earlier.

"I don't. I just met him once. I don't know what he was going on about." I laughed nervously.

"Hey, Jasmine, can you come over here for a second?" Alpha Blake called his mate over. "Sorry to interrupt," he apologized to Paige and me.

"No problem!" Paige replied, immediately grabbing my shoulders after they were gone from our vicinity. She looked at me fiercely and whispered loudly, "Did you sleep with Alpha Tyce?"

"No!" I instantly responded.

"Don't lie to me. You smelled just like him this morning. It was him. Those were his slides you were wearing."

"It's not how it looks."

"What was all that stuff about chipmunks?"

I groaned.

"Well?" She looked at me eagerly.

"Okay, I may have said some stuff to him that wasn't very nice," I admitted. "But I didn't know he was an alpha! How was I supposed to know?"

"Oh, Goddess! What did you say to him?"

I groaned again. "Please, can we not talk about this right now?"

"Okay, but you better tell me later."

And that was when I prayed silently to Artemis that later would never come. I prayed that she'd just kill and burn me.

Chapter 6

Blake

I woke to the most amazing feeling. Sparks danced up and down the shaft of my cock as it had found itself in a warm, wet enclosure. Damn, it felt so good. My eyes shot open to, similarly, the most amazing sight—my mate, completely naked, bobbing her head up and down the length of it. A guttural groan escaped from the depths of my chest. I was in awe of what was happening. My sweet, shy luna was waking me by swallowing my cock like a champ. I didn't even want to question why she was doing something so out of character for her.

Then she moaned, and it vibrated against the skin of my rock-hard cock. I must have died and gone to heaven. She glanced up at me, her eyes locking with mine, a mischievous look on her face as she slowed her pace. "I've been waiting for you to wake up. I'm so horny," she moaned. "I want your cock so bad."

What! Now she was talking dirty to me? She was using the word *cock*?

"Where is Jasmine and what did you do to her?" I demanded, a huge smile on my face.

"Fuck me, Blake. Fuck me harder than you've ever fucked me."

Holy fuck! What?

I instantly grabbed her, pulled her onto my cock, and began thrusting into her from below, pounding into her extremely wet pussy. Holy fuck, she was wet.

"Harder, Blake, harder!" she cried out. "I'm so horny." She had to be possessed. That was the only explanation.

I picked her up and rolled to get her on her hands and knees so I could better pound into her. She gripped the headboard as I shoved my cock forcefully into her, and she screamed out.

"Oh, Goddess, Blake, yes, Blake."

Fucking Artemis, the way she was crying out my name had me ready to blow my load, but I didn't want it to end. Jasmine had never been so uninhibited before, and I was loving every second of it. "Is that hard enough for you, Mrs. Alpha?" I groaned out.

"Yes, Blake, keep doing that."

"Do you want more?"

"Yes!"

"How much more?"

"More!"

I suddenly had an idea. I reached for the bedside table, pulling out a toy I'd been wanting to use on Jasmine for the longest time. I smiled mischievously to myself, delighted with the fact that the opportunity had finally presented itself. I turned it on, the vibrating noise permeating the air.

"What is that?" she moaned out.

"Trying something new," I replied, placing the wand over the entrance to her ass, allowing it to vibrate outside of it. "You like that?" I asked in a gravelly voice, so fucking turned on by what I was doing.

"That feels so good," she cried out.

"Do you want it inside?" I asked, wondering how far I could take this.

"Yes!" she exclaimed.

If this was a dream, I never wanted to wake up. I very gently inched the vibrator inside her back door as I kept pounding her front one, careful so I wouldn't hurt her. And holy fuck, if her loud moans were any indication, she was loving it, completely embracing the DP. My shy, virginal mate had transformed into a sexpot right before my very eyes.

I angled her hips until I finally found her G-spot. One huge advantage of the mate bond, especially with a shy mate, was I could feel when I hit it as her emotions transferred over to me. I pounded against it as forcefully as I could, moving the vibrator in and out of her ass. Before long, her whole body was shaking under me as she screamed so loudly I wouldn't be surprised if they could hear her on the beta floor, or the main floor for that matter.

She let out one final loud moan, the headboard in a death grip, and I quickly pulled my cock out, coming all over her back. We'd gotten much laxer with protection since marking each other. And there'd definitely been slipups. But we hadn't proactively agreed to try for a baby yet, neither of us being ready, so I tried my best to pull out. Today I was surprised I had even managed to with how incredible what just happened was. I pulled the vibrator out of her ass, turned it off, and hopped out of the bed to grab a washcloth. I quickly wet it in the sink and wiped my come off her back before throwing it into the laundry hamper and crawling back into bed with her, pulling her close to my body.

"Damn, that was so fucking hot," I remarked.

"Mmm," she moaned, snuggling into my chest.

"What else can I get you to do now that this new nympho Jasmine has appeared?"

"What do you want to do?" she asked with lust in her eyes. Holy shit, she was possessed. A sex demon had possessed my mate.

"Jasmine!" I gasped. "Are you still in there somewhere? Where's my sweet, innocent mate?"

She giggled. I pecked at her lips, baffled but thrilled by her coming out of her shell like this. I wondered what had caused the sudden change. "I love you, Blake," she said.

"I love you too, Mrs. Alpha," I replied, feeling so much affection for her, my heart warmed and grateful for her presence in my life. "So, what's on the agenda today?"

"We have training all day today," she replied. I loved how she used the word *we*. She'd kicked me out of her training group last year, but she finally let me back in after we got married. There was nothing hotter than watching her train. I lived for every second of it. She may have looked sweet and innocent, but there was a true warrior inside her—she could kick ass. She had proven herself after she basically killed the alpha of our rival pack just months earlier. A true luna.

The day started out easily enough. We had a strategy and logistics session first, where we went over all of the latest updates, mostly from my beta, Luke, but also from me. While, as alpha, I commanded everyone, Luke played a bigger role in the strategy and logistics, which suited him. He had always been much more book smart than me. I mostly liked to train, fight, deal with the political stuff such as pack alliances, and, my personal favorite, torture.

Afterward, we had cleaning duty, which neither Jasmine nor I participated in. Instead, I had her join me for a quick run of the patrol stations. I thought it was important for her to do this with me, so everyone would come to understand that she was in charge now, just as much as I was. She still hadn't completely built her confidence up as luna, so I was trying my best to get her there. I understood—she hadn't trained her whole life for the position like I had, and she was still quite young at twenty-one—but I knew she'd get there eventually. Once we were done with that, we went back to the packhouse to eat lunch together, and then it was off to physical training.

The session started with a three-mile run in our human forms. Because the weather was getting nicer now, we'd switched to doing PT outdoors. Once we reconvened as a group on the field, the trainer had us doing different body weight exercises, starting with push-ups, moving to bear crawls, pistol squats, sit-ups, and crab walks.

We then switched to cardiovascular exercises, starting with jumping jacks. But something was off. I could feel whatever Jasmine was feeling whenever I was near her, now that we had marked each other, and I could sense that she was having trouble keeping up. That wasn't like her. She was one of the best female warriors we had. I looked over to her as we switched to burpees. She'd paled, and her breathing had grown shallow as she was forcing herself to keep up. I was about to stop her and tell her to rest when she fell backward, her body almost slamming to the ground. Luckily, I caught her just in time, her body falling limp into my arms.

"Is she okay?" Sam, one of the trainers, came over.

"I don't know," I replied, brushing the loose hairs that had escaped her ponytail back, staring at her unconscious face. "Let me take her to the clinic." Sam nodded as I picked her up and sprinted over to my car. I drove quickly, worried about her, wanting to get her to the clinic as soon as possible to find out what was wrong.

I ran in and immediately sprinted to the back, not bothering to check in up front. Hey, I was alpha and my mom was a doctor, so no one ever questioned me. I immediately ran to my mom's office, but she wasn't there. I quickly found an empty exam room and deposited Jasmine onto the bed, then ran to find someone else to help her.

I finally caught a nurse. "Have you seen my mom anywhere?"

"It's her day off, Alpha," she replied.

"Oh."

"Would you like me to find you Dr. Davis?"

"Yes, but I'll still call my mom." Okay, I was being a brat, but I trusted my mom more than anyone else. Not that the other doctor wasn't competent. I just knew my mom would do a thorough job, especially with my mate.

The nurse walked away briefly and then came back to take Jasmine's vitals. "Low blood pressure," she said.

"What does that mean?" I asked.

"That's probably why she fainted."

"Will she be okay?" I asked.

"She should be. But the doctor will know for sure."

I nodded, holding Jasmine's hand and waiting for the doctor to appear. She finally moved, her beautiful amber eyes popping open.

"Blake?" she rasped.

"How do you feel? Are you okay?" I asked, brushing her hair back again.

"Yeah, I'm fine. What happened?"

"You passed out during PT."

"Oh, Goddess, how embarrassing!"

I chuckled. "There's nothing to be embarrassed about. I just want to make sure you're okay. The nurse said your blood pressure's low."

Not long after, Dr. Davis came in directly followed by my mom, who was wearing her sweats, clearly having rushed over without bothering to change. "Blake, is everything okay?" She came in panicked, letting out quick, shallow breaths.

"I'll leave it in your expert hands, Dr. Luna." Dr. Davis smiled at her, exiting the room.

"Jasmine passed out during PT today. Can you look her over please, Mom?" I pulled her in for a hug, needing my mom's comfort.

She gave my back a couple pats and chuckled. "That's it? You made me come in on my day off just because of a little PT exhaustion?" My mom seemed to be in better spirits lately. It seemed she was finally starting to get past the loss of my father.

"Please, Mom," I begged. "I think there's something wrong. Jasmine's never passed out like that before."

"Okay, Blake." She smirked, her eyes crinkling in amusement. "Jasmine, do you want your mate here while I check you over? Because I can kick him out."

"It's okay, he can stay," Jasmine said, squeezing my hand. The ensuing sparks that traveled up my arms calmed me slightly.

"All right," my mom said, taking a seat at the computer and pulling up Jasmine's files. "Low blood pressure. Jasmine, when was the date of your last period?"

"My last period?" she asked.

"Just an estimate is fine." My mom kept her eyes trained on the computer screen, clicking around. Shit, when was her last period? It had been a while, hadn't it? I would know. We were going at it every single day.

She blinked a few times and said, "It's been a while."

My mom turned to look at both of us. "A while? Like how long?"

"Definitely at least a month."

"I see. Well, in that case, perhaps you should take a pregnancy test. Low blood pressure in the first trimester is very common."

"Pregnancy test?" Jasmine asked, and I could feel all her anxiety, especially as her grip on my hand tightened. It only made my own anxiety even worse, my stomach churning and limbs tingling. Our emotions were linking together, and I sensed that the escalation of emotions was causing Jasmine to go into a panic attack as her breathing shallowed and her skin paled. I quickly pulled her toward me, trying to calm her with our mate bond.

"Mom, do you mind stepping out for a second?" I asked, barely able to breathe out the words.

"Of course," she said, giving my shoulder a meaningful squeeze as she walked past me.

"We haven't been careful," Jasmine cried out as soon as the door was shut. "We were going to wait."

I couldn't speak. I knew I should be trying to reassure her, but this was my biggest weakness. I was retreating into darkness. I knew I should've been ecstatic, over the moon, celebrating that the woman I loved and I had created a life together, but I wasn't ready. My old wounds were still raw and healing, and now they were being viciously ripped open again.

"Blake, are you okay?" she asked, her voice quiet and scared, trying to pull me back. I wanted to come back. I tried to pull myself out of the black hole I was entering. I knew she could feel everything I was feeling, and my stomach knotted with anguish that I was burdening her with that. I should have been comforting her, but I couldn't. I couldn't.

"Blake," she said again, practically in a whisper, and soft fur pressed against my palms as it sprang from her arms. I finally somehow found the strength to force myself back to reality.

"Jasmine." I gripped her body to me, not sure if I was comforting her or myself. "It's okay, Jasmine. It will be okay."

"Will it, Blake?" Her eyes brimmed with tears. "Can you do this?"

"Yes. Yes, Jasmine. I can do this. We can both do this." I rubbed her back, forcing myself to be strong.

"You're terrified," she said, her breathing shallowing again. "I can feel it."

"But that doesn't mean I can't do it. I was just shocked, that's all. But it's going to be okay. We're both going to be okay." I forced myself to believe my words. I couldn't drag Jasmine into my darkness with me. "We're just going to take it one day at a time. And we don't even know for sure yet. You still need to take the test." She nodded as I stared into her eyes. "Just breathe, Jasmine."

She took deep breaths as I rubbed the fur on her arms, and it slowly retreated. I knew that the mate bond touch was helping her, which made me feel so gratified that I could do that for her at least. Panic attacks were her biggest weakness, and I always felt like a million bucks when I could get them to stop. I kissed her on her forehead, trailing my kisses down the side of her face, onto her ear. She moaned softly, and I could sense she was feeling better. "Are you okay to take the test now?" I asked.

"Yeah," she replied.

"Whatever the test says, it's going to be fine. We have each other. Okay?"

"Okay," she replied, laying her head against my chest.

"I'll go get my mom."

Chapter 7

Tyson

"Heya, Beta!" I plopped down on a chair in the office of the packhouse, crossing my ankle over my knee as Luke typed at his computer.

"Hi, Alpha. How's it going?" he replied, not taking his eyes off his screen.

"Not bad, not bad." I paused and then, after a beat, I continued, "So, I noticed you have civilians sparring with the warriors. What's that all about?"

Luke lifted his head to make eye contact. "Blake wants everyone to be ready just in case we ever have to fight a battle on our land. He figured that if civilians sparred with warriors, they'd get better training. We still try to pair everyone based on experience and ability."

"I see, I see."

"Any other questions?"

I tried to keep my tone and body language as casual as possible. "Any chance I could see the sparring schedules for the next couple weeks?"

"Sure. Any particular reason why?"

"Just want to look, if that's okay."

"Sure, I'll forward them over to you right now."

"Great, thanks," I replied. "So, is everyone required to spar?"

"Everyone from the age of eighteen to sixty for two hours, once every two weeks."

I waited a few moments and then asked my next question. "Oh, actually, I just thought of something random."

"Yeah?" Luke raised one of his eyebrows.

"There was a young lady warrior that seemed to have potential. I think she's one of Jasmine's friends. What's her name?"

"Paige?" Luke squinted at me, tilting his head.

"Yeah! Paige! That's her! What's her last name again?" I knew I was acting very suspicious, but I had gotten this far—might as well go the rest of the way.

Luke smirked, giving me a knowing look. "McDowell."

"Thanks, man!" I said, giving him my award-winning smile.

"Do you plan to do something with that information?" he asked as I was getting up from my chair.

"Nothing in particular."

"Okay." Luke chuckled to himself and went back to his laptop. Just as I was about to exit the office, he shouted out to me, "You know, you don't need to stalk her at sparring. She's here at the packhouse all the time."

"Oh, I wasn't going to do that. Those two things were completely unrelated," I replied. Well, okay, maybe he was on to my plan. But it wasn't Paige I was interested in. I rushed out of the office and up to my room where I opened my own laptop to look through all the sparring schedules. In the end, I found four McDowells, none of whose names were anywhere close to Gigi. Paige, Heidi, Emily, Shawn.

Goddess, what the fuck was wrong with me? I really was becoming a stalker! Why was I so obsessed over this bitch? I'd even considered hooking up with some other slutty girl who'd been all over me like white on rice since I got here, thinking it would get my mind off Gigi. She was cute too. But for some reason now, after I'd seen Gigi's fucking amazing body, no one else seemed appetizing. What the hell was wrong with me? You'd think I'd met my mate or something!

I was in the worst predicament possible. I both hated and wanted to fuck this bitch. So badly that no one else would do it for me until I finally satisfied this desperate need to have her. Even her twin wasn't appealing. Okay, if they offered to both fuck me at the same time, I wouldn't decline. But her twin just wasn't my type. No, Gigi had those amazing tits and those thick thighs that I couldn't help but imagine wrapped around my hips as I pounded into her. Fuck! I was getting hard all over again thinking about it.

Not able to help myself, I made my way back into the office. Luke looked up at me, smiling as if he'd known I'd be back.

"Hey, another random question for you, bro," I started.

"Yeah?" he asked, studying me.

"Does every single person between the ages of eighteen and sixty spar? Or are there ever exceptions?"

He leaned back in his chair, putting his hands behind his head. "There are a few people with medical exemptions," he replied.

"Really? Medical exemptions for werewolves?"

He shrugged. "What, you don't have any back at your pack? Usually, it's because they're pregnant or something. But there are other reasons."

"Like what?"

"I dunno. We don't get access to that information. It's personal."

"But you get access to that list, right?"

He smirked at me again, sitting up. "I have a feeling these questions aren't random at all."

"Just doing my job and checking out the pack. Don't want people taking advantage to get out of sparring, scamming the system, you know how it is. Gotta make sure my cousin's being taken care of."

He chuckled. "I'll email you the list. At least you don't bite my head off for asking questions."

"I'm guessing Blake does."

"Sometimes. Not always. He's gotten better."

I exited the office again, making my way back upstairs. I sat down at the small desk in the guest bedroom and accessed my email again. An email from Luke was already waiting for me as soon I sat down. I quickly scanned the short list as soon as I opened it. *McDowell, Ginger.*

So either she was pregnant or there was something else she was hiding. For some reason, I thought it had to be the latter rather than the former.

Chapter 8

Ginger

"It's so nice having you back!" Paige remarked. The weather was beautiful on Paige's day off from warrior duty, so she brought me along with her and Jasmine to ride the Newport to Beebe bike path, which was about an hour from the pack. They were both much fitter than me, but they stayed at a leisurely pace so I could keep up with them.

On our way back, we stopped at a market to buy sandwiches and snacks and then hiked down to Jay Branch Gorge. Everything was crowded that day due to the nice weather, and both Paige and Jasmine complained about there being too many humans around. I had noticed over the years that most werewolves didn't really like being around humans, almost having an allergic reaction to them.

"Yeah, you're funny!" Jasmine agreed with Paige.

"She's hilarious. You should see when someone pisses her off. Some of the insults she comes up with are crazy." Paige laughed. I was suddenly reminded of Tyce and everything I'd verbally vomited all over him. Luckily, I had avoided him since the service where Jasmine had introduced us the previous week.

"Like what?" Jasmine asked.

"Like one time, she told some guy that he looked like a goat and blob-fish had mated with each other. She's savage, this Gigi!" Paige slapped me on the back. "And what did you tell me you called Alpha Tyce?" She was laughing, thinking it was the funniest thing in the world.

"Oh my Goddess, what did you say to Tyce?" Jasmine looked at me intently.

I couldn't answer. Paige cut in and replied on my behalf. "She called him a chipmunk fucker!"

"What!" Jasmine exclaimed. "You called an alpha that? I'm surprised he didn't murder you! I know if someone called Blake that, they'd be lucky to be alive. Now all his chipmunk comments make sense. Why did you call him that?"

"I didn't know he was an alpha," I replied.

"But he must have done something to provoke you, right?" Jasmine asked.

"Yeah, why did you call him that?" Paige turned to face me. "You still haven't told me the whole story."

"It's not a big deal. Let's just pretend it never happened." I tried to wave them off. Paige had really been on my case lately, trying to get the whole story out of me. I normally would have told her, but I didn't want her to know about the witch shop I was visiting on a monthly basis. I was still trying to figure out how I was going to get down to Massachusetts again before the next full moon, especially alone, without someone in my family trying to tag along with me.

"So, what's it like being twins?" Jasmine asked, and I let out a sigh of relief at the topic change. "Do you guys tell each other everything?"

"We're best friends," Paige replied, smiling. I turned to face my sister, and an affection for her overcame me. As much resentment as I had toward Paige, I still loved her and felt closer to her than anyone else. She also got me better than most people.

"It must be so nice to have a twin—to have someone you're so close to." As Jasmine said this, she seemed to space out, lost in thought.

"It's annoying sometimes too, like when they won't mind their own business," I teased Paige.

"Or when they steal your stuff." Paige laughed.

"Do you guys have any sort of special connection, like feeling each other's pain or being able to mindlink in your human forms?"

Paige giggled. "No."

"Did you ever try to switch places when you were younger?"

"Actually we did," I replied, laughing, recalling how we used to pretend to be each other back when we looked a lot more alike, before I gained a bunch of weight.

"Remember when we used to take each other's tests in middle school?" Paige asked me.

I snickered, recalling fond memories from before everything bad happened. "Yeah, we never got caught either."

"Why the sudden interest in twins?" Paige asked, studying Jasmine.

"Oh, no reason. Just curious. I always wished I had a twin when I was growing up. Or just any sibling for that matter."

When we got back later that evening, Jasmine invited us over for dinner at the packhouse and to watch some TV series they'd been watching together after. Paige basically answered for me and took me along. I figured if Alpha Tyce was there when I got inside, I could just split. Fortunately, he was nowhere to be found when we entered.

"Jasmine, Paige! Are you joining us for dinner? I'll put out some extra plates," a very tall, blonde girl said as soon as we walked in, and then I remembered that she was the beta's mate. I felt so out of touch with what went on in the pack since I'd gone to boarding school for high school and now was going away for college. "And ooh, Paige, is that your twin?"

"Yep, this is Gigi." Paige pushed me forward. "Gigi, Lucy," she said unenthusiastically. I got the idea she wasn't a huge fan of hers.

"Hi, Gigi!" Lucy said cheerfully, the contrast between her and Paige's attitude clear. "Yay! This is great! I love when we have company!"

Before long, we were all seated at the dining room table, along with Alpha Blake, Beta Luke, and Lucy's one-year-old, Libby, in a high chair. Lucy came out carrying two bottles of wine. "It's not often we have so many people here for dinner! This calls for some wine!"

She leaned over Luke, pouring him a hearty glass. Then she moved over to Blake. "I'm good, thanks," he said.

"Aw, c'mon, Blake, loosen up!" she insisted.

"I'm good, Lucy," he said much more firmly.

"Geesh, okay, grumpy!" she said, moving on to Paige and me, giving us both generous pours. She was about to pour some in Jasmine's glass when she covered it with her hand. "Move your hand," Lucy demanded.

"No, I'm good, thanks," Jasmine replied.

"Have some fun for once, Jaz! The weather's good, everyone's in a good mood, except Blake, of course!"

"She said no!" Blake bellowed at her.

"Goddess, what's with you tonight, Blake? You could use a drink!" Lucy snapped at him.

"Lucy," Luke said in a warning tone.

"Fine, whatever." She rolled her eyes and poured herself a huge glass, sitting back down in her seat. The tension seemed to settle down after that, and we all fell into lively conversation, especially as Lucy got drunker and drunker. She was actually pretty entertaining; she kind of reminded me of those California girls you saw on TV. She was very bubbly and just said whatever came to mind, hanging all over Luke as her cheeks reddened from her fourth glass of wine.

Suddenly, some loud footsteps sounded as someone descended the stairs, and I instantly knew who it was. "Tyce!" Lucy got up, running toward him. "Come join us! We need a fun alpha at the table! Blake is such a buzzkill!"

His eyes scanned the table, immediately meeting mine, and a huge smirk appeared on his face. "I'd love to," he said.

Fuck!

"Yay! C'mon! Let me pour you a glass," she said, reaching for the open bottle.

"Looks like we have some company tonight," Tyce remarked. Alpha Blake suddenly had a knowing smile on his face. And did Beta Luke have one too? Oh shit. Had they all been talking about me?

"Hey, Alpha Tyce. Have you met Paige yet?" Beta Luke was smirking as he asked Tyce that question.

"Yep, Jasmine introduced us. And looks like her evil twin came today too."

"Who are you calling the evil twin?" I snapped at him. Paige squeezed my arm, clearly trying to get me to calm down, but he was already riling me up. It wasn't even like what he said was that bad. Normally, I would have taken it as just childish teasing. But there was something about him—maybe it was how infuriatingly good-looking and smug he was. He was just looking for someone to punch him and maim his perfect nose.

"I think it's pretty obvious, but maybe your twin got the brains." He snickered.

I stood up, ready to smash the wine bottle over his head. "You're a shit person! You take advantage of unconscious girls! I wouldn't expect more from a chipmunk fucker!"

"Gigi!" Paige gasped.

Oh shit. Why did I just say that? He was completely red now, a look of murder in his eyes.

"Did you take advantage of her?" Blake stood up. And I didn't know if it was possible, but he looked even eviler, his expression that of someone who had seen some real shit.

"No! I didn't fucking take advantage of her!" Tyce yelled at Blake. "Why the fuck would I take advantage of her? She's like a three, no, a two. I have much higher standards! I don't have to take advantage of someone to get fucked! Who the fuck do you think I am?"

I knew he said all that in anger, but something about it really pained me, slashed at my heart. I didn't normally take insults so personally, but this time I did, torn apart by the fact he'd called me a two and not fuckworthy.

"Gigi, apologize!" Paige hit me on my back. "She's sorry! She didn't mean it!"

"Yeah, you better fucking apologize to me! I'm a fucking alpha, and who the fuck are you?" Tyce spat at me. Then his expression changed to something very menacing. "You thankless cunt. I should have left you in the woods to die."

My throat ached with a scratchy sensation. I'd just acted like a huge bitch after he'd helped me. Why had I snapped at him like that?

"Tyce!" Jasmine gasped. "Don't say that!"

"She fucking started it," Tyce responded.

"Okay, what the fuck is going on, Tyce?" Blake asked sternly. "I'm not going to allow you to talk to my pack members that way if you're going to continue to stay here. You're on my land now."

"Whatever," Tyce said, getting up and pushing his chair into the table, then stomping away to the living room and exiting through the sliding glass door.

"Gigi, why did you say all that to him?" Paige scolded me. "He was just teasing you."

"Because he's a dick, and he needs someone to finally put him in his place," I responded even through my awareness that I had been in the wrong. Sometimes my stubbornness got the best of me. Even though I knew I should have backed down, something kept me from doing it. I blamed it on years of feeling weak without my wolf, a constant need to overcompensate.

Blake crossed his arms and narrowed his eyes at me. "Gigi, I recommend you apologize to him. I'm not saying what he said was right, but he's an alpha, and it was wrong for you to disrespect him like that."

I nodded, slumping my shoulders.

"And just so we're clear—did he take advantage of you or not?"

"I don't think so . . ." I replied, my voice trailing off.

"What does that mean?" Jasmine asked, a concerned look on her face. "Did he or didn't he?"

"I don't know. I passed out."

"I'll find out," Blake said firmly, no bullshit, settling into this seat.

"More wine?" Lucy came over with a bottle.

"Yes, please," I replied, putting out my glass.

"Maybe you should control your drinking." Paige elbowed me.

"She's fine. She needs to relax after all that," Lucy said as she poured, not going easy. Paige let out a deep breath, shaking her head. I knew she had a lot to say, and she was probably wishing she did have that twin-mindlinking ability right now. Not that it would do much good anyway. I couldn't mindlink with anyone, twin or not.

I definitely overdid it with the wine after that. It didn't help that I didn't have a wolf, and Lucy was pouring just as heavy for me as for everyone else, obviously not knowing I couldn't handle it. While everyone else seemed to be okay, I was slurring my words and wobbly on my feet as the females all moved to the living room, and Blake and Luke went off to do something else.

When I sensed that the booze had to come up, I went searching for the bathroom. I stumbled through a hallway, opening different doors until I finally found it. I shut it behind me, not even bothering to lock it before sinking to my knees in front of the toilet, once again using one of the packhouse toilets as a vomit disposal. I still wasn't feeling one hundred after ingesting those herbs, and now I felt even worse as I laid my cheek onto the cool toilet seat, not even caring how unsanitary that probably was.

The bathroom door suddenly swung open, and I lifted my head a little on impulse to Tyce staring down at me. He took a step back at first with his eyes wide, then switched to a squint, his stare cold and hard, and finally something else. "Hey, are you okay?" He squatted down next to me, speaking really gently, much gentler than expected.

"Yeah, just too much wine," I slurred.

"How much did you drink?" he asked, helping me up as I stumbled and fell against his hard chest. Damn, his muscles felt nice against my body.

"I'm sorry for what I said earlier." I lifted my head, searching for his eyes, suddenly desperate for him to forgive me.

"Let's get you home," he responded, not exactly forgiving me but at least not seeming like he was angry at me anymore. I pulled away from him, standing on my own. He was about to reach for the door to the bathroom when a mouse sprinted across the floor in front of us.

A loud scream rang through the room, and Tyce fell into a ball into the corner, shaking, tears spilling from his eyes. I couldn't help but burst out laughing at the sight. This big, huge, muscular alpha was terrified of a little mouse?

"Shut up!" he snapped, not looking happy about the situation at all.

"Libby?" Luke yelled, throwing open the door, practically hitting Tyce. "Oh, shit, sorry." He looked at me while Tyce stayed hidden behind the door. "I thought that was Libby." He shook his head and then asked, "Was that you? Are you okay?"

"I'm okay," I mumbled. He nodded and closed the door, and I laughed some more.

"It's not funny, okay?" Tyce grumbled, standing up. But I couldn't stop the laughter. How could a big, huge alpha be afraid of a teeny tiny mouse?

"Are you crying?" I asked through my laughter.

"No, I got something in my eye." He rubbed the tears away.

Finally, I composed myself. And I'm sure I was still slurring, but I managed to say, "C'mon, you have to admit it's just a little funny."

He shook his head and looked down at the ground, crossing his arms with his shoulders slumped. Suddenly I felt a little bad, realizing he was truly upset, and something endeared me to him.

"Hey, sorry for laughing," I said, reaching out to touch his arm.

"Can you please not tell anyone that just happened?" he asked, his eyes pleading.

"Okay, I promise I won't."

"Thanks. You know, I didn't tell anyone about what happened that night either. You said you didn't want your mom to know, and I didn't rat you out." He gave me a small smile.

"Thanks, I appreciate it," I replied, softening toward him. Something inside me stirred, and my pulse quickened.

He came closer to me, only centimeters away, his body heat warming me and his eyes fierce. Something about it felt so intimate and sexual. I knew at that moment, if he touched me, I'd give in to him. As much as I thought he was a huge asshole, I couldn't help but feel an intense attraction to him, especially in that moment we were sharing. "You should get home," he said in a gravelly voice that suggested he wanted me to do exactly the opposite of that, the sound of his baritone voice shooting straight to the apex of my inner thighs, my panties suddenly wet with arousal.

"Yeah," I replied, opening the door and stumbling out, knowing that was the right thing to do. But something inside, scratching at my inner organs, told me it was also the wrong thing to do.

Chapter 9

Tyson

Goddess, what the actual fuck? How could I still want to fuck her so badly after everything that had gone down? She was so infuriating. How did she affect me so much? Why couldn't I stop seething about everything, and at the same time, want to accept her apology—the one she delivered so sweetly and vulnerably? That moment . . . she just seemed so pure, and like she was more than just some bitch hell-bent on terrorizing me with her insults.

I was in the kitchen picking at leftovers when Blake walked in. "'Sup," I greeted him.

"Look, man, I don't care if you hook up with random girls. That's your business. But I draw the line at taking advantage of my pack members. Especially if they're passed out and can't consent."

"And what, you think I'm doing that?" I replied, trying to keep my voice even, my skin and blood heating all over again at the accusation as my hands subconsciously clenched into fists.

"I wouldn't be doing my job if I didn't inquire after what was said at the table tonight. I asked Gigi, and she said she doesn't know what happened. So now I'm asking you. And you better fucking tell me the truth." His blue eyes appeared devilish and ominous, menacing. I wondered how he could do that. It was as if he had a demon living inside him.

"Look, bro, like I said at the table and I will say again, I don't take advantage of women. I have a sister for Artemis's sake! Our pack rules are the same as yours. Rape is a death sentence. What kind of hypocrite would I be if I didn't follow my own fucking rules?"

"Some alphas think they're above the law."

"Well, if you think I'm that alpha, you're wrong. I don't need to take advantage of some bitch to get my dick wet. I do things the right way."

"Fine, I'll believe you." Blake shook his head, his eyes now normal. "But I have to ask, why does she think she might have been taken advantage of? And what was she doing in your bed? I mean, the situation doesn't look good."

"She passed out in the woods, and I didn't know where else to take her, so I put her in my bed and slept on the couch in the alpha living room."

"Why'd she pass out?"

"I don't know. Maybe she'd been drinking. She doesn't seem like she can handle her liquor."

Blake chuckled softly. "Yeah, that's true. I drove her and her sister home. She was pretty sloppy."

"So, we cool now?" I looked to Blake for confirmation.

"We're cool for now," Blake replied and walked out of the kitchen.

While it was true she couldn't handle her liquor, I had a feeling that wasn't the reason she'd passed out in the woods. I would have smelled it if it was. She reeked of alcohol tonight, even with all that perfume she had on. There was definitely a secret she was hiding, and I was going to get to the bottom of it.

The next day, my younger brother, Trav, surprised me by calling. He was a couple years younger, and we got along but weren't exactly the type to have phone conversations—usually just a quick text here or there. Being the older brother, I had trained my whole life to become alpha of the pack while he had been pushed in the direction of managing the pack business.

"Hey," I answered the call while grabbing some lunch from the stove top that Connie, the packhouse cook, had left for us.

"Hey, Tyce," he replied.

"What's going on? All good?"

"Actually, I'm concerned."

"Concerned? About what? Is Grandpa acting crazy again? I told you before that's how he is—he's not becoming senile." I chuckled. I loved ripping on my grandpa, especially after having to take his shit my whole life.

"No, about JSP."

"What about JSP?" I asked, not interested in the conversation already. I liked to be involved in our pack business as little as possible. To be quite honest, I found all the board meetings about financials, net profit, investments, R & D, and assets super tedious and boring. The only part of an asset I cared about was the first three letters. I was glad to have a brother to handle it for me, so I could focus on more interesting things like training, leading, and, well, ass.

"Now that I've been added as a board member, I've been trying to gather my bearings. Just to get a better understanding of everything, I've been talking to the financial department and having them walk me through the monthly P & Ls, and there are some things that don't seem to be making sense."

This conversation was already boring me. He had lost me at board member. But, to be polite, I replied, "Like what?"

"Well, you know how Spruce Winter Pack has been handling all the green energy R & D?"

"Yeah," I replied, even though I had no idea that the neighboring pack that co-owned our business handled the research and development.

"Well, I think there hasn't been enough oversight of that on our pack's end. I think we've been too trusting. I have a bad feeling something sketchy's going on."

"Really, like what?" I asked, suddenly a little intrigued.

"I don't want to make any accusations yet. But I'm going to look into it more. Just, don't you think it's strange that they've been working on this green energy R & D project for five years now, and they haven't come back to the table with any proposals or plans for investing in any type of renewable energy yet?"

"I don't know," I replied honestly.

"I don't think Dad or Grandpa know either. They've always been a lot more into the warrior and politics stuff, so I don't think they've ever asked any questions. Especially since the money keeps coming in. But we're investing almost half our net profit into this green energy research, so I'm planning to start asking questions."

"Okay, good idea," I replied sincerely.

"So, how's it over on the East Coast?"

"Good, nice to be away from the family," I replied.

He chuckled. "Yeah, you've left me to take all their heat now. Although, thank Goddess, they hate your taste in women. They've been kept entertained by making fat jokes lately. They love dogging on Amber." Amber was my latest FWB. That actually lasted several months. Let's just say she had a gift with her mouth, and my cock had a hard time staying away. But yeah, she was definitely not my family's type. Totally my type though. What could I say? I liked 'em thick. And if they could also deep throat? Well, you got the picture.

"Okay, well, thanks for the call and update," I said, not sure what else there really was to say.

"No prob. I'll keep you posted as I dig into this more. Also, Mom said she'll be overnighting you some of her brownies. So be on the lookout. Talk to you later, bye."

"Thanks, bye." I smiled to myself as we hung up the call. I loved my mom's brownies. To be honest, my mom wasn't very mom-like except when it came to baking. It's like she took all the warmth from her cold heart and put it into her baked goods.

Just then, Blake walked into the kitchen, clearly ready for his own lunch. "Hey, have you seen my Adidas slides anywhere?" I asked him. "Did you think they were yours by accident or something?"

He suddenly broke out into a rare large smile. "I caught your girl wearing them when she was sneaking out of the house last week."

Even though I didn't have a girl, I knew exactly who Blake was talking about. And, sure, I could probably just buy another pair, but where would the fun be in that?

Chapter 10

Ginger

I'd managed to avoid Tyce for almost a whole week. But now it was Sunday, and I knew he'd be at the service that night. My anxiety was in overdrive. Not only was I stressing about seeing Tyce again after everything that had gone down almost a week ago, but I still hadn't worked out exactly how I was going to get to Salem again, and the next full moon was only two weeks away.

Our family only had one car, so asking to borrow it for an entire day was not easy. Everyone would want to know where I was going and what I was doing with it. It was a four-hour drive to get there, so it wasn't really something I could slip out for an hour or two to do. I had to think of a creative excuse.

When we finally arrived at temple that evening, I spotted him right away. It was hard not to—he was so tall and had a commanding presence. It made sense, considering he was an alpha, and I had a hard time forcing myself not to stare at him as he conversed with people at the front, near where the alpha and beta families always sat.

Paige broke off into conversation with my dad, Heidi, and her mate while my mom and I went to go take our normal seats. "What a handsome young man." My mom elbowed me, looking in Tyce's direction.

Goddess, my mom could be so juvenile sometimes! She was in her forties and yet shamelessly pointed out which guys my age she found attractive!

"You said that before, Mom!" I responded.

"Have you looked into his eyes yet? Maybe he's your mate." She gave me a devious smile. "Wouldn't make a bad mate, right?"

"I'm not mated to him!" I replied in horror. Goddess, wouldn't that be a disaster? "Besides, in the very unlikely event that I was, I would have no way to know." As I said it out loud, I could feel tears welling up in my eyes at one of my worst worries. I could have walked by my mate dozens of times already, and how would we ever know we were supposed to be together?

"You don't know that, baby." My mom wrapped her arms around me. "You have to have faith in the Moon Goddess, that she'll find a way to bring you to your mate. Those who believe, receive."

I just nodded in acknowledgment. My mom was always so optimistic, especially when it came to her faith. But I knew that life wasn't always fair—I was living proof of that.

Prior to that one bad decision, I had always been good. I'd always worked hard in school and training. I attended temple service every week with my family. For once in my life, I'd wanted to have fun and let loose. And, well, now I had no more wolf. No, it didn't seem fair at all. Plenty of people rebelled their whole lives and were walking around with a wolf *and* a mate!

When our priest, Bernard, made his way to the podium, everyone started taking their seats. As Tyce turned to do the same, his eyes locked with mine for a moment, bringing dread to the pit of my stomach. And was he *smirking*? Goddess, why had I said all that stuff to an alpha *again*? Why couldn't I just keep my big mouth shut?

After the service, I told my parents I wanted to get some fresh air and would wait for them outside, desperate to avoid our pack's alpha visitor. I walked out into the back garden and paced the area, enjoying the view of all the flowers in full bloom now. I thought that I should come here more often, maybe to meditate or journal. They did keep a really nice garden.

"Found you!" a familiar voice sounded behind me, and I jumped in shock, my heart pounding in my chest.

I instantly turned to come face-to-chest with Tyce. And, damn, the way his shirt lay against his chest, I could tell it had to be nice. I lifted my head to make eye contact with him and demanded, "How did you find me?"

He chuckled and said, "It's not exactly difficult. I just followed your scent."

"Oh," I replied, recalling werewolves could do that. I always forgot all the things they could do that I couldn't.

"Anyway, you little thief, you have something of mine, and I want it back."

"Thief!?" I glared at him. "Why would I want to take anything of *yours*?"

"Really?" He smirked. "So you wouldn't happen to have taken my Adidas slides?"

My face burned. "Oh, shit. I forgot about that." I'd thrown them in the back of my closet after Heidi had called me out and promptly pushed them from my mind.

"Do you know how hard it is to find shoes in my size? My not-chipmunk size, by the way." He laughed heartily. At least he was finding my remarks funny rather than insulting now. That was a relief. When I didn't respond, he continued, "So give them back."

And then I suddenly came up with probably one of the craziest ideas I'd ever come up with. "Fine, I'll give them back, but only if you do something for me in return."

"That seems like a big ask considering you stole my shoes and have now insulted me more than once. But okay, what do you want in return?" He crossed his arms looking at me curiously.

"You told the witch in the fortune-telling shop you'd be going back to Salem, right?"

"Right."

"I want you to take me with you when you go."

"That's a huge fucking favor, Gigi," he started. And I couldn't lie, I kind of liked the way my name sounded when he said it. "You're asking me to give you an eight-hour, round-trip ride in exchange for giving me back my slides that you *stole*."

"I didn't steal them! I just borrowed them! And you're going to Salem anyway, so you wouldn't be going out of your way!"

"Yes, but I'd have to spend over eight hours with you. And if you were nice, it might not be so bad. But you're a huge pain in the ass."

I slumped my shoulders and bit my tongue. I already had some rebukes that were not so nice to shoot back, but I needed him more than he needed me. "Please, Alpha Tyce," I said, trying to be nice and polite to show him I could behave. "I really need to go to Salem, and I don't know how else to get there from here."

"Why?"

"It's personal."

"You're asking me for a ridiculously long ride. The least you could do is tell me why."

I almost considered telling him for a second, but my pride got in the way. I still hated telling people my secret. I had been bullied in middle school because of it and was still affected by it to this day. It felt even worse to admit it to Tyce, especially after everything that had gone on between us.

"It's okay," I said, surrendering. "I'll find another way to get there. And I'll bring your slides to the packhouse tomorrow."

I turned to go when he touched my shoulder, stopping me. "It's okay. You don't have to tell me. I'll give you the ride."

I turned to look at him, my breath catching in surprise. "Really?" I brightened.

"Yeah, but you can't ask me why I'm going either. Deal?"

"Deal." I couldn't help but beam at him for agreeing to help me.

"I'll be going on Friday. That's my day off."

"That's perfect." I bowed my head slightly. "I'll meet you at the pack-house first thing in the morning. Thank you, Alpha."

"So you are capable of being respectful." He smirked.

"Don't push your luck," I replied and walked away.

Chapter 11

Jasmine

"I want you to work with a personal trainer moving forward," Blake said to me one morning as we were getting ready for the day.

"Why? Your mom said most exercise is fine as long as I just modify a few things and take a break from sparring."

He came up behind me and wrapped his arms around me, pulling me toward his warm, muscular torso, his chest rising and falling with each breath against me. "Jasmine, please, do this for me. I know what my mom said, but it's really hard for me. I can't stand the idea of anything happening to you or our pups."

"Nothing will happen to me," I replied. "My wolf will just heal me."

"But the pups don't have theirs yet."

I turned to make eye contact and instantly understood how vulnerable he was, his piercing blue eyes emotional as he peered into mine. As strong as he seemed, I'd come to learn that he constantly had a dark cloud hanging over him, that he was paralyzed on the inside from his trauma. "Okay," I conceded, letting out a sigh as I placed my head against his chest. He gently kissed the top of my head, and I could sense I'd unburdened him with that simple gesture.

I hated the idea of, once again, getting special treatment that the other female warriors wouldn't. I knew I was the luna now, but even Blake still trained with everyone else to build camaraderie. That was something I'd never quite managed to do with my fellow female warriors, with the exception of Paige. It didn't bother me much anymore, but I still wanted to be more like Blake, who had a natural chemistry with just about everyone. I knew if I ever went to battle that would be important.

"Thank you," he whispered and then went into the bathroom, continuing to get ready for the day.

I threw off my bathrobe and looked in the full-length mirror. My stomach was still flat, and the whole thing still felt surreal. Besides passing out during PT, I didn't have many pregnancy symptoms, and it was hard to believe that I was actually carrying Blake's babies.

"You're fucking sexy as hell," Blake said as he passed by me.

"It just doesn't feel real," I said. "I don't even feel any different."

"You're definitely acting different." He gave me a mischievous smile, coming close to me and nibbling on my ear.

"How so?" I practically moaned. Blake knew that was my weak spot.

"It's like you've been possessed by a sex demon. You're such a nympho lately. Can't lie, I'm hoping that's a permanent side effect." He chuckled, kissing me down my neck. "What are your plans today? Do we have time for another round?"

"Just hanging out with Tyler." My legs were weak as my body molded into his, giving in to him.

"You can be late for that. Tyler is one person who will definitely understand." Blake chuckled, picking me up in his strong arms.

"So, I have news," I said to Tyler. It was Memorial Day, so we'd made plans to hang out now that we finally had a day off together, and I'd gone over to Tyler's house for the afternoon.

"I love news!" Tyler sat down next to me on the couch, putting out some chips and salsa on the coffee table for us to nibble on. "Let me guess before you tell me!"

"Okay . . ." I replied, my voice trailing off.

"Okay, first guess." He chuckled to himself. "Dale Dog picked up his old weed habit again and got caught by your mom rolling jays."

"What!" I laughed. "Tyler, that did not happen!"

"Okay, but it would be hysterical. You can't tell me you don't sometimes think about what it was like when your mom found out she was mated to a stoner. You know Drew was probably hotboxing his dorm room in college. And your mom was, well, you know, your mom." He laughed. "So prim and proper, everything perfect all the time. I can even imagine how she probably dressed—with perfectly ironed button-up shirts and cashmere sweaters."

I laughed again at the image. "I didn't even know he did that until recently! I still can't imagine it." I shook my head. "You don't know what he was like when I was growing up. He honestly wasn't any better than my mom."

He laughed some more and said, "Okay, second guess." He had a mischievous glint in his eyes. "Lucy decided she needed to spice things up in the bedroom with Luke, so she asked Alpha Tyce to be a third, and Luke finally took a stand against her and flipped shit."

I laughed again, falling over on the couch. "Where do you come up with this stuff, Tyler?"

"Okay, that one was unrealistic. That guy has no backbone when it comes to Lucy." Tyler snickered. "How much do you want to bet that Lucy goes all dominatrix on him in the bedroom?"

"To be honest, I know far too much about their sex life." I shook my head. "Before the whole mate thing happened, Lucy used to tell me every. Single. Detail."

"Somehow that doesn't surprise me." We each grabbed some chips, then Tyler continued, "Okay, third and final guess." He swallowed a few chips. "Blake has finally been converted to enjoying cat videos and now wants to adopt a cat."

I giggled. "No, but I do think he secretly likes them. I caught him watching one of the ones you sent over recently and smiling."

"Yes!" Tyler pumped his fist. "I knew I'd convert Blake to cat videos eventually!"

I giggled some more, and we ate some more chips.

Then Tyler turned to me and said, "So, anyway, you had news."

"Yes." I put my hands on my knees. After a beat, I said, "We're not telling anyone yet, but since you're my brother, I wanted to tell you."

"Nice! I get the family privilege."

"Plus, I trust you and I need to tell someone before I burst."

"Okay, spit it out. I'm at the edge of my seat now!"

"I'm pregnant."

"Oh, shit!" He widened his eyes. "So much for not being ready and waiting a few years." He chuckled, pushing my shoulder.

"Yeah, well, things happen I guess." I shrugged.

"Can't say I'm surprised. If Blake were my mate, I'd be pregnant too by now." He laughed some more. "Damn, well, congrats, Jaz. That's great news. Do you know if it's a boy or girl yet? Is that the next alpha heir in there?" He nodded toward my stomach.

"Actually, it's twins. But we don't know if they're boys or girls yet."

"Twins?" Tyler raised his eyebrows at me.

"Yeah, I know, I was surprised too. Blake almost passed out."

"Ha, of course he did." Tyler chuckled. "Well, I'm ready! Jack and I have been practicing with Kyle and Emma's pups. We're going to be the best uncles ever to the alpha heirs once they arrive." I smiled brightly in response, and he pulled me in for a hug. "Congrats, Jasmine." When he pulled away, he asked, "So am I the first person to know for reals?"

"Yeah."

"What about your parents?"

"I know I should tell them, but I just feel so weird about it. I mean, they're going to know . . ."

"Seriously, Jasmine? You think your parents don't already know you have sex? Let me remind you, you are marked."

"Yeah, I feel weird about that too."

He shook his head. "Growing up here in this pack has messed you up big-time. This place is so backward."

"Hey! We're making changes!"

"I know, and many people appreciate it." He gave me a small smile, squeezing my shoulder. "Oh, speaking of pups, isn't Talia due any day now?"

"She's due June 15th. But Blake says alpha pups usually come early, so they're on baby watch now. He cleared his schedule just in case. He wants to make sure we're there for the baby's first full moon ceremony. And there's a chance it could be during the next one."

"Oh, wow. Time really flew. I feel like it was just yesterday that she was living in the packhouse. Did you ever find out if it's a boy or girl?"

I laughed. "No, Alpha Alex and Talia have a bet going over whether it's a boy or girl, so they decided not to find the gender out ahead of time. I guess it's gotten intense, and Alpha Alex won't even entertain girl name options."

Tyler snickered. "I can't decide if it'll be worse for an alpha to lose that bet or for a woman who just gave birth to. I'm thinking a doctor and some nurses could end up as casualties with that one."

I laughed at the thought and sat back on the couch, rubbing my belly. I enjoyed hanging out with Tyler. Blake was just so stressed about the pregnancy. I understood why, and I knew that underneath all the tension he was actually really happy about it. But it was nice to take a break and be around someone who could make me laugh and lighten the mood. I couldn't lie and say it wasn't mentally draining to be near Blake and feel all of his dark emotions when I was. I knew it wasn't his fault, and I felt a lot of empathy as he had to live with those feelings day in and day out and never got a break. I just wished so much there was a way I could help him move forward from his past.

Chapter 12

Ginger

I set my alarm for early on Friday. I didn't want there to even be a slight chance I'd miss my ride. I really had to swallow my pride for this one, and I knew I'd have to be on my best behavior. Who knew how many other rides I'd need to grovel for in the future. Although, I really hoped this would be my last one. With the sun shining, and the warm air flowing in through the window screen, I had a good feeling about this time.

I threw on a cute spring dress and stood in front of my full-length mirror. Damn, I'd forgotten how low-cut this dress was. I was sporting more cleavage than I intended. But when you were busty like me, it was pretty unavoidable. I pulled the neckline up a bit, but it didn't really do much. Oh well. It wasn't like Tyce would be interested or looking anyway. He'd made it pretty fucking clear I was a two on his rating scale. As much as I hated to admit it, his dig still stung.

After I was satisfied with my appearance, I made my way downstairs to make myself some breakfast, only to find that Paige was also up earlier than usual. While Paige was usually in a good mood, much like my mom, she seemed especially perky that morning. She was dancing around humming while putting together, what looked like, a very intricate breakfast.

"Oh, hello, Gigi!" she sang out as I made my way into the kitchen. "I'm making breakfast for the whole family today, so sit back and relax!"

"What's the occasion?" I raised an eyebrow at her.

"It's such a beautiful day! We should celebrate!"

"I see." I felt suspicious for some reason. "Did you want any help?" I asked, thinking I shouldn't just sit around while my sister put together breakfast for everyone by herself.

"No, no! I have it handled." She seemed a bit lost in her own world as she bounced from fridge to counter to stove. Then, without warning, she spun around to look me up and down and said, "Wow, you look great! That dress looks really good on you. But damn, your boobs are hanging out big-time. You should probably cover them up if you want Dad to let you out of the house like that."

I rolled my eyes and went back upstairs to throw a cropped cardigan on and buttoned it up all the way. The buttons were clearly straining against my G cups, but that was just a day in the life.

Paige eventually corralled us all to the table, and we took our regular seats, minus Heidi, of course, who no longer lived with us.

"Wow, look at this spread! It looks great!" my mom exclaimed while her eyes traveled over the stack of fluffy pancakes, crispy bacon, perfectly scrambled eggs, fresh fruit, and golden-brown toast that Paige had laid out for us.

"Great job, Princess. This all looks so delicious. Now I'll have the energy I need for PT this morning." My dad beamed at Paige.

"Yeah, it looks great!" I agreed.

"Let's say a quick prayer to Artemis, so we can dig in." My mom led us all in the prayer, and then we all began grabbing food for our plates and passing everything around.

Once we were all comfortably eating, Paige cleared her throat and said, "So, I have news, everyone!" We all looked up at her in curiosity. After a beat, she announced, "I've met my mate!"

"Oh my Goddess!" my mom cried out, tears falling from her eyes as she encompassed Paige in a huge hug.

"Wow, wonderful news, Princess!" My dad got up to do the same. "Who's the lucky man?"

I was frozen in shock. I knew I should be happy for my twin. I knew I should have been congratulating her right then, but instead, I felt nauseous, the whole room spinning around me, lead in my stomach. The food on my plate no longer looked appetizing.

"I just started a new rotation for patrol duty, and my mate is assigned to the same station as me this month."

"What's his name? Maybe I know him." My dad was beaming.

"Dylan Reynolds."

"I do know him! Good man. Hardworking. I've had him in my patrol station several times. What great news!"

"Absolutely the best news." My mom was dabbing at her eye with a napkin. "We better start planning the next wedding. Oh, I have to call Heidi. She's going to be so happy, and I know she's going to be so excited to help plan."

"Actually, I think we're going to wait for a little while before we get married," Paige said. "I mean, I'm only nineteen."

My parents gave each other looks. Then my mom turned to Paige and said, "I'm not sure that's a good idea. You're going to wait to mark each other until after the wedding of course?"

"Of course, Mom!" Paige's whole body took on a crimson hue.

"Trust me, honey. We should plan the wedding for sooner rather than later. I'll get in touch with Bernard today."

"Two down, one more to go," my dad said, smiling and taking a seat. While what he said was meant to be lighthearted, it stung. I was the third and final sister who didn't have a mate, and never would. I put my fork down and just stared at my plate, not able to eat anymore.

"Don't worry, Gigi, you'll find your mate soon too!" Paige said.

"Of course she'll find her mate. Artemis will take care of her," my mom agreed, nodding along.

"Don't be sad, Peachy." My dad squeezed my arm. "There's someone out there for you."

"How do all of you know?" I lashed out. "You all say that, but you don't actually know! It's easy for you to say that! You all have mates!" I stood up and, not even bothering to push my chair in, stomped out of the house, grabbing my purse on the way.

Although we lived pretty far from the packhouse, I was in such a foul mood I knew I needed the walk. After a few steps, I remembered I owed Tyce his sandals but didn't want to go back. I'd grab them for him when he dropped me back at home that evening. Done and done.

When I got there, Lucy let me in. "Hey, Gigi! So nice to see you!" She wrapped her arms around me.

"Hi, Lucy," I responded, returning the hug.

"Hey, if you're not busy in a couple weeks, there's going to be a really good DJ coming to the casino club. DJ Sandstorm, have you heard of him?"

I shook my head.

"Well, I ordered a table, and everything's comped since the pack owns the casino. Jasmine and Paige are pretty boring and don't want anything to do with clubbing. But you seemed so fun last time you were here! Come!"

"Sure," I replied.

"Yesss! What's your number? I'll text you when it gets closer so we can make plans."

I gave her my number and then sat down at the dining room table to wait for Tyce while Lucy ran upstairs to get him for me.

As much as I hated myself for this, my breath caught as he descended the stairs. He had a loose-fitting, thin T-shirt on that showed off every protruding muscle on his upper body as he moved. When he pushed his hand through his messy, yet in a sexy way, hair, I could have sworn something stirred inside me.

"Hey," he said in his deep and irritatingly sensual voice as his eyes locked with mine.

"Hey," I replied, practically hypnotized. Goddess, what the hell was wrong with me? Why was I always attracted to the douchey guys?

"Ready to go?"

"Yeah," I replied, standing up and grabbing my purse from the chair next to me. I followed him outside to a Jeep Cherokee and got in, putting my seatbelt on.

As soon as we were settled in our seats, he turned his head toward me and, as if I'd asked, said, "My ride back home is much nicer."

"I feel like you're dying to tell me what it is." I couldn't help but smile at how eager he was to show off.

"G Wagen."

I let out a hearty laugh. "Are you serious? Somehow I'm not surprised you drive one of the douchiest of douchey cars!" As soon as I said it, I covered my mouth, realizing that the day was already off to a bad start. I winced and said, "Sorry, sorry, ignore that comment."

"You just can't keep your big mouth shut, can you?" He looked at me with amusement. "Didn't your mom ever teach you that if you have nothing nice to say then don't say anything at all?"

"Bad habit," I replied. "I promise I'll be good the rest of the way."

"I don't believe you, but it's going to take more effort to kick you out of my car than I feel like putting in right now, so let's just go." He backed out of the packhouse driveway and pulled onto the main road.

"Why, because I'm fat?" I asked.

"What?" He glanced at me for a split second, confusion on his face.

I blushed, embarrassed by my assumption, and said, "The day you met me, you called me chubby. I figured you were making a fat joke."

He smirked to himself and shook his head as if he was laughing at some inside joke. After a beat, he said, "I don't make fat jokes. At least not normally. You just really pissed me off that day. I was already having a bad day, and then you came at me full blast. Sorry about that." After a pause, he continued, "You actually have a really nice body, if I'm being honest. It's too bad your personality doesn't match."

I turned and stared at him, completely taken aback. He thought I had a nice body? Alpha Tyce, the most jacked and, okay, probably best-looking guy I'd ever met, thought I had a nice body? After I pulled my jaw off the floor, I said, "I don't normally make small-dick jokes. Or rape jokes. I actually find them to be in bad taste. So, sorry about that too."

He chuckled. "Yet, for some reason, you dusted them off just for me."

"Hey, you called me a man-hating bitch!"

"Well, the fact you hate men explains why you're such a bitch to me."

"Because there's not a more logical explanation?" I replied sarcastically, shaking my head. "Because if I liked men, I'd clearly be all over you instead."

"Exactly." He smiled widely.

"Well, I do like men. And I'm not all over you. Maybe not every straight female is attracted to you. Did you ever think of that?"

"If you say so," he replied, an amused smile on his face. "So, where are my slides? We had a deal."

"Yeah. About that."

"Don't tell me you didn't even hold up your end of the bargain!"

"Relax!" I exclaimed. "I had a rough morning and forgot them. I'll give them to you when you drop me off later. What, were you planning to wear them in Salem today or something?"

"Okay, just making sure. Like I said, it's not easy finding shoes to fit my very, very large alpha feet." He chuckled. He was clearly in a much better mood today than he was the first day I met him.

We settled into our seats and soon found ourselves relaxed, listening to music at full blast. About halfway to our destination, I turned the music down a little. "So, Tyce, is that your real name? Or is it short for something?"

"Tyson," he replied.

"Tyson?!" I laughed hysterically.

"What could possibly be so funny about the name Tyson?" He furrowed his brows and gave me a quick glance.

"It's so fitting! Because you're a chicken!"

"What!"

"You were so scared of a little mouse! Baw ba-baw ba-baw!" I flapped my arms like wings, falling into laughter again. I glanced over at him, and he didn't look amused at all. He had his hands gripped so tightly on the steering wheel that his knuckles were turning white. "I'm just teasing." I punched his upper arm, so he'd know I didn't mean to be a jerk about it.

"You didn't tell anyone about that did you?" he asked, and he seemed very vulnerable suddenly.

"No, I wouldn't do that. I can keep a secret," I said sincerely.

"Okay, thanks. I appreciate it," he replied, letting out a deep breath and relaxing his shoulders.

"What's the deal anyway? Why are you so scared of mice?"

"Can we not talk about it?" he asked and then turned the music back up. After a beat, he said loudly, over the music, "Besides, my name is not like the chicken brand. It's like the boxer."

"Sure, okay." I snickered and squeezed his upper arm, so he'd know I was just teasing. Damn, his muscles were huge. I didn't think I'd ever been with anyone with such impressive upper arms. A shiver traveled up my legs to the apex of my inner thighs, and my stomach quivered. I rubbed my thighs together from how turned on I suddenly was.

He started sniffing, and *shit*, could he tell? Could werewolves smell arousal? I glanced over at him, and his ears were red, but he didn't say anything. Okay, relax, there was no way werewolves could smell arousal. Even if we were in close quarters in a small space. And my panties were soaked. Shit. I'd have to ask Paige later to confirm. She might not even know. She tended to be naive about a lot of things.

I forced myself to stop thinking about it and relax in my seat. We were both silent, mutually agreeing not to talk about it, thank Goddess!

Chapter 13

Ginger

The day was uncharacteristically hot for so early in June. I was relieved once we made it inside the air-conditioned fortune-telling shop. Helena greeted us, passing her hand through her dark curls—well, greeted Tyce. I may as well have been invisible.

"Oh, hello there. You're back!" She smiled widely at him as she came around from behind the register.

"Hey," he replied, giving her a flashy smile. Although it absolutely should not have bothered me, it did. No, I was clearly just annoyed that she didn't even notice my existence even though I was a regular customer—that was all. It 100 percent did not bother me that she was looking Tyce up and down and he was giving her a much bigger smile than he ever gave me. No, not at all.

"How long are you in town for? Do you have time for a drink or two this evening?" She fluttered her eyelashes at him.

"Maybe," he began to reply.

"There's a great spot. Totally underground. But I can get you in."

"I think I can make time for a drink or two. But it'll have to be early. I have a long drive back."

I was seething. What, was he just going to make me wait in his car while he had a couple drinks with this bitch? *What the fuck?* We'd see if his car was still there when he was done.

"I get off at four. Text me." She winked at him. "Take a seat for now. We'll get you in as soon as a fortune teller becomes available. Should be very soon."

"Great, thank you." I had my hands balled into fists, about to flip out, when he nodded his head toward me and said, "My friend is here to see someone too. She can go ahead of me."

She glanced over at me for a moment and said, "Oh, right, her. Yeah, we can get her in too."

"Thanks." He smiled at her again and took a seat. I sat down next to him, feeling a little calmer at his polite gesture. He then turned to me and said, "Since we have some time after we're done here, would you want to grab some lunch?"

"Why, because you need to kill time before grabbing drinks with your new girlfriend?" I said sardonically, not happy at all with the situation or how the day had been going up until this point.

"I thought it might be fun to check out the Salem underground. But if you're not interested, we can just head home I guess."

"Oh, you wanted me to come too?" I asked, realizing how totally lame I sounded saying that.

"What, you think I was just going to leave you on the streets of Salem while I went to drink by myself? Who does that?" He laughed. "You must hang out with some really shitty people."

"Ha." I gave a half laugh. He wasn't wrong. That was one bad habit my sister and I shared—our taste in people. Although Jasmine seemed to be nice. I was glad Paige finally made a good friend. Deep down I was happy for her and the positive turn her life had recently taken. But I still felt bitter about the situation and was having a hard time getting over it.

After a few minutes, they finally called my turn. I went to see my usual witch, Sybil. "Ah, Gigi, so nice to see you again," she greeted me as soon as I walked in. "Let me see your hand."

I put out my hand for her, same as I did every month. She clasped it in hers and closed her eyes, humming in concentration. I leaned forward in anticipation, my stomach in knots, hoping for good news.

"Yes, I can feel her. Much stronger now. There's definitely been a change. Whatever you're doing is working."

I let out a squeak of excitement.

"There's something in your life now that's pulling her back." She opened her eyes and stared into mine. "What has changed in your life? Something has changed."

"Umm." I tried to think. What had changed really? "I'm back at home from school."

"Hmm, I don't think that's it," she responded. "Anyway, you should take the double dose again this full moon. How did you handle it last time?"

My stomach churned, and I practically started dry heaving recalling how sick I'd been last time. "It was fine," I replied, not wanting her to reduce my dose.

"Okay, good. We'll stick with the same dose then."

After I checked out, I threw the new jar into my purse and waited for Tyce to finish up with his own appointment, wondering what he could possibly need to see a witch for. In general, werewolves stayed away from witches and only went to see them out of desperation. We'd all heard stories from a young age of witches casting spells that never turned out how they were supposed to.

Once Tyce finished, we headed out into the Salem downtown area and found a place with outdoor seating to have lunch. After the hostess sat us at our table, I pulled off my cardigan, overheated from the unseasonably warm weather. The sun beat down on my bare shoulders and partly exposed back as I leaned forward to take a sip of water.

"Wanna split an appetizer?" Tyce asked, glancing up from his menu. "Holy—!" he exclaimed, his eyes wide, trained on my chest.

"What?" I asked.

"Nothing," he replied. and looked back down at his menu, but his ears were red again. And then I recalled looking in the mirror that morning—yeah, my dress was pretty low-cut. Okay, it was really low-cut, and Paige had even commented that my boobs were hanging out. I tried to pull the neckline up again, but it was no use. The world and Tyce would just have to deal with my boobs. They were big and hard to tame, kind of like me. I snickered to myself at my thought.

"Care to share what's so funny?" Tyce glanced back up at me.

"Nothing, just laughing at something random."

"Glad I'm not the butt of your joke for once." He gave me a sheepish smile.

"Are you sure about that?" I teased. "You should be proud though. I learned not to share them out loud. I'll just make fun of you in my head moving forward."

"You're just looking to be punished, aren't you?" he said in a low, deep voice. The way he said it, I wasn't sure whether to take that as a joke or something else—a sexual joke? Was he flirting with me? Was it the weather, or did he have me all hot and bothered suddenly?

"Depends. What's my punishment?" Fuck, what was wrong with me? Why was I so hot for a douchebag fuckboy yet again?

He smirked and let out a short, mischievous laugh. And damn, something about that sound—I suddenly wanted nothing more than to know how he planned to punish me.

"Hello! I'm Amy and I'll be your server today. Can I start you off with any drinks?" A waitress approached our table, breaking the spell I was under.

"I'll have a Sprite," I replied, thinking that I'd actually prefer something harder.

"Same," Tyce said, and she walked away. He then turned back to me. "Taking a break from getting plastered?"

I blushed, recalling how drunk I'd been when he caught me in the bathroom before. "It's not so noble. I'm just not old enough to drink yet. And I didn't want it to be weird if she IDed me."

"What? Really? How old are you?"

"Nineteen."

"Damn, you're young. I thought you were older than that. Especially playing hardball with an alpha."

"Why? How old are you?"

"Twenty-seven."

"Old man." I snickered.

"I'll have you know, I have excellent genetics. My alpha grandfather is in his seventies and you'd never guess. You should see him when he tortures. Doesn't fuck around. Still has the energy of a young buck."

"Young buck?" I laughed hysterically. "You even sound old when you talk!"

"You're just asking for it." He furrowed his brows at me, but I could see that he was taking the jabs in good humor. And okay, maybe a part of me kind of was asking for it. *Fuck*, no, I totally was not.

Tyson

Holy fucking Artemis. That fucking dress. It was taking everything in me not to stare at her rack. Out of every piece of clothing she owned, why the fuck had she put that dress on? All I could think about was how much I wanted to motorboat those impressive puppies. My cock was dying for a good titty fucking. Damn, I was so horny.

By the time we made it to the underground bar, I was ready to throw her into a bathroom stall and fuck the shit out of her. My jeans were feeling fucking tight, and I kept having to get my mind out of the gutter so I didn't end up walking around with a tent in my pants.

It didn't help that I'd warmed up to her. She wasn't so bad today. She was still busting my balls (and not in the way I wanted her to), but it wasn't so aggressive anymore.

Helena met us in front of an industrial-looking building. "Thought you'd come alone. I can get you in no problem, but the boss isn't going to like multiple werewolves inside. Too much risk. I think you can understand."

I gave her the most charming smile I could conjure, one of my best assets. "I was looking forward to getting to know you and your scene today, but I can't just leave my buddy behind." I figured if I flirted a little and talked down the relationship between Gigi and me a bit (not that there was anything to talk down, of course), she'd warm up to the idea. I brushed my hand gently on her upper arm. Okay, I may have been pretty good at manipulation. Hey, it was a useful skill to have!

"Okay, I'll see what I can do. But you owe me." She winked at me. Normally, I would have more than paid my dues, especially with how fucking horny I was at that moment. But I couldn't exactly ditch Gigi while I fucked the witch sideways. Besides, I realized, the witch didn't even seem that appealing. It was so strange. While I had a preference, I normally wasn't super picky as far as casual hookups went. I mean, if she was cute—and the witch was—I normally had no problem letting her ride my cock. Like I'd said, horndog.

We entered what was, basically, an illegal gambling den and bar. It was a nice setup and actually pretty classy as far as illegal operations go. It was mostly witches and warlocks but some humans as well.

Once we got inside, Gigi took the opportunity to excuse herself to go to the bathroom. For a split second, I almost imagined—wished?—she was hinting for me to follow her and fulfill my fantasy. But then I realized I needed a reality check and should stop defiling her in my mind.

"So, Tyce, any plans for staying in Salem a little longer than a few hours in the near future?" The witch leaned over so her cleavage was on display. I mean, I looked—I was a man after all!—but I still couldn't get Gigi's far more impressive rack off my mind, or how nice it would look bouncing as I pounded into her. Fuck, I really had to stop. I was becoming obsessed.

"I haven't ruled it out," I replied noncommittally. When Gigi didn't come back immediately, we fell into conversation as I nursed my drink. Although I had a very high tolerance, I didn't want to risk it, especially with a four-hour drive back to Blake's pack. About halfway through nursing my second drink, I realized that Gigi never returned, and a protective part of me woke. My wolf's instincts were in overdrive, and I had an overpowering need to find out where she'd gone.

I excused myself from the conversation I was having and stood, my eyes tracing the room. And that's when I spotted her in a dark corner, with some blond dude. I clenched my hands into fists, not happy with the sight at all. *What the fuck?* Was I *jealous*? No, there was no way! I just wanted a piece of her pie, and it was none of my business how many others got one too.

But still, I felt on edge, my inner wolf clawing at me as I observed her companion making eye contact with her chest. Even though I normally had really good control over the animal part of me, I was starting to have doubts as my nails and skin tingled with the need to shift. Before I could consider what I was doing, I'd marched across the bar and joined the couple.

"Hey, Gigi, how's it going?" I said, taking a seat at their table. "Who's your new friend?"

"Eric," he replied, putting out his hand to me. I gripped it tightly and smelled him. Fucking human. I knew if I gripped tight enough, I could easily break his hand, but I resisted. Did Gigi normally fuck around with humans? The thought pissed me off for some reason. I didn't like the idea of Gigi riding human cock at all—or really, any cock except mine. *Fuck, what was wrong with me?*

"Eric," I repeated. "Thanks for keeping my girl company. But you can leave now." I stared him down, daring him to disobey. I knew he wouldn't. He wasn't exactly lanky, but his human body didn't even close to compare with my highly trained alpha one.

"Whatever," he said, getting up and leaving.

"Is there a reason you just cockblocked me?" Gigi glared at me.

"What, you were planning to screw that piece of human trash?" I glared back.

"Piece of human trash? You don't even know him!" Gigi threw up her arms.

"And you do?"

"I was getting to know him until you came over here acting like a jealous boyfriend. We were actually having a very nice conversation, for your information."

"What could you possibly have in common with him?" I had my arms crossed and jaw clenched, highly irritated.

"You *are* jealous!" Gigi burst out laughing. "Are you kidding me right now?"

"No, I'm not," I snapped. "It's just time to go. We have a four-hour drive, and it's getting late."

"Right." She snickered. "Anyway, what right do you have to be jealous when you had no problem sharing drinks with your girlfriend? She doesn't exactly look happy that you just ditched her to cockblock me."

"Let's just go." I grabbed her arm in a tight grip, pulling her over to the witch so I could say goodbye. I didn't want to be in bad standing since

I still planned to go back to her shop again. "Sorry, we have a long trip ahead of us. But thank you for bringing us here." I smiled at the witch. Then I waved the bartender down and closed both my tab at the bar and Gigi's (schmuck hadn't even paid before he left) and dragged Gigi out.

Once we were outside, Gigi stomped on my foot. "What are you doing?" she yelled, looking fierce with her face flushed and her eyes throwing daggers at me.

"Taking you home," I replied.

"Why are you dragging me around like you own me? Listen here, Alpha Tyce, I don't care if you're an alpha. You have no right to just boss me around."

"Really?" I glared at her. "Because last I checked, that's exactly what a fucking alpha does. Now, don't forget who did who a favor today. As far as I can see, you still need me to get back to Vermont, so I suggest you be quiet and do what I say."

She looked like she was about to explode, but she held back, clearly taking what I said to heart. I didn't fail to notice her balled-up fists and pursed lips. For a moment, I felt a little bad about being so assertive with her. But I couldn't help how irrationally angry seeing her with that human had made me.

When we got to the car, she forcefully opened the passenger door to my rental car and threw herself into the front seat, crossing her arms and staring ahead. Fine, if she was going to be a brat, I'd just blast my music and ignore her existence for four hours. I did my good deed for the day. I was done.

Chapter 14

Ginger

Tyce and I didn't talk the entirety of the ride. He just trained his eyes on the road and never once glanced my way except to merge lanes. I clutched my purse, thankful, at least, I got what I came for. So it wasn't a complete disaster.

Two emotions competed within me simultaneously. One, I was upset about how Tyce had treated me. First, he called me his "buddy" to Helena, especially after making it seem like there was something between us. I didn't even know why I thought that or why it bothered me so much, but it did. After mulling it over, I concluded that it just hurt to feel so inadequate next to someone so hot and powerful. I hated being made to feel so weak and worthless. It was a feeling that I'd carried throughout my life, and it was always so hard to kick, no matter how many friends I made or how much I succeeded at school. I still always felt like that little girl who never properly got her wolf in middle school.

Then, as soon as I disappeared, he'd gotten cozy with Helena at the bar. I didn't fail to notice how he stared down her shirt and the two of them laughed like they were two peas in a pod, my presence forgotten. It made me so angry. So as soon as some guy approached me, I took the opportunity to prove that I could have someone—anyone—if I wanted to. The guy was pretty good-looking too. Our conversation wasn't even that bad. He was a good conversationalist, and I soon found myself forgetting how upset Tyce had made me.

It actually made me feel kind of good when Tyce caught us together. And I felt so satisfied calling him out on being jealous. But the way he just dragged me around like I was an object, his fingers gripping my arm so hard I was surprised I didn't bruise! That was unacceptable. I didn't care if he was the alpha. He had no right to just grab my arm like that and make me go wherever he wanted me to. Suffice to say, he pissed me off. He was just some entitled douchebag with no respect for anyone past what he could get from them.

So, dear Goddess, please tell me why I couldn't shake the absurd desire I had for him. There had to be something seriously wrong with me. And yet, every once in a while, it seemed like he'd let down his guard and show me a different, softer, part of him. Annoyed, I pushed the thought from my head.

When he dropped me at home, I didn't even bother to grab his sandals for him like I'd promised. I was just too upset. Instead, I slammed the door to his car and rushed upstairs into Paige's room, not even bothering to say hi to my mom. I was relieved to find her inside, watching a movie on her iPad. "Do you mind if I watch with you?" I asked, needing to be near someone who could make me feel better.

"No, not at all," she replied, making room.

I crawled into the bed next to her. "I'm sorry for how I acted this morning. I shouldn't have stomped out like that after you gave us your good news," I said sincerely. "It's just so hard for me."

"I know, it's okay." She turned to face me. Paige was always so understanding and forgiving. Sometimes it annoyed me, but this time I was relieved and let out a deep breath.

"I just don't think I'll ever find my mate," I said as my voice cracked and my throat tingled. "I really fucked up, and now I'll be paying for it the rest of my life."

"You don't know that for sure." Paige wrapped her arms around me as I cuddled into her, feeling comforted by the gesture. After some time, she pulled away to look at me. "You smell kind of like Tyce. Were you with him today?"

"You can tell?"

"He's from another pack, so his scent is really distinct compared to ours. But it's pretty faint, and I probably wouldn't have been able to tell otherwise."

"Oh," I replied, considering the information.

"Is there something going on between you two?"

"No, I just saw him while I was out today, and we hung out a little."

"So I guess that means you made up now?"

"No, not really. Goddess, Paige. I just keep hanging out with assholes. I wish I could just meet my mate. You're so lucky."

"It'll happen for you too." She put her arms around me again. "You know, I sometimes pray to the Moon Goddess for you."

"I don't know if I believe in the Moon Goddess anymore."

"Don't say that, Gigi. Have faith." Easy for Paige to say—she still had her wolf *and* a mate! But I let it be, enjoying my twin's company.

"So, now that you met your mate, does that mean you finally lost your v-card?" I elbowed Paige, wanting to move the topic from something so depressing.

She turned red and said, "Not yet."

"Not yet?!" I exclaimed. "What are you waiting for?"

"Well, it's not exactly easy. We both still live at home."

"Please tell me you at least did something—anything—else!"

She giggled and said, "He fingered me during patrol duty."

"And what else!"

"Okay, okay." She giggled some more. "I gave him a blow job too."

"Damn, about time!"

"Oh my Goddess, Gigi, I love him so much! I know I just met him a couple days ago, but I can't stop thinking about him. And the way it feels when we touch each other—it's magical, like sparks! I'm so glad I saved myself for him. He's everything I ever imagined and more."

"I'm happy for you," I said, giving her a squeeze, forcing myself to be happy for her and make up for how I'd acted that morning. But my chest still ached with bitter jealousy.

I managed to avoid Tyce for over a week. I mean, it wasn't like our paths crossed that often. But still. I'd be lying if I said he wasn't living rent free in my mind. As much as he irritated me, I couldn't stop thinking about him. And I hated myself a little bit that I couldn't just forget about him.

On Sunday morning, Paige went on a cleaning spree in the house. "You know you've been overly domestic lately," I teased her as I watched her on her hands and knees in the bathroom, scrubbing the floor.

"I just like a clean home!" she replied.

"Shouldn't you have better things to do? Like, for example, mating?"

"Okay, maybe!" She threw her hands up. " But now that they know we're mates they rearranged our schedules, and we're practically working opposite shifts now. Either way, we both still live at home with religious parents and moms who don't work."

"Can't you just do it in the back of his car or something?"

"But it's my first time. I don't want to lose my virginity in the back of a 2009 Honda CR-V!"

I laughed. "Why not? You may have to anyway. You'll be going into heat soon."

"What?" She stared at me. "What does that mean?"

I started laughing even harder. "Are you serious? You don't know about heat? Goddess, Paige, you're so naive. I barely even spent my teenage years in the pack and even I know about heat."

"What are you talking about?" She narrowed her eyes at me.

"Werewolves go into heat after they meet their mates. I'm surprised you don't know. I thought at least one of the warrior girls would have told you. You become like an animal and want to fuck everything in sight. Like a man." I snickered, letting out a snort as Paige stared at me with confusion on her face.

"How do you know about heat?" she asked.

"Jocelyn told me. Her mom tells her way more than ours ever did."

"How come Heidi never told us?"

"Oh please, Heidi talk about sex?" I snorted some more. "She is the biggest prude I know. Loves to hear all my sex stories but would never tell us any of hers. Fucking puritan. I bet she cut a hole in her sheet, so she doesn't have to see Hunter naked when they have sex."

"Oh my Goddess, Gigi! You're horrible!" Paige joined me in laughter. Then she suddenly stopped and asked, "What am I supposed to do when I go into heat?"

"Fuck your mate, duh!" I pushed her on her shoulder.

"What am I going to do?"

"Looks like that 2009 Honda CR-V is going to need a full detail soon." I was now laughing so hard that tears were coming out of my eyes.

"Gigi, you're terrible!"

"I mean, you could just get a hotel room." I shrugged. "People do that too."

She then laughed, hit herself on the forehead, and said, "Oh my Goddess, you're so right, Gigi! Duh!"

"And don't forget condoms." I winked at her.

"With how stupid this mate thing is making me, I definitely need the reminder." She chuckled. "Definitely not ready for pups yet."

A couple hours later, Paige showed up in my bedroom. "I just re-arranged my whole closet. Want me to do yours too?"

"You need to do something about all that pent-up sexual energy." I laughed, shaking my head.

"Yes or no?"

"Yes." I may as well take advantage of the situation.

"Great!" She swung open the door and began pulling everything out as I watched TikTok videos on my phone. After some time, I noticed her standing over me with Adidas pool slides in her hands. "Don't these belong to a certain alpha?"

I gasped and replied, "Shit, I totally forgot to give them back to him. I probably should."

"Yeah, you probably should," she agreed. "Unless you're some weird stalker who wants to keep them to sniff when you miss him, like a dog." She snickered.

"What, wolves don't do that too?"

She appeared lost in thought for a moment and then said, "You know what, Dylan smells so amazing, I probably would. I bet even his old, dirty sneakers smell good. Goddess, there's nothing like the scent of a mate!"

I, once again, felt a pulling sensation in my gut, envious of Paige's life. I kept trying to push it away and force myself to be happy for my sister, but it was so difficult when she was able to have everything I wanted.

Chapter 15

Ginger

I wrapped Tyce's sandals in a plastic bag and threw them into my purse so I could finally return them to him. As my family piled into the car to head over to the Sunday evening temple service, I felt a bit mournful at the realization that returning them would mean he had no more reason to talk to me. Just as quickly as I felt it, I pushed it from my mind and convinced myself it was for the best. The new Gigi would no longer give douchey guys the time of day. The new Gigi only made room in her busy schedule for nice, mature gentlemen. And a gentleman Tyce was not!

I spotted him as soon as we arrived, as I always did. It was hard not to. He was just so tall and had such a naturally commanding presence. Clearly, it was an alpha thing—yes, I felt the same about Blake. Yet, somehow, I always seemed to notice Tyce first. Maybe Tyce was more alpha alpha, if that was a thing. He did, after all, come from a much larger pack.

My family took our normal seats. Heidi sat down next to me, unfortunately. I hadn't talked to her much since the whole walk-of-shame thing happened where she basically told Dad I was a slut. "Hey, Gi, how's it going?" she asked.

"Fine," I replied. *Still waiting for an apology.*

"We haven't done a sisters' potluck and game night in a while."

"Yeah, that's true."

"We should plan one."

"Sure."

"Okay, great!"

Yeah, great. As much as I used to love those hangouts with my sisters, I'd been feeling sourer about them lately. It was just so hard having their good fortunes rubbed in my face.

The service soon began. I went through the motions, barely paying attention, trying to plan how I'd be able to return Tyce's slides to him without my family noticing. After we wrapped up with our final meditation, Blake approached the stage.

"Good evening, Midnight Maple Pack!" He smiled widely, appearing happier than usual. "I have some very good news to share with all of you this evening. My sister, Luna Talia of the Pine Forest Pack, gave birth yesterday to a healthy baby girl, whom she and her mate, Alpha Alexander, have named Bianca in honor of her late mother. Both mom and pup are doing well, and I am so happy to help welcome my new niece into the world.

"As I'm sure you're all aware, the next full moon is tomorrow. So, my mate, Luna Jasmine, and I will be heading up to Ontario tonight so that we can take part in Bianca's first full moon ceremony. Meanwhile, I will be leaving the pack in Alpha Tyce and Beta Luke's very capable hands until my return later this week."

After he stepped down, the congregation all rose to their feet, and many began heading over to congratulate Blake and Jasmine on the good news. I kept my eyes trained on Tyce and watched as he chatted with some different people in the same general vicinity.

"Hey, Paige!" I grabbed my sister's arm. "We should go congratulate Blake and Jasmine."

"I was just going to say the same thing!" she agreed.

Perfect.

As we passed by Tyce, I said very loudly, "Actually, I forgot something in the garden earlier. I'll be right back!" I then glanced over at Tyce and our eyes locked for a moment. I quickly winked at him, hoping he got the hint.

I was relieved when I heard footsteps approaching a couple minutes after I got to the back of the temple. "Here." I quickly thrust the plastic bag into his hands, not wanting to make conversation.

As I brushed past him, he grabbed my arm to stop me. "Wait."

"What?" I replied, giving him attitude and pulling my arm away.

He seemed to hesitate for a moment but then spoke. "As acting alpha of your pack for the next few days, I have to consider the well-being of all pack members. And I'm assuming you're going to do the same thing you did on the last full moon, right?" He studied my face.

"Why?" I looked at him suspiciously.

"It's just, last time you passed out in the middle of the woods." He rubbed the back of his neck. "So, if the same thing happens again, I want you to have my number. Since I know you don't want anyone else to know what you're up to."

My breath caught as he, once again, surprised me with his consideration. He always came off as so rough, but maybe there was more to him than I'd assumed. "What's in it for you?" I asked, not sure I could trust him.

"Nothing." He widened his eyes as if he were surprised by the question. "I just don't want you to get hurt. And I know we can't mindlink each other. So I wanted to offer you another way to get in touch with me. Just in case." I was suddenly extremely thankful that we were in different packs.

"Fine," I replied, pulling out my phone and handing it to him so he could enter his number.

"Good, I feel better now." He gave me a small smile as he handed me back my phone. "Okay, well, I'll see you around. And remember to call if you need help." He then turned to walk away.

"Thanks," I said, watching him head back inside. He gave me a small wave and then he was gone.

Chapter 16

Blake

After the temple service, Jasmine and I jumped into my car to head north. I glanced over at her as I started the car, taking her hand in mine. "You know, you're going to need a bigger car soon. It's going to be a lot of work getting pups in and out of their car seats with a two door."

"I know." She sighed. "But I love that car."

I squeezed her hand. "Maybe we can trade cars when we have to take the pups." I smiled at her, and she put her head against my arm, sending sparks dancing up and down the length of it. I was still getting used to it, since we were hit unexpectedly by the news. I thought we'd have more time to ease ourselves into the idea of it. I always knew I'd have to provide an heir to our pack, but I just didn't think it would happen so soon.

As we drove, Jasmine drifted into sleep. I had noticed she'd been a lot more tired lately, going to bed much earlier than previously. She kept claiming she had no symptoms, but I definitely noticed them—both how horny and uninhibited she'd become in bed and how her breasts had swollen to practically double their size almost overnight. While I'd always loved her petite and taut breasts, I also appreciated the new larger versions with more prominent nipples that were now always poking through her shirts. *Fuck, I was completely obsessed.* I couldn't keep my hands off her. We were now going at it more than we ever had before.

When we finally made it to Alex's pack four and a half hours later, Jasmine stirred. "Oh, shit! Did I just sleep the whole way?" she asked, patting down her hair and blinking rapidly. "Sorry, I was going to offer to drive part of the way."

"You can make up for it with a show later." I smirked at her and then kissed behind her ear and down her neck, tracing my lips down to the top of her breasts, cupping my hand around one of them. She moaned quietly, which made my cock instantly stand at attention. "I want to get a look at your hard nipples without anything covering them." I brushed my thumb against one of them, which was once again poking through the thin fabrics of her shirt and bra.

"Blake," she moaned. "That feels so good."

I pulled down her shirt and bra so the nipple was exposed, and not able to help myself, I brought my mouth to it, licking around the perimeter. She arched her back in response and let out more quiet moans, grabbing my thigh with her hand.

A knock sounded on the car window, interrupting us, and I pulled away. Jasmine instantly reddened, pulling up her shirt to cover herself, and I suddenly remembered where we were. I rolled down my window to one of Alex's warriors on patrol at the entrance of his pack.

"Sorry to interrupt." He gave me a sly smile. I could feel that Jasmine was dying of embarrassment through the mate bond. "Are you here to visit the Pine Forest Pack?"

"Yes, my sister, Luna Talia, just gave birth yesterday, and I'm here to see her and Alpha Alexander."

"ID?" I handed him my license. "One moment," he replied and went to, presumably, check the guest list.

"Goddess, that was so embarrassing!" Jasmine cried out. "I can't believe we just got caught doing that! I can't believe I let you do that!"

"You are so much more adventurous lately." I chuckled.

"You're a bad influence."

"Always have been, always will be."

The warrior returned and said, "All set, Alpha Blake Wulfric. You're on the list. Do you need any directions to the packhouse?"

"No, I'm good," I replied, and put my foot on the gas to head over. I was anxious to get Jasmine naked in our guest room, completely riled up by what we'd been doing when we were interrupted.

Alex let us in when we arrived just past midnight, already in his pajamas. "Welcome, Wulfric," he said, shaking my hand.

"Congrats, man," I said, giving him a pat on the back. "How's Talia doing?"

"She's still recovering. She's fully healed now, but the birth took a lot out of her. To be honest, it took a lot out of me too." He cringed.

"I'm taking it you felt it?" I asked.

"I did up until she got the epidural. Those damn contractions. You can't get out of feeling your mate's intense pain." He shook his head. He then turned to my mate and kissed her on the cheek. "Nice to see you, Jasmine. Thanks for coming."

"Thanks for having us. We're both excited to meet Bianca and attend her first full moon ceremony tomorrow evening."

"It'll be good." He grinned. "We have a catered barbecue and pack run planned. I'm hoping for good weather." He then glanced down at our bags and picked them up, "Let me take you up to your room. You're probably tired after the long trip. Are you hungry? I can heat up some leftovers if you'd like."

"We're fine, we had dinner before we left," I replied.

"Okay, I'm a bit tired, so I'll be off to bed now. But don't hesitate to help yourself to anything. *Mi casa es su casa*," he said as he led us upstairs into our room. His packhouse was nice. It was much cozier than the one I'd grown up in, with wool rugs and animal hides covering the sturdy hardwood floors and wood beams lining the ceiling, and I kind of liked it. It was also much smaller than ours as his beta's family didn't live with him as was traditional in most packs.

As soon as he dropped our bags off and said good night, I had my hands all over Jasmine, desperate to have her. She instantly responded to my touch, climbing onto my lap and shoving her tongue into my mouth, letting the aggressive part of her out once again. We tried to stay quiet, keeping our lips on each other, moaning quietly into each other's mouths, careful not to wake the house.

After we finished, Jasmine snuggled up against me. "Are you worried about it hurting you when I give birth?" she asked, rubbing her hand up and down my arm.

"No. Our pack doctors are excellent. Either way, I'm not a stranger to pain. You forget that my dad was sadistic when he trained me. And I spent years building a tolerance to wolfsbane. That's not exactly painless. That shit burns like a motherfucker. I'm more concerned about you." I kissed her cheek. "But I'll make sure you're taken care of. I have connections at the pack clinic." I winked and then kissed her some more. "Are you scared?"

"Kind of," she replied.

"About the birth or other things too?" I picked her chin up with my hand, so I could look directly into her eyes.

"Everything. It's a lot. We haven't even been married a year, and we're already having pups. And I hate how anxious you've become. I can tell you're always worried. I just wish I could help you feel better."

I frowned, frustrated that Jasmine could sense everything I felt. I wanted desperately to shield her from my darkest emotions. I had gotten used to them over the years, and now they almost felt comforting in some ways—proving that I was still living and no longer completely numb as I had been. But I didn't think it was fair for my sweet, beautiful mate to be burdened by them.

"Jasmine, don't worry about me. What happened is a good thing. We've created a life together—no—lives. And we're going to love both of them so much once they're here. I know you think I'm struggling a lot with this, and I'd be lying if I said I wasn't. But I also feel really hopeful too—that I can break the cycle and be the father to them that mine never was to me."

"That's really beautiful, Blake." Jasmine teared up. "Goddess, these pregnancy hormones have me so emotional." She wiped at her tears.

"They also have you super horny." I chuckled mischievously. "I should knock you up more often."

She slapped my arm. "You act like you weren't getting any before."

"Not like this." I grinned and nibbled on her ear, knowing that was her weak spot.

Chapter 17

Blake

The next morning, I woke up earlier than Jasmine and snuck downstairs so I could surprise her with breakfast. As I approached the kitchen, I overheard a heated discussion between Alex and who I assumed was his mom.

"You've been keeping in touch with Sara behind my back?" Alex's voice boomed.

"Alex, she's my daughter. I have a right to keep in touch with her," a middle-aged woman's voice responded.

"She tried to kill my mate several fucking times!"

"Language, Alex!"

"Fuck language. I'm in a really bad mood right now."

"Alex, can you at least be rational about this? Listen to me. I'm your mother!"

"Fine, Mother. What did you want to tell me?" I could tell he was speaking through gritted teeth.

"Sara wants to meet with you. She has information about one of our ally packs. I know Sara did some things you're not happy about. But at least speak with her and give her a chance to redeem herself. She is still your sister."

"She will never redeem herself in my eyes."

"Alex"—his mom raised her voice—"you've known Sara far longer than you've known Talia. And you know how close she was to her father. I'm not saying you have to forgive everything, but at the very least have a conversation with her. You're alpha now. And while I may have never been involved much with helping your father run the pack, I do at least know that, as alpha, you have an obligation to listen to all news of threats to your pack."

"Fine!" Alex conceded. "I'll fucking talk to her. Okay?"

"Good," she said and exited the kitchen, almost walking into me. "Oh, good morning. You are?" she asked.

"Alpha Blake of the Midnight Maple Pack." I moved to shake her hand. "Talia's brother. Nice to meet you."

"Ah yes, the son of the philandering father."

"The son of the philandering father," I repeated. "Exactly what I was hoping to be known for."

"Well, if the shoe fits," she said and walked away.

"Man, your mom is tough, Adalwolf," I said as I walked into the kitchen and saw him sitting at the kitchen table with his head in his hands.

"Did you hear that conversation?" He looked up at me. I nodded. "She wasn't always like that. Losing her mate did a number on her. And I don't think she's happy with the whole Talia situation. Although, she loves her new granddaughter. She seems to slowly be lightening up."

"So, are you going to meet with Sara?" I asked, taking a seat to talk to him.

"What choice do I have? My mom is right. If she has intel, I have a duty to listen to it."

"I'll go with you if you want," I offered.

"Thanks, Wulfric, I appreciate it." He gave me a small smile.

"So what's it like with the new pup?" I asked.

"So far, not too bad. My mom's been helping a lot, and Talia had an easy delivery. She was amazing." His eyes sparkled as he spoke about his mate. "Recovered like a true luna. We got home from the pack hospital yesterday and have just been figuring it out as we go." He then gave me a mischievous smile and asked, "So, when's your pup coming? I'm sure your pack's anxious for an alpha heir now that you're mated."

I grinned and said, "Soon, very soon."

He gave me a knowing smile. "Well, I better bring my mate her morning coffee," he said, getting up and pouring some into a mug out of a carafe. "Help yourself to anything in the kitchen. Our housekeeper made sure we were fully stocked before you came."

"Thanks, appreciate the hospitality." I got up to put something together. Since I wasn't much of a cook, I kept it simple and made a couple of breakfast sandwiches.

Later that afternoon, Alex and I took his SUV out a few miles to a wooded area where he had agreed to meet with his sister. We arrived to her sitting on a tree stump. As we approached, I realized she smelled like a rogue and had clearly never joined another pack after banishing herself from Alex's. However, she didn't have the appearance of a rogue, wearing clean clothes and nice shoes, and her blonde pixie cut was well maintained.

"Hi," Alex tersely greeted his sister.

"Hello, dear brother," she replied, not appearing any happier to see him.

"You have intel, eh?" he asked, crossing his arms and widening his stance.

"No 'How are you? How have you been? How's the rogue life treating you?'"

"Let's not pretend like you didn't try to murder my mate several times."

"Not even a minute into the conversation and you're already digging up the past."

"It hasn't been that long."

She furrowed her brows, and her eyes took on an evil appearance. But then her face softened as she took a deep breath. "Look, Alex, I know we don't agree on some things. I know you might not believe me, but I still care about our pack."

"My pack," he corrected.

"Fine, *your* pack." She rolled her eyes. "Either way, Dad raised me to love that pack more than I love my own life. I still feel loyal to it even if I'm not officially a part of it anymore."

"You're not welcome back."

"Can you just let me talk?" She raised her voice. "Goddess, what is it with fucking men? They all act like they believe in equal rights for men and women, but when one of us talks, they don't even bother to listen."

"Fine, talk."

"I understand that I'm not welcome back. But I still want to help you and let you know what's going on. I've been living half my time as a human and half as a wolf, traveling through Ontario and Quebec just to keep tabs on what's going on with all the packs. The surrounding packs know that the Bois Sombre Pack no longer has an alpha. Some of them are forming an alliance to take it over."

"Why would they do that?" I cut in. Although they had formerly been our enemy, they had turned to an ally pack now that their unhinged alpha had been taken down by my luna.

She looked me up and down with a sour look on her face. She almost certainly remembered me from when I had planned to torture her. Finally, she replied, "I understand their business is very lucrative."

"Mm." Alex nodded.

"Anyway, you're probably wondering why you should care." Sara put her hands on her hips. "When a man gets a pretty girl, he's not satisfied. He thinks, If I got this pretty girl, I can get another pretty girl, eh?"

"No, not true, but I'm familiar with the concept," Alex replied.

"Well, I don't think it's far-fetched to consider that this could create a new precedent, eh? I mean, conquering another pack would only grow their own. And if they captured one pack and business, why not capture another? Either way, I know they're your allies now, so even if you don't do anything about it, you should be aware."

Alex had a faraway look for a moment and then turned his attention back to his sister. "Thanks for the info, I appreciate it. I know you didn't have to go out of your way to warn me."

She gave him a small smile and said, "Congrats on your new pup. Mom told me. I wish things had worked out differently. But, anyway, I'll let you know if I hear anything else."

"Thanks, Sara. Good luck, eh?" Alex said, and his composure softened. She then turned and walked away, not even bothering to glance back at us or wave goodbye.

After she disappeared, I turned to Alex and asked, "So, what are you thinking?"

"I mean, they're our allies now. It's only right that we help them. We also can't exactly afford to lose the Lune Nordique Pack as an ally. They're one of the biggest packs in Quebec. And I know your alliance with them goes back generations."

"Yeah, they've been with our pack since my great-great-grandfather started it. Besides our neighboring Autumn Moon Pack, they're our most loyal allies."

"I obviously wish we didn't have to get involved. I mean, I just had a pup and I hate the idea of going to battle and leaving my mate behind. But I don't think we have a choice if it comes down to it."

"No, I agree." I shook my head. "Listen, it's the same for me. We haven't told too many people yet, but you're family now. And, well, Jasmine's pregnant."

"Wow, congrats, man! Great news, eh?" Alex pulled me in for a hug and patted me on the back.

"Yeah, it's great, but it's also a huge responsibility. I don't want to battle unless it's absolutely necessary. I have a mate and two pups on the way now."

"Two?" Alex raised his eyebrows. "Twins?"

"Yep." I grinned. "Got her twice in one shot."

"Hey, good for you, man." Alex punched me playfully in the arm. "Looking forward to attending their first full moon ceremony once it's time. Do you have a due date yet?"

"It's hard to say since they're twins, and alpha twins at that. But maybe early October."

"Great time of year to visit Vermont I hear." Alex gave me a big smile.

Chapter 18

Ginger

On the evening of the full moon, I once again waited for my whole family to go to sleep. Luckily, both my dad and Paige were warriors, so they had early bedtimes. I quietly snuck out of the house, made my way into the woods, and disappeared into the darkness of the night. It was drizzling, and I couldn't even see the moon since it was covered by the clouds. I cursed my bad luck and hoped that it would be okay that there wasn't much moonlight available.

I made my way to the same place I went the last time, deciding it was a good spot. I was barely able to see in the dark, cloudy night. I wrapped my arms around my body, thinking I should have worn a jacket as the small droplets wet my exposed skin and clothing. By the time I made it to the right place, I was practically shivering, but it was so close to midnight I couldn't turn around. I was just glad my eyesight had somewhat adjusted to the darkness, but it still felt a bit ominous with everything so dark and wooded, with the only light being from the small beam of my flashlight.

Once the clock struck twelve, I went through my usual routine meticulously, making sure that everything was performed correctly. If there was one thing about me most people didn't know, it was that I was a perfectionist. I always tried to play it cool in public, but the reality was that I liked to do everything right. Paige and I really weren't so different when it came down to it. We had both always been good students and athletes, always competing against each other in everything.

But, after we started middle school, something in me shifted. Suddenly I wanted to shed my old reputation. I shunned my old group of friends that Paige and I hung out with and, instead, became friends with Jocelyn. She was one of the cool girls, and I was ecstatic once she started talking to me. Her group was fun and exciting—they snuck into the woods during lunchtime to smoke, hung out with boys, and did their makeup in the bathroom before school together. But they were also big trouble. While I couldn't fully blame Jocelyn and her friends, they were part of the reason I no longer had a wolf.

Not long after that happened, they all stopped talking to me. It was as if we'd never been friends. Even my old group joined in on the bullying. Paige was the only person who stuck up for me, even to the detriment of her own friendships.

Jocelyn actually wasn't that bad. She was probably the only reason I didn't die that night. After not talking to her for years, we finally got back in touch the summer before I left for college. She was okay, and we hung out sometimes, but I wouldn't really call her a close friend. All my close friends now were human.

When I completed the memorized ritual, I once again brought the herb drink to my mouth. As the familiar herbal smell entered my nostrils, I almost gagged right then and there, my body recalling how ill it had made me previously. But I pushed through it as I dry heaved, forcing the rotten and sour-tasting liquid down my throat, burning my esophagus and insides. My whole body convulsed, rejecting every bit of the poison. I kept swallowing, not allowing it to come back up. There was no way I was going to lose this battle.

My body weakened, and I fell to my knees, same as the previous time, gasping for shallow breaths, trying desperately to stay conscious. I crawled over to my clothing, using every last bit of strength to dress myself. I then tried to get up but instantly became dizzy, and I knew—there was no way I was going to make it home. It was either pass out here, in the middle of the woods in the rain, or take Tyce up on his offer.

Barely able to see straight, I asked Siri to call him. "Hello?" he answered after a couple rings.

"It—it's Gigi," I stuttered.

"Gigi, are you okay?" he asked, concern in his voice.

"No," I responded, wrapping my arms around myself, shivering and vision blurry.

"Where are you? I'll come help you."

"Th-the sa-same place as last ti-time."

"Hang on. I'll be right there." He hung up, and I pulled my knees to my body, sitting against a rock, trying to keep warm and awake as the drizzle intensified and turned to rain, rustling the leaves above me.

I must have drifted into sleep because the next thing I knew a wolf's cold nose was poking my cheek. I gasped in shock, practically falling over, and then remembered that it was probably Tyce. He was a huge wolf—bigger than my dad in his wolf form. I couldn't make out what color his fur was except that it was dark, reminding me of a grizzly bear. His amber eyes were more vibrant than usual, glowing, staring into mine. I assumed it must have been his night vision that made them appear that way.

He then shifted into his human form as he continued staring at me. My cheeks warmed as I realized he was completely naked, and I did my best not to look down, but I couldn't lie and say I wasn't just a little curious.

"Gigi, are you okay?" He brought his hand to my shoulder. If I didn't know better, I could have sworn I felt slightly better from his hand brushing my skin. "You're shivering. You're so cold."

"Y-you ha-have a tattoo," I said as I looked at his bare shoulder and tried to figure out what it was, struggling to see straight. I could make out maybe eyes and fangs, but not much more than that. The more I tried, the worse my vision got as black dots took over, and I was sure I was going to pass out.

He caught me as I fell over, my whole body going limp. "I'm going to carry you back to the packhouse on my back, okay? Don't worry, I won't hurt you." He gently lowered me to the ground. I put my hands out, thinking he was going to give me a piggyback ride, but then I realized what he meant as he hovered over me in his wolf form.

He flipped me onto his furry back, taking my arms into his mouth, holding me safely in place. He gave a slight shake, presumably to make sure I was secured, and broke into a run. Before long, we arrived at our destination, and he carefully lowered me to the ground again and then picked me up in his human form. I threw my arms around his shoulders as he carried me into the packhouse and upstairs before gingerly laying me down on top of his bed.

I was relieved to be on his soft bed but unable to keep my eyes open, shivering from the cold. "I'll be right back," he said softly.

I moaned quietly when he walked out of the room, clutching my stomach and trying to ignore how nauseous I felt, desperate not to throw up. When his footsteps sounded as he reentered the bedroom, I opened my eyes and saw that he'd put some clothes on.

"You're bleeding. Let me help you," he said as he sat on the bed next to me and delicately dabbed under my nose and my chin with a warm, wet washcloth. I stared up at him, surprised by how caring he was being. "The same thing happened last time."

"Di-did you clean m-me last time too?"

"Yeah, you were in even rougher shape last time." A warmth emerged inside my chest, charmed by this new side of himself he was revealing to me. He then got up and walked to his dresser. After a moment, he pulled out a heather gray T-shirt. "You're soaked. You should change into something dry. Here, put my T-shirt on."

Although I was barely able to move my arms, I found the strength to and took it from him. He turned around as I struggled to peel off the wet shirt clinging to my body. Once I finally threw it off, I unsnapped my bra, sighing with relief at freeing my breasts from the wet trap they were in. I threw the T-shirt on and noted how soft it was—much softer than I was expecting. As I brushed the fabric, I wondered if it was intentional, smiling at the thought of Tyce picking out a particularly soft shirt for me.

I tried to remove my leggings, but they were practically glued to my legs. "Do you mind helping me?" I called to Tyce.

He peeked over his shoulder. "You need help?"

"I can't get these leggings off," I replied, falling back into the bed from exhaustion. "Can you pull them off?"

He seemed to hesitate for a moment, but then he turned around and knelt down in front of me. I lifted my legs for him, and he brought his hands to my upper thighs where my leggings were stuck. As his fingers brushed my bare skin, it tingled with arousal, my breath hitching in reaction. His eyes made contact with mine as he slowly pulled my pants down, and it was so intimate and enchanting that it seemed the whole world had slowed.

Once they were off, he leaned forward, hovering over me while I looked up at him from the bed. "Is that better?"

"Yes," I replied. "Better."

"Good," he said as his mouth moved closer to mine until it was only centimeters away, as if a magnet were pulling him toward me.

My heart pounded in my chest at how close our lips were to each other. Just a small movement forward, and they would be touching. I parted my lips just slightly, my whole body alive with desire.

"Let me tuck you in," he said as he pulled away, and I felt a bit disappointed. He moved my body with his strong arms as if I weighed nothing, placing me onto the pillow and pulling the blanket out from under me. As his hands touched me, I felt marginally better, some of the nausea easing. He then covered me, patted the blanket down, and fluffed my pillow a bit. He looked down at me for a few moments, then turned out the light. "Okay, I'll be down the hall if you need anything," he said as he straightened up.

He turned away and was about to move from the bed when I called out, "Wait." He turned back to look at me curiously. "Can you stay with me? I feel better with you here."

"Like sleep in the same bed as you?" he asked, raising his eyebrow at me.

"Yeah," I replied, a comforting warmth spreading through my body at the thought.

"Goddess, you are really out of it." He smiled and shook his head. But he still crawled into the bed with me, getting under the covers.

I turned to my side and snuggled my back into his warm body as he wrapped his huge arms around me, spooning me. I sighed at how comforting it was, thinking it had never felt so right to be so close to someone before. "It's so nice," I said as strange tingles materialized inside my body, pulsing within my torso.

"The rain made your perfume really strong. What is it?" he asked quietly in my ear, his voice low and gravelly. Goddess, he had the most seductive voice sometimes.

"Perfume?" I repeated, wondering what he was talking about.

"Yeah, what perfume do you wear? It's amazing." I had to be delirious because there was no way he'd asked that. While I did own perfume, I mostly only wore it on special occasions and was definitely not wearing it then.

Determining I'd heard wrong, I decided not to answer and instead backed myself closer to him, wanting desperately to feel him against the entire length of my back. He tightened his embrace in response, his arms pulling me even closer, as if he knew how much I needed him at that moment. I shifted against him, getting comfortable.

"Is that your boner?" I asked as my ass hit something rock solid.

"Yeah, definitely not chipmunk size." He snickered.

"You're hard right now?"

"Well, I'm in bed with an attractive woman. And now you're rubbing yourself all over my body. What did you expect to happen?"

"Oh."

"I can move away if you want."

"No, I like it," I replied, my whole body heated and shivering with arousal. If I didn't also feel so ill, I wasn't sure I wouldn't have made a move, my disdain for him completely forgotten at that moment. Instead, I reveled in how his body heat surrounded me, his strong arms held me protectively, and his chest pushed against my back as he breathed.

"You're a lot nicer when you're like this." He brushed his hand through my wet hair.

"Don't get used to it," I replied as I drifted into sleep, and fluttery sensations danced throughout my chest and stomach.

Chapter 19

Ginger

I groaned, my stomach burned, my limbs were sore. I struggled to open my eyes and instantly shut them again, the light scathing my pupils. Goddess, I was in so much pain. I had to go to the hospital. I groaned again.

The pain in my stomach worsened, and acid pushed its way up my esophagus. I tried to swallow and shove it back down, wanting to fall back asleep. But it was useless. If I didn't get up at that second, I'd throw up in my bed.

I rolled until I made it to the edge, sliding out of the bed onto my knees. Finally opening my eyes, I looked around and realized I wasn't in my room. I blinked, and memories started flooding back from the previous night.

Fuck—I was in Tyce's room, wasn't I? My stomach grumbled, forcing me to my feet. I sprinted as fast as I could, recalling where the bathroom was from last time. I pulled the bathroom door open to be met with steam—someone had clearly just showered. But I couldn't think about that right then as my eyes locked with the toilet.

I pounced onto the floor in front of it and let everything come spewing out from inside my body. So much came out, I wasn't sure I hadn't also thrown up some organs. I moaned, weak and not sure I could get up again. Suddenly, I felt a presence, some warmth from a body behind me, and large hands on my shoulders.

"Are you okay?" Tyce's voice sounded. He'd squatted down beside me and was now rubbing my shoulders in a surprisingly intimate way.

"Sorry, this is embarrassing." I quickly reached to flush the toilet. I then turned my head to look at him. "You're not wearing anything!" I exclaimed, my cheeks heating.

"Well, I *was* just showering." He chuckled. "Don't worry about it. I'm used to being naked around other werewolves. Although we don't have any female warriors in my pack, so I guess this is a little new for me."

I blinked, baffled by the situation. "Sorry, guess I should have knocked."

"Guess I should've locked the door." He winked at me.

"Your tattoo," I said, seeing it properly now in the light. "Wow, it's really cool."

"You like it?" He pushed his shoulder forward to give me a better look.

"Yeah, I love it," I replied in awe. It was of an evil-looking wolf with amber flames coming from its eyes and fur, and blood dripping from its mouth. It started on his upper arm and shoulder and partially covered his peck. I touched it lightly, admiring all the details. "It must have been expensive."

"It wasn't cheap," he agreed. "But it was worth it. The guy who did it is really good."

"I can see that."

He put his hands out to me. "Let me help you up."

"Thanks," I replied taking his hands as he pulled me up as if I weighed nothing. Damn, he was strong. I wasn't exactly a small girl. "Do you maybe have some mouthwash or something?"

"I do." He gave me a small smile and handed me a bottle that was sitting on top of the sink. I quickly swished it around my mouth and spit it out. "All set?"

"Yeah, I should probably head home. Sorry for imposing," I said shyly thinking he probably had better things to do.

"Hey, it's fine. I'm just glad you called. You were in bad shape last night. You passed out in the rain in the middle of the woods. Whatever you're doing, it's not safe. What is that stuff that you're drinking anyway?"

"It's nothing."

"It doesn't seem like nothing."

"Okay, Dad!" I taunted and walked out of the bathroom, not wanting to give him any more information. He already knew too much. He'd already helped too much. When I walked back into his bedroom, I noticed he'd hung my clothes up neatly on the back of his chair to dry. I quickly closed the bedroom door and changed. As I pulled the T-shirt I was wearing off, I noted again how soft it was. He had definitely chosen a really nice T-shirt for me, and a warmth filled my body at the thought.

I threw it into the hamper, although I was maybe just a little tempted to keep it for myself. As soon as I was dressed a knock rapped at the door. "Can I come in?" Tyce's voice sounded from the hallway.

"Come in," I replied and searched around for my cell phone.

"What are you looking for?"

"My cell phone. Have you seen it?"

"Let me call it." After a moment, I heard the muffled ringtone of my phone. Tyce was standing close to his bed, pulled my phone out from inside the blankets, and took a look at the screen. "Are you fucking serious?" he exclaimed. "You put my name in your phone as *Tyson Chicken*!?"

I doubled over in laughter.

"Goddess, you're so infuriating," he said, handing me my phone.

I gave another snicker and unlocked my phone to be greeted by a few text messages from Paige. I quickly shot back a text message to her to let her know I was okay and not to tell our parents anything, hoping she hadn't already. I didn't want a repeat of last time.

"I need to get home," I said, locating my shoes and sliding my feet into them.

"Do you want a ride?" he asked.

"It's okay. I should probably just walk. My parents will ask too many questions if they see you dropping me off. It doesn't exactly look good."

"I can drop you at the end of your street. I'm good at sneaking around." He winked at me.

"Tell me you're a manwhore without telling me you're a manwhore!" I shot back at him, annoyed by the thought of him being with other women.

"You say it like it's a bad thing." He snickered, angering me more.

"Gross! I probably have an STD just from lying in your bed!"

He laughed. "That joke only works on humans. It's free and clean love for us, baby." He wrapped his arms around me playfully. "Come on, you know you'd rather be with an experienced man who knows what he's doing anyway," he said in a low, gravelly voice, and—*fuck*—my stomach somersaulted, my panties instantly wet. When he spoke in that frustratingly sexy voice, I was ready to just give it all up to him, my heart racing and my breathing erratic. His strong arms felt so good wrapped around me, and I could feel his erection growing as it poked me from behind.

"I've gotta go!" I exclaimed, breaking free of his grasp and spell. Before he could stop me, I sprinted out of the room, down the stairs, and headed straight to the woods to collect whatever had been left there the night before, probably soaked now, but it was what it was. At least I was able to complete the process, even if it hadn't ended up so great. But then, I thought, did it really end up so bad?

Chapter 20

Jasmine

"Can I hold her?" I turned toward Talia who had just sat down on the couch next to me.

"Of course." Talia smiled and gently placed her baby in my arms.

"She's so beautiful." I sniffed back tears, cradling little Bianca in my arms, staring down at her rosy cheeks, fuzz of brown hair, and bright blue eyes. Lately, everything made me want to cry. "Her eyes are so beautiful," I said as I thought, *Our babies could have the same ones.*

"I know. I hope they stay that color," Talia replied. "She's only a few days old, so the doctor said they could still change."

"How is she so far?"

"She's perfect." Talia's eyes sparkled in a way that I imagined only a mother's eyes could, making me tear up all over again. "Much better than Libby." Talia chuckled. "That baby was Satan in a onesie."

I laughed in agreement. "She's definitely a handful. I didn't realize how bad she was until I started living in the packhouse. She's gotten better in the past few months though." I rocked Bianca back and forth while we both stared at her, delighted in the little bundle of joy. After some time, I asked, "So how did Alpha Alex take it when he found out she was a girl?"

"Not as bad as I thought he would." Talia snickered. "I thought he'd be a bigger baby about it. But once the doctor put her in his arms, you should have seen his smile. She's already got him wrapped around her little finger."

"Goddess, I can only imagine how Blake will be." I smiled to myself.

That afternoon, when Blake got back to the Pine Forest packhouse, I took his hand and brought him up to the bedroom we were sharing. "I already like the direction this is heading," he said when I gestured for him to sit down on the bed.

"You've been stressed, and I thought you should have some time to relax before Bianca's first full moon ceremony. Here, Talia helped me make you some mulled wine." I handed him a mug.

He took a sip and said, "Not my normal drink of choice, but this is actually pretty good."

I smiled, climbed into the bed behind him, and began rubbing his shoulders. He closed his eyes and rolled his neck in response. "Does that feel good?" I asked quietly in his ear.

"Feels amazing," he replied. "Do I get a happy ending too?"

"Blake! You and your one-track mind!"

"Hey, you said you wanted me to relax," he teased, taking another sip from his mug.

I massaged Blake all up and down his back, and before long, he switched places with me. We worked ourselves up until we couldn't take it anymore and finished each other off. I lay snuggled up against him, listening to his heartbeat and pleased that he did seem more relaxed.

"I love you, Mrs. Alpha," he whispered. "You and our pups." He rubbed my belly gently.

"I love you too," I replied, sighing in happiness. After a beat, I said, "Blake, I've been thinking."

"Hm."

"I think it's really nice how Talia named her pup after her mom."

"Mm," he responded in agreement.

"And, well, if our pups are girls, I was thinking it'd be nice to name one of them Ria. Or something similar. Like Rita, Maria, or Riana."

His eyes shot open and he studied me. "That wouldn't bother you?"

"No, I know how much you loved Ria. And I understand. She was your mate."

"Wow, Jasmine, I don't know what to say," he replied, and I could feel the emotions flooding his body. I grasped his hand, and he squeezed mine back.

"Just an idea I had," I added so he wouldn't feel bad shooting it down if he hated it.

"Goddess, why are you so amazing? I don't deserve you." He pulled me against him and kissed me with desperation. When we pulled apart, his eyes were bloodshot. Was he crying? I rubbed his arm, hoping to soothe him. He took a deep breath and said, "It would mean so much to me if we could name one of our pups after Ria." I kissed his forehead in response.

We snuggled in silence as Blake stroked his palm up and down my back, clearly lost in thought. I put my head back against his chest and drifted into sleep.

Blake woke me an hour or so later, so we could get ready for the celebration. The evening was cool and cloudy, but luckily no rain, so the pack was able to proceed with the huge barbecue they'd put together to welcome the new alpha baby. A few live bands rotated throughout the evening while many pack members danced. Picnic tables were set out with beautiful pink flower arrangements.

"Not bad for last-minute planning, eh?" Alex leaned over to Blake and me.

"Not bad at all. I'll have to take a few tips for ours." Blake squeezed my hand.

When Alex turned away to speak to more members of his pack, I whispered, "You told him?"

"He's family now. Anyway, I wanted him to know the stakes for me. That I don't exactly want to be going off to war and leaving my barefoot and pregnant mate behind."

"Why would you be going off to war?" I asked, concerned.

"There are some issues with the Bois Sombre Pack."

"Again? I thought they all got resolved."

"Not really. I'm thinking about extending our time up here another week just so I can get a better idea of what's going on. I already spoke to Luke and Tyce, and they're fine with handling the pack for now. I'll tell you more about it later. Let's just enjoy the evening for now."

"Okay," I replied, hesitating to just let it go.

"Are you okay?" Blake looked down at me. He clearly felt the anxiety reverberating in my body.

"We're telling so many people, and we still haven't told my parents," I replied.

"So let's tell them when we get back." Blake smiled. "I'm sure they're both going to be over the moon about the news."

"I just feel so weird about it. Like, hey, Mom, Dad, you know that thing I wasn't supposed to do. Well, I did it!"

Blake laughed heartily. "You weren't supposed to reject your fated mate either. And they got over that one pretty quickly."

"Or drop out of college," I added.

"Or become a warrior." He grinned. "What a shame it would have been if you followed that rule. Or really any of those terrible rules."

I gave a small laugh. Somehow Blake always knew how to cheer me up.

"I don't think you give your parents enough credit. I know they were tough on you growing up, but I think they're more open-minded than you assume."

"You're probably right." I sighed. Blake took my hand and led me over to the buffet area, so we could grab something to eat and enjoy the festivities.

When it got close to midnight, we all headed into the woods. Blake and I found a secluded area where we both stripped and shifted into our wolves. As soon as my hands transformed to paws and thick fur sprouted from my body, I broke into a run. Blake caught up with me and the two of us sprinted side by side, eventually joining with Alex's pack. The night was dark and cloudy, and the moon barely peeked out from behind the clouds, but we still howled in delight, wishing good fortune to Bianca.

Chapter 21

Ginger

That Friday, I received a text from Lucy to remind me of the plans she had to go to the nightclub. I quickly responded and agreed to go before sighing as I fell into my bed.

Barely a minute after I relaxed, Paige stumbled into my room, closing the door behind her. "Gigi, I need your help," she cried out, collapsing onto the floor next to my bed.

I got up quickly. "What happened? Are you okay?"

"Yeah, I'm fine, but . . ."

"What is it?" I asked, getting down on the floor next to her.

"I think I'm in heat!"

"Oh!" I exclaimed. "What does it feel like?"

"Oh, Goddess, this is so embarrassing." She turned bright red. "But I'm so . . . " She lowered her voice until she was whispering. "Horny."

I doubled over in laughter. "Where's Dylan?"

"He's working until two. Goddess, I'm dying!"

"And how did you want me to help?" I snickered. "I hope you weren't expecting me to take care of you on Dylan's behalf."

She burst out laughing. "Holy Artemis, no! What the hell is wrong with you, Gigi?"

"Just making sure." I snickered.

"Dylan booked a hotel not far from the pack. I was hoping maybe you could give me a ride over. Just so I can check in and stuff. And then maybe cover for me while I'm gone. Like tell Mom and Dad you dropped me at a friend's house."

"Only under one condition!"

"What's that?"

"If you ever wake up again and I'm not here, don't tell Mom and Dad!"

"Okay, deal." She squeezed her eyes shut and squirmed a little.

"Uhh, maybe you should, you know," I said.

"I did already. Several times!" Paige cried out. "This heat thing is no joke!"

"I guess I'll never know," I said, looking away and blinking back tears.

Paige must have noticed my reaction because she wrapped her arms around me. "Gigi, don't worry. I know you have a mate out there."

"You don't know that," I replied bitterly. "Why do you and Mom keep acting so sure? It just makes it worse. You believe so much, but what if I'm just being set up for disappointment?"

"Because Mom and I both pray for you. And Artemis listens to our prayers. I know. Especially when you pray for someone else."

"But what if Artemis isn't real? What if it's just a fairy tale?"

"Have faith, Gigi." Paige touched my chest above my heart. I shook my head, deciding not to argue more. Paige and my mom were both very religious, and it wasn't worth arguing logic with them.

"You said you need a ride, right?" I got up. "Let me go ask Mom to borrow the car for a couple hours."

The next morning, Paige stumbled into the house early and crawled into bed next to me. "Well, I'm no longer a virgin." She giggled.

"Deets?" I asked.

"It was so good." She sighed. "So, so good. Better than I imagined."

"So, tell me the juicy stuff! Like how big's his cock?"

"Gigi!" She punched me playfully in the arm.

"How's his tongue technique?"

"Gigi, stop!" She giggled some more.

"Why even tell me if you're not going to tell me any of the good stuff?" I teased.

"Gigi, I'm so completely and hopelessly in love!" Paige sighed, hugging one of my pillows. "Having a mate is one of the best things in the world. I can't wait for you to meet yours too."

"Paige, please stop," I said, turning away from her. "Can we not talk about my mate anymore, please?"

"If you really want me to stop I will. But I really don't think you should give up hope."

"Stop!" I said more forcefully.

I glanced over to her nodding, but she didn't say anything.

That night, Paige helped me get ready to meet with Lucy. "You should come too. It'll be fun." I elbowed her playfully.

"Clubbing's not really my thing. Anyway, Dylan and I have plans tonight."

"In the back of his CR-V?" I winked at her.

"I'm going to regret ever telling you anything." She laughed. "Here, sit." Paige gestured to the floor as she knelt down with our shared curling wand.

"Now you know how I feel with you and Heidi always asking about my sexcapades." I sat down in front of Paige.

"Oh, please! You love telling us!" Paige twisted my hair around the wand, spraying each tendril with hairspray as she went, so it would hold the curl.

"Okay, maybe I do . . . a little."

"Though you haven't had many stories lately."

"I'm home for the summer, and you know I don't do werewolves."

"Really, not even *alpha* werewolves?" Paige questioned.

"What are you insinuating?"

"You smelled like Tyce again last time you came home after being out all night. I'm not stupid, Gigi! I know there's something going on between the two of you."

"There's nothing going on. I just slept over the packhouse and picked up some of his scent. But we didn't do anything."

"Kind of like the time before?"

"Exactly." I didn't want to give Paige any more information and hated that she already knew too much.

"Gigi, seriously, what are you up to? Your story isn't adding up. Why are you randomly sleeping at the packhouse in Tyce's bed?"

"I have my reasons," I replied, sticking to my guns. I still wasn't ready to reveal everything to Paige.

"Honestly, Gigi, whatever it is, you can trust me."

"Then trust me that there's a reason I don't want to tell you," I replied, and Paige finally let up. After my hair and makeup were done, Paige helped me pick out a dress. I pulled on a black bodycon dress with skinny spaghetti straps, and it was so tight that I didn't even have to wear a bra with it. I then slipped on some black wedged sandals and spun around in front of a mirror.

"Damn, how'd you end up with the boobs?" Paige felt up her own small pair. "So unfair!"

"I had to be blessed with something you weren't." I stuck my tongue out at her. "So how do I look?"

"You look like you're about to get laid tonight." She chuckled.

"Funny, so do you," I teased back.

Chapter 22

Ginger

"I'm so glad you made it!" Lucy shrieked as she pulled me against her in an embrace. When she pulled away, she looked me up and down and said, "Damn, you look hot, Gigi! If I weren't straight, I'd fuck you!" She stared down at my boobs. "Can I feel them?"

"Sure," I replied. I was actually kind of used to it. For some reason, women loved touching my boobs. I mean, they were kind of just out there.

She poked two fingers into the top of them, the skin jiggling in response. "They're so squishy." I laughed at her reaction. She took my arm and pulled me toward the living room of the packhouse where a bunch of people were already pregaming.

"Here, have a White Claw," she said, pulling a can out of a bucket filled with ice. I took it from her as some girls made room for me on the couch.

As Lucy walked away to go who knows where, another girl sitting on the couch next to me grabbed my attention. "Hi, I'm Erin. Nice to meet you." She put her hand out to me.

"Hey, Gigi," I replied. I looked around and realized how out of the loop I was. I didn't recognize a single person who had come. Guess going to boarding school does that to you. Erin introduced me to everyone in the room and seemed friendly enough.

"Have some chips." A muscular guy held out a bowl to me. "I'm Cody. One of the warriors. Don't think I've met you before. You're Paige's sister, right?"

"Right," I replied.

"I see the resemblance." I nodded, taking some chips from the bowl he was holding out.

I conversed politely with everyone, relieved no one from my class year had shown up. I still felt traumatized from my middle school years and wasn't quite ready to face my demons yet. After I'd put away a couple of drinks, Lucy reappeared. "Dear Goddess, I finally got Libby to bed!" she complained. "Are you all ready to go?"

Everyone cheered in affirmation, stood up, and soon started splitting up into different groups. Lucy grabbed my arm and pulled me toward her. "Do you have a ride?" she asked. I shook my head. "No worries. You can just ride with Tyce and me!" I didn't realize he'd be coming too.

As soon as I looked toward the entrance, I spotted him bounding down the stairs dressed much more nicely than usual in a yellow button-up shirt that paired well with his tan skin and brought out his amber eyes. My stomach did a somersault as I, once again, had to admit how fucking hot he was. My inner thighs tingled as his mouth raised in the corners when he spotted me, giving me a slight nod.

Lucy called shotgun, so I climbed into the back seat, a little relieved. Ever since we'd spent the night together, I couldn't stop recalling how his body felt against mine. I'd be lying if I said I hadn't imagined how his clearly not-chipmunk-size cock would feel inside me. I did my best not to think about that in the car, especially with Lucy riding along with us. If werewolves could smell arousal, Lucy wouldn't be an exception. Goddess, how awkward would that be?

"So, where's Luke tonight?" I asked, trying to make conversation.

"He's staying home with Libby. Anyway, with Blake out of town, someone has to hold down the fort. I keep trying to get him to go out with me, but he's gotten so serious lately. He's always talking about pack safety and leadership." She stuck her tongue out.

"What about you, Tyce?" I teased. "Aren't you supposed to be acting alpha or something? Looks like you're not taking your duties seriously."

"Alphas get days off too," Tyce replied.

Lucy laughed. "Yeah, someone should tell Blake that. He really needs to lighten up. If anyone needs a night out, it's him!"

"Why?" I asked curiously.

"He's so grumpy all the time. He's always snapping at the dumbest things."

"He seemed nice to me when I met him," I responded, shrugging.

"What do you think, Tyce?" Lucy touched his arm. Logically, I knew she was mated, but it still annoyed me. Some instinct within me made my fingers contort as if they were transforming into claws, which was silly because I knew they couldn't do that. I flipped my hands over to examine my palms, confused by why I had just done that.

"He seems cool," Tyce replied. "I mean, he's an alpha. All alphas are kind of dicks if my dad and grandpa are any indications."

"You're not a dick though," Lucy whined, and again I felt something bubble within me. It was the tone of voice she used, like she was flirting with him. I didn't like it one bit. He chuckled in response, making my teeth tingle. Again, my fingers did the same thing, contorting as if they were trying to form claws.

"Tyce is a dick!" I blurted out. "A chipken dick!"

"What!" Lucy burst out laughing. "A chipken dick? What the fuck is that?"

"Half chipmunk, half chicken!" I replied.

Lucy laughed some more. "What does that mean?"

"Too small to feel it and too chicken to have balls!"

"Oh my Goddess, Gigi! You're hilarious!" Lucy was clutching her stomach in laughter. "We should hang out more often!"

"Sounds like someone's been stretched out a little too much! What, have you had a train run on you or something? You seem like the type!" Tyce snapped back.

Even though I deserved his comeback, I clutched at my stomach in hurt at his words. I noted that he was gripping the steering wheel, his knuckles white. *Fuck!* Why did I just say what I did? What was wrong with me? He had been so nice to me recently. Why was I being such a bitch?

"Aw, come on guys!" Lucy playfully pushed on Tyce's upper arm. "Lighten up! It's going to be a fun night!"

Her touching him angered me, my nostrils flaring, a growl reverberating in my chest.

"Tyce! How do you feel about tequila shots?" Lucy touched his upper arm again.

"I like anything that encourages bad decisions and regrets."

Lucy giggled. "My kinda guy!"

Tyce joined in on her laughter and joking, and I couldn't help but seethe. My skin, nails, and hair follicles tingled. I forced myself to take deep breaths, doing my best to ignore what was going on at the front of the car.

When we finally arrived, Tyce pulled into valet parking. I climbed out of the back seat, and one of the valets helped me out. The three of us turned to walk into the casino, and Tyce didn't even look my way. He was definitely pissed at me. And much like something had growled within me earlier, now I felt a whimper. My body was reacting in ways I'd never felt before, as if—I gasped—as if there was something inside me. *My wolf!*

I couldn't help but smile at the thought, all my bad emotions now a distant memory. Nothing could ruin this night anymore! Lucy hooked her arm through mine, and I practically skipped down the hall. We passed by the animated sounds of slot machines and people cheering at craps tables, the whole vibe of the casino bringing a new energy to me.

"Here." Lucy slid a plastic card into my hand as we approached the line to get into the nightclub.

"What's this?" I asked, flipping it over to see it was a driver's license from Texas.

"They probably won't check since you're with me and we have the pack table, but just in case."

"Oh!" I grinned.

"Also, everything's comped tonight so drink as much as you want. Tyce promised to be our DD." I looked his way where he had found the rest of the group and was now talking to them instead of us. I flinched a little, thinking I needed to stop being sick around Tyce all the time, and made a promise to myself I wouldn't go too crazy with the booze that night.

Before long, we were seated at the table. A bunch of people began doing tequila shots, which I'd now deduced was Lucy's drink of choice. I declined, knowing I'd never be able to keep up with werewolves, instead pouring myself a Grey Goose soda water, heavy on the soda water, from the selection of beverages laid out for us. Her flirting aside, I found that I actually quite enjoyed Lucy's company. She was very good at including everyone, making sure no one was left out, something I'd realized was rare in most people hosting parties. Even though I barely knew her, it felt like we'd been friends forever.

We all soon made our way out to the dance floor. Lucy and all her friends looked out for each other, and I finally felt like I belonged in a group in our pack. I couldn't understand Paige's disdain for Lucy. She seemed quite nice to me. Then again, this also wasn't really Paige's scene. An unpleasant feeling came over me, a bad memory from when I'd first started to seek independence from Paige.

As I danced, Tyce brushed up against me and static electricity sparked from the touch. I locked eyes with him in reaction, but I couldn't read him. The unpleasant feeling from moments earlier rolled over my body, and I knew I owed him an apology. "I'm sorry!" I shouted over the music, hoping he heard me. He nodded but didn't reply, turning away toward some of the guys who had come with us.

Lucy grabbed my hips and pulled me over to dance with her and Erin. I fell into a groove with them and tried to take my mind off Tyce, but I constantly felt his presence in my vicinity. After some time, the group of girls all went to the bathroom together—not surprising after all the drinks we'd downed. I went along and was lucky to secure a bathroom stall first. On my way out of the bathroom, I told everyone I'd meet them back at the table. When I made my way out, I decided to head to the bar to see if I could get some water, thinking I should stay hydrated.

I was waiting for some of the crowd to clear when I felt a presence behind me, and someone's hands slid down the sides of my torso to my hips. A shiver traveled up my spine in response. I turned around and was about to berate whoever decided to just grab me without asking first when I came face-to-face with Tyce, my heart skipping a beat.

So, maybe he had forgiven me? Goddess, he looked good, especially with my buzz taking control of my hormones, my whole body relaxed and aroused, my inhibitions lowered. Before I could stop myself, I turned back around and ground my ass against his pelvis. He instantly fell into sync with my dance moves, but it somehow seemed more intimate than it ever had with previous dance partners. His body heat surrounded me. His fingers grazed my thighs, hips, ass. Soon his hands were against the hem of my skirt, his fingers gripping the skin of my thighs, and his palms gliding against the fabric of my dress. I was practically moaning with how good his fingers felt on my bare skin, my whole body sensitive and tingling from his touch, my panties soaked with need.

I turned around so I could face him. Before I could even process what was happening, his mouth was on mine, and hot damn! Okay, I'll be honest, I'd kissed a lot of men—a lot! But the way his lips pushed up against my lips, his tongue brushed against my tongue, his hands pulled me desperately against his body, his cock throbbed against my torso—nothing had ever made me so hot and feverish before.

His hand was soon brushing the inside of my thigh, and I arched my back in response, letting out a moan that, thankfully, no one could hear over the loud music. And I knew: if I didn't fuck him that night, I would die. He brought his other hand to my chest where the low neckline of my dress met my skin, his thumb trailing my cleavage. I exposed my neck, and he brought his mouth to it, urgently leaving a trail of kisses up and down it. I grabbed his ass in response, and fucking Artemis, it was firm. I thrust my hips into him, constraining his substantial cock to throb against my pelvis. *Fuck*, he was so hard—like a steel rod. And I knew he wanted it just as badly as I did when he grabbed my hand and pulled me somewhere. Goddess, I didn't care where he was taking me. I would let him take me there and surrender my body to him. All I wanted was to feel his cock straining inside the walls of my pussy, which was convulsing with need and practically raining down my inner thighs. I'd never felt so horny in my life.

Once we made it toward the front of the club, he opened a door by tapping a key card to a reader and pushed me inside. We hadn't even walked a couple steps in when his hand was back on my inner thigh. He pulled the crotch of my panties to the side and shoved two of his fingers inside me. I let out a loud moan as he pushed me up against the wall and finger fucked me. I threw my arms against said wall, arching my back, and gave in to him as his thumb quickly and expertly found my clit. His other hand made its way to one of my breasts, and soon his thumb was inside my dress, rubbing against my rock-hard nipple.

"Fuck!" I cried out.

"Who made you that wet?" he growled. "Huh, baby?" He pushed a third finger inside me, becoming more forceful.

I moaned in response, giving in to the magic spell his fingers were putting on me.

"Tell me, baby. Who's got you going crazy like that right now?" He added pressure to my clit, and I screamed. "Tell me with your words." His eyes twinkled.

"You," I cried out, tears practically falling from my eyes with how amazing what he was doing felt, my whole body shivering in ecstasy.

"Yeah, me? You like when I do it this way, baby?"

It wasn't long before my entire body was quivering, his fingers coaxing out every bit of pleasure they could. His eyes locked with mine as he watched me come completely undone, my whole body destroyed by the intense orgasm that ripped through me. I tried to pull away but he wouldn't let me, forcing out a second and third orgasm as he rubbed my clit vigorously. I was thankful to the wall for supporting me, because all my limbs felt like jelly when he was done with me, and I couldn't believe I hadn't fallen over. If I died that night, I would die a happy and satisfied woman.

I was left panting as he withdrew his hand from inside my panties, my chest rising and falling dramatically, my lips parted in shock. No one had ever made me orgasm like that before. Hell, even my vibrator had never made me orgasm like that before. *Who the fuck was he?*

"How'd you get in here?" I asked when I'd partially recovered.

"Since I'm acting alpha for now, and your pack owns this casino, Blake gave me an access card just in case."

"Oh, what's this room we're in?"

"The coatroom. No one uses it during the summer."

That was actually really clever. And then I realized he must have experience with fucking girls in nightclubs, which both pissed me off and just made me that much more desperate to prove myself—that I was better than all those other nameless girls he'd done this with.

I dropped to my knees and grabbed his belt, undoing it quickly and unzipping his pants, pulling out his—*holy fuck*—huge cock! So all the rumors about alphas having enormous cocks were true! I looked up at him, and he gave me an arrogant smirk. I was tempted to bite it in response. But he did just finger fuck me better than anyone had ever, well, done anything else before. So I inhaled that cock like I was in a hotdog eating contest, forcing it as far as it would go to the point I should have been gagging. But Artemis be damned if he was going to walk away thinking he was the only one who was good at this. I was out to prove myself.

I used my saliva to lubricate him and grasped his thick rod with my hand, instantly falling into a groove of gliding my mouth up and down his length with my hand trailing, pressing the underside with my tongue. I used my other hand to cup his balls, gently bouncing them in my palm. He let out a deep, loud moan. I looked up, making eye contact with him as I continued to work diligently to try to get him off. But he stopped me, pulling me up and pushing me back against the wall. He aggressively pulled the straps of my dress down until my breasts popped out the top.

"Fuck, your tits are amazing." He gasped and brought his head between them, kissing all along the inside while he used his hands to knead them with urgency. When he pulled away, he grabbed the sides of my thighs and lifted me up against the wall. He forced his body between my legs and teased me with the head of his cock, rubbing it all along the crotch of my underwear. I let out a moan, cajoling him to move my panties out of the way and push it inside.

"Fuck, condom!" he cried out, lowering me back to the ground. "One sec." He bent down to get to his pants that were now wrapped around his ankles, exposing his very muscular legs. I didn't even know I could be so turned on by a man's legs. I knelt down next to him as he dug a condom out of his pocket.

"Let me," I said. He handed me the small package and I ripped it open, putting the tip of the condom between my lips. I used my mouth to roll it down the length of his cock as he groaned in reaction. I then turned around and got onto my hands and knees, and he instantly had his fingers inside the waistband of my thong, pulling it down my legs until it was completely off. He gave my clit a quick tickle before he forced himself inside me.

"Fuck!" I gasped. He was fucking huge! I almost felt like a virgin all over again with how much his cock strained against my inner walls.

"You like that?" He growled as he thrust against me. "You like that chipken dick?"

I moaned loudly in response, affirming that I did.

"Say it, say it out loud," he demanded as he pounded against me.

"Yes!" I cried out.

He brought his hand back to my clit, and I moaned again.

"You like that? You like when I rub your clit?"

"Yes!" I cried out again.

"Tell me who fucks you better than anyone else." He brought his mouth to my ear, and Goddess, his voice was so low and gravelly, I almost orgasmed just from that. When I didn't immediately respond, he pulled his hand from my clit and spanked me playfully. "Tell me!" he demanded.

"You!" I cried out, and he instantly brought his fingers back to my clit.

"Say my name," he commanded in his deep baritone voice.

"Tyce!"

"Say it again."

"Tyce!"

He thrust into me more forcefully and rubbed my clit more enthusiastically.

"Tyce!" I moaned out again, wanting more, desperate for more. In reaction, he gave me more, becoming that much more aggressive. "Tyce!"

He let out a deep groan and pounded into me harder, all while diligently working my clit until I couldn't hold back anymore and another intense orgasm ripped through me. I was screaming so loudly I was sure we'd be discovered, even with how deafening the music was outside. A growl that was just as intense escaped his mouth as he gave his last few thrusts and collapsed on top of me, both of us falling to the floor in exhaustion.

I felt his hot breath on the back of my neck, and I rolled over. He lifted his body slightly in response so I'd have room to do so. I looked up at him and screamed in horror at what I saw. His canines had grown huge—*enormous!*—and he was about to bite down on my neck as if he were a vampire. Terrified, I kneed him in his stomach, pushed him off me, and got up as quickly as I could, pulling my dress back up over my breasts, and down to cover my bottom half. Not even bothering to look for my underwear, I sprinted out of the room to get away from him.

Chapter 23

Tyson

Oof. I clutched at my stomach.

This fucking girl!

Goddess, she is so infuriating!

She pissed me the fuck off!

And yet . . . *I might be in love?*

No, I did *not* just think that. I definitely did not just think that. There was no fucking way I was in love with the most infuriating bitch I'd ever met. But, Goddess be damned, I'd be lying if I said that wasn't some of the hottest sex I'd ever had—if I said I didn't want to do it all over again. Was it possible to be addicted to a pussy?

Everything about her was perfect. Okay, most of the time she really pissed me the fuck off. But then there were times that I saw a different side of her—a less prickly side. And, Goddess, her body, the way she smelled, the way she screamed my name, her amazingly gorgeous tits, her big, round ass, her tight, little, wet pussy. I sighed to myself and got up off the floor, peeling off the condom that contained the evidence of what we'd just done. I found a paper towel roll in a cabinet under the closed window where coats were normally collected. I tore off a sheet and quickly cleaned myself, wrapped the used condom, and disposed of it in a small trash can. I then pulled up my pants, buckled my belt, and leaned against the wall, pushing my hands through my hair.

Okay, that was really weird. My canines had never done that before. And I'd fucked a lot of girls. A lot. More than I was ready to admit. Gigi wasn't wrong—I was a manwhore. And not once had my canines ever extended and pulled me into a trance like that, ready to mark. As far as I knew, that only ever happened with a mate. And Gigi clearly wasn't my mate. I mean, I'd know if she were my mate, right? People just knew.

So why had that happened? It made no sense. I felt bad for scaring her like that. I would never mark someone against their will, and I couldn't blame her for being scared that I might when that happened. I was sure she wanted to be marked by her actual mate and not some random dude she'd just fucked in the coatroom of a nightclub. Hell, *I* wanted to mark my real mate and not some random bitch I'd just fucked in the coatroom of a nightclub.

I felt a bit bad about my thoughts. Because that wasn't how I thought about Gigi at all. She wasn't some random bitch I'd just fucked. I actu-ally—*dare I say*—cared about her. I'd never felt that way about anyone before, and it kind of both scared and confused me. Knowing I had a mate out there, I'd never allowed myself to feel anything for anyone. To be honest, I never *wanted* to feel anything for anyone. I liked the whole "wham, bam, thank you, ma'am" schtick I had going. It was simple—I got my dick wet with minimal drama. But suddenly it all felt a little old, boring.

No, I didn't want to just *bow chicka bow wow* with Gigi—I wanted to know her. I wanted to know why she was so prickly, why she was going to the witch shop, and why she was medically excused from sparring in her pack. I also wanted to protect her and keep her safe.

Goddess, I felt like a million bucks when she called me for help that night and I was able to get her out of the rain. And holding her all night while we slept—I didn't know that I'd ever slept so well before in my life. The next morning, I was singing in the shower, something I'd never done before. Suffice to say, she affected me and did something to me that I didn't really understand. And now all I wanted to do was apologize to her for scaring her like that.

I made my way to exit the coatroom and spotted Gigi's panties on the ground on my way out. I quickly bent down to grab them and shoved them in my pocket. As soon as I reentered the main room of the club, the smell of sweaty bodies hit my nose. When there were so many horny people in one room together, it was overpowering, overwhelming. It was partially why I couldn't keep my hands off Gigi, even after that shit she'd said to me during the car ride over. Well, that and that tiny, little dress she was wearing that revealed every curve of her beautiful body and pushed her breasts up, showing off that amazing rack she had.

When I got closer to the table Lucy had booked, I instantly spotted Gigi doing body shots with Lucy and her friends. And damn, what a sight. My dick was already twitching again. There was no doubt about it—she turned me on.

I approached the guys who had come along, who were all just as entranced by what was happening as I was. "That Gigi girl's not bad," one of them commented loudly, so he'd be heard over the music. "A little chubbier than what I normally go for, but she's got a nice pair of tits on her."

Another one chuckled. "You know what they say. Big girls know how to suck cock."

"I'm pretty sure she's going commando. I just caught a glimpse of her beaver." The first guy—I'm pretty sure his name was Cody—smirked.

"Easy access," his friend responded.

I clenched my hands into fists as a growl reverberated inside my chest. I didn't like how they were speaking about Gigi at all and was ready to punch them out. I took deep breaths, trying to keep my cool.

"I'm going in to make my move." Cody started to strut toward her.

"No you won't." I grabbed the collar of his shirt before I could stop myself. He was a good few inches shorter than me and not anywhere close to as built as I was. I could beat him into a pulp if I wanted to.

"Woah, Alpha. Sorry, man. I didn't know you'd claimed her." His eyes were wide with fear.

"Don't ever talk about her like that again," I added menacingly.

"Of course, Alpha. I won't."

Satisfied, I put him down. All the guys then seemed on edge. I mean, I couldn't blame them. Not only did I have a genetic advantage, I'd also been training for my job since I was ten years old—and neither my dad nor my grandpa had ever gone easy on me. I wasn't someone who was bashful about violence or killing.

My eyes didn't leave Gigi for the remainder of the night. Although, there wasn't much of a night left because, after taking all those shots, Gigi was tipsy. She had to be the lightest-weight werewolf I'd ever met. She practically fell over as she stumbled toward the bathroom. I caught her before she face-planted.

"Tyyyyccccee," she slurred looking up at me from my arms. I pulled her skirt down to try to cover her, recalling that her panties were, in fact, in my pocket.

"Fuck, Gigi, you're drunk," I said, concerned.

"I have to peeee!" she whined.

I grabbed Lucy's arm as she was walking by. "Help Gigi," I commanded.

"Sure thing!" she replied brightly, helping Gigi up.

Before they walked away, I shoved the balled-up panties into her hand. "Put these back on," I demanded into her ear. After they returned, I offered to drive Gigi home. Lucy told me she'd catch a ride with someone else, clearly in her prime at the club.

"Why'd you drink so much?" I asked once we were in the halls of the casino, out of the club and able to hear each other speak.

"I was just having fun!" she whined.

"You really can't handle your liquor though."

"Goddess, you're such a dad!"

I rolled my eyes and walked her to the valet, helping her into the front seat when they brought my car over. Once we were on the road, I decided to make an attempt at an apology. I'd have preferred for her to be soberer when I did it, but it was what it was. "Hey, Gigi," I started.

"What?"

"Sorry about the whole canines-enlarging thing earlier."

"Why did you do that?" she asked loudly. "Are you a vampire? Are you like a black widow where you fuck and then kill your lovers?"

I snickered at her theories. "No, I honestly don't know why that happened. It's never happened before."

"It's never happened before? I've heard that one before!"

"Okay, *that* definitely never happened before!"

"I like how you know what I'm referring to." She giggled. "That makes me think it has happened before!"

"You know what, you should take it as a compliment if it has happened. From what I understand, and not from personal experience of course, usually guys can't get it up when they're nervous, which means they were probably really into you."

"I doubt it," she said quietly. I glanced over to see she'd pulled her legs up toward her body and was staring out the window.

"Hey, why are you being so down on yourself?"

She sighed. "Guys will fuck anyone, even when they're a two on their scale."

I gripped the steering wheel, pained with shame at what I'd said about her to Blake a few weeks back. After constantly having to defend myself against my father's and grandfather's biting insults and digs, I'd gotten used to whipping out devastating comebacks over the years. I whimpered a little and said, "Gigi, I'm really sorry I said that. I don't actually think that. Goddess, if I had to be honest, you're a fucking ten on my scale. I mean, you're amazing. I don't even know if you'll remember I told you all this tomorrow, and maybe that's why it's so easy to say it right now. But, well, that's how I honestly feel."

She gasped, and I glanced over to see that her eyes were wide, staring at me.

"Come on, guys had to have told you that before."

"No one's ever told me that before," she practically whispered.

"That surprises me."

"Why? I don't exactly look like a supermodel like—like Lucy!"

"Lucy?" I questioned. "Lucy couldn't be further from my type. Sure, she's pretty, but I like 'em thick and juicy. I like having something to grab on to."

She gave a small laugh. "That surprises me."

"Why?"

"I mean, you're so hot. I dunno. I just thought . . ."

"That I would only go for someone society tells me is supposed to be hot?" She didn't respond. I glanced over at her, and she appeared to be lost in thought. Or maybe she was falling asleep. It was pretty late, and she had been drinking. I was tempted to bring her back to the packhouse and curl up with her again. But I knew I should do the right thing and bring her home where her family would be expecting her.

When we got to her house, I noted all the lights were off, so I decided it would be safe to drop her in front and make sure she made it safely inside. I got out of the car and went around to her door, then gently shook her. She jolted awake, confused by her surroundings. "You're home. Let me walk you to the door." I put my hand out to her and helped her out of the car.

"Goddess, I did drink too much, didn't I?" She looked up at me in a very sweet way.

When we got to her door and she was digging around for her keys in her small purse, I said, "I want you to know that I really enjoyed what happened tonight."

"Just forget it happened," she mumbled as she slid the key into the doorknob.

I placed my hand on top of hers to stop her. "Why?"

"I mean, it's just going to end in a disaster. We don't even like each other. And you're just a d-bag who's going to use me until you find your mate."

Before I could respond, she slipped into her house and shut the door in my face.

Chapter 24

Ginger

The next morning, I woke at noon to Paige bouncing on my bed, my head throbbing and my throat dry. Goddess, why did I do that again? Why did I overdo my drinking again when I promised myself not to?

"Wakey, wakey!" she sang out.

"Goddess, can't you leave me alone?" I groaned.

"Did you forget we volunteered for the temple bake sale today? Those blondies aren't going to bake themselves. Heidi's already on her way to help."

I groaned again.

"So, come on, how was last night? I've been dying to find out how it went and what you think of Lucy." She giggled.

At the mention of the prior night, all my memories came rushing back to me. Tyce's fingers inside me, him pushing me against the wall, fucking me on the floor, his vampire teeth, all the shots I took with Lucy and her friends, and Tyce driving me home. "Fuck!" I cried out.

"What?" Paige stared at me.

"Oh Goddess, oh Goddess, oh Goddess."

"What?" Paige asked again.

"Fuck, fuck, fuck."

"Oh my Goddess, Gigi, are you going to tell me or what?"

"I had sex with Alpha Tyce last night!" I blurted out.

"What!"

"Oh Goddess, why did I do that?"

"Wait, Gigi, tell me the whole story. Why did you have sex with Alpha Tyce?"

"I don't know!" I sat up, throwing my hands up and letting them crash against the bed. "He came up behind me, and I don't know, he's just so fucking hot. He took me into the coatroom and—" I groaned.

"And what?"

"Well, we did it."

"What did you do?" Paige was looking at me eagerly, staring intently.

"I can't tell you!"

"What?" She blinked. "But you always tell me!"

Something about it didn't seem right. Like we had shared something special that would be ruined if I told someone else. The images all replayed in my head—how his fingers just seemed to know what to do, how in sync we were when he slid himself inside me. Goddess, I had been wrong. He wasn't bad in bed at all. And Goddess be damned if I didn't want to do it again. That was why I took all those shots—to drown it all out. I didn't want to remember and catch feelings again. I was always catching feelings, and they never led anywhere good. Finally, I said, "It wasn't anything to write home about."

"Oh, so he's another Craig." She smiled knowingly. Goddess, why did I tell my sisters about my sex life? Craig was one of my college hookups, and Goddess, he was bad! Like, really, really bad. Like lasted five seconds and asked if I enjoyed it bad. "That's too bad. He's really good-looking."

"No, not like Craig!" I responded, thinking I didn't want to give Tyce that image. I did feel a bit bad about how bitchy I'd been toward him since I'd met him. I mean, when it counted, he seemed to be a good guy.

I'd actually kind of warmed up to him. And I didn't want my sister to think bad things about him.

"Okay, at least he wasn't that bad. So he was slightly better than terrible?"

"Can we not talk about it?" I asked. "Also, please don't tell Heidi!"

She made a gesture of zipping her mouth.

"So how was your date with Dylan last night? And when are you finally going to introduce me to him?" I asked, desperately wanting to change the subject.

"I just love spending time with him. He's so great. We didn't do anything exciting. We went out for barbecue and sat in the restaurant just talking for hours about anything and everything. I can't even explain it, but we have this connection like we're so in tune with each other." She grinned from ear to ear. "You'll meet him properly this week. We're making plans, so he can come over for dinner one night."

"Already meeting the parents," I teased.

"I mean, Mom and Dad are basically forcing me to marry him immediately. So I guess things are bound to move pretty fast." She looked out into the distance.

I touched Paige's arm. "Do you not want to marry him?"

"I do! But I don't know. It just feels so rushed. I'd like to enjoy just getting to know him longer before we seal the deal, you know? I know werewolves usually do things a lot faster than humans, and we're obviously mates, so there's nothing to question. But, I don't know. Don't you think it's weird to just rush into it?"

"I mean, there's no reason to," I replied.

She sighed. "I sometimes wish we weren't so religious. I obviously believe in Artemis and all her teachings, but it'd be nice to not feel so obligated to follow all the rules, you know?"

"Yeah, I know," I agreed. "I mean, you know I know. I'm really bad. If Mom and Dad knew how bad I was, they'd probably disown me." I chuckled. Paige laughed along with me and appeared to brighten up.

After Paige left my bedroom so I could get ready for the day, I checked my phone to see text messages waiting from Tyce.

> **Tyson Chicken**: Any chance to talk today?
> **Tyson Chicken**: I could meet you in our usual spot either before or after the service
> **Tyson Chicken**: I have a ride to Salem to offer in exchange

I stared at my phone, not sure what to make of his request. I mean, what was there to talk about? We'd gotten carried away—and, okay, it was good—but obviously we weren't going to repeat what happened, right? It was just a one-night thing.

One night of great sex with several mind-blowing orgasms . . .

Fuck, maybe this was the "it was all a mistake" conversation . . .

Curiosity got the better of me (and, okay, desperation for a ride), so I agreed to meet Tyce after the service, telling my parents I'd meet them at home. I waited until my family left and most of the congregation dispersed as well, though many stuck around later than usual to buy some baked goods. Once I made my way outside, I spotted Tyce sitting down on a bench. He stood as I approached.

"Hey, I made it." I gave Tyce a small, closed-mouth smile.

"Thanks for making it." He smiled widely in return, seeming genuinely happy to see me.

"You wanted to talk?"

He rubbed the back of his neck and said, "I'd like to start over."

"Start over?" I repeated, not sure what he meant. It was definitely not what I'd been expecting him to say.

"I'd like to get to know you, Gigi."

"Why?" I eyed him suspiciously.

"I don't know. You seem cool."

"What!" I doubled over in laughter. "All you do is make digs at me all the time. What was it you said last night? That you think I've had a train run on me?"

His ears reddened, and he flinched a bit. "Sorry about that. But in my defense, you weren't exactly the nicest person toward me either."

I looked down at my foot and kicked at the ground. "Yeah, sorry about that."

"Anyway, I think we started off on the wrong foot. So, I'd like the opportunity to make a better first impression. Hi, I'm Tyce." He reached out his hand to me.

I studied his hand, wondering why he was doing this. Was this a trick?

After a few moments of his hand being extended, he said, "You're supposed to shake my hand."

"What if I don't want to?"

"There's a ride to Salem depending on it." He gave me a knowing smirk.

"The offer for the ride to Salem was based on me meeting you. You can't just add more requirements now that I did what I was supposed to."

He let out a breath. "Okay, fine. But I'd really like the opportunity to start over. I think it will make for a better four-hour ride, no?"

I made a face like I was considering it, putting my pointer finger to my chin. Finally, I clasped his hand and shook it. "Fine. Hello, I'm Gigi. Nice to meet you."

"Gigi, you infuriate me, but there's something about you. And I'm looking forward to finding out what it is."

"How can I already infuriate you if we just met?"

"I can just tell. You give off an infuriating vibe."

"Funny. You give off a douchey vibe." I laughed.

"I'm not so bad. Maybe you should get to know me too." He winked. "There's more to me than my chipken dick and G Wagen."

"Like what?" I tried to stifle a laugh. He actually did seem to have a bit of a sense of humor.

"For starters, I'm an alpha. We're pretty big around here, in case you didn't know. I'm also quite good on a snowboard, and I make a mean carnitas burrito."

"You cook?"

"Saying I cook might be a bit of an exaggeration, but there are a few dishes I can throw together. My brother and sister are the cooks in the family, but I picked up a few things from them."

"Are you close to your siblings?"

"My parents aren't exactly the warmest people in the world, so my siblings and I kind of banded together growing up."

I began to warm toward him a bit now learning this new side of Tyce.

"Are you close with your family?"

"I'm really close to my twin, Paige. My older sister, Heidi, and I used to be closer too, but she's been pissing me off lately. My parents are great though. They're kind of strict, but they've always been really loving and supportive to all of us. I'm lucky to have them."

"I'm jealous," he responded.

"Why? What are your parents like?"

"They're tough. Really tough. I mean, it makes sense. They raised me to be an alpha. It's a huge responsibility, and both my dad and grandpa take it really seriously. And my mom, well, she's mated to my dad. You have to be a certain type of person to put up with him."

"What did they do that was tough? Like give me an example," I said, suddenly curious about him.

He shook his head a little. "That's probably a conversation for another time. Maybe once we get to know each other more. My family"—he let out a deep breath—"is intense. I think that's the best way to put it."

I nodded in acknowledgment, not sure how to respond.

"Hey, you want to sit? I purchased these blondies at the bake sale today. I took a bite earlier while I was waiting for you, and they're actually really good. Like dangerously good." He pulled some familiar packaging out of a bag he had in his hand. "I mean, they're not quite my mom's brownies, but they're pretty close." He sat back down on the bench and began unwrapping one of the cellophane bundles.

I laughed, thinking how funny the coincidence was. "I made those blondies for the sale! Well, my sisters and I did." I took a seat next to him, and he handed me a bar.

"They're excellent." He let out a moan as he bit into one, which, I can't lie, made my stomach somersault and aroused me, a shiver traveling up my body.

"But not as good as your mom's brownies?" I questioned, biting into the bar he handed me as well.

"No, my mom's brownies are out of this world. It's tough competition. But your blondies are definitely a close second. That's a compliment."

"I'd like to try the brownies sometime to judge for myself."

"I have some in the freezer. I've been rationing them to hold me over until she mails the next batch. Maybe I can bring you one for the road when we go to Salem."

"Wow, you're going to share one of your rationed brownies with me?" I put my hand to my heart. "I feel honored."

"You should." He gave me a sweet smile. "I would never share them with anyone else." Something about how sincere he sounded when he said that brought an intense warmth to my heart, taking me aback. I wondered why he was suddenly being so nice. Did Tyce like me? But how? No, he couldn't—could he?

We nibbled on the blondies quietly. After I finished mine, I asked, "When are you going to Salem again?"

"I'm not sure. Probably after Blake gets back. I've been filling in for him while he's been gone, and I didn't realize how much work he does. The thing is, back home, I have my whole family helping run our pack. Blake basically just has Jasmine and Luke. I'm actually really impressed with how much he does."

"Blake seems to be a good alpha. His dad was good too. My parents always spoke highly of him. The whole pack was devastated when he died in battle."

"I never met him. Our packs didn't have a good relationship until recently."

"Paige told me a bit about that. But it sounds like things are good between us now."

"Yeah, they are." He smiled meaningfully at me, and I wondered if he meant the packs.

Chapter 25

Tyson

On Wednesday, I filled in for some trainers in the morning, followed by a run of the pack. I had to keep shifting back and forth between my forms since I wasn't able to mindlink with Blake's pack members, which got exhausting after a while. By lunchtime, I was more than ready for a break. As I entered the packhouse and made my way to the kitchen, I wiped some sweat from my forehead and let out a deep breath.

I was pleased to see that Connie had left out my favorite for lunch—Texas beef chili. I quickly reheated it in the microwave and took a seat at the kitchen table, bringing over a bottle of hot sauce and pulling out my phone, so I could look through my calendar. I smiled to myself as I noted my evening was empty of obligations, and I'd finally have a chance to relax. I'd never worked so hard as an alpha before. Partially because of what I told Gigi—my whole family helped with running the pack, so it wasn't quite as much work.

What I hadn't told Gigi, though, was that it was also because my father and grandfather had trouble relinquishing control. My grandfather, especially, still saw me as a kid, and nothing I ever did would change his mind. I probably could have forcefully taken control from both him and my dad now that I was officially alpha of my pack, but the thing was, there probably was a part of what my grandfather thought that was true. I kind of liked just fucking around. This shit was exhausting!

But I didn't want to think about that. I sat back in my chair and pushed my family from my mind, again thankful to have a break from them for the summer, even if being part of Blake's pack was more work than I'd bargained for. As I spooned some chili into my mouth, my thoughts drifted to Gigi. I wanted to see her again. I couldn't stop thinking about her sexy body and how much I wanted to play with her perfect, firm, and beautiful tits again—to run my tongue along the perimeter of her pink nipples and place my face between them, inhaling her sweet perfume. I didn't even try to deny it anymore—I was obsessed.

I pulled up her name in my phone and sat back in my chair, considering whether or not I should text her to hang out that night. After all, I did have the night off. And we'd be the only ones on the alpha floor. Blake and Jasmine still hadn't returned. But I probably shouldn't seem so eager to just get her into my bedroom. I began to think about what I could invite her to do instead, with the obvious goal of getting her back here by the end of the night, but without making it too obvious.

Just then, the people I wasn't expecting to make an appearance did as Blake and Jasmine entered the kitchen.

"Hey," Blake said.

"Hi, Tyce!" Jasmine came over and gave me a hug.

"Hey. I wasn't expecting you guys back today." I looked between the two of them. "Welcome home."

"Thanks for holding down the fort while we were gone. Do you mind if we meet with Luke after lunch?" Blake asked, dragging his hand through his hair.

"Yeah, sure," I replied, putting my phone away. *Damn, looks like a repeat of Saturday night isn't going to happen after all.*

After we finished eating, Jasmine split up from us and went upstairs to get settled while I followed Blake into his office where Luke was already at his desk working. "Hey, welcome home, man." Luke got up and gave Blake a pat on his back.

"Thanks, it's good to be back," Blake replied and pulled out two chairs for him and me to station ourselves in front of Luke's desk. Blake dropped into his seat and dragged his hand through his hair again, letting out a deep breath. "I have some bad news."

"What is it?" Luke sat up, leaning forward.

"We need to gather a group of our warriors to bring up north. The situation I told you about with Bois Sombre isn't looking good. We've been gathering intel, and we're 99 percent sure that there's going to be an attack on their pack. They're really vulnerable without an alpha, and Luna Sofia was never really trained as a warrior, so she can't run the pack like an alpha normally would. Her brother and father are basically spread thin between the two packs, and Luna Sofia's son is only sixteen, so it'll realistically be at least another two years before he can take the alpha title."

"Fuck, man," Luke responded.

"I honestly didn't even want to come back. But I can't have Jasmine up there when this all goes down."

Luke looked at Blake. He opened and closed his mouth a few times, clearly debating whether to say something before he finally decided to. "Blake, I totally get you not wanting to involve Jasmine in battle. I wouldn't want Lucy involved either. But, I mean, why are you having her train so hard in that case? She looks really exhausted lately. Maybe she'd be better off concentrating her efforts in areas of the pack that don't require so much physical training."

Blake sighed, shaking his head. "I do want her involved. But she's pregnant."

"Oh, shit. Congrats, man!" Luke came around the desk and gave Blake a hearty pat on the back.

"Congrats!" I got up and did the same after I processed what he'd just said. "My family will be ecstatic once they hear the news. We should crack some beers open to celebrate."

When Blake didn't seem to share in our excitement, Luke shifted on his feet and asked, "It's good news, right?"

Blake put his head in his hands, an unexpected reaction, and Luke and I hovered around him, looking at each other. He finally lifted his head up. "Luke, there's something I never told you."

"What is it, man?" Luke took a seat on his desk, bringing all his attention to Blake. "We're brothers, right? You can tell me."

"You're family now." I patted Blake on the back. "Whatever it is, I'm happy to help. My pack is happy to help."

"Ria," he started, and I realized that this was going to be a heavy conversation, now well aware that was the name of his fated mate who died in battle. I shifted toward him, giving him all my attention. I definitely didn't know Blake like this, but I also didn't want to be a dick. I mean, the guy was mated to my cousin, and he was now an ally by blood. He shook his head.

"Hey, I can leave if you guys want to talk privately," I offered, wondering if he felt uncomfortable with my presence.

"No, it's okay, Tyce," he said, which surprised me. We still hadn't really bonded, so I didn't expect him to open up to me. Additionally, he always seemed really put together, which further alarmed me that he had something to share. But I should have known better than anyone else what it was like to have demons inside but still need to put up a tough-guy image all the time. It was part of the curse of being an alpha.

I patted Blake on the back. "Hey, whatever it is, I won't judge."

He sighed. "Ria was pregnant when she died."

"Oh, fuck, man," Luke said, crossing his arms. "Shit, I had no idea."

"Only my mom knew. We found out the night before. We called my mom to tell her and get advice on what to do. I was going to send her back to the pack the next day. But I never got the chance because the Bois Sombre Pack and their allies attacked early in the morning, breaking into the barracks where we were all sleeping. Ria put up an amazing fight, but it wasn't enough." He dropped his head into his hands.

Luke and I both patted Blake on the back, and I was stunned by the confession. While I'd gone through a lot in my life, it was never anything like that. And, suddenly, I was imagining what it would be like to lose Gigi, which caught me off guard. I hadn't realized how much I cared and worried about her until that moment, the idea bringing an intense and sharp pain to my chest. "Blake, I want you to know that I will help you keep Jasmine safe. And your secret's safe with me," I declared.

"Same!" Luke chimed in. "We're all in this together. Whatever you need, man, just let us know." He let out a deep breath and lowered his voice. "Also, Blake, I'm really glad you were finally able to tell me. I know it wasn't easy. I think Jasmine's been really good for you, and I'm really glad things worked out the way they did." Blake nodded at Luke.

"So, beers?" I asked. "I think we could all use some. I mean, we need to prep for war." Blake nodded, and I quickly ran to the kitchen to grab a few cans out of the fridge. The three of us cracked them open and got to business.

"I think I can manage to just go up north myself with the warriors," Blake started. "Luke, it's probably best if you stay down here since at least one of us should be here to take care of the pack. And you can mindlink with the pack members." He then looked over at me. "And, Tyce, I don't expect you to involve yourself in this. I mean, this isn't your pack's ally or problem."

"No!" I exclaimed. "First of all, if you're going to battle, I'm fucking coming with. That's what I live for as alpha. And, second of all, I already said you have my and my pack's support. I'll get some of my warriors over to the East Coast. We're a team now."

Blake gave me a big smile and patted me on the shoulder. "Thanks, man. I appreciate it!"

"Just don't accuse me of being a rapist anymore," I joked, trying to lighten the mood and giving Blake a soft punch in the arm.

Blake chuckled, and we began drawing up plans. Midway through our meeting, I realized, for the first time, I finally felt connected to my alpha role and what it meant. A renewed energy pulsed through me as I huddled with Blake and Luke and felt like a valued team member rather than just someone my dad and grandpa dragged along out of obligation.

Chapter 26

Tyson

The next day, Blake rounded up around a hundred of his enlisted warriors, and we headed up north. We bused the chosen warriors and came up with a cover story that they were part of some intramural sports teams that were going to compete in Quebec, just in case any questions got asked at the border. Blake and I took his car and rode together.

Before I left, I got in touch with my brother to keep tabs on how he was doing with arranging a chartered flight with as many of our warriors as we could fit. While I told my brother not to worry about coming, he couldn't help himself and jumped on the same flight with all of them. I smiled—my brother was a good guy, and I knew he'd always have my back. Although, I'd probably try to keep him in charge of the logistics rather than fighting on the front lines. He'd never been trained as well as I had.

"Tyce, I really appreciate all your help, both this time around and when Jasmine was kidnapped. If your pack ever needs a favor, I'll have a flight chartered from the East Coast in no time." Blake glanced over at me with a smile.

"Hey, don't mention it, bro. You know I'm going to take you up on that offer one day. That's what alpha alliances are all about."

During the drive, my thoughts shifted back to Gigi, never able to keep my mind off her for too long. I knew she was anxious to get down to Salem, so I decided to shoot her a text to let her know I hadn't forgotten about her and would be back soon. I smiled to myself thinking how much I was looking forward to spending more time with her. It wasn't even the physical stuff—although my dick got instantly hard any time I thought about her—it was also just *her*. Her spicy personality, the sweet freckles that dotted her cheeks, how her strawberry blonde hair bounced when she walked, and how quick-witted she was when it came to insults.

"What are you so happy about?" Blake glanced over at me at a red light.

"Nothing. Just thinking," I replied.

"You look like someone who's met their mate."

"Nah, no mate," I replied. And then, I thought, if I was so crazy about Gigi, what would it be like to actually meet my fated mate? *Was I in love?*

We decided to stay in the neighboring Lune Nordique Pack's territory, assuming the enemy packs were keeping their eyes on the Bois Sombre Pack. If they were planning a surprise attack, we didn't want them to know our numbers and preferred for them to believe it would be an easy battle. Our warriors all snuck onto pack land after dark, one by one, in their wolf forms. We didn't want anyone spying on us to notice a mass movement of bodies.

That evening, Blake, Blake's friends Jack and Kyle, Alpha Alex of the Pine Forest Pack, my brother, and I all met up at a pub in a town nearby. "So, how are you guys feeling?" Jack looked around at all of us. "Ready?"

"Ready or not, we're in it now," Alex replied. "On the bright side, there's no way they could possibly have more numbers than us. I mean, we have warriors from five different packs."

"You know, as much as I will never forgive your sister for what she did to mine, she's also not all bad." Blake nodded at Alex.

Alex shrugged. "After talking with her a few times during the past couple weeks, I think she might be realizing the error of her ways. But I can't ever let her back in my pack." He took a sip of his beer.

"I'm surprised she even told us anything. I mean what did she expect to gain from this?" Blake asked.

"Beats me. But everything she told us checked out. Maybe she really did just want to help her old pack."

We all took sips of our drinks. "How involved was she with planning all this?" my brother, Trav, asked.

"Not involved much at all," Alex replied. "She just gave us the initial info, and we ran with it, checking it out. And it all ended up being true."

"Okay, just wondering how much dirt she has on us and our plans. She doesn't sound like someone who should be trusted."

"Oh no, we don't trust her at all." Alex chuckled and Blake joined in. "We never even told her we followed up on any of the information she gave us."

We all nodded.

"Are you satisfied, Trav?" I clinked my glass against my brother's. Then I turned to the group and said, "He's the one with the brains in the family."

"I mean what choice do I have at this point? I'm here and we're going to battle any day now." He gave a small chuckle.

"Would it help if you talked to her in person?" Alex asked. "Maybe it'd be good to get the opinion of an impartial third party."

"That would be a good idea," I chimed in. "Trav's a good judge of character."

Alex pulled out his phone and typed something on it. "I'll have her meet us tomorrow. It'll be good to find out if she has any additional intel for us then too."

The next day, Alex, Trav, and I made our way to an isolated area of forest.

"Do you smell that?" Trav sniffed the air audibly. "Something smells amazing."

I inhaled the air and wrinkled my nose in disgust. "Not sure what you smell, but I smell rogue."

"But like, besides that faint rogue scent, something smells so beautiful, feminine, magical." Had Trav suddenly turned into a poet? I'd never heard him talk like that in my life.

After stepping a few yards into the woods and hitting a clearing, we arrived at a petite, blonde woman sitting on a stump. Her rogue scent permeated the air. After being trained in the torture of rogues for years, I instantly had an adverse reaction to the smell. However, odor aside, she had to be the prettiest, most well-put-together rogue I'd ever seen, with a perfectly trimmed pixie cut, well-tailored clothing, and a lean, muscular body, not unlike Jasmine's. She was exactly the type that my parents would have chosen for me to settle down with, which I knew because they'd made their distaste for the types of women I actually preferred perfectly clear over the years.

She lifted her head as we approached, and suddenly, Trav stopped dead in his tracks. Alex and I both looked over to note he appeared to be stuck in a trance, his eyes glued to her. I waved my hand in front of him, wondering where he went, when he suddenly spoke. "Mate."

"Mate," Alex's sister responded, a similar trance-like look on her face.

"Holy shit," Alex said.

Clearly in a world of his own, Trav stepped forward. "Travis Tikaani of the Jade Moon Pack. And you are?"

"Sara Adalwolf, my own alpha." She smiled and I could tell it was unnatural for her, the gesture seeming awkward on her face.

"Sara Adalwolf, my mate." Travis returned her smile, his whole face lighting up.

"I have a feeling any opinion he has of my sister is going to be biased at this point." Alex chuckled.

"Damn, who would have thought?" I replied, looking between the two of them.

Chapter 27

Blake

We had all expected to have more time to get settled, go over strategy, and plan before shit hit the fan. But we should have all known better than to expect war to be predictable. While our warriors stayed at the neighboring Lune Nordique Pack, the alphas, including Alex, Tyce, and Alpha Antoine of the Lune Nordique Pack with his mate Luna Marie, settled at the Bois Sombre Pack in their packhouse, so we'd be able to get to the front lines as soon as the attack hit.

And just like that, two days after we arrived, right before dawn, we got the alert that enemy troops were proceeding. We all sprinted out of bed, threw our clothes off, and turned to wolves as soon as our bare feet hit the ground outside, making our way past the border, hoping to meet them outside the territory and keep the pack safe.

We advanced with the Bois Sombre Pack warriors at our heels, knowing the others should arrive shortly. While I was against it, Alex had made sure his own troops were stocked with wolfsbane dart guns but promised to only use them if it became necessary. I was still of the belief that it was reckless, since it was nearly impossible to differentiate wolves of different packs without being close enough to smell them, and friendly fire was simply too likely. I wasn't ready to risk my own pack's lives like that.

Of course, I could be noble all I wanted, but I couldn't control what other packs did, and clearly the trend had caught on. As soon as the large cluster of enemy wolves arrived, sprinting out from behind trees and peeking out from atop hills, wolfsbane darts began raining down on us. Alex and I pushed forward, both having built up high tolerances at school, ready to start picking off their men, especially the ones in human form shooting the darts, who would be helpless against us in our wolf forms.

While they got a couple into me, I was easily able to push forward and take down a good number of their warriors. I used my sharp, lethal claws to slice through necks and pull hearts out of their bodies, slamming them to the ground as they came crashing against the dirt. Alex was right next to me, doing the same. The faster we took them down, the less darts they'd be able to get into our troops.

We tried to work as quickly as possible, but it wasn't long before my warriors arrived and I began to feel the familiar sting as a tether would be broken and a warrior would fall dead. No matter how many times it happened, it still took the air out of my lungs. These were my pack members—the people I was raised and trained to protect. This wasn't even my own pack I'd brought them to help, but an ally pack. While, logically, I knew it was the right thing because the favor would be returned one day when we needed help, it would be that much harder to explain it to their family members when I'd have to meet with them face-to-face.

While the deaths of my pack members distressed me, they also brought me a fresh wave of energy to fight harder, kill more callously. More darts pinched my skin as they were able to plunge them into me, and I began to feel the familiar burn of wolfsbane as I realized I was getting close to my limit. And then I noticed wolfsbane darts raining from the other direction. Alex had clearly given his own warriors the go-ahead, presumably as he was in similar shape to me, continuing to fight while our veins and organs were on fire, the wolfsbane blurring our vision, like acid on every pore of our body. Blood dripped from my throat, but I continued forward. I wasn't going down without a fight.

Soon Tyce was next to me, and I saw the resemblance between his wolf and Jasmine's. Both wolves were brown, but while Jasmine had a white belly and toes, his was pure brown with black-tipped fur, like a huge grizzly bear. His amber eyes glared evilly at the enemy as he fought like a maniac. I'd never seen anything like it. In his wolf form, he was completely feral and unpredictable, ready to kill mercilessly, and I suddenly understood the reputation his pack had—they were definitely not werewolves you ever wanted to fuck with. His warriors similarly followed suit, a huge advantage in our fight.

Adrenaline pulsed through my body as I tried to mimic the style of their fighting, trying to take down as many enemies as I could. Even as my whole body felt as if it were charred from so much burning. Even as sharp claws got good swipes into my body, spraying my blood into the crowd. Even as my whole being wanted to shut down from all the injuries I'd sustained.

And then, I saw it. A dart landed in Tyce's body, and he gave a loud whimper. It was safe to say that he probably hadn't ever built up a tolerance. His movement slowed as I got close to him. And as I saw another dart launched toward him, I jumped in front of it, knowing it would probably kill him, pinning him to the ground and allowing it to hit me instead. And that was what did it—the final dart that broke the wolf. I was instantly forced into my human form, immobile on the ground, the whole world going blurry and fading from my vision.

Tyson

Goddess, I loved fighting. I was built for this. In my wolf form, I was ruthless. I enjoyed nothing more than the feeling of my teeth and claws slicing through thick fur and delicate skin. I loved searching for someone's heart with my paws once I was able to plunge them into their chest. And I celebrated the crunch my teeth made when they sliced through a wolf's cervical vertebrae. Was there anything better than when I got a really good strike and was able to pull out an entire vertebral column? Oh, and biting off tails and breaking legs? More favorites. I loved all of it. I loved it even more than torturing, which was a close second.

While there were things about being an alpha that weren't necessarily my preferred activities, this wasn't one of them. I was in my natural state when it came to fighting and going to war. Even my grandfather had once commended me on how good I was out in the field—and that asshole never complimented anyone or anything. I think it was the one time he considered the idea that he could relinquish control to me one day.

I looked around in satisfaction as enemies ate dirt. We were getting so close to eradicating them. It was clear they hadn't realized how prepared we'd be and hadn't brought along enough of their own warriors. They thought it would be an easy victory, but they were wrong. We'd taken down almost every last one of them, and I was sure it wouldn't be long before whoever was left would be waving a white flag in surrender.

I was halfway to celebrating when it hit me—the dart. It was a complete shock to my system. At first, I thought I'd be okay, but it wasn't long before the liquid started spreading through my body, a burning sensation taking over all my senses. My vision blurred as I tried to push through it and keep fighting, and blood trickled from my nose, making it hard to breathe. But I forced myself to keep going. No one took Alpha Tyson Tikaani down without a serious fight, and as far as I was concerned, this was not a serious enough fight to take me down.

But even as I thought that, I knew that I had met my match with the wolfsbane. People simply never used it in wars on the West Coast. It was almost a gentleman's agreement—no one wanted to set such a precedent. But they clearly fought dirty here on the East Coast, and who knew how long it would be before it did eventually make its way west.

It all happened in slow motion. As I battled against the poison taking over my body, wobbly on my paws, I spotted another dart coming my way. It was so close, and I couldn't move fast anymore. My life flashed before my eyes, knowing if it got into my body, it would annihilate me. Right before it was about to hit me, I thought about Gigi. Her beautiful freckled face with soft pink lips and strawberry blonde hair. I imagined seeing her one last time, the sunshine reflecting off her long hair, a sweet blush spreading across her cheeks. And then—it never hit me. Instead, I was smashed to the ground by Blake who took the blow for me, shifting into a human almost instantly, his body falling limp on top of me as my fur tore through rocks and dirt.

Was he dead?

Shit, if he wasn't and I left him here, he would die and his pack would be left without an alpha. Running off pure adrenaline, I quickly got to my feet and flipped him onto my back, sprinting away from the action to take him to safety. Somehow, miraculously, although my body was pumped full of wolfsbane, I was able to retain my wolf form.

I quickly found my brother, who was atop a hill, huddled behind a rock, mindlinking instructions to our warriors as he watched on. Like I said, I wasn't about to allow my little brother to fight. He was much better at the logistical stuff.

"Goddess, isn't she amazing?" he mindlinked me as soon as I was in his field of vision, pointing his snout toward the battlefield. And then I saw what he meant. A petite but fierce white wolf was holding her own, taking down enemies twice her size. It was quite a sight to see. As bad of a reputation as his mate had, she was fucking badass. He then turned to

me and must have just noticed there was someone on my back. *"Is that Alpha Blake?"*

"Yeah, he's hurt. We need to help him," I quickly responded, putting him gently down on the ground.

But neither of us were medically trained and ended up just staring at each other. *"Is he breathing at least?"* my brother asked.

I put my ear to his chest and confirmed he was, although it was definitely labored, with blood sputtering out of his mouth and nose. *"Fuck, we need to do something. He just saved my life."*

"Run him to the pack clinic. I think that's your only option at this point."

I nodded, realizing I was being dense for not doing that from the beginning. I quickly flipped him back onto my back and ran as fast as my paws would take me, which wasn't very fast due to both the wolfsbane cycling through my body and the alpha-size man on my back. I didn't even know where the fuck the clinic actually was.

Jasmine

It started as a normal Saturday. I woke up early and, once again, felt lost and alone without Blake next to me, his side of the bed far too cold and empty. Ever since we'd marked each other, being apart felt unnatural and wrong. We were so bound together now that without him I felt like half of a whole. I understood, logically, why he wouldn't let me go back up north with him, but my entire being longed for him.

After getting dressed, I made my way downstairs for breakfast. But as soon as my foot stepped off the bottom step onto the main floor, I hunched over, the sensation of claws slicing through my skin overtaking me. I cried out, grabbing the railing so I wouldn't fall over, tears tumbling from my eyes. And I knew—Blake was hurt. His intense pain was being transferred to me. It pulsed through me again, and I let out another cry.

"Jasmine!" Luke came running down the stairs, helping me up.

"It's Blake. Blake's hurt," I cried out as Luke helped walk me to the couch and gently lowered me onto it, putting a pillow behind my head.

Lucy was right on his heels, sprinting into the living room. "What's going on?" she asked.

I moaned as more pain pulsed through my body.

"Blake's in battle," Luke replied with an empathetic frown, sharing a pained glance with me. He began to bring his hand toward my face but then stopped himself midair, likely realizing that it would have been far too intimate of a gesture—something that at one time would have been natural. I was thankful he caught himself because it would have made things very awkward.

"Don't worry, I know what to do." Lucy interrupted the moment and shoved Luke out of the way. She fluffed my pillow and got right to work. Before I knew it, she had a cold, wet washcloth on my forehead and a hot water bottle on my belly.

"Thank you," I whispered as I flinched, trying to take the blows as they came.

"My mom goes through this all the time," Lucy said as she pulled out some lotion and began massaging my hands. "I've learned all the tricks through the years. I used to help her when I lived at home." While I was grateful for Lucy's help, I was also stunned. We hadn't been on the best terms for a long time now, so I was really impressed that she didn't hesitate to help me. I knew how stubborn she could be, and after what Luke had just almost done, I thought surely she would have been livid.

"Honestly, thank you, Lucy," I said sincerely, soothed by her rubbing my palms and fingers.

"You'll do it for me one day too." Lucy gave me a small smile, and I began to wonder if maybe the crevasse between us was finally closing, and perhaps we'd be friends again.

I almost began to get used to all the different sensations as they hit me, doing my best to zone them out and concentrate on the feeling of Lucy's hands rubbing up and down my arms. Every once in a while, the sting of a tether snapping would thump in my body, and I soon realized what it was as I began to recognize the specific pack members whose connection to the pack broke off.

A tear dropped down my cheek as I reflected on the lives that were being lost, the true horror of war. But I couldn't think about it too long as, suddenly, a burning sensation ripped through me, and I couldn't help but scream bloody murder, clutching at my stomach, my whole body convulsing.

Luke came running back into the room and knelt down beside Lucy as they both stared into my eyes. "What happened?" Luke asked, putting his hand on my shoulder.

"Wolfsbane," I replied. Although I'd never felt the sensation before, I somehow knew what it was—perhaps it was built into werewolf DNA to know.

It pulsed through me again, my insides being seared, my throat and organs burning, my vision blurring. I screamed again, even more loudly, my whole body covered in cold sweat and tears pouring from my eyes. I thrashed, grasping on to the couch cushions, my whole body throbbing in pain.

"Shit, they must have got him really bad. He's got a really high tolerance." Luke got up and began pacing the room, wrinkling his brows. Then he abruptly lifted his head and looked back at me. "But he's not dead. You'd know, Jasmine."

Before I could consider what Luke said, it happened once again, this time the worst—as if a firecracker had detonated inside me. I tumbled off the couch in agony. There was nothing in the world more painful than what I was experiencing, my whole body poisoned and burning, flames drying out my blood and swallowing my organs, my eyes half blind, my fingers and toes bleeding from the nail beds, needles piercing my veins. And then, just like that, nothing. I blinked. Luke and Lucy were instantly crouched back down beside me, trying to help me up.

"What will it feel like when he dies?" I demanded from Luke, suddenly worried, rubbing my belly with cold fear that my pups would be raised without a father. The pain was gone, completely gone. That couldn't be good, right?

Chapter 28

Blake

I groaned as I forced my heavy lids open, fluorescent lights above me, a small bed below me. I shifted, but that was a bad idea. My whole body was still sore, the blood pumping through my veins still scorching me. It somehow felt heavy as I breathed, as if something was blocking the air's passage. I gave a cough, and blood trickled out of my mouth and onto my chin. *Fuck!*

"Hey, you okay, bro?" a familiar voice said next to me, more raspy than usual, probably also in pain.

I wiped at my chin, the red of the blood staining my arm. "I think so," I replied, turning my head to look at him, and familiar amber eyes stared back at me—Jasmine's beautiful eyes. But it wasn't her, although I desperately missed her and would have given anything for those brilliant amber eyes to have been hers.

"Goddess, this wolfsbane shit blows," Tyce groaned out.

"Yeah," I agreed, barely able to move because of it, thinking that all that suffering for all those years at Grey Wolf University still wasn't enough.

"You were able to take on a lot," Tyce said, as if he were reading my mind. "How'd you do it?"

"I spent four years building up a tolerance. Four fucking years, and I'm still not immune."

"I want to do it," Tyce asserted.

"It's not easy."

"I don't care. I want to do it."

I nodded and turned back to stare at the ceiling.

"Blake, you saved my life. If it weren't for you, I'd be dead now." Tyce continued on his rant. "I never want to be in that position again where someone has to risk their life for mine—where someone has to save me. I'm an alpha. I owe it to my pack to get stronger."

I nodded again but soon found the world fading as I drifted back to sleep, too weak to keep my eyes open anymore.

I woke again to find that the small room was crowded now with more beds, all the alphas in one room. "Adalwolf?" I said as I turned to face Alex, who was in the bed next to me, barely inches away, breathing heavily.

"We did it, Wulfric," he breathed out.

"What happened?" I asked, racking my brain for the last thing I remembered.

"We annihilated the enemy. They weren't prepared for all of us."

"They got some good shots into us though."

"Nothing an alpha can't handle." Alex winked at me and then fell into a coughing fit, spraying my face with blood. "Fuck, sorry about that." He chuckled and immediately winced, clutching at his stomach.

"That's one way to become blood brothers," I joked, wiping my face with my arm.

"Don't worry, the nurse will take care of you. She's really cute, with a decent rack," Tyce called out. "She wiped me down earlier."

"I think Tyce was about to ask her to wipe in some places that weren't even soiled." Alex smirked.

"Hey, if she's willing, why not?" Tyce grinned.

"At least wait to ask for your happy ending until we're not all in the room with you!" I chuckled.

"It's a free show. You're only seeing live what you watch on your phones anyway. And don't lie and say you don't," Tyce taunted us. We all laughed, immediately groaning from the pain it caused.

"Blake, Alexander, Tyson, I owe all of you," Alpha Antoine said in his French Canadian accent. "Both Lune Nordique and Bois Sombre are at your disposal. Any time you need help, our warriors are yours."

"That's all we ask," Alex responded. "You can never have too many friends when it comes to war."

"Agreed," Tyce chimed in.

"Why are so many people in this tiny room?" I asked, looking around the room that was barely the size of a closet with almost no space for someone to move.

"They needed the bigger rooms for all the injured. They ran out of beds and are using nap mats from the preschool now," Alpha Antoine replied. "There were a lot of casualties. But most were on the enemy side and not ours, thank the Goddess. I have my warriors burning the bodies now."

I nodded. We wouldn't be able to bring back any of the bodies. It would be too risky. Another problem with fighting battles on someone else's territory, especially one in a foreign country—the families wouldn't be able to hold a proper funeral. Much like Ria's hadn't.

I frowned as the memory rushed back to me—a memory I'd done my best to suppress but would still find its way back to my nightmares when I least expected it. While my father had commanded the warriors to burn the bodies of all the dead, there was one I couldn't leave to someone else. I dragged her body deep into the woods, to the top of a rocky hill, where I gave her the funeral we wouldn't be able to, chanting the prayers that I'd memorized over the years, the same ones I was sure the warriors would have chanted. The image of flames engulfing her sweet face and the coils of her hair would never cease to haunt me. I could have given that image to someone else—someone who wouldn't have been so affected by it—but it just didn't seem right.

Before I choked up and gave in to my emotions, I asked, "Have they counted the dead?" I tried to keep my voice even, but I'm sure the others must have noticed the crack.

"One warrior from each pack volunteered to take a count for their own pack. I believe the one for yours was named Jack Owen."

"Jack," I repeated back the name of my friend. "How is he? Did you see him?"

"Yes, he looked okay. Not too injured. Nothing that shouldn't heal overnight."

"Thank you." I let out a sigh of relief.

Chapter 29

Jasmine

Once Luke was finally able to get in touch with one of the warriors, he came back. "Is there news?" I asked him, desperate with worry. "Do they know what happened to him?"

"They're finding out and will get back to me. Jasmine, try not to worry." Luke sat down next to me on the couch.

"How can I not worry?"

"I know." He let out a sigh. "But you'd know if he were dead. Trust me, Jasmine. The fact that he's no longer feeling pain and you haven't sensed him losing his life, it means he's okay."

"Okay." I let my voice trail off, unconvinced, putting my hand on my belly for comfort.

"Jasmine, you should go to the clinic," Luke suddenly blurted out. "I mean, all that stress. It can't be good for . . ."

"You know?" I asked, raising my eyebrows at him.

He looked down at the floor. "Yeah, Blake told me before he left." Then he looked toward my stomach and added, "Plus, you're kind of starting to show."

I had mostly been sticking to baggy T-shirts lately, but that day I had on a tank top as I hadn't been planning to go out. "Is it obvious?"

"Not super obvious. I mean, I guess someone could just think you had a huge burrito for lunch." He chuckled. "Why? Is it a huge secret?"

"I haven't told my parents yet," I confessed, putting my head in my hands. "Oh, Goddess. Why have I waited so long?"

"Why haven't you told your parents?"

"It's really stupid. The more I think about it, the more I realize how ridiculous I'm being. But—" I paused with shame.

Luke blinked at me a few times. "But?"

I let out a sigh. "It's just so weird for your parents to know that you've, well, made a pup!"

Luke let out a hearty laugh. "Goddess, I always forget how religious your family is!"

"I know, Lucy's and your families are so different."

"I mean, my family's religious too. But I guess we're just more open about that stuff."

"Yeah, I remember." I let out a small laugh.

"Hey, come on, let's go to the clinic, just for peace of mind. I wouldn't be being a good friend to Blake if I didn't take you." Luke got up and put his hand out to me. I took it and he helped me off the couch. I wobbled a little and he caught me.

"Shit, I feel kind of dizzy."

"Yeah, we should definitely go then." He walked me to his car and then grabbed me a water before he drove the short distance to the clinic. It was surprisingly busy that day with tons of families in the waiting area. "Busy day," Luke stated the obvious to the woman at the front desk.

"Yeah, something's going around with all the pups. So what brings you in Beta, Luna?"

"We were hoping to have our luna checked over, make sure everything's okay with the pregnancy. She just had a very stressful day. And you can never be too careful with these things."

"Oh! Of course! We'll get her right in. Don't want any harm to come to our future alpha." She winked at me.

True to her word, we were escorted right in. I lay down on an examination table while Luke waited in a chair close by.

"Luke, how are you? Nice to see you. How are Lucy and Libby?" Blake's mom greeted him as she walked in.

"Both good, Luna," he replied politely. "Libby's getting a bit more manageable these days."

"That's good. She was always quite spirited."

"That's one way to put it." He chuckled. "Do you mind taking a look at Jasmine? She's had a stressful day, and we just want to make sure everything's okay."

"I don't mind taking a look at my grandpups at all." She gave a wide smile. "Jasmine, do you mind just lifting your shirt up and lowering your pants a little? Just down to your pubic bone and up below your breasts."

"I'll avert my eyes." Luke turned so he was facing away, and I did as she asked.

"Oh my, Jasmine, you've popped!" Blake's mom stared down at my stomach. "You must be so excited." I nodded in confirmation. "So tell me, why were you so stressed today that you had to come in?"

"Blake was in battle," I replied, thinking it was best to be as vague as possible. I didn't want to worry his mom. But I clearly wasn't vague enough because her whole face took on a downturned appearance, and a deep crease formed between her eyebrows.

"Is he okay? Have you heard from him?" She took my hand, giving it a firm squeeze.

"Not yet. But the pain stopped. Luke said that means he's recovering," I replied, trying to comfort her, even though I didn't feel one hundred about it either.

"Luke?" she called out.

"I've reached out to the warriors. They're checking." He pulled out his phone to show her. "They should be getting back to me any minute now."

"Oh my, I hope he's all right." I could tell that the excitement she had just shown at seeing my belly had been completely wiped away. "Let's at least make sure the pups are doing all right. I'm just going to feel your belly, okay?" I nodded. She brought her hands to my stomach and felt around it while I tried to zone out, the whole situation felt a bit surreal. "Everything feels normal. Let's just do a quick ultrasound to make sure."

A ping sounded from Luke's phone. We turned to face him while he had his back to us. I'm pretty sure both Blake's mom and I stopped breathing. After what seemed like far too long, Luke finally said, "Got word. They found him at the clinic with Tyce. He's okay. Got shot with wolfsbane pretty bad, but he's recovering."

"Thank Artemis." Blake's mom breathed out, and a tear rolled down her cheek that she quickly wiped away. "Goddess, I don't know what I'd do if he wasn't okay." She sniffed a bit and then said, "Okay, let's focus. Blake's okay. Let's make sure his pups are too." She squirted some jelly on my belly and then pulled out the ultrasound machine. I looked on as she studied the black screen. Suddenly, she turned to me and said, "I can already tell the sex of the pups!" Her eyes were shining, and she appeared as if she was trying to keep a straight face. "But I'm assuming you'll want to find out with Blake during your next appointment? It's not always 100 percent accurate this early on."

My eyes widened, thinking how real it was. Blake's mom knew what we were having. "Oh my Goddess!" I gasped. "Yes, we should probably wait."

"I know, it's very exciting." She gave my hand another squeeze. "I remember when I was pregnant with Blake and we first found out he was a boy. It was such a wonderful moment." Another tear slid down her cheek. "There's nothing in the world like having a pup." She turned away, and it seemed that maybe she'd begun crying.

"Are you okay, Dr. Luna?" I asked.

"Oh, yeah, I'm fine." She turned back around and had a smile on her face, but her eyes were bloodshot. "Just worried about Blake. As a mother, you never stop worrying. But everything is fine with the pups."

"I'll ask Blake to give you a call once he's able to," Luke said.

"Thank you, Luke. I'd appreciate that." She handed me some paper towels, so I could clean myself.

After I was decent again, I said, "You can turn around now, Luke." I went to hop down from the table and my vision began to blur again. I brought my hand to my head, trying to steady it, my whole body beginning to lean sideways. Luke clearly noticed because he came over to support me, putting his arm around me before I tumbled.

"Jasmine, are you okay?" Blake's mom rushed over.

"Just a little dizzy," I replied. "I think I just need to eat."

"Make sure you get some electrolytes. Do you have Gatorade at the packhouse? If not, I have some here at the clinic."

"We have some at the packhouse," Luke confirmed. "We always keep it on hand."

"Okay, good. Saltines are good too."

"Have those too."

"I see Connie's been keeping you well stocked." Blake's mom smiled.

"She's the best," Luke replied. "Anyway, it's obviously busy here today. Sounds like something's going around. I'll go ahead and take Jasmine home so she can get some rest."

"Thanks for being such a good beta." Blake's mom gave Luke a friendly squeeze on his arm.

"Of course!" he replied and led me out the door. As we exited, we came face-to-face with one of my mom's temple friends holding hands with her young grandson.

"Oh! Hello, Jasmine!" she exclaimed.

"Hi, Mrs. Thompson," I replied, hoping she wasn't expecting a long conversation because I really wasn't feeling well and wanted to lie down.

"Hello, Beta." She nodded at Luke.

"Good afternoon." He put his hand out to shake hers.

"Is everything okay, Jasmine?" She studied me, getting very close to my face and making me feel uncomfortable.

"Yeah, it's fine. Just stopping by the clinic," I replied.

"What's wrong? It must be serious if you're at the clinic." The way she said it made me believe she wasn't concerned at all and just looking for some gossip. "Unless . . ." Her voice trailed and she looked down at my belly.

Shit!

"Jasmine was just visiting her mother-in-law. Nothing to be concerned about," Luke swiftly replied. "Now if you don't mind, we have some pack business to take care of and will be on our way."

"Of course, Beta." She backed away.

Once we were outside, I said, "Thanks for your help back there. My mom's friends are all super nosy."

"So I've heard." He chuckled. "Pretty sure I've gotten caught in their crossfire before." I joined in his laughter and realized how what seemed like the worst thing ever at the time was actually kind of funny now. I was glad I could finally laugh about it.

Chapter 30

Tyson

After my body was able to metabolize all the wolfsbane and finally heal properly, my brother and I started planning the memorial service we'd have to hold later that week. The final count for our pack was ten dead, which was a very good number considering, especially since we had never trained for battle with wolfsbane. The experience still traumatized me, and I was determined to follow through on my dedication to becoming tolerant. No more fucking around. Practically dying out on that battle-field was a huge wake-up call.

The Wednesday following the battle, after all our warriors had a chance to recover, we boarded the chartered flight back to Alaska. A part of me was desperate to get back to Vermont and see Gigi again, but as alpha, I knew it was my duty to visit all the families of the fallen warriors and give my condolences. Considering it was my idea to fight this battle, I knew it would be wrong to expect my dad and grandpa, or even my beta or gamma, to do that. No, it was time I started taking my responsibilities seriously.

"Welcome home, Alpha, Trav." My beta, Liam, greeted us at the airport. He was about ten years older and far more mature than me. He gave us both hearty slaps on the back and led us out to the pack bush plane that was waiting for us, which he often piloted. Although we lived off the beaten path, we did have our own roads we maintained so that we could drive to civilization. However, during wintertime, maintenance often became difficult, and the bush plane was really the only way to get out and bring supplies back in. Even during the summer months, it was a lot quicker, which was probably why Liam had chosen to take it rather than his car.

Once Trav and I got settled and we were on our way, Liam made an attempt at conversation. "So, your family must be excited you're coming back, Tyce. What's it been? Two months now?"

"You act like they missed me." I gave a chuckle even though it wasn't really funny.

"I mean, they're your family. Even if they are the way they are, that doesn't mean they don't care about you."

"Wise as ever, Liam."

"C'mon, Tyce. Liam's right. I mean as tough as Dad and Grandpa are, it comes from a good place." Trav unsurprisingly took Liam's side.

"Please, Trav, you know they couldn't wait to get rid of me when the opportunity came up."

"That's not true." Trav's voice trailed off. He knew it was true. When I was there, I was in their way. Sure, they acted like I was in charge to outsiders, but in reality, I wasn't. Trav then suddenly looked like he wanted to say more, opening his mouth slightly, but he clearly decided against it and turned back toward the window.

"Did you want to say something, Trav?"

"No, I didn't say anything."

"But you wanted to."

"No."

"I know you did. What did you want to say?" I definitely wasn't going to let this go, and I was growing irritated because clearly, whatever he wanted to say, he was too scared to say it.

He let out a deep sigh and finally came out with it. "Maybe you should stop fucking around so much."

"What does that mean?" I narrowed my eyes at him.

"I mean, the way you took charge recently, you're obviously capable of being alpha. You did great leading everyone out in Quebec. I was really impressed."

"But . . ." I said, clenching my jaw.

He sighed again. "But when you're home, you're always off screwing around instead of taking any initiative. I mean, come on, a week before you left, Dad walked in on you getting a blow job from some girl in *his* office, with your bare ass in *his* chair."

Damn, I almost forgot about that. I couldn't lie, it was satisfying seeing the look on my dad's face when he walked in on us. Pretty sure that chair went into the trash the next day.

Liam broke out into laughter. "Goddess, classic Tyce! That almost beats the time that the priest found out you were hooking up with his granddaughter and had a talk with your grandfather about it."

Oh shit, that happened too.

"What about the time when Dad was doing a run of the patrol stations, and he caught you with some girl bent over a fallen tree trunk instead of, you know, *patrolling*." Trav snickered.

"Okay, I get it. Sometimes my dick leads and I follow."

"*Sometimes?*" Liam and Trav both asked at the same time and broke into laughter.

By the time we made it home, the two of them had regaled me with a list of my stories that were as long as the scriptures of Artemis. Okay, it wasn't like I ever denied being a horndog. But, fine, it looked pretty bad.

I walked into the packhouse where my mom was seated in the living room.

"Hi, Mom," I greeted her. Most people probably would have hugged or kissed, but we weren't really the touchy-feely type.

"Hi, Tyce, welcome home," she replied, giving me a closed-mouth smile—about as much as I could have expected from her.

My brother came in right after me. "Hey, Mom."

"How was your trip, Trav? Are you boys hungry? Let me go heat something up for you." She got up and walked toward the kitchen. I supposed that was her way of showing her love.

"Heya, big brothers!" My sister bumbled into the room. "Welcome back! How was the big fight?" She was definitely the bubbliest out of the whole family. To be honest, she was kind of the black sheep. While most of the family was cold and uninviting, she was always smiling and brought a certain warmth to the packhouse. I sometimes wondered if she was even related, but her matching amber eyes indicated she was. She had clearly gotten some recessive genes none of the rest of us had.

"Heya, Terri." I messed up her hair and walked off toward the stairs to head to my room, not bothering to answer her question and instead leaving Trav to deal with her. Most of the time I actually enjoyed her presence, but I wasn't in the mood. I still wasn't feeling great after everything that had gone down, and Trav and Liam digging up my past indiscretions brought a weird ill feeling I'd never felt before. I fell into my bed and decided to mindlessly scroll through my Instagram feed.

Then, I suddenly got curious. Perhaps Gigi had an Instagram. Most girls did, right? Hadn't Jasmine followed me recently? I quickly navigated to my Activity where I saw the update that Jazzy.DW had followed me. I clicked over to her profile. Private. *That's okay*. I quickly requested to follow her back.

It only took a minute or two for her to accept the request, and I was in. And there she was in the first picture of Jasmine's feed. It was Jasmine with Paige and Gigi, posed with their bikes somewhere out in the wilderness. I smiled at how wholesome it was. I quickly noted that SpicyGi was tagged and navigated to her profile, also private, which made sense since most packs had strict rules about keeping social media accounts private. I requested to follow her.

"Tyce! Come eat!" my mom called up to me.

"Coming," I replied, shoving my phone into my pocket. As I descended the stairs, I felt it vibrate in my pocket. She had both accepted my follow request and made one for my account. I couldn't help but smile, quickly accepting her request, although I didn't post too much on my own account, so there wasn't much to see.

After rushing through my meal, I ran back upstairs and pulled my phone out again, navigating back to Gigi's Instagram account page. I quickly noted that it seemed most of her friends were oddly *human*. I didn't even know exactly how I could tell. But they were definitely pictures from her college.

Once I started, I couldn't stop, completely hypnotized by her feed and wanting to know everything about her. She had tons of pictures with girlfriends, but then there were also many with guys, which irritated me. In one, one was affectionately kissing her cheek. I clicked in to read the comments.

craigyboy22 *sexy cum over tonight*

I was ready to punch him through the screen.

I kept scrolling. In another, she had her cleavage hanging out and one of her friends was wrapping her arms around her, grabbing her tits. Fuck, what an amazing picture. But I couldn't help myself as I clicked to read the comments.

stantheman11 *Beautiful and sexy*
bobbyboss01 *Check your dm @spicygi*
jjcoolj *I want a repeat of last night*

My knuckles were turning white from grasping my phone so tightly. I began to wonder how many of these guys leaving her comments had slept with her, my thoughts spiraling. I mean, okay, I was totally being a hypocrite. It wasn't like I'd exactly kept it in my pants. But I still couldn't help how much it pissed me off that she was possibly spreading her legs for all these dudes—these *human* dudes. No, she should be sticking to her own kind—a werewolf who could take care of her every need and leave every single part of her perfect body revered and satisfied. A werewolf like me.

I kept scrolling and was surprised to see she went to a boarding school with humans for high school. I began to wonder why she didn't go to the pack school. It wasn't common for werewolves to spend so much time outside their pack. And it was clear that her twin sister hadn't done the same. There was definitely something up, and it was bothering me more and more as time went on that I didn't know what it was and that she wouldn't tell me.

A DM came through. I quickly clicked into it.

SpicyGi: Are you enjoying stalking my insta?
AlphaTT: You give a good show
SpicyGi: How so?
AlphaTT: You should know, you get plenty of comments from admirers
SpicyGi: Is someone jealous?
AlphaTT: No why would I be jealous when I know I'm better?
SpicyGi: Someone's a bit full of themselves
AlphaTT: The night at the club was only a preview. When I come back to VT you won't walk straight for a week

After that, she didn't respond, and I wondered if maybe I came on too strong. Maybe I should tone it down moving forward. But, *fuck*, I couldn't help how badly I wanted to see her again and really make it so she couldn't walk straight for a week.

Chapter 31

Ginger

My heart pounded in my chest as I read Tyce's DM over and over again. I kept wondering what it meant. I mean, duh, I knew what it meant. But what did it *really* mean? Was he just looking to fuck me, or did he maybe want something more? Why did I do this to myself? Reading his message, it was clear as day he was only looking for one thing. But still, sometimes it just seemed . . .

No, I had to stop overanalyzing. Plus, either way, it was going to end in disaster. While I would probably never have the opportunity to meet mine, Tyce had a mate out there, and he was going to eventually meet her. And one thing was very clear—getting involved with Tyce was going to get me hurt. He was not the type of guy you called a *fuckboy* and just moved on from. No, he was the type of guy who could give you four orgasms in a matter of minutes, and, yes, could most likely literally make it so you couldn't walk straight for a week.

I let out a deep breath and threw my phone across the bed from me where I couldn't reach it and couldn't reply to Tyce.

"Ginger! Come help me set the table for dinner!" my mom called out. Saved by the mom! I left my phone in my bedroom. There, now I definitely wouldn't respond.

My dad and Dylan had both returned from battle the day prior, so we were finally having the official meeting tonight. Paige hadn't been one of the chosen warriors to go and had stayed behind. She'd been jittery all day, scrubbing the bathroom, vacuuming the whole house, and reorganizing my closet again. I think she was half expecting to find more evidence in it, but the slides were now safely returned.

Not long after I put the last glass on the table, Heidi entered the house with her mate, Hunter. He was very well put together as usual, with a crisp, perfectly ironed collared shirt that was tailored to his actually quite nice body.

"Oh, Heidi, good, you're here!" My mom came into the hallway. "You can help me with the potatoes."

"Good evening, Mrs. McDowell." Hunter gave my mom a big smile and pulled her in for a hug.

"Hello, Hunter. Actually, do you mind picking out a wine? You always do such a good job!"

"Absolutely!" he replied, following my mom into the kitchen.

"How do I look?" Paige called out from the stairs, coming down.

"Let me see!" Hunter came out to take a look. "Do a spin."

Paige spun around in a floral sundress she chose for the evening.

"Change the shoes," Hunter said after looking her up and down.

"Really?" Paige looked down at her feet.

"Yeah, put on a pair of wedges. Those flats aren't doing your legs any favors."

"I don't have any . . ."

"You can borrow mine," I said, heading back upstairs so I could pull a pair out for her. Once I opened my closet and went to reach for a pair that would match her dress, I hesitated. "Damn, I almost feel bad moving them. They're all so nicely organized."

"Don't worry, I can fix it for you later." Paige took the shoes from me and pulled them on her feet. "Better?" she asked once she had them on and was standing back up.

"Actually, yeah. Hunter's really good at this stuff."

Not long after, Dylan arrived with two bouquets of flowers—one for Paige and one for my mom. *Nice touch!* We all sat down for dinner. I couldn't help but feel envious during the meal as I watched Dylan and Paige continuously sneak glances at each other and noticed their arms move as they were clearly touching each other underneath the table. They both glowed with infatuation.

I then glanced over at Heidi and Hunter and couldn't help but compare. They seemed friendly enough with each other, but really more like friends than lovers. Was it because they'd been together for a while? I thought back, racking my brain. Had Heidi and Hunter ever really seemed infatuated with each other? Even on their wedding day, their body language seemed to indicate they were just friends. At the time, I supposed, I'd just chalked it up to Heidi's personality. But it wasn't like she had ever been any more religious and sanctimonious than Paige—if anything, Paige was more sanctimonious than Heidi. And yet, she was now touching Dylan under the table in front of the whole family, possibly even in an inappropriate way, although it was hard to tell with the tablecloth.

After we finished dessert and everyone decided to call it a night, Paige, my parents, and I walked all our guests to the door and said good night. I was about to head upstairs and fall into bed, exhausted from the evening, when my dad pulled me aside. "Can I talk to you, Peachy?"

"Sure, Dad," I replied and followed him into the living room.

Once we sat down, he put his hand on my knee and said, "Peachy, I want you to know that your mom and I are really proud of you. You've done so well considering the circumstances, and we're both so happy with how well you're doing in school."

"Thanks, Dad."

"And I know tonight probably wasn't easy for you. I'm really impressed with how you handled yourself at dinner."

"Dad, it's okay."

"No, it's not okay, Peachy. I'm your father, and I feel all your pain. I know it's really hard for you to be without a wolf. But you've done so well, and I know you're going to meet a good man one day who will really appreciate you, wolf or no wolf. You've got a lot to offer, and any man will be lucky to have you. So don't worry. Okay?"

I nodded, a scratchy feeling at the back of my throat at how much my dad cared.

"Your mom still believes very strongly you'll find your mate. But even if you don't, you will find someone, so please, Peachy, don't worry." He pulled me in for a hug, holding me against his body and patting my back. I almost began sobbing but held my tears at bay. After we pulled apart, he said, "Now have a good night, honey, okay?"

"Okay. Thanks, Dad," I said and got up to go to bed.

Once I picked up my phone, I couldn't lie—I was a little disappointed Tyce had never followed up on his message.

Chapter 32

Tyson

Thankfully, it was just my dad this time. He was at least semirational. My grandfather, on the other hand, was a total nutcase.

My dad was giving me an intense stare, his forearms flat on his desk, fingers intertwined. "So, care to explain why you had Trav load up a good chunk of our warriors and send them to the East Coast for a battle that had nothing to do with us?"

"I'm the alpha. I'm allowed to make decisions for the pack now. Technically, I don't have to run it by anyone."

He let out a deep sigh. "Yes, but battles are a huge cost to our pack. We can't be making rash decisions."

I cut him off. "Why do you assume the decision was rash?"

"Tyce," he said in a very patronizing way. "What else am I supposed to assume when you don't even discuss this with your grandfather and me? We're the ones who have been running this pack while you're off fooling around with your porky skanks."

"Don't call them that!" I bellowed, clenching my hands into fists. I'd always let my family's insults of women they perceived as less desirable roll off my back. But now, I couldn't help but recall Gigi's insecurities, and I began to imagine how they'd perceive her if I ever introduced her to them. I loved her exactly as she was, and I hated how my parents had certain expectations about everything, especially about the types of women I could and couldn't like.

"What?" My dad looked at me confused, blinking a few times.

"Don't call them porky skanks. I'm sick of you dogging on people's weights. There's nothing wrong with them, and you're just being a huge dick for no reason. What does it matter to you what kind of women I prefer?"

He shook his head. "Okay, this isn't what this conversation is about."

"But you still found the need to be a dick."

"Okay, that's enough, Tyce!" My dad banged his hands onto his desk, his face red and brows furrowed. "Goddess fucking damn it! Can we just talk about the fucking battle?"

I crossed my arms and let out a huff, realizing my dad was not going to admit fault. But I still felt proud of myself for finally calling him out on his shit. I was done just being kicked around by him and my grandfather.

After taking a couple deep breaths, my dad resumed. "So, why the fuck did we lose ten of our pack members? Why do I now need to go visit ten different families and explain to them why we needed to sacrifice their lives—?"

"You don't have to do anything. I'm going to go see their families." I cut my dad off again. "The battle was my idea, so I will explain it to them. I'm the alpha, and I'm going to take responsibility."

"Okay, then explain it to me. I want to hear what you're going to tell these families."

"Why?"

"Because, Tyce! This kind of conversation takes a lot of tact! Do you think I'm just going to trust you're going to handle it delicately? These are grieving families. And while you're off running around using them like pawns, to these families these are brothers, fathers, sons—"

"I know that, Dad!"

"Do you though?"

"You act like I didn't risk my own fucking life being out there! You act like I didn't fight the battle with them!"

"Tyce."

"Alpha Tyce! I am alpha, not you! I have a fucking title!"

"Tyce, my patience is running thin with you."

"What are you going to do? Fight me? Because you know I'm stronger. You know I could tear you to shreds if I wanted to. Both you and Grandpa! That's why you had to hand me the title. You can't have it both ways! You can't just use me to strengthen the pack and not allow me to lead!"

"Holy fucking Artemis! You will lead when you're ready to lead! And I am not seeing that you're ready!"

"Fuck you, Dad!" I got up and stormed out of the office.

"Tyce!" he bellowed, and I could feel his alpha aura rolling over me. But I was far stronger than him, and he was no longer the alpha. It was useless on me. I slammed the door to his office and stormed off.

I knew better than to think that was the end of it. My father brought in his attack dog next—a.k.a. my grandfather. They both burst into my bedroom while I was lounging in my bed on my phone. I had been thinking about beating off to blow off some steam, but now that plan was ruined by two people I definitely didn't want to think about while I did.

"Tyson, what the fuck is going on with you?" my grandfather asked menacingly, his shadow covering me as he looked down his big nose at me. "Why are you disrespecting your father?"

"Respect is earned, and Dad hasn't earned it," I replied.

"I ought to whip you!"

"Fucking try!" I glared at him. "Because you and I both know you would have to have a death wish. Your days of being the top dog in this pack are over!"

"Goddess, what the fuck has gotten into him?" My grandfather turned to my father, shaking his head.

"Clearly sending him out to the East Coast was a bad idea. Now he thinks he runs this place," my dad responded.

"I do run this fucking place!" I got up, ready for a fight. "You're both just trying to manipulate me to think I don't!"

"You ungrateful piece of shit," my grandfather said through clenched teeth. "After everything we did to train and raise you so you could become alpha."

"I would have been better off without your fucking excuse for physically abusing me for over a decade!" I lashed out.

"Okay, guys, come on, let's calm down. This is getting out of hand." My dad clearly must have realized how much this argument was escalating now. "Why don't we go back downstairs to my office so we can talk this out like adults?"

"Fine!" I said, my fists clenched tightly.

Once we were all seated, my dad let out a deep breath and said, "Okay, Tyce, I'm sorry. I shouldn't have accused you of not having a good reason for the battle. So let's start over. Can you please tell us why you thought this battle was a good idea?"

I stared at my dad wide-eyed, completely taken aback. This was the first time he'd ever apologized to me. I was suddenly wondering if he'd been possessed at some point during our walk downstairs from my bedroom. After I finished pulling my jaw off the floor, I finally replied, "Well, thank you for allowing me to explain."

My father nodded.

My grandfather looked like he was about to jump at my throat, but he controlled himself.

After taking a deep breath, I said, "Seeing as how we've now formed a blood alliance with the Midnight Maple Pack, I wanted to show our dedication to the alliance and do right by them. Additionally, the battle was to help the Lune Nordique Pack, which is one of the largest, if not the largest, packs on the East Coast. I thought it was time we started thinking bigger. Right now, almost all our allies are on the West Coast, but why can't we build alliances with packs farther away? It'll give us an edge when we go to battle because I'm pretty sure no other pack in the area is doing that. I mean, all it takes to get their warriors over here is a chartered flight, so why not?"

My dad nodded, putting his hand to his chin. At first, he didn't say anything. Then he surprised me and said, "Tyce, you know what, I think you're finally growing up. I honestly wasn't expecting such a mature and well-thought-out explanation, and I should have given you more credit. I think helping out with Alpha Blake's pack has been good for you."

"I'd like to go back," I replied. "And finish off the summer there."

"I think that's a good idea. And maybe once you're back, you can start taking on more of a leadership role around here. I know sometimes we're hard on you and don't trust you, but your grandfather and I are most concerned with this pack. It's a lot of responsibility to run it with so many lives on the line. And you can't deny that there have been many incidents where you didn't show up as a leader." He gave me a meaningful look. "Look, I understand, Tyce. I was once young too. But you're the alpha now. And when you're fooling around with some slut instead of doing your patrol duty, it makes our leadership look bad."

I swallowed and nodded. The ill feeling returned. I was beginning to realize how much I'd really fucked up. It seemed funny at the time, but now looking back, I had a completely different perspective and had a hard time laughing about it.

"Your father tells me you're going to go see the grieving families today?" my grandfather asked.

"Yeah."

"I'll come with you. It's not an easy job. My grandfather took me the first time I went too." He gave me a small smile.

"Thanks." Something inside me warmed as I realized I'd taken the first step toward finally earning my father's and grandfather's respect.

Chapter 33

Jasmine

Tears of happiness welled up in my eyes as Blake stepped into the pack-house. I ran and jumped into his arms, wrapping my legs tightly around his body, attacking his mouth with mine. "Blake, I thought I lost you. I honestly thought I lost you." Tears ran down my cheeks as I choked out words between my kisses. I shoved my tongue into his mouth, wanting to taste him again desperately.

"I'm still here, Mrs. Alpha," Blake whispered between kisses. "I'm home now. You don't have to worry anymore." He carried me up the stairs until we were in our bedroom, and he lowered me onto the bed.

He crawled in and hovered over me, his piercing blue eyes staring into mine. I slid my hands under his shirt, feeling every groove of his well-defined torso, memorizing the structure of how each muscle felt under my fingertips. I moved my hands up his body, easing his shirt off him, wanting desperately to feel his whole naked body against mine, to reunite with him.

"Well, this is a nice welcome home gift." Blake smirked in a way only he could, his blue eyes twinkling mischievously.

"Take it all off!" I demanded.

"Mrs. Alpha!" he gasped. "Yes, ma'am." He began peeling off his clothes and chuckled. "I feel like I'm getting a new Jasmine every time lately. I kind of like this one."

"Undress me," I commanded, smiling.

"With pleasure." He brought his mouth to my ear, nibbling gently on it as he eased my shirt off me. Blake knew that was my weak spot, and I arched my back, letting out a loud moan. He moved his mouth to where the waistband of my shorts met the skin of my waist and kissed upward, taking his time. My whole body came alive with arousal as the sparks from his kisses danced to every limb. He unsnapped my bra and began sucking on my left breast, taking his time, flicking his tongue along the tip of my erect nipple, which was now more sensitive than ever.

I cried out in ecstasy as he moved across to the other one, doing the same thing. It felt so good that I was practically orgasming, my panties and shorts soaked. I brought my hand down to Blake's erection, wrapping my palm around it. He instantly began thrusting into my hand, clearly just as desperate as I was to be back together.

"Take everything off. I want to feel you inside," I moaned.

"Who can say no to that?" He brought his mouth back to my waist, letting it follow as he pulled my shorts and underwear off at the same time, kissing down my pubic bone.

"No foreplay," I said. "Just put it in."

"Holy fuck. Maybe I did die and go to heaven." He followed my instructions, pulling my shorts and underwear clean off my legs. He then nestled himself between my thighs, easing himself inside me and getting down onto his forearms. I looked up into his eyes and wrapped my legs around him as he thrust in and out of me. Desperate to have him even closer, I pulled his head down against mine, crushing his lips against my own, then taking his bottom lip between my teeth. I savored everything—the friction of his hips against my legs, the movement of his thick member inside me, the taste of his breath on my mouth, and the sparks that moved along my body with each movement.

"Please don't ever leave me, Blake," I moaned out.

"I won't," he reassured me.

"Please, I love you too much to lose you."

"Jasmine, I'm here, I'm home. Don't worry." He lifted himself slightly and slipped his fingers between my legs, instantly finding my clit. Sparks danced up and down my thighs as he stroked it gently at first and then became more aggressive, drawing out every bit of pleasure he could. I moaned against his mouth as we continued to kiss each other, our tongues twining viciously, both fighting to take from the other what we needed.

Soon I couldn't hold back anymore. My whole body convulsed against his, my thighs shaking, sparks overtaking my whole body. Before I knew it, I was at the point of no return as fireworks danced inside me, and I let out a loud moan, my whole body overwhelmed with carnal gratification. Blake rode out his own orgasm, letting out a loud groan as I felt his come fill the inside of me.

He collapsed next to me, instantly pulling me against him. "Goddess, that was fucking amazing," he cried out. "Definitely made it worth almost dying. Maybe I should do it more often."

"I felt all of it." Tears trailed my cheeks.

"Jasmine, I'm sorry. I didn't want you to feel any of that."

"It's not your fault. But I was so worried. I'm just so happy you're home."

"I'm home, I'm home," he reassured me, kissing my cheeks. "Please don't worry. I came home to you and our pups." He rubbed my belly. "Shit, Jasmine. There's no question you're definitely pregnant now."

"I know. I was so worried. Luke took me to the clinic after you got hit with the wolfsbane. He was afraid all the stress might have hurt them.

But your mom checked me over and they're okay." I tried to sniff back the tears that were now flowing freely.

"Fuck, I'm so sorry, Jasmine. I'm so glad they're okay." He kissed me up and down my cheeks.

"We need to tell my parents."

"We will. I just have to go around and inform all of the families of the fallen warriors." He furrowed his brows, letting out a deep sigh. "And plan the memorial service."

I grasped his hand. "I want to help you. The luna does that stuff too right?"

"Yes." He gave me a smile and kissed me on the forehead, getting out of bed to head to the bathroom.

"How many?" I asked.

"Twelve."

"Blake, I'm your teammate. I know why you wouldn't let me go to battle with you. But I want to be a good luna to our pack. I want to help with everything I can. I'll go with you to see the families, and I'll meet with Bernard to plan the service."

He turned around and threw his arms around me. "You're an amazing luna."

It was a difficult day. I knew speaking to all the families would be challenging, but until I actually did it, it was really hard to imagine what it'd be like. Telling families their loved one had died twelve times in a row was the type of mental exhaustion I would never even wish on my worst enemies.

I tried to comfort them as best as I could—but what did you say to someone? There was nothing I could say that would bring their sibling, parent, or mate back. And that was what made it the most difficult.

There was no comfort in the world I could truly bring to someone who'd experienced loss. By the end of the day, I had fallen into a depression.

Knowing how much Blake had gone through, I forced him to go home and rest while I pushed through it and met with Bernard to plan the memorial service we'd be holding the next evening. We worked together to enlarge portraits of the fallen warriors and place them in frames, we went through different prayers and chants to use for the service, and finally, we called around to order flower arrangements that I would pick up the next day.

The sun was already setting by the time Blake arrived to pick me up. My stomach was grumbling as I'd completely missed both lunch and dinner, being so preoccupied with all the day's events.

"I got us some subs." Blake smiled at me. "Why don't we go around back and sit in the garden to have a picnic dinner?"

"Sounds good to me. To be honest, I'm starting to feel a little dizzy from not eating all day," I replied.

"I know, I haven't eaten all day either." Blake took my hand in his, and we walked around back, sitting down on a bench.

"You know, it's so pretty back here. They do such a good job with the garden. I should really spend more time here."

"It is nice, isn't it?"

We ate silently, both somber from the day's events. But it was a comfortable silence of being with my best friend—the one person in the world I truly felt like I could be myself around, without judgment.

Chapter 34

Jasmine

The service was held the next day. I spent an inordinate amount of time trying to find an appropriate dress to wear that would disguise my baby bump. In the end, Lucy came through and let me borrow one of her pregnancy dresses.

I could sense that she was finally coming around and getting over the whole Luke debacle, bringing me a sense of relief. Although she had done a lot of hurtful things since Luke and I discovered we were mates, it was hard to push aside a long-term friendship. There were still so many memories from the time we'd met in kindergarten until the eventual dissolution of our friendship that I thought back on fondly. Could things be normal between us again one day?

"Can you tell?" I kept asking Blake. He was probably super annoyed with me after being asked the same thing for the hundredth time that day. But I was in anxiety overdrive. My parents still didn't know, and we had to tell them before other people started noticing.

"Jaz, don't worry." Blake pulled me against his body. "It's a memorial service. No one's going to even be looking at you." He then pulled away, looked down, and shook his head. "That thing is like a potato sack and I hate it. Can't a man who almost died at least get a chance to admire his mate's fine ass?" He smirked. "I can't even believe Lucy owns something so frumpy."

"Blake." I pushed on his chest.

"Okay." He rolled his eyes. "Let me see again." I moved away and did a spin. "Nope, can't see any part of your body at all. Fucking hate it."

"Okay, good." I smiled, and he pulled me back against him, giving me a kiss.

"After the service is over, we'll tell your parents. Don't worry, okay?" I nodded, then snuggled into him.

When it was time to go, I went to pack up my small purse. I was about to throw my cell phone into it when I noticed I had some missed calls from my mom. My finger hovered over the call button when Blake shouted out to me, "Ready to go, Jaz?"

"Yeah," I responded, throwing the phone into my purse and going over to where he was waiting with Luke, Lucy, and Libby to walk over. I figured I'd see my parents that night anyway.

As soon as we entered the temple, I could sense something was wrong. Everyone's eyes were on our group, whispering. Blake walked away to speak with Bernard, and I was left with Luke, Lucy, and Libby. I took deep breaths, telling myself it was all in my head, but my instincts were going into overdrive.

Suddenly, Mrs. Thompson approached our small group. "Oh, hello, Jasmine! Are you feeling better after your visit to the clinic?" she asked with a huge smirk on her face. "What a good friend you were, Beta Luke, taking her. I could see how much you care about our luna."

"Excuse me?" Lucy cut in. "Are you insinuating something?" Thank Goddess for Lucy never taking shit from anyone.

"No, why would you think that?" Mrs. Thompson put her hand to her chest and widened her eyes. "I was simply worried and coming over to check on my friend's daughter after seeing her at the clinic."

"I'm fine. Thanks for checking," I said, trying to act as normal as possible but freaking out on the inside. What had she told people?

Lucy looked like she was about to say something else, but Luke cut in front of her and patted Mrs. Thompson on the arm. "Luna Jasmine's completely fine. Like I told you on Saturday, we were just visiting the former luna. Now please go have a seat. The service is about to start."

Luke then led Lucy, Libby, and me to our seats, where Blake soon joined us, taking a seat next to me and grasping my hand in his. *Blake, I think they're talking about me,* I mindlinked him.

"Jaz, it's okay. Just relax, all right?" he mindlinked me back and squeezed my hand, sending sparks up my arm that instantly helped me calm down. I traced his palm with my thumb throughout the service and soon began to forget about the incident.

The service was hours long as every family had a chance to give a eulogy, and we went through the different prayers and chants that I had helped Bernard pick out the prior day. As the sky outside descended into darkness, Blake finally got up to give his final speech. My heart warmed with pride as I watched him. He was always so good at working a crowd, a true leader.

But the good feelings I had were short-lived. Once the service was over, and Blake got pulled away, I started to notice all the snickering and whispering again. My heart raced, and I began to really worry I was going to have a panic attack.

Paige came running over. "Jasmine! Come with me." She grabbed my arm and led me away.

"What's going on?" I asked as soon as we stepped outside. Paige shook her head and had her brows furrowed. I took deep breaths, trying everything I could to steady my heart rate, knowing whatever she was about to tell me wasn't good.

"I know the rumors aren't true."

"The rumors? What rumors?"

"I just want you to know that I told everyone they're definitely not true."

"Paige, please tell me. What are people saying about me?"

"They're saying you're pregnant! And Luke's the father. Crazy, right?"

"Oh Goddess." I thought I was going to throw up and began to dry heave. The world started going blurry, and my chest tightened. "Oh Goddess, oh Goddess, oh Goddess."

"Jasmine, anyone with half a brain would know those rumors aren't true!"

Fur was now sprouting up my arms and legs, my canines were extending. I wasn't sure that I'd be able to stave off the panic attack. Kicking off my shoes, I ran, trying to get as far as I could before I'd be forced to shift.

"Jasmine, wait up!" Paige followed after me. I didn't get far before the dress I was wearing tore into pieces as my body transformed into a wolf. I sprinted away, Paige's shouts echoing in the background. "Jasmine, wait!"

Blake

"Hey, man. Nice speech." Jack gave me a friendly punch in the arm.

"I'm liking the suit." Tyler grinned. "I always thought less was best, but there's just something about an attractive man in a well-tailored suit."

I rolled my eyes and laughed.

"So, where's my sister?" Tyler looked around.

I, similarly, began looking around, wondering where Jasmine was, and then I sensed that she wasn't nearby. "Where *is* Jasmine? Shit, I need to go find her."

Just as I was about to mindlink her to see where she went, her parents strolled over, and I realized it wasn't good. Her mom had her sour face on, one that I'd become familiar with. While I had a good relationship with Jasmine's mom, she was tough, and it was easy to put her in a bad mood.

"Hey, Blake!" Jasmine's dad greeted me, but he didn't seem as jubilant as he normally was. *Fuck.*

"Hey, Drew, Miriam. How's it going?" I went to hug both of them, acting normal.

"Where's Jasmine?" Miriam asked. "She's been ignoring all my calls. I haven't seen her for weeks. Is she avoiding us?"

"No, she wouldn't be avoiding you," I instantly replied. "We were planning to invite you to the packhouse tonight for tea. I know things have been busy with my sister giving birth and the battle. But we were looking forward to finally seeing both of you tonight."

"Why isn't she here?"

"She's probably just in the bathroom. I'm sure she'll be back soon."

"So there's nothing Jasmine might have been hiding from us?"

"Nothing she was intentionally hiding from you."

"But she was hiding something?"

"Miriam, stop interrogating the man!" Drew jumped in.

"Honestly, Dale Dog, I think your mate missed her calling as a cop!" Tyler snickered.

"That she did!" Drew gave his son a pat on the shoulder. He then turned back to me. "Blake, we're just concerned. There have been some interesting rumors around the pack. And we're just trying to figure out if any part of them is true."

"What are the rumors?" I asked.

"Oh, shit! You mean the rumors that Jasmine got knocked up by the beta! That scandalous girl!" Tyler fell into laughter.

"Wait, what?" I almost choked.

"Maybe we should talk about this somewhere else," Drew said. "Somewhere more private."

"I agree," I replied. "This isn't really an appropriate conversation for a memorial service." I glared at Tyler, hoping he got the hint. As much as I loved him, he had a knack for making the most awkward jokes at the worst times.

"Alpha!" Paige came tumbling toward us, her skin flushed, panting as if she'd just gone for a run. She then looked around at the group. "Hi, everyone!" She forced a smile to her face and then turned to me. "Alpha Blake, I need to talk to you."

"Sure, one moment, everyone." I looked around apologetically at Jasmine's family while I followed Paige over to a semiprivate area, not that any area was that private with the large number of pack members currently crowded inside the temple.

"What's going on, Paige?" I asked quietly as soon as we seemed to be out of earshot of the others.

Paige fidgeted with her hands, looking down for a bit. Then finally looked up and whispered, "Jasmine shifted into her wolf and ran away. I'm so sorry. Please forgive me, Alpha. It was all my fault. I wasn't thinking."

"Why did she shift into her wolf?" I asked, even though I already knew why, my chest heavy at the thought of how distressed she'd been all day and how I probably should have taken her concerns more seriously.

She looked down, not making eye contact with me. "I thought she should know the rumors going around about her. But when I told her, she freaked out."

"It's okay, Paige." I put my hand on her shoulder. "I'll go find her." Not looking back at everyone I had obligations to, I walked out of the temple, feeling my way to my mate. As soon as I stepped into the woods, I threw off my suit and shifted into my wolf, following the mate bond to her.

I finally found her curled up in her wolf form in a pile of leaves. I used my snout to poke her cheek, giving her a little lick on the cheek. *"Jasmine, baby,"* I mindlinked her. *"It's okay. Everything will be okay."*

She looked up at me, giving me the saddest puppy eyes I'd ever seen. I couldn't help myself as I licked her again, planting wolf kisses all over her cute little wolf face. *"Link me, Jasmine. Tell me what's wrong."*

"The whole pack knows I'm pregnant. And they think it's Luke's." She put her head down in a defeated gesture. *"My mom's probably heard the rumors by now. She's going to be so pissed that she didn't find out from me."*

"If I'm not mistaken, this isn't the first time your parents are finding out something important about you through the pack rumor mill instead of from you directly." I chuckled as much as I could in my wolf form, which came out more like a half bark. *"I'm pretty sure they found out about Lucy's pup that way too. At this point, it's a trend that that's how they get their pregnancy announcements."*

She gave out a pained whine.

"Come on, Jasmine. The world didn't end then, and it's not going to end now. We'll explain why we took so long to tell them. I'll even do the talking. I'll take the blame, okay?"

"Goddess, I feel so ashamed. I'm supposed to be the luna and look how I'm acting." She gave out another whine.

"No one knows about this. Okay? And they won't find out. We'll just tell everyone you had really bad pregnancy symptoms and had to go home and lie down. See, problem solved. Like you said before, we're teammates. We'll help each other out. Alphas help each other out too."

"How do you mean?"

"When I passed out during the battle, Tyce carried me off the field and brought me to safety. Even as alpha, I'm not immune to being weak sometimes. That's why we create alliances. So we can help each other."

She nodded her cute head.

"Ready to go back to the packhouse now?"

"*Okay,*" she mindlinked me back, letting out a deep breath, and slowly got up. Even in her wolf form, I could see that her belly had become more rotund, just slightly curved. My body warmed. While it had been terrifying when I'd first been given the news, I was finally starting to get used to it and smile about it. Part of it almost felt healing in a way—something that had been taken so violently from me previously was finally handed back to me, giving me a second chance at love and a family. Overcome with emotion, I nuzzled her neck for a moment before breaking into a run and looking back to make sure she was following.

When we made it back to my clothes, I threw my dress shirt over her. And, I can't lie, it was actually kind of hot, seeing her beautiful naked body cloaked in my button-up. I smirked looking her up and down.

"Please don't tell me you're getting horny right now." A smile came to her face.

"Well, you're finally out of that hideous potato sack. My cock and I are in agreement that this is a much better look."

"Blake!" She pushed on my chest.

"What? Am I not allowed to be turned on by my sexy-as-fuck mate?"

She gave me a small laugh. "You'll be glad to know that I tore that dress when I shifted."

"Artemis has answered my prayers!"

Chapter 35

Tyson

I sat with my family for an early dinner before I'd be flying back to Vermont later that evening.

"Miriam called this morning," my grandmother said.

"What's it been? Months? What, did she have a cancellation in her busy schedule or something?" my mom remarked.

"Must have been important?" my dad added.

"Yes, she had absolutely wonderful news to share." My grandmother broke out into a huge smile, and I instantly knew what it was. But I stayed quiet, not wanting them to know I already knew.

"Well, what is it, Catherine?" my grandfather asked.

"Our little Jasmine is pregnant. With twins!" she gushed.

"With twins?" Terri repeated, leaning forward in her seat. "Wow! How exciting!"

"Hmph." My mom didn't look pleased. "Well, Artemis knows best I suppose." She paused and then, clearly not able to help herself, continued, "It's not like I don't have my own grown alpha son who's far older than Miriam's daughter. And it's not like our pack isn't depending on him to give us an alpha heir before he gets too old. And it's not like I don't have two other perfectly wonderful pups of breeding age who are more than ripe enough to find their mates and give me some grandpups! But, no, even though Miriam allowed herself to be marked before marriage, and even though her mate had a bastard son out of wedlock, and even though her daughter rejected her mate, she's the one that gets not just one but two grandpups!"

"Now, Julia!" my dad started.

"Don't 'now, Julia' me! Maybe Tyson should just take a chosen mate! I mean, why not? He's going to be thirty soon, and it's not like he hasn't slept with half the pack as it is. At this point, why even bother waiting for his mate?"

"Over my dead body!" My grandfather stood up slamming his fists onto the table. "What Jasmine did is an abomination! I will not allow anyone in this family, in this pack, to do the same thing! And, Julia." He looked at my mom menacingly. "If you ever suggest Tyson take a chosen mate again, I will banish you from this pack. Just because other packs have allowed sin and evil into their packs does not mean we will do the same in ours. We are a holy pack, blessed by Artemis. Take a look around. Three generations of alphas are still standing. We can't say the same about Miriam's pack." He took a moment to glare at all of us. "Now, does anyone else have any other sinful thoughts they'd like to confess tonight?"

"Dad, calm down. Julia was just upset. There's no need for that outburst. And there's no need to threaten to banish her." My dad spoke up, clearly instinct driving him to stand up for his mate. "Tyson knows to wait for his fated mate."

"I should fucking hope so," my grandfather spat out as he fell back into his chair.

"I take it you haven't told Mom about your mate yet?" I mindlinked Trav, who was also staying quiet.

Since he wasn't an alpha, beta, or gamma, he wasn't able to mindlink back in his human form, but he gave me a nod and then peeked his cell phone out from below the table. I watched as his head turned downward. It wasn't long before I felt mine vibrate in my back pocket. I quickly pulled it into my lap.

Trav: *Going to hold off for now. Not sure how Grandpa and Dad will feel about her being a rogue.*

I nodded at him in understanding and put my phone away before someone noticed. My family had strict rules against cell phones at the dinner table. And chosen mates. And, well, rogues. Then my mind began to wander, considering what my grandfather would do had I, say, been sent a male mate. What would be worse? Telling my grandfather I was gay and my fated mate was a male or rejecting my male mate and taking a female chosen mate instead? Something told me he'd prefer the latter option. Would it be the same with rogue mates, or, I thought, weak mates who had a medical reason for not sparring with their pack?

Goddess damn it, Gigi. I couldn't stop thinking about her, my whole body physically wanting to return to her. I'd already beaten off three times that day thinking about her spectacular rack and luscious thighs. I was a goner. Was taking a fated mate so important? I mean, I was alpha now. What if I did decide to take a chosen mate? And, realistically, how would my grandfather even know if I did?

Luke picked me up from the Burlington International Airport the next morning, after my almost-ten-hour red-eye flight with a layover. Suffice to say, I was exhausted, having barely slept.

"Welcome back, Alpha." He greeted me with a friendly handshake.

"Thanks, Beta. It's good to be back."

"Did you enjoy the time with your family?"

I let out a chuckle. "Yeah, not sure 'enjoy' is the right word."

"I've heard your family's tough."

"That's a nice way to put it. But, anyway, enough about my fam." I clapped and rubbed my hands together in an excited gesture. "Tomorrow's the Fourth. What's going on at your pack? Are we setting off fireworks or what?"

"Normally we do something fun for the pack for the fourth. But with all the lives lost recently, Blake thought it would be in bad taste. So we're just going to have a small cookout at the packhouse for our families."

A big smile on my face, I turned to Luke and asked, "Hey, since I'm away from most of my family, does that mean I get to invite a friend or two?"

He laughed. "Sure, if you have someone you'd like to invite, they're welcome to come."

"Great!"

Once we had settled in his car and were on our way, Luke said, "Before I forget, Blake had me order the stuff and it came in yesterday. We're storing it down in the basement."

Chapter 36

Ginger

I stared at my phone. He contacted me again after I'd done my best to ignore his existence since he'd followed me on Instagram days earlier, as fruitless of an exercise as it was. I was definitely getting in too deep.

> **Tyson Chicken**: *Have any plans for the 4th?*
> **Tyson Chicken**: *We're having a BBQ at the packhouse.*
> *Bring your sisters too*
> **Tyson Chicken**: *We can discuss Salem. Blake's back*

I let out a heavy sigh. I did want to go, and yes, I absolutely wanted to discuss plans for Salem. The next full moon was now just over a week away, so we were cutting it really close. But I had an internal battle, wondering if I should continue seeing him socially.

Finally, my hormones gave in. I found Paige in the living room watching TV. "Hey, do you have warrior duty tomorrow?"

"No, why?"

"Wanna check out the barbecue at the packhouse? We were invited."

"Invited through you?" She narrowed her eyes at me. "I didn't realize you'd become closer to the people who live there than I am."

"Why? Are you jealous?" I teased.

"Who invited you?" She crossed her arms.

"Fine! Alpha Tyce invited me!" I threw my hands up. "He invited you too."

"You two seem to be getting suspiciously close."

"What's it to you? It's not like I have a mate to save myself for!"

She let out a deep breath. "Okay, it's your life, Gigi. I'll go. Dad and Dylan have duty tomorrow anyway, so it's not like I have anything better to do."

Paige and I spent the morning putting together enough spicy deviled eggs to feed an army of warriors. I, additionally, made a small special batch of extra spicy eggs for Paige and me to share, which I marked with red-topped toothpicks, knowing most people didn't have our spice tolerance. After we finished, I spent probably far too long deciding what to wear, eventually settling on an A-line blue-and-white-striped summer dress. It felt very Fourth of July, and I slipped on a pair of red sandals as a final touch.

"You look cute!" Paige remarked as she came into my room to borrow a pair of shoes. She had simply put on a red top and white shorts and decided to borrow the same wedges she'd worn for the dinner when Dylan came over. "Do you want me to curl your hair?"

"Sure, that would be great!" I agreed. I curled hers in return when she was done.

When we were ready to go, our mom drove us over and dropped us off, telling us both to have fun and call when we were ready to come home.

Jasmine greeted us at the door when we arrived. "Paige! Gigi! I wasn't expecting you!" She looked back and forth between the two of us, eventually pulling us each into hugs.

"Gigi apparently has a connection at the packhouse who forgot to mention we were coming." Paige chuckled.

"Did Blake invite you?" She squinted in a way that made it clear she was racking her brain trying to figure it out.

"You're getting warm!" Paige giggled.

"Lucy?"

"Colder."

"Umm . . ." She put her index finger to her chin. "I can't figure it out. Who?"

"He's also an alpha."

"Tyce?" Her eyes bugged out. "What? Tyce invited you?"

"Yep!"

"Wait, he invited you or Gigi?" She looked between us.

"He invited both of us!" I responded.

"But he was obviously only interested in one of us coming." Paige elbowed me in the rib cage.

"I see." Jasmine looked a bit dazed. "Okay, well, let me take those for you. You didn't have to bring anything. We have plenty of food already."

"It's okay, Jaz. We'll take them. Just lead the way to where to put them."

Jasmine turned and walked toward the living room, and we followed, going out the glass door into the backyard of the packhouse.

My eyes instantly found his amber ones as soon as we stepped outside. He was standing by the grill, sipping beers with Beta Luke and a blond man with a clear resemblance to Lucy. I glanced at Beta Luke for a moment and secretly wondered if there could be any truth to the rumors. I mean, I didn't think there was, but crazier things had happened. Beta Luke was actually quite handsome, in a movie star sort of way, and Paige had told me he had been Jasmine's fated mate before she ended up with Alpha Blake. Furthermore, the pregnancy portion of the rumor had ended up being true. So could Jasmine have been having an affair?

I turned away and continued to follow Jasmine to a table laid out with food, but I could feel Tyce's eyes burning into me. "Hey, ladies, thanks for coming!" He came over to greet us.

"Tyce, I didn't realize you were so close to Paige and Gigi." Jasmine crossed her arms and looked him up and down.

"He's only close to one of us," Paige said.

"Do you have a crush, Tyce?" Jasmine teased, poking him in the chest.

"I think he does." Paige snickered.

"Hey, Luke said I could invite a friend or two. And it looks like my friend or two came," Tyce replied with a playful smile. "Can I get my lovely friends anything to drink? We've got a really nice selection of beverages, and Lucy made some punch I hear is famous around here. Although, I'd go easy on that one. One of her younger brothers drank a little too much of it about an hour ago and isn't doing so well."

"I think it's best we stay away from the punch then," Paige replied, giving me a look.

"How about some rosé then?"

"Sure," I replied. He led us over and poured some rosé into plastic cups for us, adding a couple ice cubes so it would stay cold. Paige went over to hang out with Jasmine, and Tyce led me around to introduce me to everyone. I found out the blond man that was standing with Luke was Kyle, one of Lucy's four brothers, and had graduated in the same year as Luke.

A small kiddie pool was set up, and Lucy and her friend Emma, who was Kyle's mate, were playing with their pups in the pool along with Luke's sisters' pups. There were so many pups, I couldn't keep track of all their names. Scratch that, I couldn't keep track of all the people in Luke's and Lucy's large families at all, pup or grown-up.

Tyce's family, on the other hand, was much smaller and easier to remember. Jasmine was an only child, so I only had to remember her parents and grandparents, until her brother showed up with his mate.

We soon began putting together our plates of food. After Tyce got me a burger we went over to grab side dishes. "So what'd you bring?" Tyce asked.

"Paige and I made the deviled eggs. But be careful, the eggs are spicy, especially the ones with the red toothpicks."

"Oh, then I definitely want one with a red toothpick," he said, putting one on his plate.

"You like spicy food?"

"Love it! The hotter the better!"

"Okay, I'd love to see you eat one of those eggs then," I challenged.

"I'll eat it right now." He pulled the toothpick out and plopped it in his mouth. After chewing and swallowing, he smiled and said, "Damn! That's spicy, but good!"

"You have to be the first person outside our family I've seen be able to handle one of those eggs!" I said, astonished.

"I can handle much more than that." He winked, and I had a feeling he wasn't talking about food. My stomach somersaulted and my thighs tingled. He grabbed another and put it on my plate. "Chips?" he asked, pouring some on his plate.

"I'm good," I replied, grabbing some salad instead, thinking I shouldn't go too crazy with eating junk food. I looked over at Paige who was leading the pups in games, bouncing around with her skinny, toned limbs.

We took a seat at a picnic table. After I finished my burger, I picked at my salad and watched as Tyce popped a chip in his mouth. I decided to do the same, as they looked far more appealing than what I'd put on my own plate. I pulled one off his plate and stuck it in my mouth. Crunch.

"Hey, those are my chips!" Tyce exclaimed. "You didn't want any when I asked."

"I changed my mind." I smiled and took another. Crunch.

"Stop stealing my chips!"

"Sharing is caring." I gave him a devilish smile and popped another into my mouth. Crunch.

"Alphas don't share." He gave me a mischievous grin. Then he brought his face down to his plate and began licking them. "My chips!"

"What, are you five?" I couldn't help myself as I doubled over, laughing at how ridiculous he was being.

"Caden knows what's up!" He turned toward Luke's eight-year-old nephew who began doing the same thing, then gave him a high five. I rolled my eyes and went back to picking at my salad.

"Holy shit! What's in these deviled eggs!?" We suddenly heard someone cry out. We turned to see Kyle with tears and snot running down his face. "Emma, get me water!"

"Oh no, did you eat one of the ones with a toothpick?" Paige rushed over. "Gigi marked those for her and me!"

"Wuss!" Tyce called out, chuckling.

"There is no fucking way you can handle those things!" Kyle retorted.

"Already did." Tyce went back over and popped another in his mouth. "Who else wants to challenge me?" He beat his chest with his fists.

"Oh, Goddess. I've tried Paige and Gigi's spicy food before. I definitely can't handle it!" Jasmine laughed. "Tyce, I'm really impressed."

"Okay, no more spicy eggs. The last two are for me!" Paige took them and put them on a plate for herself. "I better eat them before we get in trouble for poisoning everyone."

"You're such a buzzkill, Paige." I laughed. "I was waiting for someone else to get their mouth burned!"

"Come on, let's get some more drinks." Tyce led me back over to the drink stand.

"Actually, I need to use the bathroom," I replied.

"No problem, let me walk you over." He took me into the packhouse where there was a line for the downstairs bathroom. He took my arm and led me in a different direction. "No need to wait in line. You've got a bathroom hookup here." We walked up the stairs to the third floor so I could use his.

I quickly ran in to do my business and wash my hands. I also splashed some cold water on my face, wondering if it was the weather or Tyce that had me so overheated. I couldn't lie. Being in such close proximity to him had me all riled up. I mean, how could it not? He'd recently become much less dickish, and damn was he hot! And now that I knew how skilled he was . . . Fuck, I really needed to stop thinking about it. I was definitely getting in too deep and catching feelings.

Just friends, we could just be friends, who take long car trips together . . .

and who hooked up one time . . .

and left me desperate for more . . .

After taking a few breaths and pulling myself together, resolving not to let anything happen, I finally stepped foot outside. But clearly Tyce was not on the same page as me, because before I even had a chance to close the door behind me, he grabbed me and had me pinned to the wall, his body heat surrounding me, and his massive arms on either side of my face. I stared into his intense amber eyes for a moment, my whole body alive, my breathing shallow. Fuck, he was so hot, and if he kissed me, I knew I'd totally give in.

And then he did, closing the space between us, crushing his mouth against mine. My hips jutted forward in reaction as he wrapped his arms around me, grabbing my ass and pressing me closer to his body. I ran my fingers up his chest to his neck and then his face, memorizing the feel of his cheekbones and stubble, knowing I'd always want to remember everything, including how his cheeks felt as our tongues twined and how his hard steel rod of a cock pressed up against me.

I let out a moan. Liquid pooled in the crotch of my panties, and the whole bottom half of my body pulsed with desperation. I was a goner. Every part of me wanted to have Tyce again. And again. And again.

"Let's go to my room," Tyce whispered into my ear, his warm breath tickling my ear and sending a shiver down my spine. He took my hand and led me inside, pushing the door closed. I walked a few steps backward until my legs hit the edge of his bed.

He came closer, looking down at me, his gaze intense. "Take your panties off, baby," he said in a low, gravelly voice that did things to me that even someone's skilled tongue had never done before. I instantly followed his command, burying my hands underneath the skirt of my dress, hitching my thumbs into the waist of my panties, and pulling them off, bringing them down my legs until they dropped to the floor.

"Lie on the bed, baby, and bring your legs up," he said in that same voice. I, again, followed his instructions, throwing off my sandals, plopping onto his bed, lying back, and holding myself up on my forearms. I scooched back a bit and brought my legs up until my heels were practically touching my ass.

"Now spread your legs for me, baby. Show me your pussy." Holy shit. I wasn't normally one for taking orders, but the way he was doling them out had me so overheated and wet that there had to be a puddle forming under me on Tyce's bedsheets.

I pulled the skirt of my dress up, exposing myself, and stared up at him as I slowly spread my legs. I watched him as he brought a fisted hand to his mouth and bit down on it, his eyes not moving from my body.

He stared at me intently, not saying anything—just staring. I'd never known silence to be so intense before. I didn't fail to notice his cock throbbing and straining in his khaki shorts, and I wondered if it was painful. Finally, he moved his fist from his mouth and said, "You need a werewolf to ravish that body. Once I'm done with you, you'll never go human again."

"Not sure what a werewolf can do that a human can't," I teased.

He knelt down at the foot of his bed, put his hands on my knees, and in a very husky voice, replied, "A werewolf can hear you better, see you better, and"—he smirked—"eat you better." A shudder raced down the length of my back, ending at the apex of my inner thighs.

He slowly slid his palms down the inside of my legs until his fingers were grazing my ass. He grasped my hips aggressively and pulled me toward him until my ass was right at the edge of the bed. "Goddess, your pussy smells delicious," he groaned. "I bet it tastes even better."

Then fucking taste it. I was screaming on the inside, the anticipation killing me.

Finally, he brought his head between my thighs, touched his tongue to me, licked me slowly from bottom to top, and pulled away. With a mischievous smile, he said, "I licked it, now it's mine."

"Fucking possessive alpha!"

"Alphas don't share, baby. Your pussy is mine." Before I could protest, he brought his mouth back onto it and instantly found my clit, sucking it into his mouth. I let out a loud moan in response. He plunged his fingers inside me and instantly began working them in and out of me. I screamed, grabbing for his bedsheets. "Who's got you screaming like that, baby?" he groaned out.

"You!" I cried, now familiar with his game.

"Say my name, baby."

"Tyce!"

Clearly satisfied, he brought his tongue to my clit and began flicking it back and forth.

"Tyce!" I screamed out again, and his strokes turned aggressive, his tongue moving more rapidly, lapping at me heartily. *Fuck, it feels so good.* "Tyce!" His fingers became more forceful as they plunged in and out of me. I wasn't sure how it was possible, but somehow his fingers felt even better this time than they had in the club.

Overcome with pleasure, I let out more moans, my legs shaking, my toes curling, my insides on fire. He kept going, not stopping. "Tyce!" I screamed again, and he growled, working that much harder, bringing me to the point of no return.

He pulled away for a second. "Come for me, baby." Then was right back at it.

"Who the fuck comes on comma—" I couldn't even finish my sentence as I grasped for his blankets, my back lifting off the bed, an intense orgasm rolling through my body. His fingers and tongue drew my soul out of me as I shuddered, a loud scream escaping my lips. And he wouldn't stop. He just kept going, forcing more orgasms out of me. By the end, I had lost count of how many times the sensation had ripped through my body, leaving me half-numb.

"Baby, I want you to remember that every time you even think about looking at a human again."

I panted, barely able to move.

"Now, come on, put your panties on and let's go back downstairs." He turned to move toward the door.

"No."

He spun back around to face me, cocking an eyebrow.

"Not until you finish."

"You really think you have the energy to do that after what I put your body through?"

"Someone thinks they did a better job than they did." I sat up smirking. "I was promised not to be able to walk straight next time, and I still can." I got up and began pacing the room in straight lines, though I had to admit I did feel a bit wobbly on my feet. But Tyce didn't need to know that. "Now take your clothes off!" I demanded, pointing my finger at him.

"Someone thinks they're an alpha now."

"Let's get something straight, Alpha Tyce. You don't control my pussy. My pussy controls you. Now take your shirt off."

He gave me a mischievous smile. I wondered if he'd go along with it, until he finally did, pulling his polo shirt off his body. And, *fuck*! I was totally caught off guard by how much his bronzed body turned me on. My eyes traced his massive traps and shoulders, impressive pecs, and abs that must have been carved by the Goddess herself, with bulging muscles straining against the crisp crevices that separated each one. His V-cuts pulled my eyes southward where his cock was still trapped, straining inside the confines of his shorts.

"Take everything off," I commanded.

His eyes didn't leave me as I watched him undo his belt and then unbutton his shorts. His fingers found his zipper, and he very slowly pulled it down, gradually revealing the gray boxer briefs he had on underneath. He pulled everything off, dropping it to the ground until he was completely naked, his massive cock standing at attention, precome dripping from the end of it. Fuck, I didn't think I could be any hornier, but Tyce somehow made it possible even after he'd pulled several orgasms out of me.

"Now what?" he asked with a glint in his eyes.

I unzipped my dress and let it drop to the ground. Then I unsnapped my bra and did the same thing. He let out a groan, clenching and unclenching his hands. I smiled, suddenly feeling really powerful. "Fuck me, Alpha Tyce. And I don't want to walk straight when you're done."

I didn't have to ask twice because he threw open his bedside table drawer almost immediately, ripped open a condom, and pulled it on. He grabbed me and lifted me up against the wall. "You think you can handle it?" he growled.

"Fuck yes!" I replied. And in milliseconds, his cock was inside me, pounding into me.

He banged me against the wall, my legs wrapping around him, one of his hands hitched under my ass and the other against my breast. Before I could get too used to the position we were in, he threw me on the bed and we wrestled for who got to go on top, rolling from one to the other. Tyce would get some strokes in from above until I'd fight for control, forcing him onto his back, bouncing on his cock. Back and forth, we repeated this power struggle several times until he finally pushed me up against his headboard and took me from behind. He gripped my hips and enthusiastically pounded into me. "You like that, baby?"

"Tyce!" I screamed, and he went even faster and harder, his fingers gripping even more firmly.

This only lasted so long before I pushed my ass forcefully back into him until he fell backward, and then I fucked him reverse cowgirl while he kneaded my breasts and rubbed my erect nipples between his fingers.

When I didn't know how much more energy I had to keep going, he pulled me down next to him until we were side by side, facing each other, and he pulled my leg over him. Somehow the position felt more intimate than expected as he tugged my body against his and brought his fingers to my cheeks, kissing me. "Goddess, you're a fucking goddess," he said between kisses. "I will never fuck anyone more amazing for the rest of my life."

Wait, what?

Did I just hear that right?

He brought his hand down between my legs, and before I had a chance to think more about what he'd said, my whole mind went blank, giving in to the power of his fingers as he expertly stroked me and brought me to orgasm once again. We moaned against each other, our lips touching as we both came at the same time, Fourth of July fireworks being set off from the guest bedroom of the packhouse. And fuck, I couldn't move. Nope, Tyce would have to carry me downstairs. I was completely spent and my legs no longer worked—my mind no longer worked!

When I regained some consciousness, I turned toward him to see that he'd rolled onto his back and had a pillow covering his face.

"What are you doing?" I laughed. After a minute or two, he finally moved the pillow, feathers floating into the air. "Did you just bite the pillow?"

He chuckled and said, "That was weird. Let me get cleaned up. And we should probably go downstairs before your sister starts worrying that you're having massive diarrhea."

"First of all, Tyce, that's disgusting!" I chuckled. "And second of all, my sister is on to me, and that's definitely not what she's going to think."

Chapter 37

Tyson

"Is this the best way to do it?" I asked Blake, staring at the small, partially filled shot glass in front of me.

"Yeah, that's how we started. First we drank small vials until we regained our ability to shift into our wolves. And that's when the injections started."

As I brought the shot glass to my face, stomach acid traveled up to my throat in reaction. I didn't know if I'd be able to get it down without retching. "Fuck, this shit smells horrible."

"I mean, it's natural, right? It's our kryptonite. We're going to be averse to it. Maybe you can put it in a smoothie or something to help get it down. We didn't even have the option. They'd just whip us if we didn't drink it or threw it up." Blake shrugged. "I still can't decide if swallowing that shit or getting whipped would be worse. I never threw up, so I can't say for sure."

"Fuck, bro. And you did this shit for four years?"

"It got easier once they started injecting us."

I nodded, continuing to stare at the shot glass. This wasn't going to be easy. But then I thought back to how I had been milliseconds from death, and I finally took a deep breath, pinched my nose, and threw back the shot. I almost instantly fell to my knees, the intensely bitter flavor immediately burning my tongue and numbing my taste buds. *Fuck!*

"Hey, are you okay, man?" Blake came over and helped me back into my chair.

I swallowed a few times, making sure it settled into my stomach. "Fuck, man. That was brutal!"

"You should probably take a few days off from patrol duty. It's going to be hard to shift into your wolf for the first couple weeks. Although, you were able to stay in your wolf form after you got shot with the dart, so maybe it won't affect you as much."

"I'll take it easy. I actually have errands I need to run tomorrow."

"Hey, no problem, man. I appreciate all your help this summer, but this isn't your pack. So take all the time off you need."

I smiled and patted Blake on the shoulder, then decided to head upstairs and lie down for a bit. My tongue, throat, and insides were all burning, flames scorching my stomach and intestines. Before I made it to my bedroom, I took a detour to the bathroom where I took a moment to cough up some blood. *Fuck! I was in bad shape.*

I fell into my bed and pulled out my phone. Before I passed out, I shot Gigi a text.

Me: *Hey are we still on for Salem tomorrow?*
Gigi: *Absolutely! Be there first thing!*

I smiled as I drifted into sleep.

Ginger

Ever since the Fourth of July cookout two days earlier, all I could think about anymore was Tyce. He completely consumed my waking and dreaming thoughts. He was doing to me exactly what I thought he would, and I couldn't help the nagging anxiety that kept beating at me, telling me these feelings were only temporary. He was going to break my heart.

Realistically, he would eventually find his mate. Also, realistically, he was an alpha and would want a strong luna to lead with him. I was just some girl with no wolf—all I would do was weaken his pack—and that was assuming he'd even be willing to take a chosen mate, which he probably wasn't.

Furthermore, if I never got my wolf back, I'd likely never be able to give him an heir. It was dangerous for a human to carry a werewolf baby, especially considering the werewolf genetics would be on both sides. Werewolf pregnancies progressed in two-thirds of the time of human ones, and carrying his pup would likely kill me. The whole relationship was doomed before it had even begun.

I wiped tears from my eyes as I got dressed, devastated by my predicament. There was no question about it, I was in love, and it was with someone I couldn't be with. I always wondered what love would feel like, and now I knew. Once you were in it, you just knew. And I was completely in fucking love with him. This was a disaster.

But I was strong, and I would get through it. He was only here until the end of the summer. Eventually, he'd go home, and I'd go back to school. Maybe I'd even get my wolf back, and I'd still be able to meet my fated mate. I just had to think logically about it and hold on to hope. My wolf had already shown signs of coming back, so it wasn't totally a lost cause.

I took deep breaths and snuck out of the house. It was going to be hot that day, but in the morning, it still wasn't too bad. I made my long walk over to the packhouse from the outskirts where we lived. The walk felt therapeutic as I listened to the different birds make their mating calls. Sometimes, when I'd walk with Paige, she'd describe all the smells. I tried to inhale them. There was a wilderness, foresty, wet wood, and crisp plant smell out where we lived, but I could never quite describe the different scents in as much detail as Paige could.

My whole body felt a bit damp by the time I arrived after walking underneath the sun's rays in the New England humidity. I was looking forward to finally getting into an air-conditioned car. I walked up the steps to the front door of the packhouse and rang the doorbell.

After about a minute, Blake pulled the door open. "Oh, hey, Gigi." He gave me a knowing smirk. "Is someone expecting you?"

"Yeah, Tyce," I replied. I was pretty sure the whole packhouse and their families were privy to what had gone on a couple days earlier. The two of us had disappeared for quite some time. I wondered how long it would take to get around the pack. Hopefully, it wouldn't. My parents definitely wouldn't be happy about the rumors. And, I thought with annoyance, Heidi would probably love to repeat them to my family with glee. I had no idea what was up with her lately, but she was really bothering me big-time.

"Come in. I'll go see how he's feeling and see if he can come down," Blake replied. What did that mean? He hadn't told me he wasn't feeling well. How was that even possible? Werewolves, especially young werewolves, couldn't get sick.

I took a seat at the dining room table as Blake sprinted up the stairs and I took out my phone to scroll through my Instagram feed. Minutes later, Blake came back down with Tyce following. He seemed to look okay. He was dressed well and had the same smug look on his face he always did.

"Hey, ready to go?" he asked as I stood up. I nodded and followed him outside. He held the door open for me as I passed through. I waited as he closed it, and before I had a chance to walk toward the car, he pulled me toward him so our bodies were touching. I looked up at him and he smiled. "Damn, I want to kiss you so badly right now."

While initially my stomach fluttered, as soon as his breath hit my face, I went into an internal panic. I'd never forget the scent of it. I almost vomited right then and there, my heart racing, my palms sweating. I'd never had a panic attack before, and I wondered if that was what was happening to me. I pushed him away and cowered, completely overtaken with terror.

She's lucky she'd almost fully developed her wolf already.

It only takes two milligrams to kill a human.

Her wolf died so she didn't have to.

"Why do you smell like wolfsbane?" I screamed.

He had his arms around me almost instantly. "Gigi, it's okay."

"It's not okay! It's not okay at all!" Tears were spilling from my eyes. I had already been emotional that morning, but now that scent was putting me over the edge.

"Gigi, listen to me. It's fine." He had his mouth close to my ear, and the scent was touching my skin. I began to sob, imagining my skin boiling from his breath touching it. "I'm just drinking it to build up a tolerance, so I can get stronger. I know it smells bad, but I won't kiss you, I won't hurt you, don't worry."

"Get away from me!" I screamed again, pushing him off me. "Don't touch me!"

"Okay!" He instantly backed away and put his hands up. "I promise I won't touch you again for the rest of today, okay?"

"Thank you," I replied, wiping the tears from my eyes.

He walked to his car and opened the passenger side door, gesturing for me to get in. I climbed in and collapsed into my seat, taking deep breaths. *It's okay, it's okay.* He wasn't going to touch me. I would be fine.

He closed the door and climbed into the driver's seat. As soon as he sat down, he put his head down on the steering wheel. Then, he threw his door back open and leaned over, letting out loud, wet coughs. When he sat back upright, he had blood dribbling down his chin. He instantly reached into his pocket and pulled out a handkerchief that he used to wipe himself. "Fuck."

"Are you okay?" I asked.

"Yeah, I'm good now. Just needed to get that out," he replied as he put his car into drive. But I wondered if he really was good. It wasn't every day that you just coughed up blood. I was tempted to touch his hand and comfort him, but my whole body rejected the idea of it, my skin crawling at the thought.

We drove quietly, with just the music on the radio to fill the silence. There were a few times I thought about saying something, but I was still recovering from what happened earlier, the thought of it choking me. After about two hours, he said, "I have to pull off at this exit. I'm really not feeling well." I nodded and he got off, finding a McDonald's parking lot to pull into. We parked in a back corner of the lot, and he put his head back onto the steering wheel. "Gigi, I hate to ask. But can you drive? I don't think I can make it. Otherwise, maybe I can just nap a little."

"It's okay, I can drive," I replied almost instantly. "I have my license. I just don't have a car."

"Thanks, I appreciate it." He got out of the car and then climbed into the back seat. "I need to lie down. I hope you don't mind." He clutched his stomach and curled up into the seat on his side. The position couldn't have been comfortable, considering how tall he was and how much space he took up. He looked severely cramped.

"It's fine. I don't mind at all," I said, pulling open the passenger door, so I could get into the driver's seat. As soon as I'd gotten settled and adjusted the seat for how short I was compared to him, I put my phone into the holder and set it to navigate to Salem. It wasn't long before I heard his snores from the back. He was totally out. I wondered how long he'd suffered before he'd given in. I should have offered to drive from the moment he'd coughed up blood. And then, I wondered, was he only going to Salem for me? Would he have gone in such bad shape otherwise?

I eventually made it to the downtown area of Salem. After driving around, I realized there weren't really any parking lots, and I didn't know how to parallel park very well. "Tyce!" I called out.

"Wh-what?" He shot up.

"Sorry for waking you." I winced, feeling bad. Why did I do that?

"It's okay. I didn't mean to just pass out like that."

"No, I'm really sorry. I know you're not feeling well. But, oh it doesn't matter. Go back to sleep."

"Gigi, what is it? Tell me."

"I don't know where or how to parallel park," I blurted.

"Well, good thing you woke me then." He chuckled. "Just pull over somewhere and I can handle that part."

I did as he asked and found a place to pull over so he could take over. He was able to find a side street to parallel park on almost immediately, and then we were on our way.

"How are you feeling?" I asked.

"I needed that nap. Thanks for driving. I'm starting to feel better now."

"Is the only reason you came for me?" I stopped and turned toward him.

He rubbed the back of his neck. "It's not the only reason. I have my own reasons for coming too."

"But are your reasons contingent on the full moon? Like you could have come when you were feeling better, right?"

"My reasons are technically contingent on the full moon. All werewolf spells take effect during the full moon due to our nature. I suppose I could have skipped this one. But it doesn't matter, Gigi. I knew this trip was really important to you, so I would have made it happen no matter what. And you were able to drive anyway, so it all worked out."

"Thanks," I mumbled. "I appreciate it." Goddess, he was going to make it difficult to keep my head in the game. As much as I kept trying not to fall for him, it was becoming more and more impossible.

"I'd hold your hand while we walk to the witch shop, but I made a promise." I looked up at him and he winked. Fucking Artemis. Why did he turn sweet all of a sudden? And why did my panties have to be soaked from just a wink? *Maybe because he fucked you practically unconscious the other day?*

When we got there, I was pleased that Helena wasn't manning the register as usual. Instead, it was the Sybil. "Ah! My favorite customer!" She smiled as we entered the small shop. "I was wondering whether you'd be back again this month. And who is this handsome man you're with?"

"Hi—Tyce—nice to meet you." He put out his hand. "I normally see Maria when I come."

"Ah, yes, my mother. She's just with a customer right now but should be out shortly." She then turned to me. "And you, my dear, come right this way."

I followed her to the usual room and took a seat, looking around the small room, refamiliarizing myself with it. "Do they work?" I asked, nodding at the tarot cards behind her.

"Ah, yes, most definitely." She nodded. "Why don't you and your boyfriend stick around after, and I'll do a free one-card reading for both of you. It'll be fun." I was about to correct her and tell her he wasn't my boyfriend, but she kept speaking. "Now, darling, give me your hand. Let's see what's happening. I was really hoping you wouldn't be back again. You were so close last month, but alas! There's always the upcoming moon. One nice thing about the moon. It's predictable and always follows the same cycle. The same can't be said for most things!"

I put my left hand out and she took it in between both of hers. She closed her eyes and hummed. My heart raced. If I was so close last time, why didn't it work? Was I trying to accomplish the impossible? Did they just keep stringing a carrot of hope in front of me to separate me from my money? But no, those feelings I had the evening we went to the nightclub. They felt familiar—the same feelings I'd had at twelve years old, right before everything happened.

"Yes, it's definitely working!" Sybil's eyes shot open. "If she doesn't come back this full moon, then she won't. But I believe she will. She is clawing to come back, fighting against the darkness of death. She has a reason now, and it is giving her the will."

I whimpered. Was it really going to happen finally? I sniffed back tears at the thought.

"Let's go ring up that double batch."

I followed her out, and she rang me up. I handed her my credit card, cringing at the cost. I hadn't been working at all during the summer, so I wasn't sure how I was going to pay off the charge. I'd just have to take on extra shifts once I went back to school.

Tyce came out not too long after. "Come, my dears. Let me do a one-card tarot reading for both of you." Sybil led us back into the same room, gesturing for us to take a seat, and pulling a deck off the shelf. As Tyce and I sat down next to each other, she pulled the cards out of the box and turned toward Tyce. "Okay, my handsome werewolf friend. Think of a question you want the answer to." She waited a moment. "Do you have one?"

"Yes," Tyce replied.

"Wonderful." She shuffled the cards then handed them to him. "Now you shuffle until you feel they are in a good place." He finished shuffling and nodded, handing them back to her. She fanned them out onto the table. "Okay, now pick one and turn it upward." He did as asked, turning it over so we could all see it.

"Very interesting." Sybil nodded. "Seven of wands. I take it you are in a position of power?" She looked up at him.

"I'm the alpha of my pack."

She smiled. "But you do not currently lead?" He didn't respond, but she continued anyway. "There are challenges coming your way, and you will have to stand up and fight, hold on to and protect what you have, defend what you believe in. You have the talent, drive, and ambition to do so, but your convictions will be tested."

Tyce nodded, keeping a poker face.

She took the card back and put it back in the pile. "Okay, my darling. Your turn now. Please think of a question."

The only question I could think to ask was, *Will my wolf come back?*

"Okay, dear. You have your question?"

I nodded.

"Wonderful, now shuffle please." She handed me the deck. I did as asked, shuffling for a few seconds, and then handed it back to her. Again, she fanned out the cards. "Please pick one and turn it over."

I hovered my hand over the deck for a bit until I finally found one to pull. I flipped it over. *Death.*

I let out a cry and ran out of the room, unable to listen to what Sybil was going to tell me. I couldn't bear to hear it. I ran until I was outside, down the street, and then I leaned my back against the brick wall of a building and began sobbing. I'd already been so emotional all day, and that had finally put me over the edge. All I wanted to do was go home and pretend I'd never seen that card.

"Gigi!" Tyce's voice rang out. I looked up to him jogging over to me. Once he got close enough, he asked, "What was that all about? Why did you run out like that? Are you okay?"

I shook my head. "Let's just pretend that never happened."

"Why though?"

"Did you see that card?"

"I did but—"

"Just pretend you didn't!" When I said that, he shut his mouth and nodded his head.

He made a gesture as if he were reaching out to touch but then stopped himself and backed up. "Okay, why don't we just go for a walk and grab some lunch then, before we head back? It's a long drive."

I nodded in response.

"I googled some places to eat beforehand, and there's a place called the Howling Wolf Taqueria." He laughed. "I mean, I don't know about you, but I love Mexican. And if it's got *wolf* in the name, I mean, who can say no to that?"

"Yeah, sounds good," I replied, wiping at my tears.

"Come on, Gigi, cheer up. It can't be that horrible to spend the day with me." I lifted my head, sniffing back tears. "Goddess, I want to touch you so badly. You are killing me with this no-touching thing you have."

"Why do you want to touch me so badly?" I asked, wrapping my arms around myself.

"Because you're so fucking beautiful. And when you're sad like you are right now, all I want to do is make it go away. It's like something inside me is practically forcing my hand to reach out and touch you to cheer you up. But I made a promise, and I'm not going to break it."

My breath caught by how candid he was being. Why did he have to make this all so fucking difficult?

"Come on, ready for some lunch?" He smiled at me, gesturing for me to walk forward.

"Okay," I replied, and began walking. He led us around the Salem downtown area for a bit until we eventually reached the restaurant. They sat us at a high top once we got inside.

"How do you feel about chips and guac?" Tyce glanced over his menu at me.

"Are you going to be able to share or do we have to put in two orders?" I teased, finally starting to feel better after our walk.

"I suppose I can try to learn to share with you." He gave me a cute half smile.

"The bacon-wrapped jalapeños look good."

"You should get them. It's killing me, but I'm going to lay off the spicy food for a little while. My stomach's not feeling great." He frowned.

"Are you okay?" I asked. "I can drive home if you want to sleep again."

"I think I should be able to make it home. The nap really helped."

"Good."

"Damn, they have chile con queso here? That's one of my favorites! Fuck, I wish my stomach wasn't basically bleeding right now!"

I laughed. "Seriously?"

"Yeah, I love it. I mean, cheese and spicy? And carbs to dip in it? What's better than that?"

"My sisters and I make it all the time, with chorizo. Maybe once you're feeling better, I'll make some for you. Actually, your cousin Jasmine tried it once when she came over. It didn't go well." I laughed.

"I'd love to try your queso. And make it as spicy as you normally eat it. Don't judge my tolerance based on my cousin!" He paused for a moment, then continued, "Actually, speaking of which, I almost forgot. I have dessert waiting in the car. So save room."

"You brought your mom's brownies?"

"She made a fresh batch while I was out there. And I promised I'd let you try one next Salem trip. I'm a man of my word." I smiled, my heart warming.

After we placed our orders and were waiting for our food to come, I commented, "You're being really nice today. I'm starting to get suspicious."

"Why?"

"You're usually kind of a dick."

He rubbed the back of his neck. "I'm sorry. But honestly, a lot of it was in reaction to you being kind of nasty to me."

"What about that first day you met me? The first thing you did was snap at me and ask what I was looking at."

He let out a sigh. "That wasn't personal."

"What was it then?"

"Okay, I'll tell you. But you have to promise not to tell anyone. Deal?"

"I promise. I'd pinky swear but, you know."

He chuckled. "Yeah, your whole not-touching thing."

"Air pinky swear?"

"Sure." He gave a really big smile that made my stomach somersault. He had to have one of the nicest smiles I'd ever seen. We both made a gesture of pinky swearing. He then let out another sigh and lowered his voice to a whisper. "It's really stupid. That day, when I was walking the downtown area of Salem on the way to the witch shop, a huge rat sprinted out from a dark corner, and I completely freaked out, screaming like a little girl. People started laughing at me because I'm sure it looked ridiculous. I mean, I'm this huge guy and I'm crying like a baby over a rat." He slumped his shoulders. "So when you were staring at me, I just got really defensive. I honestly didn't mean to be a jerk. You just caught me at a really bad time."

"Oh, shit. Now I feel really bad about what a bitch I was."

"Hey, you didn't know, right?"

"Right, but I guess I should have known better than to assume. I just thought you were being a douche to me because you thought I was below your standards for the types of girls you normally like."

"That couldn't be further from the truth. When I first saw you, I thought you were one of the most beautiful women I'd ever seen. I instantly felt bad for snapping at you and was going to apologize, but then you went on your tirade." He chuckled, shaking his head.

"I totally fucked up, didn't I?" I laughed.

"Hey, it still worked out in the end though, right? I mean, here we are, having lunch together, after having some of the best sex two days ago. I'm admitting things to you I'd never admit to anyone else. And I'm planning to *share* my chips with you. I mean, an alpha sharing?" He chuckled.

"You are so weird with your chips."

He stuck his tongue out at me. "Anyway, since I'm being honest, I'll tell you why I've been going to see the witches. It's because of my fear of rodents. I've been so embarrassed about it my whole life, and my dad and grandpa shit on me for it all the time. So when I found out that witches can hypnotize you to get rid of your worst fears, well, sign me right up!"

"Why are you so scared of rodents?"

He gave a small laugh. "It started out kind of silly. As a joke, my younger brother threw a decomposing mouse at me when I was a little kid. It really freaked me out. And then it got worse when my dad and grandpa used to take me down to the dungeons to torture people. There used to be so many mice down there. Sometimes I'd pass out on the floor, and when I'd wake up, they'd be running right past my face."

"Why would you pass out?"

"Because the shit my dad and grandpa did." He shuddered. "I mean, I enjoy it now, but at ten years old, it was really fucked-up."

"You enjoy it?" I stared at him wide-eyed.

"I mean, sure. You eventually start to get a sick pleasure from it. It's hard to explain."

"Holy Artemis."

"Maybe I can train you in the art of it sometime?" He winked at me.

"I think I'm all set with that."

"Okay, well, if you ever change your mind . . ."

"I'll know who to call," I finished his sentence for him. Then, suddenly, I considered revealing my secret to him, especially after he'd opened up to me. But when I was about to open my mouth, I reconsidered and chickened out. Maybe it wouldn't be my secret much longer anyway. I straightened up and tried to push all the negative feelings from seeing the tarot card earlier away.

"Did I mention you look really cute today and I want to touch you?"

"Tyce."

"Just seeing if you changed your mind. I mean, the whole torturing thing had to give me points, right?"

I laughed. "You are so weird."

"But you love me anyway."

Fuck, I did love him.

Chapter 38

Ginger

The evening of the full moon finally came. This was the night of all or nothing. Either my wolf came back, or I'd finally have to accept that she was gone for good and any life I'd continue to live would be as a human. I took a deep breath, preparing myself for the moment of truth.

After all the lights in my house were out and everyone was asleep, I snuck out once again, as I had since I'd come home for the summer. It was the perfect night with a cloudless sky and the full moon in all its glory shining down onto earth. I crossed my fingers and hoped it was a good omen as I slipped into the forest to make my way to my usual spot.

My stomach squeezed with nervousness. I didn't know if I was ready. What if all of this pain and suffering I'd endured had been for nothing? What if my wolf really was never coming back? No! I straightened my shoulders. That was the wrong attitude. She would come back. She had shown signs, and even Sybil told me she wanted to come back. So what if I'd drawn a Death tarot card? Tarot wasn't real. They were just some paper cards laminated in plastic that were probably printed in some factory in China. What I felt inside me was real.

I quickly stopped by the lake to fill my jar with water and carefully screwed the top back on, giving it a good shake, then I proceeded to my regular spot. Same as all the times prior, I began to unload my tote bag, putting the stones I had out for the five points of the pentagram. As it got closer to midnight, I undressed, folding my clothes neatly on top of the usual rock. The air was nice that evening, with a slight breeze to cut through the heat. It was actually a great night for taking a swim in the lake that I'd passed. But I knew it was closely monitored by warriors, so unless I wanted to show off to them, it was best that I didn't.

As soon as my cell phone showed 12:00, I went through my usual ritual, now well memorized after almost a year of practicing it. But halfway through performing, I froze. Ferns nearby boisterously rustled, making clear it wasn't just the wind. I stared in terror as a furry creature popped out of them. It took me a moment to figure out what it was.

A bobcat sprinted toward me, ready to pounce. I screamed in horror just as it leaped. It was as if it all happened in slow motion. The bobcat opened its mouth in midair. I instinctively put my leg out as if I were going to kick it, and it promptly latched onto it.

As its teeth sank into my skin, the jar that held my concoction slipped out of my hand and shattered against the ground, spilling all of its contents onto the dirt. I let out another blood-curdling scream, from both the pain of the bobcat's teeth tearing into me and the loss of the potion that held all my hope. In just milliseconds, that small jar turned from my only chance at happiness to plant food.

Tyson

At around eleven thirty in the evening, my phone rang. I grumbled, turning over. My mom. My parents constantly kept forgetting that I was four hours ahead of them. I was still affected by all the wolfsbane being fed into my body daily, so my bedtime had become quite early in the past week. I had passed out probably around six or seven.

I rolled over and took the call. She realized her mistake as soon as I answered and only kept me on the phone for a few minutes before hanging up. My stomach grumbled. I'd totally missed dinner. I decided to go downstairs to scavenge for leftovers.

In the end, I just made myself a roast beef and cheddar cheese sandwich and grabbed a beer, deciding to eat out on the back patio since it was a nice night. As soon as I stepped outside and looked at the sky, I recalled what night it was—the full moon—and my mind instantly went to Gigi. Was she okay? She had my number, so she would call. Maybe if I didn't hear from her at ten minutes past, I'd go looking for her. Whatever she was drinking wasn't good, and I was starting to wonder how trustworthy those witches were. I mean, their shop had a good reputation. We even knew of it out in Alaska. But still. I didn't like what happened to Gigi when she drank whatever potion they were selling her.

A few bites into my sandwich—I saw it. A vole was sprinting across the back lawn. And before I could even consider what I was doing, my wolf took over, turning savage, forcing me to shift. I tore through my clothes as fur sprouted from my pores and claws pushed themselves out of my nail beds. With a bloodthirst I'd never felt before, I leaped onto the vole and pierced my teeth into its delicate skin and bones. Before I could even comprehend what I'd done, it was torn into shreds. *Holy shit!*

After uncharacteristically losing control of my wolf, I was about to shift back when I suddenly had another impulse. *Danger.* I knew exactly where to go in this form. I raced into the trees and hightailed it until I caught Gigi's perfumed scent. And I followed it. My instincts were in overdrive.

What I found turned my blood cold. A bobcat, completely out of character for its species, attacked my Gigi, getting a bite right into her leg. Why hadn't she shifted into her wolf to defend herself? With even more savage anger than I had felt toward that vole, I similarly leaped onto the bobcat, cutting my teeth into its body, shredding it with my claws, and finally beheading it.

When I was satisfied it was dead, I shifted back into my human form and ran to Gigi, who was crying frantically, crawling around on the ground with a stream of blood coming down her leg.

"Gigi! Why didn't you shift into your wolf? Why didn't you defend yourself?" I pulled her into my arms, holding her body tightly against mine.

She sobbed uncontrollably. I could barely make out what she was saying as she tried to speak between her sobs. "Gigi, why? Why did you let that bobcat do that to you?" I asked, burying my face into her hair, smelling her perfume, wanting to comfort her.

"Tyce, I need to go to the hospital!" she finally cried out.

"Yes, good idea. I'll take you to the clinic. They'll give you some painkillers for the pain. You'll heal in no time."

"No, Tyce!"

"Okay, I can just take you to the packhouse and you can heal there then. I can wrap your leg for you. We might even have some painkill—"

"No! I need to go to a human hospital. For humans!"

"What!" I pulled away so I could look into her bloodshot eyes. "Why would you go to a human hospital? You can't go there."

"Yes, I have to go there." She began sobbing again. "I think I need a rabies shot."

"Gigi! You don't need a rabies shot! Your wolf will just heal you! You don't have to worry! I'll take care of you. You'll be fi—"

"I don't have a wolf! I'm not going to heal! I need stitches and a rabies shot. Please just take me there. Otherwise, I'll have to wake my parents up and tell them everything." She sobbed into my shoulder in a way I'd never heard anyone sob in my life, as if her heart was breaking into a million pieces. It impaled my chest, and every part of my being was tormented by her cries.

I finally understood that I had to do what she was asking even if I didn't understand the request. I quickly gathered her clothes and helped her dress. I shifted into my wolf and flipped her onto my back, then I sprinted to the packhouse. Once we were there, I ran inside where I found a bandage that I used to wrap around her leg. Then I threw on some clothes and carried her into my car, so I could take her to the human hospital. I didn't even know where one was, so I googled it and put it into my navigation.

She quietly cried in the front seat, her tears spilling down her cheeks, chin, and neck. Seeing her like that pained me and broke my heart. I absolutely hated it and was ready to destroy entire cities to make her happy again. Once we were on our way, I asked, "When you said you don't have a wolf, what does that mean?"

"It means exactly what it sounds like. I. Don't. Have. A. Wolf. I can't shift. I'm basically just a human."

"But how? How is that possible? Your twin has one and you smell like a werewolf . . ."

"Because I made a dumb mistake seven years ago. I was only twelve and really stupid, and now I don't have a wolf anymore." Her voice broke into a sob, and I decided to stop with the questions for the time being. But I still wanted to know more. I wanted to know everything. And, most of all, I wanted to make it better. I wanted to fix whatever was making Gigi cry so much.

I went into a place I'd never been before—a human hospital—and I hated it. It was so depressing, filled with injury and the threat of death, and strong smells of disinfectant and decay. It was not a good place for Gigi to go at all, and I hated that I had to take her there. But I stayed with her the whole time, holding her hand while they gave her stitches and a rabies shot. I told them I killed the bobcat with a shotgun, and they told me the Vermont Department of Health would want the body to test its brain for rabies. I promised I'd bring them the head, which I said I'd sawed off out of anger. They probably thought I was fucking insane, but, well, it wasn't like I was going to tell them what really happened.

They asked for Gigi to come back for three more doses of the vaccine, and I promised I'd bring her, putting the days she was due back into my phone so I wouldn't forget.

I drove Gigi back to the packhouse, and she continued to look completely devastated, tearing my heart up again. I carried her into my room and laid her down on my bed, pulling her body against mine. I wanted to kiss her, but I was still drinking the wolfsbane, and I didn't want to risk poisoning her in case there were any traces of it left in my mouth.

"You smell like wolfsbane." She finally spoke again.

"I'm sorry. I can't help it, Gigi. But please let me hold you. I want to take care of you," I whispered into her hair as I spooned her against my body. "Please don't make me stop touching you."

"Why though, Tyce? I have no wolf. What use am I to you?"

"Why do I need to have a use for you? Why can't I just enjoy being with you?" I moved my fingers through her hair, brushing it out of her wet face.

She began sobbing again. "Because you're an alpha."

"So what?"

"So what?! I don't have a wolf!" she cried.

"Gigi, tell me why you don't have a wolf. Please. I want to know."

She sniffed a few times and then finally spoke. "In our pack, we go to elementary school here with just other pups from our pack. But then, when we get to sixth grade, we go to the middle school at the Autumn Moon Pack, our neighboring pack, where we combine pups from both packs.

"When I was in elementary school, Paige and I were inseparable, and we played with the same pups. We were both kind of religious nerds growing up, so most of our friends were too. But then, when I got to middle school, I began to meet pups from the other pack. I became friends with a girl named Jocelyn, who was one of the cool girls. Because I wanted to be cool too, I stopped hanging out with Paige and my old friends and got a whole new group of friends.

"They were bad news though. They did stuff like smoke in the woods during lunch break, kiss boys, and sneak out of their houses at night. Pup stuff. Anyway, I basically went along with a lot of it, mostly because I thought it was fun, but also because I wanted to be cool. I never kissed any boys though, because at the time I was still religious and wanted to save myself for my mate like Paige. But I pretty much did everything else they did.

"One night, we all snuck out and met up at a boy named Pete's house. His parents were out of town. His dad was a wolfsbane dealer, and he had tons of it down in the basement. Like crazy amounts! We all started daring each other to eat some. Everyone was too much of a coward to do it. But the thing is, I've always been super competitive. I always competed against everyone, especially my sister.

"So what did I do? I was the idiot who took a bunch of dried wolfsbane petals, shoved them in my mouth, and swallowed. It was horrible. It burned so much that I thought I was going to die. Everyone got really scared, and they were thinking about just dumping me in the woods because they didn't want to get in trouble. But in the end, my friend Jocelyn helped me. She called her dad who came and got me to the pack clinic.

"The problem was, everyone did get in trouble, and they stopped talking to me after that. And because I'd basically shunned my old group of friends, they didn't talk to me anymore either. But that wasn't even the worst part. The worst part is that I had just started getting my wolf. If I had just made it to the next full moon, I would have shifted for the first time. That became clear when I got my period a week and a half after. I'd finally grown my wolf, and she was gone before she'd even arrived.

"It wasn't long after that that everyone started making fun of me for being the wolfless girl. That's why my parents sent me to boarding school for high school. Because I was bullied in middle school, and they thought it would be better for me to go to school with humans. The old alpha, Alpha James, agreed, and the pack helped pay for me to go away for school for four years.

"So that's what happened in a nutshell. Now you know my big secret. You know why I'm the wolfless girl." She teared up again, sniffing and hiccuping.

My chest ached, and heat flushed through my body. "I wish I could go back to your middle school and claw all of those pups that ever made fun of you. I wish I could behead all those pups who even thought about leaving you in the woods to die. If you ever tell me who they are, I swear to Artemis that I will fucking kill them! Not only will I kill them, but I will torture them and watch them suffer under my knife. I will carve them into little pieces until they're begging to die. Trust me, Gigi, when I torture, I don't fuck around. Anyone who ever hurts you will regret the day they did."

Gigi sniffled, not responding.

"Is that why you've been going to the witch shop?" I asked.

"Yes. And tonight was supposed to be the night that my wolf could finally come back. But because that bobcat bit me, I dropped the potion I was supposed to drink, and now I don't know."

"There's the next full moon, Gigi. I'll take you back to Salem, and we'll get more of that potion."

"I don't know."

"What don't you know?"

"The witch told me that if my wolf didn't come back this time, she wouldn't come back."

"But she meant if you drank the potion, right? But you didn't drink it. So you still have one more shot, right?"

"I don't know, Tyce. What if my wolf doesn't come back? What if I'm cursed to be wolfless for the rest of my life?" She let out a pained cry.

"Then we'll figure it out. But don't lose hope, Gigi. There's still a chance, and I'll help you."

"I'm losing hope," Gigi choked out in a way that pierced me in my soul.

"C'mon, Gigi," I said, grasping at things to say to cheer her up. "Let's think about something else right now. Insult me instead. Tell me I'm a chicken. Make fun of me for being a big bad alpha who's scared of tiny little rodents."

She chuckled a little but immediately went back to crying, her tears drowning me in her misery.

I held Gigi tightly and listened as she sniffed until she finally drifted into sleep. It was only then that I allowed myself to doze off, not letting her go, tucking her beautiful, curvy body safely against mine. My final thoughts as I began to lose consciousness were that, as far as I was concerned, she was mine. And I vowed that I would always protect her and keep her safe and do everything in my power to make her happy again.

Chapter 39

Blake

As I descended the stairs, a faint smell of decomposition wafted toward me—the scent oddly feline. I scrunched my nose as the aroma got stronger. I was planning to continue following it to see what it was when I was distracted by the ring of the doorbell.

Jack and Tyler walked in as soon as I opened the door and similarly began sniffing. "What's that smell?" Jack asked, scrunching his own nose.

"What, are you using the packhouse as a torture chamber now?" Tyler asked. "Do I need to call CPS on you for traumatizing my nieces or nephews before they're even out of the womb?"

We followed the scent into the dining room, where a plastic bag was left in the middle of the table. I untied it immediately, only to be greeted by the bloodied head of a bobcat. "What the fuck?"

"Blake! I know you don't like my cat videos, but you don't have to go all *Godfather* on me!" Tyler chuckled.

Jack joined him in laughter and added, "For someone who likes pussy, you sure don't respect it."

Tyler laughed some more. "Right? When rappers say, 'beat the pussy up,' they don't mean literally."

I shook my head and couldn't help but laugh along with them. "I wasn't the one who left this here."

"Who else has a knife hobby?" Jack asked.

I lifted the head up and inspected the bottom. "Don't think this was a knife. Judging by how jagged the cut is, I'd say someone bit it off."

"And saved the head for a prize!" Jack added.

"Those damn pregnancy hormones. I bet it was Jasmine!" Tyler snickered. "Sounds like you're doing more than just physically rubbing off on her."

I glared at Tyler, not happy with his joke.

Just then, Tyce came down the stairs to us all staring up at him. "Was this you?" I asked, holding the cat head up to him.

He gave a small laugh and said, "Yeah, I was just about to take it out."

"May I ask why?"

"Long story. Short version is it was rabid. Just doing my duty to keep your pups without wolves safe."

"How'd you know it was rabid?" I tilted my head, studying him.

"Because it attacked me. Good thing I had a wolf to protect myself."

"I see. I just hope you're not going to tell them you caught it in our territory. The last thing we need is humans sniffing around here."

"You think I don't know better than that?" he asked with an edge to his voice, swiping the cat head from my hands and placing it back in the plastic bag. Then he turned and walked out with all of us staring after him.

"Maybe you should send out an email to the pack to be on the lookout for rabid animals. That sounds like it could get dangerous," Jack said.

"Yeah, I'll have Luke do that and get the warriors to start keeping a lookout," I said and then mindlinked Luke to repeat exactly that to him.

My mom arrived not long after, and we all walked down to the office and each took a seat.

"So, Tyler, Blake tells me you're quite good with building software?" My mom leaned forward in her chair.

"He's great. Just finishing up his master's degree," Jack boasted.

"Oh, wonderful. Congratulations, Tyler!"

"It's no big deal," Tyler replied modestly. "Just looking for a fat paycheck."

"Well, unfortunately, I'm not sure what I have in mind will pay very well, or really at all, but I hope you'll consider working on it anyway."

"Don't worry, I also take payment in chicken pad Thai and crab rangoons." Tyler grinned.

"Can you get pad Thai around here?"

"Well, not really. But there are a couple spots in St. Albans."

"St. Albans?" My mom widened her eyes. "That's what, thirty miles away?"

"It's okay. I'll ask Connie to learn the recipe," I offered.

"Now that I like! Maybe I can finally get my favorite food more than once a week!"

"You go to St. Albans every week?" My mom studied Tyler. "Just for pad Thai?"

Jack elbowed him and gave him a look. "It's our weekly date night."

"Well, that's nice I suppose. Something to look forward to each week." My mom nodded. "Anyway, I'm hoping you'd be willing to help our clinic, and well, all the other pack clinics and hospitals, with something. As I'm sure you're aware, the humans have software, websites, and apps they can access for information on their different injuries and diseases. Unfortunately, werewolves don't have the same thing. As you can imagine, part of the reason is the risk of humans discovering it if it's not secure enough. But the other problem is just tradition. Each pack clinic has mostly always operated as a completely separate entity, and many records we have are handwritten or typewritten and just passed down through the generations.

"While we've tried to organize all the information we have, it's honestly quite a mess and difficult to reference, especially when something new happens that no one who's currently working in the clinic has ever witnessed. Sometimes we'll call around to other pack clinics and hospitals we have relationships with, but there are so many in just this country alone, not even considering the ones overseas. And everyone's information is so disjointed.

"What I'd like for someone to do is create a secure database that every pack clinic and hospital could have access to. We could just start with our records, and perhaps the Autumn Moon Pack's since we have a very close relationship with them, and slowly expand to other packs as they agree to buy into the system. What do you think?" My mom looked at Tyler meaningfully.

"I like it! And I'm sure my old pack would participate too once I brought it to them."

"So you'd be willing to help?"

"I could definitely build the software and put it on a very secure server. It won't necessarily be cheap to maintain though, depending on how big the database gets and how many packs are going to access it simultaneously."

"If other packs are accessing the database, it's only fair to charge them too," I said.

"I agree." Tyler nodded. "We also have to think about who would enter all the information. I'm assuming it's pretty sensitive, so you'd need to find someone trustworthy who's willing to do tons of data entry and is also a werewolf. So we can't just hire a firm from India like most companies do these days. And that could get expensive too because I'm going to assume whoever does it is going to want to be paid, and you'll probably want multiple people working on it."

"Maybe we could hire high school and college students over the summer who are looking for work. We could absolutely vet them for trustworthiness. And I don't foresee us entering personal patient information, at least not yet. This would be more of a general database of ailments."

"Perfect!"

"How long do you think this would take?"

Tyler pulled out his phone and peeked at it quickly. "I could have the software ready in a couple weeks, maybe early August? The software itself should be pretty basic to start, and we can add to it as you think of features you'd like to see."

"I'm so happy, Tyler! This will make our jobs at the clinic so much easier!" My mom smiled widely.

"Hey, if it helps take care of our pack members, I'm happy to help."

Connie brought us over some tea and cookies, and we all stayed and chatted for a little while until Jack and Tyler headed out, so Tyler could get back to work. My mom stayed behind, and the two of us went into the living room. She took a seat in one of the chairs while I sat on the couch.

"Blake, there's something I'd like to tell you." My mom reached out to take one of my hands.

"Yes, Mom?" I asked, leaning forward.

"I'm sure you've noticed I've been feeling better. And while I'll always miss your father, I've had a bit of a distraction lately, which has helped a lot."

"A distraction?" I asked, instantly knowing what she must mean. And although I'd always wanted my mom to find happiness away from my father, the idea of her being with someone else still felt a bit strange.

"Yes, I've met someone. A widower."

I blinked a few times. "Who?"

"His name is Raymond, but he goes by Ray. He's a part of the Autumn Moon Pack. I've actually known him for years. We were in middle and high school together. We lost touch over the years but recently reconnected. To be quite honest, I used to hope we were mated to each other. But after I realized we weren't, I figured it was for the best anyway because I was able to concentrate on school and become a doctor without any pressure to be with my mate.

"I reached out to him recently and found out that he used to have a crush on me too. Isn't that funny?" She beamed. "I feel like I'm getting a second chance at happiness now. I call him my Ray of sunshine."

I stared at my mom, speechless. I'd never known, or even thought about, the fact she could have harbored feelings for anyone but my father. I wondered what else I didn't know about her. Had she had boyfriends before she met my father? She was almost thirty by the time she met her mate, so it would be hard to believe she hadn't. It wasn't exactly something I wanted to think about, but she also rarely ever spoke of her life before becoming the luna.

"Blake, would you and Jasmine be able to come by Saturday for dinner to meet him?"

"Yes," I replied. I would definitely want to meet him and make sure he was good enough for my mom. If he wasn't, well, I was an alpha, right?

"Great! Also, you and Jasmine should come by the clinic soon again for a checkup. She's far enough along now that we can tell the sex of the pups." She gave a sly smile.

"You already know what they are, don't you?" I asked, her demeanor giving her away.

"My lips are sealed."

"You know I could use my alpha aura to get it out of you." I sat forward on the couch, wondering if Jasmine was carrying my heir, the thought somehow divine and transcendent.

"But you won't. You'll find out with Jasmine, so you can share the moment together." She stood up and then leaned forward to kiss me on my forehead. "I have things to do but come by the clinic on Friday with Jasmine and we'll fit you in for an ultrasound."

Chapter 40

Ginger

On Friday morning, I turned over and glanced at my phone to find another text message from Tyce waiting for me, and my stomach did a somersault.

> ***Tyson Chicken***: *Hey how's your leg?*

Fuck, I was in way too deep. I was trying my best to ignore him, but he definitely wasn't getting the hint, and I couldn't lie and say I wasn't having a very hard time keeping my mind off him. I moaned into my pillow. He now knew my big secret, and he had to understand why we had to stay away from each other, right? I mean, this was clearly a one-way street to heartbreak.

My phone pinged again.

> ***Tyson Chicken***: *In case you forgot you're due for your next shot today. Do you need a ride?*

I moaned again. He was right. I could probably just ask to borrow the family car and go myself without him. But something inside me was desperate to see him again. No, I couldn't stay away.

I was about to get out of bed when Paige burst into the room.

"Holy Artemis, Paige! Haven't you ever heard of knocking? You could have just walked in on me ringing the devil's doorbell!"

"Wha—what?" Paige laughed. "Doing what?"

"You know, petting the beaver, flicking the bean, clicking the mouse, pleasuring myself."

Paige burst into laughter. "Okay! I get it! You don't need to give me any more euphemisms or visuals!"

"Just making sure you realize what you could have just subjected yourself to."

"Noted!" She shook her head. "I just wanted to remind you we're having the sisters' potluck tonight. I'm going to take the car to go grocery shopping for my dish. Did you want me to pick anything up for you too?"

"I'll just pitch in my usual chips. Pick whichever ones you want."

Just then, I realized that Paige was no longer making eye contact with me but had her eyes on my exposed leg. Fuck! I'd done such a good job hiding it from the family, but she'd caught me with my shorts on. "What happened to your leg?"

"Nothing." I threw my blanket over it.

"That didn't look like nothing. That looked like you had stitches. When did you get stitches? *Why* did you get stitches?"

"Don't worry about it."

"How am I supposed to not worry about it? It's not like people normally get stitches around here!"

"I just fell on a rock and got a bad cut, okay?"

"So why is it such a big secret then?"

"It's not. You know I'm just sensitive about everything that makes me human."

She narrowed her eyes at me, making a face like she clearly didn't believe me, then letting out a sigh. "Okay, Gigi," she finally said and walked out of the room. I fell back into my bed in relief. At least she didn't fight me for more information.

"Look who finally decided to stop leaving my texts on read." Tyce greeted me as soon as I met him in front of the packhouse. He moved closer to me and looked like he was about to hug me but stopped himself. My heart raced, suddenly wanting nothing more than to feel his tree-trunk arms wrapped around me, to snuggle up against his hard, muscular body. Fuck, I wanted him so badly.

I moved toward him and made the move he'd hesitated to make by wrapping my own arms around him. He returned the hug and pulled me against him. Before I could stop myself, I pressed my lips against his, pushing my tongue into his mouth. He deepened the kiss, our tongues twining viciously as if it had been months since they'd touched. His cock twitched against me, coming to life, and I pulled back before we got too carried away. "Your breath doesn't smell like wolfsbane anymore."

"Blake's injecting it into me now."

I stepped back. "Doesn't it hurt?"

"It hurts like a motherfucker. Both going in and the side effects. It's like my blood's on fire. But I'm getting more used to it now."

"Why are you doing that?"

"Because I don't want to be a weak alpha. I want to be able to lead my pack into battle fearlessly. I don't want a couple shots of wolfsbane to take me out." His eyes were intense as he said all this to me, and I felt a strong affection for him.

"You mean like what happened to me," I said, and a tear dropped down my cheek. I sniffed, ashamed of myself and how I was acting, rubbing the wetness from my face.

"Gigi," he said softly, putting his hand on my arm.

"Don't you fucking dare pity me!" I shouted. "Just take me to the hospital, okay?" I turned on my heel and walked toward his car.

I heard him let out a breath behind me, but he didn't say anything and followed, unlocking his car. I pulled my door open as soon as I heard the beep, throwing myself into the passenger seat.

"Gigi, I'm not pitying you," Tyce said as soon as he sat down. "I want to help you. I'm going to take you back to Salem. We'll figure it out."

"Tyce, we may never figure it out. I've been trying to get my wolf back for almost a year now—something that's not even supposed to be possible. Trust me, my parents tried. The pack clinic tried. Dr. Luna called every pack clinic and hospital she had a connection to, and not only am I one of the few werewolves in thousands of years who lost their wolf and lived to talk about it, but there was also no record of anyone recovering their wolf. For all intents and purposes, my wolf is dead. The only way to bring her back is to bring her back from the dead." I couldn't help myself as I started sobbing, tears and snot running down my face, full-on ugly crying.

"Fuck, Gigi," Tyce said as he brought his arms around me, pulling me toward him, at least as much as he could with the center console between us. If I were being honest, his touch actually made me feel better. I felt so relieved that I could finally unburden myself to someone else.

I slowly composed myself and pushed away from Tyce, wiping at my face. He reached into the center console and pulled out a napkin that he handed to me. "How's your leg?" he asked.

"It's fine. It's healing." I sniffed. "Human speed, of course."

"I take it that's why you're wearing pants when it's over ninety degrees out?" He nodded toward my legs where I had on a pair of loose linen pants.

"They're not too bad. Summer pants." I looked up at him and noticed his ears had reddened. "Did you just think of something dirty?" I asked him.

"What?" he choked out, a blush spreading across his cheeks.

"Your ears go red every time you get turned on."

He let out a laugh. "For a second I thought you were a mind reader."

"So you did think of something dirty! Come on, tell me! What were you thinking about?"

"Taking your pants off. Do you need more detail?"

"Yes, I want more detail," I replied. I initially wasn't going to ask for it, but, well you know, a cat had already died and I couldn't lie and say I wasn't curious.

He leaned toward me, and in a low, deep, gravelly voice said, "I was thinking about how I want to bite into the inside of your thick, delicious, naked thighs, especially now that you're letting me touch you again." I stared at him, my lips parted and breathing turning heavy. A warmth spread through my inner thighs, every part of me awakening with need. "Anyway, we should get to the hospital." He put the car into drive as if he hadn't just overheated my whole body.

Fortunately, the wait for my booster wasn't long, and Tyce insisted on holding my hand while they injected me. "Are you going to give me a lollipop too?" I teased him.

"The lollipop's for me." He smirked. Then he leaned closer and whispered in my ear. "Be careful, I don't just lick. I also bite." I'm pretty sure my ears turned red from that comment. Scratch that, my whole body was flushing. Tyce was on a roll with teasing me, and I was dying of anticipation.

On our way back, he took a turn I wasn't expecting and parked at a hiking trail. I looked around as we got out. It was crowded with people that I assumed were humans. "You're taking me hiking?" I asked as he pulled his door open to exit the car.

"Kind of. But we're not taking the hiking trail."

"Where are we going then?"

"It's a surprise." He came around to open the door for me and took my hand, leading me into the woods. We soon parted from the trail and headed into the forest, not following any sort of path, walking on dead leaves. It seemed that Tyce knew where he was going as we came upon a large, rocky hill with no clear way around it.

"Obviously we didn't dress for rock climbing, and this will be easier in my wolf form anyway. Lie down, and I'll flip you onto my back." He began pulling his shirt off, revealing his very jacked body. I couldn't help but stare as he gazed back at me, giving me a smug smile. He threw his shirt into a bag he'd brought along with him and then pulled off his shorts and boxer briefs, kicking off his sandals, until he was completely naked. Dying of lust, I could barely pull my eyes away so I could lie down.

He squatted over me and slipped the bag around my arm, clearly to hold while we got to our destination. Then he backed away and shifted, revealing his wolf form to me in daylight. He was an absolutely stunning wolf—huge, with brown fur tipped in black. At a quick glance, I could have easily mistaken him for a grizzly bear. His thick, lustrous fur fluttered in the breeze as he strutted toward me on his humongous paws, which I quickly noted were tipped with lethal-looking claws. I wouldn't ever want to mess with him in this form.

He flipped me onto his back with ease, bringing my arms into his mouth so he could hold me in place. It was actually nice being so close to him, his soft, thick fur caressing me. I did feel a bit hot, but the shade of the trees helped.

He climbed over the rocks, and I could see how this was easier using four legs rather than two. Plus, I'm sure his sharp claws helped. I felt a pang of envy that he could just shift into his wolf form whenever he needed. My family tried not to shift too much in front of me, since they knew it hurt to see them as wolves. We soon made it over the rocks into an area with a grassy clearing and a stream with huge stones sprinkled throughout, its water sparkling from the sunlight. I was just about to try to climb off Tyce's back when a chipmunk sprinted out from beyond a rock.

And something completely unexpected happened. Instead of lowering me gently onto the ground, Tyce threw me off his back as he sprinted toward the chipmunk, and I went crashing against some small stones which cut into my bare arm. I cried out as blood spilled from the shallow cuts. But Tyce didn't stop, growling as he ran into the forest, the chipmunk squeaking as he scooped it into his mouth, shaking his head murderously as he tore it into pieces. He turned back to look at me as I lifted myself up to a sitting position, with blood spilling from his huge mouth, his eyes evil.

I let out my own squeak at how scary he looked as he sprinted back toward me—terrifying and monstrous in his wolf form. But when he made eye contact with me, his eyes instantly softened, and he shifted back into his human form, kneeling down next to me. "Fuck, I'm sorry, Gigi. I didn't mean to do that. Are you okay?" He examined my arms, staring up into my eyes, his amber eyes taking on a pained expression. "Here, let me clean you." He instantly pulled his T-shirt out of his bag, ran to the stream to wet it, and came back. I was speechless as he diligently wiped the blood from my arms, making sure he didn't miss a single spot.

"If you didn't mean to do that, why did you?" I asked.

He looked up at me, staring into my eyes. "I don't know."

"It seems you do a lot of stuff that you don't know why you're doing it. Like when you almost bit my neck with your fangs, or now when you threw me off your back to murder an innocent little chipmunk. Is there something wrong with you? Do you just go into weird murderous rages? Should I be worried? I mean, you did tell me you like to torture."

He let out a deep breath and said, "Honestly, none of this stuff ever happened before. I usually have really good control over my wolf. Well, actually . . ."

"Actually?"

"During the last full moon, I did do the same thing. I saw a vole, and I was forced to shift into my wolf so I could tear it into shreds." He then looked out into the distance as if he were deep in thought.

"You were forced to shift?"

"Yeah . . ." He blinked a few times and continued, "It must be the spell. It must have taken effect during the last full moon. Instead of being scared of rodents, now I go into a murderous rage when I see them."

"But that's dangerous, Tyce! What if that had happened while we were still on the human trail? You would have shifted in front of all of them, and then we'd be forced to kill them all after what they witnessed. And there were so many of them!"

"Fuck, you're right."

"Tyce, you have to do something about that. Otherwise, you won't be able to go out in public anymore. Did the witches tell you that that would happen to you?"

"No, they didn't say anything except that they could hypnotize me into losing my fear."

"But your fear got replaced with this! Weren't you worried that could happen? I mean, everyone knows that no one's wish ever comes true like they expected."

"I guess I was so desperate to get rid of my fear that I didn't care. I mean, do you worry about what bringing back your wolf would mean for you?"

"No, I guess I don't." I sighed. "I don't care. Having my wolf back is more important to me than anything else. I'd be willing to give up just about anything."

"Like what. What's something you love that you'd be willing to give up." Tyce turned toward me.

"I want my wolf back so badly that I'd be willing to give up sex!" I blurted out the first thing I could think of.

"Damn, what a shame that would be. I hope you don't have to give that up." He leaned in closer to me, bringing the back of his fingers to my cheek. "Because that would mean I'd have to give up sex too. And I definitely don't want that."

"Why would that mean you'd have to give it up?" I gulped. His lips were practically grazing mine they were so close.

"Because you're the only person I want to have sex with anymore." And, just like that, his mouth was on mine, kissing me hungrily. I brought my hands to his torso, tracing all the contours of his muscles, a desperate need to not leave a single part of his body untouched.

Soon he was lifting my shirt off me and unsnapping my bra, quickly and desperately kissing his way down my neck and to my chest. His large hands encompassed my breasts, kneading them as he kissed his way out from the center of my chest until his mouth latched on to one of my nipples, sucking gently, then he flicked his tongue against it, tracing his way around. As I let out a soft moan, he grazed his teeth against my breast and very softly bit down onto the nipple. I let out a loud moan and shoved my nails into his skin as he did this, and he pulled away. "That was just a teaser bite."

He carefully lowered me onto the ground, and I didn't even care that I was laying my hair directly onto grass and dirt. He brushed his fingers down my soft belly. I tried to suck it in, insecure about the good few extra pounds I carried compared to his perfect, hard, athletic body. His fingers found the waistline of my pants, unbuttoned them with urgency, pulled them off my legs, and threw them to the side. Then he brushed his palms up the sides of my thighs and hooked his fingers into my panties, dragging them slowly down my legs, making sure to avoid the stitched area. He lightly kissed the area around the stitches, which warmed my heart a little.

When he looked up, he commanded in a deep, sensual voice, "Spread your legs for me, baby." I instantly did as asked. He watched intently from his kneeling position, his eyes half-closed and lustful, and his huge erection rock-hard and pulsing. I was swollen and desperate, longing for it to stretch and fill me.

My breathing shallowed as he brought his mouth to my inner thighs, at first kissing up and down them. But, before long, those kisses turned into nibbles as he gently bit into the skin of my thighs. I let out soft moans, shocked by how pleasurable it was feeling his teeth graze the sensitive skin.

"You like that, baby?" he rasped.

"Mmm," I moaned out.

"Does that make you wet, baby?" I slid my fingers through his hair and pushed his head down farther between my legs. He pulled away and looked up, smiling at me. "You know the rules, baby. Tell me who makes you wet and crazy to be tasted."

"Tyce," I whined.

He immediately moved his head back down, slowly licking from bottom to top.

"Tyce!" I said with more passion, and he sucked my clit into his mouth and then sped up the movement of his tongue.

"Tyce!" I screamed out even more fervently, and he flicked more vigorously, concentrating all his effort in exactly the right spot, my whole body overheated and sweating, the pleasure inside me building.

"Fuck me, Tyce!" I screamed out, desperate to have more.

He pulled away. "Fuck! I didn't bring a condom."

"Just pull out." He glanced down at me, and I could tell he was hesitating, balling and unballing his fists, taking deep breaths. His chest rose and fell dramatically with each inhale and exhale.

Finally, he said, "I can't risk it, Gigi. What if you got pregnant? I mean, without . . ."

"A wolf." I completed his sentence and got up, a sharp pain in my chest and a scratching at my throat. I brushed the grass and dirt out of my hair, the moment ruined. A feeling of unease came over me. "This was a bad idea," I blurted out. "We're going way too far and getting way too close when this is never going to work out." He was about to say something when I cut him off. "Let's just go home."

He suddenly had a pained expression on his face, his eyes downturned. Was he pitying me? He must have been. I was overcome with nausea as I thought about how much he knew about me—how much I'd let him know about me. And how much I'd let him get under my skin. I'd fallen for fuckboys before, but I knew that Tyce was going to hurt me far more than any of the others ever had. And I was giving him the go-ahead to wreck me every time I allowed him to get close to me, as I had foolishly been doing.

I grabbed for my clothes, dressing frantically, wanting to cover myself.

"Why do you say it won't work out?" Tyce asked as I pulled my shirt over my head.

"C'mon, Tyce. Why would it? You're an alpha and I'm a wolfless girl. Anyway, you have a mate out there somewhere who's meant for you."

"I don't care," he said, grabbing my arms. "I don't care."

"Well, I do!" I yelled, probably far too loudly. I softened my voice. "Can you just take me home, please?"

He appeared like he wanted to say something, opening and closing his mouth. But then he finally nodded, shoving his wet shirt back into the bag and shifting into his wolf form.

Chapter 41

Ginger

I rolled into the house around three to Paige with her hands on her hips. "And where have you been?"

"Hi, Mom, nice to see you too," I replied, rolling my eyes.

"What happened to your arms?" She came closer. "And your pants?" I looked down to find my linen pants were dirt streaked and torn. Well, there went one leg-covering item.

"Nothing. Just another spill."

"You're not usually that clumsy."

"Maybe I'm getting old."

"Seriously, Gigi?"

I shrugged and turned to walk upstairs to change. Before I got too far, she said, "You smell like Alpha Tyce. That wouldn't happen to have anything to do with what happened, would it?" I stopped for a second, caught off guard. But I decided to just ignore her and continue on my way until I was safely in my room and able to close the door.

Fuck, I didn't think I'd be able to get away with wearing long sleeves too. I examined the scratches along my arms and wondered how long it would take them to fully heal. I groaned as I pulled a maxi dress out of my dirty laundry and sniffed it. It still smelled okay, at least to my human nose. I let out a sigh and undressed. If I smelled, I smelled, and my sisters would just have to deal with it.

I quickly ran into the shower, scrubbing the dirt and Tyce's scent off me. Then I threw on the maxi dress and a light cardigan, giving Artemis thanks for air-conditioning in our house. I could just feign being cold, even though the whole day had truthfully left me overheated and on edge. My chest was heavy as my heart beat forcefully against it. Feeling torn about Tyce, I tried to push him from my mind.

I finally made my way downstairs to Paige working diligently in the kitchen. "So, what's for dinner?" I asked.

"I decided to make chicken marbella. I'm just throwing the chicken and marinade together now, and I'm going to bake it once it gets closer to time. You're actually supposed to marinate it overnight, but oh well."

"Oh well? What happened to the usual overachiever Paige I know and love?" I tilted my head at her.

In an outburst that was completely out of character for her, she threw her hands up and shouted, "Maybe I don't want to be an overachiever! Maybe I just want to enjoy my life! Maybe I should be allowed to wait to get married, and maybe it's actually not that big of a deal if we mark each other before marriage! Why am I following such stupid, antiquated customs anyway? It's the twenty-first century for Artemis's sake! Birth control exists! People have sex before marriage!"

I backed up, not sure how to react. I was the one with random bursts of emotion. Paige was the patient, stable anchor. Paige was predictable. Paige always had good days! Paige was the one who always comforted me, not the other way around. Then, I realized, I had to say something. I coughed a little and asked, "So, are you planning to do that? Mark each other before marriage?"

"I don't know, maybe!"

"Wait, what?" I widened my eyes at what Paige was saying. Should I be concerned? Was she having a psychotic break? "You're going to show up at home with a mark on your neck for Mom and Dad to see before you're married?"

"Why not? What are they going to do? Disown me?"

"Paige." I put my hand on her shoulder. "Maybe you should sit down and think about this before you do something completely crazy and rash. Once you're marked, that's it. There's no taking it back. You're going to have to live with Mom and Dad's disappointment."

"Mom and Dad's disappointment? That's it? You mean Artemis isn't going to strike me down with lightning? I'm not going to be banished from the pack? They're not going to put a big letter *S* on me for *slut*? Disappointment is my only punishment?" She burst out into laughter, falling to her knees on the kitchen floor.

"Paigey, I'm really concerned," I said, staring at her, unsure of what to do. "Is it really that bad not to mark each other until you get married? I mean, why don't you just make it clear you want to wait longer to get married?"

"Because I found out why Mom and Dad want to rush the wedding!"

"Why?"

"I talked to Jasmine, and she told me that the urge to mark starts out not that bad, but it eventually gets really hard to resist. She told me that she was biting into her hand toward the end, bleeding onto Blake's pillows. It was really painful." She shook her head. "Don't you see? Mom and Dad are afraid that I'm not going to be able to resist at some point and bring shame onto the family! But they can't even fucking tell me that! They just act all weird about it! Don't you think that's messed up? That they are so ashamed of the whole mating process that they can't even have a conversation with us about it? They couldn't even warn me about heat!"

"I mean, to be honest, I don't *want* to have a conversation with them about the mating process." But then something about what Paige said didn't sit right. "Wait, Paige. What you said about the urge to mark.

What exactly happens? Like when you have the urge? When does it happen?"

She sat back on the floor and wrapped her arms around her legs. "Our canines extend after we have sex. And I go into this trance where I'm pulled toward his neck."

"That happens every time you have sex?"

"Isn't that what I just said?"

"When you say your canines extend, do they turn into like, vampire fangs?"

"I guess, yeah. That's a good description."

"And it happens to Dylan too?"

"Yeah, why?"

"Oh, I was just curious. I just want to understand."

"Well, you're lucky you don't have to worry about it. You can just live your life. And you don't have to worry about heat. I'm due any day now, and I have no idea when it's going to strike! I just better hope it's not while I'm in training or on duty! I mean, how awkward for all the guys I work with to sense it. And dangerous!"

I suddenly felt unsteady on my feet, everything Paige was saying going in one ear and out the other. I dropped into one of the kitchen chairs, feeling like the whole room was spinning around me. Could Tyce—?

"You said your mate smells really good to you too, right?"

"Yeah, the mate scent."

"Can you describe it?" I clenched my hands around the chair.

"It's hard to really describe it. It's not like anything I've ever smelled before. It's really musky and sexy, very sensual. The best way I can think to describe it is like maybe the best cologne or aftershave you've ever smelled but better—more natural and not so chemically."

"Or perfume," I added.

She giggled. "Actually, it's funny. Dylan once asked me what perfume I wear. I was like, you dum-dum, that's not perfume!"

My breathing shallowed.

"Are you okay, Gigi? You look like you're about to pass out." Paige got up and walked toward me.

"Yeah, fine!" But I wasn't fine. My heart was beating at quadruple speed, and I didn't know what to make of all the thoughts and emotions suddenly flowing through me. No, it couldn't be. There was just no way. Was there? And if there was, what did it mean? "I'm going to lie down for a little bit," I said, getting up and heading toward the stairs. But then I stopped, realizing I was being a little selfish. After all, wasn't it Paige who had freaked out first? Shouldn't I be a better sister? I turned around and asked, "Will you be okay? Or do you want to talk about the whole marking thing more?"

She waved her hand and said, "I'll be fine. We can talk about it later, after Heidi leaves. I have too much to do before then."

"What do you have to do besides make the chicken?"

"I have stuff to do. Anyway, it's fine. I just freaked out a little. But I'll be fine!" She stood up with a smile on her face. "Just be down here by six. That's when Heidi should be showing up."

I wondered if I should press her more. I could tell the smile she'd plastered on her face was completely fake, and I made a mental note to press her after Heidi left. Then another thought came to me. "Why is Heidi coming here?"

"What do you mean? Why wouldn't she? We planned the potluck. Are you sure you're okay?"

"No, I mean, why does she always come here instead of us going to her house? I mean, she has her own house now. Don't you think it's really strange she almost never invites us over? And when we do go over, it's always really weird. Like she's always super on edge."

"Is she?"

"Yeah, you can't tell me you never noticed. And then, like Hunter always seems so clueless about everything."

"What do you mean?"

"Like, one time I asked him where they keep their glasses, and he had to open a bunch of cabinets until he figured it out. Like I could see him not knowing where they keep, say, the serving platter they pull out once a year for Thanksgiving, but the *glasses*? And then I asked him if they get the travel channel, and he said he thinks so. Why doesn't he know what channels they get?"

"I don't know. Maybe he doesn't watch much TV. And, I mean, there are so many cable channels. It's hard to keep track of all of them."

"What about the glasses?"

"Maybe he drank too much that night?"

"I don't know, Paige. The more I think about it, the more I think something isn't adding up with Heidi and Hunter."

"What are you implying?"

"I don't know!" I threw my hands up. "But I think Heidi is hiding something from us."

"Why would Heidi hide something from us? I mean, what does she have to hide from us? She's always been like the most normal one in the family. I can't imagine her having any weird secrets. And they marked each other, right?"

"Yeah, I guess."

"Why would they be mates and mark each other but not live together? And if they don't live together, where does Hunter live? His car is always parked out in front of their townhouse when he's home. I would notice. I pass their place every day on my way to training."

"I don't know. I'm just saying, something's weird. Anyway, I'm going to rest for a little bit, but I'll be down for the potluck."

Chapter 42

Jasmine

"Blake. Blake, wake up." I gently shook my mate's shoulder. He stirred and opened his mesmerizing blue eyes to me. His lips turned upward into a smile as he brushed my hair out of my face. "Blake, the pups—they're kicking."

He instantly moved his hand to my belly, sparks drifting across my skin as he kept it there to feel the little pops inside me. His smile widened. "I can feel them! Already alpha warriors." He pulled me against him and kissed me. "I wouldn't expect any less of course, with two alpha parents."

I snuggled into him, listening to the drumming of his heart in his chest. "You've been getting better, Blake."

"Maybe you're just getting used to it like I have."

"No, I definitely think you're getting better." He didn't say anything and rubbed his hand up and down my back. I could barely bring myself to get out of bed to get ready for the day. It didn't help that I was constantly exhausted. Growing twins in six months was taking a toll on me, and I imagined alpha ones likely took even more energy, although I had no way to compare. After a long pause I said, "I think my parents have finally forgiven me."

"Your parents forgave you from the night they found out." Blake chuckled.

"I think getting my dad drunk helped." I laughed. "I don't think I'd ever seen him drink so much actually. Or my mom."

"I have. Well, your dad at least."

"When was that?"

"The night we bonded over torturing that piece of shit Charlie. Fun night. And the fact that you were the one who finally finished him off after convincing me not to just makes my memories of that evening so much better." He rubbed his nose against mine and brought his mouth to my ear. "Maybe next time you'll join in. Nothing hotter than a woman wielding a knife."

"I'm having trouble keeping up with all your fantasies." I shook my head.

"You've been indulging so many of them lately though. Just adding another one to the list for when your pregnancy hormones possess you again." He gave me a playful smile and began nibbling my ear. Dear Goddess, he knew my weaknesses way too well.

After we got ready for the day, Blake held my hand as we walked to the clinic. I was very much showing now and was going to need to buy more clothes since almost nothing fit anymore.

"Hello, Alpha, Luna." The young woman at the front desk greeted us with a slight bow when we arrived. "Dr. Luna told me you'd be coming today. How are you feeling, Luna Jasmine?"

"I'm fine. How are you?" I replied.

"I'm good. The whole pack is so excited about the news. I know everyone is dying to know if you're having boys or girls!"

"I'm looking forward to finding out too," I replied.

"What do you hope they are?"

"Well, if they're boys, I won't have to do this again." I chuckled. But then, I thought, it would be so sweet to see Blake with daughters, and my heart warmed at the thought. There was no question that they'd have him wrapped right around their little fingers.

"It would be so exciting to have an alpha heir!" The young woman smiled. I smiled back politely.

After we checked in, we sat down to wait until we were called.

"What do you hope they are?" I asked Blake.

He smiled and said, "Obviously I hope at least one of them is a boy, as our pack needs an heir, and it would take the pressure off to produce one now. But if they're both girls, it just gives us more excuses to keep trying." He brushed his hand through my hair.

"Typical Blake, always bringing it back to sex," I said quietly and snickered.

"You love it."

We were called in not long after we sat down. A nurse brought us back to an examination room and checked all my vitals. Blake's mom came in not long after. She gave both of us hugs and then went to review my file. "Well, Jasmine, you seem to be right on track with your weight gain. I'm not surprised since you haven't had any nausea?" She said it like a question rather than a comment.

"None at all," I replied, confirming.

"Lucky. Blake gave me all the worst pregnancy symptoms. Clearly he had a knack for torturing, even in the womb." She snickered and punched him lightly on the arm. His mom seemed much more jovial than I'd ever known her to be, and I began to understand where Blake got that part of himself. "Anyway, there's not much to worry about as far as your health is concerned, Jasmine. That's one of the nice parts about a werewolf pregnancy. I had to do a rotation in Obstetrics and Gynecology during my residency, and there is so much to consider with human pregnancies. But we just need to worry about your pups. So that makes at least half my job easier!"

I nodded.

"You've been exercising, I assume?" she asked.

"Yep, I'm still training but with a private trainer now."

"Good, that's probably helping a lot with your symptoms. Exercise is very good during pregnancy. And I highly recommend that you keep shifting forms, especially during the full moon. It'll help keep your wolf strong."

"We'll make sure we take long full moon runs." Blake grasped my hand, squeezing it harder than I was expecting, and I could instantly sense his anxiety.

"Make sure they're not too strenuous," Blake's mom added. "Her blood pressure is low, which is normal for pregnancy, so I'd keep it to a jog. No racing your mate for now." His mom smiled and jabbed at him. "Although I know she can beat your butt. So it'll probably also spare a bruise to your ego." She winked.

Blake chuckled and said, "I'll wait until after birth to show her who the alpha is."

"Clearly not as fast as the luna," I retorted.

"Clearly." His mom gave me a big smile.

"I'm starting to hope they're boys in there because I'm seeing that having girls means I'm always going to be ganged up on."

"I think it'd be good for you," I said, amused by the thought. Blake definitely wasn't used to being challenged.

"Well, why don't we find out?" Blake's mom stood up. "Jasmine, hop up on the table, and I'll pull out the ultrasound machine."

Same as the previous time, she had me pull down the waist of my shorts, which were now being held on using a belly band. Blake pulled his chair up next to me and took my hand again, giving it a quick kiss when his mom wasn't looking. She rubbed the ultrasound gel on my belly and moved the transducer against my skin, watching the screen intently.

After some time, she gave an amused smile. "Well, Baby A is certainly giving us a very clear view and is dying to tell us the gender."

"What is it?" Blake leaned forward.

After a beat, his mom replied, "A boy."

"I knew it!" Blake shot up. "Of course my son would want us to know he's the alpha already."

"*And be proud of his male anatomy.*" I rolled my eyes and mindlinked Blake, not wanting his mom to hear. "What about the other pup?" I asked out loud.

His mom moved the transducer every which way as Blake and I waited in anticipation. His grip on my hand strengthened as time went on. Finally, his mom looked back over at us and said, "I can confirm that Baby B is a girl. A perfect pair of twins."

"Of course they're perfect. I have the perfect luna to carry them." Blake stood up and kissed me on the forehead. And while he said this calmly, I could feel how emotional he was from the news, all his sentiments heightening my own. I looked up into his eyes, and we couldn't bring ourselves to break eye contact, locked in a silent conversation.

"Well, I'll let the two of you process the good news." His mom stood up with a big smile on her face. "See you both tomorrow night for dinner."

Chapter 43

Ginger

"Aren't you hot dressed like that?" Heidi asked only seconds after arriving.

"It's cold in here."

"Cold?" She looked around as if she could actually see the temperature. I rolled my eyes.

"Yeah, I'm cold."

"Maybe you caught something. Do you have a fever?" Heidi asked, putting her hand to my forehead. I swiped it away.

"I'm fine."

"Maybe you got mono." She snickered.

"Haha! So funny! Why don't you get all your slut jokes out of the way now, so I don't have to endure them all night," I replied. "We can't all be Miss Mated and Married perfect housewife."

"I'm not a housewife!" she scoffed. "I told you, I've decided to start taking classes in graphic design at the local community college. There's just not a lot of job options out here in the middle of nowhere. But I think this will be good for me."

"Weren't you trying to conceive?"

"Yes, so?" she asked. "I can be both a mother and in school. Or working."

"Who's going to watch the pup?"

"I'm sure Mom will help. What, were you planning to quit your job once you have a baby?"

"I'm not planning to have a baby," I replied.

She let out a laugh. "I don't think you'll have much of a choice with how often you practice making one."

"Fuck you, Heidi!" I yelled at her, tears threatening to fall from my eyes, reminded of earlier that day. "You're such a bitch! It's not enough for you to come over here and rub your perfect life in our faces, but you have to act so fucking pompous about it too."

"What just happened?" Paige came running into the entryway where we were stationed.

"I'm done with Heidi! Tell me when she leaves and I'll come back down!" I began to stomp away toward the stairs.

"It's not like the whole pack doesn't know what you've been up to!" Heidi yelled out to me. "You're just bringing shame on Mom and Dad and the family!"

I knew I should ignore her, but I couldn't help myself, eager to know what she'd heard and what was being said about me. "And what have I been up to?"

She let out a small laugh and instantly straightened her face, but I could tell she was trying not to laugh as her nose wrinkled in amusement and her lips slightly puckered. "The whole pack is talking about how Alpha Tyce puts on your panties and gives you golden showers right before he puts it in your butt."

"What!" Paige gasped. "Where did you hear that?" Then she turned to me. "Do you actually do that with Tyce?"

I didn't know whether to laugh or cry at the elaborate and outlandish rumors Heidi had heard. Part of me wondered if she'd made it up, questioning if she was even creative enough to come up with something like that. "No, I don't do that with Tyce! How would someone even know if I did!"

"But you are involved with Alpha Tyce, aren't you?" Heidi questioned.

"None of your business."

"Heidi, stop!" Paige burst out. "Why are you shaming Gigi? You know the pack constantly makes up untrue rumors. Just the other week they were saying Jasmine was pregnant with Beta Luke's pup. And Jasmine is 100 percent faithful to Alpha Blake. These are obviously just bored people with nothing better to do than make up crazy lies for entertainment."

"Yes, but there is some truth to the rumors about Jasmine. She *is* pregnant. And isn't there truth to Gigi's rumors too? I mean, seriously, Gigi, it's one thing to hook up with random guys in college when the pack will never find out about it. But now you're screwing around with an alpha, and alphas are known for just picking up easy, slutty girls. Plus they're practically celebrities, so everyone talks about it. And you're not just dragging yourself down—you're dragging down our family!"

"No, she's not!" Paige came to my defense. "Stop slut-shaming Gigi! Seriously, Heidi. She's your sister. And why shouldn't she be allowed to have some fun before she meets her mate? Just because you and I decided to save ourselves doesn't mean everyone should be forced to do the same. Gigi's already gone through so much. She deserves to be happy too!"

"Gigi's gone through so much," Heidi mocked and rolled her eyes. "Yeah, because she didn't follow the rules! Because she was being rebellious! Can't you see? Gigi would still have a wolf if she'd just done what she was supposed to instead of sneaking out of the house all the time. I'm so sick of having to censor myself to spare Gigi's feelings. It's time for Gigi to grow up and take responsibility for her actions."

"You stuck up, sour, miserable bitch!" I yelled at Heidi. "I hope you fall off your high horse onto a sharp rock that cuts your head from your body and you die a painful bloody death! If I never speak to you again it will be too soon. You are not my sister but some prude cunt who's just bitter because your mate doesn't want to stick his dick in you while you lie there like a dead fish in the dark."

She gasped. "What!" A blush burned across her face and chest, and her breathing shallowed.

"Clearly that's why you're such a miserable cunt," I screamed. "Because you're not getting fucked. That's why you've been trying to conceive for a year now with no results!"

"Gigi!" Paige yelled as a tear slid down Heidi's cheek. She quickly brushed it away, and I almost felt bad, but then I recalled everything she'd said to set me off.

"Don't you fucking dare defend her!" I glared at Paige. "You heard what she said to me, and I'm done." I turned back to my other sister. "Heidi, don't ever come here when I'm home again!"

I tried to walk away again when Paige stepped in front of me. "No!" she yelled, putting her hands on my shoulders and stopping me. I tried to shake her off, but she grabbed hold. "No, Gigi. I'm not letting you go upstairs. We're all sisters, and I'm not going to let both of you fight like this. There's no reason for it!"

"Stop being such a diplomat," I demanded, trying to move toward the stairs as my throat ached. I knew I wouldn't be able to hold the tears off much longer. But she had a strong hold and wouldn't let me. "Just let me go upstairs!" I implored more loudly.

"No. We're all going to sit down and talk. I'm not letting either you or Heidi leave and get out of this."

Tears were spilling down my cheeks at this point, and I was completely embarrassed and uncomfortable, desperate to get away from both of them and be alone where I could reflect on everything that had happened and had been revealed that day. "Heidi! Apologize to Gigi now!" Paige yelled.

"Why should I? You heard what she said to me. And she's the one who's acting inappropriately."

"Fucking Artemis!" Paige uncharacteristically yelled. "Why are you both acting like this?"

"Just let go of me." I tried to shake Paige off again.

"It's okay. I'll go home," Heidi said.

"No!" Paige finally let go of me and grabbed Heidi. "Not until we talk this out."

"There's no point," Heidi said. "I don't regret anything I said. Gigi knows it's true. That's why she's crying about it now. Because she knows that Mom and Dad are going to be ashamed once they hear about what she's been up to."

"Even if it's true, you didn't have to say it the way you did, Heidi! I don't understand why you've been so mean to Gigi lately. What's she done to you?"

"Because!" She raised her voice. "Because she just does whatever she wants whenever she wants, without any care about who she's hurting or how it's affecting anything. Whenever we say something that even slightly triggers her at the dinner table, she just runs away, not caring about how upset it makes Mom. You don't know this, Gigi, but Mom cries when you do that! And then goes on for an hour about how much she wishes she could help you get better. But you wouldn't know that because you just fucking leave!

"And then! Then you go around screwing every guy with a heartbeat, acting like a ho. Which, okay, your stories are entertaining. But why are you now doing it with an alpha, the most prominent fucking person you could possibly choose? You know they're just going to blame Mom for raising you improperly and drag our whole family down. And you know Mom loves the temple. And those ladies at the temple are the biggest and cruelest gossips.

"Don't you think that I sometimes want to not have to act so proper all the time? But I don't. Because in a pack, it's not just me who gets affected. It's our whole family."

Paige tightened her grip on our older sister. "Heidi, you can't just put that on Gigi's shoulders! There are people in this pack who act perfect all the time, and they still don't avoid the rumor mill. You should know that!"

"Yes, but she could at least try."

"I have tried!" I cried out. "I didn't pursue Tyce! It just happened. And now." I sat down on the stairs. "And now he's just going to hurt me. He's going to hurt me more than anyone else could ever hurt me. I wish I'd never met him."

"Why are you saying that, Gigi? Why are you saying he's going to hurt you?" Paige sat down next to me.

"Because you know as well as I do that we can't have a future together. He's an alpha, and one of his biggest obligations is to give an heir to his pack. Something that I could never do. Even if we were meant to be together," I sobbed, "we can't."

"Gigi, you don't know that you can't have pups."

"But is it worth the risk?" I asked.

"You could find a way. Maybe a surrogate or maybe someone else would just give him an heir."

"Oh, okay. So I'm supposed to be okay with him fathering a pup with someone else—someone who will always have to be a part of our relationship for the rest of our lives?" My blood boiled at the thought. "Anyway, even pups aside, everyone knows a luna strengthens an alpha unless she's weak! And then she just drags the pack down with her. And what would I be but a very weak, wolfless luna?"

Heidi let out a breath. "Gigi, I hate to be the one to ask the obvious, but why did you ever think you had a future with Alpha Tyce to begin with? Why are you even considering it now?"

"You're right, it's really dumb," I said and shot up the stairs until I was safe in my room, locking the door behind me.

"You're right, it's really dumb," I said and shot up the stairs until I was safe in my room, locking the door behind me.

Chapter 44

Ginger

A few hours after my exit, Paige burst into my room. "What did I tell you about knocking!" I yelled.

"As long as I don't walk in on you getting a golden shower or having anal sex with Tyce, I think I'm good." She snickered.

"What about him wearing my panties?" I couldn't help but let out a chuckle.

"Well, I'm thinking the important things would be covered in that case. And, anyway, I've already seen him naked."

"What! You have?" I was furious at the thought, and my fingers began contorting themselves to turn to claws, similar to the night I went to the club.

"I am a warrior, you know. We're constantly shifting back and forth between our two forms." I calmed down after she gave her explanation, relieved that nothing more nefarious had gone on. "Especially Tyce since he can't mindlink with us. And it's literally all the other female warriors can talk about. You should hear them. I think they're worse than the guys!"

"What do they say?" I asked, my ears perking up.

She scrunched her nose. "They give really detailed descriptions of everything they want to do to him. Especially this one girl, Tina. Just the other day she was going on and on about how she wants to lick and suck his balls." My blood boiled at Paige's words, the visual physically paining me. "Actually, you know what, don't tell Jasmine this, but I think Tina slept with Blake before he left for Siberia. I think that's why she's always so cold toward her."

"What!" I gasped.

"I know, awkward, right?"

"But she hasn't slept with Tyce, has she?" I knew I'd be sick if Paige said she had.

"Actually, no, I don't think he's slept with anyone in the pack except you. At least he hasn't slept with any of the warriors. I'd know if he had because those girls are shameless." I let out a sigh of relief. "Gigi, maybe he really does like you."

"It doesn't matter." I wrapped my arms around my legs.

"Of course it matters."

"Paige, I don't know why you're trying to put a positive spin on this. Heidi's right. I'm not supposed to date anyone who's not my mate. It'll only be a matter of time before it gets back to Mom and Dad. And I can't stand Dad's disappointment. I was able to get out of the whole shoe incident, but now all the lies and deceit are adding up."

"What you said downstairs. When you said, 'if we're meant to be together.' That made it sound like there's a reason you think you are. Gigi, do you think Tyce is your mate? Because if he is, Dad couldn't be disappointed in you. He might not like the rumors, but you can just tell him the pack made some crazy stuff up."

"I don't know."

"Are there signs?"

"Even if there are, we wouldn't be able to confirm them. I've thought about it, and I don't want to know. It's easier than to have to live the rest of my life knowing I can't be with my mate."

"Gigi, that's absolutely crazy!" Paige shot up and began passionately pacing the room. "If the Moon Goddess thinks the two of you should be together, then you should trust her judgment. Why are you being such a martyr? And worse, why are you giving up before you've even *tried* to make things work with Tyce? That's not the Gigi I know! The Gigi I know fights for what she wants and doesn't surrender."

"Because, Paige." Tears trailed my cheeks. "Because it hurts so much. I am in fucking love with him. Completely over my head in love with him. And if he rejects me, I don't know how I'll be able to just move on. At least if I reject him, then I'll feel some control over the situation. At least then I don't have to feel what it's like to be totally, hopelessly in love with someone and have them stomp on my heart."

"So you honestly think that if you're the one to reject him, and you never see him again, never even give the relationship a chance, that you'll be okay? That you'll just be able to move on like nothing ever happened? Because that is some hardcore delusion right there."

"You know what! You don't know what it's like!" I cried out. "You have it so easy. You were able to live *my* dream and become a warrior. You don't have to hide your shameful secret from everyone. And you were able to just meet and know who your mate is, like it's the most natural thing in the world. And your biggest worry is just whether you get married now or in a couple of years. Either way, there's no question about who you'll marry or who you're meant to be with. You're just trying to create drama by putting off the inevitable and getting marked before you're supposed to."

"I know it may not be a big deal to you, but it's a big deal to me!" Paige fought back. "I love Artemis, and I'm devoted to her 100 percent, but sometimes I question why we do certain things the way we do. Like, for example, why are gay people supposed to reject their mates but it's a sin if straight people do? And why does it matter if mates mark each other before or after the wedding? And why is it that it's always religious people who are the most judgmental when Artemis teaches us love and acceptance of others?" She inhaled and exhaled deeply then continued, "And do you know why I became a warrior?"

I looked at her and didn't say anything.

"It's because I always wanted to be able to protect you. Especially if there were ever a battle on our land. I know you always like to act so strong, but you're still more vulnerable than all of us."

"You don't have to protect me!" I burst out.

"You know if the roles were reversed, you'd do the same for me, Gigi. You're my twin. And losing you would be like losing a part of myself."

I put my head onto my knees and sobbed, feeling so much pity for myself and how out of control I felt. It was like I was twelve years old all over again, becoming aware of the fact that I'd completely and permanently destroyed my life.

Chapter 45

Jasmine

On Saturday morning, I was upstairs in my office looking through some reports on the casino, when I recalled that Blake had recently printed out the PowerPoint slides from a presentation we'd been given earlier that week. He had taken some handwritten notes, and I wanted to make sure I took them into consideration before I responded to the director of finance's email that was awaiting a reply, so I descended the stairs to go find them in his office.

As I approached, I noticed the door was slightly ajar with light trickling into the hallway and voices in a passionate conversation, possibly an argument. Curiosity getting the best of me, I snuck closer so I could better hear what was going on.

"Fucking Artemis, Lucy, now is not the time. Blake could come back any second. Put your clothes back on."

"C'mon, Luke, don't you think it's time we get started on the beta heir? You know the pack's going to be expecting one now." It was quiet for a moment and then Lucy's voice continued, "That's right, baby, just sit there like that. I'll do all the work. Let me get your cock nice and warmed up."

I was about to walk away, feeling a bit nauseous from what I'd almost walked in on, when Luke's voice boomed, "Lucy, for the love of Artemis, just stop, okay? You barely even mother Libby as it is. We shouldn't be having another pup who you're just going to throw to the nanny."

"I don't just throw Libby to the nanny!"

"Seriously? I don't even remember the last time you wanted to spend the evening with your family instead of going out with your friends. When the nanny goes home, I'm usually the one who has to take care of Libby, and it puts me in a bad spot because I'm the fucking beta of the pack, and I have obligations. Luckily, my parents don't live far from the packhouse, and my mom is far too nice and willing to take her at a moment's notice. But this can't keep going on like this."

"I watch Libby a lot of nights too! I'm not *always* out with my friends!"

"Quite frankly, I'm not happy with your behavior either. You're a beta's mate, Lucy! You knew that when we chose to be mates! That title comes with a lot of obligations. It looks really bad when the pack is constantly whispering about how you're grinding up on different warriors at the club and doing body shots with pack members. It doesn't just make you look bad—it makes the whole pack leadership look bad. Can you imagine if the first lady was behaving the way you are?"

"So, what? I'm not allowed to have a job or any fun? I have to just devote the rest of my life to being some fucking proper beta's mate?"

Luke let out a loud sigh. "We clearly rushed into things. You weren't ready to be a mother or take your responsibilities as a beta's mate seriously. And Goddess knows I wasn't ready to be a father."

"What are you saying, Luke?"

"Nothing. We chose to be together, so we should just make the best of it. There's no going back now."

"Don't you love me?" Lucy's voice was shaky.

"I do love you, Lucy. But sometimes I wonder if it's enough. I have a lot of responsibilities. When Blake's out of town, I stand in as the alpha. Everything I do and you do is put under a microscope. And I thought you understood that, but it all just seems to be some big joke to you. You're constantly on the remediation list for training, you behave like you're still in high school, and any time I try to involve you in pack business you space out or tell me you're too busy. Can't you even put in a slight effort to show you give a shit at all? Can't you be more like—" Then he stopped, and my stomach dropped.

"Like who?" Lucy gritted out.

"No one."

"You were going to say someone's name. Fucking say it!" Lucy screamed. "Tell me who you wish I was more like!"

My heart pounded against my chest. I couldn't believe what I was overhearing and wasn't even sure how to feel about it. I'd finally gotten over Luke for good after Blake marked me, but it was news to me that he ever compared me to Lucy or second-guessed his choice.

I was about to turn to leave when Blake's scent drifted into my nose and I turned to almost crash into him. *"What's going on? You're anxious,"* he mindlinked me.

I was about to reply with a mindlink back when Luke's voice sounded into the hallway. "I don't wish you were more like anyone. I just wish you'd grow up."

"I'm not fucking stupid, Luke! I know exactly whose name you were going to say. And, as usual, you don't even have the balls to actually say it!"

"Lucy, just let it go. We don't need to fight about this."

"We do need to fight about this! You won't even touch me anymore!" Her loud sobs echoed into the hallway, and I knew I should give them privacy, but I couldn't pull myself away from the drama. Blake must have felt the same because he stayed right there, also not moving. "I'm a woman. I have needs, Luke. I just want things to go back to how they used to be when we couldn't keep our hands off each other."

"Don't cry, Lucy." Luke's voice softened. "Shhh, Lucy."

"*We should get out of here,*" Blake finally mindlinked me. "*Before they figure out we're eavesdropping.*" I nodded and walked back down the other way with him.

"Wow, that was pretty crazy," I said to Blake as soon as we were back in the main part of the packhouse.

"I missed most of the conversation. What were they arguing about?"

"I probably shouldn't repeat it. But essentially Luke's getting fed up with Lucy's behavior."

"I'm not surprised." Blake rolled his eyes. "She's out of control. How he ever chose her over you, I'll never understand. But hey, it worked out great for me." He gave me a huge grin. "One man's terrible taste is another man's priceless treasure."

"I know I shouldn't feel bad for her, but I kind of do," I said. "I mean, Luke's not wrong. She doesn't take her responsibilities of being a beta's mate seriously, and she has basically replaced herself with the nanny as Libby's mother. But I don't know. Sometimes she does step up to the plate. Like when you were in battle, she was a good friend and helped ease the pain when I felt you get hit by the wolfsbane."

"It's hard to stop seeing someone as a friend when that's the only way you knew them for so long. I think that's part of the reason why I had such a hard time finishing Charlie off. He wasn't always that bad. I probably should have been there for him more after his father got put to death. That's when he started to change and got mixed up with some shady people."

"How old was he when his father got put to death?"

"Fifteen, and I witnessed the whole thing. My father was brutal. He hated rapists, and I think they were his favorite to torture. Charlie asked me what was done to his dad, but I could never tell him. As much as I hated my father, I don't think I'd ever want to know if the same thing had been done to him."

"What was done to him?"

"Do you really want to know?"

"I'm trying to get used to the idea of torture. Maybe if you tell me, I can start to feel more comfortable with it."

"Jasmine, you don't have to get used to torture. I'll take care of that part of the job." He wrapped his arms around me.

"Okay, tell me one really bad thing that your father did to him."

Blake's eyes turned evil, and I could suddenly feel a flooding of pleasure in his emotions as he was seemingly transported back to that day. I put my hand on his chest, now realizing that torture really did give him some sort of sick enjoyment. While I knew this on a logical level, now I could feel it, and it all became so real. "He sliced his dick into small pepperoni slices using one of his sharpest knives and then fed them to him one by one. When he refused at first, he shoved his blade into one of his balls. After that, Charles Sr. ate every single piece, chewing and swallowing them."

"Holy shit!" I replied, feeling a bit nauseous.

"Want to hear more?"

"No, I think I'm good. That was enough."

"When you're ready again, I'm happy to regale you with more torture stories anytime."

That evening, Blake and I took a walk to his mom's house. She had relocated to a small house in the center of town after Blake had taken the alpha title and his parents retired.

"Hello, Blake, Jasmine." His mom greeted us with a big smile on her face. She wrapped Blake in a hug and gave him a kiss on the forehead.

Then she pulled me in for a hug. "How are my grandpups doing?" she asked, looking down at my belly.

"Amazing," Blake replied.

"Come in, come in, I have someone to introduce both of you to." His mom waved us in. We followed her into the living room where a middle-aged man with a bald head and brown eyes was sitting. He stood up as soon as we walked in. "Blake, Jasmine, this is Ray."

"Nice to meet you, Ray." Blake stepped forward with an intense look.

"Likewise, Alpha," he replied.

"This is my luna, Jasmine." He pulled me forward, and I shook Ray's hand as well. I noted he had a very firm and confident handshake.

"Pleasure, Luna." He gave me a warm smile.

"Pleasure's all mine," I replied politely.

"Sit, everyone." Blake's mom gestured at the couches. Blake and I took a seat on the loveseat, and his mom sat down with Ray on the main couch.

"So, Ray." Blake leaned forward. "I understand you and my mom knew each other in high school. What made you get back in contact with her now?"

Ray gave a big smile and replied, "She reached out to me through Facebook, and we agreed to meet. Seeing her again, it was almost like no time had ever passed at all." He gave Sienna's hand a squeeze.

"I see," Blake replied, and I noted he was glaring at their hands. "What do you do for work?" I almost laughed out loud at how much like a dad Blake was acting.

"I'm the chief innovation officer at the pack lab."

"Oh, you must know my parents then!" I exclaimed.

"Yes, I do actually. It was big news when you were married to the alpha. It's nice to finally meet you in person, Luna Jasmine. I understand your mom also comes from an alpha family?"

"Yes, my cousin, who's the alpha of the Jade Moon Pack, is actually visiting us for the summer."

"Very nice. I can't say I'm surprised at all that Sienna was mated to an alpha, nor am I surprised that her alpha son would find himself a mate from an alpha family." Ray smiled at her. "Sienna was always the smartest, prettiest, and sweetest girl in school. I constantly had to work up the courage to talk to her, but I was a shy boy back then. On my eighteenth birthday, the only thing I wanted to do was look in Sienna's eyes. I can't even tell you how disappointing it was when I asked her to borrow a pencil and I didn't feel anything." He chuckled.

If I wasn't mistaken, Blake's mom was blushing and her eyes glistening. "There's nothing like young love."

"Nothing like young love at all, with only hope and your future ahead of you," Ray agreed.

Chapter 46

Ginger

The morning after the sisters' potluck disaster, I woke up to find the house empty. Paige was nowhere to be found. I figured she must have had Saturday duty along with my dad. My mom also wasn't home, and the family car was gone. I breathed out a happy sigh. It was nice when I got the house to myself. I could just wallow in my misery alone without anyone bothering me.

I spent the entire morning and early afternoon in the backyard, laying out in the sun while reading and listening to music. The sun was blazing without a cloud in sight—the perfect day to sunbathe. I knew I'd regret it later since my fair skin didn't take well to the sun. But my sunburns eventually faded into tans, so I suffered through it.

Around midafternoon, a group text came in from Lucy with a bunch of phone numbers included that I didn't know.

Lucy: Club tonight! Packhouse 10 sharp!

I was going to ignore the text at first, but then I thought, it would be nice to get out and ignore my problems. I double-checked, and Tyce wasn't included as part of the group. So, maybe he wouldn't be there, which would be ideal. While a part of me that I tried so hard to ignore was dying to see him again, I also wanted to clear my head, get drunk, and let loose—stop worrying about my wolf, or lack thereof, and him for one night.

Me: *I'm in*

After about another hour of sunbathing, I heard the family car pull into the garage, and I decided to make my way inside. My skin was starting to feel a bit hot anyway, and I didn't want to overdo it, although I wasn't sure that I hadn't already.

I wrapped my towel around my legs, making sure the stitches were covered. I'd made sure to choose a big towel exactly for that reason.

"Oh, Gigi! There you are!" My mom greeted me, but she didn't look happy to see me, and my stomach dropped. The rumors must have finally made their way to her.

"Hi, Mom."

"What happened to your arms?" she asked.

"I got into a fight with some branches while walking in the woods," I replied with my prepared answer. "Didn't realize they were covered in thorns."

"It looks painful." She flinched. "Maybe we should put something on them."

"It's okay, I already did. I've been rubbing them with Neosporin."

"Okay, good." She nodded and gave me a small smile.

"Okay, well, I'll be heading upstairs."

"Wait, before you go, Gigi. There's something I need to talk to you about."

"Okay," I replied, preparing myself, my stomach churning and chest tightening.

"There's apparently been rumors around the pack."

"I know, Mom. I'm sorry." I looked down at the floor, my lips quivering.

"Are you apologizing because they're true?"

"No! I'm just sorry that there are rumors and you had to hear them." I flinched a little at the lie, but I told myself that the majority of the rumor wasn't true, so I wasn't really lying.

"Okay." She let out a breath. "I know Tyce is very good-looking, and he's an alpha. So I could see how you might be tempted, especially if he pursued you. But don't fall for anything he says. Alphas are known for being very manipulative because they know they can get away with it. Alpha James was the same way."

"I thought you loved Alpha James!"

"I loved looking at him. But I know women who fell for his lies. And sinned, thinking he'd leave his luna for them. But alphas don't ever take chosen mates. So don't be fooled, Gigi." I nodded. Then she added, "Also, don't ever let a man pressure you into doing anything degrading, okay? Have some respect for yourself." My face burned with shame, horrified that my mom had to hear those things about me.

I considered whether maybe I should confide in my mom that I thought Tyce was my fated mate, especially after speaking with Paige the day prior, and hadn't my mom even suggested it at one point? Had she just been wistfully thinking out loud, or did she have some weird motherly instinct? But then, I realized, that meant telling her he got vampire fangs when we had sex, and that was definitely not a conversation I wanted to have with my mom. The conversation had already gone way out of my comfort zone. Instead, I asked, "Is Dad really disappointed?"

My mom wrapped her arms around me. "Don't worry about your dad. I'll talk to him. He knows you're a good girl, baby." A small part of me felt a bit sick from my deception, but I tried to push it away. What they didn't know couldn't hurt them.

By the time nine o'clock rolled around, Paige still wasn't home. I quickly shot her a text to make sure she was okay. I then showered, noting my skin had not taken well to the sun at all and it would definitely be peeling soon, only adding to the injuries to my body that I'd need to cover. Pretty soon my only option was going to be a full-on burqa. I made sure to keep the water cool in order not to scald myself.

I tried to put a bra on and found it painful where parts of it touched the skin my bikini hadn't covered. It was becoming quite clear what a bad idea it was to go clubbing that night as I'd also have to cover my legs and arms. I hadn't thought this through fully. But I'd already committed to go and didn't want to back out now.

In the end, I pulled on some fishnet stockings and wrapped a scarf creatively around my stitches, thinking maybe I could set a new trend and chuckling to myself. On top, I had on a pair of black shorts and a blouse with long, loose sleeves and a dangerously low neckline. Without a bra, it looked even more scandalous with my girls practically falling out. I knew I'd have to be careful or I'd be giving everyone a show that night. I flipped through my tops again and decided this was the best option as it met my criteria of being sexy, having sleeves, and not being too hot in a club. And the third criterion I wasn't even quite sure it met, but it was the best I could do.

I rubbed some glittery bronzer cream all over my neck and décolletage to try to camouflage my lobster skin. I also went super heavy on the makeup, completely smoking out my eyes.

As a finishing touch, I grabbed the tallest heels I had along with my small crossbody bag. After slipping into a pair of flat sandals, I crept out of the house, deciding to text my parents on my way over so they wouldn't be privy to my outfit, which I was certain wasn't Dad approved.

"Look at you!" Lucy greeted me with a big hug as soon as I arrived after making the long walk over.

"I just have to change into my heels," I said.

"I'm loving the outfit! But you won't be too hot in that shirt?" she asked, looking me up and down.

"I'll be fine. I get cold easily."

"Guess you'll just need to find a warm body to rub up against tonight." She winked and giggled.

I similarly looked her up and down taking in the dress she had on, which I noted I'd never in my life be able to pull off the way she did with her skinny, modelesque body. It was very short and tight with what was essentially two pieces of fabric covering her breasts, tied in the center with a small bow holding them together.

I was about to follow her toward the living room when Luke appeared from the hallway. If I didn't know any better, I'd say he looked less than pleased. His brows furrowed, and he pinched the bridge of his nose. "Lucy, what are you wearing?"

"Doesn't it look so awesome?" She gave him a big smile. "It just came in today. Perfect timing—I needed something new to wear tonight!"

"So that's not lingerie?" he asked with a bite to his words.

"No, silly!" She continued to smile, and I tried to determine what was happening. Lucy's reactions weren't matching Luke's clear distaste.

"And where is Libby?"

"Oh, don't you worry, baby." She continued to smile and pushed on his nose. "My mom is taking her for the night. She's been wanting to spend more time with her granddaughter anyway. It worked out perfect!"

"Fucking Artemis," Luke said under his breath, rolled his eyes, and walked away.

"Is Beta Luke okay?" I asked Lucy.

"Of course he's okay! Now, c'mon, put your shoes on! We're going to head out soon. Let me go grab everyone else!"

I pulled out a dining room chair to pull off my flats and put my heels on in their place. When I'd buckled the second shoe and was about to get up, I came face-to-face with Tyce standing over me. I almost fell out of my chair in shock, not expecting to see him.

"So I take it you're going out with Lucy tonight?"

"Is it that obvious?" I teased.

"I'm coming." His eyes looked intense, and I wondered what he was thinking.

"You don't look like you're dressed for clubbing," I responded, raking my eyes over his T-shirt and gym shorts.

"Lucy! I'll be your DD. Give me a sec to change!" Tyce called out.

Luke walked back into the room and grabbed Tyce's arm before he climbed the stairs. "Do you mind keeping an eye on Lucy tonight?" he asked.

"Sure, bro," Tyce replied and then headed upstairs. I let out a breath.

When we gathered into groups to split into cars, Tyce grabbed my hand, pulling me toward him. "Someone's a bit possessive tonight," I remarked.

"You think I'm going to let you out of my sight looking like that?" His eyes lingered on my chest.

"Why not? It's not like you don't let it all hang out regularly. Even my sister's gotten a look."

"Because I can't keep my eyes off you even if I wanted to."

My stomach flipped. "Tyce . . ." I started.

"Gigi, can you at least listen to what I have to say?"

We were soon interrupted by Lucy pulling us toward Tyce's car. "Thanks, Double D!" she said to Tyce. "And you're really Double D!" She turned to me, blowing her alcohol breath in my face as she giggled.

"Double G actually," Tyce said in a low voice as Lucy bounced away, and he chuckled at his own joke. "Now I know why they call you Gigi."

"How do you know my size?" I asked, staring at him as a blush spread across his cheeks.

"I may have peeked at a tag a while back."

"You dirty little dog!"

"Wolves *are* a part of the canine family." He stuck his tongue out at me playfully.

"Shotgun!" Lucy yelled from Tyce's car.

"What do you think, should we just let her drive and I'll get in the back seat with you?"

"You think I'm going to let Lucy drive in that state?"

"Good point. Her pregaming put a damper on things. But the night is young anyway." He wiggled his eyebrows suggestively and opened the back door for me after he unlocked his car. Things were definitely not going to plan, and Tyce already had me riled up and aroused. I knew with 100 percent certainty that if he touched me I would give into him yet again, the pain from the previous day forgotten.

We were soon at the club, where Lucy had a table waiting for us yet again. Tyce stood next to me, and everyone's eyes shot over to us. Fuck, they'd probably all heard the rumors. Were they wondering right then if Tyce regularly pissed on me? Did they wonder if it hurt when he shoved his alpha cock in my ass? Goddess, it would probably kill. I'd be wondering the same thing myself, and I suddenly couldn't stop thinking about it.

We barely even got settled when Lucy started pouring drinks for everyone. She shoved a vodka OJ in my hands, which was clearly much more vodka than OJ, judging by the translucent color of the drink. I vowed to nurse it.

I noted Tyce similarly nursed a beer while everyone soon switched to shots. Lucy tried to force me to take one with her, too, but Tyce grabbed it from her before she could hand it to me, which I was secretly thankful for. Once everyone began heading to the dance floor, Tyce came up right next to me and yelled into my ear, "Can we please talk?"

"Fine," I replied, and he took my hand, leading me back to a familiar location. Did "talk" really mean *talk*? I couldn't decide which option I preferred. My loins were on fire, but my emotions were also in a fragile state.

As soon as we were behind the closed doors of the empty coatroom, I opened my mouth to say something, but he put up his hand. "Gigi, before you say anything, I just want you to know that I really really like you. I know you might not be my mate—and odds are you probably aren't. But I don't care. I choose to be with you."

"What are you saying?" I felt weak, very weak. All my intentions to reject him were now on shaky ground.

"I want to be with you, Gigi. Be with you for real. Give this thing between us a fair shot."

"But werewolves don't do that. They don't date, not really."

"Werewolves also don't really go see witches either, but we both did that. So let's break some more rules and do this too."

"I don't know, Tyce." I looked down.

"Why are you hesitating?" he asked, putting his hand under my chin and lifting it so I looked up at him. My skin tingled from his touch, every part of my being begging me to just let go and be with him.

I took a deep breath and backed away, so he was no longer touching me. "Okay, say I do agree to give this a shot, where do you see this going? It's not like I can be your luna."

"Why not?"

"C'mon, Tyce. You know why."

"Gigi, look at me!" My eyes locked with his. "Did you seriously already give up on getting your wolf back? Because I won't accept that. You are going to get your wolf back, and I'm going to help you. Even if you don't want to be with me, even if you break my heart and tell me you'd rather be with your fated mate, I won't give up until you have your wolf back."

I blinked back tears, amazed at his kindness. He instantly wrapped his arms around me, pulling me against his body. "Don't cry, Gigi." He spoke into my ear. "It'll be all right."

I almost considered telling him my suspicions right then and there, confessing that I thought we were mates. But then some weird insecurity nudged at me and I didn't, deciding to wait until I felt more confident about Tyce's intentions. Maybe it was my mom getting in my head after she told me about how manipulative alphas were. I didn't actually think Tyce was manipulating me, but it was so hard to completely shake years of insecurities.

"I can't cry. It'll be a disaster. Do you see how much mascara and eyeliner I have on?" I chuckled, wanting to lighten the mood.

"Yeah, I definitely noticed. I like this seductive vixen look you have going on today." He smirked. "By the way, I know things ended not great yesterday, but I do have a condom today. No pressure, but wanted to throw it out there, just in case."

"You don't need a condom for anal," I joked. "At least not with a werewolf."

"Wait." He held me away from him. "Are you saying . . . Did you want it in the back door? Because, I can't lie, when I heard those rumors, I kind of wished they were true. Well, that part of them at least."

"What about the other parts?"

"Not as into the other stuff. But if you were, I wouldn't judge." He gave me a big grin.

"No, I'm not into being pissed on!"

"Okay, but back to anal—"

"I'll think about it. But definitely not in here."

"Of course, I'll make it very comfortable for you. In a soft bed, with tons of lube, and I'll be really slow and gentle."

"Oh my Goddess, Tyce! I can't believe you've already thought this all out."

He gave me a shy, sweet look. "No one's ever let me try anal with them, and I've always wanted to."

"Well, you're not exactly anal size. Even from the front it's a lot to handle."

"You handle it so well though." He moved closer to me, brushing his fingers along my cheeks, moving them to my lips, gently tracing the contours of them. My breathing shallowed, my lips parted, and he slipped two fingers inside my mouth. I sucked softly on them as he pushed his other hand into my blouse, stroking my bare breast. "You have to be hot in that shirt." He groaned. "You're so covered up."

I moaned against his fingers. He pulled them out of my mouth and was about to move to kiss me when I stopped him. "Weren't you supposed to be keeping your eye on Lucy tonight?"

"Lucy?" he asked. "Fuck. Yeah, I did tell Luke I'd do that, didn't I?" He grumbled. "Fine, we should probably do the right thing and rejoin the group. But this isn't over."

Chapter 47

Ginger

I didn't know what I was expecting when we stepped out of that room, and part of me probably should have expected what I witnessed, but it was still quite shocking. Lucy was completely sloshed—especially considering she was a werewolf. If I didn't know better, I'd think she was one of my college friends rather than a beta's mate.

She was grinding up on all the guys that had come with us, wobbly on her feet, practically falling over as she flung her body against theirs. One of them took a bottle of beer and started pouring it from above into her mouth while everyone looked on cheering.

"Oh, fuck," Tyce shouted next to me and headed toward the group.

"Alpha Tyce!" Lucy yelled so loudly I could hear her over the music. "Pour some more in my mouth."

I couldn't hear what was said after that, but I watched as Tyce clearly tried to persuade her to go with him. There was a struggle between the two of them as he put his arm around her shoulders, and she pushed him away. It seemed like he'd finally grabbed a firm hold of her when she slipped out from under his arm and rapidly walked away—surprisingly fast on her heels.

I maybe should have been more worried, but I was actually dying of entertainment. Soon Lucy had disappeared into the crowd. Tyce and the group went to follow, stopping in their tracks when they could find no sign of her, as if she had completely vanished.

I came up next to Tyce and yelled, "Where'd she go?"

"I don't know." His eyebrows drew together. "I should probably get management involved. She reeked of alcohol."

He was about to move when a female voice rang out from the speakers. "Who's having fun tonight?"

We all tilted our heads up toward the big screen behind the DJ booth as the club cheered. Lucy had a microphone in hand and was shaking her hips. The DJ looked on appreciatively. To be fair, Lucy was very beautiful, almost in an otherworldly way. She had clearly hit the genetic jackpot and could have easily been a famous model had it not been forbidden by our pack, or likely most packs. Her dress revealed her perfectly flat stomach, clearly unaffected by having had a pup—was it the werewolf healing, or was she the Moon Goddess's favorite?

"Who wants some more fun?" Lucy's voice boomed out to the crowd. She held up a shot glass that had come from who knows where. She tipped it back and then threw it down onto the DJ stand. "Here's more!" She smiled widely as she used her free hand to pull the strings that were holding the front of her dress together and flashed the entire club, her bare breasts and pink nipples on display for everyone to see.

"Holy shit!" one of the guys in our group yelled out. Another one whistled and another cheered.

"Fuck!" Tyce exclaimed, marching over toward the stand, and I followed. Two large bouncers came up from behind Lucy and tried to wrestle her away as she called into the microphone, "You can't stop me! I own this club! This is my club! I own this club and casino!" One of the bouncers finally pulled the microphone out of her hand, and the other grabbed her around the waist, pulling her off the stage and to a back room as she kicked and screamed, her entire body flailing.

I stayed on Tyce's heels as he practically sprinted to where she'd been taken. He was able to easily open the door with his key fob, and he held the door open for me so I could follow inside. The bouncer had Lucy restrained, holding her arms behind her back.

"You can't do this to me! Wait until the beta hears about this!"

"The what?" The two bouncers laughed. "The *beta*? Sounds intimidating. I'm so scared!"

"You will be once he bites your balls off!"

They laughed even harder.

A man in a suit was pulling out his phone and looked up. "Ah! Mr. Tikaani! I was just about to call Mr. Hemming and Mr. Wulfric. But it looks like I don't need to."

"No, I'll take care of her," Tyce replied.

"Take care of me how? Do I need to wear my dress while you do it?" She giggled at her joke.

"Okay, that's enough, Lucy!" Tyce went up to her with his arms crossed. "Just stop, okay?"

"Oh, please, Tyce! You know you liked the show."

I was about to claw her to death at her comment, my ears pounding, my fingernails and teeth tingling.

Tyce rolled his eyes and said, "Tie your dress together so I can take you home."

"You're just as boring as Blake. Bo-ring!" she screamed out.

He let out a sigh. "I don't want to carry you out of here. But I will if I have to."

"Oh please, you know you want a feel. They're real!" She puffed out her chest.

"Fucking—" Tyce said under his breath. All I could think was that I wanted to murder Lucy.

"Can someone tie her dress back together?" Tyce asked. The bouncers and who I imagined must be the club or casino manager all looked at each other, clearly wondering if it would be appropriate. "Never mind, I'll do it."

"It's okay, I got it," I said, diving in front of Tyce, not liking the idea of him touching her the least bit.

"Traitor!" Lucy glared at me.

"Lucy, seriously, this is embarrassing," I said as I pulled the strings of her dress together.

"Embarrassing?" she cried out with a laugh. "You almost fell into the toilet last time! I had to go into the stall with you! And you're calling me embarrassing? Just because Tyce fucked you in the ass a few times doesn't make you a luna all of a sudden! Bitch!"

I gasped, backing away.

Tyce grabbed her shoulders and pulled her away from the bouncers like she was a rag doll. With the most threatening voice I'd ever heard, he roared, "Don't you ever insult Gigi again. I don't fucking care who your husband is. I will murder you."

She let out a squeak and was suddenly quiet.

"Let's go to my car, now. I will let you go, and if you behave, I'll let you walk on your own. If you don't, I will drag you out of here by your hair. Got it?"

She nodded with her eyes wide and skin pale, a single tear sliding down her cheek. I couldn't lie—I was both terrified and awed by Tyce's outburst.

He slowly let her down onto the ground and removed his hands from her upper arms. At first, she rubbed at them, but then she walked toward the door with her head hung.

"Follow me, there's a back way to the valet," the man in the suit said. He spoke into a microphone attached to his suit jacket, asking them to pull up Tyce's car for us, and it was already waiting by the time we arrived.

Tyce helped Lucy into the back seat, where she lay down, and the valet opened the passenger door for me so I could get in. Most of the way back to the pack was pretty quiet. Tyce played music on low, and Lucy was soon passed out. As we pulled into the packhouse driveway, Tyce took my hand in his and asked, "Would you want to hang out a bit longer before I take you home?" I nodded. He gave me a big smile and said, "Great! Let me just get rid of Lucy. Wait here."

Not long after, Tyce came out with a tired-looking Beta Luke. They opened the back door, and Beta Luke peeked into the car. "All right, Lucy, let's go."

"Lukey!" She stirred from the back.

"How much did you drink?" he asked, scrunching his nose.

"I was just having some fun, baby!" she replied, getting up and stumbling as she tried to climb out of the car. Luke easily caught her, pulling her up by her arms.

Luke heaved a sigh. "Okay, let's go inside." I watched as he practically carried her back toward the packhouse. I then turned to where Tyce was climbing into the driver's seat.

"Is Lucy normally like that?" I asked. She had seemed okay previously, but I was now beginning to understand she might be a bit of a train-wreck.

Tyce gave a small laugh. "Lucy's definitely an interesting character. I think Luke has his hands full with both her and his pup."

"Paige told me that Lucy wasn't actually mated to Luke and that they're chosen mates."

"Yeah, it was a big controversy in my pack. My grandfather was especially pissed when he heard his granddaughter rejected her mate. It's practically a crime in our pack to take a chosen mate. It's a lot more conservative back where I'm from."

"So why are you okay with taking a chosen mate?" I asked as he pulled out of the driveway.

"I'm the alpha, aren't I? Technically, I make the rules. And anyway, how would my family ever know the difference? It's not like they can feel it for themselves. For all we know, there might be more people who take chosen mates than we know."

"I guess I never thought about that."

"I never thought about it either until recently." He took my hand in his and emotions flooded my body.

"If you were to take a chosen mate," I began, "would you want to know who your fated mate was first, so you'd at least know what you were giving up?"

"No, I'd rather not know." I was surprised by his quick response. But then, I realized, hadn't I basically said the same thing to Paige?

"Because it's easier not to miss or regret something you never knew, right?" I asked.

"Right. Plus, what I want is already right in front of me. I don't need to wait and see if something better comes along. I know what I want." He glanced over at me and gave me such a mesmerizing smile that I thought my heart was going to beat right out of my chest.

He parked his car at the entrance to the party lake. "Did you want to go for a midnight swim or something?" I asked when we were both out of the car and he took my hand, leading me into the forest. I was a bit wobbly walking in on the uneven terrain in my heels.

"Not a bad idea, but no. I have better plans. And, again, you didn't wear your hiking shoes." He snickered, looking down at my feet. "Not that I'm complaining. I like the whole look. And I need to borrow that thing you have strategically wrapped around your leg." He bent down and untied it. "How is your leg, by the way?"

"It's fine." He stood up and tied the scarf around my eyes. "Why are you blindfolding me?"

"Because I have a surprise for you. Now, no peeking. I'm going to bend over so you can get onto my back." He gently backed into me and took my hands with his, leading me onto his back. I climbed on and he got up, his arms wrapped around my legs. "Now hold on. It's a little bit of a walk. Are you comfortable?"

"Yeah, I'm good. I should really be asking you."

He chuckled. "My dad used to make me carry sandbags that weigh a lot more than you do. Basically until I passed out."

"Sounds intense."

"It was. My family is the definition of intense." He walked me farther into the woods, and I snuggled into his hard, muscular back, inhaling the smell of his shampoo.

"Tell me more about your family."

"My younger brother, Travis, or Trav as we call him, is basically the complete opposite of me. He's always been super nerdy and serious."

"What about your sister?"

"Terri is great. She's basically sunshine, kittens, and all things happy and warm. The worst possible thing could happen to her, and she would still see the good in it."

"She sounds great. I'd love to meet her."

"I'd love to introduce you."

"And where do you fit in with your siblings?"

"I'm the screwball fuckup." He let out a laugh.

"I'm sure that's not completely true. You are the alpha."

"Only because I was born first."

"Do you think your brother should have been alpha instead?"

"Nah, he can't fight like me. And he was never as good at the alpha training stuff as I was. My dad made him train too, just in case, you know. But he never went as hard on him. I think because he knew he wasn't really built for it. Anyway, he loves all that business stuff. He's discovered some shady stuff going on, and he's been investigating it."

"What kind of shady stuff?"

"Our pack runs an oil company with a neighboring pack. He thinks they might be embezzling."

"That sounds pretty serious."

"Yeah, I'm glad my brother's investigating instead of me. I can barely even stay awake during our board meetings." We continued walking and chatting, and I realized how nice it was just hanging out with him. It just felt comfortable. And I couldn't lie—I really enjoyed snuggling up against his rock-hard, muscular body. It was both exactly what I needed and somehow too much, almost like crouching too close to a campfire on a cold night.

After some time, he stopped walking. "Okay, we're here." He put me down gently.

"Can I take the blindfold off?"

I felt his presence behind me as he untied the scarf. I immediately opened my eyes to the most breathtaking sight. I was in complete awe as hundreds of fireflies surrounded us, like tiny, sparkling yellow fairies floating against the dark forest backdrop. It was as if we'd entered a mystical fairy tale. Tyce took my hand in his and we looked on, our bodies surrounded by the hot, humid night. "Oh my Goddess!" I gasped.

"I discovered them the other night while doing a run of the patrol stations. Pretty amazing, right?"

"It's so magical!" I replied and turned to look at him. His amber eyes were glowing like two particularly large fireflies.

"You know what, I should have realized sooner," he said as he stared into my eyes.

"Realized what?"

"Your eyes don't glow in the dark. That should have tipped me off. I guess I just thought it was because whatever you drank weakened you and you lost some of your abilities."

I breathed out a sigh. "I think we all find explanations for stuff to confirm whatever we want to believe. It worked in my favor, obviously."

And then I wondered if I was doing that with the mate bond evidence. I mean, as far as confirming a mate bond, it was pretty weak, right? Just two clues. Maybe I was so desperate to believe we should be together that I'd grasped at whatever straw there was. Kind of like looking up some minor symptoms on WebMD and thinking you needed to go to the hospital pronto or you'd die of an exploding kidney.

"Sometimes it's easier to just believe something you want to be true. It's less work than digging deeper and really questioning your preconceived notions." He leaned in and kissed me, gently pressing his lips against mine, pushing his fingers into my hair.

I pulled away from him for a second to say, "I think there's some nerd in you too, screwball."

"I can put some into you, too, if you want." He snickered against my lips. "Preferably in your ass, but the other options work too."

"And it was such a nice moment."

"C'mon, Gi. Everyone knows that happy endings are really just the prologue to porn."

"I thought happy endings were the epilogue."

"Now that you mention it, I suppose they're both."

Chapter 48

Jasmine

"It hurts, baby. Everything hurts," Lucy whined to Luke from the living room couch, wrapped in a robe with sunglasses on. Blake and I were in the dining room having breakfast, overhearing the whole conversation between the two of them.

"How much did you drink last night that you were actually able to get a hangover?" Luke looked her up and down.

"I dunno. A lot. A lot!"

"Clearly."

"Can't you do something, baby?"

"I've never had a hangover, so I don't even know how to fix one. Where's Libby?"

"My mom will be bringing her over soon. Can you watch her today, baby? I'm in so much pain, and the nanny doesn't come on Sundays."

"Lucy, I have work to do today. I don't get days off like everyone else."

"Please, Lukey?" she whined, giving him puppy eyes.

He let out a deep sigh and said, "Fine. I'll be back to watch her." He then opened the glass door and stomped outside before Lucy could even thank him.

"Jasmine, Blake, can you get me some coffee and painkillers?" Lucy called out to us.

"What are we, your servants?" Blake yelled back.

"I was just asking for a favor!" she whined.

"Goddess, I feel like you just get worse as time goes on," Blake replied, shaking his head.

"What's that supposed to mean?" Lucy asked with a bite.

"It means get your own damn coffee and painkillers," Blake replied, picking up his plate and heading into the kitchen. I looked at her with pity and followed him. When we were behind closed doors, he said, "Luke's pissed."

"I mean, I could tell."

"Not just because of that," Blake continued. "We went by the civilian gym yesterday to check on how everyone's doing maintaining their fitness standards, figuring out if we need to set up some sort of small group training classes, and we found out she's been skipping out. Not even going to her required sparring."

I gasped. "I can't believe Lucy's not even showing up. I mean, she's always hated school and training, and her punctuality's never been great. But I've never known her to just completely skip."

"I don't know what's going on with her, but I'm letting Luke deal with it." Blake opened the dishwasher and put his and my dishes inside.

"Maybe I should talk to her," I offered.

He gave me a side-eye. "If you want."

"I feel like I should try to help. I am the luna, right?"

"Maybe wait for her to get over her hangover." Blake snickered.

"Yeah, good idea."

When we returned to the main part of the house, Lucy was gone, seemingly having gone back to bed. Blake turned to go toward his office, and I pulled out my laptop, opening it on the dining room table so I could research baby stuff I'd need in a few months.

About a half hour into my research, Tyce came down the stairs with a big smile on his face. "Good morning!"

"Good morning," I replied. "You're in a good mood."

"It's a nice day." He kept smiling, and it seemed like he was definitely happy about something other than just the weather. When he got to the bottom of the stairs, he continued, "Grandma called yesterday, by the way. She wants you to send your baby registry to my sister so she can help her order stuff for the pups. Don't go cheap. Grandma's generous with that stuff, so take advantage." He winked.

"It seems like your pack does really well," I replied. "I mean, it's not like ours doesn't. But the casino revenue definitely fluctuates, especially seasonally. We always have to be careful with our spending."

"Oil's where it's at."

"Yeah, I can see that. Maybe I should talk to Blake about investing in some new businesses or something." I tapped a pen against my chin. "Tourism is just so dependent on the season and the economy."

"That's why our pack started investing in green energy. Who knows how much longer everyone's going to depend on oil."

"Good idea. Diversifying!" I nodded.

"It seems like you're into this business stuff." Tyce took a seat at the dining room table.

I let out a chuckle. "Honestly, I didn't think it would be interesting, but the more I get into it the more I like it. I might go back to school part-time after the pups get here so I can finish up my degree. I was originally going to do something like biochemistry like my parents, but now I'm thinking I want to be more involved in running the business side of the pack."

"Goddess, nothing bores me more!" Tyce sat back in his chair and put his hands behind his head. "You should talk to Trav. He's a nerd like you. Thank Goddess I have him! I can concentrate on what I'm actually good at—fighting."

"I like fighting too. But with becoming a mom now, I'm just thinking that maybe both their mom and dad shouldn't be putting their lives in danger." I rubbed my belly. "I keep having anxiety about them being left without parents."

"So, how's it feel?" Tyce nodded at my stomach.

"Honestly, it hasn't been too bad so far. I guess I'm lucky. Most people I've spoken to have told me horror stories of pregnancy symptoms. Blake's mom thinks it has to do with how much I exercise. I'm still keeping up with my training, so I guess it must be helping." He nodded. "Why, will there be a baby Tyce sometime soon?" I teased.

"Not too soon." He gave a sly smile. "But my pack will be expecting an heir soon. I'm getting close to thirty, and that's around the time everyone starts to get worried."

"So, what are you going to do if you don't meet your mate by then?"

"I will." He smiled widely, his eyes sparkling.

"You seem really confident about that."

"I just have a feeling." He got up. "Anyway, time for some coffee and eggs." He headed toward the kitchen.

After some time the doorbell rang, and I went to go answer it. "Oh, hello, Jasmine!" Lucy's mom greeted me with Libby in a stroller. "Wow, look at you! You're so pregnant now! How are you doing?"

"Hi!" Libby put up her hand and smiled at me. She was actually quite adorable, especially today with her hair put up into pigtails and a watermelon dress on. She could easily be a baby model.

"Hi, Libby." I smiled at her, then looked up at Ivy. "I'm not bad."

"You look great. You're glowing!" Lucy's mom pulled me in for a hug. "I'm so happy for you, Jasmine." After she let me go, she brought the stroller into the house. "Where's Lucy?"

"She's not feeling well. Maybe I should take Libby for a little bit," I replied. "I need to learn how to take care of pups anyway, right?"

She snickered. "Hopefully yours aren't as rambunctious as this one. I love my granddaughter, but she's definitely a handful. Not much different than Lucy, actually. Out of my five, she was always the one who kept me on my toes the most. Especially when she went through her spilling phase." Lucy's mom rolled her eyes. "Anyway, I already gave Libby her breakfast. She normally has a snack around ten and lunch at noon, followed by a nap. If you have any problems, just give me a call."

"I'm sure we'll be fine." I smiled. "Right, Libby?"

"Hi!" Libby said, putting her hand up again. I picked her up and took her out of the stroller, placing her gently on the ground. "Why don't you go find your puppy?" I said to her.

"It was nice to see you, Jasmine. I hope to see more of you, honey." Ivy gave me a smile. "Don't be a stranger, bye!"

I waved goodbye as she walked away, and then I closed the front door.

"Dada!" Libby showed me her stuffed wolf.

"Is that your dada?" I asked her, taking a seat on the dining room chair. "It does actually look a lot like him," I noted, taking in the coloring of its fur.

"Dada!" she said again.

"Do you want to draw?" I asked. "Let's go get you some paper and something to draw with." I took her hand and we walked over to the office, so I could find something for her.

Blake looked up as we entered. "Did you get suckered into watching the pup?" He chuckled.

"No, I offered," I replied. "I'm not always a pushover! I just wanted to practice a little. Our pups will be here before we know it."

Blake got up and pulled me against him, rubbing my belly. "You'll be a natural."

"Dada!" Libby yelled as Luke walked in.

"Good run?" Blake asked, stepping away from me.

"Yeah." He rolled his eyes, then looked down at Libby. "Hi, baby!" He smiled at her, his whole face lighting up as he picked her up.

"Baby!" Libby repeated.

"I can watch Libby today, Luke," I said. "I know you're busy, and I have the day off. I don't mind."

"You don't have to do that," Luke replied. "She's not your responsibility."

"It's okay. I'm sure we'll start trading pups at some point."

"I'll help you." Blake smiled at me. "Why don't we take her to the park? I'm due for a day off anyway. It might be nice." Blake then turned to Luke. "Maybe you can talk to Lucy while we're out."

"Yeah, thanks." He looked down and let out a sigh.

"Good luck." Blake took Libby from Luke and gave his shoulder a pat. "Ready for the park, Libs?" Blake gave her a really endearing smile, and my heart fluttered. He put her on the ground and took her hand. "Maybe we can start your beta training early. Let's see how you compare to your dad. How's your kick?" Libby kicked her foot up. "Not bad. Not bad. But we can definitely work on that." She kicked again.

When it was time to attend temple service, Lucy had finally recovered and made herself presentable. I was impressed with how well she'd managed to clean up from how she'd looked that morning. She had a cute summer dress on, and her long blonde hair was freshly washed and glossy. Libby was dressed in a matching outfit. If I didn't know better, I'd think Lucy and Libby were the perfect mom and daughter duo—possibly Instagram influencers with a huge following.

As a fun little surprise for after the service, I'd arranged an ice cream social with some of the other women who were heavily involved with the temple. Lucy reluctantly agreed to help out last minute. I assumed it had something to do with her talk with Luke. We got there early to begin setting everything up to make it easy to roll out once the surprise was announced. Lucy was shockingly helpful, working efficiently to pull everything together, likely well practiced from working in pastry for the past few years.

"Did you see the pictures?" a middle-aged woman's voice sounded. I looked around to try to figure out where it was coming from. "The ones where she's flashing the entire nightclub?"

A laugh was returned. "Goddess. I think everyone's seen them by now."

"That beta's mate really is a hoochie mama, isn't she? Nothing like Robin."

"It's like night and day."

I finally figured out that it was coming from some air vents.

"Look at those tatas hanging out. Must have formula fed. There's no way they'd be that perky otherwise."

"Maybe she had a lift." A woman snickered.

"As pretty as she is, I wouldn't blame Beta Luke at all for straying and knocking up his actual mate."

"I heard he got baby trapped anyway." A bunch of laughter resounded.

"I mean clearly. Can you imagine a beta actually choosing a tramp like Lucy?"

"Her whole family is trash."

"Just look at the son and what he's into." The voices began to fade as they seemingly exited the room they were stationed in. I looked over at Lucy who was uncharacteristically quiet. Her eyes were bloodshot, and she swiped a hand across one of them.

"Don't fucking look at me like that, PJ!" she lashed out. "It must feel nice to be so fucking perfect all the time! Ooh! I'm Jasmine! I love Artemis, and I'm so sweet and innocent. Everyone thinks I saved myself for my mate even though I was going at it with Blake and Luke at the same time."

"What!" I screamed.

"Don't act so fucking innocent. I know what you were up to!" She waved her finger at me. "You knew I was in love with Luke, and you fucked him anyway. You didn't even have the decency to tell me he was your fucking mate before you did! I can't believe I ever trusted you!"

I clenched my fists. "First of all, I never had sex with Luke! Second of all, I didn't *choose* to be mated to Luke. In fact, I wish I never was. Because it's created nothing but a mess for me. And now I have to not only live with him but also live with his chosen mate who used to be my best friend, but even though she's known me since kindergarten, she still thinks so lowly of me that she believes I'd be a two-timer!"

"You know what—fuck you, Lucy!" I got closer and pointed my finger at her. "You *chose* a beta for a mate. You wanted to get pregnant with Luke's pup because it would 'just speed things along,' right? And you know what, I felt kind of bad for you with how hard you were handling the transition. But now I've realized that I don't feel bad. Because you *chose* all of this. You could have waited for your actual fated mate, who would have been perfect for you, but you decided it was worth sacrificing that to be with Luke—the fucking beta of the pack! It's not like it's a big secret that leadership is held to a higher standard than everyone else." I looked her up and down and scoffed. "Luke's right, you need to grow up."

"How the fuck would you know that Luke said that to me?" Her eyes darkened, and her hands began to contort themselves as if they were going to turn into claws. I was ready. I knew if it came down to it, even pregnant I'd easily overtake Lucy. "Maybe the two of you really are going at it behind my back! Are those *really* Blake's pups in there or are you actually carrying the beta heir?"

"You're delusional! When Luke and I rejected each other, I never looked back! You can have my rejection and keep him. I got the alph . . ." My voice trailed off as I inhaled Luke's scent, and my stomach dropped. I turned around to him entering the room.

"Bad timing?" he asked, rubbing the back of his neck. "I was just coming to let you know the service is starting soon." He shuffled his legs.

"Oh, thanks," I said looking between him and Lucy. "I'll head over now." I turned away and practically sprinted to my seat at the front. Goddess, that was awkward.

Chapter 49

Ginger

"Where were you yesterday?" I asked Paige when she got home from patrol duty late on Sunday afternoon.

"I went into heat again."

"Damn. Where'd you go?" I asked.

"Hotel again. If this keeps going on like this, I have a feeling the hotel staff are going to get to know us a little too well." Paige shook her head. "Don't get me wrong—not that I have much to compare it to—but the sex is *incredible* when I'm in heat."

"Incredible how?" I asked, curious to learn more.

She blushed. "Goddess, I can't tell you, Gigi."

"I tell you all the time!"

"I know, but don't you think it's weird that we're sisters and share that info with each other?"

"No. I want to know." I pushed Paige's shoulder.

She sighed and smiled to herself.

"You're dying to tell someone, I can tell." I giggled. "And you know you're never going to tell anyone else. So tell me!"

"Okay, fine." Paige stuck her tongue out and smiled playfully. "It's just like, we're so perfectly in sync. It's like we know what the other person wants, and, Goddess, like the urge comes on so strong, and when we—you know—" She laughed nervously.

"You come."

"Yeah." She giggled some more. "It's like the most amazing feeling in the world times one hundred. I mean, if heaven exists, that has to be it."

"Damn."

"What's it like with Tyce?" She smiled mischievously. "Your maybe mate."

"I wouldn't know. I don't go into heat."

"You know that's not what I meant!"

"And I've thought about it. I don't think he's my mate anymore."

"One, you're lying." She narrowed her eyes at me. "And two, why are you saying that?"

"Because he's an alpha. It doesn't make any sense. If Artemis really exists"—I rolled my eyes and continued—"why would she mate me, someone who's practically a human, to an alpha?"

"I feel like every conversation with you is just going around in circles." Paige's gaze flicked upward. "But I'll tell you why. Because I know why."

"Really, you know why? Do you have some divine connection I'm unaware of? Are you a medium or something?"

"No, but I know you."

"Okay, and?"

"Because, first of all, Artemis knows things about us that we don't even know about ourselves. It doesn't matter how we see ourselves. What matters is how Artemis sees us. That's one. And second of all, you're tough, Gigi. Back before everything happened, you were so passionate about becoming a warrior, and it was before they even *allowed* women to be warriors! You used to go outside and practice everything they taught us at school in training until you'd practically pass out, completely unprompted. You used to beg Dad to spar with you on his days off from work. And nothing made you happier than to watch him train with the other warriors. Gigi, wolf or not, you have the heart of a warrior." She touched my chest, right above my heart. "So maybe you can't be a warrior, but you still have the genetics, right? You can still pass them on to the future alpha of Tyce's pack."

I stared at Paige in shock. I couldn't believe how well she knew me and how much she *saw* me. Really saw me.

"So." She smiled. "How is it with Tyce? But I already know."

"What do you know?"

"It's always good with a mate. So I know it's good with Tyce."

"Maybe."

"And what was it that you asked Jasmine about Blake that time she came to our sisters' potluck?" She laughed heartily. "About a certain body part alphas are known for."

"I did ask that, didn't I?" My mouth spread into a smile. "I was pretty drunk that night."

"You would have asked anyway."

"Who am I kidding? I probably would have." I scrunched my nose in amusement.

"You're just as bad as the other female warriors."

"Let's change the subject," I said, wanting to get off the topic. "You were going to say something before."

She let out a deep breath. "Yeah. I just keep thinking about it. And I don't want to wait to mark each other until we're married. I mean, yeah, we could just get married now, and then we'd be free to mark each other, and I wouldn't have to go into heat anymore. But I'm only nineteen. I'm not ready to be married yet."

"What's the big deal, though?" I studied her. "I mean, it's just a piece of paper. And you know you're meant to be with Dylan, so it's not like there's any risk that it's a huge mistake and you're going to get divorced at some point."

"Okay, let me ask you something. Hypothetical."

"Yes?"

"Say Tyce was your mate and you knew for sure."

"Okay."

"Would you marry him now?"

"Well, that's a totally different situation. If I marry him, I'd have to also move to Alaska, probably drop out of school, and basically become a luna instead of whatever I was planning to do. With Dylan, you don't have to change anything. Well, I mean, you'd move in with him. But that's it. You'd still stay in this pack and be a warrior. Nothing else would change except maybe your last name and the fact you'd be marked." As I said all that, it really began to hit me what it would mean if Tyce were my mate. I'd have to upend my whole life for him, and my heart began to race at the thought. How did I feel about that? Even if I were okay with all the other things, I'd be moving across the country from my family and my twin. Even though I'd gone away for school for the past several years, I was still in New England and only a car ride away. Now we'd be separated by not just one, but two huge countries.

She sighed. "I know you're right. But I'm just not ready." She suddenly appeared really vulnerable, rubbing her arm and looking down at the floor.

Wanting to comfort her, I threw my arms around her. "All I'm saying is, just think about it before you go through with marking each other. Did Jasmine say how long you have until the urge becomes really bad?"

"She said it was about six months until it got bad, and about nine before it got to the point where she didn't think she'd be able to resist much longer."

"So that means you have time. Don't make any rash decisions yet, okay? There's no reason to."

"What about heat?"

"Well, you have a hotel you can go to, right?" I gave her arm a squeeze. "And you said the sex is really good when it happens. So why worry about it?"

"But what happens if my heat kicks in when I'm around a bunch of unmated males? I told you what happened with my trainer Charlie last year, right? I'm scared now. I never thought him acting creepy and asking me to have drinks with him would ever escalate to that. And now, after it did, I can't help but always feel that something like that could happen again. There are so many Charlies out there. All I need is for one of them to smell me when I'm in heat."

"Goddess, I guess I never thought of that," I said.

"Dylan told me that all unmated males can sense it, and it's really hard to resist."

"That is dangerous." I gave Paige a hug. "Plus, men are scum. I bet someone wouldn't even try."

"Like Charlie."

"But he's gone now, right?"

"Yeah, Jasmine killed him."

"She comes off so innocent. But I guess there's a killer in there." I chuckled.

"Jasmine's really sweet. But she's also badass in the field and doesn't even realize how good she is. I honestly think she's better than some or most of the guys. What she lacks in strength she definitely has in skill and brains. I sometimes think that would have been you too. You were always so good and dedicated before . . . well, you know."

A sharp pang pierced my chest, a deep mourning for my wolf and everything I lost with her. I knew there was still another chance to get her back. But ever since I dropped the potion in the woods and got bitten by the bobcat, I couldn't help but allow pessimism to overtake me, suddenly thinking that maybe it'd be easier to ready myself for the idea that it really was over rather than deal with the deep disappointment if it didn't work.

We were all surprised when some of the ladies who were heavily involved with the temple wheeled out a buffet of large tubs of Ben & Jerry's ice cream and toppings, scoopers ready. Jasmine went up to the podium and announced that they were throwing an ice cream social for us. My whole family got in line, and I was delighted to see that they had a few fun flavors to choose from rather than just plain vanilla and chocolate. I got the Chunky Monkey and Paige got the Gimme S'more, and we agreed to share so we could try each other's.

They opened the back door, and soon, everyone was spilling out into the garden. Paige and I took a seat on a bench and scooped out of each other's ice cream cups. I noted Heidi stayed close to our parents instead, which I was thankful for. She still boiled my blood every time I looked at her.

After some time, Jasmine came by. I got up so she could sit.

"No, no, it's fine! I don't mind standing. Please sit." Jasmine waved her hand.

"You're too nice, Jaz." Paige stood up too. "You're carrying the future heir plus another! You've earned the right to sit."

She finally took a seat. "So, what do you think. Do you think people are enjoying the event?"

"Yeah, it was a great surprise. Especially when it's been so hot lately!" Paige replied. "I really hope they take sparring and training back indoors because working out in this heat outdoors is brutal! Especially in our wolf forms with all that heavy fur."

"Unfortunately, I don't think it's going to happen." Jasmine gave a compassionate look to Paige. "Blake and Luke discussed it, and they both agreed they want everyone to get used to fighting and surviving in all temperatures. Actually, Blake had it even worse when he was away at school. They made him survive in his wolf form in the dead of winter in Siberia. So, unfortunately, I don't think you're going to get much sympathy from him."

"It seems like alphas really train to the extreme." I commiserated, thinking about Tyce.

"Alpha Blake or other alphas too?" Paige gave me a knowing smile.

"I'd assume other alphas also train hard, of course," I replied, narrowing my eyes at her.

"Sounds like you might know." She giggled.

"I have a feeling you're both talking about Tyce in code." The corners of Jasmine's mouth lifted. "He does train really hard. Blake's been injecting him with wolfsbane. He's been having a really hard time with it, but he's still pushing forward and still goes to train with Blake and Luke. I'm really impressed by his dedication."

"Hard time how?" I asked. Besides that one time, he'd seemed to be doing okay.

"Oh, it's bad. He coughs up blood a lot. And sometimes he'll just fall asleep in the most random places. Once I found him asleep on the stairs. He didn't even make it to his bed. And I thought pregnancy made me tired!"

"Oh, wow," I replied, feeling a lot of empathy and a sadness that I had no clue how much he'd been suffering. My chest panged with tenderness for him, and I suddenly wished I could wrap my arms around him and make him feel better, a strong urge to comfort him coming over me. I looked up, and his eyes locked with mine, a big smile spreading across his face. Goddess, he did have the most amazing smile.

Before long, he was standing next to Paige. "Can I come join the cool group too?" He gave us all a friendly smile.

Jasmine laughed. "Sorry, it's only for cool people."

"No breaks for family?"

"I'll think about it. And it's not only up to me. You have to get agreement from the other members too."

"Don't worry, Alpha. I know someone who will give you their vote." Paige elbowed me playfully.

"Really, and who might that be?" Tyce stared into my eyes.

"Not me," I replied.

"Really? I bet there's a way I could convince you." He gave me a mischievous smile.

"How so?" I asked, already imagining all the ways he could convince me, a vivid image of his face between my legs playing in my head as I stared at him, trying my best to keep a poker face.

"Blackmail."

"Blackmail?" Jasmine asked. "Do you have dirt on Gigi?"

"Yeah, she has a sick obsession with chipmunks." He snickered.

"First of all, I think you have the two of us confused. And second of all, that's not how blackmail works!" I exclaimed.

"No?"

"No, you're not supposed to just tell everyone my secret! You're supposed to threaten me with it to get my vote."

"I think you'll give me your vote anyway."

"Nope. You've already stood here too long. Now leave."

"Or what?"

"Goddess! Can't you guys get a room!" Paige pushed me away. "Jasmine and I don't need to be a part of your foreplay! You're scarring her pups before they're even out of the womb!"

I rolled my eyes. "Thanks for encouraging the rumors, Paige."

"With any luck, they won't be rumors much longer." She winked at me and then turned back to Jasmine.

"Which rumor?" Tyce smirked at me as we were now standing together, just the two of us. Definitely not helping the situation at all.

"Enough with the anal sex!" I said, far too loudly, especially as Tyce's eyes shot to something above my shoulder, and I turned to see Alpha Blake standing there. *Fuck!* My face burned, and I quickly turned away, not able to look him in the eye.

"Don't worry, he walked away."

"Fuck, why did I just do that?"

"I guess you couldn't smell him. I've gotten so used to being able to tell people are behind me before I blurt dumb shit out." He laughed. "But you have to admit that was pretty funny."

"Why are you coming over here where the whole pack can see us together? Where my parents can see us together!"

"I was actually hoping I'd be able to join the group and make it less obvious, but looks like your sister had other plans."

"My sisters are so frustrating lately!" I squeezed my fists tightly in annoyance.

"Well, at least she's on my side."

"Trust me, the other one isn't. I can't even look in her direction, but she's probably shooting daggers through her eyes at me right now."

"Why?" He leaned closer to me.

"She basically called me a slut to my face the other day and told me I'm bringing shame on the family."

"Damn."

"Fuck my life."

"I'll walk away now. Just tell your parents that I came over to talk to Jasmine about some temple or Artemis scripture stuff, and she suggested I talk to you because you knew more about it. But, while I'm here, I did have something to talk to you about."

"What?"

"Well, two things. You're due for your next booster on Tuesday, in case you forgot. And I told Blake I wouldn't be able to help out that day so we can go back to Salem. So, what do you think?"

I smiled. "Honestly, Tyce, thanks so much. You've been such a lifesaver, and I don't know what I would have done this summer without you."

"Wow, so you are capable of being sweet." Tyce's eyes crinkled in amusement.

"Don't get used to it."

"Don't need to. I like spicy better, Spicy Gi." He winked and walked away.

"Paige, I am seriously going to kill you!" I stormed into her room that night.

She laughed. "You guys were about to tear each other's clothes off in front of us. Even standing in the group it was obvious, with you guys shamelessly eye fucking each other."

"We were not!"

"Goddess, the tension between the two of you. There is no possible way you aren't mates. I can't believe I didn't see it sooner."

"Mom and Dad just interrogated me downstairs for almost a half hour!"

"And, what happened?"

"Tyce came up with a good cover story. And Dad bought it. After Dad bought it, Mom just went along with it. She hates disagreeing with him."

"See? It wasn't the end of the world."

"You're just lucky I'm Dad's favorite." I stuck my tongue out at Paige. "Otherwise you'd be dead."

"Why not kill Alpha Tyce? He's the one who can't stay away from you, even in public."

"He'd be dead too."

"He's totally in love with you. I can tell."

"Stop!"

"I'm just stating facts. He's got it bad!"

Chapter 50

Ginger

"I was thinking Salem first and hospital after?" Tyce asked when I showed up on Tuesday morning.

"Yeah, that's fine."

"And I'm also thinking we should buy two of those potions this time, just in case."

I cringed.

"What?" He looked intently into my eyes.

"Nothing. Yeah, you're right," I replied, not wanting him to know how poor I was. I would just insert my credit card. This was more important than money and credit card debt. This was about the rest of my life.

He gave me a smile, took my hand, and then pulled me toward the car, opening the passenger door for me. Once he was seated in the driver's seat, I asked, "Are you okay to drive?"

"Yeah, fine, why?"

"You're still getting the wolfsbane injections, though, right?"

"Yeah, but I'm getting more used to them now."

"Are you though? Or are you just acting tough?"

"I'm fine, Gigi." As he said this, he backed out of the pack driveway and onto the main pack road.

"You're helping me. So if there was anything you needed help with, I'd be happy to help too." I touched his arm.

"What kind of help are you offering?" He smiled.

"Not anal sex."

"Then I don't want it."

"What about the rodent thing? Have you gotten help for that?"

He let out a deep breath but didn't say anything.

"I'm going to take that as a no." After a minute, I continued, "You know, from what I recall when I used to go to training, meditation helps a lot with having control over your wolf. Maybe we could meditate together. I'm actually really good at it. In school, I got assigned as the meditation lead in sixth grade because the teachers thought I was so good at leading in it. That's what I told my dad you asked about actually. I told him you were helping Alpha Blake find some volunteers to lead meditations in the elementary school, but I also told him I informed you that I wouldn't be around during the school year."

"I'm actually pretty shocked to learn you're good at meditation."

"Why?"

"Because you have one of the hottest tempers out of anyone I know." We both laughed. "Okay, I'll take you up on the offer. I've actually always been pretty bad at meditation, to be honest."

"Well, maybe it's a good thing this happened then." I smiled. "Maybe it was just a sign that you need to become more one with your wolf, especially as an alpha."

He grasped my hand. I looked up at him in reaction, but I couldn't read him. If he felt anything like I did at that moment, I didn't know how he could keep such a stoic face. My whole body was alive, my stomach tumbling, my lungs heavy, and my heart racing, a warmth spreading across my skin, and a strong tingling deep within my body, as if something inside me was fighting to be freed.

We drove like that, and I realized there was a sort of comfort with him. Even though we hadn't known each other long, we just got each other—almost like we'd known each other over a span of millions of years and were reunited once again in another life. There was just a certain ease between us that I didn't know if I even felt with Paige.

When we were well into our drive down to Salem, I asked, "Why won't you be honest with me about the wolfsbane and how much it's affecting you?"

He crinkled his eyebrows. "Why do you think it's affecting me that much?"

I didn't want to throw Jasmine under the bus, so I said, "I just know how bad wolfsbane is, remember? It killed my wolf. So I'm just thinking about what it might be doing to you. I mean, I'm assuming you know what you're doing and you're dosing yourself so that doesn't happen. But well, I just want to make sure you're okay." I gave his hand a squeeze.

"Goddess, when you go sweet, it's too sweet." He wrinkled his nose. "It's hurting my teeth. Can't you go back to calling me a chipmunk fucker or something?"

"Tyce, I'm serious."

"Okay, yeah, it sucks. I just hate being seen as weak. It feels unnatural when you train your whole life to be alpha. Actually, it's even worse than that. My dad and grandpa both spent my whole life beating the weakness out of me, both figuratively and literally. They trained me like a pit bull in a dogfighting ring."

"How so?"

"Trust me, it's better I don't tell you. Let's just say that my pack's reputation doesn't come from nowhere."

"I want to know. I can handle it!" I said with enthusiasm, but also questioning whether I could. How would I feel to learn about how they'd hurt Tyce? Probably the same way he felt when I told him what happened to me—when he vowed to kill every person who ever hurt me. I'd never thought of myself as the torturing type, but suddenly I could see a world where I'd be okay with it. If anyone hurt Tyce, nothing would bring me more pleasure than to watch them suffer.

"Maybe one day." He squeezed my hand. "I don't want to talk about it right now."

"This is the second time I asked and you avoided the question," I said. "How am I supposed to get to know you if you don't tell me anything?"

He let out a deep breath. "I don't like talking about it. I think out of everyone, you'd understand."

He was right. I did.

When we arrived in Salem and finally parked, I stepped out of the car, taking a deep breath, readying myself. "Goddess, I feel sick," I whispered.

"What was that?" Tyce asked.

"Nothing," I replied. The ease I'd felt in the car had dissipated, and I was left feeling nauseous, my palms sweaty and my throat dry. *I can do this. I can do this.*

Tyce took my hand in his, and we walked toward the shop. I couldn't lie—his hand had an instant calming effect on me. "It's nice being able to hold your hand and not worry about who might see us." Tyce gave me such a sweet smile.

"Now look who's hurting *my* teeth," I responded, but I secretly loved it, my heart fluttering.

I was dismayed to find Helena at the register when we made it inside the shop. Her eyes instantly fell on our hands. And something about it gave me so much satisfaction. *Take that, bitch! He's mine!*

Mine. I kind of liked the ring of it. I'd never thought myself the possessive type, but Tyce had me feeling all sorts of ways I'd never felt before. Vengeful, possessive, murderous.

"Oh, hello," Helena said, looking between us.

"I made an appointment for Ginger McDowell yesterday," Tyce said. *He had?* Damn. It seemed he cared more about this than I did now.

"Your buddy?" she asked.

"My girlfriend," he replied. *What?* Okay, while he did say he wanted to do this for real, I'd never really proactively agreed to it. Did he really see me as his girlfriend now? How did I feel about that?

Before I could fully process what just happened, Helena's mom stepped out. "Ah! My favorite customer. And her handsome man. Come on in, darling! And, handsome man, you may come in too, of course." She gave him a playful wink.

"Do you mind?" Tyce asked me quietly.

"I guess not. The cat's out of the bag at this point." I gave a small chuckle.

We both walked in and took seats, bringing back the memories of the tarot cards. "So, darling, what happened? Still no wolf?" she asked.

"No wolf," I replied, looking down at the table, not able to make eye contact.

"But the next full moon, she'll come back!" Tyce chimed in.

"I'm afraid not," Sybil replied. "It's been ten moon cycles now. Ten is the number of rebirth. If her wolf did not come back, she is too far gone and there is nothing we can do. I'd hoped otherwise, but continuing to try would be theft on my part. I even checked her wolf's location in the death realm, and she was so close, practically through the veil. If she couldn't step through when she was so close, well, pardon my phrasing, but it's much like beating a dead wolf to keep trying."

Tears dropped freely, splattering onto the skirt of the maxi dress I was wearing, and I quickly brought my hands to my eyes, trying to wipe them away.

"That potion you give to Gigi to drink," Tyce asked, "what does it do?"

"It slices open Gigi's human soul so that the wolf half can connect to it. It is a violent process, and I'm sure Gigi must have felt ill when it took place. The deeper the cut, the longer the wound will stay open to allow another to connect to it."

"But if she didn't drink the potion, her soul wouldn't have been sliced open, and her wolf wouldn't have been able to connect, right?" Tyce asked.

"Correct. It would be an incomplete and ineffective spell. You could call the wolf, and even if the wolf stepped through the veil, she wouldn't be able to connect to our realm and, consequently, she would be pulled back behind it."

"So, in that case, would Gigi have another chance? If the tenth cycle was never fully completed?"

"I have a feeling that you're asking this for a reason." I looked up and she was giving Tyce a half smile.

"I am, in fact. Gigi spilled the potion before she was able to drink it. So perhaps the tenth cycle hasn't officially happened yet."

"Very interesting." She rubbed her chin. "Well, I suppose in that case, we can give it one more try."

"That's all I ask." Tyce put his palms down on the table.

"Gigi, let me see your hand," Sybil said to me. I held it out to her, unable to speak. After a minute, she said, "Yes, well, the wolf is definitely persistent. She is desperate to come back and is still in the same place she was last time, waiting to pass through the veil. I often find that persistence of this sort has a motive. A strong motive. She wants something."

"Like what?" Tyce asked.

"Let me see your hand, my handsome werewolf friend."

Sybil took it and hummed, suddenly a big smile appearing on her face. "Yes, it's exactly as I thought."

"What is it?" I asked, leaning forward in my chair.

"Not my place to say. But it will certainly be revealed if she comes back. All I can say is, werewolves quite fascinate me. Your human side is so naive and unobservant, spending too much time overanalyzing. Your wolf side, however"—she smiled more widely—"is very instinctive and wise. It notices and understands things your human side never will. Most werewolves spend their whole lives living as two halves. Only few dedicate the energy and effort to allow the two forms to effectively communicate.

"But don't worry—even when the communication is not effective, your wolf always finds ways to tell you what you absolutely must know. Whether you listen or not, well, that's where the overanalysis comes in. If you're too far in your head, you're too far from your ears."

"Can we buy two bottles of the potion this week? Just in case," Tyce inquired. "I want to make sure that even if there is an accidental spill, we have a backup."

"I will sell it to Gigi, but only if she promises not to drink both. I said she needs to cut the wound deep enough for her wolf to connect. But I certainly don't need to tell you what happens if the cut is too deep, do I?"

I gulped.

"She won't drink the second bottle unless she spills the first."

"Of course not." Sybil smiled, getting up.

We made it to the front, where Sybil placed the two bottles on the counter for her daughter to ring in. "

"Eight hundred and sixty-four dollars," the bitch witch, as I'd dubbed her in my mind, said.

I almost had a heart attack. I pulled my credit card out of my wallet with shaky hands. That was a lot of money. I could buy a new laptop for that kind of money. Or two or more semesters worth of textbooks.

I inserted my card into the reader.

After a moment, Helena said, "Declined."

"Let me just try again," I said, knowing for sure I was over my limit, and it would be fruitless. Then what? I'd have to borrow it from Tyce. And it would take me forever to pay that kind of money back. Fuck, I was screwed.

"Declined," Helena said again. "Do you have another card?"

"I have one." Tyce gently pushed me aside. It went through with ease. "Can you give us two bags?"

"Sure," Helena replied, packaging the jars separately.

"I just figured, we should each carry one, just in case. You know that saying: Don't put all your eggs in one basket." Tyce smiled at me.

"You seem way too prepared and thoughtful for how you present yourself. I'm starting to get suspicious that the whole screwball thing is a cover-up for the real Tyce." I studied him.

"This is just really important to me," he replied. "I don't want it to get screwed up."

"Why are you so invested in my wolf?" I asked as soon as we exited the shop.

"Because I know it means a lot to you. And I care about you. When I said I wanted to help, I meant it. I'm your teammate in this now."

I looked up at him, staring into his amber eyes, which were glowing under the sun of the day. Then I looked down. "Thanks for paying for the stuff by the way. I promise I'll pay you back. It might take me a while, but I'm good for it."

"It's a gift," he replied. "So don't worry about it."

"I can't accept it. That's way too expensive of a gift! You don't even give someone that much at a wedding!"

"Honestly, Gigi, don't worry about it. I was happy to pay it. These potions are on me. You can pay me back by getting your wolf back."

"Like I said, I don't accept."

"Well, I won't accept any of your money if you even try to pay me back."

"You can't not accept my money!"

"And you can't not accept my gift."

I groaned.

"Anyway, you should probably call your bank to figure out why your card wouldn't go through."

"I know why it wouldn't go through." I looked down at the ground, my cheeks burning.

"Why?"

"I'm over my limit. And I sort of skipped out on my last credit card bill."

"Why would you do that?" Tyce asked, his eyes wide.

"Because I don't have any money right now. I haven't been working since I left school, so I ran out of money to pay my credit card bill."

"What! Gigi, how did that happen?"

"Well, these potions aren't cheap, and there aren't exactly ample jobs opportunities back at the pack, especially when you don't have a car to go off pack land. But it's okay, I'll fix everything once I'm back in school. I have a decent job at the cafeteria, and I can always pick up extra hours if I need to. See, it'll all be fine! I'll even make enough to pay you back too."

"I'll find you a job now."

"How are you going to do that?"

"My cousin's mate is the alpha of your pack, right? If there's not a job already available, he's able to make one." Tyce gave me a big smile. "Plus, he wants to keep my family happy, so he won't say no."

I rubbed my arm. "I mean, it would be really helpful." I felt my anxiety melting away by the thought.

"Consider it done. Now come on, let's go grab some lunch." He took my hand again. We began walking through the downtown area when he stopped suddenly. "Hey, look! A haunted house! What do you think? Should we go in?"

"Are you sure you can handle it?" I teased, pushing on his chest. Damn, his chest felt nice. I didn't even want to remove my hand—wanting the rub it all over, discover every part of his hard, muscular body. A hot shiver was overtaking me.

"Oh, please. Everyone knows the only reason guys like haunted houses is because it makes the ladies grab onto us in fear. And then we can be their knight in shining armor. While your boobs are pushed up against us." He gave me a playful smirk.

"Haha, okay, Mr. Big Tough Horny Alpha," I teased.

"Feel free to call me that from now on."

"What's my nickname then?"

"Miss Sexy Beautiful Spicy Damsel."

"Damsel?"

"Yes, damsel in distress who's going to push her boobs up against me in the dark haunted house."

I rolled my eyes. "We'll see about that."

We got in line to purchase a ticket to enter. "Quick tip." The clerk smiled at us. "When you go in, give it a minute to let your eyes adjust. It's really dark in there, and you'll probably be sunblind at first. That way you won't miss any of the first attraction."

"I guess that's something you don't have to worry about," I said to Tyce as we headed toward the entrance where they were gathering people into groups to enter. "Now I can see why your only motivation of going to a haunted house is to cop a feel."

"Probably doesn't help that I'm a real monster too." He gave me a playful smile. "But I'll take copping a feel any day. Especially if they're yours." As he said it, I already began imagining it in vivid details—his palms crushed against my breasts, his thumbs tracing my areola, his teeth softly nibbling on my nipples. Damn, was it wrong to be more turned on by than scared of monsters? Especially when they had monster-sized cocks? And thick, capable monster fingers?

We entered with a good-sized group. This was clearly a popular attraction. And, true to the clerk's word, it was dark inside. I wrapped my arm around Tyce's, so he could lead the way, and we stayed toward the back of the group.

The attraction didn't start out too bad. It was mostly animatronics, strobe lights, dry ice machines, and scary sounds. But it slowly became scarier as they'd darken and quiet the entire room, leaving us in anticipation. I squeezed Tyce's hand for comfort. Without warning, strobe lights danced. The first time this happened, a man in a terrifying clown costume jumped out in front of me. I screamed in reaction, and pushed my whole body (including, yes, my boobs) against Tyce's body. Damn, he was right. This was a great form of foreplay.

My adrenaline was rushing. The two of us laughed and continued. This happened again, and this time a man done up in stitches and bloody makeup jumped out at me. Again, I screamed in terror and Tyce laughed heartily. The attraction was better than expected as we walked down a hall with more animatronics.

We turned a corner, and the room went pitch black again. And Tyce, who had stayed practically glued to me the whole time, very suddenly and forcefully pushed himself from me. I practically fell over, tumbling against a couple in front of me. "Sorry!" I shouted, apologizing for accosting them, in shock from him unexpectedly doing that.

Suddenly, the strobe lights came on again. And while actors dressed in horror costumes were jumping out at us, that wasn't why everyone began screaming bloody murder. Tyce, in his wolf form, let out the most terrifying growl I'd ever heard, tearing a rat into pieces, his lethal teeth and claws on full display, blood flying from his mouth as his teeth crushed its body and bones. Even I was terrified, and I knew it was him.

When the room went dark again, I heard mumblings through the crowd.

"Did you see that werewolf?"

"It looked so real!"

"I've never seen such a realistic-looking animatronic."

"It was so scary!"

Shit! I was worried, realizing why that must have happened. Luckily, no one had seen him shift, and they thought he was part of the show. But this couldn't be good. He would have ripped his clothes when he did that. I stayed behind and did my best to feel around for where it would have torn. My fingers found a shopping bag. *My potion!* I picked it up and my stomach dropped as it made the sound of broken glass. But maybe it was still okay. It was just dried herbs, after all. I hadn't added the water yet. *And I still had mine.* I quickly felt for the one I'd slipped into my purse. It was still in one piece.

"Hey, what are you doing?" One of the costumed men, dressed in a Dracula costume, found me.

"I dropped something," I replied.

"What did you drop?"

"My wallet. And cell phone." I began listing off things that Tyce would have lost. "And car keys." *Shit, we definitely had to find those, or we'd be stuck here.*

"You dropped all those things?"

"Yeah, it's scary in here!" I said, maybe a little too exaggerated.

"Okay, let me get them to stop the tour so we can turn the lights on for you."

"Thanks!" I replied as he walked away. But then, what about Tyce? If they turned the lights on, would they see him?

Suddenly, I felt a poke into my leg, and peered down to find a creature with dark fur. "Tyce!" I exclaimed and quickly noted he had his wallet, cell phone, and keys in his mouth. He tilted his head in a gesture to follow him, and I did. He brought me toward the end of the tour and tapped a door with his paw. I easily opened it, and we walked into a bathroom.

As soon as we were inside, I locked the door, and then he put the things that were in his mouth down and shifted into his human form. "Fuck, that was bad."

"That was horrible!" I agreed, throwing my arms around him. "Tyce, you need to get control of your wolf. We're just lucky they all thought you were part of the show."

He let out a deep breath as I backed away. "I guess this is where me needing your help comes in." I looked up into his eyes, and he couldn't hide how devastated he was if he tried. It pained everything inside me to see him suddenly so vulnerable. He shook his head and bent down, picked his wallet up off the ground, and handed it to me. "Can you get me some clothes? I'm usually a size 2XL in T-shirts—large in shorts. I'll just hang out in here and wait for you . . . and make lots of constipation noises." He gave me a small smile.

"Be right back. I'll be quick. Just watch my stuff," I said, as I left the things I was carrying on the sink counter and dashed out of the bathroom.

"There you are!" The man in the Dracula costume spotted me. "We looked around and were only able to find some torn clothes. That wasn't yours, was it? Not sure where it came from. Big tripping hazard though. Good thing we caught it before someone fell."

"Oh, no, those weren't mine. I actually found all my stuff and I'm good." I put up my thumbs and quickly sprinted away.

I ran into the first shop I saw with clothing in it. It was definitely some sort of souvenir shop. But no matter. Tyce made it clear money wasn't an object, so surely he wouldn't mind if I paid tourist prices for his clothing. I quickly grabbed a T-shirt and shorts.

I then sprinted back and found the exit, slipping in as a group slipped out. I knocked on the bathroom door, and a bunch of deep moans resounded. "Are you constipated or masturbating in there?" I chuckled at my own joke.

He quickly opened the door and pulled me in. "Well, now that you're here, no need for masturbation anymore."

I pushed the shopping bag into his chest. "I got you clothes. Now put them on before I report you for sexual harassment, chipmunk fucker."

He smirked and grabbed the bag. "Spicy Gi is back. I like it." He quickly pulled out the shorts and slid them up his legs. Then he pulled out the T-shirt and held it away from him to look at it. "You got me a shirt that says, 'I don't need therapy. I just need to get f#ed in public by thirteen werewolves?'"

I burst into laughter. "It's great, isn't it?"

"I can't fucking believe I'm going to wear this."

"Next time don't rip up the T-shirt you're wearing, and you won't have to walk around sharing your kinks with everyone."

"Ha, funny." He smiled and rolled his eyes.

"Seriously, Tyce, I'm putting you on a meditation schedule. I'm coming over every day from now on until you can control your wolf again." I put my hands on my hips and gave him a stern look.

"Damn, sexy teacher. I like it. Can you put your hair up in one of those clips and put on the nerdy glasses too? And pencil skirt. You gotta have the pencil skirt."

"This isn't sex ed, Tyce!"

"Your ass would look fantastic in a pencil skirt."

"Stop casting me in the porno in your mind!"

He smirked and went to pick up the rest of his possessions, throwing his cell phone and keys into his pocket and grabbing the shopping bag from the counter. As he lifted it, the glass and ground-up herbs came tumbling out—the bag had apparently been cut by the sharp shards. "It broke? Fuck. I'm really sorry, Gigi." He continued to stare at the bag and the mess it left on the counter.

"It's okay. I still have another one," I replied, feeling bad about how down Tyce looked and showing him the one in my purse that was still in one piece.

He let out a breath and said, "I totally sucked at my backup plan, didn't I?" He quickly brushed the mess into the trash, clearly unconcerned if one of the pieces cut him.

"Hey, you thought of having a backup in the first place, so you didn't totally suck." I gave him a reassuring smile.

Chapter 51

Ginger

When we got back out into the sunlight, we decided to just grab a couple sandwiches and drive home, agreeing it was too risky to stick around out in public. "Hey, thanks for helping me out back there." Tyce squeezed my hand as we walked.

"What was I supposed to do? Just leave you naked and helpless?" I snickered.

"I may have been naked, but I wasn't helpless."

"You had literally two choices. Go out naked or as a wolf, in the middle of tourist central."

"There was another option."

"Which was?"

He gave me an evil smile and said, "I mean, desperate times call for desperate measures. I could have just knocked out a human and grabbed his clothing, if it came down to it. It was pretty dark in there. Great place for a real monster to lurk."

"Damn, you're psycho."

"You don't even know the half of it." I looked up, and he had the most ominous look on his face I'd ever seen. I was taken aback—it was the look of someone you did not fuck with. The way he'd manhandled Lucy flashed in my mind, and it suddenly clicked that he'd definitely had a soft spot for me the whole time I'd known him. I'd clearly gotten away with far more than I would have otherwise.

When we got to the hospital, Tyce again insisted on holding my hand. When the nurse left us alone, I said, "You know, I'm not a little kid. I can handle a little shot. Does Alpha Blake hold your hand while he injects you?" I snickered at the image.

"No, but you're welcome to come over and hold my hand while he injects me any time. That shit kills like a motherfucker, and it'd actually be nice to have you there as a distraction."

"What's it like? Are you constantly in pain?" I asked.

"It burns the most when it first goes in. But yeah, I'd say it's like a dull burning or stinging sensation all day. It basically feels like my veins are constantly scorched. I have no idea how Blake did this for four years. But, you know, it's interesting. When you touch me, it seems to feel better. I don't know if it's psychological or what."

"When I touch you where?" I teased.

"I'll tell you where it feels the best," he whispered into my ear in his deep, gravelly voice. And, yep, I was a goner. After a beat, he continued, "So does meditation start today?"

"Definitely today," I replied.

"Good, let's get the hell out of here then."

We'd barely stepped into his bedroom when he slammed the door shut and pushed me onto the bed. "Do you know how crazy you've had me going for the past few days?" he practically growled.

"How crazy?"

"You've been far too covered up. I'm ready to rip it all off. Every last piece of fabric." He aggressively pulled the long skirt of my dress up, his fingers grazing my skin, sending shivers up and down my legs.

"No, don't. I need it," I whined.

"Take it off then, baby. Do it slowly. Give me a show." He got up from being on top of me and moved off the bed, crossing his arms and looking down at me. His lack of underwear was clear, as his massive boner tented his shorts, practically ripping through the fabric.

I got up onto my knees, grabbed the hem of the maxi dress I was wearing, and slowly peeled it off my body. I didn't break contact with him except to lift it over my head.

"Show me your tits, baby," he commanded in a deep, husky voice that was doing all sorts of things to me.

I instantly unsnapped my bra but didn't let it fall right away, holding my hands over the cups.

"Take it off. I want to see you play with your bare titties, baby."

I gave him a mischievous smile and moved to slip the straps off my shoulders, but then stopped, sliding them back in place, keeping myself covered. He continued to stare at me, keeping a poker face. I moved the fabric of one of my cups, giving him a glimpse of my nipple and then moved it back to cover me.

"You little tease."

"You take off yours and I'll take off mine," I responded.

"Deal," he replied, smirking, and threw off his T-shirt, revealing his upper body that was so perfect it had to be illegal. Fuck. Yep, goner. I let my bra drop.

"Now play with them for me, baby. Do everything to yourself you want me to do to you. Teach me how you like to be touched, baby."

I arched my back, thrusting my breasts forward, rubbing my palms over them, pushing them together, brushing my thumbs over the erect nipples. I let my hands trail my entire body, completely turned on by how he was staring at me—like he was starving and I was the first meal he'd been offered in weeks. No one had ever looked at me like that before, especially not anyone so fucking hot.

"Come closer, baby," he rasped as he pulled his shorts off, allowing his massive erection to spring free. Had it always been that big, or had it grown? "Sit on the edge of the bed." I did as he said, taking a seat as he moved closer. "Goddess, you have the most amazing pair of tits." He moved toward me until his cock was pushing against the middle of my chest.

He moved his hands to my breasts, brushing his thumbs against my nipples the same way I had been moments earlier, his cock throbbing between them. "They're so perfect, and firm, and massive." He kneaded them gently. "I've been imagining how my cock would feel between them since I first saw them."

I arched my back again, moving my chest forward, and he pushed my breasts together, allowing his cock to be wrapped inside them. I grabbed his ass as he thrust between them. "How does it feel?" I asked.

"Heaven," he replied. "Like I'm fucking the tits of an angel."

I snickered. "Romantic."

He grinned, stopped what he was doing, picked me up, and threw me back into the bed, crawling in after me. He had me surrounded, his forearms on either side of me as he hovered over me. "I can be romantic."

"Really?" I lifted an eyebrow.

"Yes, really." He moved his mouth toward mine until our lips were practically touching. "I can be very romantic." As my lips parted, he gently pressed his mouth against mine, giving me a soft kiss. "And tell you how bad I have it for you. How my cock instantly gets hard at the thought of you."

"That's not romantic."

He kissed me again, this time not pulling away, easing his tongue into my mouth. My own tongue twined with his, hungrily tasting him. I wrapped my legs around his hips, pulling him closer to me, not able to get close enough. As he deepened the kiss, I moaned into his mouth.

He pulled away and kissed toward my ear, bringing his mouth to it as he spoke. "You are the sexiest, sharpest, and savviest girl I've ever met. You are so beautiful that I can't believe you're real, and there's not a single thing I don't like about you. You are absolutely, 100 percent, perfect."

Before I could respond, he brought his lips back to mine and began feverishly kissing me again. I gave in completely and knew for a fact that I didn't have enough willpower to reject him. There was not enough willpower in the world for me to reject him. I was playing with fire while drenched in gasoline, and I no longer cared. I had fallen hard and was now Tyce's prisoner to do with whatever he wanted.

He kissed down my body. "Soft, perfect skin." Then he kissed across the top of my underwear. "Beautiful, luscious, grabbable hips." He hooked his fingers into the thin fabric of my panties and dragged them down slowly, kissing over the top of my pubic bone. He continued his journey as he kissed onto my legs. "Thick, mouthwatering thighs." I let out a soft moan, and he pulled my panties farther down my legs until they were completely off.

He kissed his way back up, bringing his lips back to the inside of my thighs, taking his time kissing up the inside of each leg. Soon kissing turned to nibbling, and my moans loudened, affirming how amazing it felt. When I thought I would burst if he didn't move farther north, I pushed myself into his mouth. He pulled his face away and gave me a mischievous smile. "No, baby. I want you to show me what you like. Play with yourself for me, baby. Show me what you do when you're alone at home and thinking about me."

I let out a whine. I'd never done this in front of anyone before.

He rubbed my thighs in a soothing gesture. "Come on, baby. I want to watch."

What was it about him that had me ready and willing to do anything? I brought my fingers between my legs, spreading them wider for him, pushing my fingers inside myself, then finding my clit, rubbing it the way I'd only ever done in private with a blanket covering me.

"Fuck, baby," he groaned. "I love watching you do that. My dick is so hard right now." He stroked the long length of it.

"Put it inside me," I moaned out.

He immediately pulled open his bedside drawer and slipped on a condom, and soon he was back between my legs, the head throbbing against my pussy. I looked up into his eyes, and he pushed his massive length into me as I groaned while my insides stretched to accommodate his substantial girth. Fuck, he was huge. It surprised me every time. He instantly began plunging in and out of me, his hips brushing against my inner thighs, his chest rubbing against mine, his hand weaving into my hair, and his other hand stroking my clit. I let out passionate moans, digging my nails into his back.

"Tyce!" I screamed out, and he quickened his thrusts, becoming more rough, slamming his pelvis into mine.

"Tyce!" I screamed out again, and his fingers rubbed more vigorously. Although I never wanted to leave that moment, I soon found my whole body shaking under him, my thighs quivering, the fire inside me building to the point of no return.

"Come for me, baby," he growled, and that was all it took to tip me over the edge as an orgasm overtook me, my insides tumbling and releasing. He let out his own loud groan and collapsed on top of me, our bodies sticky against each other's skin.

Suddenly, his body tensed.

"Are you okay?" I asked. And then he lifted and turned his head to face me, and again, he had fangs.

"Fuck," he said in a muffled voice. "I'm not going to bite you."

I blinked. "It's okay. You can't help it, right?" He shook his head, then got off me, and moved next to me, turning his back to me.

I discovered something I'd never noticed before, because, surprisingly, up until that point I'd never actually seen his bare back, which I noted was rippled with muscles. But what I really noticed was he had a series of tattoos lining it, which looked like barbed wire at first glance. But when I looked more closely, I realized it was branches that were drawn to look like barbed wire.

I brought my fingers to the tattoos, an impulse to feel them. While I'd expected them to be smooth, I was surprised to find the skin was raised. I moved my fingers along one of the barbed branches. "Did you just get these tattoos on your back?" I asked.

"No, why?"

"They feel fresh." He didn't respond. "Your skin is raised." When he stayed silent, something clicked. "Are those scars that you're covering?"

"Yeah," he finally replied.

"Those are scars? But how? I thought werewolves couldn't scar."

"They're from before I got my wolf."

"What happened?"

He sighed. "My grandpa used to whip me."

"He whipped you?" I exclaimed, horrified by the thought. "But, why? Why would he do that? How old were you? You couldn't have been that old if you didn't have your wolf yet."

"It started when I was ten."

I moved closer, spooning him. "But why, Tyce? Why would your grandpa hurt you like that?" Tears threatened to spill from my eyes as I thought of Tyce as a little boy being whipped by a person he likely loved and trusted.

He sighed again. "He did it whenever I didn't react correctly when he'd torture. It's an old-school form of alpha training. So like, if I'd cry or throw up, he'd whip me. When I told you I passed out, that was usually why. And he'd just leave me there, in the dark, until I woke up."

"Goddess, Tyce." I snuggled up against him, pressing my body against his, desperate to be close to him and comfort him. I was slowly realizing how little I knew him and just how much I'd misjudged him.

"Don't worry, Gigi. It happened so long ago now. And I'm fine. It helped me become a better, stronger, more ruthless alpha."

"But it's horrible, Tyce." I could sense in my heart that the scars were just as much inside him as they were outside.

"Let me get cleaned up," he said, prying himself from my body, sliding out of bed, and sneaking out of the room.

He returned moments later, getting back into the bed and pulling me in his arms. "By the way, I got you a gift." I turned to face him and he gave me a smug smile. "Turn around and look on top of the dresser."

I did as asked. "The plant?"

He pulled me closer against him, spooning me. "Yeah, it's an aloe vera plant. I looked up what's good for sunburns and healing cuts and that came up."

"Tyce, are you kidding me?"

"What?"

"You are such a closet nerd. I can't even!" As I said this, a warmth spread inside me, and I couldn't help but smile a little—only a little.

"I'm going to take that as you like it." He nuzzled into my hair.

"It was a very thoughtful gift," I replied noncommittally, trying to keep my face straight.

"So you like it?" He pressed.

After a beat, I replied, "I love it, okay? Do I have to be sappy now?"

"No, I like you better when you're prickly. Kind of like the aloe vera plant. Prickly on the outside and gooey and soothing on the inside."

"Nerd."

He chuckled. "So, meditation?"

"Yes, meditation. It's why we came in here."

"Ms. McDowell, sexy meditation teacher, please lead the way."

Chapter 52

Jasmine

"Tyce! Tyce! Tyce!" Gigi's moans echoed through the room. It had been going on for a few days at that point.

"These walls aren't soundproof at all, are they?" I asked Blake, who was lying in bed next to me.

He smirked. "Nope, clearly not."

"And anyone who ever slept in that room, including Tyce and Talia, have heard us, haven't they?"

"Yep." Blake chuckled.

I groaned. "Goddess, that is messed up! My cousin and your sister have heard us have sex!" My entire body was burning with embarrassment. "They've heard us have sex so many times! Tyce has been listening all summer and never even said anything!"

"What was he going to say? 'Nice job, Alpha, wink wink. You railed my cousin good last night.'"

I groaned again. "Blake, you're not helping!"

He laughed. "Aw, c'mon, Jaz, you have to agree it's kind of funny." He pulled me toward him.

I made a face and said, "Okay, maybe it's kind of funny." Then after a beat, I asked, "So did you really not know? You used to sleep in that room, right?"

Blake had a faraway look and then—was that a blush? "Now that I think about it, I do remember when I was a little kid, my parents used to make noises. I kind of blocked it out. And they stopped doing it by the time I would have figured out why they were making those noises." He was quiet for a moment and continued, "And now that I think about it, Ria and I were never that good at keeping it down, especially when she was in heat."

I then let out a hearty laugh. "So did your dad congratulate you in the morning?" I teased, and in a deep voice, said, "Wink wink, son, you railed your mate good last night."

"You little—" He began tickling me. I screamed in laughter. "You are really going to get it good now."

"If you think I'm ever going to scream or moan again, you are out of your mind!"

He scrunched his nose. "First order of business, soundproofing the walls of our room, A-SAP!" He snuggled close to me and rubbed my belly. "Second order of business, putting the pups in the farthest rooms from ours."

"We probably should start getting their rooms ready." I nuzzled into his neck, inhaling his luxurious mate scent. While I always loved the scent of Blake, it became that much more potent and intoxicating after we marked each other, and even more so now that I was pregnant. I craved smelling him and often found myself snuggling into his pillow or picking up one of his sweaty gym shirts when he wasn't around. "They're going to be here before we know it."

"Mm," he affirmed, kissing me on my head.

"Blake, what kinds of things would Ria have liked? I'd like to decorate the girl's room in something Ria would have liked too."

His body tensed, and a dark cloud descended over him that I instantly sensed. "You don't have to do that, Jaz."

"I want to. I feel like she probably checks in sometimes from the other realm. And I don't want her to feel like I'm pushing her away. She was supposed to have your pup first. And she never got the opportunity. So I don't know. Maybe it's really dumb." As I rambled, I began to second-guess myself and my thought process, feeling a little embarrassed for being so candid with Blake. But after I stopped, I felt his emotions change as a warmness spread through him, and I looked up into his eyes.

A sweet smile spread across his face. "You are the most thoughtful mate I could ever ask for." He kissed me very gently, just barely touching his lips to mine, rubbing his nose against mine. Affection overtook his whole body. I instantly knew I was doing the right thing and helping him move past the loss of his mate. He then kissed me again, this time with more pressure, pulling me toward him, my large belly pressed against his torso. "She loved tigers. And the color yellow. She was warm but fierce. And had so much energy. I could barely even keep up with her."

"I will make our girl pup's room one that Ria would love."

He didn't say anything, but I could sense how he felt about it, the affection overtaking his body being transferred to me, our emotions running together side by side. I rubbed my palm down the length of his arm and sighed happily into his chest.

The next morning, Blake mindlinked me and asked me to come into his office as I was finishing up getting ready for training. I made my way over. Both he and Luke were at their desks, and I was surprised to find Lucy inside as well, sitting in a chair at the center of the room. I'd been avoiding her since the whole temple debacle.

"Mrs. Alpha." Blake smiled at me. I walked over to him, and he got up to give me a kiss. "Do you mind sitting for a second?"

"Sure," I replied, taking a seat in a chair he pulled out for me.

Luke then stood up with his arms crossed. "Lucy has something to say."

I turned toward her, and she appeared uncharacteristically vulnerable, her shoulders slumped and her face blotchy as if she'd been crying. She continued staring at the ground. "Jasmine, I'm sorry for all the mean things I said at temple last week."

It probably should have satisfied me that she was apologizing, but it didn't. She had clearly been coerced into doing so, and I knew she didn't regret anything she'd said, especially with such a generic apology. But I decided not to dwell on it.

Luke nodded then made eye contact with me. "Lucy's going to join you during your private training sessions a couple times a week moving forward. We all agreed that it would be good for her to start working harder and proving herself as a beta mate." Clearly, I was not included in this "we," and it almost sounded like they were hoping I'd be a babysitter to make sure she wouldn't skip out. I was a bit peeved, especially that Blake would agree to such an arrangement, and even more so that he hadn't consulted me first.

"Your session starts in a half hour, right?"

"Right," I replied, holding in the annoyance that was bubbling under the surface.

"Great. Lucy, are you ready to go?" Luke gave her shoulder a squeeze.

"Yep." She rolled her eyes and got up. "Let me just change." She showed herself out of the room.

"I'll go do a run of the patrol stations," Luke said and exited, leaving just Blake and me in the office.

Before I was able to get up, I felt his hands on my shoulders, rubbing them. "You're so tense," he said, working his thumbs under my shoulder blades.

"I was just assigned to babysit someone I'm not exactly the biggest fan of at the moment," I replied with an edge to my voice.

"I know. I'm sorry and I promise I'll make up for it somehow."

"But *why*? Why can't Luke babysit his own mate?" Blake let out a deep breath and I continued. "Why wouldn't you even ask if I'm okay with it? Why would you just volunteer me like that? You heard her lame excuse for an apology. She's obviously not sorry about anything she said to me and only did it because of whatever she has going on with Luke right now."

"Jaz, I'm sorry. You told me you wanted to talk to her as luna before, so I, obviously wrongly, assumed you'd be okay with it. And you're not a babysitter, so don't worry about that. I mean, yeah, I think Luke is hoping it'll encourage her to show up if you're going too. But her performance isn't your responsibility. Luke agreed that he'd be in charge of that. I've wiped my hands clean of it."

"Don't you find it semiridiculous that Lucy is being treated like a little kid?"

"Like I said, it's not my call. That's between her and Luke."

I shook my head. "I don't understand what happened. They seemed to be doing okay."

"I mean, did they? Or did Luke just let Lucy walk all over him all that time? I think he's finally standing up for himself, and Lucy doesn't like it."

As soon as we entered training, Lucy did a 180 and went from being a sulky brat to her usual bubbly, flirty self. "Oh, hello there, Xander. Your arms are looking much bigger than the last time I saw you!" She touched his bicep. "You've clearly been working really hard."

"Hi, Lucy," he replied flatly, clearly not amused.

"So, what's on the schedule today?" She gave him a big smile. "Let me get stretched out so I can be ready." She bent over and reached down to touch her toes, basically shoving her butt in his face.

He barely paid her any attention and said, "Get stretched out because it's going to be a tough one today."

"But Jasmine's pregnant!" Lucy exclaimed.

"Luna Jasmine's been doing great. We've just been modifying anything that's not safe for pregnancy. But the doctor has cleared her to stick with her regular routine otherwise. Why don't we start with some floor exercises to get warmed up?" Lucy groaned as I got into position on the mat.

At noon, the bell signaled it was time for lunch, and Lucy and I headed into the locker room. "Do you seriously do this every single day?" Lucy asked, groaning.

"No, just three times a week."

"Goddess, this is torture! My legs are on fire and my arms are like jelly," Lucy whined.

"Welcome to warrior training?"

When we exited the locker room, she followed me as I walked toward the indoor sparring court. "Wait, aren't you going back to the packhouse to eat?"

"No, I eat here with Paige on the days she has training too."

"Why didn't you tell me? I didn't know you did that."

"Because I wasn't aware you needed to know that information."

"What if I wanted to join in too?"

"I didn't realize we were friends now," I replied, annoyed with the conversation.

"Hmph!" She seemed to finally get the hint and turned on her heel to leave.

"Were you just with Lucy?" Paige came up from behind me.

"Yeah." I rolled my eyes. "She's apparently training with me now."

Paige burst out laughing. "I mean, I know she deserves to get her ass kicked. But that's just way too easy of an opponent for you! It's practically cheating!"

I laughed along, and we took our usual seat on the bleachers. "So, Gigi and Tyce?" I asked.

"Gigi and Tyce," Paige repeated with a big smile. "They're good together, don't you think?"

"I thought they hated each other. But now Gigi's at the packhouse every night. And I'm pretty sure whatever they're doing together is not hate." I giggled.

"It's a really thin line between hate and love. I think Gigi got the feelings confused at first." Paige snickered.

"Love?" I asked. "But doesn't Gigi want to meet her mate?"

"I guess we'll find out soon enough. Tyce has to go back to Alaska at the end of the summer. So they're going to have to make some decisions."

"And you think there's a chance they may go back to Alaska together?" I studied Paige, feeling like there was something I was missing.

"I think there's a big chance." She grinned.

I blinked. Did Paige know something I didn't? Was Tyce really considering taking a chosen mate? The idea seemed absurd. He was an alpha, from a very religious pack no less. My mom's side of the family had made their thoughts on what happened between Luke and me very clear. I couldn't imagine Tyce just sticking his middle finger up at his family like that.

Then I wondered if maybe Gigi just had her hopes up. My heart ached for her if that was the case. I would definitely have to talk to Tyce and figure out what he was doing. Because if he was leading her on, I'd have some choice words for him.

Very surprisingly, Lucy returned after lunch. We'd done weight training all morning, and after her complaints, I figured she might give up on this turnaround Luke apparently expected (forced?) her to have.

"Since we had an intense morning, I figured we could go lighter in the afternoon. How do you feel about yoga?" Xander asked us.

"Yes!" Lucy cheered.

"Now, I said lighter, not easier. I still expect you to have good form and follow all the instructions."

"Sounds good to me!" Lucy said, pulling out a mat.

After we finished an hour of yoga, Xander gave us a break while he had to step out.

"So, when are the babies due again?" Lucy asked as we took sips from our water bottles. Before I could even consider answering, she continued, "We should plan you a baby shower."

I blinked, completely taken aback by her acting like nothing had gone down recently. "Werewolves don't have baby showers," I replied, having no desire for one, especially not one thrown by Lucy.

"So? That doesn't mean you *can't* have one. I still had one for Libby, and it was so much fun. I'll even make you cute boy and girl cupcakes."

I turned to look at her, putting my hands on my hip. "Why do you want to throw me a baby shower, Lucy? Especially when I'm allegedly carrying your mate's pups?"

"Well, I wasn't going to bring *that* up again." She rolled her eyes. "And I said sorry!"

"Why should I just forgive you for everything you accused me of and said to me? Why should I forgive you for anything you've done for the past two years?" I was really fired up now, anger pulsing through my veins. "You've not been a good friend to me at all."

"What about you?" She raised her voice at me. "Why do you act like you're completely innocent in all of this?" She waved her arms around.

"What exactly have I done?" I glared at her. "Luke was my mate! I didn't ask for us to be mated to each other! And I'm sorry that I hid it from you at first, but it also wasn't just me!" Relief flooded through me as I was finally getting everything off my chest. "Luke asked me not to tell you! Right or wrong, I was trying to be considerate of him until we were both on the same page."

"But you knew I was in love with Luke. You knew he was my boyfriend! And maybe you didn't have full-on sex with him, but you still did something with him before you even told me! I smelled you all over him, and I smelled his fingers!"

My body burned at the thought. "I went into heat. I couldn't help it," I practically whispered.

"Heat? That's your excuse for being a shitty friend!"

"You know what, Lucy—you've never even gone into heat! So you literally don't know what it's like at all!" I probably could have stopped there, but anger was pulsing through my veins. Lately, I was having trouble controlling my emotions, so I continued. "You also knew how important it was to me to be with my mate and have a temple wedding. You knew how strict my parents were. But none of that mattered to you when it came to getting what you wanted, even though we'd been friends since kindergarten. Lucy, you are selfish. You are selfish toward me, you are selfish toward Luke, and you're selfish toward your own daughter!"

"You bitch!" she yelled. "I should claw you for that!"

"I'd like to see you try!" I yelled back. "You haven't even been going to sparring for the past month. How the fuck are you going to fight me?" She glared at me, her arms shaking.

"I'll fight you right now!" she yelled, and I was thankful we were in a private room of the gym where no one could witness what was happening.

I just stood there and watched, wondering whether she really would attempt it. And then she let out a loud groan and charged toward me. I easily dodged her attack, jumping out of the way as she stumbled.

"Don't be a coward and dodge me! Fight me!"

Goddess, had Lucy gone insane? Did she really want me to fight her?

She, again, charged toward me, fists ready. As she went to punch me, I grabbed her arm and flipped her in the air onto her back. She landed with a thud and let out an *oof* sound.

I looked down at her pancaked on the ground. "Paige is right. Fighting you, even while pregnant, is practically cheating. You're a sad excuse for a beta mate." What had gotten into me? I'd never said anything so cruel to anyone before. But something about it also felt so good.

Xander walked back into the room, and Lucy got up. "I don't feel well. I think I'm getting my period," she said and sprinted out of the room.

He shook his head. "I'm impressed she lasted as long as she did."

Chapter 53

Tyson

Goddess, she had me—she had completely dominated an alpha. I was addicted, spending all day going through the motions, waiting for my next fix. And I wouldn't be fully satisfied until I had her marked as mine. The urge had grown stronger with every time we did the deed, which was now every night, several times a night. I was barely sleeping, and I didn't care, greedily keeping her in my bed until she firmly insisted she had to go home.

"Good night?" Blake smirked at me as I entered his office. "Seems like you were up pretty late."

I couldn't help but smile to myself. "Sorry 'bout that. Will try to keep it down moving forward."

"I have someone coming in an hour or so to soundproof my bedroom. Jasmine and I realized the sounds go both ways." Blake smiled and shook his head.

"Guess I probably should have given you a heads up. Just felt a little awkward about it." I rubbed my neck.

"Hey, no worries. You're not the only one who never said anything. My sister is just as guilty." He chuckled. "Mind helping me move the

bedroom furniture around? We can put you in another room temporar-
ily since they'll probably need to break down your wall too."

"Yeah, no prob."

Blake pulled out a fresh syringe and a vial full of violet liquid. "Are you
ready?"

I flinched. "No, but let's go."

"Honestly, if my mate and I hadn't marked each other, I'd be doing
it with you. I still don't feel immune enough." Blake pulled back the
plunger on the syringe, keeping his eye on the barrel to make sure he filled
it with the correct amount of liquid. He was slowly adding more to the
dosage each day.

"This shit sucks," I said, taking a seat in my usual chair.

"Trust me, I know."

I nodded. After a pause I asked, "Hey, while I have you here, quick
question. Are there any job openings you know of around the pack?"

"Actually, we will be hiring soon. But it's for something really specific."

"Really?"

"Yeah, we're going to hire high school and college students to do some
data entry. It sounds really dull and tedious. But it needs to get done."

"College students?"

"Well, that age range. Someone who would be okay with getting minimum wage."

"Oh, I have someone perfect then." I smiled. "What do you need? A
résumé?"

"Sure, a résumé would be great. You can just give it directly to my mom
or Tyler. They'll be the ones hiring."

"Sweet."

Blake got up and walked over to me. I turned my head away, and he
stuck the needle into my left deltoid. I groaned, biting into my right
hand as he pushed all of the liquefied wolfsbane into me, the intense,

sharp, burning sensation instantly spreading to my whole arm, practically numbing it.

"Fuck!" I yelled when he finally removed the needle from my arm.

"I think Luke keeps stickers for Libby in his desk drawer if you want one." Blake gave me a friendly smile.

I chuckled. "I'll pass. But you should probably get a stash for your own desk soon." After disposing of the syringe, Blake sat back down and leaned back in his chair, putting the back of his head in his hands, with a big smile on his face. I rubbed at my sore arm and asked, "So, what's it like? Becoming a father?"

"Still getting used to it. But it's nice. Gives me the opportunity to be the father I never had."

I nodded in understanding, considering all the things I would do differently from what my grandfather and father did when raising me. My grandpa had been heavily involved in raising me, almost to the point where my dad had basically handed over all his responsibility. I wondered about that. Why had he done it? Did he feel like his own father had done a better job raising him than he would have done himself? Or was it just easier than fighting him to do it his way?

And I instantly knew—I'd never relinquish control over raising and training my own pups to either my grandpa or dad. If it came down to it, I'd be willing to kill for any of my pups—Gigi's pups. I smiled to myself at the thought of Gigi carrying my pups.

"I think someone's in love," Blake teased.

I straightened my face. "What?"

"You were just zoning out with a smile on your face. So what's the deal? She's not your mate, right?"

"No," I replied. But then something clicked. If she didn't have a wolf, then I wouldn't really know for sure, would I? All this time, I'd been assuming I'd just know if someone was my mate—I mean that's how I'd grown up understanding it, not even considering that there was a remote possibility that my mate could have an incapacity that prevented the mate bond from being recognized. *Could we . . . ?*

"I know how it feels," Blake said. He got up, giving me a friendly punch on the good arm. "Good luck, man."

I exited the office not long after he did and traveled the hallway to the main part of the packhouse to find Jasmine on her laptop at the dining room table. She looked up as soon as I entered her vicinity. "Oh good. Tyce!" she exclaimed, getting up. "Exactly who I wanted to speak to."

"Yes?" I replied, going over, pulling out a chair, and taking a seat. I was starting to feel a little dizzy and sitting helped.

She crossed her arms and came closer to me. "What are your intentions with Gigi?" she demanded, and I could see she was trying to make an alpha face. I snickered.

"What's so funny?" She glared at me.

"Your face!" I laughed.

"Why is my face funny? Do I have something on it?" She rubbed at her cheeks and chin.

"No, no. But if you want to learn how to make the alpha face, I can teach you. I'm surprised Blake hasn't. His is hardcore."

"Oh!" She laughed. "Yeah, I don't think I've seen enough torture to ever make my face as good as Blake's." She shook her head. "Okay, back to the topic. Tell me your intentions with Gigi."

"Goddess, you're such a mom already."

"Stop avoiding the question."

I almost laughed to myself, thinking that I wanted to tell Jasmine I had every bad intention with Gigi, wanted to explore every last bit of her curvy body, put her into every position physically possible, fuck her until she couldn't speak or walk anymore, find out every fantasy she had and make it come true. "My intentions are good."

"Can you be more specific?" She glared into my eyes.

"I want to make her happy."

"And if being your mate would make her happy, how would you feel about that?"

"That's a really prying question."

"Well, someone has to ask. I don't want Gigi to assume you're going to invite her back to Alaska to live with you at the end of the summer when you have no intention of doing that."

"Woah woah woah!" I was taken aback. "Did Gigi say that she thought I was going to do that?"

"Well, no." Jasmine twirled her hair, and her face reddened. "Shit, I probably said too much, didn't I?"

"It depends. Why did you just say that? That was an oddly specific statement."

She let out a deep breath and took a seat, rubbing her stomach, which seemed like it had practically doubled in size overnight. "The two of you seem to have gotten really close. And I'm just afraid that Gigi is expecting you to take her as a chosen mate when you're planning to wait for your fated one."

"I have no intention of hurting Gigi," I replied, not having any desire to elaborate. "I care about her and, like I said, want to make her happy. So you don't have to worry."

"What about your family?"

"What about my family?"

"You know how they feel about chosen mates. You heard what they said to Blake."

"Jaz," I said.

"Yeah?"

"I've got news for you. I'm the alpha. I make the rules."

"Hey, Tyce!" Blake's voice sounded from the top of the stairs. "A hand, please."

"Sorry, gotta go," I said to Jasmine and headed upstairs to help Blake.

After we finished rearranging all the furniture upstairs, all my limbs felt weak and my head was pulsing. My vision was starting to blur a bit too. My lungs ached, and the familiar wet sensation flooded my esophagus. I quickly ran into the bathroom just in time to hack up blood into the toilet. Fuck, I really had to lie down.

I flushed the red liquid, quickly rinsed my mouth out, and then stumbled into my new bedroom, falling onto the pillow that had the strongest scent of Gigi. I inhaled deeply, taking in all her amazing perfume, thankful it clung so well to fabric and lasted so long. It was the most amazing scent I'd ever smelled, and I knew I'd have to ask her what it was again. I couldn't even believe it kept slipping my mind to ask. I supposed I'd always been thinking about other things when she was with me.

And even as my whole body burned with the wolfsbane pulsing through it, and my head ached in a way it never had in my life, I still had a smile on my face as I drifted into sleep.

My phone ringing jerked me out of sleep. I groaned and reached for it, seeing my brother's name on the caller ID. "Yo!" I said as I picked up the phone.

"Were you sleeping?" he asked.

"Yeah, but it's fine," I replied, figuring I shouldn't waste the whole day in bed.

"But it's noon over there. Do you normally sleep this late?"

"No. Long story," I said. "So what's up?"

"Just wanted to give you some updates. I've started asking some questions about the green energy investments, and I don't think the Spruce Winter Pack is happy about it. They keep dodging my questions or giving generic answers, basically reiterating that our pack's share of dividends are up so we shouldn't worry."

"Sounds like we should worry," I replied.

"Exactly. I'm starting to wonder if they're somehow inflating the profit numbers to make it work out so they can pay out more dividends, figuring if we're consistently receiving more money, then we won't question what's going on."

"Seems legit."

"The other thing. This is just an instinct thing, but I don't trust their new alpha, Alpha Vic. Ever since he succeeded his dad, something's felt off. He seems to spend excessively. Granted, both our packs do well with JSP, but he just seems reckless. He showed me the watch he was wearing and boasted about it being a Rolex Submariner Date White Gold. I didn't know what that was, so I looked it up, and do you know what those things sell for?"

"What?"

"Like forty K."

"Maybe he's a watch guy. I mean, I put down some serious cash for my car."

"Yes, but that's not just it. He constantly throws all these crazy parties with hired strippers, told me he put down a deposit for a yacht and wants to invite me out once it arrives. He told me a party's not a party unless there's Cristal. I don't know. The vibe I'm getting from him isn't good. I mean, fine, he's alpha, and it's up to him how to spend the money his pack earns. But it just seems really excessive and irresponsible." He paused and then added, "Even *you're* not as bad as him." Trav chuckled, making it clear he said that in jest.

"Ha ha ha," I replied.

"Has your reputation caught up with you on the East Coast yet?" he teased.

"If you must know, the old Tyce is no more. I'm a changed man."

"Really? What, have you suddenly chosen a life of celibacy?" He snickered.

"Hey, I wouldn't go that far. But I am, well, I'm now monogamous."

"Monogamous? Where is Tyce and what have you done with my brother?"

"I think I'm in love," I confessed.

"Holy shit! In love? Who's this incredible woman who's tamed the wild Tyce?"

"Her name is Gigi." I couldn't help by smile to myself.

"And she's your mate, I assume?"

"It's complicated."

"Complicated? It's a yes or no question. Either she is or she isn't."

"I'll tell you another time," I said, now suddenly questioning whether maybe she was. Was it wishful thinking, or could she be? And, if she wasn't, well I had every intention to pretend she was. Although I did trust my brother and would come clean to him. "But what about you, bro?" I asked. "How are things with your mate?"

"It's complicated." He let out a small laugh.

"Apparently it's not so simple then."

"You got me there." He let out a deep breath. "She's here now, living in one of our apartments in Prudhoe Bay. I'm still trying to figure out how to break the news to Dad and Grandpa. You know how they feel about rogues. It's not going to go over well."

"Hey, when I get back, we'll figure it out. I intend to take my rightful place as alpha then. I'm done with Dad and Grandpa pushing me around. I'm ready. And if I have to fight them, I will."

"You're going to fight them?" I couldn't miss the shock in Trav's voice.

"I don't want it to come to that. But I've been doing a lot of thinking. I'm sick of not being trusted. I've been helping Blake run his pack here all summer, and I honestly don't know why I let Dad and Grandpa convince me I'm not ready for all these years. I was built and raised for this. And it's time for them to step aside."

Chapter 54

Ginger

I smiled to myself, continuously checking the text messages as they came in. Goddess, what was wrong with me? I'd never let a guy wrap me up so much in him before. Okay, every time I even looked at a guy, I tended to think he was going to be my boyfriend and maybe future husband. But not to this level!

Tyson Chicken: New geography to explore tonight ;)
Me: What, did you grow a second cock or something?
Tyson Chicken: Damn, think witches can make that happen?
Tyson Chicken: Second one I'll ask to be anal size
Me: You're obsessed
Tyson Chicken: With your ass? Yes
Me: Don't you have some important alpha stu ff to do or something?
Tyson Chicken: Like fuck your ass?
Me: That is not even remotely sexy or convincing
Tyson Chicken: Come over and I'll convince you another way

> **Me**: *No can do. My parents are complaining I'm never home anymore. Promised I'd hang with them tonight*
> **Tyson Chicken**: *Damn cockblockers*
> **Me**: *You have a hand :)*
> **Me**: *Two if you need one for your second cock too*
> **Tyson Chicken**: *Will you be using your hands tonight?*
> **Me**: *Wouldn't you like to know*
> **Tyson Chicken**: *Will find a way to find out ;)*

"What's so funny?" My mom took me out of a trance I didn't realize I was in.

"Nothing. Just some funny comments on an Instagram post," I replied.

"Clearly her phone is more entertaining than us." My dad gave an amused smile.

"Even when she's here, it's like she's not here." My mom snuggled into my dad a bit more. "All my chicks are flying the coop, honey." She sniffed a little.

"Paige and Heidi aren't far. And we still have our Gigi. She'll be back from school again next summer."

"That's true. All our girls are still in our pack. It could be much worse." She sighed. "When my brother found his mate at the Autumn Moon Pack, and they decided to move there, you'd think he'd died with how my mom reacted. And that's only the pack next door."

"Not like moving across the country," my dad agreed. "Or to another country."

"I don't know what I'd do!" my mom cried out. She then glanced my way and wagged her finger at me. "Gigi, don't you even dare look in any man's eye who's not from around here."

"But what if my mate ends up being from somewhere else?" I asked.

My mom made a choking noise and my dad cut in. "Then we'll support the match." After a beat, he added, "And I'll have a talk man-to-man about why he's to join our pack. After all, a woman needs her mom to help raise her pups." He smiled at my mom. My stomach squeezed with guilt.

"Absolutely!" my mom agreed. "Oh, I can't wait until Heidi finally gets pregnant. It'll be so nice to have a little pup in the family again!"

The gears in my mind rotated at sonic speed. My first thought was, if my mom was expecting to help me raise pups, then she had to know that I'd need to find a human to be my partner. And it wasn't like I could exactly move a human into the pack. But then my second thought went to Tyce. What was going on between us was definitely moving in a certain direction. And whether or not I'd get my wolf back was still uncertain. If I never got her back— I couldn't think about it. The thought was just too painful. Not only would I have to say goodbye to my wolf forever, but likely Tyce too.

Sometime around midnight, I'd begun to drift into sleep when the sound of a pang jerked me awake, my heart thudding against my chest. I blinked a few times, looking around the dark room. What was that?

Tap tap tap.

Something rapped against my window. I looked up and almost screamed at the monster outside my window before I realized the two glowing orbs were a familiar amber color. I quickly got up and opened the window, and a very fluffy, huge wolf crawled in.

He first pushed his snout into my hand and spit out a small, aluminum packet. Before I could even process what it was, he dragged his huge tongue from the bottom of my cheek to the top, leaving a layer of drool behind. I scrunched my nose in disgust, wiping the wetness from my face. He then shifted into his human form.

"What are you doing here?" I whispered loudly. He put his index finger to his mouth and then crawled into my bed, pulling me against him. "This is crazy!" I whispered again.

"Shhh," he hissed in my ear and then began nibbling on it. Quickly becoming powerless, I instantly gave into him, letting out a light moan. "Shhh!" he hissed again and covered my mouth with his hand. I turned to face him, and he had a huge smile on his face.

He brought his mouth to mine, and soon his hands were traveling to the bottom hem of my sleepshirt, pulling it off me with urgency.

He kissed back down my chin, neck, and chest, soon latching on to one of my nipples. His hands assertively kneaded both my breasts, the suckling of his lips turning into gentle nibbles. I pushed my hands into his hair. He moved to my other breast, doing the same thing, driving me crazy. My heart was pounding and tingles flooded my body.

When I didn't think I could take any more of his nibbles on my now very erect and very sensitive nipples, he began his descent farther down my body, kissing his way along my belly. As soon as he reached my sleep shorts, he didn't even bother taking his time—he just ripped them off my legs with my underwear. Soon his mouth was on my clit, sucking it into his mouth, and I swear the whole bed shook.

He shoved his fingers inside me and licked his tongue back and forth, settling into a rhythm. I clenched my hands, my right one wrapping tightly around the condom packet he had brought, the feel of him both inside me and licking at my clit overwhelming me. My breathing turned heavy and very audible, and I almost wondered if it could be heard through the walls of the house.

Now well aware of the condom scrunched in my hand, I shoved it into his face, desperate to have more than just his fingers inside me. I wanted to be filled, to ache from the telling soreness the next day, to walk around conscious of what had happened the night prior.

He instantly complied, ripping the packet open and rolling it onto himself. Tyce was soon on his forearms, his body heat surrounding me, his skin brushing against my skin, and his lips on my lips. I tasted myself as he shoved his tongue into my mouth, and I loved it. I loved that he lapped at my pussy every night, and I loved how his huge cock stretched and packed itself inside me. I could never get close enough to him. I pulled him closer to me with my legs and grabbed on to his ass.

He got lower, practically squishing me, the friction of our sweaty bodies igniting us. Goddess, we had to be on fire. Every time we had sex, it was better than the previous time. He kissed me with a scorching desperation that I matched when I kissed him back. More, more, more. That was all I ever wanted was more kisses, more closeness, more Tyce.

As he thrust vigorously and rubbed my clit methodically, I breathed into his mouth, our gasps almost turning to moans. Before long, we were convulsing against each other, finally giving in to the building sensations within us. He gave his final few thrusts as an intense orgasm rolled over me. We clung to each other, using our lips to quiet the other, the silence somehow more intimate than it had ever been. He immediately rolled off me and turned away. And I knew—he must have grown his fangs again.

After I caught my breath, I turned and traced my fingers along his back, following the raised lines. I recalled the intricate tattoos in my imagination, not able to properly see them now, especially living this deep in the woods with a waning moon.

"Hey, do you have a tissue?" he whispered. "And a trash?"

I quickly opened my nightstand and pulled one out for him. He immediately cleaned himself and wrapped the condom. I pointed toward the trash under my desk, and he instantly found it, clearly the dark wasn't an issue for him. But before he turned away from the trash, he covered his mouth and coughed, muffling the wet hacking sound. He rounded his back over the can, staying like that for a few moments. Then he turned back to me, reached back into the nightstand, and pulled out more tissues.

I got up, trying to get a better look as he wiped at his mouth. He finally returned to the bed, and I handed him the cup of water I kept on my nightstand for when I got thirsty during the night. He gulped it all down. "Thanks," he whispered as he snuggled up against me.

"Are you okay?" I whispered.

"I think so," he replied, pulling me closer to him.

I brushed back his hair as he closed his eyes, and before long, his breathing turned into soft snores. I knew I should kick him out, but it felt so nice having him close to me, and I felt bad waking him after witnessing him hacking, what I assumed was, blood into my trash can. Before I could reconsider, I drifted into sleep as well.

"Oh shit!" Paige's voice rang out, the sound of my door slamming soon following.

I jerked awake and gasped, and a male groaned next to me.

"Oh fuck!" I said quietly. "Fuck, fuck, fuck."

Tyce's eyes flew open and he shot up, looking around. Morning light flooded the room, and he was very much in my bed, very much completely naked.

"You have to leave—now!" I whispered loudly. "Fuck, this is bad. Let me figure out how to get you out. Stay here." I pushed my pointer finger into his forehead and then quickly dressed, throwing on sweatpants that would cover the cut on my leg that was still healing.

I sprinted into Paige's room. "Why is Tyce in your bed?" she demanded as soon as I walked in.

"Keep your voice down," I said, pacing her room. "Fuck, how do I get him out?"

"Why is he in here to begin with?"

"Because he snuck in last night." I plopped down on her bed.

"And, what, he forgot to sneak back out?"

"Yep." I let out a chuckle. "Goddess, I can't believe that just happened. Mom and Dad are going to flip the F out!"

"Especially once they get a sniff of you." She giggled. "His scent is all over you."

I groaned.

She rolled her eyes. "Fine, I'll do you yet another favor and distract Mom. And you and Tyce can figure out how to get him out without the neighbors seeing."

"I'll make him climb out the bathroom window." I got up off the bed. "It faces the back of the house."

I quickly sprinted back into my bedroom to find it completely empty once I arrived. Where'd he go? I searched around and looked out my window. He'd disappeared as if he'd never been there. Well, I supposed, he was probably trained in being stealthy. I went back into the hallway, where Paige was exiting her bedroom. "He's gone," I said.

She laughed. "Looks like you freaked out for no reason."

"Well, you freaked me out! Haven't you ever heard of knocking?"

Chapter 55

Blake

"Baby, can you watch Libby for a few hours today? Me and Erin want to go get some mani-pedis." Lucy threw her arms around Luke as he worked at his desk across from me. His look said everything. His shoulders tensed, nostrils flared, and he moved his hands from the keyboard, tightening them into fists.

Honestly, I had to give him credit for being possibly the world's most patient person for having dealt with Lucy for so long. She did have some positive qualities—she was very pretty, had bigger balls than most men, and wasn't a bad person overall. But, damn, she was fucking annoying, irresponsible, and had turned out to be a huge lush, especially in the past few months.

"Are you serious?" Luke snapped.

"What?" she asked innocently, fluttering her eyelashes.

He let out a deep breath. "I've been going through the training rosters today."

"And?" Lucy pulled away from Luke.

"And did you have something to tell me?" He turned in his chair so he was facing her.

She rolled her eyes. "Okay, so I may have missed a few sessions. But it's just not my thing. And I have a strong, sexy beta to protect me and keep me safe." She got closer to him. "I basically don't need training. And it's about time we start trying for pup number two anyway. I can't be sparring if I'm carrying your pup, baby."

"We are not having another pup," Luke said through gritted teeth.

"But we have to, baby! The pack needs a beta heir!"

"We'll talk about this later. Just go." Luke sighed and turned back toward his laptop.

"No, we'll talk about it now! What does Blake think about the fact that you won't make a beta heir?" I looked up at the sound of my name, and Lucy turned to face me. "Blake, don't you think it's time we start working on it? The pack is anxious! Especially with the alpha heir on the way!"

"Lucy, for the love of Artemis, stop!" Luke got up. "Just stop, okay!"

"Stop what, Luke! You're the fucking one who won't start. Does your dick even work anymore?" She reached for his crotch and he blocked her, pushing her hand away.

"Fucking Artemis, Lucy! Do you really need to air out our dirty laundry to Blake? What the fuck!"

"Yes, I do!"

"Yes, clearly. You clearly can't keep anything private, including your tits."

"So fucking what? It's not like the same people don't see your dick all the fucking time when you're shifting back and forth between your two forms!"

"I do that for fucking work, Lucy! I don't get completely sloshed and start putting on shows for an entire fucking nightclub! Especially not while I have responsibilities at home. Especially not while I'm out with a bunch of horny, unmated warriors."

"Well, at least someone's horny. Because you're clearly not! Fucking old man! You can't even get it up anymore!"

"Fucking Artemis." Luke shut his eyes and balled his hands into fists.

"Are you fucking someone else? Is that why?" Lucy shouted. "Are you fucking Jasmine?"

"What?" Luke shouted.

"There's always truth in rumors, right? Is that what you've been up to? Having regrets about the choice you made? Because I'm not perfect like perfect fucking Jasmine? I'm not a boring, nerdy, flat-chested, religious freak like you wish I was!"

I stood up and banged my hands on my desk, causing Lucy to jump. "Excuse me?"

Lucy flinched and took a step back.

"Don't you ever fucking talk about your luna like that again. I don't fucking care if you're my beta's mate. I have a knife in my desk, and I will fuck you up."

Lucy sniffed a few times, and then tears slowly began to tumble down her cheeks. Luke stiffened, and his features softened as clearly the mate bond must have forced him to sense and empathize with Lucy's distress.

"Lucy, I think you should go," Luke finally said in a tender voice. She nodded and walked out of the room. He sighed loudly and fell into his seat, putting his head into his hands.

"You okay, man?" I asked.

"Look, I'm sorry about that." He shook his head, looking down. "I just don't know what's up with Lucy lately."

"Lately?" I asked.

"Yeah," he replied. "I don't know. She's just so out of control. I mean, she was never exactly a Jackie O, which I knew going in. I loved her for who she was. But she's just been acting out so much lately. Her partying is out of control. She never wants to mother Libby. And how can I push everyone else in the pack to go to sparring when my own fucking mate doesn't?"

"Do you regret it?" I asked, semicurious myself, wondering if Luke did feel like he chose wrong. Did I want to know if he felt that way? Was there a part of him that pined for my mate now?

He groaned. After a beat, he finally said, "No. I love her. I just wish she'd fucking grow up. I mean, I get it, she's only twenty-one, things happened much more quickly than I'd ever expected them to. And I know you don't like her, but she is a good person inside. I honestly think she's just going through some growing pains adjusting to all this responsibility." He sighed. "I just don't know what to do. I mean, those pictures of her flashing the club have gotten around to the whole pack now, and she can't even do the bare minimum to at least keep up appearances. I don't want to control her, but—" He let out another deep breath and put his head into his arms.

"Luke, it's not that I don't like her— Okay, maybe I don't. But she's annoying as fuck. And even though she was supposedly best friends with Jasmine for all those years, you heard how she just spoke about her. That's not cool, and I'm not okay with it."

He sighed. "I'm sorry, man. I'll talk to her. Although she was pretty terrified when you gave her your evil eyes. I could feel it." He chuckled a little. "Not sure I need to say anything more."

Chapter 56

Ginger

On Tuesday morning, I woke to my cell phone vibrating next to me.

> **Tyce**: *Don't forget last shot today. I'd take you but promised Blake I'd fill in for training. But lmk if you can't get there and I'll make it work.*

I took a deep breath. I did enjoy Tyce's company when he brought me to my appointments. And as much as I acted tough, I really wasn't a big fan of hospitals. And, okay, I selfishly wanted to spend more time with Tyce. But I didn't want to take him away from his duties. I could find my own way there.

After I showered, I checked my leg once again. It was starting to look much better and was well on the way to healing, although I supposed I wouldn't really be enjoying any beach days or pool parties this summer, at least not around other werewolves. But there was always next year, and I'd be back at school around humans soon enough, where I wouldn't have to be so diligent with hiding all my wounds.

After getting dressed, I made my way downstairs, where I found my mom busy in the kitchen.

"What's all this?" I asked.

"It's your dad's and my wedding anniversary tonight." She smiled. "I figured I'd put together a nice cake to celebrate."

"Carrot cake?"

"Of course, it's your dad's favorite. Pass me the eggs, please."

I handed her the carton of eggs. After considering for a moment, I decided to get Paige's back and help her out. "Do you ever regret getting married to Dad right away instead of waiting?"

She tilted her head. "Why would I regret it? He's my mate. We're meant to be together."

"But do you ever wish you had more time to get to know yourself and who you are without a mate?"

"Of course not, honey!" She studied me. "Gigi, you shouldn't worry. When you meet your mate, it will feel completely right. You'll see. And you can still do everything you're doing now. Having a mate doesn't have to stop you. You may just need to make a few adjustments. But there's no reason you can't finish school and do everything else you planned. I'm sure your mate will appreciate how intelligent and hardworking you are."

"Oh, the question had nothing to do with me." I blushed.

"Who did it have to do with then?"

"I've just been thinking."

"Honey, your father and I have a great relationship. Artemis sends everyone their perfect match. And she's going to send you yours too. It's one of the most wonderful things about being one of us. I can't wait until you meet yours." She pulled me in for a hug and brushed her hand through my hair. "Just keep being you. Your mate will love and appreciate everything you have to offer."

"But, theoretically, if I wanted to wait for a few years after I met my mate to get married, how would you feel about that?"

"Gigi, honey, you won't want to wait. Trust me. You'll be excited and ready to spend the rest of your life with him! He's going to complete you. Be your other half."

"But if I did."

She shook her head with a smile on her face. "Gigi, it's best not to wait. Just trust me on this. You are best off placing your trust in Artemis's hands. She won't lead you astray."

"I suppose," I replied, letting out a breath and wondering whether I should argue more for Paige's sake. But, the problem was, I honestly couldn't think of any good reasons to wait. Like my mom said, our mates were supposed to be our perfect match, and it wasn't even like Paige doubted her match with Dylan. So what points could I actually make to convince my mom otherwise? It wasn't like my mom was even close to a feminist activist or someone who ever remotely questioned her religious beliefs. My mom was, well, my *mom*. As much as I loved her, she wasn't exactly with the times, especially the human times. I couldn't even imagine what she would think if she ever stepped foot in a human boarding school or on a college campus.

Deciding to pick up the conversation another time, when I had some better talking points, I asked what I'd really originally wanted to ask. "Mom, do you mind if I borrow the car for an hour or so today? I wanted to check out a new bookstore that opened not far from here. It looks really cool, and I was hoping to pick up some new books. Plus, they have a cute café inside too." *Too much, Gigi! That's too much. Stop acting suspicious!*

"Of course, honey. But can you do me a favor when you take the car, please?"

"Sure," I replied. *Good, very good. Favors will make her happy I borrowed the car.*

"I picked up some groceries for Heidi this morning when I went to the store. Can you please drop them off to her?"

Fuck! I did not want to see Heidi. It's okay—I could just hand them to her and GTFO. "Of course! No problem!"

"Thank you so much, honey. Let me go grab them for you." She pulled some items out of the fridge and put them into shopping bags that she handed to me. I smiled and took them with me to the car.

I was home free! I quickly sped to Heidi's home and arrived in no time. I got up the front steps of her townhouse and the sound of music flowed out the open windows on the second floor. A part of me had been hoping she wouldn't be home, but the music said otherwise. I tried pressing the doorbell and then recalled it was broken and that Heidi had told us she and Hunter were too lazy to get it fixed. My dad was supposed to go over to look at it at some point, but it appeared that hadn't happened yet.

I then knocked and waited. No answer. Okay, I knew she had to be in there so I knocked again, this time more loudly. I waited but still no answer. I finally decided to try the knob. It turned with ease, and the door opened. Okay, maybe I could avoid Heidi altogether and just sneak the groceries into her fridge. *Sweet!*

The floorplan was a bit odd with a garage and den on the first floor. I quickly sprinted up to the second floor where the kitchen was. Once I got to the top of the first landing, I was about to swing to the left to head in the direction of the dining room and kitchen when something caught my eye in my peripheral vision.

I turned right instead, and my jaw honestly must have hit the ground, crushed on impact. My eyes bugged out of my head, and all I could do was stand there and stare like a deer in headlights.

On the couch in the living room was Heidi, completely naked, with a woman with short, brown hair's head between her legs. I let out a squeak. I didn't know what to do.

Both of them looked up at me and screamed, quickly fumbling to cover themselves with blankets. Was that Heidi's friend Kelli? *Kelli? And where is Hunter?*

"It's not what it looks like!" Heidi finally got up and moved toward me, wrapping a throw around her.

I blinked, still too shocked to speak. Finally, I came to. "So Kelli wasn't just going down on you?"

"Okay, it looked really bad."

"What other explanation for what I saw could you possibly have?" I demanded. "Was she helping you insert a tampon with her mouth?"

Heidi's mouth opened and closed, and she let out a pained sound.

Anger bubbled inside me. "So all this time you were judging me for what I've been up to, and here you are, screwing your friend while your mate's not home. What the fuck, Heidi? Does Hunter know about this? Do you have some weird swinger relationship? Or are you just a dirty cheater?" I glared at her. "Are you bi? Because that's definitely against the scriptures of Artemis."

She blinked a few times. *Look at Heidi and her big mouth now!* Not able to help myself, I reamed into her. "Okay, Miss You Should Have Followed the Rules, what do you have to say for yourself now? Because I'm pretty sure none of what I just witnessed was you following the rules. What's going to be your punishment now, huh? Should we take your wolf away too? Bitch!"

"Don't call her that!" Kelli stood up with murder in her eyes. "Who are you coming in here talking to Heidi like that? Why'd you even enter our house without knocking?"

"Our house?" I blinked.

The two of them looked at each other, their cheeks reddening. What did that mean? I thought Kelli lived next door in the connecting townhouse. Something weird was definitely going on.

Heidi looked back at me, and tears tumbled down her cheeks. "Gigi, I know I wasn't that nice last time we talked. But please, don't tell anyone about this. Please." Her eyes pleaded with mine.

Kelli rubbed Heidi's back in a very affectionate way, and for a second, I considered if maybe I was being too harsh. But then everything that she'd said to me the last time I saw her replayed in my memory, and I decided I wasn't. "Goddess, you are such a huge hypocrite, Heidi! What are you gonna do when this gets out? How will Mom and Dad feel then?" I gave her one last glare and dumped the grocery bags on the floor. Then I sprinted out of the house and back to the car, so I could get to the hospital.

Chapter 57

Ginger

I'd managed to avoid Heidi for a whole week. Don't ask me how that was even possible when I had to see her at temple services both Sunday night and Monday morning, standing there like a perfect goddamn mate to Hunter, as if I hadn't caught her friend between her legs days earlier. I had only the Moon Goddess to thank that Heidi would never confront me about what happened in front of our parents, especially at temple where anyone could easily overhear.

But she kept texting and calling me. *Ignore, ignore, ignore.* I never wanted to talk to that hypocritical bitch again. She was no longer my sister. I didn't even care what explanation she had for what I'd walked in on. Okay, I was dying to know. I mean, clearly there was way more to the prude Heidi than I'd ever imagined. But still—my blood boiled at the thought of being near her.

I was grateful to finally have something to take my mind off everything. I'd be starting my new job that day. Tyce had taken my résumé to the former luna of the pack. And after she spoke to me for about a half hour, she offered me a job working on a new project for the pack clinic. It was like a huge boulder had rolled right off my shoulders. I'd finally be able to pay back my credit card bills, and I now had something to keep me occupied during the day so I didn't have to spend every waking moment stressing about my terrible luck—no wolf, sister from hell, and the waning time I had left to spend with Tyce.

Every time a new day started, I'd take in the fact that it was one day closer to possibly never seeing him again. My chest would tighten at the thought. I knew I'd never meet anyone else who would ever compare to him. He'd always be the one I'd evaluate other men against. I'd have to settle. I mean, sure, he acted like he was really into me too, but once the next full moon rolled around, and it was clear my wolf was gone for good, there was no way he'd stay with me. He was an alpha. And I could never be a luna.

But today was a good day. I had a job!

I spent extra time showering and getting ready, smoothing out my hair, putting on a no-makeup makeup look, and throwing on the cuter of the two maxi dresses I had on rotation.

As I was about to head out, my mom pulled me into a hug and said, "Good luck at your new job, honey!" and handed me a lunch bag.

"What's this?" I asked, taking it from her.

"Your favorite." She winked. My mom was just too good to me. I had definitely gotten lucky in the parent lottery. Even though I couldn't talk to them about most things, they never made me feel unloved or uncared for.

I arrived at the clinic fifteen minutes early. Both Dr. Luna and Jasmine's brother, Tyler, were already there. "Ah, great! Our first employee!" Tyler rubbed his hands together after the woman who had greeted me at the front desk led me into a small room.

"Hi, Gigi! Thanks for coming." Dr. Luna gave me a warm smile. "I'm interviewing a few more candidates today. So after Tyler gets you trained, I hope you won't mind taking the lead on this project."

"I don't mind at all!" I replied eagerly.

"Great. I've heard wonderful things from your parents. It sounds like you've been doing very well in school."

"Straight As."

She nodded approvingly. "Looks like we made a good hiring decision then."

"I won't disappoint!" I smiled widely. "I'm ready to get started."

"Great!" Tyler beamed. "So Dr. Luna will walk you through these files and how to read them, and then I'll show you how to get them entered into the database."

"I figured we'd start from the oldest records." Dr. Luna picked up a book that had the appearance of something that should be in a museum. "This is from the seventeenth century, brought over from Europe and preserved from before our pack even existed. As you can see, we value documentation of our kind's ailments and medical observations highly, especially as it is so rare and hard to come by. If our pack ever came under attack, I can tell you that I'd rush to the clinic first to make sure these records didn't get burned to the ground. They are invaluable to our medical practice. We can't get this information from a human medical school or any of their databases and records. We have to preserve them ourselves."

She opened up to the first page. "Now, these old records are much less organized. They were kept mostly as notebooks and added to as new observations were made. With this new database, I'm hoping we'll be able to get them more organized and easily searchable." She glanced over at Tyler.

"Absolutely!" He nodded. "So here's where you come in, Gigi. Come sit." He patted a chair next to him. I took a seat, and he turned a laptop to face me. He then showed me the steps to open the database and add a new entry. "Now here's where you'll add the tags. If it has to do with a certain body part, include that. Add any pertinent symptoms, like cough, bleeding, whatever. And anything else you think deserves a tag. I'll review your work today with Dr. Luna, and we'll see if we need to make tweaks to how you're entering everything."

"Okay! That sounds easy enough!" I replied, eager to show my enthusiasm.

"Great." Dr. Luna nodded. "Now as for the actual text, just enter it as written."

"What about diagrams?" I asked, looking at the page she had opened.

"Ah! Good point!" Tyler brightened. "Yes, we can't lose those. Maybe the next hire we can put in charge of scanning, cropping, and uploading all the pictures to your entries."

"Perfect!" Dr. Luna smiled.

After we finished going through everything, Dr. Luna left the room, and Tyler continued to show me how everything worked so I could navigate my way around.

"There are some dirty entries in there." Tyler snickered, glancing over at the large, old book in front of me.

"What!" I looked up at him. "Like what?"

"Flip to page 157."

I quickly did, dying of curiosity. As soon as the book was laid open, my hands flew to my mouth and I gasped. "Holy Artemis, it's an illustration of two wolves *doing it*." I burst out laughing. "Why is that in a medical book?" Then I looked up at him. "Oh my Goddess, and you memorized the page number!"

"How could I not?" Tyler grinned.

I began reading the entry. "Oh my Goddess, they literally describe two people in their wolf forms mating and then compare it to two actual wolves in the wild mating. Someone actually sat there and observed people *mating*. And *wrote about it*. In detail!" I giggled. "How do I get that job?"

"Seriously, sounds way more interesting than building a database."

"Are there more entries like that?"

"Not sure. That's the only one I've come across. But you better let me know if you find more. Don't keep it to yourself!"

"I didn't realize I was getting hired to read werewolf porn. Now this job got a whole lot more interesting." I giggled some more, not able to help myself.

"I love the enthusiasm. Now get to work." Tyler got up. "And here, I'll give you my number if you have any questions, since I'm going to head home to do my real job." He quickly scribbled his number on a Post-it Note.

After he left, I turned back to the task at hand and got started. The first entry was about an elderly werewolf who had begun to lose his fur. The doctor who had observed the phenomenon concluded it was due to old age, although it had never been observed previously in other werewolves.

A little after noon, someone came up behind me, startling me. I jumped in my seat and turned to come face-to-face with Tyce.

"What are you doing here?" I exclaimed.

"I always forget how easy it is to sneak up on you." Tyce snickered and bent down to give me a kiss. "I wanted to stop by and bring you lunch for your first day of work."

"Oh, my mom already had that covered. She beat you to it."

"Damn, and I thought I'd be the hero of the day."

"What'd you bring anyway?" I asked, looking up at the tote bag he had in hand.

"Okay, I can't really take credit for it. Connie, the packhouse cook, made it. I just cut you a slice. She made some meat lasagna."

"Oooh, that sounds really good!"

"I even brought a container of red pepper flakes for us to share." Tyce thrust out his chest and had a gleam in his eyes with how proud of himself he was.

"Wow, that does sound really good. Maybe we can just put everything out on the table and share, potluck-style."

"What'd your mom pack you?" he asked, taking a seat next to me.

I pulled out the lunch bag and opened it up, taking out a huge Tup-perware container that I popped open. "No way! My mom made me my favorite beef stir-fry. She always makes it extra spicy for my sisters and me."

"Nice. I know where the break room is. I'll heat everything up real quick and grab us some waters." Tyce got up, taking the three Tup-perware containers. He returned moments later, balancing everything carefully. We dug in, eating bits out of each other's containers.

"Damn, this stir-fry is awesome!" Tyce beamed.

"The lasagna isn't bad either. I'll give you some half-hero points."

"Okay, well, the lasagna wasn't the main attraction anyway." He winked.

"Tyce, I'm not hooking up with you in the clinic."

"That wasn't what I meant, but now that you brought it up, it doesn't sound like a half-bad idea." He elbowed me playfully and then moved closer to me. "Perfect place to play doctor." He nibbled on my ear.

"Stop!" I giggled. "Okay, what is the main attraction then?"

He smirked and dug around in the tote bag he'd brought in, then placed a plastic-wrapped item on the table.

"Is that your mom's brownies?"

"I'm sacrificing another one for you."

"Tyce!" I put my hands to my heart.

"Don't expect it again. This is twice now. And there aren't many left. Who knows when she'll send another batch." He made direct, probing eye contact with me.

"I'll be sure to savor it, taste every bit of it, run my tongue all along it," I teased in a seductive voice, leaning closer to him.

"If you don't stop, I'm about to yank a stethoscope off a nurse and make good use of it. And the part where they use the wooden stick?

That's not what I'm using. So you better be ready if you're going to talk like that."

I snickered and went right back to eating. After we finished, I walked him to the door of the room we were in. "You'll be by later for meditation, right?" he asked as he ran his hand down my arm, goosebumps trailing.

"Has it been working at all?" I asked. "Because I feel like you don't take it seriously. Tyce, this is a big deal. If a mouse popped out right now, you'd be forced to shift. I'm really worried."

He let out a deep breath. "I am taking it seriously."

"I'm honestly about to go out and buy a pet rat to start testing you."

"Oh fuck."

"Yeah. So no more sex until you can control your wolf!" I pointed my finger into his chest. "And that pet rat thing. I'm not joking. Shit's getting real! I have money now. So if you don't want to make friends with a cute wittle wat, you better start working your ass off at meditation."

"Noted. But I think we need to negotiate some of the terms."

"No negotiation." I crossed my arms, giving him a stern look. "And no sex. That's final."

"Really?" He gave me his most killer smile, and I was so ready to backtrack on everything. Damn. How did he do that? But no, I'd stick to my guns. I wouldn't let him fail.

"When you can control yourself around chipmunks, then you can touch me again."

"You won't last a week." He moved closer and brought his mouth close to my ear. "Did you forget that thing I did last night already?"

"It wasn't that good." I kept a straight face, although my body was already abandoning my side. The fabric of my panties was definitely moist against my skin and slowly becoming wetter.

He smirked. "If you say so." I glared at him. "I'll see you tonight for meditation. And we'll see if it's just meditation."

After work, I made it home after my half-hour trek through the pack. Before I could go inside, Paige came out and stopped me on the doorstep. "Gigi, you need to stop avoiding Heidi." She crossed her arms and glared at me.

"You've got to fucking be kidding me!" I responded in exasperation.

"She's your sister, Gigi."

"So I take it she told you what happened?" I let out a sigh and took a seat on the steps.

"Yeah, she did," Paige replied and sat down next to me. "I know you're mad at her, but honestly, she's been going through a lot. She's been hiding a lot. From all of us. And you should listen to her and let her explain herself."

"Why should I? You heard how she talked to me."

Paige sighed. "I know, and honestly, I think she feels really remorseful about it now. I think she was projecting some of her own stuff on you. Can you at least just talk to her? You don't have to forgive her, but at least let her explain what you saw."

I groaned. "She doesn't deserve it at all whatsoever. But fine!" I threw my hands up and stomped into the house.

Chapter 58

Ginger

On Friday evening, I came home to Paige and Heidi both staring at me from the kitchen table. "Don't you dare run!" Paige got up and I swear she was ready to use one of her warrior moves on me.

"Goddess, okay! I'm here!" I replied.

"Now sit." Paige pulled out a chair and gave me a hard stare. Damn, she was actually pretty good at giving a warrior look. Did she learn that in training?

I rolled my eyes and plopped myself down. Heidi didn't say a word. Her whole posture was stooped, and her chin trembled. Served her right.

Paige started, "I'm disappointed with both of you."

"Disappointed with me?" I shouted. "What have I done? Besides defend myself against Heidi's slut-shaming? Especially when she was the one who was slutting it up all along, acting like she's Miss Innocent!"

"Gigi," Paige warned.

"It's okay, I deserve it." Heidi spoke up, her voice cracking. "I'm sorry, Gigi. I shouldn't have been as mean as I was."

"You're only sorry because you got caught," I snapped back at her.

"No, that's not true," Heidi replied, solemnly, and I almost believed her.

"Gigi, can you just chill for once in your life?" Paige eyeballed me. I huffed. Okay, I was being a brat. But, Goddess, could you blame me? After a beat, Paige continued, "Gigi, you've obviously been going through a lot, for many years and this summer. And we probably could have supported you more. Right, Heidi?" She looked at our older sister meaningfully.

"Yes, right." Heidi nodded. She sighed and then continued, "I haven't been a good older sister because I've been going through my own stuff. And the way you're always just doing whatever you want without a care in the world, and then the rumors about Tyce, it just triggered me." She looked down at her hands, fiddling with them. "The thing is that I've been keeping a huge secret from everyone. From both of you, from Mom and Dad, and from the whole pack. I thought it wasn't a big deal and I'd be fine keeping it the rest of my life, but it just got to the point where I couldn't do it anymore." Her voice cracked, and a tear slid down her cheek.

She sniffed, wiping at her face. "I was pretending to be someone I'm not every single day of my life. I was just playing the part of Hunter's perfect little housewife who's trying to conceive a pup. And I am trying to conceive . . ." Her voice trailed off. "But not the normal way."

"What do you mean?" I leaned forward.

She took a few deep breaths. "The truth is, Hunter isn't my mate." I blinked, letting this new fact sink in. She sniffed and tears streamed down her face. She choked out, "The truth is that I'm gay."

Paige got up and threw her arms around Heidi. She then affectionately moved Heidi's hair out of her splotchy face. "Heidi, I love and accept you, and so does Gigi, even if she can't express it right now."

"Thanks, Paige." Heidi sighed. I knew I should say something, but I was having a hard time processing this. Even though I had witnessed what I'd witnessed, and already had almost two weeks to let it sink in, for her to admit it was just so definite. I'd never known Heidi this way, and now I had to basically unteach myself everything I had taken as fact.

And even though I probably should have been more empathetic and loving like Paige was, the only thing I could think to say was, "And Kelli is your real mate?" It suddenly all clicked. When Heidi began hanging out with Kelli just years earlier, I had always thought they were overly touchy-feely with each other. At the time, I'd chalked it up to them just being very close friends. But now I realized that she was affectionate with Kelli in exactly the way she never had been with Hunter.

She nodded slowly. "Yes." She sniffed. "The thing is, I didn't even know I liked girls until we met each other."

"But how could you not know?" I asked.

Paige handed her a napkin, and she wiped at her face. After a moment, she replied, "I guess maybe part of me knew. Like there'd be girls I really wanted to be friends with, and now I realize that they were crushes. And then like, when you'd talk about boys, I could never relate. Like I might think a guy was cute, but then when I'd think about doing stuff with him, I'd feel uncomfortable and anxious about the idea of it. I kept thinking it was because he wasn't my mate—of course I wouldn't feel comfortable being with someone who wasn't my mate! I never questioned the belief that my mate would be a man. The thought that it wouldn't be just never crossed my mind. I guess that's what happens when you grow up in a place where that's the expectation."

She paused, a small smile coming to her face. "But then when Kelli and I looked into each other's eyes, it all just made sense. Well, sort of. I also felt so sick and anxious about it. I used to throw up every morning when I'd think about what it meant, having to tell Mom and Dad and disappoint them, and wondering what I was going to do. I used to just shift into my wolf and run for miles. Sometimes I'd even dream about going rogue and running away with Kelli, so I wouldn't have to face any of it."

"But what did Kelli think about all of this?" I asked. "Were you guys actually planning on going rogue and never seeing us again?"

Heidi wiped at her eyes. "She'd known for a long time, so she'd had more time to get used to the idea. And she really talked me off the ledge."

"But you never came out though!" I said. "She talked you off the ledge, but you both just stayed in the closet? Were you planning to live in the closet forever?"

"Yes, I was planning to."

"But how? Why?"

"Isn't it obvious why?" Heidi cried out. My face burned, realizing how stupid the question I'd just asked was. After spending most of my time in the human world, where people were much more accepting of the LGBTQ+ community, I'd sometimes forget how conservative our pack was. Even though it was no longer banned in our pack, only a handful of couples had come out. That had only been in the last year, and they weren't exactly welcomed with open arms either. I couldn't expect Heidi, who had been raised so conservatively by parents who couldn't even fathom the idea of waiting to get married, to just accept this bombshell with open arms.

"Tell her the rest of the story." Paige patted Heidi's arm affectionately.

Heidi put her head into her hands for a moment as we both stared on. Finally, she looked up at us again and continued, "Kelli was friends with Evan. And after Evan met his mate Hunter, a plan just started to form between all of us. We figured we'd all just marry each other's mates. Then Hunter found out about the side-by-side townhouses being available, and it all just seemed to click into place. We'd all live in townhouses attached to each other, and we could easily just switch from one house to the other through the back. We even thought about building a doorway inside to connect the two houses to make it even easier.

"It seemed so perfect at first. None of us had to come out to our parents or the pack, and we could be with our mates. But after a while, it just started to wear on me. I realized that no one really knows who I am. Not even my family. And I always have to be so diligent. I can't randomly invite people over. Hunter and I constantly have to cancel plans to show face to each other's families. Hunter hates going to temple with me because he hates the whole institution, but he does it anyway because how can he not? And at the end of the day, I want people to know who my mate is—the person I really love. The way Paige is able to be with Dylan. I want that too. And I realized I'd never ever have that. I could potentially die without anyone ever really knowing the real me." At that, she began sobbing. Paige handed her more napkins, and she wiped at her face some more. Paige rubbed her back.

Finally, Heidi stopped and gave me a small smile. "Honestly, part of me was happy you walked in on us, Gigi. While it made me want to crawl into a hole and die, another part of me was just so relieved that someone else finally knew."

I felt like shit for having ignored her for all that time, not allowing her to even have a chance to explain her side of the story. I really had been a shitty sister, completely wrapped up in my own issues, not realizing how much Heidi had been struggling with all this time. "So what are you going to do now?" I asked. "Are you going to tell Mom and Dad?"

"I can't!" she choked out. "Plus I have the pact with the other three. This isn't just about me. This is about all of us. If one of us gets outed, we all do!"

"Gigi, you better not dare!" Paige glared at me.

"Relax!" I defended myself. "I wasn't going to! I just wanted to know what Heidi was planning to do."

"This stays between us." Paige gave Heidi a hug.

Overcome with guilt and emotion, I got up and did the same. "Heidi, I'm really sorry. I should have let you explain yourself. I didn't know what you were going through."

"It's okay, Gigi. I know why you didn't."

"I know I've met Kelli plenty of times before, but I'd like to finally meet her properly, as your mate."

Tears flooded Heidi's eyes. She sobbed out, "I'd love that, Gigi."

"Potluck at your house next week?" Paige asked. "This time with our sister-in-law too."

"Kelli will be so happy. She's been dying to finally be a part of my family. I've been dying to be a part of hers too. But small steps."

"Why don't we make spicy pasta and have some wine now? And have an impromptu potluck tonight? Mom and Dad are out for their date night anyway." Paige got up, pulling a pot out of the cabinet.

"I can make the rattlesnake sauce," I offered.

"I'll cut up a salad." Heidi smiled, getting up and wiping at her face.

"I'll just get the water boiling and pour everyone some wine," Paige said.

"Heidi, I just have one more question," I said as I opened the pantry to pull out the jar of jalapeños."

"Yeah?" she asked, looking over her shoulder at me as she headed for the fridge.

"How are you trying to conceive? Does that mean that you and Hunter . . . ?"

Heidi giggled. "No, we use a turkey baster. Hunter just, well, you know." She blushed.

"So you were actually going to have a baby with him?" I asked, eyes wide, unable to move.

She let out a small laugh. "Yeah. Both our parents have been on our cases. And I mean, I always wanted a pup. I still do. So does Kelli."

"But like, won't it create a bunch of complications?"

"We'll just figure it out. It's not like the pup will be able to talk right away anyway."

"But there are just so many logistics to consider."

"I know." She sighed, a painful sob following. "I'll live the rest of my life in the closet and give up my identity. But how can they make me give up being a mom too? It's what I've wanted my entire life." She gasped for air, laying a cucumber out on the cutting board.

"You won't give it up!" Paige rushed over to her. "Gigi and I will be the best aunts ever to your pup. And we'll help you keep your cover if that's what you really want."

"And maybe one day you won't feel like you need to hide your identity anymore," I added. "I know it's tough now, but times are changing."

"That's it!" Paige exclaimed. "I've decided! I'm going to let Dylan mark me. I am going to be the change that I want to see! I'm going to show Mom and Dad that the world won't end because I didn't follow the rules!"

"Paige!" Heidi gasped.

"Don't you dare talk me out of it. I've made my decision, and it's final! I'm doing this for all of us. Taking one for the team. It's about time Mom and Dad start living in the twenty-first century. And worst case, they disown me. But I have a job and a mate. And I have both of you! So it won't be that bad."

"Mom and Dad won't disown you." I went over to hug Paige. "It'll definitely be a shock for them, but they'll eventually get over it. And I'll stick up for you. I promise."

"I'll stick up for you too." Heidi also hugged Paige.

"See how much better it is when we're not all fighting?" Paige giggled.

"Yeah, yeah." I waved her off.

"So what's the deal with you and Alpha Tyce? Are you still seeing him?" Heidi asked.

Both my sisters stared at me. I let out a deep breath. "For now."

Chapter 59

Jasmine

I was upstairs in my private office when a loud banging sounded on my door. I got up to open it, and Lucy's scent drifted into my nostrils. I swung the door open to her in a raggedy T-shirt and leggings, her normally glossy hair tangled and unbrushed, and her face red and blotchy as if she'd been crying for hours.

"Please, Jasmine," she choked out. "Please, help me."

"What happened?" I asked, looking her up and down. She walked past me and took a seat in the comfortable chair I'd set up next to my bookshelf.

After sniffing a few times, she finally blurted out, "Luke's kicking me out of the packhouse."

"What?" I stared at her wide-eyed, not knowing what to say.

"Jasmine, I love him. He's the only reason I get up in the morning. Without him, I'm nothing. I don't know what to do." She began sobbing.

"But why?" I asked. "What happened?"

"I don't know. I don't know where it all went wrong. After we had Libby and got married, everything seemed so perfect. It was everything we'd always wanted. But now—now, he's changed! He's so demanding.

He wants me to be this perfect beta mate that I'm never going to be. He was never like this before."

"Lucy, are you serious?" I stared at her. Was she really this delusional?

"What do you mean, am I serious?"

"You act like I don't live in the same packhouse as you. Like I haven't witnessed everything that you've been up to."

"What do you mean?" She looked up at me with her bright blue eyes. Was she just playing dumb, or did she really think she'd not done anything wrong?

"Lucy, you've been acting so horribly toward Luke! You've been manipulating him for all this time, always trying to get your own way. And now that he's finally telling you that he doesn't like how you're behaving toward him or the reputation you're giving him with your behavior around the pack, you're acting even worse!"

"That's not true!" she yelled.

"Okay, then tell me your side of the story." I crossed my arms, glancing down at her.

She wiped at her cheeks and sniffed. "I've always loved Luke, ever since the day I met him. He's the best thing that ever happened to me. I used all the money I made working at the café to send him care packages and to travel to visit him when he was away all that time. And when he told me that he was going to be with his mate, my heart broke into a million pieces. There was never any doubt in my mind that he'd choose me, and for him to just do that so easily—it hurt so much."

I took a seat in the office chair, so many thoughts running through my mind. Was she just going to ignore the fact that she'd known he wasn't her mate for years prior? That he, in fact, was *my* mate? Did she just completely wipe all that from her memory?

She continued, "But when I got pregnant with Libby, it all became obvious. We were meant to be together. The Moon Goddess knew she'd made a mistake. When he finally came back to me, it was all so clear that he'd come back to the person who was really supposed to be his mate."

I clenched my fists, anger pulsing through my veins. How could she just sit there and say all that to me when she knew how much she and Luke had hurt me? But I decided to just let her speak, curious to know where this was going.

She sighed, and then continued, "But after I had Libby, I just didn't realize how hard it would be. She cried all the time, nonstop. I was barely sleeping, and I was still working, taking care of Libby whenever I was home. I got barely any help from Luke because he was always working. He was obsessed with work. It was like he did it on purpose—gave himself more duties and more work so he didn't have to deal with Libby crying and being fussy all the time. I became so depressed. He took me to the clinic, and I got put on antidepressants. But still, it was so hard. I just didn't know being a mom would be so hard." She sobbed. "It's still so hard. I'm really trying, Jasmine. I really am."

"But you're not, Lucy. Maybe you did at the beginning. But lately you're always going out and dumping Libby on Luke, Luke's mom, or your mom. I never see you with her anymore. You're not even with her now."

"Because it's just gotten so bad between Luke and me. I was so exhausted, and it became so overwhelming, that I didn't feel like I could keep going. You know how much I loved my job at the café, but I asked Valerie for a leave of absence. Because none of it brought me joy anymore. And going to training was just more tiring. I kept up with it for so long, but I couldn't do it anymore. And the more I tried to do small things to stop being so tired and exhausted all the time, the more Luke would get mad at me. And then he stopped having sex with me. We haven't had sex in months." Tears flooded her eyes and streamed down her cheeks. "I just don't know what to do. I feel like I'm going crazy."

"So what did you tell Luke about all of this?" I asked.

"I told him. But he doesn't care anymore. He said that he'd maybe be more understanding if I wasn't out with my friends all the time. But, Jasmine, that's the only thing that gives me any joy anymore. When I'm out with them, I can just let loose and not have to be a beta mate or perfect mom. I can just be me."

"But you have responsibilities now, Lucy. You can't just keep living like you don't have a mate and pup. They're both depending on you."

She nodded, her shoulders slumped.

"And, Lucy, if it's so hard with Libby, why do you keep pressuring Luke to have another pup with you? You can barely even handle this one."

"Because I think it will make things better. Luke and I will have a new pup and a bigger family. It will bring us closer together."

"That's not how it works, Lucy! Just like Libby didn't bring you closer together, this new pup isn't going to either."

She let out a whimper. "I don't know what to do."

"So, what did Luke say? He told you to just pack your bags and leave? What about Libby?"

"He said he wants a break. He asked me to move out for a while and said we could work out an agreement for Libby. He told me that being around my emotions is making it hard to think with a clear head, and he thinks I need to figure out what I really want."

"Maybe he's right," I replied. "I mean it doesn't sound unreasonable. You're clearly going through a lot right now, and maybe you should take some time away from being a beta mate to focus on getting better."

"I don't want a break from Luke though." She sniffed. "He's my mate, Jasmine. You know what it's like. It's hard being away from your mate. When we're apart, I feel like half of me is missing. How can I get better without him?"

"Lucy," I said sternly, "once again, you're only thinking about how this affects you and not how it affects Luke or Libby. Do the right thing and respect Luke's wishes."

"But what if he decides he doesn't want to be with me?" she whined.

"You can't force him to be with you."

"How can I convince him to stay?"

"You can't, Lucy! I was his fated mate, in case you forgot."

She winced.

"And the same way you can't force him to be with you, I couldn't either. Why would you want to anyway? If he doesn't want to be with you, why would you want to be with him?"

"But we marked each other!" she cried out. "It's not like I can just go out and find someone else now. We're connected for the rest of our lives."

"Well, then, maybe it's about time you started making more of an effort. It's not like he asked you for a divorce and said he never wants to see you again. Maybe you need to just honor his wishes for now, get better, and prove to him you're capable of being a good mom and good beta mate. For once in your life, you need to think about someone other than yourself. Then if Luke sees you're capable of caring about him and his pup, then he'll ask you to come back."

She nodded and put her head in her hands, not saying anything.

"Is there anything else?" I asked. "Because I have a lot of work to do. I know you think Luke is just making up work to stay away from you, but running a pack isn't easy. Maybe if you pitched in sometimes, you'd see how much goes into it. And that's just the paperwork. That doesn't include all of the physical stuff Luke has to do with training warriors and students or overseeing all the patrol sites. Plus, he has to train and stay in shape himself, which takes a lot of dedication, especially since he has much higher standards for himself than everyone else."

She hiccuped and looked up at me, appearing completely defeated. I couldn't recall ever seeing her so vulnerable before. While Lucy was a lot of things, she was also a fighter. She was the type who wouldn't rest until she got her way. Was she actually giving in for once and admitting defeat?

After a moment, she lifted herself out of the chair. "I'm gonna go," she said and walked out of the room, closing the door behind her.

Chapter 60

Ginger

"Ommm," Tyce said in an exaggerated way as he sat next to me in a lotus position.

"Tyce, you're not even trying!" I pushed on his arm.

"How do you know?"

"Because it's obvious!"

He snickered.

"Tyce! You're killing me! I'm doing this for you."

"I did something for you too." He gave me a huge smile.

"What did you do?" I asked. "And it better not be anything sexual."

He moved closer and took my hands in his. "I know this meditation thing is really important to you, so I've actually been working really hard at it, outside of when you and I meet up at night, because, let's be honest, I'd rather be doing something else with you."

"I don't believe you." I pulled my hands out of his and crossed my arms.

"I'm being honest. I have. I don't want to be out of control of my wolf. I'm taking my job as alpha really seriously now. That's why I've been doing everything I've been doing to help Blake with his pack, getting injected with the wolfsbane, and now meditating every day, a few times a day whenever I have time." He smiled and grabbed my thighs, bringing me even closer to him so we were now touching. "I don't talk about this stuff with anyone else—not even my brother. But I feel like you get me and you don't judge me. When you get on my case, it comes from a good place. And it makes me want to work harder and be a better alpha."

"This is treading on really mushy territory." I gave him a playful glare but couldn't help but smile, a warmth spreading through me.

"Can I fuck you now?" He winked.

I pushed on his chest. "Not until you can look at a rodent without shifting. I need to make sure you have some motivation." But then I felt a pang in my chest. What if he couldn't do it by the time the summer ended? Would we never be intimate again? Damn, what had I done?

"Okay, get that pet rat then, and we'll start practicing," he said, brushing his hand through my hair. "I'd offer to go with you to pick one out, but, you know."

"Really?" I looked up into his amber eyes, which were intently staring back into mine.

"Yeah, I want to do this." He trailed his fingers along my cheeks. "And the faster I can do it, the faster I'll be back in your pants."

"Tyce!"

"What? Is there something wrong with how badly I want you? Because you can't tell me you don't feel the same way."

"I do feel the same way," I said quietly, looking down at the ground, my face burning from my admission.

"Gigi, do you ever think that maybe we could be mates and we just can't know for sure?"

I looked up at him and my breath caught. He finally said the thing I'd been avoiding because I didn't want him to know how bad I had it for him—bad enough where I started to believe I could be fated to an alpha, which still seemed crazy to me. After blinking a few times, I said, "Yeah,

I have thought about it. I mean, there are signs, I guess." I tried to play it off like it wasn't a big deal.

"Tell me what signs you've noticed."

I got up on my knees and moved my neck close to his nose. "How do I smell?" I asked.

He inhaled deeply. "Amazing. Best scent I've ever smelled in my life. What perfume is it?"

I moved away. "It's not perfume. That's just how I smell to you."

"You're not wearing any perfume at all?"

"No." I shook my head. "And after we have sex, you get the vampire fangs. You said that never happened to you with anyone else right?"

"Right. Honestly, that's what made me start thinking maybe we were mates. But it's hard to know why it's happening without knowing for sure."

"Yeah." I slumped my shoulders. "I guess the only way we'd know for sure is if I get my wolf back."

"You will!" He took my chin in his hands. "You will! I won't stop fighting for your wolf until you have her back. And this isn't even about knowing you're my mate or not. I want you to have a wolf, Gigi, because you deserve to have one. You deserve to be happy."

My throat prickled. "Thanks, Tyce."

"Also." He gave me a mischievous smirk. "I know another thing we could do to test if we're mates or not." He paused for a moment. "But it's painful."

"How?" I asked, my ears perking up.

"To be honest, I don't even know if it would work since you don't have a wolf. But if you have an open wound, and your mate licks it in his wolf form, it should close up right away, no matter how bad it is."

"Let's test it!" I said.

"Are you serious? I was half joking."

"I think we should do it. Don't you want to know?"

"I do, but . . ."

"No, I'm serious. Let's try it and see if it works."

His head tilted to the side, and he gave me a smile that was half terrifying, half appreciative, his eyes taking on an almost evil appearance. Damn, he actually looked super dangerous and hot! He got up, pulled open the drawer next to his bed, and pulled out a huge switchblade that he flicked open. "Really?" he asked.

"Yes." I straightened up, half horrified, and half turned on. He did look very sexy handling a knife.

"Well, since you don't have a wolf, we should be safe about this." He closed it back up again. "Be right back."

I waited and he returned with a bottle of rubbing alcohol and a bag of cotton balls. He quickly and diligently cleaned his knife, then he turned to me. "Take off your clothes, baby," he commanded in his husky voice, and I was a goner. I peeled off the maxi dress I was wearing and then quickly removed my bra and underwear until I was completely naked.

"You are so fucking sexy. I love your beautiful, curvy body." He came closer and began kissing on my neck. I moaned quietly—the feeling of his lips so nice on my skin. "And how you're just so uninhibited and wild. Fuck, so amazing." He brushed the back of his blade against the same place where he'd just kissed my neck. I closed my eyes and inhaled, taking in the sensation, listening to his breathing. Something about the cool metal stroking my warm skin flooded my body with tingles. I moaned more loudly as he traced the dull part of the blade up and down the sides of my neck, and down the center, along my throat.

He closed his knife up again and trailed his lips onto my shoulder blades and to my collarbone, provoking my whole body to shiver with pleasure and desire.

He pulled away and slowly removed all his clothes, revealing his jacked body and massive erection. I was regretting my decision to abstain from sex even more now. "Lie down on the bed, baby, face down," He said softly, his voice gravely with lust.

I immediately got onto his bed. He moved on top of me, straddling my legs. "Baby, do you trust me?"

"Yes," I replied, my heartbeat quickening with anticipation.

"If you want me to stop, just say so, okay? Because I'd never want to hurt you against your will."

"Tyce, just do it."

He chuckled. "I've never had such a sexy and willing victim. I'll be gentle, I promise."

He bent down and began kissing one of my ass cheeks. "It's going to kill me so much to cut this beautiful ass. But I will lick it better," he moaned out. I began to feel a bit nervous. Would it hurt a lot? I closed my eyes, not wanting to think about it too much. Wet cotton touched my skin. Tyce dabbed at me up and down. "Are you ready, baby? This is going to sting."

"Do it, Tyce. It's okay," I responded. "Don't ask me again because it's making me hesitate."

He didn't say anything, but soon cold metal was being brushed softly against my skin. I was completely aroused—my pussy throbbing with desire. I never thought I'd ever get so turned on by something so crazy.

I just concentrated on my panting, not allowing my mind to wander to what he was about to do. The only noise in the room was our labored breathing. After what felt like forever, a sharp pain radiated from my ass as metal tore through the delicate skin. I whimpered, and tears flooded from my eyes. I did my best to keep myself from screaming at how much it stung, the metal practically burning me.

"Are you okay?" he asked, gently.

"Yeah," I forced myself to reply through my tears.

A puff of wind blew on the wound as Tyce seemingly transformed into his wolf form. I felt the brush of his fur against my legs as he moved closer to me. Soon, his tongue was on my skin, and it actually felt very soothing as he licked me, brushing his tongue up and down the bare, broken skin. I moaned at how good it felt. He continued the movement of his tongue all along the wound. Something about it was so intimate and sexual, and I knew that even though it had initially hurt, I wouldn't be against him doing it again.

After some time, I felt another puff of wind.

A human Tyce lay down next to me and kissed me on my forehead, pulling me closer to him. "It didn't work." He furrowed his brows. "You're still bleeding, but I didn't cut too deep. I'll get a bandage for it."

I nodded and he got up, returning moments later. "Luckily, there's a pup in the packhouse, so they keep a fully stocked first aid kit. Just stay still and I'll clean you up."

"Looks like you got your wish to play doctor," I joked.

"I can't lie. That was really fucking hot. I'm upset I couldn't lick you better. But fuck! You are so fucking amazing, Gigi, that you let me do that. And you were so fucking strong—took getting stabbed like an alpha. I really hope you get your wolf back because then you'll really be fire."

He diligently dabbed at my wound and spread a cream on it, finally covering it with some gauze and a Band-aid. He lowered his mouth back to my ass and gave it a big kiss. "You'll be okay, Spicy Gi," he said, then lay down next to me, pulling me against him.

"Tyce, I trust you," I said, and I realized what I really wanted to say was I loved him. But I wasn't ready for him to not return the sentiment.

"Baby, I will always take care of you," he replied.

Always? Did he see this as a long-term thing? Maybe all hope wasn't lost. I kissed him, settling for him showing me for now, until I was ready to beg him to tell me how he truly felt.

Chapter 61

Ginger

"How are things going?" Tyler asked after I'd been doing my job for a couple days.

"Really good, actually!" I replied cheerfully.

"So you don't mind all the tedious data entry?"

"No, not at all! The stuff I'm learning is so interesting. Like, I always thought werewolves were immune to almost anything, but there are all these crazy things that can happen to them. Like one doctor observed a werewolf who stopped being able to heal quickly, except when there was a full moon. The doctor decided the wolf had bad blood, and they ended up chopping off his balls so he couldn't reproduce and pass on the defect."

"Yikes!" Tyler cringed. "Glad there are more humane sterilization techniques these days."

"And then, even though most wolves can only heal their mates, there was one wolf who could heal anyone, mate or not. But that wolf never ended up meeting her fated mate, so it was both a gift and a curse."

"Huh. Interesting."

"I honestly wish I could stay and continue doing this into the school year, because all the stuff I'm learning is so cool. I'm even thinking about changing my major in school and going into premed. Or at minimum nursing. Because it would be so interesting to learn all this stuff and work at the clinic."

"You should definitely talk to Dr. Luna then because that's exactly what she did."

"I know!" I replied. "I can't wait to talk to her and learn more about it."

"Well, I'm glad you're enjoying it." He smiled. "We were afraid this would be really boring and tedious work."

"No, I love it!"

"Great. Dr. Luna and I reviewed your work, and you're doing an excellent job. She thought you made some great judgments with the tags, and there were very minimal errors in the data entry, just a couple typos. Honestly, I think we're also upset you can't continue into the school year. But we have some new people starting next Monday, so I hope you don't mind taking them under your wing."

"I don't mind at all!"

"Great, thanks so much, Gigi." He got up. "I'll be heading home now to do my real job, but definitely call if you need anything."

"Sounds good, thanks," I replied and opened the old book up again. I was now nearing the end of it. Dr. Luna had brought in a few more books for me to get started on after this one.

I opened the book up to a new section that was all about werewolf pregnancy. My chest panged. I didn't think it would be so triggering, but I was once again reminded of the fact that I wouldn't be able to carry werewolf pups. Then again, Heidi was making her crazy situation work, so maybe I could make mine with Tyce work too. I began to wonder if there was anything in the books about humans carrying werewolf babies. There had to be, right? From what I'd heard, it was dangerous and the mother was unlikely to survive it. But that was all he said, she said. There weren't any official sources—well, besides maybe these books.

I got to work and began typing the notes the doctor had recorded of different women he'd observed.

Tyce

"I haven't seen Lucy in a while," I commented to Luke as we were sitting in the packhouse office together.

He frowned, rubbing the back of his neck. "We're taking a break."

"No shit, really?" I jerked my head, surprised at the news. "Wow, sorry to hear that, bro."

He took a deep breath and said, "Yeah, I think we need to take some time apart, just to clear our heads and get our priorities straight."

"Was this your idea or hers?"

"Mine," he replied, sighing. "It was just getting to be too much."

"I'm surprised you didn't have to drag her out kicking and screaming," I remarked. Lucy didn't seem like the type to just accept getting dumped by her mate.

"Honestly, I'm surprised too." He brushed a hand through his hair. "At first, she was pretty hysterical, but in the end, she just packed her stuff and left. Her parents helped her move out, and she's got Libby for the time being."

"Damn. I know they say fated-mate relationships usually work out the best, but I didn't think that chosen mates would have the same issues human relationships do."

He sighed again. "I still love her, and I care about her. But yeah, I guess I didn't realize how different our values and personalities were until we started living together. It just changes how things are when you're suddenly with someone all the time. And having a pup together just exacerbated everything."

"So what are you gonna do if it doesn't work out?"

He shook his head slowly. "I don't know. We've marked each other. We're mated for life. And honestly, Lucy is a good person. I know she can be a lot to handle, but I'm holding out hope we'll find our way back to each other. If not, I don't know. I guess I'll just have to figure it out."

"Hey, good luck, man. I hope it works out."

"Me too." He gave a small smile. "Thanks again for keeping an eye on her at the club that night. Things probably would have gone worse if you weren't there."

I chuckled. "I don't even want to think about what my parents would say if my beta's mate acted like that. Pretty sure my dad and grandpa would consider murdering both the beta and his mate."

Luke laughed. "Yeah, I guess at least Blake isn't as harsh as his dad. I honestly don't want to know what he would have done if he were still alive. Luckily my parents are a bit more understanding. Though they're not happy about the whole situation." He let out a deep breath.

At that, Blake entered the office. "Hey, you ready?" he asked, striding toward his desk.

"Not at all, but let's go," I replied.

"So what do you think? Is it getting easier?" Blake asked.

"Nope."

He chuckled. "Yeah, it was the same for me. I still don't know how I did it for four years."

"Hey, it's worth it. It sucks now, but it'll pay off."

He filled a syringe with the violet liquid. "So how much longer are you staying here for?"

"I'll probably leave right before Labor Day weekend. Head back and get back into the swing of things at home."

"So what do you think? How'd you find my pack? I hope you're not going to send a bad report to your family."

"Nah. Let's be honest, I only came here to take a summer break." I snickered. "I'll give the fam a perfectly good report of your high standards and excellent warriors."

"Great." Blake nodded. "Last thing I need is bad blood with our pups being due soon."

"No bad blood. Just a new ally."

"Hey, if you guys ever need my pack's help, I'm only a phone call away. We'll figure out how to get a flight chartered from here and be on our way. You've been a big help this summer, and I see you as a friend now."

"Same," I replied. "Fuck!" I yelled, groaning as Blake injected me. "Except when you stab me like that."

"Tough love." Blake pulled out the needle after emptying the fluid in me. "Any chance you can pick up a shift tonight?"

"Yeah, tonight's fine. But I'm going to need tomorrow night off," I replied.

"Big full moon plans?"

"You could say that," I replied, cringing with the pain pulsing through my arm, rubbing at where Blake had just injected me.

"I think either Luke or I can handle tomorrow night," Blake replied, then he looked over at his beta. "Luke, get him a sticker."

Luke opened his desk drawer and held out a couple sheets of stickers. "I have Barbie and Little Mermaid. Which do you prefer?"

I smiled. "Barbie. She's got bigger tits."

Chapter 62

Ginger

I woke up the morning of the full moon, my stomach already queasy. I thought last time it was now or never, but this time it was *really* now or never.

Trying to keep my mind off it, I crawled over to the cage sitting on the floor of my room. "Good morning, Splinter," I said to the brown rat, opening the cage and pulling him out. I let him climb onto my shoulder as I added pellets into his food bowl. I'd gotten him over the weekend and had already fallen in love. He was just so darn cute and fun to watch.

Recalling how Tyce had destroyed the chipmunk in the woods, I began to hesitate about the idea of introducing him to Splinter. Tyce was lethal as a wolf, and I wasn't ready to watch him pulverize my new friend.

I put Splinter back into his cage and then changed out his water bottle. This was now quickly becoming my morning routine. My parents weren't thrilled about the new addition to the family. Paige tried to meet him, but it was as if he could sense the predator inside her. He instantly peed all over me. So, for now, he was just my friend.

After getting ready and having a quick breakfast, I headed to my new job. I did my best not to think about the crushed-up herb that was sitting inside my dresser drawer. Every time my thoughts would drift that way, my stomach churned, and I felt a little bit dizzy. It was a good thing that my job only required sitting, because I wasn't sure I wouldn't pass out from all the anxiety if I had to stand.

The day seemed to drag. I could barely concentrate on what I was typing, which was okay. I really only had to copy letters over. But not being able to concentrate on what I was reading also meant my mind kept turning to worst-case scenarios. I kept imagining how disappointing it would be once it was made final that my wolf was never coming back. All that money, sickness, and hope over the past year wasted, only to end up in the same place I was before.

My phone pinged next to me.

> ***Tyson Chicken****: Stop thinking about it.*
> ***Me****: How do you know what I'm thinking about?*
> ***Tyson Chicken****: If it's my cock, definitely don't stop thinking about it ;)*
> ***Tyson Chicken****: Feel free to expand that thought to my cock inside your ass*
> ***Me****: You've already penetrated my ass enough*
> ***Tyson Chicken****: How's it feel? :(*
> ***Me****: Never trusting you near my ass again*
> ***Tyson Chicken****: :(*
> ***Me****: :)*
> ***Tyson Chicken****: Glad you're smiling. Meet at your usual spot at 11. Don't be late*

I let out a deep breath and got back to work. Did I really want Tyce there to witness the worst moment of my life? I kept considering whether I should tell him not to come. But I felt so sick already, and I knew I'd need the moral support. He was the only person who knew what I was up to. And maybe he'd finally fully wrap his head around what I'd been trying to tell him—my wolf wasn't coming back.

I knew I was being negative, but it was so hard not to be. I'd felt so positive about it in the beginning, but as time wore on, it became harder and harder to hold on to hope. And now I knew it would only hurt that much more if I actually expected my wolf to come back. It was definitely best to expect the worst.

At 10:45, I began my trek over to my usual spot. Thankfully, everyone had early bedtimes, especially my dad who'd recently begun taking on super early patrol shifts. It was a perfect night, without a cloud in the sky, and I was almost convinced that things weren't as doom and gloom as I'd forced myself to believe.

When I arrived, Tyce was already waiting for me on a rock and I stopped, looking around. He'd spread flower petals and glass jars with lit candles. "Holy shit, Tyce!" I exclaimed.

He smirked. "I hope that's a good 'holy shit' because I've literally never done anything like this before. I was trying to be romantic. Did I pass?"

"Too sweet! Too sweet! I think I'm getting a stomachache, like I just ate way too much ice cream with chocolate syrup and whipped cream and crushed Oreos." I laughed.

He stuck his tongue out and pulled me against him. "Okay, well, I hope you're not too sick. Because I also got a gift for Splinter."

I playfully punched him in the chest. "Tyce! You got a gift for my new pet rat? Goddess. You need to stop before I throw up."

He chuckled. "The exact reaction I was expecting. I'd give Splinter his gift myself, but you know. I'll get him another one once I'm ready to meet him."

"You mean, your gift isn't crushing his bones between your teeth?"

"Close actually." He snickered. "More like the opposite. I got him some chew toys. Maybe he can sharpen his teeth, and it'll be a fairer match once we finally meet." He handed me a small gift bag and pulled me over to sit next to him on a large rock.

I opened the gift, and it was exactly as he said. "This is really sweet. But you didn't need to do all this. Honestly, I think it's just making it harder." I inhaled deeply and let it out.

"Why?" he asked, looking intently into my eyes.

I slumped my shoulders, considering how much I wanted to admit to him. "Making a big deal about this is just making me more anxious," I replied, deciding that was an appropriate amount of information to share.

"Okay, well, tonight is a big deal to me," he said, taking my hands in his. "So please don't throw up, but I prepared a speech."

"Holy Artemis."

He snickered. "I thought you females were supposed to eat this shit up."

"Us females?" I scoffed. "At least call me a woman."

"Okay, woman." I narrowed my eyes at him. Then he added, "Soon-to-be only half woman."

"Okay, continue with your speech, Alpha," I said.

He straightened his shoulders. "First of all, I wanted to tell you that, after you ran out from the shop, I asked the witch what the Death card you pulled meant."

I groaned, my chest tightening with anxiety from the reminder.

"It doesn't mean what you think it means, Gigi." He squeezed my hand. "The Death card in tarot symbolizes transformation. It's putting the past behind you to allow for something new. So you don't have to worry. It's actually a good thing."

I looked up at him, and he rubbed my arm up and down in a soothing gesture. "Was that your speech?" I asked, hiding how comforted I was by what he told me. "Because I think an hour early was overkill for that short speech."

"I'm not done," he replied.

"Okay, continue."

He cleared his throat and gave me a big smile. "Gigi, you drive me absolutely fucking crazy. You are so prickly, infuriating, and short-tempered."

I was about to say something, but he put his hand up, not letting me.

"And if my choice is to spend the rest of my life with you busting my balls, hopefully in the good way, but probably in the bad way, I choose that. Because, Gigi, you are perfect. You are everything I ever wished for in a mate and more. You are sexy, beautiful, witty, and so damn spicy. And, most of all, you are a fighter.

"I believe in my heart you'll get your wolf back tonight. But if you don't, I don't care. Because I love you." He paused, and my heart froze and my breathing stalled. "I love you with or without a wolf, and I want you to be my mate, my luna. I don't care if we are or aren't fated to each other. I choose you, Gigi. And I hope to Artemis you choose me too. Because if you don't, I might have to cut a few rodents up, and maybe some bobcats too. Fuck that, I'm going totally insane and cutting up any and every animal in this state."

I giggled. "As long as you don't cut up Splinter . . ."

"Fuck Splinter. I'm cutting him up too. Splinter is getting splintered."

Tears dropped from my eyes uncontrollably, my whole body shivering. I choked out, "Okay, well, I am kind of an animal lover, and I can't be responsible for the mass murder of every animal in Vermont . . . and Splinter." He squeezed my hands, not breaking eye contact with me. I took a deep breath, my throat aching with emotion. "I love you too, Tyson."

"Fuck yeah!" He fist pumped.

"Goddess, you make it seem like you just won some sort of sports competition."

He moved closer to me, bringing his lips so they were practically touching mine. "Forget sports. This is a million times better than winning a war. I won a luna."

"Okay, slow down there. We've barely even known each other three months." My lips brushed against his as I spoke.

"I don't need more time than that to figure out what I want. I'm an alpha. I want it, I conquer it." He pushed his mouth onto mine, pulling my body against his. I gave in completely, deepening the kiss, taking in how his hard muscles pressed against my soft body, how eager his hands were as they grabbed on to my hips, pulling me closer to him, and how good he smelled to me—a woodsy soap mixed with a fresh aftershave. I was certain it wasn't as good or strong as the mate scent, but I loved it anyway.

"So what is with all the decor?" I asked, pulling away.

He snickered. "I told you. I was trying to be romantic. You know, setting the mood. Hoping if I get the vibe right you'll let me slide myself into the back door."

I pushed on his chest. "Goddess, no one knows how to ruin a moment like you!"

He smiled. "So you have everything you need for tonight?"

"Of course!" I replied. "And I moved the crushed-up herbs into a plastic bottle to avoid any mishaps. Can't be too careful."

"Good."

"I already mixed it with water. So now I just have to set out my crystals and wait until midnight to perform the ritual."

"Are snacks beforehand allowed?" he asked, pulling out a backpack.

"Sure, why not?"

"Okay, good. Because I brought some homemade jalapeño poppers. I can't take credit though—it was all Connie." He pulled out a container and opened the top. "She also doesn't really understand spicy. She took out the seeds. Who does that?"

I laughed and pulled one out of the container, taking a bite. "They're still really good. But yeah, not very spicy."

"Probably better for me anyway. That wolfsbane has thrown me off my game completely. One thing too spicy and I'm puking blood." I gave him a soft rub on the back, and he gave me a sweet smile.

We sat together like that, nibbling at the poppers, waiting for time to tick by. It was actually really nice and comfortable—like sitting with a best friend I'd known forever.

When it got close, I got up, my stomach in my throat. It would be so much easier if Tyce weren't there. I felt so vulnerable having to undress and run through the process with him observing me.

"Hey, it's okay." He also got up, then stood close to me and brushed his hands along my arms before turning me so I was facing him. "Whatever happens, I'm on your team. And if your wolf doesn't come back tonight, I'm not going to give up unless you want me to. And if you want to give up, that's okay too. I told you—I love you and I accept you with or without your wolf."

I swallowed and nodded. "Do you mind turning around and not watching? You're giving me performance anxiety."

"Yeah, I'll turn around. I'll just be sitting over here. Is that okay?" He walked over to the rock and took a seat, turned toward the woods.

"Yeah, that's fine. Thanks." I took a deep breath and began laying everything out before pulling off my clothes.

Here goes nothing.

I followed the ritual, which I'd memorized by now to the point that I could do it in my sleep. I chanted and shook the bottle, then quickly unscrewed the top and gulped it all down, choking down the acidic, rotten taste. I threw the plastic container to the side and turned slowly, allowing the moonlight to catch every inch of my skin.

Only moments in, the familiar sickness began to come over me. My throat burned, practically closing up as I clutched at my neck and gasped for air. I fell to my knees as the world spun around me and caused me to lose my balance. I pushed my palms against the dirt, holding myself up and fighting to stay conscious.

I choked on the air as I inhaled it, gagging. My stomach churned, acid spilling into my esophagus. I swallowed, forcing it to stay down. Tears involuntarily flooded my eyes and spilled onto my cheeks. Everything was blurry. "T-t-t," I tried to choke out, needing him. But almost nothing came out.

I compulsively grabbed for anything I could on the ground—pine needles, leaves, tree roots. I again tried to call out Tyce's name but ended up falling onto my stomach with a thump. That finally got his attention and he turned, rushing over immediately.

"Gigi, Gigi!" he yelled. He got down and pulled me up against him. "Gigi, are you okay?" he shouted, brushing my hair back with one hand and pulling me into his lap with the other. He cradled me as I couldn't do anything but stare at him, pleading with my eyes for him to help me. "I don't know what to do. Should I take you back to the packhouse? Gigi, nod if you want me to take you from here?"

I was about to move my head when another sensation pulsed through me, and every limb in my body simultaneously felt as if it were being broken. A cracking, stabbing pain penetrated all my bones, crimson flooded my eyesight as I screamed out with agony, convulsing.

Tyce tried to hold me still, but I thrashed hysterically as if I'd been possessed by a demon and no longer had any control over my body. I continued to beat against him, but he wouldn't let go, holding me with his strong arms. And soon, the world faded to black as I began to lose consciousness. The last things I saw before my eyes finally closed were Tyce's amber ones, his brows furrowed with worry.

Chapter 63

Tyson

Fuck, I was panicking!

Gigi flailed against me, bruising every part of my body as she smashed against it. Her screams may as well have been swords with how deeply they pierced and agonized me. I used every bit of strength I had to hold her and keep her with me, not allowing her to drop to the ground.

I didn't know what to do. Was she transforming or was she dying? I had first shifted not long before I turned twelve. The first time was always painful. My bones ached, and it felt like another being had possessed me as my body went through the process, forcing me to change from human to wolf, my bones popping into new positions, my teeth and nails growing into weapons, and fur sprouting from every pore of my skin. But it wasn't anything like this—her pain was clearly on another level.

I groaned, doing my best not to let her go, tensing and using every muscle in my body. I didn't know how much more strength I had to keep holding her.

She finally went limp in my arms, and I cried out a howl that came from deep within me—a sound I never made except in my wolf form. How would I ever forgive myself if she died? Especially after I had pushed her to try one more time. Even though I'd never been especially religious, I silently prayed to Artemis she would be okay.

I laid her gently on the ground and brought my ear to her chest to make sure her heart was still beating. Her body still smelled alive. I sniffed, making sure. It only took moments for decay to set in and for my nose to be able to sense it. I lay down on the ground next to her, pulling her against me, brushing her hair, and inhaling her amazing scent.

I was about to get up so I could bring her to the clinic when it started up again. Her eyes popped open and she, again, thrashed uncontrollably, screaming bloody murder. I was about to pull her back against me when it finally began to happen. Her body snapped, popping slowly from human to a semihuman-semiwolf form. I was in awe as I watched the process of someone's first shift. It was rare that anyone observed this phenomenon as it was usually done in private. I, myself, had shifted in my bedroom. I'd locked myself away as soon as I began to feel the symptoms we were told about in school. I wasn't even twelve yet, and not exactly comfortable with the idea of my family watching this take place, especially while I was completely naked.

But something about her transformation seemed off. As she shifted, bits of her skin would tear when she'd turn into a semiwolf, revealing the bones and tissue underneath. I couldn't recall this having been the case with my transformation, although I wasn't an observer either. Bits of tawny fur finally sprouted, which I recognized as being the same coloring as her twin's—something I'd taken note of, wondering if Gigi's would be the same. But it didn't sprout everywhere, and I grew concerned as her figure became more monstrous with every turn.

I continued to watch the back and forth, as she'd pop from one form to the other. I could tell it was fucking painful—definitely more painful than my transformation had been. She was hysterical, howling into the night. I felt helpless watching, unsure what I could do to help.

This went on for an agonizingly long time as I could do nothing but watch and pray she'd be okay and it would all be worth it.

And then she shifted one last time—emerging as a fully formed wolf—but not like one I'd ever seen before.

My first instinct was to attack the monster she'd turned into—she had the appearance of a decaying wolf coming back from death. Her skin was loose and broken on her body, revealing her ribcage and the radial bone on her front left leg, and femur bone on her back right leg. Her eyes were clouded over, and her night vision glowed in a terrifying red color.

Every instinct in my body was telling me to shift and fight her—to destroy the beast that had emerged. But then, I really looked into her eyes, and a different feeling came over me, a sympathetic and tender feeling. My heart raced, and warmth flooded my body.

And something else happened—new feelings emerged that I realized were not my own. I could sense a vulnerability and fear permeating me. I could sense what Gigi felt as she looked at me. Her feelings quickly changed to the same affection that I'd begun to feel as we continued to stare into each other's eyes.

"Mate," I said, the word forced to my mouth, confirming everything.

She wagged her tail in response. As I approached, she got down and rolled onto her back, fully revealing her exposed, bony ribcage, the organs inside of it, and fortunately still-intact skin covering her underbelly. She whimpered in a submissive sound, and I squatted down next to her.

I rubbed her belly, and she purred affectionately. I was suddenly thankful for how used to carcasses I was from the years of torturing, because her form was not for the squeamish. But then, another thought came over me, and I realized how amazing she was. She was terrifying and would be so perfect in a battle. The other side would be terrorized by this demon wolf, and I was flooded with pride that she'd be my luna, fighting beside me.

I then pulled all my clothes off and transformed into my own wolf. Her eyes glowed an even brighter red as our two animal forms were finally united. In this form, I instantly got into a play bow, encouraging her to join in some fun with me. Once she got up, we fell into a game of chase, running through the dark forest together, dodging trees and jumping over fallen branches. I could tell she was still getting the hang of this, so I went easy on her, making sure she was able to keep up with me.

The game was so natural and effortless—it was as if we were two halves of a whole finally reunited, chasing each other through the woods, the moonlight guiding our way, much like we may have done in previous lives.

We sprinted outside the pack land and came upon a pond, sparkling from the moonbeams reflecting off of it. We approached it, both taking drinks as the water rippled toward us. Once I was satiated, I shifted into my human form, wanting to properly communicate with my mate.

I approached her and patted her behind the ears, wanting to feel her fur against the palm of my hand, a light buzzing traveling up my fingertips as my hand touched the skin under her fur, almost like soothing sparks. "Gigi, do you know how to shift back?" I asked. "Do you remember what they taught you in school?"

She blinked a few times and then finally emerged back in her human form. I immediately grabbed her into my arms, holding her tightly to me, embracing the new feeling as I held my mate against me, all her joy radiating around us. "Are you okay?"

"Yeah," she replied quietly.

"You fucking did it, Gigi! You got your wolf back!"

"And we're mates," she replied, her mouth agape as if she couldn't believe it.

"Let's go for a midnight swim," I said, pulling her into the water, feeling like a little kid again, before my father and grandfather had fucked me up, back when life stretched ahead of me in a landscape of color.

She laughed joyfully as I pulled her in. When we were deep enough, she wrapped her legs around me, and I put my mouth on hers—and I swear, just knowing she was my fated mate made her taste that much sweeter.

We swam and splashed each other, completely losing track of time. I thought I loved her before, but now it was as if I would die if she no longer existed—as if anything without her was meaningless.

She tried to splash away, and I caught her, pulling her back against me, nibbling on her ear. I couldn't get enough of her and her beautiful body. Her skin felt so much better, softer, smoother against mine now, and I was desperate to have her again. I rubbed my palm up her thigh, and against her thick, beautiful ass. "Goddess, I want you so badly," I groaned out, my cock throbbing with more desire than I'd ever felt before.

"You know the rules!" she teased, playfully splashing me.

"You said no sex, but you didn't say no this," I said softly into her ear as I slipped a finger between her thighs. She let out a moan against my shoulder, and I slipped another finger inside her, thrusting them in and out of her warmth. "Do you like that, baby?" I rasped out.

"Tyce," she moaned out, and I knew I had her.

I brought my thumb to her clit, circling it gently. Her moans grew louder, and before long, her hand was on my cock, which I'm pretty sure had never been so hard before in my life. The sparks from her hand as she touched it almost made me blow my load right there and then, but I didn't want it to end. I held back.

"Tyce," she cried out again as she miraculously stroked my cock exactly the way I liked it, her thumb finding my weak spot at the head. I groaned, in awe. I usually wasn't one to like a handy, but Goddess be damned, Gigi was perfect. She rubbed it like a porn star, using exactly the right firmness in her grip.

I rewarded her in return by fingering her even more enthusiastically, curving my fingers. And it was like magic as I could practically feel once my finger hit her G-spot through my new ability to sense her emotions. She cried out, her body vibrating against mine. "Fuck, Tyce!" she screamed. I'd never been so turned on by hearing my name before.

Goddess, she's something else.

Before long, she threw her head back, letting out a final loud moan as she stroked me to completion. I groaned as I spilled my fluids into the abyss of the black water.

Fuck, that was so amazing.

I embraced her, inhaling her beautiful scent, and kissed her on her forehead. We stayed like that for a while, the only sound from us was our breathing as we recovered.

Finally, Gigi broke the silence. "How is my wolf? What does she look like? Does she look like Paige's?"

My pulse quickened and heart ached, knowing I'd have to be honest.

"Something's wrong, isn't it?" she asked. *Fuck, she felt that, didn't she?*

"Gigi, I love you no matter what."

"What does that mean?"

"It means that even though your wolf doesn't look like a conventional wolf, I still think you're beautiful. And your wolf will be absolutely fucking perfect in battle. I can already imagine it. You will be the star on the field, kicking ass in your form."

"Why in battle? Tyce, what aren't you telling me? You're obviously dodging the question. This is like when a woman asks her boyfriend if he thinks she's fat!"

I hesitated, not sure how to start to tell her.

"Please tell me, Tyce. I can handle it! I think." Her eyebrows drew together and anxiety emanated from her.

I let out a deep breath. "Your wolf—well, she obviously died and went away for a long time. And I don't exactly know what happens after death, but it obviously changed her."

"Changed her how?"

I sighed. "That's how she looks—like she died and came back."

"How does a wolf that died and came back look? Please tell me, Tyce."

"I mean, she looks kind of like a demon wolf."

"A demon wolf?"

"Yeah."

"What does a demon wolf look like? Is she scary?"

"Kind of."

"Kind of or yes?"

"Yes. But, Gigi, you got your wolf back. It's incredible. And now I feel like my pack has gained a secret weapon with your wolf. I'm going to train you to be the most badass luna ever, and, Goddess, when other packs see you, they're going to be terrified. It's going to be so fucking amazing."

"Your pack," she repeated, and another wave of anxiety rolled off her.

"What's wrong?" I asked.

"I'm going to have to leave my family. Heidi is going to have a pup soon, and I won't be here to be the best aunt ever like I promised. And Paige is going to get married. Not right away, but eventually. And I'm not going to be here to help her with that either. And my mom is going to be so upset . . ." Her voice cracked. "And what about school? I won't be able to go back to school because you have to be alpha of your pack, and we can't live apart or your pack will grow weak."

"You can go to school in Alaska. You can go to the same school my brother went to. It's not even a two-hour flight from our pack."

"Two-hour *flight*?" I exclaimed.

"Yeah, we'll figure out the living situation."

"But, my family."

"You can still come back here to visit them. They're only a plane ride away. And they can always come out to our pack. My packhouse is huge—way bigger than the one in this pack. There's plenty of space for everyone to stay there when they come out." Her anxiety was increasing. I tried to calm her, rubbing my palms down her arms. "Gigi, we don't have to figure everything out tonight. It'll all be okay, though. It's meant to be. You're meant to be a luna, Gigi—my luna."

She nodded, but she still seemed hesitant. I grabbed her hand and pulled her to walk with me to the shore. "Come on, Luna Gigi, let's go for another run to dry off. I want to see what your wolf is made of."

She finally smiled and shifted, instantly breaking into a run. I did the same, chasing after her. My perfect mate.

Chapter 64

Ginger

I closed my eyes and transformed, my bones unsnapping and snapping back into place, fur tingling as it sprouted from my skin. I hesitated. Did I want to see myself? The description of demon wolf scared me. Was my wolf really that terrifying?

I finally opened my eyes. I couldn't help but whimper at what I saw.

While my face seemed okay, and I could see all right, my eyes had an eerie, clouded-over appearance to them. I turned to get a look at my torso and sniffled at the sight of the bones of my ribcage sticking out from my skin, hollowed out, my organs visible through my bones. Bile rose to my throat, and I gagged at how horrifying it was to see my innards revealed like that. My skin was broken in patches throughout my body, including on two of my legs.

I got my wolf back, but she was exactly as Tyce said—a wolf that had risen from the dead, as if I were in a horror movie. I couldn't go out in public like this.

I glanced over at Splinter. He was frozen, unmoving. I smelled the fear from him. He was just as horrified as I was. What was I going to do?

Suddenly, my bedroom door swung open and Paige walked in, then froze. Her eyes bulged and she screamed, instantly shifting into her own wolf form, tearing everything she was wearing. I barely had a chance to react when she pounced on me, pushing me to the ground and shoving her sharp claws into my shoulder. I howled in pain as she brought her wolf teeth to my throat. I didn't know how to fight her off. Was she going to kill me?

Then she stopped.

"*Gigi?*" her voice sounded in my mind. Was this . . . ? "*I can mindlink you?*"

I whimpered as she pulled her claws out of my skin and got off me. I shifted back into my human form, and she did the same. I rubbed at my shoulder, wincing, my hand sticky with blood from the large wound Paige had given me.

"Oh my Goddess! I'm sorry, Gigi!" Paige cried out. "Let me get you a wet towel!" She fumbled to her feet and didn't leave the room right away, staring at me. I reddened, realizing I was completely naked.

"Can't you give me some privacy?" I shouted, and she moved. As soon as she was gone, I quickly threw my pajamas back on. She returned moments later, with a bathrobe on and a wet towel that she handed to me.

"I don't understand. You got your wolf back?" she asked. "But how? And why does your wolf look so scary?" She shook her head. "Sorry, I'm just still trying to wrap my head around this. I keep thinking I'm dreaming."

I sighed, taking a seat on my bed. "Paige, I've been hiding something from you."

"Well, clearly!" she replied. "But why?"

"Because I was afraid you'd try to talk me out of what I was doing. And I didn't want that."

"What were you doing? How did you get your wolf back?"

"I went to the witch shop in Salem—the one I know we're not sup-posed to go to."

"What!" Her eyes practically popped out of her head.

"Paige, I was desperate! I know everyone told me they'd still love me no matter what. But I didn't want to live the rest of my life without a wolf. I was ready to make a deal with the devil. I didn't care what it took—"

"—or if it killed you!" She cut in. "Gigi, you could have died! You can't trust witches! They are conniving, and things never work out the way they're supposed to! I mean look at the wolf they gave you! She's horrifying! They turned you into a monster! It's like a horror movie! When I came in here, I thought some evil zombie wolf thing had come to kill you! Thank Goddess I smelled you. Because I was about to kill you!"

I choked out a whimpering sound that I didn't think came from me. "How can you say that to me, Paige? That's me! That's my wolf!" My throat burned, and I did everything I could to keep the tears from flooding out.

"That's not you! The witches gave you a monster wolf! Can't you see what happened?"

I got up, my heart pounding and my muscles quivering, my chest on fire. "This is exactly why I didn't tell you! Because look at how you're reacting! First you tried to kill me, and now you're calling me a monster! Get out of my room!" I pushed her. "Get out!"

"Gigi, I'm not calling you a monster! I'm calling the wolf the witches gave you a monster!"

"That wolf is my wolf! She died, okay! What do you expect? She's been dead for seven years. She's obviously not going to come out perfect like your wolf! She's been through a lot. And that's who she is now! Beggars can't be choosers. I wanted my wolf back, and I got her back. So I'm going to have to learn to accept her for who she is." The tears I'd been trying to hold back trickled down my cheeks uncontrollably. "So if you only have bad things to say about her, then please leave. Because I don't want to hear it. I get enough people calling me fat. I don't need my wolf being attacked too!"

She paused and bit her lip, looking down at the ground.

"Please, just leave," I said more quietly.

She looked up at me and winced. "I'm sorry, Gigi. I didn't mean to hurt you."

"Well, you did. Both verbally and physically. Okay? I know, I fucked up. I made a huge fucking mistake. And I'm sick of it always being rubbed in my face. At least now I have my wolf back. And okay, I probably won't go out in public as my wolf, but at least I can heal quickly now. Like look at my leg." I thrust it forward and turned it to show Paige where just a light scar remained. "It's completely healed."

She nodded.

"And Tyce! He's my mate, Paige! Just like you thought!"

"What!" Her eyes brightened. "You're kidding! You were able to confirm it?"

"Yeah, he was there when I shifted. And when we looked in each other's eyes, I finally felt it, that we were mates."

"Oh my Goddess, Gigi! I'm so happy for you!" She wrapped her arms around me. "You're going to be a luna! This is amazing! And Tyce isn't going to hurt you!"

I choked up a little, some stray tears falling down my cheek. "But I'm going to have to leave. I have to move to Alaska now. We're literally going to have an entire country between us. And I won't be here for Heidi and her pup. And mom is going to be so upset."

Paige held me tighter. "It's okay, Gigi. The Moon Goddess knows what's best. We're going to stay in touch. You can be there for Heidi through Zoom. And we'll come visit you."

"My pups are going to grow up barely knowing their cousins and grandparents."

"You'll have Tyce's family though, right? And, like I said, we'll still visit each other."

I sighed. "I guess. But it hurts so much. I haven't even left yet, and I'm already devastated about it. It's just all happening so fast."

"That's how it happens with mates. One day you have your whole life ahead of you, and the next you're intricately connected to someone else, and now everything is a compromise."

"Are you still planning to ask Dylan to mark you?"

She let out a small laugh. "I asked him to mark me but he wouldn't do it."

"Why not?"

"Well, he doesn't want his parents to get upset about us marking each other before marriage. I guess I can't be a dictator and force him to do the same thing I'm doing."

"Honestly, Paige, I'm glad you guys haven't marked each other. You don't have to make some crazy grand gesture to Heidi and me or stick your neck out for us. We'll both be okay. We might not be warriors, but we're strong women!"

She smiled and gave me another squeeze. "Can we please hang out as much as possible before you leave for good? I'm going to miss you big-time."

"I'd love that."

"Good."

Chapter 65

Jasmine

"How'd you sleep last night?" Blake pulled me against him after shutting off the alarm, his hand instantly finding my belly.

"Horrible," I replied. "I think my pregnancy symptoms are finally kicking in. I kept waking up to pee all night, and I can't seem to get comfortable."

"We'll do a moon run tonight. Maybe it'll help."

"I doubt it, but it won't hurt anyway. Your mom did say moonlight is good for me now."

"Mmm." Blake nuzzled into me. "You know, something weird happened when you got up to use the bathroom in the middle of the night. I felt something."

"What?"

"A new wolf."

"Don't you feel new wolves most full moons, when the pups finally shift for the first time?"

"Yes, but this was different. This was an adult. For a second, I was wondering if I dreamed it, but I can feel her now, and I don't think I did before."

"Do you know who it is?"

"Yeah, when it happens, I can also tell who it is."

"Who?"

"Gigi."

"What? Gigi? Like Paige's sister Gigi?"

"Yeah. I'm going to ask Tyce about it. Because I don't think I've ever felt something like this before. Maybe he knows. He said he had full moon plans, and I wonder if this had something to do with it."

I thought back and suddenly recalled something. "You know, remember that night you picked me up from their house, around the time we got married?"

"Yeah, when you booty called me?" Blake snickered. "Which, by the way, feel free to booty call me any time. I'm at your service, Mrs. Alpha."

"I'm not sure how booty calling works when we live together!" I gave him a playful smack in the arm.

"The same way when we didn't. You just tell me you're horny, and I'm ready. Any place, any time."

"I never had any doubt about that."

"Feel free to test your theory." He gave me a mischievous smile.

"I will, later." I moved to the edge of the bed. "It's time to get up now." I got to my feet and moved toward the dresser to pick out my clothes for the day.

"I'm the alpha. I won't get in trouble if I'm late." He winked.

I giggled. "Blake, do you ever think about anything else?"

The corners of his eyes wrinkled in mischief. "Nope."

"Anyway, before this all somehow went off track, unsurprisingly." I rolled my eyes and continued, "I was going to say something."

He chuckled. "Okay, okay."

"When I was over at Paige's house with her sisters, something seemed off. It seemed like Gigi was hiding a secret. I didn't know what it was at the time. But do you think maybe it has something to do with this?"

"I don't know but I'll find out." He got out of bed and headed toward the bathroom but stopped in front of me for a moment. "You look so beautiful carrying my pups." He moved closer to me and kissed me on the forehead, and I felt both his pride and a slight sadness behind it. I knew he must have been reminded of Ria. I wrapped my arms around him, trying to comfort him.

I sat with Blake at his desk, going over some financials, when Tyce darkened the doorway. We both looked up as he strolled in with a big smile on his face. While he was never quite as gloomy as Blake, it was very noticeable when he smiled like this.

"Good morning, Alpha, Luna," he said as he plopped himself down in a chair.

"Good morning, Alpha Tyce." I smiled at him.

"How are the pups doing?" he asked. "And our grandma called to ask if you got her gifts."

"Oh yes!" I replied. "I actually just finished writing her a thank you card and was about to put it in the mail. The two cribs she sent are perfect! And I absolutely love the double stroller. She must have spent a fortune."

"I told you she's generous with gifts." He winked. "She's dying to meet the pups soon. I think she's hoping you'll come visit our pack with your parents once they're here."

"That would be lovely. You'll have to tell me the best time of year to come to Alaska."

"Definitely July."

"Okay, then maybe we can plan a trip for next year." I looked up at Blake. "What do you think?"

He smiled at me and then turned to Tyce. "Before we start planning our next vacation, I have some questions."

"Shoot," Tyce said.

"I felt a new wolf in my pack last night—an adult one." When Tyce didn't say anything, Blake continued, "I have a feeling you know who it is."

"I guess we can't get around your alpha senses."

"Is it a secret?" Blake tilted his head.

"Yeah, it was actually."

"Why didn't she have a wolf until last night?"

"I'm surprised you don't know. But I suppose it's a private medical record."

"My mom takes her job very seriously. She doesn't share any pack members' medical information with me."

Tyce sighed. "This is really her story to tell, and this better not leave this room."

"Neither Jasmine nor I would ever break your trust."

He nodded. "I can give you the short version. She basically killed her wolf when she was twelve by eating wolfsbane. And she got help from some witches to bring her wolf back from the dead."

"Is such a thing possible?" I asked, leaning forward in my chair, amazed. I'd never heard of someone losing their wolf and definitely hadn't heard of them getting it back. I wanted to learn more, but I could tell Tyce wasn't going to be open about it. Maybe Gigi would eventually feel comfortable enough to open up to me.

"Seems so," Tyce replied.

"And is her wolf *normal*?" Blake asked.

"Blake!" I exclaimed at his rude question, but he didn't flinch.

"Why wouldn't her wolf be *normal*?" Tyce responded with a bite to his voice, crossing his arms. "Anyway, she's no longer your concern. As of the end of the month, she's going home with me and joining my pack."

"Tyce! Is she going to be your mate?" I got up, ready to give him a congratulatory hug.

"She *is* my mate," he replied. "It's confirmed now that she has her wolf back."

I ran over to him and wrapped my arms around his shoulders. "Wow, congratulations! What great news! I guess we do have a vacation to plan then—for your wedding!"

Blake cleared his throat and said, "She's still here for the next few weeks. And she hasn't had training. I'm concerned that she's not going to know how to control her wolf."

I gave him a glare, annoyed by how grumpy he was being. I would talk to him about it later. "Blake! I'm sure it's fine!"

"Yeah, I understand your concern." Tyce nodded. "I'll train her. Starting today."

"Why don't we all train together?" Blake asked. "You owe me that since she's still a member of my pack. And we can do it after dusk, so we won't have an audience."

Tyce seemed to hesitate. He didn't say anything for a while. Finally, he replied, "Fine, but this stays between us. I don't want people talking about her around the pack. There's already been enough rumors."

"I agree," Blake replied. "Okay, ready?" He pulled open his desk drawer.

"Yep, gotta get my shots in while I still can." He rolled up his T-shirt sleeve.

"Hey congrats, man, on finding your mate." Blake gave him a small smile. "She seems like a good girl."

"She's the best."

I had training in the late morning and broke for lunch at twelve with all the other warriors. Paige and I met up and decided to eat outside that day, since the weather was so nice. "So, what'd you bring today?" I asked her.

"My mom made pasta salads for everyone this morning. You?" Paige looked over at my lunch bag.

"Looks like Connie made me some turkey pinwheels and cut-up fruit." I pulled everything out.

"That must be nice to have a cook do all that for you. I guess I have my mom for now, but soon I'll be on my own!"

"When are you and Dylan finally tying the knot and moving in together?"

She sighed. "Don't you think it's weird that I'm only nineteen and already getting married and moving in with a *husband*?"

"Why is that weird?" I studied her. "Everyone gets married and moves in with their mates when they meet them. I guess it takes longer for some than others. But you're one of the lucky ones! You don't have to wait and worry that you'll never meet him and will have to settle for a chosen mate."

"I guess." She sighed again.

"What's wrong?" I thought things were good between Paige and Dylan. They seemed perfect for each other. But now I was wondering if there was something I didn't know. It seemed like there could be a lot Paige didn't tell me. Take, for example, that her sister didn't have a wolf.

"Maybe it's stupid." She looked down.

"Your feelings are valid, Paige! You know my story. I knew the whole time things weren't right with Luke, but I was so set on being with my mate that I completely ignored the obvious. Do things seem off with Dylan?"

She looked up, her breath catching. "Oh, Goddess, no! I love Dylan! It's not that!"

"Then what is it?"

She let out a small chuckle. "I guess I'm just really getting into this whole warrior thing now. And I want to be like my dad—work up the ranks and become a senior warrior like him. I'm just afraid that if I get married, I'm going to end up getting sucked into becoming a mom, and my whole career will just go out the window. I'd like to at least establish myself as a warrior first. I mean, for men, it's so easy. No one expects them to just stay home when they become dads. But with women, like you basically lose momentum when you get pregnant, and then after pups, you become the primary caretaker. I don't know. Maybe I'm overthinking all of this. I guess I was just sometimes jealous of Gigi and how she was able to go away to school and not have to worry about all this mate business."

"But she ended up with a mate anyway!" I pointed out.

"Oh, so you know?"

"Yeah, Tyce told us this morning. Isn't it amazing? Your sister's going to be a luna!"

She smiled. "Gigi always had the heart of a warrior."

"Wow, I'm looking forward to training with her tonight then!"

"You're training with Gigi tonight?" Paige raised her eyebrows.

"Yeah, Blake wants us all to train together. With him and Tyce too."

"Oh, okay . . ." Her voice trailed off. "In your wolf forms or human forms?"

"I guess human to start. But maybe wolf too. I'm not sure." Paige was biting her bottom lip and brushing her hands through her ponytail. She seemed a bit spaced out. "Why?"

"I'm just afraid her wolf might be unpredictable. And with you being pregnant, I don't know. It seems dangerous."

"Dangerous?"

"Yeah. Be careful, Jasmine. Please. Maybe you should just train in your human forms."

That evening, after dinner, Blake and I were changing to head out. "Why were you asking Tyce if Gigi's wolf is normal, Blake?"

"I don't trust witches."

"So you think they gave her some crazy, uncontrollable wolf?"

"I don't know, but I'm going to find out. I don't like the idea of there being someone in my pack with an unpredictable wolf. It's dangerous, especially with so many pups around. All it takes is one incident."

"So what are you going to do if her wolf is unpredictable?"

"If she's going to stay here for the rest of the summer, then she's going to have to take something to suppress her wolf. After she leaves, that's up to Tyce. He can deal with his own pack."

"Blake, that seems so extreme! She can't learn to control her wolf if it's being suppressed!"

"She's only here for two or three more weeks if she leaves with Tyce. Two or three weeks isn't going to make or break anything."

"Please don't do that to her, Blake. They injected me with tranquilizers in middle school, to try to help me with my panic attacks, and it was horrible. I was so happy when we started training in our wolf forms and I didn't have to take them anymore." I shivered from the memories that I tried to suppress. Blake wrapped his arms around me, clearly feeling them too now.

"What was it like?" he asked gently.

"It felt so unnatural. I could sense my wolf frozen inside me, heavy. I became depressed. It wasn't that different from that year after Luke and I rejected each other. And my anxiety got even worse. But my parents didn't care. They thought it was best for me. They didn't understand. They only cared that they'd cured me from uncontrollably shifting into my wolf when I had a panic attack. And they pointed out that I was still getting good grades. But I had to work twice as hard, and I was so exhausted."

"Jasmine," he whispered.

"When they finally stopped injecting me, it was like a really heavy coat had finally been taken off me. My wolf sprang back to life, and I was finally able to be happy and laugh again."

Blake kissed me on the head and said, "I'll try to be open-minded tonight, okay?"

"Thank you."

After we finished getting ready, we headed out. "I told Tyce we'd meet him in the smaller field since it's more secluded. And we have the woods right there for privacy." I nodded, and he took my hand, leading the way.

When we arrived, Tyce and Gigi were already there.

"Awesome job, Gi! You're a natural!" Tyce exclaimed with a big smile on his face as he observed her front kick. "Not rusty at all."

Her face reddened, and then they turned as we approached.

Blake nodded at the two of them and asked, "How's it going?"

"Great, Gigi's a natural luna, an amazing addition to my pack. You don't know what you're losing." He gave her a big wink.

"Have you done any training in your wolf form, Gigi?" Blake asked, looking her up and down.

"Hey, hey! We're starting slow!" Tyce replied. "Let's ease our way into the wolf training. Just human forms today."

"Good idea, Tyce!" I responded before Blake could say anything. "There's no reason to rush things. Everyone starts out learning in human form first and then moves into wolf form once they master the basic moves. So let's make sure Gigi is ready before we do that." I glared at Blake, and he crossed his arms but didn't say anything.

Gigi let out a deep breath and looked down at the ground. Tyce affectionately rubbed her on the back. He then looked down at her and smiled, and my heart must have melted. It was so obvious how deeply he cared for her. "Come on, baby. Let's show them what you've got," he encouraged her. "You're doing great."

"Okay, let's start with the seven basics then," Blake said. "Ladies fight, men defend."

"Come on, baby, you know these." Tyce got into a defensive stance next to Blake as he did the same and nodded at me to start.

I went through the motions. I'd been practicing these moves since kindergarten, so I had long mastered them. Partway through, I noted Blake was barely even paying attention to me and was more focused on what Gigi was doing. So I decided to be a little trickster. I smiled to myself and went full force on the double-leg takedown, grabbing Blake with both arms around his legs while keeping my chest close, forcing him to come crashing to the ground.

"Booyah! You're down!" I teased, laughing. "Not so tough now, Mr. Alpha. Taken down by a pregnant lady."

Blake playfully glared at me and Tyce burst into laughter. "Yeah, she definitely has Jade Moon blood."

Gigi clearly took a cue from me because she did the same thing, taking Tyce down as soon he let down his defenses. "For an alpha, you're weak!" she teased, getting up.

"Oh yeah?" He pulled her back down, and she tumbled on top of him. He quickly flipped her onto the ground until he had her pinned down. "Who's weak now?" She tried to wrestle him off, but he kept her trapped, sticking his tongue out at her. "Time to learn your place, Luna. Under your alpha."

"That's not what you said the other week when I rode your cock so hard you started screeching like a chimpanzee." She tried to push him off her. I covered my mouth, trying not to laugh. I looked over at Blake who had an amused look in his eyes.

"We said we wouldn't talk about that again." He held her down as she struggled. "Or should we also talk about that time you started naming all the presidents while you were coming."

"To be fair, Monroe seems like he'd be a good lay."

Tyce wrinkled his nose. "Is that what you want? Presidential roleplay?" She giggled. "Because I'm ready to watch you swallow my cock in a blue dress."

Blake cleared his throat very loudly, and Tyce finally let Gigi go. The two of them got up, and Gigi brushed herself off. "Is that how you two train?" Blake asked. The way he said it was all business, but I could tell he was trying really hard not to smile, just as amused by their interaction as I was.

"We train in both physical and verbal attacks," Tyce replied without even batting an eye. "Words cut deeper than knives and all that." He then turned to Gigi and said, "Although, I wouldn't mind putting knife training on the roster." He winked at her, and she blushed.

Blake cleared his throat again.

"Okay, let's go again. This time pay attention to your own mate." Tyce gave Blake a hard stare.

"I was distracted by her eyes," he replied. I glanced over, and her eyes seemed normal, but then, I realized all of us had our night vision on and she didn't.

"Do you know how to switch to night vision?" I asked Gigi. "My eyes usually just switch automatically when it gets dark, but maybe you're suppressing it without realizing it."

"Oh, no. I like to train without my night vision," Gigi responded. "It's more challenging."

"It flickered on, though," Blake elaborated. "That's why I was distracted." He gave Tyce a look I couldn't interpret.

"So what? It flickered. She's still learning how to control everything, and she's doing great. Mind your own mate," Tyce replied with his jaw and fists clenched.

"I want to know what you're hiding," Blake responded, getting closer to Tyce.

"I'm not hiding anything that's your business. She's my fucking mate, and as far as I'm concerned, she's already a part of my pack."

"She's on my pack land." Blake raised his voice. Gigi whimpered, and Tyce's features softened as he touched her arm affectionately.

"Blake, stop it!" I grabbed his arm. "Why are you acting like this?"

He opened his mouth. He was clearly about to say something when, for no obvious reason, Tyce tore through his clothes, the sound of ripping fabric echoing through the air, and turned into his grizzly bear of a wolf. Before any of us could react, his claws tore through the grass as he chased a rat that had sprinted out of some ferns. Gigi instantly followed suit, doing the same thing.

I barely processed what had happened when a scream left my lips at the monster that emerged. Her form was that of a wolf that had begun decaying, skin eaten away by bacteria exposing the bones and organs inside her on her chest and legs. Her eyes switched to night vision and glowed a terrifying red. It was as if a zombie had climbed its way out of the earth in order to feed on all our pack's pups.

As soon as Gigi's paws hit the ground to chase after Tyce, Blake shouted, "Stop!" And I sensed a vibration secondhand as his aura was reflected back toward him, as if she were shielded. "Stop!" he tried again. But the same thing happened, and she kept moving.

Within seconds, Blake had his clothes peeled off, and he sprinted after the two of them as they went to retrieve the rat out of the ferns where it had run to hide. He was midpounce onto Gigi when Tyce suddenly abandoned his mission to chase the rat and turned to meet Blake in the air. The two of them fell into a fight, tearing into each other with their claws and threatening each other with their teeth.

Not sure what else to do, I also threw off my clothes quickly and shifted into my own wolf. I pounced onto Blake, trying to get him to stop.

"*Get off me!*" Blake mindlinked me.

"*No! Stop it, Blake!*" I mindlinked him back. "*Stop it right now! I'm not letting go until you stop!*"

I knew he wouldn't throw me off, so his only option was to listen to me. But I could tell he wasn't happy. He was raging on the inside, seeing red. I'd never felt him react so angrily before, especially not toward me. I was actually a little terrified.

I released my claws and climbed off him, but I refused to let him intimidate me.

"*Jasmine, let me deal with this!*" he mindlinked me.

"*No, shift back!*" I replied, not backing down. "*Shift back now!*"

Tyce ran in front of Gigi, gesturing with his head for her to stay behind him. Yes, her form was horrifying, but it was clear that Gigi wasn't a danger. The only danger was Blake as far as I could see, and I couldn't understand what had gotten into him. Also, why had Tyce suddenly shifted, and why had Gigi followed, doing the same?

I glared at Blake and we ended up locked in a staring contest. Finally, he gave in and shifted back. He breathed out a huff as Tyce also shifted back.

"*Apologize now!*" I demanded of Blake.

I could tell he was hesitating, but I knew he'd do the right thing. He balled his hands into fists, but finally nodded at Tyce. "Look, sorry about that, man. I wasn't going to hurt your mate. I was just trying to restrain her—"

"Why would you try to *restrain* her?" Tyce replied with cold, hard eyes and flared nostrils.

"She didn't stop when I used my aura on her."

"And why the *fuck* would you use your aura on her?"

"Because she shifted without warning—clearly unintentionally seeing how she tore right through her clothing. With Jasmine being pregnant, I'm going to be on edge when someone doesn't have control of their wolf. And her form." He gestured to Gigi. "Her form caught me off guard. I wasn't expecting, well, *that*!"

"She's fucking amazing!" Tyce responded defensively. "Look at her. She's going to be fucking brilliant in battle! The other side is going to be whimpering like little pups when they get a look at her. You have no right to lay a single paw on her. She did nothing wrong except not look the way you expected her to!"

Blake sighed.

"You already had it out for her this morning. What's your problem, bro?"

"Look, I just don't trust witches!"

"Well, take a look at her. What do you think? She's not attacking anyone, and she's not out of control. Satisfied?" He gestured toward her, and she turned her muzzle downward, drawing her tail between her legs as we all stared at her.

"*Gigi, it's okay. Blake is sorry. I can sense it,*" I mindlinked her. "*There's nothing wrong with you.*"

She looked up and locked eyes with mine. It would definitely take some getting used to, but I also felt a tightness in my chest and devastation at her predicament. It wouldn't be easy to look like her wolf. Blake was only the first person who would react as he did. Even her own twin was wary of her. I promised myself that I would do the best I could to make her feel accepted.

"Satisfied?"

Blake gave Tyce a nod. "Look, let's just forget about what happened. Obviously, I overreacted and need a run to cool off. Why don't we call it with the training and do a moon run together instead?"

Tyce didn't say anything and shifted back into his wolf form. He gestured to Gigi to follow him, and the two of them sprinted off. Blake similarly shifted, and he waited until I followed to break into a run as well. "*Jasmine, I'm sorry,*" he mindlinked me.

"*You should really be apologizing to Gigi,*" I replied.

"*I know, and I will.*"

Chapter 66

Ginger

After we got back to the packhouse, all I wanted to do was hide—hide away forever. My heartbeat thrashed in my ears, and my chest felt tight. Was our alpha really going to attack me because of how I looked? Was this going to be my life now? And my sister too. Everyone I thought would protect me was now impulsively turning on me.

I burrowed underneath Tyce's blankets while he went to use the bathroom, thankful they kept the air-conditioning at close to freezing in the packhouse. I was safe in the dark where no one could see me. I inhaled his linens. The smell was mesmerizing—like nothing I'd ever smelled before. A musky, warm, almost burned-vanilla scent I couldn't quite put my finger on. All I knew was that I wanted to snort it and hold it in my lungs. Under his sheets, I was surrounded and safe in my little cocoon. I was now able to experience so many wonderful things because my wolf came back, but she was also dangerous—not dangerous because she was a demon like everyone thought, but because she made people want to hurt me.

"Hey." Tyce crawled inside the covers, joining me. "What are you doing in here?"

"Hiding," I replied.

"Why?"

"Because no one can see me in here. I can be ugly all I want and exist in peace."

"You're not ugly. You're the complete opposite of ugly."

Tears flooded my eyes. For someone who never cried much before, I definitely let it all out this summer. "Be honest, Tyce. You only like me because of the mate bond. You just didn't realize it before. But if you weren't pulled toward me, you'd think I was fat and ugly."

"What? That's not even close to true." He pulled my chin up, forcing me to look into his glowing amber eyes. He slowly and delicately brushed my hair out of my face.

"How can someone like you who's so in shape and muscular and hot ever like someone like me?"

"Gigi, I've told you before—you're exactly my type. Even before I met you, I always hooked up with thick women. I'll show you pictures if you want, though I don't know why you would. I could have anyone I wanted, and that's what I wanted. I love everything about you. I love your G cups, your big, round ass, your delicious thighs that are so perfect for biting into, your soft belly that I just want to bury my head into and sleep on—everything. You're so beautiful." He touched his lips to mine, gently kissing me. "You're beautiful. You are so beautiful." He kissed me again. "You're beautiful."

"I don't feel beautiful."

"Feel my cock."

"Tyce!"

"Feel it—it's rock-fucking-hard right now. My cock don't lie. It doesn't get up for just anyone."

I brought my hand to his crotch and brushed against it. He wasn't lying. It was a pulsing steel rod. I continued to glide my hand along it, and he let out a groan.

"Now do you believe me?"

I sighed and snuggled against him.

"I will tell you every day for the rest of my life that you're beautiful if you want me to. Because I don't ever want you to doubt it."

"But my wolf," I choked out.

"Your wolf is amazing too. People just don't understand yet. But they will. Your wolf is special, and I'm lucky as fuck that you're my wolf now too. Warriors try to make themselves look scary and intimidating by growling and baring their teeth. But you—you're already intimidating without even trying. You're absolutely perfect."

He held me and we lay like that in silence, snuggled up against each other, the sparks from our bodies traveling along our skin. I wanted to stay like that forever, safe with Tyce's arms wrapped around me. Finally, I broke the silence. "You were forced to shift."

"I know. Is that why you shifted too?"

"Yeah, I felt all your emotions secondhand. And they were so strong that it caused me to change too. I don't know. Maybe if I had more control over my wolf it wouldn't have happened, but it's so new to me. I'm still learning."

"Fuck, I'm sorry, Gigi. I really am trying. I promise."

"But you stopped. You didn't chase the rat all the way."

"Yeah, a stronger instinct took over to protect you. This mate bond—it's something else. You hear about it your whole life, but I don't think anything could have prepared me for what it's really like."

I kissed him and he pulled away.

"Also, I have to thank you. Your wolf totally distracted Blake and Jasmine from the fact that *I* was the one who wasn't in control of my wolf." He chuckled. "Goddess, I have to laugh about it because it's almost ridiculous. I'm supposed to be the most trained and in control person in my pack, and all it takes is a fucking rodent to sprint across my field of vision."

"Tyce, it's not forever." I kissed him again. "I believe in you. You're going to conquer this. It's just going to take some patience and time. You're so dedicated. I know you don't tell me everything, but even how you willingly get injected with wolfsbane on a regular basis shows how much you care about being alpha and leading your pack. And someone with as much heart as you will never fail. You got this!"

He smiled but didn't say anything, and I wished so much I didn't have to go home and could just stay wrapped up in him all night.

The next day, I headed to my job, still a little down from the night before. I got right to work as soon as I got in, flipping open to the next page to transcribe, sticking my headphones in to block everything else out.

I probably hadn't been working for a half hour when the scent of someone entering the room traveled into my nostrils. Now I finally understood what Tyce meant about it being hard to sneak up on a werewolf. I instantly turned around to see Blake's tall figure stepping through the doorway.

I pulled my headphones out, straightening up.

"Hey," he said. "Do you mind if I sit down?"

"Uh, sure," I replied. I knew, logically, I was going to be a luna soon, but I still couldn't get over my timidness around our alpha. I mean, I'd been raised my whole life to show our alpha the utmost respect.

"Thanks," he replied, taking a seat at the table across from me. "So, how are you, Gigi? How's the job going?" he asked.

"It's good. Tyce told me you helped me get this job, and it's been going really well, so thank you."

"You're welcome." He nodded humbly.

"How are you and your job going?" I asked, not sure what to say and feeling awkward, wondering if I was expected to make conversation.

He gave me a small smile. "I'm good. The job is, well, it's a job. But I get to order people around, so it's not half bad."

"Doesn't sound bad at all," I replied, nodding.

"Sounds like you'll have the same job soon." He gave me a friendly smile. "Anyway, Gigi, I came in here for a reason. I wanted to come in person and apologize for my atrocious behavior last night. I was completely out of line, and everything Tyce said to me was right. Not trusting witches didn't give me an excuse to do any of the things I did, especially to a luna of another pack. So I'm sorry, and I hope you'll forgive me."

I took a deep breath, let it out, and responded, "I forgive you. But please, be honest. Is my wolf really that bad?"

He clenched and unclenched his hands. "No. But let me elaborate. My fear was that your wolf would be feral and bloodthirsty. I had already prejudged your wolf, so when you shifted, I just made an impulsive assumption. I was on high alert, especially with Jasmine being there. I obviously made a lot of mistakes. But it wasn't your wolf—it was me."

I nodded.

"And, for what it's worth, Tyce is right. You will be brilliant in battle. Half the fight is intimidating the other side, and you've already got that covered." He gave me a big, encouraging smile.

"Thanks," I replied.

"Also, I haven't said anything to anyone, including my mom. But, if you feel comfortable, I'm sure she'd love to take notes on your wolf and how you got her back. It can't be common for something like that to happen. My mom is really trustworthy. She'd never tell anyone anything you told her, including your parents or even me."

"Yeah, I'll think about it."

"Cool. Well, I've got to get back to work. But let Tyce know if you ever want to do couples training again. I promise to behave next time." He got up and headed toward the door.

"Thanks, Alpha." I waved goodbye and got back to work.

Chapter 67

Ginger

"Paige, I've been speaking to the priest, getting some dates he has open for your wedding," my mom announced at dinner. "I also called Dylan's mom, and she's right on the same page."

"You called Dylan's mom?" Paige replied, much more aggressively than I was expecting.

"Well, of course! We need to make sure everyone's in agreement. Since she only has sons, and this is the first of hers to find his mate, she's dying to be included. But don't worry, I let her know you're very agreeable and will be more than happy to involve her. How do you feel about her coming with us to look at wedding dresses?"

Paige blinked rapidly, her mouth agape.

"You know, she actually has great taste. She helped decorate for the winter solstice celebration at the temple a few years back, and she had some wonderful ideas. Maybe we should include her in picking out the flowers too."

I glanced over at Paige again, and her whole face was red, her hands balled into fists. Shit, maybe Paige and I were more alike than I thought.

"Oh Goddess," our dad joked. "How much is this going to cost me this time around?"

"Good news!" my mom responded. "The temple had a last-minute opening for a Saturday in mid-September. Seems that Becky girl got herself knocked up, so her family rushed the wedding before she started showing. If we do it then, it'll still be warm enough to do a backyard wedding, so we won't need to rent an indoor space."

I was uncomfortable with how oblivious my mom was to the clear breakdown Paige was having right next to me. Wanting the awkwardness to stop, I blurted the first thing that came to mind. "I won't be here in September."

"Don't worry, Gigi. We'll pick you up from school for the wedding. We obviously don't want you to miss it!" my mom replied.

"I'll be in Alaska."

"Alaska?" my dad exclaimed.

Shit, I had planned to ease them into the subject. Fuck fuck fuck.

"Why would you be in Alaska?" my mom asked with a blank look on her face.

Okay, I was practically hyperventilating. Time for the big reveal with absolutely no tact. "I got my wolf back and found out that Alpha Tyce is actually my mate. So he asked me to move to Alaska with him, so I can be luna of his pack."

I'm pretty sure I'd never seen my parents so shocked in their life. The whole room was completely silent when my mom went pale and dropped out of her chair.

"Emily!" my dad shouted, diving after her. Paige and I rushed over as my dad hoisted her into his lap. My mom slowly opened her eyes, staring up at all of us looking down at her. "Honey, are you okay?" my dad asked my mom tenderly.

She blinked a few times. "Oh my." She slowly got up and climbed back into her chair with my dad helping her. "I feel a little weak, but I'll be okay."

"Gigi," my dad said sternly.

"I'm sorry, Daddy!" I replied, feeling guilty about what had just transpired.

"There's nothing to be sorry about," he replied, not seeming that forgiving. "But you just dumped a lot of information on us that's going to take some time to process. Did I hear you correctly? You got your *wolf* back?"

I nodded.

"How?"

"Please don't be mad, Daddy."

"Why would I be mad? This is obviously a good thing." His eyes shifted between my mom and me.

"I asked for help from some witches."

"You what?" He raised his voice and I flinched.

"They're not that bad, Daddy. I promise."

"Gigi, for the love of our Goddess, why would you ever involve yourself with witches? Haven't you learned what happens when you don't obey the rules? You can't trust those conniving *things*. You could have died, Gigi! Is that what you wanted? To hurt your family like that?"

I shook my head, feeling like I was twelve years old all over again, getting lectured by my parents when they found out I'd been smoking behind the school and sneaking out of the house.

"But Dad! She got her wolf back!" Paige surprisingly came to my defense, even though she had acted the same way when she first found out. "It's a miracle! Shouldn't we be celebrating?"

"It's all the praying we've done, Paige!" my mom chimed in. "The Moon Goddess listened. It's amazing! And what a mate she brought to our Gigi! An alpha! Can you believe it? Our daughter is going to be a luna!" For a second it seemed like everything would be okay, but then the waterworks started as my mom's excitement turned to sobbing. "And she's going to leave me. My Ginger is going to leave me. My little baby Ginger is leaving me," she choked out through her tears.

My dad leaned toward my mom, taking her hand in his. "Emily, it's okay. I'm sure Ginger will still come back to visit."

"Of course I will!" I tried to console her. "Heidi's going to have a pup soon, and of course I'll come back when her pup is born and for all the other important life events."

"And we can always go visit Gigi too. Right, Gigi?" Paige pushed on my back.

"Yes, of course. I'm going to be an alpha's mate, so I'm sure that means I'll have plenty of money to pay for everyone's plane tickets. And Tyce said his packhouse is huge with plenty of room for everyone to stay."

"How much have you and Alpha Tyce discussed all this?" my dad asked.

"Not much yet. I mean, we only just found out," I replied.

"Is he planning to meet us?"

"Of course."

"Has he even asked you on a date?"

"What?"

"Well, normally he'd ask you on a date to get to know you before he asks you to move to be with him. Doesn't he want to get to know you?"

Shit, this conversation was totally derailing, and not going the way I was hoping at all. Not that I knew what to hope for, but I was panicking. How was I supposed to answer that? *Tyce and I have already been fucking for over a month now?*

"Dad, chill!" Paige intervened. "Gigi and Alpha Tyce were already friendly with each other. They felt the bond before they were able to confirm it."

"Just friends though!" I clarified. "And barely even that. We just talked sometimes. About scriptures mostly. He's really into temple and scriptures. And religious meditation. Actually, really into religious meditation and pursuing religious enlightenment." Okay, I was acting super awkward and obvious.

"And didn't Tyce tell you he wanted to come over for dinner this week?" Paige added. "And meet your whole family and both your sisters' mates?"

"Yeah, he did." I nodded along.

"This Sunday after temple, right?"

"Right."

My dad seemed to relax in his chair. "Great. Tell Alpha Tyce we'd love to have him over."

"Of course."

"And your wolf. Can we see your wolf?" my dad asked.

"You want to see my wolf?"

"Of course we do!" My mom nodded enthusiastically. "This is what we've been praying for all these years."

"Y-yeah," I replied, sighing.

"What's wrong?" my dad asked.

"Daddy, you're not going to like my wolf," I replied, my voice cracking. "Paige saw her by accident, and she was terrified. My wolf was dead for a long time, and that's exactly how she looks." I slumped my shoulders.

"Is that true, Paige?" My dad questioned her.

"Her wolf is pretty scary," she agreed, "but seems to be harmless."

"My wolf *is* harmless!" I insisted.

"Okay, well, now I definitely want to see it," my dad said.

"Please don't judge her, Daddy, please." I blinked back tears, already imagining what my father would think once I revealed her to him.

"Peachy, I'm going to keep an open mind, okay? I don't love that you went to see witches to get your wolf back. But as long as she doesn't harm anyone, then I won't be upset, okay?"

I nodded and stood up. "I'll go into the living room to shift, and then come into the kitchen, okay?"

"Okay, we'll all wait here."

I dragged my feet, barely able to take the necessary steps into the living room, my stomach acidic. I steadied myself, taking deep breaths, my shaky hands pulling off my clothes. I stood there, naked, hesitating. *I can do this, I can do this, I can do this.* Finally, I forced myself to shift.

I slowly dragged myself back to my kitchen as my wolf, my head hung. I finally entered and looked up at everyone. My mom gasped, bringing her hand to her mouth. Paige sat still, not saying anything. Finally, my dad got up.

"Holy Artemis. Well, your wolf is something," my dad said, his eyes downturned and sad. I hated disappointing him. I could tell he hated my wolf. But there was nothing I could do.

I nodded, deciding my family had enough, and turned back around, going back to the living room. It took everything in me not to cry when I shifted back, throwing my clothes back on. I wanted to throw up. They were clearly disgusted.

I returned to the kitchen silently, falling back into my chair. My dad put his hand on mine and said, "Gigi, we still love you, okay?"

I nodded, swallowing.

"And we're very happy you found your mate," my mom added.

"Yes, we all look forward to having Alpha Tyce over this weekend." My dad smiled, patting my hand.

Chapter 68

Ginger

Sunday evening came far too fast, and I was a mess. In just days, my life had completely changed. Now, instead of preparing to head back to school in Boston in a few short weeks, I was withdrawing, researching schools in Alaska, and pulling together a list to apply to so I could start up again in the spring.

Between that, work, and not getting enough sleep because Tyce and I were still meeting up most evenings, I was stressed to the max. And now I was super nervous about Tyce meeting everyone.

My mom fluctuated between being ecstatic and randomly crying. My dad had to live with the fact that he wasn't going to be able to have his man-to-man talk with Tyce about relocating to our pack. I guess my dad hadn't considered the possibility of my potential mate being an alpha—literally the one job that couldn't relocate. And also the one person my dad would never try to convince of anything.

I went back and forth on what to wear several times. "Goddess, I wish Hunter were here!" I whined to Paige. "He'd know!"

"I don't know why you're stressing about this so much," Paige said from my bed.

"It's just all happening so fast. I've barely had any time to let it sink in. Tyce is meeting Mom and Dad today, and I'll be gone before Labor Day."

"Hey, it's been great for me!" Paige snickered. "Mom's totally forgotten all about the wedding. Let's just hope someone else gets knocked up in the meantime and snatches up that mid-September date before Mom remembers to book."

"You know you're going to have to address it at some point. Mom's not going to let it go."

"Yeah, I know." Paige sighed. "And now Dylan is on everyone's side too. He thinks we should just get married now and not fight it. Goddess, why doesn't anyone get it?"

"Oh my Goddess! I've figured it out!" I exclaimed.

"Figured what out?" Paige studied me.

"You're Jojo in *Mystic Pizza*!"

"What?"

"You know! That old eighties film! We watched it at a potluck a couple years back with Heidi! You're Jojo!"

"How am I Jojo?" Paige stood up with her hands on her hips.

I doubled over in laughter. "How don't you see the resemblance? You're so ridiculous." I laughed some more. "You and Dylan are in love, and there's no reason you wouldn't get married. Even Dylan wants to get married. And for some unknown reason, that no one can understand, you're making a big deal out of it, and you're just going to end up married in the end anyway!"

She huffed.

"Admit it! You're Jojo!" I kept laughing, not able to help myself.

"Fine! Maybe I am Jojo! But . . ."

"But what?"

"Aren't I allowed some breathing room? To get used to the idea of being with my mate. To get to know each other, etcetera, etcetera?"

"Easy for you to say. It's not like Dylan has a whole pack that could become weak if you go off to do your own thing," I replied. "I mean, I am literally a prisoner to this mate bond. Everything I've planned is now over. I'm being torn from my family and have to find a whole new school to go to. Plus, who knows if I'll even be able to finish school. Tyce is going to have to start having pups soon, so he can pass title before he gets too old." I sighed.

Paige sat back down on my bed and put her elbows on her lap and her head in her hands.

"Honestly, it's fine," I said. "I'm so happy Tyce is my mate. It's just a lot to process in so little time."

"But it is kind of romantic," Paige said. "I mean, you're literally running away with your mate. It's actually kind of cool."

"It is, isn't it?" I smiled.

In the end, I settled on a green sheath dress that emphasized my curves and Paige said brought out my eyes. I was so happy to be done with all the maxi dresses and pants I'd been wearing.

Tyce saved all of us seats up front where the alpha, beta, and their families normally sat. Blake came by to greet all of us as we took our seats. "Looks like I was justified in pulling some strings to get your family front row seats to my wedding." He winked at my mom, and she definitely blushed. Gah, my mom could be so juvenile sometimes!

"How's your luna doing?" she asked Blake.

"She's doing great. Thank you for asking."

"She looks great—glowing! Pregnancy really suits her. Such a blessing."

"Yes, definitely a blessing." Blake nodded.

It wasn't long before Tyce arrived and came around to shake hands with my whole family. He then took a seat next to me just as the service started.

After the service ended, we all headed back to our home. Tyce drove back with me. "I guess I probably shouldn't meet the *whole* family tonight," he remarked.

"What do you mean?" I asked. Did he somehow know about Kelli?

"Well, unless you don't mind a casualty."

"What?" I was totally lost now.

"Splinter," he replied.

"Oh, right." I chuckled at how dense I was being. "Honestly, Splinter is pretty scared of me now, but he's starting to get more used to being around our kind."

"That makes two of us then." He smiled. "I'm getting used to his kind too."

When we arrived, there were way more people than I was expecting to be there. My parents had apparently taken it upon themselves to invite their parents, their siblings and their mates, and our cousins. The small house we lived in was completely packed when Tyce and I arrived.

My dad greeted us as soon as we walked in and took Tyce away to go pick out a drink.

"Mom, I thought this was going to be a small, family dinner," I whined.

"Honey, you're mated to an alpha! Don't worry, Nana and Grammy both helped out and made tons of food," my mom replied.

Just then, the doorbell rang, and Dylan walked in with his parents and brothers. As soon as my mom greeted everyone and they went farther into the house, I turned back toward her. "Mom, you invited Dylan's family too?"

"Of course I did! His family is our family now. Now go bring Alpha Tyce around to introduce him to everyone. We're all dying to meet your alpha mate!"

Fucking Artemis—I couldn't believe my mom had gone ahead and done this! Then again, maybe I shouldn't have been surprised. She'd begun planning Paige's wedding without Paige even being aware. I headed into the kitchen where my dad was deep in conversation with Tyce and my grandfather.

As soon as I walked into the room, they all turned to look at me. "There's your mate, Alpha!" my grandfather stated the obvious. He must have already been a few drinks in.

"Sure is," he replied with a big smile and gave me a wink.

"Tyce, let me bring you around to meet everyone," I said, seething on the inside. This was not how the small family dinner I'd envisioned was supposed to go.

"Hey, Gi, it's okay," Tyce whispered as I grabbed his arm and pulled him away. "I can feel how anxious you are, and it's fine. Your dad and grandpa are both great."

"Sorry, this wasn't supposed to be a huge family reunion thing."

"It's okay. I kind of like it. Your family is so much friendlier than mine. I was expecting to be interrogated and challenged to a duel in the backyard when I walked in."

"Is that something that happens in your family?"

He chuckled. "My family is intense. If you can't fight, you don't get a seat at the table. Don't worry—you've already got the warring with words mastered, so you'll fit right in."

I brought Tyce around to meet everyone as people started spilling out into the backyard where my uncle had gotten the firepit going. I made my way over to Paige who was standing next to Heidi in the back corner of the yard.

"You've met Paige of course," I said to Tyce. "This is my older sister, Heidi."

Tyce shook Heidi's hand and then turned to my twin. "Nice to see you again, Paige."

"Tyce!" Paige exclaimed in a way that was completely out of character for her. "You should get married to Gigi in mid-September." Was she slurring her words?

"What?" He looked at her in confusion.

"Don't mind Paige. She's had a little too much to drink." Heidi grabbed a cup out of Paige's hand.

"Already?" I asked. The gathering had barely been going on an hour at that point.

"Maybe it was all the Southern Comfort shots she did after Dylan started talking about engagement rings." Heidi giggled. Now that she mentioned it, I could smell the alcohol seeping out of Paige's pores.

"Maybe you should have a drink, teetotaler!" Paige pointed her finger into Heidi's belly.

"Hey, stop!" Heidi backed away.

"You're always the first one with the wine! Where's your glass?" Paige exclaimed loudly.

"I don't feel like it." Heidi blushed.

"You don't feel like it?" Paige asked. "What!"

"Paige, calm down," I said. "This isn't like you." No, it was definitely more like me. How did my sister and I suddenly switch places?

"Heidi is judging me! She thinks she's better than me because she's not drinking!" Paige burst out.

"I don't think that. I'm just not drinking tonight," Heidi replied.

Then I had a thought. "Are you—" I looked at her stomach.

"Keep it down," Heidi replied, gesturing with her hands.

"Is she what?" Paige shouted.

"Paige, why'd you drink so much?" I asked.

"Here, let me go grab you some water," Tyce offered.

"No! I don't need water! I need tequila!" Paige grabbed Tyce's arm.

"You need tequila like a wolf needs to buy a fur coat!" I replied. Then I turned to Tyce. "Do you mind grabbing her some water?"

"Sure." He turned to go.

"I told you, I'm fine!" Paige said way too loudly.

"What's gotten into you?" I asked.

Just then, Dylan approached our group. He was actually quite a good-looking guy—very well-built with light brown hair and light green eyes. "Hey," he said shyly, making eye contact with all of us.

"Hey," Heidi and I replied.

"Are you okay, Paige?" He looked over at her with furrowed brows.

"No, I'm not okay!" she replied. "I've got duty for the next five days, and I'm due for my next heat anytime now. If you'd just mark me, then I wouldn't have to worry about being raped every time I go to work."

He took a step back and his mouth fell open. After a beat, he finally replied in a loud whisper. "I do want to mark you."

"So why don't you?"

"Because, Paige, I want to do things the right way." She opened her mouth to speak, but he continued, "I want to marry you in the temple where we were both raised, in front of our families and friends. And I don't want people to whisper about how you sinned and shouldn't be wearing a white dress, and for that to overshadow the commitment we're making to each other."

"Wow, Paige, you've got a really good guy!" Heidi said. "Who are you getting marked for anyway? I really hope it's not for me or Gigi. I mean, you've always been the most devoted to Artemis out of all of us. Why are you suddenly rebelling now?"

"Can't I just have some more time?" Paige retorted.

"But why?" Dylan asked. "I love you, Paige, and I'm not going to rush you. But I'm also not marking you until we're married. I saved myself for my mate, and it was worth it. And after all that waiting, I'm not just going to mark without giving it the respect it deserves."

I'm pretty sure that Heidi and I both swooned.

Just then Tyce arrived, balancing water bottles for all of us. "Hey, Reynolds, right?" Tyce put his hand out after he handed out all the bottles.

"That's right. Dylan Reynolds. Nice to meet you in a more informal setting, Alpha." Dylan shook his hand.

"Sounds like we'll be seeing a lot more of each other." Tyce gave him a friendly smile.

"Yeah, if Paige ever gives up the bachelorette life." I snickered.

Chapter 69

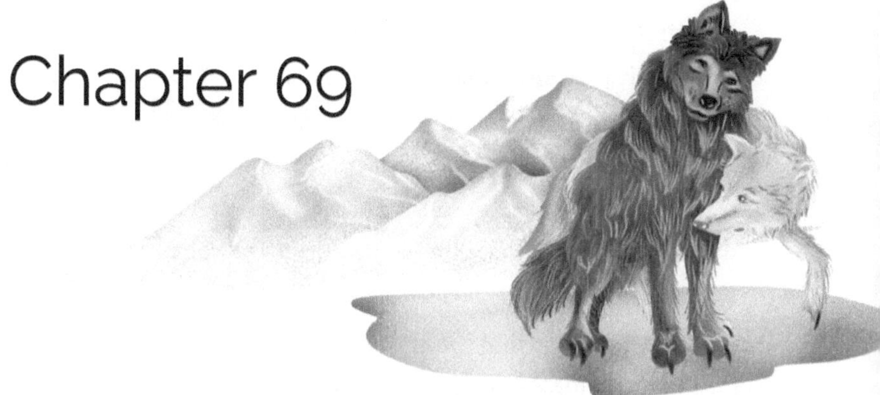

Blake

We were encroaching on late August, and Jasmine was very pregnant now. She was starting to look as if she could pop any moment.

"Goddess, I'm so tired," she said when she came home from training for the day.

"Jasmine, I think you should cut back on your training hours and focus more on paperwork instead," I said gently.

She yawned, plopping down on the couch and rubbing her big belly. "I really don't want to, but I don't know if I can keep going at this rate."

"There's no reason to push yourself. You can always get back to it after the pups are here." I took a seat next to her.

"I'm ready for them to be here already. I don't know if I can take another month of this. I've been feeling so much pressure on my pelvis lately."

"Maybe you can ask my mom about it tonight when we go see her. Unless you're too tired?"

"No, I'll be fine. Just let me shower."

"Okay." I leaned in and gave her a kiss.

"By the way, I'm definitely going to take you up on that booty-calling offer tonight," she teased, running her hand down my chest, leaving a trail of sparks. "These hormones have been making me so horny. I feel like all I could think about during training was sex."

"Really?" My ears, and something else, perked up. "Tell me more."

She giggled, her face reddening.

"Goddess, you're killing me, Jaz. I want to hear all your dirty fantasies."

"I was thinking about that time we did doggy, and you put the vibrator in, well, you know." She giggled some more.

"Fuck! Why am I not doing that to you right now?" I moved closer to her, inhaling her amazing scent, kissing down her neck, and practically growled, "I'm so fucking hard." She let out a light moan as my fingers found the elastic of her gym shorts, trailing the soft skin underneath her belly. "You keep moaning like that and I'm going to take you right on this couch."

Just then, the sound of the glass door opening interrupted us. I pulled my hands from her shorts, and Jasmine pulled away from me. Luke stepped inside, giving us both a nod.

"I should get showered," Jasmine said, getting up. "We told your mom we'd be over at six." She walked off, heading toward the stairs.

"Did I interrupt something?" Luke asked as soon as she was out of earshot.

"Yeah, you damn cockblocker." I gave him a friendly punch in the arm.

"You know, you seem to be doing a lot better. You're joking a lot more now. Kind of like you did back when you were younger."

"How are you doing?" I asked Luke, giving his shoulder a squeeze.

"Well, you know, could be better." He let out a breath.

"Obviously it's none of my business, but for what it's worth, I think you did the right thing. I have to commend you for how patient you were with Lucy for so long. But you're always trying to be the good guy, and Lucy knew that and took advantage of it. I'm proud of you for finally sticking up for yourself."

"Yeah." Luke sighed. "I know it's for the best, but *fuck*, it hurts."

I put out my hand and he took it, and I pulled him in for a hug, much like he had almost a year earlier when I was fighting my own demons. We probably hugged for far too long, but I was so glad to have the brother I'd pushed away back.

"What's in the backpack?" Jasmine asked as we exited the packhouse to take the short walk over to my mom's house.

"Just something for my mom," I replied, clasping her hand in mine. It had been over a month since I'd met her boyfriend, and even though she seemed happy, I couldn't seem to get comfortable with it. I was pleased that she was inviting us back over, because I wanted to have a talk with him now, especially since they were still together.

My mom greeted us at the door as soon as we arrived. "Look at you, Jasmine! How's the beginning of the third trimester treating you? You already look full-term."

"I feel full-term," Jasmine replied.

"Why don't you come by this week for another exam? We can check you over and make sure everything is progressing as it should. I'll give you a call tomorrow once I have access to my schedule and can figure out where I can fit you in."

"That'd be perfect," I replied on Jasmine's behalf, anxious for her to be seen.

"Blake, that question wasn't for you." My mom gave me a friendly punch. "Is he being overbearing—that alpha." She winked at Jasmine.

Jasmine let out a small laugh. "No, he's good. Just a little anxious, which is understandable." She gave my hand a squeeze. "He's been through a lot."

"Yes, he has." My mom leaned forward, pulling my head down to give me a kiss on the forehead. "Anyway, come in, come in. Ray is so excited to see both of you."

Something about hearing his name brought an uncomfortable, primal, protective feeling to the surface. Maybe it was the years I had witnessed my dad's philandering and abuse—but I couldn't stand the idea of another man hurting my mom. She seemed happy for now, but for how long?

Jasmine and I followed her into the kitchen where Ray was pulling a chicken out of the oven. "Good evening, Alpha Blake and Luna Jasmine!" Ray sang out as he placed the chicken onto the stove top.

I smiled to myself as I approached, pulling my switchblade out of my pocket. When I got close enough, I flipped it open, almost slicing the tip of Ray's nose. "Need someone to do the carving?" I gave Ray a hard stare. The look that he gave back to me wasn't so different from that of the many people I'd tortured, and it gave me a sick satisfaction.

"Blake, what are you doing? That's not a carving knife." My mom rushed over. "Go sit. Ray will take care of that."

"*What was that?*" Jasmine mindlinked me as I put down my backpack and we took a seat at the table.

"*Just protecting my mom,*" I replied. "*She's been through a lot.*"

"*Goddess help our daughter.*"

"*If you think any guy that isn't her mate is coming within twelve feet of her, think again.*"

"*You're worse than my parents.*"

"*I mean, your mom did come from an alpha family. Alphas don't exactly play it fast and loose with their families. She probably went easy on you compared to how her parents were with her. You should ask Tyce about his upbringing.*"

Ray and my mom placed the now-carved chicken onto the table and took their seats. After a quick prayer to Artemis, we began passing food around the table. "How are you feeling, Luna?" Ray politely asked Jasmine.

"Very pregnant." Jasmine chuckled, rubbing her belly, and Ray and my mom joined in.

"I remember when Fiona was expecting. She only had one at a time though. I'm sure it's a lot more work with two."

"Especially alpha pups," my mom added. "I only have Blake as reference, but he was a huge baby—eleven pounds five ounces—and came two weeks early." She then turned to Jasmine. "Don't worry, twins tend to be smaller, so it's highly unlikely you'd have to birth two eleven-pound babies at once."

Jasmine winced, and I squeezed her hand.

After we finished up dinner, Ray and I helped my mom put the dishes into the dishwasher. She turned to us and said, "Why don't you boys head into the living room, and Jasmine and I will bring the tea out in a bit?"

I smiled to myself and grabbed the backpack I'd left under my chair, bringing it into the living room. As soon as we both got settled on adjacent couches, Ray leaned forward and asked, "Anything special in that backpack?"

"Glad you asked." I smiled mischievously. As I began unzipping it, I remarked, "So, it's been about a month since I last saw you. How are things going with my mom?"

"Things are going quite well," Ray responded.

I pulled out what I had brought over and placed it on the coffee table so Ray would have a good view.

"W-why do you have a human skull with you?" He fumbled over his words a bit, and I could tell he was trying to remain calm.

"Just an artifact from one of my tortures. Two ex-warriors were accomplices of the man who fucked with my brother-in-law. I was initially going to let them live, but after their ringleader tried to rape my mate after I took mercy on him, the risk was too high to let his lackeys live too. And instead of burning their bodies like I normally would, I decided to keep a couple souvenirs."

"I see."

"I figured my mom might like to have one for her clinic."

"Why would she want that for her clinic?"

"Educational purposes, I suppose." I smiled. "So, Ray, it seems things are getting pretty serious with my mom."

"Indeed. We quite enjoy spending time together."

I scooched forward in my seat, leaning closer to Ray. "Tell me, what are your intentions with my mom?"

He rubbed his hands along his pant legs. "I really quite like your mom. She is a wonderful woman. Smart, kind, beautiful."

"My mom is the best. And she only deserves the best."

"I absolutely agree." Ray nodded.

"Good, then it sounds like we're in agreement." I nodded. "And trust me, Ray, you want to be in agreement with me. Because if we're not, well . . ." I swiftly pulled out my switchblade and stabbed it into the skull, piercing through the bone. I gave him a hard stare in the eyes, noting he had markedly paled, then pushed down on the skull with my other hand so I could retrieve my knife. "Capisce?"

"Capisce," Ray replied, and I placed the knife back in my pocket, subsequently crossing my ankle over my knee and relaxing into the couch with my hands behind my head.

At that moment, my mom entered carrying a tray of mugs, teabags, and cookies followed by Jasmine with a kettle. "Blake, why is there a skull on my coffee table?" My mom glared at me.

"It's a gift for the clinic."

"Why would I want a skull for the clinic?"

"Don't doctors normally have skeletons around?"

"Yes, replicas. Not actual bones."

"Hmm, my bad. I'll take it back." I shoved it back into my backpack. Jasmine sat down next to me giving me a look. I gave her an innocent smile in return.

Chapter 70

Ginger

It was nearing the end of August, and I was stressed beyond stressed, trying to decide what to bring with me to Alaska. On a rare day when no one would be home, I invited Tyce to come by and help me pack.

I went downstairs to greet him when the doorbell chimed. As soon as I opened it, my heart skipped a beat. How did he do that? Every time I saw him, it was like the first time. He greeted me with a big kiss, and I didn't want to let go, wishing I could just stay wrapped in his arms forever.

I finally pulled away. "Okay, so before I take you upstairs, should I move Splinter into another room?"

He rolled his shoulders back and puffed out his chest. "No, I can do it. I'm ready."

"Are you sure?"

"Well, okay, maybe I'll take my clothes off just in case. There's no one home, right?"

I laughed. "No."

"Okay, because that would be pretty awkward if your dad popped out while I was buck naked. I mean, on the field it's okay. But very awkward when visiting his daughter at his house." He chuckled and began pulling his shirt over his head. I watched as he removed everything, not able to tear my eyes away, still in disbelief that someone so jacked and fucking hot could actually be my mate.

"Okay, ready," Tyce said, handing me his clothes.

We slowly made our way up the stairs, and I showed him to my room. "Okay, please don't kill Splinter," I said, my stomach dropping at the thought. "I know I originally got him as bait. But I've bonded with him now."

"Don't worry. I got this," Tyce said, giving my arm a squeeze.

"Okay, here goes nothing." I swung the door open. And I should have known better, because as soon as Tyce's eyes met with Splinter's, he transformed into his wolf.

"No!" I screamed, dropping his clothes and rushing in after him. He had his claws and teeth bared, and I knew it was over. That cage was no match for a werewolf, an alpha one at that. Splinter's short life with me flashed before my eyes as I kept screaming in terror.

And then something amazing happened. Tyce stopped and backed away, transforming back into his human form. "I didn't kill him!" he exclaimed.

"Oh my Goddess!" I cheered. "Oh my Goddess, Tyce! You did it!"

He let out a breath. "I couldn't do it. When you screamed like that, I couldn't go through with it. It killed me too much to make you suffer like that."

I threw my arms around him. "Tyce, I'm so proud of you. You're not 100 percent there, but you're so close. Just give it a few more months, and you'll be cured I bet."

"Honestly, it's all thanks to you, Gigi." He hugged me back. "You came up with the idea to meditate to get better control, and it's been a game changer. Plus, you being here makes my wolf better. Goddess, I'm so fucking lucky to have you as my mate."

Tyce agreed to fly home Saturday, so I could have one last potluck with my sisters before we left. Since it was my last day at work that Friday, Tyler and Dr. Luna decided to get everyone pizza from the local pack pizza and sub shop. Two others had joined since I started, so the five of us sat around the break room table in the clinic for lunch that day, Tyler cracking jokes the whole time. He was actually pretty hilarious.

After we finished, I pulled Dr. Luna aside and asked if I could talk to her.

"Of course, Gigi."

"I guess I have two things," I said.

"Yes?"

"First of all, thank you so much for this job opportunity. I've learned so much, and I'm seriously considering going into the medical field now."

"That's wonderful, Gigi!" She pulled me in for a hug. "I know you do very well in school, so I'm sure you'll do great. If you ever need any help or advice, I'm only a phone call away. It's too bad that we won't be able to hire you here at our clinic, of course." She gave me a friendly smile. "Sounds like you may be stationed at a different one for the foreseeable future."

I returned her smile. "Yeah. But I'll definitely let them know about this database once I get to know everyone over there. Hopefully they're willing to hire me once I get done with school."

"Of course they will! Medical professionals are always in demand in pack clinics and hospitals. So few go into the field, and different clinics are always recruiting from other packs to come to theirs."

"Good to know."

"And you said you had something else?"

"Yes, it's about my wolf."

"Your wolf?"

"Yes, thank you for all your help when I first lost my wolf, especially with trying to get her back."

"Of course, Gigi. I honestly tried my best. I must have called around to fifty different clinics. I can only imagine how hard it is to go through life without your wolf." She gave me a pained look.

"Yeah, it was tough," I admitted. "And I did the thing my parents told me not to. I went to see a witch for help."

She brought her fingers to her mouth, her eyebrows drawn upward. "You did?"

"Yes, and, well, it worked. The witch was able to bring my wolf back."

"Oh my. I didn't know it was possible."

"They weren't even sure if it would work. But it's my wolf!" I said far too loudly. "I was desperate."

"Honestly, Gigi, I understand. And I probably would have done the same thing. Just don't tell your parents."

That made me smile. "I'm so glad you understand."

"Of course. None of us can know what we'd do if we lost our wolves. But I don't think it's far-fetched to imagine someone would risk everything. You essentially lost half of your being. Do you mind if we sit down and you tell me everything? I'll clear my schedule for this, because I definitely want to take note before you leave. This is a big deal."

I nodded. "Yeah, that's why I wanted to tell you."

"And I'd love to see your wolf, if you don't mind."

"I don't mind. But . . ."

"But what?"

"She's kind of scary. But don't worry, I won't hurt you in my wolf form. I promise."

"Well, okay then. Let's go into a private room."

I told her the whole story as she asked me detailed questions and typed rapidly on her laptop. After we were done with story time, Dr. Luna exited the room so I could remove my clothes and get into my wolf form.

I took a deep breath, readying myself, and transformed into my wolf. I whimpered, my muscles quivering. People didn't have good reactions to my wolf, and I was still getting used to it. But I stayed strong. Moments later, I heard a knock at the door, and Dr. Luna walked back into the room.

I had to give her credit because she kept a really good poker face and definitely didn't overreact like her son had.

She walked around me, and I shivered a bit. I knew she was trustworthy, but it was still hard for me to be so exposed like this.

"Gigi, can I touch you?" she asked. I nodded. She pulled on latex gloves and approached. She gently moved her hands through my fur and ran her fingers along my exposed ribs. I stayed still, my heart racing as she gently examined my whole body. She grabbed an ophthalmoscope and shone a beam of light into each eye.

"I'm going to turn the lights off so I can observe your night vision, okay?" I nodded, and she flicked the light switch. After a few moments, she said, "This is the first time in my life that I'm seeing someone with red night vision. Amazing."

She then turned the light back on and turned back to her laptop. After typing for a few moments, she said, "Okay, Miss Gigi. I think I have all the notes I need for today. I'll exit the room so you can have some privacy to shift back. Then I'll come back in if you have any questions."

Once I was dressed and she returned, I sat down in one of the chairs, my stomach still in knots. Finally, I squeaked out, "Do you think my wolf will always look like that?"

She looked down and shook her head. She then looked back up and said, "Honestly, Gigi, I'm not sure. But I would assume so. It seems that your wolf has become permanently disfigured. Otherwise, she would have healed herself by now, and it doesn't seem there's anything to heal." I nodded, taking a deep breath. After a beat, Dr. Luna asked, "Anything other questions?"

"With my organs exposed like that, does that mean my wolf is more vulnerable?"

"It does seem so. You don't have a protective layer of skin in some places. I'd also assume you might be cold in the winter in your wolf form, as your fur doesn't cover your entire body. But, honestly, I'm not sure. From what I've heard from my son, there's a wolf he met who can swim miles in freezing water, so some wolves appear to be immune to cold. The only way to find out is to go out in your form during wintertime. And definitely let me know once you find out."

I nodded, digesting the information. "Why do my eyes glow red?"

"That I'm just as baffled about as you are. I don't have an answer for you, and I don't want to make guesses or assumptions. However, with this database being built, perhaps we'll be able to eventually search and see if other wolves have had similar night vision. I will let you know once I'm able to more easily research."

I nodded again.

"Any other questions?"

"You don't mind?" I asked, confirming I wasn't wasting her time.

"Not at all, Gigi. Please, ask away. And if more come up later, you can always call or email."

"Okay, there is something I've been worrying about." I fidgeted with my fingers. "Obviously, Alpha Tyce's pack is going to expect an heir. But I'm worried. With my wolf the way she is, will there be issues?"

She sighed. "Gigi, I'm not sure. What I will say is that I believe the odds are in your favor. First, we've found that werewolf pregnancies are mostly carried on the human side. While werewolves can reproduce with humans, they cannot reproduce with wolves. So you shouldn't have any issues with fertility. Second, your uterus and other reproductive organs appear to be fully enclosed when in your wolf form, so the fetus would not be exposed when switching forms. The only hesitation I have is that after the embryo implants in the uterine lining, it begins to shift with the mother. So, essentially, as you shift between human and wolf form, so will your pup zygote or fetus.

"There are a lot of unknowns, as we don't know exactly how your wolf was affected during the time she was gone. My guess is, your wolf is probably at the same point of development as you were when you lost her, and I have no idea if she's going to catch up now that she's back. As we previously discussed, you had already begun to feel the symptoms of her coming when she disappeared. And you had your period after the following full moon. That leads me to believe that your wolf had been able to build up a uterine lining at the point at which her development was halted. So perhaps there won't be any issues when shifting back and forth.

"However, we also need to prepare for the possibility that shifting forms will cause you to miscarry. If we find that's the case, then you'll need to be diligent about not shifting forms throughout the entire duration of the pregnancy, from the point of conception until delivery. This isn't ideal, as you'll likely have severe pregnancy symptoms if you can't shift. Werewolves gather their strength from being able to run in their wolf form, especially under moonlight. And if you're not able to, well, it will certainly be a hard pregnancy." She frowned and shook her head.

"But you think I should still be able to get pregnant?" I asked. While I had no way to know what Dr. Luna meant by severe pregnancy symptoms, I knew in my heart it would be worth it. I wanted to be with Tyce, and I wanted to have a pup with him—hopefully more than one.

"If humans are able to get pregnant with werewolf pups, then I think it's highly likely you'll be able to as well. We'll just have to monitor the situation, of course. And I'll be happy to speak with your doctor once it comes time if you think that would be helpful."

"Thank you, Dr. Luna. I appreciate it." My throat was scratchy because of how helpful she was being. After a beat, I asked, "And how will the wolves of my pups look? Would they also look scary?"

She gave a small half smile. "I don't think so, Gigi. You'd pass on the genetics within your eggs. It wouldn't be any different than someone who had an amputation having children. Their children wouldn't be born without a limb. So you don't need to worry about that."

I let out a sigh. "That's a relief."

"Can I answer anything else?"

"Just one more question. Do you think it'd be possible to do a skin graft while I'm in my wolf form?"

Dr. Luna sat back in her chair, putting her finger to her mouth, clearly deep in thought. After some time, she finally replied, "Honestly, it's an idea. I wouldn't be able to perform the surgery as I don't have much training in that area. We'd need to find someone who could. It'd probably have to be done over multiple sessions, and you'd likely need to be awake so that you wouldn't accidentally shift into your human form while unconscious. But before we do such an extreme surgery, I'd like you to first spend some time outdoors during the winter to see if it's necessary. I understand why you want it for cosmetic reasons, but perhaps see if you get used to your form first before we seek out this option."

I brightened from her response. So maybe all hope wasn't lost and there was a way to regrow my skin! "I will. Thank you, Luna. No more questions from me today."

"No, thank you, Gigi. Thank you for letting me examine you in your wolf form. And please, don't be a stranger. You have my email address and phone number. I'm happy to try to answer any other questions if you think of them later." She got up and pulled me in for a hug. "Take care, Gigi."

I felt really emotional that evening as I put in more effort into the potluck than I had for the past few years. I went all out and deep-fried extra spicy buffalo wings and cut up carrots and celery to go along with them. Paige, the overachiever, made beef empanadas.

Our mom gave us a ride to Heidi's house, where we were greeted by both Heidi and Kelli. They both gave us big hugs, and we made our way upstairs to the kitchen where we laid out our spread.

"I can't eat as spicy as you guys, so I made a mild potato salad," Kelli said.

"That's okay. I made a few milder empanadas. You can have those ones," Paige offered.

"I made some mild honey-barbecue wings," I added. "Just stay away from the buffalo ones."

"I went mild this time too," Heidi said. "My acid reflux has been acting up a bit, so I made Mexican street corn. But there's hot sauce if anyone wants to make it spicier."

"Acid reflux?" I asked.

"It's one of the symptoms," Heidi said coyly.

"So you are then! Congratulations!" I exclaimed, giving her a hug. And then moved to hug Kelli. "And congrats to you too."

"We're not telling anyone because I'm not two months yet. But yeah—we're both so excited." She smiled, and her whole face glowed as she squeezed Kelli's hand.

Paige then pulled Heidi and Kelli both in for hugs. "Congratulations, and sorry again for how drunk I was at Gigi's mate meeting thing."

Heidi laughed. "What got into you?"

Paige let out a chuckle. "It's like you said. Dylan started asking me about engagement rings, and I panicked. And before I knew it, I'd downed like five shots, one after another."

"So have you talked with him since then?" Heidi asked.

"Yeah, of course," Paige replied quietly.

"And?"

"We've decided to compromise. Since we have about six months before the urge to mark each other will start to get bad, we've agreed to put off the wedding until December. He promised to talk to his mom. And I'm going to talk to our mom as well. She can't be too upset. I mean, it's still happening really soon, but at least this will give me some breathing room. I mean, I'm still kind of scared about the whole heat thing while I'm on duty, but I talked to Jasmine about it, and she completely agreed with me that it's dangerous. And she's actually planning on establishing accommodations for female warriors who have met their mate but haven't been marked yet—making sure we're only put on patrol duty with marked male warriors. And she said she wants warriors to start having sexual harassment training anyway, so she's working with Alpha Blake and Beta Luke now to make that happen."

"Wow, it sounds like Jasmine's making tons of positive changes!" I commented.

"Oh definitely!" Paige nodded. "She's changing the school health programs to teach about heat and birth control, and she's been working with her brother to try to push for acceptance of the LGBTQ+ community in our pack, although it's been really slow moving unfortunately. Too many people stuck in their ways."

"You can say that again," Kelli agreed and let out a deep sigh. Heidi gave her hand a squeeze. The mood of the room turned somber, none of us knowing what to say.

After some time, Heidi broke the silence with a devious smile. "Well, we do have one unanswered question!"

"What?" Paige asked.

"When's the big alpha wedding happening?" She looked at me meaningfully.

"Chill! We just found out we're mates!" I replied.

"So now you know how it feels!" Paige teased, poking me in the stomach.

"It's not so bad," Heidi said. "I know I sort of married someone else, but living with my mate has been great." She smiled at Kelli.

"The best," Kelli agreed.

"Why don't we dig into the food before it gets cold?" Heidi led us toward the table and Kelli began pulling out bottles of wine and lemonade. Before long, we were seated on the floor with plates of food in front of a game of Catan.

After we were well into the game, and I'd downed quite a few glasses of wine, I looked around at my sisters and my sister-in-law and couldn't help it as tears streamed down my face. Goddess, what was wrong with me?

"Gigi, are you okay?" Paige asked, turning toward me.

"Seriously, I'm the one who's supposed to be hormonal right now!" Heidi added.

"I'm going to miss all of you so much!" I cried out. "You too, Kelli!"

Everyone moved to give me hugs. "Don't worry, Gigi, we'll FaceTime all the time," Paige said.

"And have Zoom potlucks," Heidi added.

"And we'll make sure that our pup knows all about their cool luna aunt," Kelli chimed in.

"Goddess, I love all of you. And for the love of Artemis, please don't be this sappy again after tonight."

Everyone laughed and we hung out, ate, and drank for the little time we had left together. Unfortunately, we couldn't stay as long as we wanted-ed. A little after ten, my mom came to bring Paige and me home since I'd be waking up in only a few hours to make the trek to my new home.

Chapter 71

Ginger

My alarm woke me at two thirty that morning, and I groaned, forcing myself to roll out of bed. I had put together three suitcases of stuff to bring—three suitcases to transport my entire life across the country. I quickly dressed in the outfit I'd laid out for myself the night before. I had decided on a simple jersey dress since it'd be comfortable for several hours of travel but would still look cute for when I arrived to meet his family.

I moved Splinter into his special travel carrier and added some fresh fruit to hopefully help him stay fed and hydrated throughout the journey. Then I looked around my bedroom and sighed to myself.

At around three, Tyce texted me to let me know he'd be there in a half hour. I dragged everything downstairs. My parents came down just as I was placing Splinter's travel cage by the door.

My mom pulled me in for a hug and began sobbing for the millionth time since she found out I was leaving. "Make sure you eat all your veggies and always wear clean underwear."

"Mom!" I groaned.

My dad pulled me in for a hug after. "I'm gonna miss you, Peachy," he said as he wrapped his strong warrior arms around me.

Right at three thirty, Tyce arrived as promised. He greeted both my parents, giving my mom a friendly hug and shaking my dad's hand. My dad gave Tyce a pat on the shoulder and said, "Take good care of her, Alpha."

"She doesn't need it, but I will." Tyce winked at me. "She's already tough as wolf claws."

"That she is." My dad chuckled. "Even without a wolf she was always a fierce one."

"That's what I love about her."

My dad helped Tyce move all my luggage to the back of his SUV. I had to pry myself from my sobbing mom, so we could leave on time. They both stayed outside and waved as we drove away. "Don't look at me," I said to Tyce.

"Why?" he asked, glancing my way.

"I said not to look at me!"

He laughed. "Why, because the fierce Gigi is crying?"

"I just have something in my eye, okay?" I laughed through my tears, and he grabbed my hand in his.

"I won't tell anyone."

"You seem to be okay even with Splinter's smell in the car," I remarked.

"It mostly affects me when I see a rodent. But I'm getting used to Splinter and his smell now. I think I'm slowly becoming desensitized."

It was an hour drive to get to the Burlington airport, where Tyce returned his rental. We checked in, giving Splinter up, and made our way to the terminal. "First class?" I exclaimed as I looked at the ticket.

"It's a long flight," Tyce replied.

"Do you normally fly first class?"

"Actually, yes."

"Damn, alpha lifestyle! I like it!"

I dozed off during the two-and-a-half-hour flight to Chicago, leaning my head against Tyce, soothing sparks hypnotizing me into sleep.

When we landed, I woke feeling uncharacteristically warm and pulled the sweatshirt I'd put on for the flight off me. "How long is this layover?" I asked.

"One hour."

We grabbed a quick breakfast sandwich and some coffee before boarding the next flight. "Goddess, something about traveling is making me horny," I whispered to Tyce.

"What are your thoughts on joining the mile-high club?" he asked, snickering.

"I mean, you're still not fully in control of your wolf. But I'll think about making a special exception." I gave him a flirty smile, and I couldn't lie—the thought of it was very tempting.

"How often do you get the chance to have sex at over 5,280 feet in the air?"

"Closet nerd."

"What?"

"How do you know how many feet are in a mile?"

"Okay, so I know some random facts, especially when they pertain to sex." He stuck his tongue out at me.

We soon boarded the plane and found our first-class seats—these ones were legit. Plush and huge with plenty of leg room. Tyce had really hooked us up. As soon as we sat down, the flight attendant came around to bring us coffee and water. "Damn, this is nice," I remarked. "I could get used to this."

"See, being with a douchey alpha comes with some perks."

"Okay, I don't hate it anymore." I snuggled into my seat, but a part of me still felt uncomfortable. "Is it just me or is it really warm in here?"

"Here, let me turn up your air." Tyce adjusted a knob above me.

"Thanks." I positioned myself so it was blowing onto my face.

Tyce played some games on his phone while I read a book on mine. But as the flight wore on, the less at ease I began to feel. My skin was definitely on fire, and the whole area between my thighs felt sensitive and engorged, pulsing with need. I could no longer concentrate on my book because visuals of Tyce destroying me in every position possible kept flashing in my mind. I wanted to fuck in a way I'd never wanted to fuck before.

Tyce sniffed and he suddenly tensed. "Fuck," he said quietly next to me.

I looked up at him.

"Fuck," he said again. He had a pinched, pained expression on his face, his eyes squeezed shut. After a beat, he choked out very quietly. "You're in heat."

"That's what this is?" I asked, and fuck, he was right. I was ridiculously horny—more horny than I'd ever been. I was ready to risk going to jail for unzipping Tyce pants and fucking him right on his plane seat.

"This has to be the world's worst timing. We still have four hours left of this flight."

"Looks like we're about to join the mile-high club."

"Fucking Artemis, if we don't, I can't guarantee I'm not going to take you in front of this whole plane." He groaned.

"How's it feel?" I asked, brushing my hand against his crotch.

"Don't do that!" he exclaimed far too loudly and flinched in reaction to his tone as some of our neighboring passengers turned to look our way. He clenched his hands into fists and took a few breaths. In a softer tone he said, "Sorry. I didn't mean for that to come out like that."

After the other passengers finally seemed to lose interest, he brought his mouth to my ear and whispered, "It doesn't look like anyone's using the bathroom now. Just go in and wait. I'll knock three times when no one's looking. Okay?"

Fuck, the way his scent surrounded me and his warm breath tickled my ear did things to me that I didn't even know were possible. A hot shiver overtook my whole body, and I wasn't certain that my wetness hadn't fully soaked through the skirt of the dress I was wearing onto the seat under me. I nodded and made my way to the bathroom on wobbly feet. I quickly threw myself into the bathroom, locking it behind me.

If Tyce didn't hurry, I was ready to take matters into my own hand. I'm pretty sure my wetness was dripping down the insides of my thighs. I'd never felt such an intense urge before. The only thing I could concentrate on was how badly I wanted to be filled at that moment. I rubbed my thighs together.

Just as I was about to say fuck it and shove my hand into my panties, three knocks sounded on the door. I instantly tried to push it open before recalling I'd locked it. I fumbled to unlock it and moved back so Tyce's huge body could fit inside. This was definitely not going to be easy. Neither of us were exactly small.

"Quick and dirty," I blurted out quietly. "No foreplay."

"Fuck, I forgot the con—"

"Tyce, if you walk out of this bathroom, I will seriously fucking kill you," I whispered loudly. "Just pull out."

He clearly understood because he had his pants unzipped and his boxer briefs pulled down in nanoseconds. His cock was rock-hard, precome dripping from it. I gave it a light stroke, and he groaned in a way that it almost sounded painful. Before I could stroke it again, he had his hands under the skirt of my dress, and his fingers hitched into the sides of my panties. The sound of fabric tearing echoed in the small room as he ripped them clean off me.

I could barely even process what he'd just done when he lifted me up onto the small counter. I spread my legs to give him access. He didn't bother to take his time as he pushed his full length inside of me as far as it would go, stretching my insides to their max to accommodate him. It had been a second, so I had forgotten how big he was. A tear fell from my eye from the pressure of him not holding back and going all in. But even so, I couldn't deny how fucking good it was to finally feel the sweet relief of him being inside me.

Soon, I felt nothing but immense pleasure as he thrust himself in and out of me. He placed his mouth on mine as we moaned into each other, and it was clear that this was exactly what we needed. His huge hands gripped my hips tightly as his hips glided against my inner thighs, and he slowly began to reposition me until he was hitting exactly the right spot. Sparks danced in front of my eyes with every stroke as he hit my G-spot over and over again. It took everything in me not to scream from how amazing it felt.

In a matter of seconds, I was convulsing, my whole body shivering with pleasure. I bit down on his lip as an intense orgasm exploded inside me, overtaking my whole body as it made its way to every limb. Blood filled my mouth and a sick part of me thirsted for it. Just as the aftershock of my intense orgasm was subsiding, Tyce pulled out just in time to spray my inner thighs with his warm come, stroking his cock until he got every last bit out. "Fuck, that was amazing," he whispered.

I was panting, recovering from the intense experience, when suddenly a trance came over me. My gums tingled as my canines expanded. And then I spotted it—the perfect place to pierce. I was moving my head toward his neck with every intention to claim him when he blocked me with his arm, and my teeth punctured his bicep instead.

He groaned quietly, and I could sense he was in pain as I did that. As soon as I could grasp what I was doing, I pulled my teeth out of his skin. I blinked, confused by why I had just done that, and noted he had grown his vampire teeth. And then I came to. *Oh Goddess, I just tried to mark him!*

He pulled out a bunch of paper towels, handing me some. The ones he kept, he dabbed against his arm where I'd left two bite marks. "Fuck, sorry about that, Tyce," I whispered, my whole face burning with shame for having just done that as I used my own paper towels to wipe at my leg that was now covered in his semen.

"Just be glad I didn't kick you in the stomach for that," he teased, his words a little muffled by his teeth.

"Yeah, sorry about that too."

"I heal fast." He grabbed another paper towel, wet it, and dabbed the blood away. Once I climbed off the counter, we did a little dance so he could get to the sink and wash out his bloodied mouth. "Now that there's a demon wolf inside you, you've gotten kind of violent."

I scrunched my nose and tried to stifle my laughter.

"Anyway, that should hopefully hold us over for the next few hours," he said, but his brows were furrowed with concern. "Okay, you go out first, and I'll follow. But hold on, let me check and make sure no one is waiting to come in." He sniffed at the door, and when he seemed satisfied, he gestured for me to leave.

I scurried out and took my seat as I watched a man in our first-class section get up. I cringed as he pulled open the door to Tyce inside. Tyce winked at him and pushed past him to take his seat next to me.

"I have a feeling that once we're done with this flight, we're going to have the mile-high club down to a science." Tyce quietly snickered. "Also, looks like we'll be spending a night in Anchorage because it's not exactly the best timing to introduce you to the family."

"I'm glad you find this so funny."

Chapter 72

Tyson

So, things may have started out a bit awkward. It's not exactly the best timing for your mate to go into heat while you're stuck in a moving vehicle that you can't exactly get off in the middle of the sky. Well, we did get off, more than once—just in a different meaning of the word. And, holy shit, sex in heat is like sex on steroids. I mean, everything just feels that much better and that much more intense.

That was the first time I ever raw-dogged (what? I couldn't exactly risk bastard children)—and holy fuck—the way I could really *feel* her body, the way the bare head of my cock brushed against her inner walls, all the sensations. Damn. I was officially done with condoms. And considering I'd met my mate, I saw no more purpose for them.

After we got off that plane, we hightailed it to the closest hotel where I proceeded to fuck the living daylights out of Gigi in every position known to man on every surface of that room. Suffice to say, it would not pass the black light test.

My alarm went off far too early the next morning. We definitely needed more sleep after the marathon the prior day. But we had to catch the five forty-five flight to Deadhorse Airport.

"Mmm," Gigi moaned as I gently shook her.

"Mmm to you too," I said pulling her toward me for a kiss. "Are you ready to meet the family today?"

"Is there anything I should know before I meet them?"

"Don't take anything they say personally, okay? Both my dad and grandfather are dicks."

"Should I be worried?"

"No. I'll be there with you. I'm stronger than them now, and they know it."

"Okay . . ." Her voice trailed off, and I kissed her again, wanting her to know how great she was. "I should get showered. I'm pretty sure I smell like nothing but sex right now."

"I'll join you," I responded with a smile, moving out of the bed.

My beta, Liam, met us at the airport when we landed. "Plane or car this time?" I asked.

"Plane—it's quicker," he replied. I nodded. "So, is this your mate?"

"Yes, meet your future luna, Gigi. Gigi, this is Beta Liam."

"Very nice to meet you, Gigi." He shook her hand.

"Nice to meet you as well, Beta Liam," she replied politely.

"He's probably the nicest person you'll meet today," I joked.

"Trav's not too bad either. And Terri's fantastic—everyone loves her. You'll also meet my mate, Nina, who's wonderful. My pups on the other hand"—he chuckled—"they have their good and bad days."

He helped carry Gigi's bags while I took my own, and she carried Splinter. As we were walking, Gigi turned to me and asked, "Your pack has a *plane*?"

"It's not as special as it sounds," I replied. "Most villages in the middle of nowhere have a bush plane. Our pack is bigger—it's really more a town than a village—so we have roads that lead to the main highway too. But during the winter they get really hard to maintain, so we mostly hunt as a pack to make sure everyone stays fed. Our full moon runs are epic during wintertime. We also have a huge greenhouse for vegetables. However, sometimes we need to get off pack land or need other supplies, so we have this plane."

She looked around, wide-eyed, as we approached the plane. I had gotten so used to the way we lived, never having known anything different, but it was really cool seeing it through fresh eyes. "It's so chilly," she finally said.

"Yeah, average high around here this time of year is around fifty. Perfect weather for getting close and keeping warm together," I said suggestively.

"Get a room!" Liam shouted from in front of us.

We made it back to the pack in no time, and Liam drove us over to the packhouse from the runway. I observed Gigi as she stared out the window at everything. A lot of our pack wasn't too different from Blake's—it was just a bit bigger and even more in the middle of nowhere. Because it was so hard to get to civilization, our pack subsidized the whole downtown area so people would have something to do. It still wasn't much—a grocery store, restaurant pub, café, movie theater, a couple gift and clothing shops, and an ice-skating rink. I pointed everything out to Gigi as we drove by.

Liam helped us bring all the luggage in, and my mom greeted us at the door. "Tyce, you're home." She gave me a nod and closed-mouth smile. "And is this your mate? Come in, come in." We all walked into the packhouse with our luggage.

"Mom, meet Gigi, my mate. Gigi, this is my mom, Luna Julia."

"It's so nice to finally meet you, Luna Julia!" She opened her arms, ready to attack my mom with a hug, who flinched as Gigi threw her arms around her. Shit, I forgot to tell Gigi that we were kind of a no-touching family. But it was pretty funny watching my mom be hug attacked. She awkwardly patted Gigi until she finally pulled away.

"Yes, nice to meet you too. I'm so happy that Tyce finally found his mate. Why don't I have Tasha make some breakfast after you get settled?" She looked at us for confirmation.

"Sounds great," I replied. "Where's Dad and Grandpa?

"Well, I suppose you haven't heard the news yet. Trav apparently met his mate too. And we found out she's a *rogue*." My mom wrinkled her nose in disgust. "He's been keeping her in our housing in Prudhoe Bay by the rigs. Trav never came home last night, so they've gone out to surprise them this morning."

"Why are they doing that?" I asked. *Fuck, I should have come home sooner.* I already knew this was not going to go over well.

"Because you know your grandfather doesn't like secrets." She shook her head.

"Where's Terri?"

"She went back to school a few days ago. You just missed her."

"Damn. I wanted to introduce her to my mate."

"She'll be back for Thanksgiving. Anyway, go get settled. Alana already set up Gigi's bedroom for her. We put her in the main guest bedroom. You're going to sleep in separate rooms until marriage, I assume?" Like fuck we would, but I wasn't going to inform my mom at that moment. She then sniffed the air. "Why does it smell like a rat in here? What's in that container?" She looked toward Gigi.

"That's our new pet rat," I replied.

"Your *what*?" My mom's eyes almost popped out of her head. "Your *rat*?" She said the word like it tasted foul in her mouth.

"My packhouse, my pet," I replied and turned to help Gigi bring everything upstairs.

I showed her to her room, which was definitely not where she'd be sleeping. "Your mom has an accent," Gigi remarked.

"Yeah. She grew up in Ukraine."

"Oh really? How'd she end up here?"

I chuckled. "It's actually kind of a scandal. My Uncle Gabe, who no longer lives in this pack, met her when he went away to college. She was the beta's daughter in her pack, and they sent her to school in the US so she'd get an American education. Although, my grandfather always jokes that they sent her here to get a green card.

"I guess the story goes that they fell madly in love, and he brought her home over Christmas to announce to the family that he was going to take her as a chosen mate. Except, joke was on him, because she ended up being fated mates with my dad."

"Holy shit!"

"Yeah, so my dad and Uncle Gabe basically became estranged after my mom chose to be with her fated mate. I'm sure it didn't help Uncle Gabe's case that my dad was the alpha and Gabe was just next in line, but only until my dad made an heir. And my dad didn't even take long to do that. They conceived me before they'd even been married a year."

"Damn, that's so crazy," Gigi responded.

"My family likes to pretend they're all high and mighty and religious, but don't let them fool you," I said. "There are tons of scandals from throughout the years."

I helped Gigi reassemble Splinter's cage. "You're doing great." Gigi smiled at me.

"I told you—I'm used to Splinter now."

"Does that mean he can get a friend soon? I read that rats are social creatures and do better with friends."

"You can get anything you want." I pulled her toward me and kissed her. "As far as I'm concerned, you're already the luna of the pack, which means you're in charge now."

We made our way downstairs where my mom had laid out some food. I pulled out a chair for Gigi in front of a huge plate of scrambled eggs, sausages, and home fries.

"Tyce, that's your food." My mom rushed over and moved the plate out from in front of Gigi. She then moved a soft-boiled egg and a grapefruit in front of her instead. "Gigi, I figured you'd want to eat the same thing I do for breakfast."

"Why would you assume that?" I asked.

"Us women have figures to maintain," she replied, giving Gigi a once over, and Gigi looked down at her lap, her face reddening. I could instantly sense how uncomfortable she was.

"Gigi already has a naturally beautiful figure," I responded. "Here, Gigi, have some of my sausages."

"It's okay," she replied. "The egg and grapefruit are fine."

"We had a pretty active day yesterday, maybe you should eat some more." I put a couple sausages on her plate. "And these potatoes are fantastic. Tasha should open a diner they're so good." I dropped some onto her plate too.

"Tyce, why are you giving her more food? She said she was fine with just the egg and grapefruit. She knows." My mom gave me a hard stare.

"Knows what?" I asked with a warning tone. If she weren't my mom, I wouldn't have been so restrained with my response.

My mom shook her head and walked out of the room. At least she had enough tact not to say what she was thinking in front of Gigi. My mom didn't exactly shy away from jumping in on conversations when my dad and grandfather made their usual jokes.

"Honestly, Tyce. It's okay. Your mom is right. I probably should watch what I eat more." She moved the sausages and potatoes back on my plate.

"No, she's not right. Is that honestly what you would have wanted to eat for breakfast if our cook, Tasha, had come out here and taken your order? You would have seriously asked for a bland-as-fuck soft-boiled egg and *grapefruit*?"

"Well, no, probably not."

"Gigi, you're going to be the luna soon. I understand being polite to my parents, but don't let them walk all over you and convince you to eat or do anything you don't want to. If they're going to be assholes, they're going to answer to me. Now, what did you actually want to eat for breakfast?"

"This is fine." She smiled. "I'll have a bigger lunch later today."

"I don't believe you, but fine." I then smiled and took a bite of the sausage. "Mmm, this is sooo good!" I said loudly. Then I shoved some of the potatoes into my mouth. "Mmm, so good!"

"I thought alphas didn't share," Gigi teased.

"I'll make an exception for the luna," I replied, giving her a wink.

"Okay, fine, give me a bite of your sausage." She finally gave in.

I put one on a fork and brought it to her mouth. She nibbled a piece off. "Damn, that is good!" she exclaimed. "It even has a little bit of a kick to it."

"Tasha knows how I like my food. More?"

"More," she agreed with a big smile on her face.

"I'll let Tasha know you have the same taste in food as me and not my mom."

My dad and grandpa came home a few hours later with Trav and his mate trailing behind. I brought Gigi downstairs to introduce her to everyone. "Looks like we get to meet two mates in one day," my grandpa said. "One rogue." He scrunched his nose in disgust. "And one, well, I shouldn't be surprised by Tyson's mate."

"What's that supposed to mean?" I glared at him. Trav gave me a look that I tried to interpret but failed.

"Dad, it's been a long day." My father shook his head. He then stepped toward Gigi. "Hi, Alpha Lance, and you must be Gigi?"

"Yes, nice to meet you, Alpha." She shook his hand.

"Pleasure is all mine," he replied politely. At least my dad wasn't going full dick right off the bat. "This is my father, Alpha Bruce."

"Nice to meet you as well, Alpha," Gigi responded and shook his hand as well.

"Hi, I'm Trav." My brother pushed forward. "So nice to finally meet the woman who's tamed this guy over here." He elbowed me and then shook her hand. "And this is my mate, Sara."

"So nice to meet both of you!" Gigi shook both their hands. I couldn't help but notice that Gigi scrunched her nose a bit when Sara approached her. I was certain that was probably her first time ever smelling a rogue, and they didn't exactly have the most pleasant scents.

"Let's sit down to a nice family meal. What do you think, Dad?" My father looked to my grandpa.

"I'm starving. Let me get Tasha to bring out the food." My grandfather walked away toward the kitchen.

"I need to go do something in my office real quick. Call me once the food is out, will you?" My dad looked toward Trav and me.

"Yeah, no problem, Dad," Trav replied. After my dad was gone, he let out a deep breath.

"What the fuck happened?" I asked Trav.

"Some asshole working the rigs tipped Dad off about Sara. So, obviously not the way I was going to let them know."

"I don't even know what I'm doing here." Sara rolled her eyes. "Your grandpa's a huge dick, and I don't fucking care if he's a former alpha. He has no right to talk to me the way he did during that one-hour car ride.

He's lucky I didn't cut him into pieces." She flicked open a Benchmade Autocrat with a red handle. Damn, Trav's mate was no joke.

Trav let out another breath. "Let's just get through lunch. And then I'll take you back." He laughed a bit. "Welcome home, Tyce!" He patted me on the shoulder. "Home sweet drama home." Then he turned to Gigi and with a big smile exclaimed, "Welcome to the family!"

Soon everyone was seated at the large table in the dining room. We all said a quick prayer to Artemis and then began passing around the food. Tasha had made chicken parm and a huge bowl of pasta. My mom and grandma both took small pieces of chicken and filled the rest of their plates with salad. I noted both of them watching Gigi like hawks as she helped herself to some chicken and pasta.

"Red pepper flakes?" I asked Gigi.

"Yeah, of course," she replied.

"Looks like your mate has the appetite of an alpha," my grandfather joked.

"Why wouldn't she? She's going to be training like one too," I replied, rolling my eyes. "Hey Grandpa, your arms are looking flabbier than last time I saw you. What, are you slacking in your training or something? Or are you just getting old?"

My dad laughed.

"With how lazy you are, boy, you won't even have half the strength I do when you get to my age. You're just lucky I'm still around so this place hasn't gone to complete shit yet."

"Dad, Tyson, let's just enjoy our meal, okay?" my dad said.

"You act like I was the one who started it. I've only been home a few hours and Grandpa's already acting like a dick," I rebutted.

"He was a dick before you got here," Sara chimed in.

"And who the fuck are you to speak that way?" My grandpa got up, throwing his napkin on the table.

"I'll speak however the fuck I want," Sara retorted.

"Learn some fucking respect, you dirty, savage rogue. I'm a fucking alpha."

"First of all, no, you're not. And second of all, even if you were, you're not my fucking alpha. I'm my own fucking alpha. And no crusty old man holding on to some title he didn't even earn is going to disrespect me. I've had enough of your shit for today. If you think I'm ever joining this shitty pack, then fuck you."

"Why don't we take this outside?" my grandfather asked, his eyes taking on an evil appearance, the veins in his forehead popping.

"I'd love to!" Sara got up. "You don't intimidate me. You're not even half the alpha my father was."

"Okay, okay, let's all calm down." My grandmother got up. "Bruce, let's not fight." She gave my grandfather a stern look.

"Catherine, sit," my grandfather barked at her as if she were a dog, pointing downward to her chair.

"Dad, come on. There's no need for this." My dad tried to pat my grandpa on the shoulder in a calming gesture.

"Fuck off, Lance!" My grandpa pushed my dad's arm off him. "You're just as lazy and useless as your sons." He then stomped off down the hallway.

Chapter 73

Ginger

Goddess, what had I gotten myself into? Tyce had told me that his family was intense, but I still hadn't exactly known what to expect. And never in my wildest dreams would I have expected what I'd witnessed.

After lunch, Trav and Sara left almost immediately to head back to where Sara was staying. I went upstairs to take a nap. I hadn't gotten much sleep in the past couple days, and I was pretty exhausted. Tyce walked me to my room. "Hey, sorry about that." He brushed his hand through my hair. "I told you, my family is all assholes."

"Is that how you all communicate with each other? Through insults?" I asked, baffled.

"Yeah, pretty much, actually."

"Wow, that's horrible, Tyce!"

"I mean, what am I gonna do? It's my family. I can't exactly just kick them out of the packhouse."

"Alpha Blake and Beta Luke's families don't live with them back in my pack."

"Yeah, but the tradition is different here. It's always been like this. That's why our packhouse is so huge. We have the alpha, beta, and gamma families all living under one roof. It's an old-school pack mentality."

I let out a breath. "It is kind of nice to have family around all the time. But I mean . . ." I didn't know how to complete my sentence.

"Yeah, I know, my family is the worst kind of dysfunctional."

"Yeesh."

"But Gigi." He looked me intently in the eyes. "I promise I'll always treat you well, and I'll never let my family get away with insulting you. I'm the alpha now, and it's time for me to start taking charge and making changes around here."

I smiled and touched Tyce on the arm. "Your grandpa is wrong. You're not lazy at all."

He gave me a small smile. "He's half right. I did fuck around a lot before this summer. I won't bore you with the details, but I'm ready to take charge now and prove myself."

"I believe in you," I said, throwing my arms around him. "You're going to be an amazing alpha."

After he left to get back into the swing of things with his pack, I crawled into the bed they'd made for me. They'd actually made it quite cozy with brushed cotton sheets, a beautiful crocheted blanket, and a velvety comforter. The room had a wood-burning fireplace, which I imagined was like heaven during the Alaskan winters. The whole pack-house smelled of pine and cedar and gave me the feeling of being right at home, even if home was actually over four thousand miles away. It didn't take me long to drift into sleep.

I woke sometime later to the door creaking open and Tyce carrying a tray into the room. "Hey," he said as he put down the tray onto the dresser and came over to me.

"What time is it?"

"Eight. You slept through dinner, so I figured I'd bring some up for you."

"It's still light out," I replied.

"Yeah, sunset is at around nine this time of year." He came closer as I sat up, hoisting myself up onto my forearms. "Also, this isn't going to be your bed moving forward, just so you know."

"I kinda like it though."

"Yeah, well this bed is lacking some important features." He took a seat on it, bouncing a little.

"Like what?"

"It gets pretty cold around here, even during the summer. The bed down the hall is much better equipped for someone who's not used to the temperature in these parts."

"Really?" I squinted as if confused.

"Yes, really." He moved his face closer to mine until we were practically touching. "It comes with a built-in heater that will keep you warm all night."

"I can just get an electric blanket."

"But does an electric blanket come with a stiff cock as a bonus?"

"I have a rechargeable vibrator." I stuck my tongue out at him.

"But can a vibrator do this?" He pushed his hands under the blanket and began to glide them slowly up my legs, sparks dancing along my skin, shooting straight to the apex of my inner thighs. I was about to give in when—

"Tyce, there you are!" His brother walked into the room. "Sorry, was I interrupting something? The door was open."

"Not anymore," Tyce replied and stood up off the bed.

"Sorry. I just wanted to talk to you about JSP. Do you mind if we go downstairs to the office for a bit?"

"Yeah, okay," Tyce replied. "Gi, you wanna come?"

"Sure!" I replied. "What's JSP?"

"It's the name of our oil company that we co-own with another pack called Spruce Winter Pack."

"Oh, is this the whole embezzlement thing?" I asked, recalling Tyce mentioning it to me before.

"Yeah, actually," Trav responded.

Tyce and I followed Trav downstairs to a good-sized office with three desks. "This is where Trav sits with Beta Liam and Gamma Brayden," Tyce explained as he pulled out a chair for me. "I'm sharing an office with my grandpa, though we don't really use our office much. We're usually out in the field. My dad shares his office with my mom, who does most of the bookkeeping and admin stuff for the pack." He then turned to his brother. "So what's the latest?"

His brother pulled out some papers and handed them to Tyce. "Ghost vendors."

"Ghost vendors?" Tyce asked.

"Yeah, those are some of the invoices that were entered into our accounting system for the green energy consulting and investments. I've done a bunch of digging, and these companies don't exist. The EINs go to completely different companies, the phone numbers ring, but no one picks up. I checked the website for this Green Monstera Consulting, and someone did a half-assed job setting it up—very amateurish for us to choose them for our consulting when we're running an almost billion-dollar business. Also, what kind of name is Green Monstera Consulting?" He chuckled.

Trav picked up another paper from his desk. "This is supposedly the investment statement from one of our investments. What in Artemis's name is this? It looks like something someone typed up on Excel when they barely even know how to use Excel."

Tyce took the paper from Trav's hand and gave it a once over. "To be honest, I don't know how an investment statement is supposed to look."

"Yeah, neither does Dad or Grandpa." He rolled his eyes. "Long story short, not *that*. Anyway, I typed 'sample investment statement' on Google and clicked through the images. These numbers match exactly to one of the top results."

"Damn. It's like they're not even trying."

"I'm putting pressure on them now. I talked to Alpha Vic and told him I want more information about this green energy R & D. He told me that they've already started construction of windmills on some island he claims our company purchased."

"Our company supposedly purchased an island?" Tyce raised his eyebrows.

Trav chuckled. "Yeah, I can't wait to see that one. How the hell are they planning to prove the existence of an entire island?"

Chapter 74

Tyson

After about a week, things seem to be getting more settled. I taught Gigi how to inject wolfsbane into me, and she began taking the task on. She was much gentler than Blake, which was kind of nice. I knew my time was limited, so I was trying to get as resistant as possible for now, before we finally marked each other.

After breakfast, I'd gotten into the habit of training Gigi for at least two hours every day, and I was planning to set her up with a full-time personal trainer once I figured out whom I trusted to take on that job. We'd gotten back to the packhouse for lunch when Gigi split from me to go take a shower since she was done for the day. I wasn't going to bother because I'd be right back outside after I was done eating.

"I get the idea she hasn't trained much," my dad remarked as soon as she'd disappeared at the top of the stairs.

"What gives you that idea?" I asked.

He let out a chuckle. "C'mon, Tyce, just look at her. Her ass could have its own zip code."

"What the fuck makes you think I'd be okay with you saying shit like that to me about my mate?" I snapped at him.

He shook his head. "Goddess, you're so sensitive."

"No, Dad, I'm not. You're just a fucking dick. I've tolerated you putting me down my whole life, but I draw the line at Gigi. I'm not some little kid anymore who you and Grandpa can just bully. I'm done putting up with your shit. You diss either me or Gigi one more time, and I will do what Trav's mate didn't. I'll take it outside and we can fight it out for who's going to be in charge around here moving forward."

"Tyce, take a joke."

"No, Dad, you shut the fuck up!" I walked away, my blood boiling. Gigi was right, it was totally fucked-up how my family communicated with each other.

I decided to go cool down by hanging out with my brother while I waited for Gigi to finish up in the shower and come down for lunch. He was busy typing on his laptop when I took a seat in one of the chairs in front of his desk.

"Hey, what's up?" Trav asked as soon as I sat down.

"I never asked you—what exactly did Grandpa say to your mate that day in the car?"

"What didn't he say?" Trav rolled his eyes. "Basically any and every insult you can think of for rogues, he said it. I didn't know what to do. I tried to ask him to stop, and he just laughed and told me to be quiet. I feel like he's just getting worse with age."

"Damn."

"Yeah, I don't think she's ever going to set foot in this pack again." He shook his head, frowning. "I don't know what to do now. I want to be with my mate. Should I just go rogue too and try to survive out there in the wild with her? Find a pack that's willing to take me in and try to convince them to let in a rogue too? I mean, everyone knows that rogues have been banished from other packs, so no one wants to take the risk of housing them."

"To be fair, the story of how your mate got banished isn't exactly great. She tried to kill both Blake's sister and her own brother. She hasn't really made a great case for why she *should* be trusted."

"I know." He sighed. "But Goddess, I just get her. She's so badass. And the thing is, Blake's sister murdered her father. I can kind of understand why she'd want revenge."

"Didn't Sara's father also murder Blake's sister's mother?"

"Okay, yeah, that happened."

"Dude, I don't know how to tell you this. But your mate isn't exactly a saint."

"I know. But she feels remorse over everything now. Honest. I think being estranged from her family and having to survive as a rogue has brought her some new perspective. Plus, now she finally understands the mate bond and why her brother protected his mate so fiercely."

"I mean, you're also going to be a little biased."

"Okay, well, obviously my word isn't going to be enough, but maybe she'll be able to prove it somehow."

"Don't get me wrong, I've wanted to kill Grandpa plenty of times before too, but her pulling that switchblade didn't exactly help her case." I snickered.

"Hey, she'd fit right in with the family." He shrugged.

"Can't argue with that."

"Anyway, mate aside, I'm planning to tell Dad and Grandpa about the embezzlement tonight."

"Just let me know when you're doing it. I'm happy to be in the room with you. I think everything you've found so far is pretty sus, and I'll back you up 100 percent."

"Thanks, bro." Trav gave me a big smile.

"Anytime." I got up to head to lunch. I made it out just in time to catch Gigi coming down the stairs with wet hair.

"Are you from the moon?" I smirked.

"What?" she asked, tilting her head.

"Because your beauty is out of this world."

She gave me a shove. "Goddess, you are such a nerd, I just can't!"

"So, when do you go back into heat?"

She crinkled her nose. "You'll have to wait another three weeks."

"Damn. Why's it so long away? I want my exception now."

"There's a way to get what you want sooner." She gave me a mischievous smile. "I hope you haven't been slacking on your meditation."

"Tough to concentrate on meditation when my mind keeps wandering to how blue my balls are."

"Hmm. Sounds like you'll be waiting then." She stuck her tongue out.

That evening, after dinner, Trav and I sat down with those I'd now dubbed *the elders* in my mind. Trav went through all the same evidence he'd presented to Gigi and me with Grandpa and Dad, answering all their questions.

To say they were pissed would be an understatement. I'm pretty sure they were both ready to murder.

"So how much, Trav, would you say they've stolen total over all this time?" My dad leaned forward in his chair.

"Around two hundred million."

"Two hundred million?" My grandfather shot up, crimson, nostrils flared. "You've got to be *fucking* kidding me!" He grabbed a paperweight off Trav's desk and threw it against the wall, leaving a gaping hole in its wake. "Do you know how much money we've lent those assholes throughout the years? Do you have any clue how many battles our pack has helped defend them in? The dirty scoundrels!"

"What the fuck are they using all that money for?" my dad raged. "Their pack is a fucking dump. Every time I go there, their roads need repairs, their houses look like they're from a third world country, they have fishing boats that have fallen into disrepair after years of neglect."

"Just a hunch, but I think Alpha Vic is using it to pay for his lifestyle," Trav replied. "Every time he comes into a board meeting, he's showing off his designer clothes and watches. He treated me to lunch one time, and tipped the waitress one hundred dollars on a fifty dollar tab."

"What the fuck? This is madness!" my dad fumed.

"If you think I'm going to let that asshole Alpha Vic and his good-for-nothing alcoholic father get away with this, you've got another thing coming." My grandfather stormed out of the room.

My dad sighed. "Fucking Artemis." He shook his head and after a beat continued, "Trav, thanks for all the hard work you did to uncover all this. We're going to have to figure out how to handle this. They've been our ally going back generations. But, from this point forward, we're enemies."

He then stomped away, leaving Trav and me alone.

"What do you think Grandpa and Dad are going to do?" Trav asked.

"Honestly, I wouldn't be surprised if they want to declare war at this point with the intention to take the alpha out and eliminate the pack. Because you know Alpha Vic won't give up his portion of the business, and I can't see either of them getting humans involved to do it the legal way. He's fucking dumb, because his pack is a fifth of the size of ours, and there's no fucking way they have enough allies to beat us in battle. The fucking coward will probably go run and hide while his pack battles it out." I shook my head.

Chapter 75

Tyson

"Tyce, I feel like we should show your family my wolf form. I'm finally starting to learn to accept it," Gigi said to me as I dodged her right hook.

"We will. But tension is really high right now. I want to find the right time. You know they're going to have something to say."

"It's okay. I can handle it, I think. I mean, it's not like they haven't been calling me fat without calling me fat the whole time I've been here. Your mom and grandma both give me looks every time I serve myself, and then I look over at their size-two bodies with their bowls of salad and, Goddess, I feel so gross sometimes."

"Don't, Gigi, don't. You're so beautiful. Do you really feel unhappy with how you look?" I moved closer to her, brushing my palm against her cheek that had become rosy from the chill. We were now in mid-September, and the temperature had noticeably dropped since arriving. It wouldn't be long until the first snow of the season.

"I mean, I didn't. I honestly didn't really think there was anything wrong with my body. But then, sometimes guys at school would make certain remarks, and then I'd compare myself to my friends who would always get their attention, and now with how your family is." She sighed.

"I'm trying so hard to be happy with how I look, but it's difficult sometimes when the rest of the world isn't."

"A few assholes aren't the rest of the world. The people who matter love you just the way you are. Honestly, I was so envious when I met your family. Everyone was so nice and caring. They lift each other up. My family just kicks you and laughs when you land on your ass. It's terrible. I mean, not to toot my own horn, but I'm pretty fucking sexy, and they still find shit to harass me about."

"I miss my family." Gigi sniffed. "My family isn't perfect. I mean, there are so many things my sisters and I can't tell our parents, and they're super old-school. But they also never made us feel anything but loved and accepted. Even after I fucked up and lost my wolf, my whole family was there for me so much, telling me how they'd always love me no matter what. Paige basically lost all her friends sticking up for me when I got bullied in middle school."

"Honestly, I wish we could live with your family instead of mine. But my family isn't all bad. I wish you could've met Terri because you'll love her. You got to meet Trav, of course. He's too nice—he lets Dad and Grandpa walk all over him. And both my beta and gamma and their families are great. They'll always have your back."

"I can understand now why you were so insecure about your whole rodent thing to the point where you went to see a witch."

"Yeah, you can only imagine the shit I got for that." I chuckled.

"I love you." Gigi wrapped her arms around me, and I'd never felt so much fondness for someone before. It was like all the affection and love I'd been missing from my parents my whole life was finally being gifted to me a hundredfold by her. I didn't even know it was possible for someone with so much warmth to exist. At times it almost felt painful, similar to how my hands felt when I'd come in on a cold, snowy day and run them under warm water.

"I love you too," I whispered into her hair.

Later that afternoon, as I was running patrol stations, a sharp pain ripped through my body, as if a thick tether was being snapped. I stopped in reaction, and then I knew—my grandfather was dead. At first, I didn't know what to think. Although he'd tormented me my whole life, he was still my grandfather, who raised me the best way he knew how. And deep inside, as much as I hated him, I also loved him in the complicated way you can only love a family member.

While there had been many bad memories, the happy ones suddenly started flooding in. My grandfather holding my hand and walking me to kindergarten every morning before he went off to training. My grandfather carrying me to the clinic after I fell out of a tree and broke my arm when I was six years old and then staying with me and telling me funny stories while they set my arm and put it in a cast. My grandfather patiently sparring with me when I was seven for weeks and hours on end during the summer until I mastered the basic seven.

And while the physical ache of a tether being broken had passed, a different kind of agony ripped through my body. He was gone—the man who raised me, and even if he did continuously call me worthless and lazy, he also continued to train me from the time I was a little kid until now, preparing me to finally take on the alpha role one day when I was ready. I threw my head back and howled sorrowfully, giving myself over to my wolf.

When my throat was hoarse and I had no more howl in me, I sprinted home, abandoning my patrol station run. I quickly threw my sweatpants on when I approached the packhouse, not even bothering with any of my other clothes.

As soon as I entered, the only thing I heard was my grandmother's hysterical crying. I followed the sound to where she was screaming on the floor of the dining room. "Bruce!" she screeched. "Bruce!"

My mom and Gigi were both trying to help her, but she kept slapping them away. "Don't touch me!" she screamed. "I want my Bruce!"

I squatted down in front of her to try to lift her up, and she slapped me too. "Where is my Bruce?" Her bloodshot, devastated eyes made contact with mine.

"Grandma, he's dead," I replied, stating what she obviously already knew.

"They tortured him, Tyce! They tortured him! They didn't just let him die!" She began sobbing again.

I got up and looked at my mom and Gigi. Finally, my mom spoke. "She's been like this for a half hour. I tried to get a hold of your father, but he's at the board meeting with Trav, probably with his phone on silent. I was about to get into my wolf form so I could mindlink you, but you made it home on your own."

"Fuck. Do you know who did it?"

"No. We offered to drive her so she could point the way to him, but she was too hysterical."

I let out a deep breath. "Who the fuck was actually able to capture and kill that man?"

"He's been getting old, Tyce. He wasn't as strong or quick as he used to be. He was over seventy."

My father made it home with Trav a few hours later. We had finally gotten a nurse from the clinic to come by to inject my grandmother with some heavy tranquilizers. My father and I carried her into her bed and tucked her in.

My dad looked at me for a moment over my passed-out grandmother and sighed. "Tyce, your grandfather, my father, was tough. He wasn't perfect by any means. But he loved you and he respected you. I know he complained about you all the time, but"—my father gave me a small smile—"he believed in your ability to lead and be alpha one day."

"What about you?"

"I've always believed in you, Tyce. From the moment your mother and I conceived you. That's why your grandfather and I trained you so hard. Because we know what it's like. Being alpha breaks you sometimes. And it's easier to piece yourself back together when you've already learned to do it before. One day you'll understand."

I nodded, not knowing how else to respond.

We made our way downstairs to my father's office and Trav joined us. I took in my father's grief-stricken face, his eyes clouded over and his brows drawn downward. Of course, he must have been taking it pretty hard. He had always been close to his father, as fucked-up as their relationship was. Even I felt a numbing devastation, and I didn't even like the man.

After we all settled into our seats, I asked, "Grandpa didn't go to the board meeting with you today?"

My dad shook his head. "No. We told him we'd address the fraud during the meeting today, but he decided to take matters into his own hands and confront Alpha Vic and his father at their pack this morning. I tried to stop him, but you know your grandfather." My father sighed. "He doesn't—didn't—take well to people telling him what to do. He was supposed to make it home in time to go with us, but when he never showed, we just left without him"

"So what happened between this morning and the board meeting?"

"I don't know. Alpha Vic and his father were both there, denied every-thing—those motherfuckers. Never once mentioned your grandfather coming to see them. Either they lied or he never made it to their pack."

"Who else would have had motive?" Trav asked.

"Beats me. We haven't had conflicts with any other packs in a couple years now. And if your grandfather never made it to the Spruce Winter Pack, then they wouldn't have known that we know about the fraud," my dad replied.

"But what if he did make it to their pack?" I asked.

"Still, both Alpha Vic and his dad have alibis. They were at the meeting with us while the murder occurred."

"Unless they handed off their dirty work to someone else," I added.

My dad tapped his chin with a pen. "Unfortunately, there's no way to prove it. He's dead, so our chance to track his whereabouts using his mate is now gone. And while I do plan to put some trackers out to do it the good old-fashioned way, it's going to be tough since he traveled by car, and there's a lot of mileage to cover."

"My mate is a very skilled tracker," Trav chimed in. "I bet she could find him."

"Your psychotic mate?" My dad turned toward him, squinting.

"Dad, give her this chance to redeem herself," Trav said with more intensity. "Yeah, she's a little extreme, and her past isn't exactly clean, but she's learning from her mistakes."

My dad blew out a breath. "Fine. We'll give her this chance to prove herself."

Chapter 76

Tyson

The three of us piled into my G Wagen and made the hour drive to Prudhoe Bay, where Trav's mate was staying. We'd built up housing there for the rig workers, and my family kept a couple of nicer, slightly larger units for ourselves, one of which was currently being occupied by Sara.

As soon as we parked and stepped out, we all simultaneously began audibly sniffing, catching whiffs of what was very clearly Grandpa's blood. We followed the scent, the strong wind making it impossible to miss as it blew our way. After following the smell for about a quarter mile, a trail of blood appeared, undoubtedly his. We looked up and in the distance was an olive-green Toyota Sequoia, the same car that my grandfather drove.

We rushed over to find it partially submerged in one of the many bodies of water that peppered the North Slope.

"What the fuck?" I gasped.

"Tyce, Trav, help me pull it onto land," my dad commanded, getting a grip of the back bumper. Trav and I both found different parts of the back of the car to get a good hold of next to him and helped my dad pull. Luckily my father and I were very well-built, and Trav wasn't anything to sneeze at either. Even if he didn't train as hard as us, he still had the natural alpha genetics. Between the three of us, we were able to hoist all of it onto land.

My dad threw open the passenger door. "What the fuck? Trav, why does his car smell like your mate? She hasn't been in this car, has she?" He sniffed audibly and pulled up a few stray blonde hairs off the front seat, handing them to me. I sniffed, and they were unmistakably hers—her disgusting rogue scent permeating each strand. I promptly handed them to Trav.

But that wasn't the most shocking part. The next thing my dad pulled out of the cupholder did not make Trav's mate look good at all. He flicked open a bloodied red Benchmade Autocrat. I gasped, immediately noting the color. I knew knives, and I had distinctly noted the color of the one Sara had as I had not known this particular switchblade to come in red.

"Dad, that's Sara's knife," I said, stating the fact out loud.

"I gathered. Smell it." He held it up to my nose and the rusty smell of blood drifted into my nose. I instantly recognized my grandfather's scent.

"I know it looks bad, but she didn't do it," Trav asserted. "She wouldn't kill Grandpa." We both looked over at him, and he had noticeably paled. He rapidly ran his hands through his hair. "It's just too messy. I know her. She would have been meticulous. She's not the type to leave a trail and an unclean weapon. Someone wanted you to find this and frame her."

"Tyce," my dad said firmly, "I need you to use your alpha aura to command Trav to follow us to your car *now*."

I turned toward Trav and hesitated. I knew why my dad was asking me to do this. Trav's mate had motive, and the evidence didn't look good. Plus, I knew Trav would turn on all of us for his mate, as I would do the same for Gigi.

Tightness in my chest and pain in my throat, I commanded, "Trav, follow us." Never did I imagine I'd betray my brother, but I had been put in an impossible situation. Bile rose to my throat at my disloyalty.

He just stared at me wide-eyed, blinking, and he couldn't hide his devastation. He knew what was going to happen, and he had been put in a position where he was helpless. He couldn't override his alpha's command—no one could, except possibly Gigi with her demon wolf, I recalled. My dad reached into Trav's pocket and pulled his phone out.

"Ask Trav his password." My dad nodded at me.

"Trav, what's your password?" I asked with my alpha aura.

Trav flinched, and I could tell he was fighting it, his whole face turning red as he strained not to speak. "314159," he finally choked out.

My dad scrolled through the phone for a bit and then activated speech-to-text. "Hey, Blondie Badass Baby." My dad winced as he said the pet name he must have found in the text trail.

I tried not to laugh because it was so unlike Trav to come up with a pet name, especially one so ridiculous.

"Are you in the room, question mark. My dad's going to come by so you can help him track my grandpa."

Trav followed us quietly back to my car, where I opened the back door, commanded him to get in and stay.

We popped open the trunk and pulled out the chains I always kept on hand for exactly this.

"If she really killed Grandpa, don't you think she'd try to run now?" Trav called out as my dad slammed the trunk closed.

My dad turned to me, making severe eye contact. "There are only two ways to exit that room. You take the fire exit stairs in the back with the chains—and make sure you're quiet. I'll go to the door and act like everything's normal. I'll text and then knock. When she goes to answer the door, break into the room, and we'll take her down and chain her up.

We'll knock her out and throw a sheet over her to get her body out. Got it?"

"Got it." I swallowed. My shoes felt like they were filled with lead as I followed my father's instructions and stealthily climbed the back stairwell. I waited out of sight with the metal chain wrapped around my knuckles. As soon as the text from my dad came in, I popped up, and punched my metal-wrapped fist through the large, single window to the unit.

I had to hand it to her. She was good. As soon as I shattered the window, she sprang into action and gave my dad a good fight. She got a good punch right into my dad's face, leaving behind a very prominent black eye. My dad fought back, attempting to trip her, but she had an impressive jump and recovered, getting right back into it.

As good as she was, there was no way she'd be able to match up against both of us. I pulled the chain I was carrying apart, removed all the slack, and quickly flipped it over her head. This was easy to do since she was a good foot and a half shorter than me, if not more.

She tried to backkick me, but I was already expecting it and dodged. I tightened the chain around her neck, which caused her to instinctively reach for her throat. If she could have, she would have shifted into her wolf now, but it would be useless to even try with a steel chain wrapped so closely to her body.

My dad took this as his cue to knock her out, giving her several blows to her head, bloodying her nose and lip and leaving bruises around both eyes. "What a pity. She did have a pretty face," my dad commented as her body slackened. "It's okay, she'll heal."

I let her down gently onto the floor, then my dad and I quickly did the chains up around her wrists. Once we were satisfied she was restrained, we covered her with a blanket, threw her over my shoulder, and climbed out the back window.

My only solace was that she and Trav hadn't marked each other. I checked. Because if they had—I honestly don't know that I *could* have gone through with it. It's one thing to hurt someone who's practically a stranger. But if I knew that Trav would feel everything—no, I wouldn't be able to do it. Even as it was, Trav made good points. Someone who kept such an impeccable appearance with her perfectly trimmed blonde pixie cut and clothing that seemed tailored to her body didn't seem like the type to do such a messy job murdering someone. Hell, even I, who was not the most organized person, wouldn't have done such a shoddy job.

But, at the same time, I could understand my father's point of view. The risk was too great that she'd flee if we didn't grab her right then and there.

Chapter 77

Tyson

I'd never felt like such shit in my life. My dad took the wheel, and the hour ride to the pack was fucking painful. We ended up dumping Trav's mate into the trunk. I stayed facing front, but it didn't stop me from feeling the agonizing daggers Trav was shooting into my back. I had to be the worst fucking brother in the world. I could only imagine if our places were switched and he had gone with our dad to knock Gigi out and dump her in the back of our trunk, transporting her to . . . well, Trav knew exactly what her destiny was.

When we made it back to the packhouse, my dad finally broke the silence that had suffocated us the entire car ride. "Trav, I'm sorry."

"She didn't do it. I know she didn't."

My dad shook his head. "You're being influenced by the mate bond, son. Look, I understand. But no one gets away with murdering someone in my family."

"That asshole deserved to die. You know it, Tyce knows it, and I know it. Whoever did kill him did this family a favor."

"Get out," my dad said firmly and threateningly. "Tyce, command him out now." If I didn't know better, it seemed my father's voice may have even broken a little as he said it.

I sighed, my stomach sour and acidic. "Trav, get out." He had no choice but to do what I said.

Before he closed the door, his pained amber eyes bore into mine. "Tyce, ask her to join the pack. She won't be able to lie if you use your alpha aura on her." He blinked, and I think a tear may have even slipped out, only driving the daggers he'd shot further into me.

Once Trav slammed the door to go into the packhouse, my dad blew out a breath. Then he put the car into drive and headed toward the pack's detainment center.

We pulled her out of the trunk, and I hoisted her small body over my shoulder. Once inside the torture chamber, we chained her up to the wall. My dad had beaten her pretty bad. Her nose, mouth, and chin were covered in crusty dried blood, but the swelling in her face was slowly going down—the bruises around her eyes now more of a murky brown than the initial deep purple they had been. Her blonde hair had traces of more crusty blood from where my dad had clearly cracked some of her skull with a hit to the side of her head.

Moments after we'd gotten her set in place, she finally began to wake, blinking at us staring back at her. She flexed her arms and legs—clearly seeing if she could move them from the restraints she was in. I instantly noted how built she was—all lean muscle.

My dad gave her a very ominous smirk, his whole face taking on an evil appearance. "So, you seem to be well versed in knives, Sara." He pulled out a case and dropped it on the metal table in the center of the room. "Which blade should we use today? A clip point, tanto, or maybe a straight back?" He looked up at her. When she didn't respond, he continued, "Sounds like it's dealer's choice then. Straight back it is." He pulled it out of the case.

As my dad walked toward her, I put up my hand. "Wait!" They both stared at me. I approached Trav's mate and looked her up and down. I could smell the fear emitting from her pores, even if she kept a good poker face. "Sara, join the pack so I can question you. Then we'll know you're not lying."

Not even a second after I asked, she launched a huge ball of spit in my face. Rage ripped through me at how considerate I'd been—offering her an option not to be tortured—and that was how she replied. At least I could keep a clear conscience when I had to face Trav later. I'd tried to do exactly as he'd asked. I wiped the disgusting liquid off my face as my dad patted my shoulder and moved in front of me.

"Someone thinks they're tough, huh?" my dad said in the most condescending voice.

"Tougher than you, motherfucker." She rolled her eyes.

"Just a little lesson. Don't bite the hand that feeds you." Before she could even respond, he drove the knife into her mouth. She spluttered as blood dribbled down her chin and onto her chest, choking out gasps. "Hmm, seems this one can't deep throat. I'll let Trav know he can do better."

At the sound of his name, she let out a sad, choked whimper, as my father withdrew his knife.

My dad then pulled out a chair and took a seat in front of her. "My bad, now we'll have to wait for this bitch to heal before she can speak again."

As much as I normally enjoyed torture, something about this was making me nauseous. I couldn't get the look Trav gave me out of my head. Plus, I'd never really tortured females before. Even if Sara seemed capable of holding her own against a man, and her past was sketchy, it still felt wrong.

While we waited for her to heal, my dad picked up several different knives and began flinging them at the wall, just narrowly missing her body. The stench of fear permeated the entire room with each swish of the blade through the air and thud as its pointed tip penetrated the wall.

My dad was an excellent shot, and he'd normally use his torture subjects as target practice. I wondered if perhaps he was going easy on her.

"Ready to talk, bitch?" my dad asked after some time.

"Fuck you," Sara responded.

"Hm." My father gave her a sadistic smile. "Thanks for the offer, but my sons' pussy is where I draw the line."

"All you men are the fucking same." She cackled. "Don't pretend like you actually have a fucking line." He got up and walked toward her. When he got close enough, in an almost seductive voice, she said, "You'd shame fuck me and love every fucking second of it. You'd love to prove your old cock fucks better than your son's."

"You sick fuck."

She cackled some more. "Somehow your dick is more virtuous than your hand? You have no problem stabbing the fuck out of your son's mate. Just not with your dick! Too far!" she taunted him. Was Trav's mate completely unhinged? Everyone knew not to poke the sleeping dragon. Seriously, what the fuck was up with her?

"Okay, bitch, that's enough!" My dad glared at her. "Let's make this fast so we don't have to spend the night here. Admit you killed my father now, and I'll make it quick and painless. Just one slice of the neck."

She rolled her eyes. "You think I'd waste my time killing that old geezer when he was ready to drop dead soon anyway?"

My dad pushed his knife into her stomach, blood spurting out of her innards, down onto her legs. I had to hand it to her. She was fucking tough. She didn't even scream. Just grimaced and groaned, clenching her fists, and flexing all her hard muscles. Damn, she really was ripped.

"Tyce?" My dad offered his knife to me.

I looked at it, and that same sour feeling in my stomach returned, bringing bile to my throat. "Dad, I can't do it," I said. "I can't torture Trav's mate."

"Pussy."

"She's Trav's *mate*!"

"Trav's mate is unhinged. You think your grandfather and I didn't check into why she doesn't have a pack?" He gave her a quick glare and then turned back to me. "We reached out to the Pine Forest Pack and talked to their alpha. She isn't someone you should feel bad for."

I shook my head. Trav's pained eyes burned into my mind. I couldn't push them out. Fuck, if he ever tortured Gigi. The thought made me want to vomit. *My own fucking brother torturing my mate.* And how could I be more loyal to my asshole grandpa who had no qualms whipping a ten-year-old kid? Trav had always had my back my whole life.

"I won't," I finally said firmly.

My dad rolled his eyes. "Your grandfather was right. You're too soft. We were too easy on you."

"No, you're an asshole!" I replied. "You don't know that she actually killed Grandpa. You're just assuming."

"If I assumed, she'd already be dead. This is how we find out." He turned away from me and dug his knife into her bicep, running his blade along each arm, making red streaks that spilled blood from the seams as her milky skin was slowly torn apart. She grimaced, her whole face clearly pained, but still didn't cry, grinding it out with her teeth. My dad smiled, an evil glint in his eyes. "So, admit it now. You killed my father."

"No, I didn't fucking kill him."

He shook his head and made slices into her cheeks. "Tell the truth."

"I didn't fucking kill him. I'd admit it if I did."

He yanked at her hair and she shrieked. "Admit it!" my father shouted.

"I didn't do it!" she cried out.

He broke the skin on her neck, dragging the blade onto her chest, blood soaking her shirt as it spilled down her body. "Tell the truth, bitch! You fucking killed him!"

"No!" she cried out again, tears finally tumbling from her eyes.

"What's this then?" He pulled her switchblade out of his pocket and flicked it open, bringing it close to her nose. "Do you smell that? That's his blood on your weapon."

Her eyes widened in recognition, now bloodshot and tear filled. When she didn't immediately answer, my dad dragged his blade down each one of her legs, tearing her pants and skin

"That blade was in my dresser," she cried.

"No, it was in the car of the man you killed."

"I've never been in his car."

"Your hair was in it too."

"Question the housekeepers then, you dumb fuck!"

"Dad, stop!" I yelled, having had enough.

"What now?" he sighed.

I turned away from him and approached Sara. "Please, just join my pack, and this will stop. My dad can and will go all fucking night."

"Make him stop then." She glared at me accusingly.

"No. We don't know that you didn't do it, and there are only two ways to find out. Either my dad keeps going until you break down and admit to it, or you join the pack. Trust me, I don't offer this to anyone. I suggest, if you ever want a chance at seeing your mate again, you take option B because I can't guarantee you'll live if I hand you back to my father."

She whimpered, her whole expression downturned. "Fine!" she gritted out.

I nodded, putting out my hand. My dad handed me his knife. I quickly sliced my palm and then sliced her restrained one. "Say it."

"I, Sara Adalwolf, hereby solemnly pledge my loyalty and allegiance to the Jade Moon Pack and Alpha Tyce Tikaani."

I placed my hand against hers until the warm sensation of her becoming tethered to my pack passed between us. I then stepped away and looked her up and down. "Did you kill Alpha Bruce Tikaani?"

She tensed in reaction and finally replied, "No."

"Sorry, Dad. Fun's over." I handed him back his knife.

"I'll get some warriors to put her in a cell for now until we can feel confident that letting her loose isn't a risk," he replied, leaving his knives out for someone else to clean.

Chapter 78

Ginger

I sat with Tyce's mom all afternoon while she made funeral arrangements and kept up communications with the beta and gamma of the pack as they searched for the body of Tyce's grandfather. I saw Trav momentarily when he came in and stomped upstairs, locking himself in his room.

I got the gist of what happened between everyone's conversations. It had to be one of the most messed-up situations I'd ever heard of. Tyce's brother's mate had supposedly killed Tyce's grandfather.

"Anything you need, I'm here to help." Beta Liam's mate Nina joined us. She was a beautiful woman with long black hair she kept in a ponytail, smooth white skin, cheeks that were constantly blushing with emotion, and kind, dark brown eyes. She was also tiny like all the other women who lived in the packhouse, even after pushing out two huge boys who already looked every bit to be beta heirs at only five and seven years old. I'd never felt so huge in my life as I did in Tyce's packhouse.

"My poor son," Luna Julia said, sulking. "He won't answer his door when I knock, and he ignores my mindlinks. I don't know what to do."

"It must be hard for him. I mean, his own mate killing his grandfather? How do you move past that?" Nina responded.

"Why did the Moon Goddess bring him such a horrible mate? My sons deserve the best. Oh, I'm so disappointed. I've waited so long and . . ." She shook her head, not finishing her sentence.

"He can always find a better chosen mate. And look, Tyce got a wonderful luna!" Nina smiled at me. "He looks happier than I've ever seen him before."

Luna Julia glanced at me and didn't say anything. My heart sank. Even though I knew logically she didn't deserve me devoting any energy to her attitude toward me, I couldn't help but feel devastated by the fact my future mother-in-law wasn't happy with me and thought Tyce deserved someone better. It only reinforced all my insecurities. And I couldn't even fight back. How could I disrespect my mate's mother? Especially knowing I'd be living with her for many years to come.

"I'll have Tasha make Travis chicken teriyaki with rice. It's his favorite." Luna Julia got up. "And I'll have her make me chicken Caesar salad. Gigi, Nina, would you like the same?" The look she gave me was one of, *don't you dare to ask for what Trav's eating even if it sounds better than salad.*

"That would be lovely!" Nina replied.

"Sure, thank you," I answered quietly, looking down at my lap.

"So, how are you liking the Jade Moon Pack so far, Gigi?" Nina asked as soon as Julia left the room.

"It's nice," I replied, deciding it was best not to be completely forthright.

"The wildlife in Alaska is so beautiful. Definitely make sure Tyce brings you out to see it. And the winters are majestic. Sure, the sun doesn't rise for several weeks, but the northern lights are spectacular. And our full moon runs are unparalleled during the winter months. We hunt the night before, and throw huge parties, roasting our kill over open flames with live music and dancing the night of the run. You and Tyce will be leading them, of course."

"Wow, sounds amazing," I replied, brightening a bit.

"Once this whole situation is sorted out, I'm going to show you around the pack more. This packhouse can be really intense sometimes, but the pack itself isn't so bad. Lots of great people. You're going to be very happy here, Gigi." She gave me a big smile, and for once I didn't feel hopeless when it came to my future here.

Once the food was ready, Luna Julia tried to bring some upstairs to her son. We could hear her knocking on his door and calling for him, but he was clearly ignoring his mom. Goddess, he must have been devastated. I didn't know what would make me completely ignore my family like that.

After some time, she finally descended the stairs without the food. "I left it next to his door," she simply stated, her shoulders slumped, and took a seat in front of her salad.

Just as we dug into our food, her phone went off, the ringer echoing in the large dining room. "Hello?" Julia answered. A muffled male voice could be heard as she intently listened. "Dear Goddess," she finally said, bringing her hand to her mouth. "Well, bring him home so we can have a proper funeral." After a few moments she finally hung up the phone and stared off into space.

"What happened?" Nina asked.

"They found Bruce's body."

"Where was it?"

"Dumped into a body of water, weighted down with a pair of forty-pound dumbbells."

"Holy Artemis."

Tyson

My father and I got back to the packhouse that evening to find my mom, Nina, and Gigi situated in the office. "Hey." I nodded toward everyone and then went over to Gigi to plant a kiss on her cheek. Just the touch of my lips to her skin instantly calmed all the tension that had built up inside me from the day.

"I'm sure you heard that your grandfather's body was found?" my mom asked.

"Yeah," I replied. "Dad and I are planning to go view it in a bit after we get a chance to eat."

She nodded. "And Trav's mate is dead now?"

"What?" I asked.

"Well, I'm assuming you took care of the murderer."

"She's not the murderer," I replied, not in the mood to elaborate. "Come on, Gigi, come with me." I turned to my mate, no desire to go through an interrogation with my mom. I helped Gigi up and pulled her hand to take her out of the office.

When we were at the stairs, Gigi said, "Trav hasn't come out of his room all day. He won't talk to anyone." She looked down at her feet.

"Fuck," I replied. "I need to talk to him. Do you wanna come?"

"Will I be in the way?"

"No, of course not." I gently pushed on her back, so she'd walk in front of me.

When we got to Trav's room, I knocked. "Hey, Trav, it's Tyce. Open the door. We need to talk."

After a few moments, Trav swung the door open and my heart dropped. He looked like complete shit, his face haggard with dark hollows under his eyes. "Trav," I practically whispered.

"How could you do it, Tyce? You're the fucking alpha. All that shit about you finally stepping up and leading the pack, and when it came down to it, you still let Dad order you around and tell you what to do like you always have."

I hung my head, ashamed that Gigi was witnessing this. Why did I ask her to come into the room with me? I didn't want her to know me like this. I defended myself. "Trav, all the evidence pointed to her being the one who did it. If she weren't your mate, you know you would have thought she did it too. I mean, she tried to kill her own fucking brother, for Artemis's sake. What makes you think she wouldn't murder an asshole like Grandpa?"

He wrapped his arms around himself, taking a seat on his bed. "She didn't do it. I know she didn't."

"Listen," I said, taking a deep breath. "I did what you asked. I asked her to join the pack. And you know what she fucking did? She spat in my face, Trav! I was offering her a lifeline, and that's how she responded."

He sniffed, not saying anything.

"Yes, Dad tortured her. But I didn't—I couldn't do it. Okay? I never touched her once except when she finally broke down and agreed to join the pack. Then I was able to ask her, and she said she didn't do it. So your mate is officially not guilty, cleared of all charges."

"Where is she now?"

"In a cell. Until we know for sure she can be trusted."

"Can I see her? Please?" he asked in an emotion-choked voice.

"Only with escorts."

"That's fine. I just need to see her, please."

I nodded.

He continued, "Listen, I'm going to talk to her. Tyce, I can't live without her." His voice was shaking.

"I know," I replied, empathetic to what he was feeling, wishing things had gone differently. But now that my father had tortured her, how could we trust she wouldn't try to take revenge?

"Just go," Trav said in a defeated voice. "And let the guards know I'll be by the detainment center tonight."

I nodded, taking Gigi's hand and bringing her to what had become our bedroom. When we entered, I gestured for her to take a seat on the bed and followed, doing the same.

"Why did your father torture her?" Gigi asked.

"I wasn't lying when I told Trav I'd offered her an option so we wouldn't have to. But she didn't take it," I replied sincerely.

"Why not?"

"Who knows. She seems pretty unhinged. Goddess, I have no fucking idea why she was mated to my brother. He is such a nice, nerdy guy. It's just baffling."

"Your mom feels the same. About her and about me." Gigi fell back into the bed, sighing.

"What?" I asked, lying down next to her and pulling her to me. "My mom doesn't think that."

"It doesn't matter. I get the idea that no one will ever be good enough for her sons. I'll just have to learn to deal with it."

"My mom just doesn't know you yet. But she will." I kissed Gigi, my heart heavy at how miserable she seemed living in the packhouse with me. I knew my family was intense, but I guess I hadn't thought it all through enough. I'd grown used to them over the years. But now I could see how hard it could be for someone coming in who hadn't dealt with it their whole life.

She sighed again. "It's okay. Let's just leave it. But there's something I don't understand. If you can just have someone join your pack and force them to tell the truth with your aura, why do you even torture to begin with?"

"For a few reasons. One, most won't join a rival pack willingly. Most are loyal to their own packs and have to be worn down either way. But there are other reasons too. Like killing our own pack members is actually painful for alphas, and only done under extreme circumstances. Because our role is to protect and nurture our pack, it goes against our nature. Plus it's rumored that killing too many of your own pack members can make you go insane. There's some pretty unhinged alphas out there, and I wouldn't be surprised if it's because they killed too many of their own."

"I didn't know that," she responded, snuggling closer to me. "I want to learn more. All this alpha stuff is really interesting. I never told you this, but I big-time wanted to be a warrior before I lost my wolf, and I feel like with becoming luna, I'm finally kind of getting my chance."

"You're definitely getting your chance." I smiled. "I'm going to find you the perfect private trainer, and you'll be kicking ass in no time. I can't fucking wait until we go to battle together and you fuck up our enemies with your demon wolf."

Chapter 79

Jasmine

I was about to call it a day with pack work when my cell phone lit up on my desk. I glanced over to see it was my dad. Odd. My dad didn't normally call. He'd text. That was the first thing that tipped me off that something was wrong.

"Hello?" I answered.

"Hey, Jaz," my dad replied somberly. "How are you? How are the pups?"

"Everything is good. Progressing as normal."

"Great, great." The way he said it didn't sound great at all. "Are you sitting?"

"Yeah, why?"

"Okay, good. Your mom got some bad news today."

My stomach sank. I hated bad news. What could it be? Did my mom somehow get an illness? Was she at the age yet where that was possible? I tried to steady my heart as I waited for him to tell me what it was.

"We got a call from your mom's old pack, and it seems her father was murdered."

"Murdered?" I gasped. "By whom?"

"They're not sure yet. But they're making funeral arrangements. We're looking up flights now. Your mom thinks it'd be best if you and Blake go too. After all, they came out here for your engagement, your wedding, and Alpha Tyce was out here all summer. It would look bad if you and Blake didn't show the same courtesy."

"Of course! I completely agree!"

"I know it's cutting it close with your due date, but you still have some time, right?"

"Right," I replied, wondering how much time exactly. Dr. Luna had told me to expect the pups to come in early October, maybe late September. I could certainly take a long weekend to attend my grandfather's funeral. There was still time. "How's Mom doing?"

"It's never easy to lose a parent." My dad sighed.

"Should I come by?"

"Why don't you come by tomorrow? Let your mom process everything tonight."

"Okay, love you."

"Love you too."

I hung up and reflected on the call. I'd never known my grandfather well. My mom mostly shielded me from that side of the family, so they always felt very distant from me, barely family at all. Even now, it was hard to feel anything about the news, besides empathy for my mom who, I was sure, must have been taking it hard. I could only imagine how difficult it would be to lose my own father. It would be absolutely devastating. And for him to be murdered? That was unthinkable.

I made my way downstairs, gripping the railing as I wobbled my way to the main floor. Blake was already setting the table when I entered the dining area. "Hey, I was just about to call you downstairs." He came over and wrapped me in his arms, pulling me in for a kiss.

I snuggled into his chest, inhaling his scent and allowing the sparks of his touch to travel along my skin. "Hey, is everything okay?" Blake asked, gently rubbing my back.

"Let's sit down for dinner and I'll tell you," I replied.

Luke popped out from the kitchen, carrying plates with meatloaf, mashed potatoes, and broccoli, putting everything out. After Blake finished setting the table, we all sat down, and everyone took some food. Once we were all quietly eating, I finally spoke. "Blake, we may need to move up our Alaska vacation by a lot. Like to tomorrow."

"Tomorrow?" He raised an eyebrow at me.

"Yeah, tomorrow."

"Is there a reason why? It's not exactly the best time to be vacationing right now."

"The vacation was actually a joke. I know, I'm not as funny as you."

"So, was the whole thing a joke, or . . . ?" Both he and Luke looked at me funny, and my cheeks burned at how awkward I was being.

I let out a nervous laugh. "Okay, seriously, we do need to leave for Alaska because my grandfather was murdered."

"Murdered?" Blake and Luke said at the same time.

After a beat, Blake asked, "Was that a fucked-up joke?"

"No, he actually was murdered. My dad just called to tell me. My parents are looking up flights now to go to the funeral. And, obviously, we should go too. It would only be right."

"Hold up, your grandfather—one of the most notorious alphas—was *murdered*? Are you going to tell me the rest of the story?"

"I don't know the rest of the story. From what my dad told me, I don't think my family even knows the rest of the story."

"Damn. Are you okay, Jaz?" Blake reached across the table to touch my hand.

"Yeah, I didn't really know him that well, to be honest."

"I'm going to talk to my mom and make sure you're okay to fly."

"I'm sure it'll be fine. We'll only be gone for a few days. I'm not really due for another couple weeks, which is like a month or something in human. Plus, worst case, I'm sure Tyce's pack has a perfectly good clinic."

I could sense how tense Blake had become from the conversation. But he knew as well as I did that it would be a huge insult if we didn't go. My parents were right. They had come all the way over here several times already. Besides the fact that Tyce had spent the whole summer with us, he'd also flown dozens of his warriors to the East Coast to help fight a battle his pack had nothing to do with. Twice. I knew Blake was definitely weighing all those things against the small risk of me taking a couple flights.

"I want to take a private jet," Blake finally blurted. "I don't feel comfortable with the idea of you being so pregnant on a plane full of humans. Even if it's unlikely, I don't like the risk."

"How much is that gonna cost?" Luke asked.

"I don't care. It's worth it. This is our luna. She's carrying the future alpha. I don't think anyone in the pack would begrudge us." He then turned to me. "Tell your parents to stop looking up flights. They're coming with us."

Two days later, early Saturday morning, we boarded a private jet to Alaska—well, to be exact, first to Spokane, Washington, to refuel and then to our final destination of northern Alaska.

"Here's a nice comfortable place for you to sit, Mrs. Alpha." Blake had his hands on a very plush seat.

I plopped down in it and stretched out. "I could get used to this. I don't even know why I ever flew commercial."

My mom took a seat across from me, acting quieter than usual, as my dad looked around. "So, what d'ya think, Drew?" Blake asked, giving my dad a pat on the shoulder.

"Very cool. Just wish we could enjoy it more under better circumstances," my dad replied, looking toward my mom.

"Blake, thank you for doing this," my mom added. "I know my father could be difficult, and he wasn't one to hold back. You've always been very gracious to my family."

"Your father wasn't much different from my own," Blake replied. "So I get it."

She nodded, and a look of understanding seemed to pass between them.

After traveling for over twelve hours, we finally arrived in northern Alaska a little after three in the afternoon, thanks to the time difference. We climbed down the stairs of the jet and were escorted into the airport where Alpha Tyce and Gigi were already waiting for us.

"Gigi!" I exclaimed, giving her a big hug. "How are you? How do you like Alaska?"

She hugged me back tightly. "Still getting used to it. It's so nice to see someone familiar." She pulled away. "Look how big your belly is now. You look like you could pop at any second."

"Don't say that too loudly," I joked. "That's Blake's worst fear right now."

She gestured that she was zipping her lips.

I smiled at her and said, "Hey, I know we're far away from each other. But if you ever want to just chat luna-to-luna, maybe we could do a regular FaceTime or Zoom happy hour. I mean, I'll have to stick to just juice for now. But it could be nice to have someone else to talk to about the unique stuff we have to deal with."

"I'd love that so much." Gigi threw her arms around me again.

Tyce went around, greeted everyone, and introduced us to his beta Liam. "I hope you're not all flown out, because we still have one more flight to get to our pack," Beta Liam said as he began helping with the luggage.

"Hard to get 'flown out' on a private jet," my dad joked. Beta Liam led us to the small plane, and he and Tyce loaded all our luggage inside. It brought back memories from years earlier as I recalled the small plane we'd flown on before—that had to have been at least ten years ago, when Tyce was still in high school and his father was still very much the alpha.

"So, how's it going? How are you settling into your new pack?" I asked Gigi once we were all seated inside the plane. It was nice but not quite as big and luxurious as the one we'd flown here on, and it was clearly made more for practicality than luxury travel.

"I've been getting used to everything. It's really different from back home." She looked down at her lap.

"Really? How so?"

"I just miss having my family around. Tyce's family are all such strangers to me. But I'm sure I'll eventually get to know them more and it'll be okay." I could sense she was holding back and not telling me everything.

"Any time you want to talk, I'm happy to listen," I offered.

"Thanks, Jasmine. You're a good person. I can tell." Gigi smiled. "I'm so glad you're here. I wish you could stay longer."

Chapter 80

Tyson

The past couple days passed by like a bullet train. After my grandfather's body was found, my father and I went to the pack clinic to take a look at it. And although I had grown used to seeing dead, mangled corpses, it still shocked the fuck out of me to see my grandfather like that. I had grown up with him being the enforcer, ex-alpha, most terrifying and strongest person I knew. He had to be one of the most notorious alphas in recent history. He'd always been ruthless and brutal and fought in battles like nobody's business. I hated, loved, admired, feared, and respected him.

But seeing him reduced to a bloodied corpse with his heart ripped out of his chest—well, that was sobering. It reminded me of meditating on impermanence in school and at temple. Nothing, not even the man who seemed undefeatable, was impervious to death. My grandfather had been tortured and killed the same way he had done to likely hundreds before him.

"Closed casket," my father said, and I nodded. We both knew he'd never have agreed to his pack seeing him this way.

The next day, Friday, I went with Trav to the detainment center after he begged me to release his mate. "Trav, I swear to Artemis, if I release her and anyone, a single fucking person in this pack, including Dad, ends up hurt by her, I will banish you from this pack. I don't want to do it, but this decision is falling on me as alpha, and my ultimate job is to keep the pack safe. I'd never do this for anyone else. But you're my brother, and I can't deny you your mate."

Trav did something we didn't ever do in our family and pulled me in for a hug. "The mate bond goes both ways, Tyce. I would never do anything that would lead to her getting hurt, and she the same for me. I know she'd never break my trust like that."

"Goddess, for the pack's sake and your sake, I hope that's true." I sighed.

"Tyce, just think. You have a mate too, right? If Gigi's dad tortured the fuck out of you but eventually released you, and you could take revenge on him but knew it would hurt Gigi if you did, would you?"

I blew out a breath. "No." I didn't even hesitate. I would let her father stab me a hundred times, and I still would never fight back if I knew it would hurt her. And then I recalled how my grandfather had reamed into Blake almost a year earlier about Jasmine, and how he had just stood there and taken it up the ass. At the time, I'd remembered thinking I would have had some choice words, and possibly fists, if it had been me. But now it all made sense.

I walked into the jail with Trav, and with barely a word, I unlocked her cell door. We had put her in one of the nicer ones, not that any of them were particularly nice. But this one at least wasn't missing a toilet seat, and the bed had a newer mattress, as the previous one had gotten stabbed and soaked in blood.

Trav pulled Sara into his arms, practically suffocating her. I cleared my throat and said, "Sara should probably continue to stay in Prudhoe Bay for now. I'm thinking it'd be pretty awkward to have her in the packhouse. Maybe we can figure out a more permanent housing solution at some point."

"Tyce, thanks." My brother pulled me in for another hug. He then took Sara's hand and led her out to freedom. I knew my dad would be pissed when he found out. But Trav was right. I'd talked the talk, but I hadn't walked the walk. And that was going to change from this point forward.

After that, I finally did what I should have done much sooner. I picked Gigi up at the packhouse, and I took her on a ride to the Spruce Winter Pack. "Are you ready for your first diplomatic visit as luna?" I smiled at her.

"What should I do?" She looked up at me with her eager eyes. Goddess, she was so cute and so enthusiastic about her new job, it was contagious, and it only made me want to be better at my job as alpha.

I clasped her hand in mine as we drove. "Just act super charming. Let out your sweet side. And you know I love your spicy side, but definitely reel it in today."

"So no calling this other alpha a chipmunk fucker?" She snickered.

"While that line may have worked on me, I don't think this alpha will appreciate it as much." I grinned. "Anyway, we're going to pretend that the reason we're going over is so I can introduce my new luna to him. But the real reason we're going over is twofold. I'm trying to get more information about this embezzlement. He supposedly bought an island with the money that's gone missing, so he's going to have to come up with some proof this island exists. And, second, at this point, the only lead we have on who murdered my grandfather is him. My grandpa had gone over that same morning to confront Alpha Vic about the embezzlement and ended up dead hours later while Alpha Vic was at a board meeting. I know that motherfucker is involved somehow."

"Wow, okay," Gigi replied.

"Don't worry, I already know you'll do great."

Alpha Vic's beta escorted us to the packhouse. My father and grand-father weren't wrong. His pack was a shithole. The roads were all in terrible need of repair, and many weren't even paved. You could easily tell who had money and who didn't with one glance at the houses. Clearly the pack didn't subsidize or help with home repairs like ours did. The packhouse, however, was in pristine condition and even appeared as if it had some additions made to it since the last time I'd visited, which had to have been barely a year earlier.

"Alpha Tyce!" Vic greeted us from his doorstep. "And who is this beautiful young lady?"

"Alpha Vic, this is my mate and soon-to-be luna, Ginger. But she goes by Gigi," I replied once we got closer.

"Gigi, my pleasure." He took her hand and kissed the back of it. This dude was something else. Who the fuck did that except in movies?

"Pleased to meet you as well," Gigi responded.

"Come in, come in." He opened the door for us. "Let me take your jackets," he said, sliding Gigi's jacket off her. I pulled my own off and handed it to him. He hung both of them up in the entryway closet and then gestured for us to come in.

"Your packhouse is absolutely beautiful!" Gigi exclaimed.

Damn, he'd really done this place up. The entryway was crazy fancy, with marble tiles, a huge chandelier, and a bougie glass table with a huge fresh flower arrangement displayed. "Did you recently have this place remodeled?" I asked.

"Oh yeah, with how well business has been going, it only made sense," he replied. "Let me know when you remodel yours. We have some pack members who do great work. I'm sure they'd love the business."

"I'll keep that in mind," I replied as he gave us a quick tour of the downstairs of his packhouse. Now I knew where the road repair funds had ended up.

We took a seat on possibly the most plush leather couch I'd ever sat on, and suddenly I wondered why my packhouse didn't have the same one. It must have cost a fortune just to get it over here. Shipping to Alaska alone was half the battle. His cook came out and served all of us some tea and put out pastries on the coffee table.

"I heard the news, of course." Alpha Vic put on a show of a sad face. "My father and I both give our condolences. We obviously knew your grandfather a long time, and will, of course, be attending his funeral tomorrow."

"The whole family is so broken up about the loss!" Gigi blurted out. "I'd only known him a short while, but wow, even I feel a bit emotional about it." I had to force myself not to snicker. I knew Gigi never liked him, but man, she was a great actress.

"I can only imagine," Alpha Vic replied. "Tragic how he died too."

"Murdered!" Gigi, sniffed. "Who would do such a thing to such a well-respected and beloved alpha?"

"Great question. My father and I have wondered the same thing since we heard. If it happened to him, it could happen to any of us. And now there's a murderer out there on the loose." He shook his head. "Do you have any leads?"

"None yet," I replied. "Do you have any thoughts?"

"What about that rogue that you have staying at the complex? What's the deal with that? I never trust rogues myself. They tend to be feral and unpredictable."

"What makes you think that rogue did it?" I asked, my instincts in overdrive, my wolf practically scratching at my chest. Damn, this guy really was horrible at this. "Rogues usually aren't very well trained, and I can't see one taking down my grandfather."

"Hmm, true. So there were no signs of anyone doing it? No DNA evidence or murder weapon?"

"No, none. We had our warriors scour the area for hours, and they didn't find anything."

"What about his car?"

"No, they didn't find that either." I was trying so hard not to laugh, and I couldn't believe how dumb this guy was as he kept naming everything he'd used to frame Sara.

"Hmm, I'm out of ideas then."

"If you think of any others, definitely give me a buzz."

"I will." He nodded. "But in some more positive news, as you've heard, JSP has purchased an island and we're building windmills. This is the first of many projects we'll be taking on to invest in green energy. And, as a celebration, after all this funeral business is over, I'd love to take you, your mate, your brother, and anyone else that wants to come on a little cruise to visit. We'll take my new yacht. So it can be a little mix of business and pleasure."

"Your yacht?" I raised my eyebrow.

"Oh yes, I mean, business has been so good. I'm sure Trav's shared the latest figures with you. It was time I started reaping some of the benefits."

"I see."

"So, you'll join me of course? Gigi?" He looked toward my mate.

"I've never been on a yacht before," she replied.

"Oh, well, you must come on mine then. Do you have any friends? Bring them along as well!"

"We have another alpha and his luna visiting for the funeral. Maybe they could come too," Gigi suggested.

"Fabulous! And what about your siblings? Trav? Terri?" He looked toward me.

"Trav maybe," I replied, a bit protective of my sister. I didn't trust this motherfucker around her. He'd always given her creepy looks. Besides the fact that she was very pretty, my sister was also far too friendly, and it always attracted the wrong kind of attention. Men mistook her kindness for flirting, and I didn't like it one bit.

"Great, great. So what do you think? How's Monday? A nice way to spend the lunar sabbath, no?"

"Sure, Monday works. I'd like to see this island in person."

"Great, I'll get the crew ready for then. Let's plan for everyone to meet at the packhouse at eleven, so we can set sail by noon. My yacht's docked right on our shore, and it's only about a half hour ride out to the island, but we can take the scenic route and spend a bit more time out at sea. They've already started construction on the windmills, so you'll get to see all the action."

"Great, looking forward to it."

"Well, if that's all." Alpha Vic stood up. "I've got quite a busy day ahead of me. Thanks for visiting, and I'll see you on Monday."

When Gigi and I were back in the car, Gigi turned to me and said, "That guy is wicked sketch."

"He's also dumb as a rock," I agreed. "He basically all but admitted to framing Sara. Now we just need to figure out how to prove it. Which shouldn't be hard considering."

"But it seems there is an island?" Gigi added.

"Yeah, we'll see on Monday. I'm really curious to see where the fuck he's going to take us and if there are any windmills to speak of when we get there."

On Saturday, I spent the early morning training and running patrol stations. It was nice getting out and doing something active to get my mind off things. After a late breakfast, I trained Gigi for over two hours. "I'd like to start training you in your wolf form," I said. "But in order to do that, you're going to have to join my pack so I can communicate with you."

"Okay," she replied, but I could sense hesitation and maybe even sadness.

"Do you not want to join my pack?" I asked, coming closer, taking her hands in mine. Her skin was like ice. Even though we'd kept warm by staying active, her hands were still cold, and I didn't want to let them go, trying to warm them for her.

"I do . . ."

"But?"

She sighed.

"Please tell me, Gigi. I won't be upset. I just want to know what's wrong."

"It'll just be so final. I'll lose the last bit of attachment I have to my pack and family." She put her head on my chest, and I pulled her closer to me.

"I want you to feel at home here, Gigi. What can I do to make it better for you?"

"I'm just homesick. I'm sure I'll eventually get more used to it." She sniffed. "I'm going to be luna of your pack soon, and I need to start acting like it. The first step is to become a member."

"I don't want to rush you, Gigi, so it can wait. I'm just really anxious to get you trained. And it'll be tough if I can't communicate with you."

"Then let's do it, Tyce. Let's do it today." She smiled. But even with her bright, beautiful smile, I wondered if I was pushing too much.

When we got back to the packhouse, we both went upstairs to shower so we could leave to pick up Jasmine and her family from the airport. Gigi pulled all her clothes off, and I couldn't help but stare. She was so stunning—I couldn't believe my family couldn't see what I did when I looked at her. The way her body curved, her large, beautiful breasts with sweet little pink nipples, her round ass with tiny freckles dotting it, her whole womanly figure—she just exuded sex.

"What?" she looked up at me as she slid her panties off.

"Goddess, you are so fucking sexy," I replied. She reddened and I got up. "You're not taking that shower alone." I picked her up and carried her directly into the steamy, walk-in shower I'd left running to warm up moments earlier. I practically threw her against the tiled wall and instantly had my mouth on hers, our tongues twining.

Fuck, I can't get enough of her.

My dick pulsed against the crack of her ass cheeks. It had been far too long since I'd been inside her. She let out a slight moan. I didn't think I could be any harder, but that did it.

I let her down to the ground and pumped some soap onto my hands. "It's time to get you clean, baby," I whispered into her ear. I brought my fingertips to her neck, taking my time gently massaging the soft skin, moving slowly down to her shoulders, making my way down her arms.

I added more soap to my hands and slid them down the side of her chest until they found her breasts, gently massaging each breast from the outside in, until my fingers were on the stiff peaks of her nipples. I decided to go a little rougher, pulling them between my fingers. "Tyce," Gigi moaned out.

"You like that, baby?" I smirked as she let out another loud moan. I took that as my cue to bring my mouth to her left nipple. I started by rubbing my tongue around the whole perimeter, as she let out her sweet moans. I grazed her nipple along my teeth and then bit down gently.

"Tyce!" she cried out.

I moved to the other one and did the same thing. She had her back and arms pushed against the wall and her head thrown back, her mouth agape and her eyes shut, the appearance of ecstasy. *Goddess, I love the way she reacts to my touch.* I kissed down her body, down the center of her soft belly, taking my time and indulging in every moan and twitch that Gigi made. I got down on my knees, wanting to worship her Goddess-like body.

I grabbed her ass, pulling her hips toward me. "Spread your legs for me, baby." I coaxed her legs slightly apart as I grazed my fingers along the inside of her thighs. I moved closer to her pussy, inhaling her intoxicating mate scent. I'd never smelled anything so majestic before, my mouth watering with the need to devour it. I instantly had my mouth on it, sucking on her pussy like it was my first meal in months.

"Tyce!" Gigi screamed and pushed her fingers into my wet hair, sparks sprinting across my scalp. I slipped my tongue out, running it against her, from back to front, promptly finding her clit. She cried out, and I slipped two fingers into her pussy, working them in and out of her as my tongue flicked back and forth against her little bean. Soon her legs were convulsing. "Tyce!" she cried out again, and I pushed my fingers into her more aggressively, adding a third and, deciding to see how far I could take it, letting my pinky brush against the entrance to her ass.

She clearly liked it because her hands tensed in my hair, and she let out a final deafening scream as her whole body convulsed against my mouth and fingers, completely coming undone. I kept going, forcing out more orgasms, not wanting it to end. Goddess, there was nothing as satisfying as watching Gigi like this and knowing I did that.

When she couldn't take it anymore and pushed my head away from her, I got up, turning the water off. She panted as I wrapped a towel around her. "So, when can I finally do that with my dick?" I asked. She looked down and gave it a slight stroke, the sparks like electricity as her skin made contact with mine. I groaned in reaction, completely worked up now.

"Have you been meditating?" she asked, giving me a mischievous smile.

"Yes."

"So what would happen if a little mouse popped out right now?" She giggled, stepped out of the shower, and ran out of the bathroom. I quickly dried off and wrapped a towel around my waist, exiting the bathroom. As soon as I stepped onto my bedroom carpet, I found her sitting on my bed, completely naked, her towel abandoned. "How much control do you have?" she asked seductively, spreading her legs slowly, revealing her perfect pink pussy.

"I clearly have a lot considering how much you're fucking teasing me right now." I growled and moved closer to her. "That pussy is begging for my cock," I gritted out and dropped my own towel. She stared at it, rock-hard and throbbing, and gave it another teasing stroke. When she didn't keep going, I groaned. "You fucking tease."

"I'm not a tease. This is for your own good. I'm giving you some motivation, lighting a fire under your ass."

"Goddess, you are so infuriating." I crawled into my bed, pulling her down against me, and nibbled on her ears. "Most infuriating, stubborn, ball-busting woman."

"I told you I'd join your pack." She offered, fluttering her eyelashes, giving me the look of innocence.

"Now?" I asked, getting up onto my forearms, balancing myself above her, and pulling open my bedside drawer.

"Yeah, I'll do it now," she whispered.

I pulled out my switchblade and flicked it open. She gave a mischievous smile, pushing her palm into my face. I got up onto my knees, straddling her body. "Are you sure?" I asked.

"Do it," she said, and I sensed that something about this really turned her on, not unlike the last time I'd had my knife out. This girl was definitely kinkier than I would have initially thought.

I licked my lips and gently pierced my knife into her skin, dragging it down the center of her palm. I then did the same to my own. "Do you know what to say?" I asked.

"I, Ginger McDowell, hereby solemnly pledge my loyalty and allegiance to the Jade Moon Pack and Alpha Tyson Tikaani." We pushed our palms together and the sensation of her becoming tethered to me tingled within me, something more intimate and warm about this connection than any other I'd ever made. Once the feeling passed, Gigi pulled my hand, pressing my palm to her mouth, and gently licked it, lapping up my blood. My dick hardened from the image, already painfully stiff. But she just knew how to drive me completely crazy.

She let go and smiled, a mischievous glint in her eyes. I lowered my blade to her face, and ran the back of it along her soft, pouty lips. She let out a slight moan, and I'd never been so turned on. I moved it gently down her chin and onto her neck. As I did this, she grabbed my cock and began stroking it. Not unlike the time in the water, she knew exactly what to do, running her hand along it just the way I did, miraculously knowing exactly how I liked it. I let out a moan.

"You like that, baby?" She gave me cute smirk.

"I love it," I gritted out, groaning.

She stopped and stuck her tongue out. "Who makes you feel so good, baby?"

"Gigi," I moaned, grinning.

She continued stroking me, up and down, her thumb finding exactly the right part of the head to press into. I moved the back of my blade along her soft, smooth skin, the cold metal tracing her hard nipples. Fucking Artemis, even if she wasn't having sex with me, this had to be the best consolation prize I'd ever been given.

I was in fucking heaven from the pressure of Gigi's hand, sparks gliding up and down my shaft, and the vision of my knife dancing along her beautiful naked body. The sensation built up inside me, and my whole body tensed and released, the orgasm ripping through me.

"Fuuuuck!" I cried out as I blew my load onto her stomach. I inhaled and exhaled, recovering from the intense release.

"Am I still a cocktease now?" Gigi questioned, looking at me through her eyelashes.

"You are but only the best kind," I replied, catching my breath.

Before the end of the day, the packhouse had filled up with Blake, Jasmine, and her parents. Terri made the trek back from school. And then we got word that my uncle, whom we hadn't seen in years, had arrived for the funeral with his family. I supposed death was the one thing that really brought everyone out.

I barely had the chance to introduce Terri to Gigi, or even process everyone who was making an appearance, before it was time to leave for the service. Gigi and I rode over with my mom, dad, and grandma. I got shafted to the middle seat with Gigi and my grandma on either side of me. My dad was uncharacteristically quiet during the drive. I got the idea that he was taking this a lot harder than he let on. My grandma, on the other hand, didn't hide her feelings at all as she sobbed quietly the entire ride.

Blake pulled up in my car next to us as we parked. I'd given it to him to borrow for the duration of their trip. As my dad held my grandma's arm and pulled her along toward the temple, with my mom trailing, I hung back with Gigi.

"Very nice ride," Blake commented as he climbed out of the car.

"Thanks," I replied.

"What do you think, Jaz? Should we trade my Wrangler in for one of these?"

"I like your Wrangler," Jasmine replied.

"I'm on board! But only if you let me drive it every once in a while." Jasmine's dad chimed in, elbowing Blake in a friendly manner.

"Drew, my car is your car." Blake winked.

"Goddess, how typical, men and their love of douchey cars," Gigi said quietly to me, laughing.

The contrast between Jasmine's family and my family was clear. While, okay, her mom was a bit cold, probably a symptom of having been raised by my grandparents, everyone else joked and laughed with each other in an easy way, without resorting to mean-spirited humor. I imagined that was probably what Gigi had with her family, and I understood why the transition had been so difficult. I suddenly longed for the same thing—a happy family—one where people actually liked each other.

I squeezed Gigi's hand as we made our way inside. We arrived early to make sure any last-minute issues were addressed. Trav was already waiting inside next to Terri, without his mate. It made sense—his mate certainly would have felt unwelcome.

As the priest went over a few last things with my father, the big, heavy door to the temple swung open and a man who looked so similar to my father it was eerie entered, followed by a woman and two grown children.

"Gabe?" Jasmine's mother stood up, bringing her hand to her chest.

"Gabe," my father repeated, looking toward the man who made his way toward us. "You made it."

"He was my father too," the man replied. He then looked toward my mother and said, "I see you've still got your alpha and your citizenship, Julia."

"Gabe, he's my mate. And I see you found yours as well. It's time to let it go."

"He's not your mate and you fucking know it," Gabe replied cryptically, then turned to the woman next to him. "Come, Donna, let's go take our seat over there." He gestured toward the other side of the temple and moved over there with his family.

I looked toward Gabe and back to my parents. They didn't say anything, and I wondered what that meant. Had my parents not been fated to each other? Then I recalled how my mother had suggested I find a chosen mate. Had there maybe been more belief behind those words than it had seemed at the time?

People began trickling in, and I had to put my thoughts aside as I went around with my father to greet everyone. My dad kept up a good facade, but a part of me could sense he was struggling, in a way that one only could when they knew someone really well—like the way his voice would break slightly, or how he seemed slightly out of it and following a script.

The service was long and difficult. My grandmother sobbed next to me the entire time. And I began to recall more good memories—my grandparents taking me to the park and taking turns pushing me on a swing, my grandfather giving me rides in his wolf form around the house, my grandfather watching horror movies with me late into the night, then waking me as a wolf when I'd fall asleep, terrifying me. We had had a better relationship when I was younger, before the alpha training had really started. And that part of me that loved him reawakened, burning my chest, and scratching at my throat again. Fucking Artemis, why'd he have to die?

I went up to give a short speech, and even my voice cracked a little as I recited it. My dad clasped his hand on my shoulder, and then gave his own, much longer speech.

After we had our final meditation, the priest led us outside, where my father and I doused the casket in gasoline and then both brought lit candles to each end of it, watching as the flames engulfed the wooden box. His body burned as my family stood in a circle, observing as his spirit was released into the otherworld. And fuck, was that a tear that dropped down my cheek? I clenched my hands into fists, forcing myself not to cry but—Goddess be damned—he was my grandfather.

Chapter 81

Ginger

"Mmm," Tyce moaned into my ear as the alarm went off, waking us early on Monday morning. I was still getting used to waking up before the sun rose. But this seemed to be Tyce's schedule, and I couldn't believe that he'd functioned all summer like this considering how late we'd stayed up on many nights.

"Do we have to get up?" I moaned, snuggling closer to him.

He chuckled. "Time for my morning injection. Then breakfast and morning run before temple."

"Goddess, your schedule is so intense."

"I thought you wanted to be a warrior," he teased, nibbling on my nose. "But if you wanted a quickie, I could be persuaded to stay in bed a little longer."

"When I see proof you have complete control of your wolf, that'll be on the table again." I gave him a playful shove.

"Hopefully on the table, the counter, the wall, the floor, the chair . . ." his voice trailed off. He chuckled again. "And in the back door."

"Okay, Tyce." I grinned to myself. "I'll make a deal with you. I'll let you put it in my ass."

"Really?" He brightened.

"But."

"But?"

"You have to let me put a dildo in your ass first. And not just any dildo. One that's alpha size."

"Damn."

"Well?" I snickered, wondering if he'd go for it.

"My credit card's all yours. Order that shit up. But make sure you get some lube too."

"What, really?" I widened my eyes staring at him.

"And maybe some muscle relaxant."

"How much research have you done on anal sex exactly?"

He laughed. "I didn't want to fuck it up and then you never agree to it again."

After a busy morning, Blake, Jasmine, Tyce, and I gathered at Tyce's car and drove over to the Spruce Winter Pack. It was a windy day with gloomy, gray skies and the crisp smell of fall in the air. "Weather says no rain, so I guess there's that," Tyce commented as we waited for everyone outside Alpha Vic's packhouse.

Blake groaned in a pained way from the back.

"Are you okay?" I asked, looking behind me.

"Yeah," Blake replied.

"It's just false contractions," Jasmine explained. "I talked to Dr. Luna this morning, and it's nothing to worry about. But yeah, they're not fun."

"Oh, I just learned about those!" I brightened. "It was part of my data entry work. I read a whole section about werewolf pregnancies. Apparently, false contractions are thought to be even stronger for werewolves than for humans."

"Yeah, that's exactly what Dr. Luna said." Jasmine nodded.

"And same with real contractions," I added.

"Yeah, Goddess, not looking forward to that." Jasmine cringed. "Even these ones are pretty bad. Can't imagine the real thing. I've already agreed to the epidural, mostly for Blake's sake." She grinned and patted his leg.

"I've felt a lot worse than childbirth before. I could handle it au naturel no problem."

"Sure. I'm pretty sure you were the one who was just groaning, not me," Jasmine teased.

After some time, Trav finally arrived with his mate in the passenger seat. Once we confirmed everyone had made it, Alpha Vic went to grab his car and pulled out of the garage in a bright red Porsche 911.

"What the fuck?" Tyce exclaimed. "Who the fuck drives a Porsche in the middle of fucking nowhere Alaska, especially when half the roads aren't paved?"

"Someone with fuck-you money?" Blake offered.

"His pack is in shambles! And he's buying a fuck-you car?" Tyce scoffed. "That's definitely a 'fuck you' to his pack, that's for sure."

Tyce switched his car into drive, and we followed the red Porsche on some of the few paved roads toward the shore. Alpha Vic's pack had a beautiful piece of property right on the water. It was probably nice here during the summer months. I could imagine spending the warmer, sunny days sunbathing out here, especially to get away from the chaotic packhouse.

We all got out of our cars and gathered at one of the docks. Alpha Vic stepped out of his flashy car with who I now knew was his father and the former alpha. "Weather could have been better. But no worries. We've got a beautiful climate-controlled yacht waiting." Alpha Vic smiled in what I think was supposed to be a charming way, but all I could think was *creepy*. "Alpha Tyce, nice to see you again. And you brought your beautiful luna with you as well. Nice to see you again, Gigi." He took my hand and kissed it like he had last time. I cringed as his lips touched my skin.

"This is Alpha Blake and his luna, Jasmine." Tyce introduced our companions.

"Pleasure, Alpha Blake." Alpha Vic shook his hand. "And my, look at your pregnant luna. You must be ready to give birth any moment now."

"I've still got a couple weeks to go," Jasmine replied. "But I'm definitely ready. They're pressing on all my organs, and it's not comfortable. I hope you have a bathroom on board."

"I absolutely do. They?"

"Yep, twins—boy and girl."

"Are these your first?"

"Yes."

"Oh, so that's the future heir you're carrying. Very nice." He then turned to Trav. "Ah, Trav! So glad you could make it. And who's this?" He sniffed. "Hm, she looks familiar, but this is one of your pack members?"

"Yes, this is my mate, Sara."

"Oh, so new joiner to your pack?"

"Why would you assume that?" Tyce asked, butting in.

"I just thought I knew her from somewhere else. But perhaps I'm misremembering," Alpha Vic replied. "Anyway, let me introduce everyone who hasn't met him yet to my father. Dad!" He called him over, and he approached the group.

Once we finished the meet and greet, Alpha Vic led us past a bunch of dilapidated-looking fishing boats. "Many of our pack members are fishermen," Alpha Vic explained.

I wondered if the boats were even capable of starting or would stay afloat out at sea. And what a contrast once we got to his yacht which, even in this terrible weather, shone and sparkled. Not only did he have a fuck-you car, but he clearly also had a fuck-you boat.

As soon as we boarded, we were all handed champagne flutes. The servers scrambled to get Jasmine some apple juice. Once the boat set sail, Alpha Vic showed us around, and servers came out with hors d'oeuvres. "Bacon-wrapped scallop, miss?" someone asked. I pulled it off the plate and bit into it as Tyce did the same.

"Damn, this shit is good," Tyce remarked, reading my mind. "Maybe I should look into a yacht and crew for myself."

"Private jet, private yacht. I feel like I'm dreaming," Jasmine commented. "This trip was worth it just for the experience."

"Come back and visit anytime," I responded. "I could use the company."

"Blake and I will definitely be back once the pups are here. I'd like them to get to know this side of the family. I feel like I really missed out growing up." Jasmine gave me a friendly smile.

"We can probably come out to your pack for the first full moon run too," Tyce offered.

"Really?" I asked, my pulse quickening at the thought of seeing my family again so much sooner than I expected.

Tyce gave my hand a squeeze. "Definitely."

"Ugh, I already have to use the bathroom again!" Jasmine exclaimed, walking away.

I noticed that Trav and Sara pretty much kept to themselves. I felt bad that things had turned out the way they had and they felt they couldn't be part of the group. It seemed that perhaps even Blake had some bad history with Sara based on some of the looks she shot at him.

After I'd gotten quite a few champagne flutes in me, I started to feel a comforting buzz, my body warm with emotion. "I love you, Tyce," I blurted out, throwing my arms around him. As soon as the sparks touched my skin, I wondered why I'd ever cut off sex. His scent and body heat surrounded me, mixing with the cloudy, woozy feeling of wine in my blood. "Is there a term for having sex a mile out at sea? Mile-wide club? Mile-length club? Nautical-mile club?"

"Offshore drilling," Blake offered with a smirk.

My face burned, not realizing he'd been close enough to hear me. Tyce chuckled.

"Okay, I should have known he was right there. But it's tough to distinguish scents and how close they are when there are so many people in one small area."

"You'll get better at it with time," Tyce responded. "And I love you too." He kissed me on the forehead, my stomach fluttering in reaction.

About an hour after setting sail, Alpha Vic came around to let us know we were approaching the island. "You're gonna love it!" he exclaimed to Tyce. "We just haven't built a dock yet, so the crew is going to anchor the boat. Then everyone should fit in our dinghy, so we can get safely to shore without getting wet."

We all bundled up in our coats and watched as the crew anchored the boat. It seemed the wind had simmered down a bit, and some sunrays peeked through the clouds. Before long, Alpha Vic and his father began helping everyone into the dinghy. Blake went first so he could help Jasmine down from below. Trav and Sara followed, then Tyce, me, Alpha Vic, his father, and one member of the crew who had on what looked like a wet suit. This made sense, as once we got close, he had to get out into the freezing water to drag the dinghy the rest of the way to shore.

Alpha Vic and his father got out first and then helped the rest of us. "Are you ready?" Alpha Vic asked us. I looked around at the thick forest of pine trees ahead of us, wondering how they had already begun building windmills without having cleared the trees first.

"Let's go," Tyce replied. We followed Alpha Vic down a path into the forest, and I had a bad feeling that instantly sobered me. My stomach flip-flopped, and something scratched inside me, my instincts in overdrive. This didn't seem right. I could sense that Tyce felt the same way.

Our emotions were syncing, which only brought on more anxiety. The walk seemed to be never-ending as we made it farther and farther into the lush forest.

"Where the fuck are the windmills?" Sara shouted from the back, putting into words what the rest of us were thinking. "I thought you said you'd already started construction on windmills. All I fucking see are trees!"

"Patience, patience," Alpha Vic replied. "We're getting there."

"Admit it, this is just as much of a farce as your shit framing job," Sara aggressively yelled.

"What the fuck are you talking about?" Alpha Vic turned to glare at her.

Before Sara could answer, a loud explosion rang out far ahead, as if a bomb had gone off. We all covered our ears, the smell of explosives thick in the air.

"Oh, shit! What was that?" Alpha Vic shouted.

Suddenly, a large group of mice sprinted under our feet, likely running from whatever that explosion had been. I tensed and looked toward Tyce. And I couldn't believe it, but he hadn't shifted. He stood there, still as a stone, his hands clenched, and it took everything in me not to celebrate right then and there.

"The windmills!" Alpha Vic's father yelled, snapping my attention back to reality. Before anyone had time to react, Alpha Vic and his father began running in the direction of the boom.

"Gigi, stay here with Jasmine," Tyce shouted to me and then took off with Blake, Sara, and Trav.

Once everyone disappeared beyond the trees, leaving the two of us behind, I turned to Jasmine and said, "I have a really bad feeling about this."

"Me too," Jasmine agreed. "We should get into our wolf forms just in case." She tugged on my arm, pulling me toward the tree line. "Here's the plan." She spoke quickly. "If anything happens, you jump out first and try to spook them with your wolf, and I'll jump in right after to fight, okay? Hopefully they'll be so intimidated by your wolf that they'll be an easier fight for me."

She tugged off her jacket and then pulled off her shirt. I followed suit, removing everything I was wearing. Before shifting, Jasmine showed me how she tied all her clothes together, so it'd be easy to carry in her wolf form if we had to later, throwing everything into her jacket and tying up the sleeves. I did exactly as she had, and we left the two parcels of clothing next to each other in a spot we'd hopefully remember later.

Once we shifted into our wolf forms, she gestured up a hill and I followed her, climbing up the pine-needle-littered slope. Clever. We had a much better view from up here. My eyes traced the small clearing where we'd been and then the trees that surrounded it.

"Alpha Vic and his dad disappeared," Tyce mindlinked me. *"We lost them! Keep your eye out!"*

I looked toward Jasmine and imagined Blake must have linked her the same thing because she gave me a nod and turned back toward the area below.

It wasn't long before the slight movement of tree branches tipped us off that someone was approaching. Jasmine tapped me with her nose and got into a pounce position. She gestured for me to get in front of her. I moved forward, getting into what I thought was a pretty good fighting position, although I had no way to know. As soon as two wolves made their appearance, I sprinted down, noting instantly who they were as their scents permeated the air.

They stopped in their tracks at the sight of me. Yes! The plan was working! Jasmine sprinted down the hill, coming in with her sneak attack, pouncing and digging her claws into Alpha Vic's back. He was like a wild bronco as he tried to throw her off, but Jasmine was so fucking good and kept a tight hold on him, not allowing him to knock her off. Even pregnant, she was a badass.

I was obviously distracted by the amazing show, because the next thing I knew, claws were tearing through my skin, and I let out a pained yelp. Alpha Vic's father had taken the opportunity to attack me. I tried to fight back, but I was useless as he kept biting into different parts of my body. I whimpered, wondering if he'd kill me, when he was suddenly thrown off me. Tyce and Trav arrived, and they both took him on as I moved to the sidelines to nurse my injuries and watch.

Jasmine, Blake, and Sara ganged up on Alpha Vic and, before long, had him down and in his human form. Sara also shifted, found a rock on the ground, and smashed it into his skull a couple of times, splattering blood along the dirt.

Before long, Tyce and Trav had similarly taken down the former alpha, and Sara did the same thing to him, crushing the rock against his skull. "Love the sound of bones shattering," she remarked.

"Are you okay?" Tyce mindlinked me. *"Lie down. Let me see your wounds."*

I whimpered, doing as he asked, and he got low, sniffing and checking me all over, gently licking everywhere that I'd been injured. His tongue ran along the gashes in my skin, soothing and closing them. *"Goddess, I really gotta train you,"* he remarked.

Blake shifted back into his human form and approached Tyce. "Let's carry these motherfuckers back to mainland where we can really deal with them."

Tyce nodded and followed Blake to where their bodies were limp on the ground. Tyce flipped the former alpha onto his back, and Blake did the same with Alpha Vic.

Jasmine approached me and gestured over to our clothes. I followed her to where she picked her own up into her mouth. I did the same. Once everyone gathered, we all ran back toward the shore, following Blake and Tyce.

When we got there, the dinghy and the anchored yacht were gone, not a boat in sight and only blue water ahead. Tyce shifted back into his human form and threw Alpha Vic's father off his back. "Fuck, they must have had some sort of getaway plan."

Blake followed suit. "This sucks. With how knocked out they are, it'll be hours before they wake up to tell us what it is."

"Shit, what do we do?" Trav asked after he also shifted, his brows furrowed.

"Let's go back and get our clothes and cell phones for now," Tyce said.

"I'll stay here. Can you grab mine, too?" Blake asked.

"Yeah, sure," Trav said. He and his brother shifted and ran back into the center of the forested island with Sara.

Jasmine gestured into the trees, and I followed her so we could shift back and dress. Once we were clothed, we returned to Blake in his wolf form, keeping guard over the two bodies.

The three of us sat down on a grassy patch of land and waited until the other three returned, jogging back with Blake's clothes in hand. Blake shifted back into his human form and threw his clothes on while everyone tried to make calls with their phones.

"Anyone have service?" Trav asked, waving his phone in the air.

"I got nada." Tyce sighed.

"Nothing." Blake shook his head.

"Nope," Sara replied.

"Nothing for me either," Jasmine said.

"Nope, nothing," I agreed, trying to spin in circles to catch a signal, but it was useless.

"Fuck, so we're really stuck," Tyce lamented. "And it's fucking cold. Goddess, I'm so sorry, Blake. I didn't know this would happen." He pulled his brows together in a pained expression.

"Hey, it's not your fault," Blake responded. "None of us knew what to expect. And you've helped my pack out twice when we had problems. I owed this to you. I just wish my pregnant mate wasn't here."

"It's okay. If it gets too cold, I can just get into my wolf form. I'm fine for now in my jack—" She was cut off as both she and Blake groaned, clutching at each other.

"False contraction?" I asked.

"Yeah, that one was bad." Jasmine sounded winded as she replied. "Must be the stress of the day."

"I have an idea!" Sara suddenly exclaimed. "I can swim in cold water. It might take me a while, but I can swim to shore and grab one of those shoddy boats and come back for everyone."

"That's right!" Blake jumped up in excitement. "How the fuck did I forget?"

"Are you sure you'll be okay?" Trav went over to her, concern on his face.

"Yeah, I'll be fine. I do it all the time," she replied, pulling off all her clothes and shifting into her fluffy white wolf form. And before anyone else could say anything, she dove into the water.

"See, I told you my mate would redeem herself." Trav gave Tyce a friendly punch in the arm. "She's fucking amazing!"

"Let's not celebrate too soon. Who knows if she'll come back for us," Tyce responded.

"Oh, she'll be back. You'll see."

Another groan came from Jasmine and Blake. "Shit, that one was bad," Jasmine exclaimed, and they shared a wincing expression.

We sat around for about a half hour, just chatting, and the contractions seemed to stop. But then, midsentence, Blake was cut off as they clutched at each other with pained expressions on their faces. The both groaned, and their reaction seemed to last over a minute.

"That was a pretty long contraction," I commented. "False contractions are supposed to be short."

"What are you saying?" Blake asked in a panicked voice.

"Well, if the contractions are thirty to seventy seconds long, it could be a sign that Jasmine's going into labor."

"What?" Blake barked out.

"Fuck." Tyce's jaw tightened. "This can't be happening."

"Fucking Artemis." Blake didn't look well. His face had noticeably paled, and he was running his hands through his hair nonstop, ruffling it all up.

"Blake, it'll be okay." Jasmine touched his arm in a gentle manner.

"The pups. Our pups," he said in a heartbreakingly pained way.

Before she could respond, Jasmine moaned again, digging her nails into his arm—Blake let out a distressed whimper. The two of them appeared agonized.

"Shit, Gigi, what if Jasmine really is going into labor? What are we supposed to do?" Tyce asked me.

"Umm . . . umm . . . umm . . ." I began thinking, trying to remember what I'd read. "She needs to stay in her human form, because the pups can only be birthed in her human form. And a mate's touch will help ease the pain."

"Okay, what else?"

"She's probably still in early labor, if anything, and that can last hours or days. So it might be okay."

"How will we know if it's not early labor?" Blake demanded.

"She'll be in active labor once the contractions become stronger, closer together, and regular."

And just then, another contraction clearly rolled over Jasmine as she let out a moan and Blake did the same. After a good amount of time, Jasmine choked out, "They're definitely getting stronger."

"Is it possible for her to go into active labor so quickly?" Tyce asked.

"I don't know," I replied.

"They're alpha pups," Blake added. "I think things progress much faster with alpha pu—" He didn't finish his sentence as he let out another moan. "Fuck!"

"Blake, I think I might be going into active labor," Jasmine cried out.

"Try walking," I said. "I think walking is supposed to help."

She nodded, and Blake helped her back up. She paced in circles as we stood around and watched. Every few minutes, another contraction would roll over her, and she and Blake would flinch in pain.

This went on for a good amount of time, Tyce, Trav, and I all looking on and at each other, not sure what to do.

"Okay, we need to make a plan," Blake finally said. "It's very fucking possible she's going to give birth here on an island, in the middle of the ocean, in the woods." He winced, clenching his hands into fists. "Goddess, what are the fucking chances? And I thought giving birth on an airplane would be bad." He was shaking, and Jasmine rushed over to rub his back.

"Gigi, I think you're going to have to help deliver the babies, because you know literally more than all of us," Tyce said.

"Okay, I can do it," I replied. "I'm going to fucking do it!"

Blake took a few breaths, shook his head, and seemed to finally come to. "Tyce, Trav, when it's clear she's going into labor, get into your wolf forms so you can keep her warm with your fur," Blake said. "Because she's obviously going to have to, well, remove her pants."

"Got it," Trav said.

"Yeah, we're on it," Tyce agreed.

"I'll probably be completely fucking useless because I'm going to have to feel everything she feels." Blake flinched as another contraction rolled over Jasmine, a pained expression on both their faces for at least thirty seconds. Jasmine let out a pained moan.

"Are you okay?" I approached her, rubbing her back.

She nodded, her eyebrows furrowed, and in a shaky voice she said, "That was really bad."

"Take some deep breaths maybe," I said, continuing to rub her back.

Blake blew out a breath. "No epidural."

"People gave birth for thousands of years like this. She can definitely do this." Trav patted Blake on the shoulder.

"Plus, she's got werewolf healing on her side," Tyce added. "Quick recovery."

"But the pups." Blake let out a strangled cry of frustration while scrubbing a hand over his face. He then doubled over, moaning, just as Jasmine did the same.

I timed the reaction on my cell phone. "That was almost forty-five seconds," I said. "They're getting longer, and they seem to be getting more regular."

Jasmine took a few deep breaths and began pacing again as we stared on. Suddenly she stopped, and a large wet spot formed on her light-colored jeans. She reddened, looking down.

"Jasmine, I think your water just broke," I exclaimed.

"Shit, shit, shit," Blake fretted, running over to her. Just then, a really bad contraction must have rolled over her as she clutched Blake's body, moaning loudly.

"Tyce, Trav, shift," I commanded. "Jasmine, you're going to have to take off your pants!"

Blake helped her pull her shoes and pants off, as they muscled through the contractions that continued to roll over her. Tyce and Trav sprang into action, pulling off all their clothes and throwing them into a heap, instantly taking their places next to her. "Should she lie down?" Blake asked in a pained voice as I approached.

"No, from what I read, it's better to give birth in a standing or squatting position. Gravity is on her side," I said, but they were barely listening. He got behind her, helping hold her up, as she let out a primal growl.

Not knowing what else to do, I squatted in front of her and rubbed her bare legs, hoping that might bring her some comfort.

"They're really bad." Blake groaned. "Really. Bad."

Jasmine growled again, her whole body convulsing. She dug her nails into Blake's arms as he stayed behind her, helping steady her. We went through several rounds of this as Tyce and Trav stayed close to her legs, and I stayed in position. "You can do this, Jasmine. You can do it," I said, not sure what else I could say to comfort her.

"I don't think I can do this," she cried out, tears soaking her face. "I can't do this."

"Fuck, fuck, fuck." Blake fell to his knees, but kept hold of her hips. "Fuck, Jasmine. What are we going to do?" He seemed to be breaking down. My former alpha had completely collapsed on himself.

"Jasmine, you can do this." I took her hands in mine and looked deeply into her pained eyes. "You can definitely do this. You're a luna."

She nodded and began groaning again, getting back into her squatting position.

"Alpha Blake! Get up and help her!" I barked at him.

He shot up and got back into position behind her as she squatted. "I swear to fucking Artemis, if anything happens to either of these pups or Jasmine, I am going to peel Alpha Vic's dick like a banana, one layer of skin at a time." His eyes took on a demonic appearance, and I can't lie, I was a little scared.

But the look left his face just as quickly as it appeared as he let out another guttural groan. Jasmine leaned up against Blake, her whole face strained, and her nails dug so far into Blake's arms I was surprised she hadn't either broken his skin or snapped his arm in half. Her well-formed muscles tightened as her limbs trembled. I knelt down, practically under her, in a position I never imagined I'd be in.

"You're doing great, Jasmine." I looked up at her. Her face was covered in sweat and tears as she let out more groans, the contractions waxing and waning as she breathed through them. I continued to rub her legs, hoping it was helping, as Tyce and Trav stayed snuggled close to her.

"Baby's coming." Blake groaned, breathing heavily, doing his best to keep Jasmine steady. She squirmed in discomfort, grunting, every muscle in her body tensing.

"You can do this, Jasmine. You're doing so great." I tried to encourage her, hoping I was saying the right thing.

Finally, a fluff of black hair appeared between her legs. Jasmine gave a loud, agonizing cry, pushing it out some more. As soon as it slipped out enough that an arm emerged, I helped Jasmine by guiding the pup out as gently as I could, careful not to hurt him or her. Once the baby was fully out, I cried out, "It's a boy!" as he let out a wail.

"A boy," Blake echoed. "Our son."

"Our son," Jasmine repeated, tears streaming down her face as she gasped for air.

"You did so well, Mrs. Alpha," Blake said gently to her.

Springing into action, I grabbed Tyce's sweater off the ground, so I could wrap it around the pup to keep him warm, and handed him to Jasmine. She wrapped him in her arms and held him close to her, both she and Blake completely focused on him.

"I have to cut the cord," I said.

Tyce mindlinked me, *Do you need my help? Do you know how?*

"I need some sort of string," I replied, biting my lip. Then my eyes stopped at Tyce's abandoned shoes. "I'm going to need to remove your shoelace."

"Do it," Tyce said.

My pulse quickened, and I fumbled as I undid the lace from Tyce's sneaker. Once I had it freed, I gently grabbed the thick, bloodied cord and looped the lace around, creating a knot. I thought back, remembering I needed to wait for it to stop pulsing.

When it was time, I commanded, "Tyce, bite the cord off."

I held it out slightly, and he used his teeth to chop through.

"Jasmine, how are you doing?" I asked.

"He's amazing," she whispered with watery eyes. "Perfect."

"Beautiful," Blake added, kissing her on the head. "One more, Mrs. Alpha."

After not long, Jasmine let out another growl as the labor restarted, and more fluid leaked down her legs—her second water breaking. Tyce shifted into his human form to take the baby from her, and I got back into position. This time it went much faster. Again Jasmine grunted, squirming against Blake. But very soon the second pup crowned. I did the same thing again, guiding her out as soon as an arm emerged.

"Jasmine, you did it!" I cheered.

"You did it, Mrs. Alpha." Blake kissed her on the head. "You were fucking amazing."

I handed Jasmine the second baby after grabbing Trav's sweater from the ground to wrap around her. Trav shifted back into his human form and laid out his jacket. "Here, Jasmine, lie down over here," he offered.

Blake helped her move, kneeling down behind the jacket so she could lay her head on his lap. Blake pulled off his own jacket to cover her legs. Tyce gently laid the boy pup onto her chest, so she was holding both. Tyce then pulled his own jacket off the ground to cover the pups and keep them warm.

I tied the second cord, using Tyce's other shoelace. Tyce shifted back into his wolf form, so he could bite it off.

"Why isn't she crying?" Jasmine unexpectedly yelled out. "Why isn't she crying?"

"What?" I glanced over at Jasmine who was practically hyperventilating. She began rubbing her baby vigorously, kissing her. Blake picked up the male pup, keeping his whole attention on the female one who Jasmine was actively trying to resuscitate. We all crept closer, instinct taking over to try to help however we could.

Finally, the girl pup let out a loud cry, and everyone simultaneously let out a relieved sigh.

"You fucking did it," Blake said gently to Jasmine, handing her back the pup he'd taken from her and brushing her hair back out of her face.

"Our pups are here and they're fine," she replied, kissing each of their heads.

"You did fucking amazing. A true luna."

"Jasmine, how are you feeling? Do you feel okay?" I asked.

"Yeah," she rasped out, smiling at her two pups, clearly lost in her own world.

"You just need to deliver the placentas and you'll be done. They should come out in the next few minutes."

She nodded, her eyes still on her two pups.

Just then, the horn of a boat sounded in the distance, and we all looked up. A fishing boat was approaching. Once it got closer, we were able to make out Sara, wearing clothes that were definitely too big for her, at the helm.

Chapter 82

Tyson

"Okay, so what's the story?" I asked Sara as she navigated the boat back to the Spruce Winter Pack.

"There's not much to it. I swam back like I said I would. I found a storage closet, that I was easily able to break into and steal some clothes. Then I walked the dock, picked the boat that looked the least fucked-up, and hotwired it. And here I am."

"Damn!"

"She's amazing," Trav remarked. "Best mate."

Sara glanced his way and gave him a smile.

"You did really good, Blondie Badass Baby." Trav swooned.

I choked, trying so hard not to laugh. I couldn't believe that was actually the nickname he'd come up for her and she was okay with it. But, I supposed, that was the mate bond.

"Tyce, they're waking!" Blake called for me.

I walked past Gigi and Jasmine, who were snuggled up together with the pups. We'd found a spare blanket in the boat that we'd wrapped around them to keep them warm.

I entered the inner part of the boat, closing the door behind me, and made my way to the victims. I squatted down over Alpha Vic who blinked his eyes open. "What the fuck?" he shouted as he tried to free himself from the rope we'd tied around him.

"Don't you dare try to shift into your wolf, or I'll beat you to a pulp again," I threatened.

"And it's a good thing I keep my knife handy at all times," Blake added with an evil glint in his eyes. Before Alpha Vic could say anything, Blake pushed his knife into his stomach. Alpha Vic let out an agonizing scream as dark red blood pulsed out of him with each heartbeat. "That should keep him from shifting for a while."

"So, where do we start this interrogation?" I asked. "May I?" I put out my hand to Blake, and he placed his knife in it.

"Why am I being interrogated? I didn't do anything!" Alpha Vic cried out.

"Really? So you didn't embezzle millions of dollars?"

"I told your brother! I didn't do anything!"

"Liar!" I yelled and stabbed the knife into his thigh.

"I didn't do anything!" he shouted.

"Hmm, a stubborn one," Blake said. "Looks like this torture could go on for hours. Lucky for him, those are my favorite."

"I didn't do anything! I'm innocent!" Alpha Vic cried, tears streaming down his face.

Both Blake and I stilled as the familiar sound of pups crying penetrated the walls of the room. "Hmm. Maybe we should continue this on shore when ladies and pups aren't present," Blake said and gave him several blows to his face until he was knocked out again.

Just then, Sara appeared. "We're close to shore now," she said. "And there's one problem."

"What?" We both looked up at her.

She pulled off all her clothes, and before we knew what was happening, she shifted into her wolf form and lunged for Alpha Vic, severing his head from his body.

"What the fuck!" I shouted. Before I could even process what she'd just done, she did the same to the father. Just as quickly as she'd done that, she shifted back to her human form.

"Why'd you just do that?" Blake demanded, standing up.

"Why do you think? We need to be able to dock this boat, get to our cars, and get off the pack land. If we show up with their alpha as a prisoner, we're going to be outnumbered, and his pack will destroy us. But now that I've killed the alpha and his father, and he has no luna nor heir of age, *I'm* the alpha of this pack."

"Holy shit! She's right!" I studied her, not sure whether I should be impressed or horrified by what had just happened in only a matter of seconds.

"How are you doing, Jasmine?" Gigi asked, sitting down at Jasmine's bedside in the clinic.

"I'm fully healed now. Just tired," Jasmine replied, kissing the heads of the two pups that were situated on her chest.

"And how are the pups?" I asked.

"Perfect," Jasmine whispered.

"Alpha pups, so surviving just fine, thank the Goddess," Blake chimed in. "Thanks again for all your help, Gigi."

"I'm just so glad I was able to help," she said humbly. "And Jasmine really did all the work. I just jumped in as needed."

"You were great," Blake added. "You stayed calm under pressure and gave everyone directions. We needed you out there today."

"Thanks." Gigi blushed.

Once we were done visiting, I took Gigi's hand, and led her out of the clinic. "You did such an amazing thing today." I wrapped my arms around her.

"The whole thing was so incredible," I replied. "It made me realize something."

"What?"

"I already had a hunch, but now I know for sure. That's my calling—that's what I want to do with my life. I want to be like Dr. Luna back home."

"You're going to do it. I believe in you. We'll figure out the college and living situation. It's really important to me that you don't have to give up your dreams to be my luna."

"But what about your heir? And my training?"

"We'll figure that out too. I know it'll all work out." I squeezed her hand.

"And, Tyce!" She stopped, giving me a push on the chest. "You did something amazing today too. When all those mice ran out, you didn't shift."

I grinned. "You know what that means."

"Yep, I know exactly what that means." She stepped closer to me, running her hand down the center of my chest, leaving a trail of sparks as her fingers brushed against me, the sensation flowing straight to my cock. "I want to know why you still have your clothes on."

"I didn't know you were an exhibitionist. But if outdoor sex is what you want, well, who am I to deny you that?" I teased, peeling off my jacket, a big grin on my face.

She gave me a friendly punch to the chest. "Tyce, let's go inside before the making of the alpha heir becomes a pack activity."

"Might not be terrible. Everyone could chime in and give us constructive criticism on our technique so we can improve." I snickered.

"Speak for yourself. I'm already fucking great. You could use some work though."

"Really?" I nibbled on her nose as she giggled. "I could use some work?"

"Lots of work," she teased.

"We'll see about that," I said, picking her up and throwing her over my shoulder in a fireman's carry, and she let out a joyful scream. I quickened my pace as I sped toward the packhouse. "I want you to count how many orgasms I get out of you today, because it won't be less than twenty."

Chapter 83

Almost three weeks later

Jasmine

"Gigi!" Paige and Heidi screamed as their sister made her way out into the airport arrivals area. They both rushed over, wrapping their arms tightly around her. Her parents followed, doing the same.

Blake grabbed her luggage from her, and then I gave Gigi my own hug. "Welcome home, well, sort of."

"Thanks." Gigi hugged me back. "And how are the miracle pups?" she asked, looking into my double stroller. "Wow, they're so big compared to the last time I saw them!"

"Do you want to hold one of them?" I offered. They were staring up at her with their big blue eyes.

"I'd love that," she replied, with a big smile on her face. I pulled Aria out of the stroller and handed her to Gigi. "You're so much cuter in person than over Zoom, Aria." Gigi swooned, cradling her in her arms.

"Welcome, Tyce," I said, pulling my cousin in for a hug next.

"Congrats, again, Jaz," he replied, hugging me back. "We've been looking forward to this run since you left to go home."

"So, when's it your turn?" I gave him a playful punch in the arm.

"Not for a while. Gigi's going back to school in the spring, and I'm now taking on a lot more pack responsibilities."

I snickered. "Well, I thought the same. Pretty sure Alex and Talia did too."

"Come on, let's head back to the pack," Blake called.

Gigi handed me Aria, and I gently placed her back in the stroller next to her brother, Ryker.

Tyce rode back with us, his huge alpha body squished between the two baby seats, while Gigi went with her own family. "So, no car upgrade yet?" Tyce asked from the back.

"Nah, double the expenses now," Blake replied.

"Guess you're not one to dip into your pack funds."

Blake chuckled. "Prefer that my crazy sister-in-law doesn't bite my head off and take over my pack."

"How has that been, Tyce?" I asked. "I mean, she now co-owns the business with you, right?"

"Luckily, she's similar to me in that business doesn't interest her, and my brother is an honest guy. So it could be worse."

"So what's your brother's official title then?" Blake asked.

"Luno, I suppose."

"Luno," Blake repeated. "Hm, well, I guess it's time that women start becoming alphas too."

That afternoon, Alex and Talia arrived with their five-month-old daughter. "Her eyes!" I exclaimed as soon as Talia lifted her up so I could hold her.

"Yeah, black as Alex's now. Guess my eyes didn't take."

"They suit her though," I replied.

"And where are your two little alphas?" Alex asked.

"Blake's got them in the office. I gave him baby duty today." I snickered. "He won't admit it, but he secretly loves it."

I handed Talia back her pup and gestured for the two of them to follow me down the hall. My heart swelled to probably twice its size when we entered the office. Blake and Tyce each had a pup in their arms, gently swaying them.

"I don't know, Tyce," I teased. "You act like you don't want pups, but then I walk in on this."

"What? I like being an uncle," he replied. "Who's the best alpha uncle you ever had?" he said in a baby voice to Ryker. "Say Tyce. Ty-yce."

"Okay, my turn!" Talia said, handing Bianca to Alex and taking Ryker from Tyce.

"Hey, nice to see you again, bro." Tyce stood up, giving Alex a pat on the shoulder. "Or bro-in-law I should say now."

"Yeah, crazy." He shook his head. "I guess my sister finally got to become alpha like she always wanted."

"It's honestly not much of a pack. The whole place is in shambles. She's going to have a lot of work cut out for her. From what I've heard from my brother, the pack isn't happy. A lot of them have been slowly leaving for years. And they're in a ton of debt now due to all the mismanagement of funds."

"Well, can't say she doesn't deserve it," Alex replied. "So where's your luna?"

"Her family's a bit conservative, so she's staying at their place while we visit. But you'll definitely see her tonight."

I added, "As the one who delivered my pups, she's going to help lead the run tonight."

That evening, Blake and I walked around, mingling with the whole pack as live music played and catering was set out. It was the perfect fall day—a little chilly but perfectly sunny, with the Vermont foliage in full bloom, all the leaves turned rich reds, oranges, and yellows, blending with the sky as the sun set in the background. Everyone was anxious to get a peek at the two newcomers fast asleep in their stroller.

During a lull, Blake pulled me aside. "Apple cider donut, Mrs. Alpha?" he asked, pulling two of them from the dessert table.

"Can't say no to that," I replied, taking one from him and biting into the fresh, local donut. I swear, they didn't make them better anywhere else.

"I want to tell you again how amazing you were when the pups were born. I know you constantly have doubts, but whenever it comes down to it, you handle everything like a pro."

"You weren't so bad either. Especially without an epidural."

"Yeah, definitely not doing that again. Next time, no traveling."

"Next time? We have an heir now, and the last time scarred me for life."

"I don't know. I kind of miss when you were pregnant." Blake began nibbling on my ear. Damn, he knew how to get me riled up, instantly going for my weak spot.

"Stop, everyone's watching." I pushed Blake off me, even though my whole body was saying keep going.

"These ones are barely out and you're already starting on the next one?" Tyler snickered as he approached with Jack.

"Knowing them, there's already another on the way," Jack added.

"Maybe you should stay away from the stork for a little while and make friends with the swallow instead," Tyler quipped.

Blake chuckled. "Tyler, what would we do without you and your awkward jokes?"

"All jokes aside, I love my little niece and nephew pups." Tyler grinned widely. "Congrats again." He pulled me in for a hug.

After a couple more hours of mingling, my mom took the pups, so she could keep watch over them during the full moon run. As it got closer to midnight, I found Gigi and Tyce in their own world.

"I can't believe you still have me in your phone as *Tyson Chicken*." Tyce held Gigi's phone above her head.

She let out a hearty laugh. "Sometimes when you come it sounds like you're clucking, I swear. I think the name fits."

"As opposed to when you come, and it sounds like you're waking the whole neighborhood with your rooster call?"

"Oh please, you love it. Or do you not want morning sex anymore?" She stuck her tongue out at him.

"I want you to cock-a-doodle-do while you ride my cock-a-doodle-do every morning and every night please."

She slapped him on the chest, and then they both turned to look at me. I had to try so hard not to smile. "Um, it's almost midnight."

"Right," Gigi responded.

"You'll do great, baby." Tyce pulled her in for a hug and tenderly kissed her cheek. "Just remember, no matter what anyone says, your wolf is the fucking greatest thing."

"Right," Gigi said then turned to me. "Okay, let's go. Lead the way. I've never done this before."

I brought her over to where Blake was waiting for us. "Here, we can go behind those big bushes over there to shift so no one sees us," Jasmine said.

"Yeah, great," Gigi said. "Although, I guess I'll have to get used to it if I'm going to be training with the warriors."

"Don't worry. I'm still not," I replied, giving her an encouraging smile. "And don't ever let any asshole make you strip in front of him. Don't be like me and wait to kick his ass. Do it right then and there like I should have."

She laughed. "Got it."

"Also, Blake let the pack know ahead of time about your wolf, so everyone's aware and won't be surprised."

She took in a deep breath and let it out. "I can't lie, I'm still really nervous. But I'm really trying hard to accept my wolf and how she looks. And I hope this will help."

I gave her arm a squeeze. "There's nothing wrong with your wolf at all. You're able to do the same things all the other wolves can do. You just look a little different. And, honestly, I think it helped a lot when we were out on that island and you were able to pop out and shock those guys into stopping. There's no way they would have ever expected to see a wolf like that."

She gave a small smile and nodded. It didn't seem like I'd fully convinced her, but I was proud of her for accepting the invitation to do this run with me. I knew it couldn't be easy. Gigi had opened up to me more in the past few weeks about her struggles with our pack growing up, and I couldn't blame her for feeling insecure after what she went through in middle school.

When midnight struck, we made our way to the front of the group where the whole pack was waiting, everyone shifting into their wolf forms until we were all just a big group of colorful fur, our eyes glowing, the moonlight shining onto the tips of our hairs. When it seemed just about everyone had shifted, the three of us leaped into a run and ran into the night, dodging trees and rocks, jumping fallen branches, and hopping over tree roots.

Everyone let out howls into the night, welcoming the new alpha pups into the pack.

Chapter 84

Three weeks later

Ginger

"Goddess, it's been such a long week!" I flopped onto the bed after showering and throwing on some sweats on a Saturday night in late October. "Your alpha schedule is no joke," I griped to Tyce. "I'm ready to go to bed now."

"Do you think you could stay awake for a little bit longer?" He came over and sat on the bed. "Because I have a surprise that just came today."

"A surprise? Have I been so busy that I didn't even realize it's my birthday already?" I joked.

"It's a 'just because' kind of surprise."

"Goddess, stop, Tyce. I can't do all this sweetness. I need a dentist! I think I'm getting cavities."

"Okay, the surprise isn't really for you. It's for Splinter anyway. Are you ready for me to bring it in?"

"Well, if it's not for me, you should ask Splinter," I teased.

"Splinter already said he's ready."

"Okay, rat whisperer."

Tyce gave me a cute little smile that made my stomach flip-flop. Fuck, why did he affect me so much? Even though we'd now been living together for two months, it still felt like it was the first time every time he walked into the room. "You should go get Splinter, so he can open his surprise," Tyce said.

I hoisted myself out of the bed and went into the other room, which was technically my bedroom for appearance's sake, but had really turned into Splinter's bedroom at this point. Fucking spoiled rat.

When I returned to the room I actually slept in, I found that Tyce had set up a little playpen.

"Where the heck did you get that?" I asked.

"Amazon," Tyce replied. "You can order anything on there."

"Okay, Splinter." I giggled. "Looks like Tyce spends more time ordering you gifts than me. Now I know who he really loves more. I shouldn't be surprised. I mean, before you, he was all about the chipmunks. Guess now he's upgrading to rats." I placed him into the playpen carefully.

"I don't see Splinter complaining about me being too sweet. He actually appreciates when I do nice things for him." Tyce reached over the side of the playpen and gave Splinter a little pat on the head.

"Okay, so what's Splinter's 'just because' surprise?"

"Is he ready?"

"I thought you told me he was ready already."

"Okay, be right back." Tyce smirked mischievously.

I waited and watched Splinter run around the playpen, sniffing in different areas. "I wonder if he got you some playpen toys. The nerd!"

Tyce walked back into the room with a cardboard box with holes and a huge red ribbon. "Is that what I think it is?" I sniffed the air, the smell of another rat very clear.

"Why don't you open it and find out?" Tyce gently placed the box on the ground.

I crawled over and undid the big red bow. Then I lifted the top of the box off. "You put a ribbon on the rat too?" I asked, peeking into the box, a rat with a white body and dark gray head staring back at me.

"It's a gift for Splinter, so why not? You said he needed a friend, so I'm gifting him a friend."

My heart banged against my chest, a warm tingle moving from my chest to my limbs. "Splinter loves it already," I replied, lifting the new rat out of the box. "Wait, what's this?" I asked, noticing as the light in the room sparkled against a stone attached to the ribbon. I untied the bow, and a ring dropped to the floor. I stared at it, my mouth agape, not sure what to do.

"Aren't you going to introduce Splinter to his new friend?" Tyce asked, a big smile on his face.

I blinked a few times, and gently placed the new rat into the playpen, my eyes not leaving the ring that had dropped to the floor. "Is that . . ."

Tyce picked the ring up off the ground, getting down on one knee, and I couldn't stop staring at the huge diamond rock in the center, an intricate design surrounding it with tiny little milky green and sparking red and yellow stones. "Gigi, from the moment you called me a chipmunk fucker, until now when you accuse me of having relations with our pet rat, you have infuriated me like no other. You are hot-tempered, quick-witted, and damn do you fight ugly. But you are also so loving, so caring, and you make me want to be a better person and alpha. With you, I feel like I finally found what I was lacking my whole life, which is a family that makes me feel loved and accepted.

"And I know we don't plan to have pups for some time, but once we do, you will make an amazing mother. You'll bring warmth that's been lacking in this packhouse, at least for all the time I've lived here. Gigi, I love you. You are more perfect than any mate I would have ever thought to ask for. I know it hasn't been smooth sailing with you coming to my pack, but I promise I will always do my best to make you happy here. So, will you do me the honor of making me the happiest man in the world and marry me?"

I was shaking all over, my heart racing, my legs so weak I thought I was about to fall over. "Yes," I choked out. Tyce grabbed my jittering hand and pulled it toward him, slipping the ring onto my finger.

"You could look a little happier." Tyce tilted his head.

"I'm trying so hard not to cry," I choked out. "Tyce, this is too sweet! Too sweet!" Tears escaped and trickled down my cheeks. "Fuck." I wiped at them, trying to stop the waterworks.

He leaned closer to me. "I forgot to add that you're also amazingly sexy, give the best hand job I've ever had in my life, and your blow jobs are—" He pinched his pointer and middle finger to his thumb and kissed them, tossing them dramatically from his lips.

"No one knows how to ruin a moment quite like you." I chuckled.

"I didn't ruin it. I'm just warming you up for the next one where I peel off all your clothes and we do a honeymoon dress rehearsal." He pressed his mouth against mine, spreading soothing sparks from my lips, down my body, shooting straight to the apex of my inner thighs. I pressed my body against him in reaction, shoving my tongue into his mouth, deepening the kiss.

He soon had my sweatshirt off, uncovering my bare breasts. He kissed along my neck and down the center of my chest while cupping my breasts and running his thumbs along my nipples. I let out a soft moan, my nipples hardening under his touch, and grabbed the fabric of his T-shirt, desperate to pull it off.

As soon as he lifted the thin cotton shirt over his head, I jumped onto him, pushing him to the ground, straddling him. I rubbed my crotch against his rock-hard cock, which was tenting his sweatpants, not able to get enough of the dulled sparks that zapped along the inside of my thighs. He shut his eyes and let out a loud groan, hooking his fingers into the elastic of my sweatpants, tugging them off. I lifted myself slightly off him so he could pull them down my ass and thighs, and I quickly kicked them off.

I leaned forward, my lips crashing against his. He dug his fingers into my hips as our tongues twined, desperate with hunger for each other. I pulled away, panting, and kissed my way down his body, indulging in the feel of my lips against his hard muscles, the intoxicating mate scent that permeated from his pores, the taste of his tanned skin. I kissed down his happy trail that turned me on like no other, until my mouth found the fabric of his pants.

I slipped my fingers down the side of his body to his hips, and into the band of his pants, dragging them slowly down his body until his throbbing erection popped free. I slid my fingers around it, slowly working them up and down the soft, velvety skin as I pushed my mouth onto the head and lowered it down the shaft. He let out a satisfied groan, and I looked up, locking eyes with his beautiful amber ones, not breaking eye contact as I bobbed my mouth up and down, syncing it with my hand.

I quickened my pace as he dragged his fingers through my hair, gently lifting it out of my face.

"Fuck, Gigi!" he groaned out. I kept going, sensing how good it felt for him—*so fucking amazing*.

He suddenly stopped me and lifted himself up onto his elbows. I looked up and he grabbed me, flipping me onto my back as he rolled on top of me. "Your blow jobs are fucking excellent, but I want to hear you scream as I fuck the shit out of you."

He gently eased my legs apart and pushed his massive cock inside me. I gasped in reaction, digging my nails into his shoulders. He began working it in and out of me, slowly at first and then speeding up. He brought his nose to mine, and I moaned into his face.

"You like that, baby?" he asked in his gravelly voice.

"Yes," I moaned out.

"You want me to fuck you harder, baby?"

"Yes."

He stopped. "You know the magic word, baby."

"Tyce!" I screamed, grabbing his ass to force him to thrust again. He quickened his speed, the friction of his hips rubbing against my thighs setting off electrifying sparks. "Tyce!" I cried out again and he became more aggressive, banging against me with complete abandon. I gripped his ass tighter, wanting more, not able to get enough of him.

He then pulled out, grabbed my waist, and forcefully flipped me over. His fingers dug into my hips as he pushed them upward and pushed his cock back inside me, falling back into the same rhythm.

"Tyce!"

He gripped my thighs, digging his fingers into the skin and jackhammering into me.

I let out a loud moan, seeing stars as he positioned himself to hit my G-spot. Every limb was convulsing with ecstasy, and I screamed more loudly, wild with lust. "It feels so good," I moaned out. "Keep fucking me like that, Tyce."

Before long, every part of me was tingling as all the pleasure built up in my core, my legs vibrating. And soon I found myself at the place of no return as fireworks and stars exploded inside of me, releasing all the tensions I'd been holding from the week, warmth and static traveling to my fingers and toes. Tyce pulled out and let out a final loud groan as he spilled his warm come all along my lower back. I practically collapsed onto the floor, completely spent.

Tyce got up and ran into the bathroom as my canines expanded. I took a few breaths and clutched my hands into fists, now more used to controlling the urge that came on to pierce my enlarged canines into Tyce. Paige let me know it would get worse with time, but it wasn't too bad for now.

Tyce returned with a warm, wet towel just as my teeth began to shrink back down, and he dabbed along my skin. He then threw it into the laundry basket and lay down next to me, pulling me on top of him. I rested my head on his shoulder as he brushed his fingers along my back. "That was amazing," he whispered.

"Thank you for the ring. It's beautiful," I said.

"The stones have meanings. I got jade put in for the Jade Moon Pack of course, but then the yellow citrines and the red rubies are for our wolves' eyes."

"Nerd." I grinned, secretly loving it, a warmth spreading through my chest and my stomach fluttering at his thoughtfulness.

"I'm starting to think you have some sort of nerd fetish."

"Time for you to get some nerdy glasses then." I lifted my head and stuck my tongue out at him. "Maybe then you'll be able to actually see what you're doing for once."

"You act like I've missed."

"Pretty sure you've been aiming at my ass for months. Haven't seen you hit the target yet." I snickered.

"Next time, baby. Get ready, because I'm coming for it."

"Hey, we had a deal. I hope you're ready for the alpha-size dildo I ordered."

"Oh, I'm ready." He nibbled on my nose. "Whatever you want, baby, I'm game."

THE END

To be continued: **Wolfbitten***, Book 4 of the Wolfbane series.*

Epilogue

Tyson

I picked up my ringing phone. "Sara caught the culprits," Trav said, not even bothering to say hello.

"Damn," I replied.

"She's already tortured them but offered to let you finish them off. You know, for pack alliance reasons."

"I have a feeling that allowing someone else to do the final deed is a gift of generosity in her eyes." I chuckled to myself. Trav's mate was something else. But I'd be damned if I didn't want to watch the motherfuckers that killed my grandfather take their final breaths. Before I hung up, I asked, "Can I bring Dad?"

"Obviously that's still a bit of a touchy subject but . . ."

"But you know that Dad, more than anyone, would want to be the one who does it." I finished his sentence for him.

Trav let out a breath. "Bring Dad."

After Sara had taken some time to get settled in her new position, she finally began her search for Alpha Vic's minions who had done the dirty work for him while he was in the board meeting with Trav and my dad. It hadn't taken long. She'd only started searching the prior day. I mean, it couldn't be too hard when you had an alpha aura.

After informing my dad of the news, we headed out to his car. "One sec," he said as soon as we stepped outside into the crisp, cool air, snow flurries floating around us. I threw open the passenger door, let myself in, and watched out the windshield as he approached with a chainsaw.

"What the fuck?" I asked as soon as he deposited it into the back seat and got behind the wheel.

"I've always wanted to go *Chainsaw Massacre* on someone." He gave an ominous smile and put the car into drive.

My dad turned up his nineties rock music as we drove, not saying much. When we arrived, Trav escorted us to their cells and brought us down into their dungeon. It wasn't quite as large as ours, and the collection of weapons wasn't quite as extensive, but it would do the job.

The one small light in the room flickered overhead, and my dad and I ran our eyes along the prisoners—two chained to the wall and the other two chained to metal tables.

"Very nice." My dad lifted the corners of his mouth, nodding approvingly.

"They're all yours," Trav said and turned to ascend the steps. Torture had never been his thing. But it was definitely my dad's and my thing.

Sara had already maimed them quite a bit. The ones on the table were missing their fingers and toes, which were currently lying in a puddle of their dried blood. The ones on the wall were missing their eyeballs and noses. The whole room stank of blood and burned flesh and hair.

"What do you think, Tyce? Where should we start?" He clasped his hand on my shoulder. "After all, you're alpha now." He gave me a fatherly wink.

"Looks like their dicks and balls are still intact," I replied, sharing a look with my father.

He chuckled in a menacing way. "Indeed they are. Probably means their assholes haven't been played with either."

We both pulled knives off the wall and got to work, approaching the shivering motherfuckers. What was it about pitiful, scared warriors that gave me so much pleasure?

My father and I spent hours finding creative ways to torture them, going at it until we'd bled them dry and practically cut off every last limb, their screams echoing throughout the small chamber. In the end, they begged for their death, admitting everything.

"I had to do it! He was my alpha!" one of them cried out.

"How'd you do it?" my dad asked, his knife at his throat.

"We surrounded him, took him down, beat him until he was uncon-scious. And when he woke again, we took turns punching and stabbing him."

"And then?" my dad bellowed, his whole face red, the veins in his forehead and neck popping.

"We tore his heart out."

My dad went ballistic, stabbing the man in much the same way it sounded like my grandfather had been stabbed. Tearing his skin and muscle to shreds. And when there was practically nothing left of him, my dad pulled a couple safety goggles off the wall.

"Tyce, it's time. Safety first," he said as we both adjusted the goggles onto our heads.

He yanked the start cord on the huge chainsaw that was probably normally used to cut down massive trees for firewood. And then he went right at it, shredding each body one at a time as blood splattered all over us, as if we were just having a fun day at a waterpark. And although my dad and I had never been particularly close, I knew I would have done the same for him if he had been the one who had been murdered.

Once my dad put down the chainsaw, pulled off his goggles, and took a few breaths, he said in a choked voice, "Damn it, I still miss the asshole." He shook his head. "Let's go, Tyce. We did our job."